S0-AKC-068

RIVA—Seeking a new life far from the terrors of Eastern Europe, she was determined to shield her child from poverty and persecution . . . but denied what her daughter needed most.

EVELYN—The proud mother of martyrs, she held two ravaged families together with an unbreakable will and an indomitable heart.

JULIA—Swept up in a seething storm of hatred and injustice, she chose to follow her convictions . . . at the price of her daughter's love.

ROSA—Wounded by her mother's cool indifference, she saw cruel history repeated when her own child turned from her.

MARTHA—Betrayed and abandoned, she spurned her family's bitter legacy to forge her own identity in a violent, changing world.

TIES OF BLOOD

GILLIAN SLOVO

AVON BOOKS ◆ NEW YORK

AVON BOOKS
A division of
The Hearst Corporation
105 Madison Avenue
New York, New York 10016

Published in hardcover by William Morrow and Company, Inc.; for information address Permissions Department, William Morrow and Company, Inc., 105 Madison Avenue, New York, New York 10016.

First Avon Books Printing: May 1991

AVON TRADEMARK REG. U.S. PAT. OFF. AND IN OTHER COUNTRIES, MARCA REGISTRADA, HECHO EN U.S.A.

Printed in the U.S.A.

RA 10 9 8 7 6 5 4 3 2 1

Acknowledgments

Ties of Blood draws its inspiration from real people and real events, from those involved in the long struggle against apartheid. However, all the characters (except for well-known names such as Mandela) are fictional and although many of the episodes are modeled on actual events, I have taken some liberties with them.

The process of writing has been a long one, and I am grateful to the people who helped me during it. My thanks to Winnie Dadoo, Lindiwe Guma, Wolfie Kodesh, Riva Krut, Joe Slovo, Beryl Unterhalter, and Jack Unterhalter, all of whom gave generously of their time and experiences.

There are people who I did not consult but whose books greatly contributed. I owe a debt of gratitude to Mary Benson, Brian Bunting, Michael Dingake, Charles Hooper, Tim Jenkin, Ellen Kuzwayo, Hugh Lewin, Winnie Mandela, Todd Matshikiza, Mbulelo Vizikhungo Mzamane, Indres Naidoo, Molefe Pheto, Edward Roux, Albie Sachs, Jack and Ray Simons, Can Themba, Eli Weinberg, and many others for their unwitting cooperation.

Thanks also to Susie Orbach and Jud Stone for their support and encouragement, to Susie and Luise Eichenbaum for their ideas, which helped me to give psychological solidity to some of the stories in this book, and to Joseph Schwartz for helping me out during sticky times. Thanks also to my editor Susan Watt, who brought a much needed and intelligent eye to the process.

Finally there are three people to whom I owe special thanks.

Caradoc King, my agent, was the person who first encouraged me to write this book. He was a source of enthusiasm and good advice throughout.

Elaine Unterhalter supplied me with background, research materials, and references, contributed many good ideas, and spent hours of her precious time going through the manuscript to weed out historical inaccuracies.

And Andy Metcalf lived through this book with me, tolerating the bad patches, celebrating the good, and spending his time reading, reading, always reading. My thanks to him.

Prologue

Lithuania: 1902

"WELL, MAMA, YOUR WISH HAS BEEN GRANTED. YOU ARE FINALLY at peace."

As Riva gazed down at her mother, she noted with detachment that the colors of life had already drained from Esther's face, replaced by a kind of yellow tinge. She saw a blandness in her mother's visage, a neutrality, that a live Esther would never have displayed. And she saw defeat. During her lifetime Esther had withstood many battles; but even she had been powerless in the face of death.

All this did Riva Cyn see, and yet it meant little. Around her the *shtetl* women were putting into motion the rituals of death. Somebody had gone to break ice, to bring water that would be used to wash Esther. The body had been laid on the floor, the shroud was lying ready. "Blessed be the true judge," said Hannah Toplin, as she walked into the room, repeating those age-old words that were supposed to give comfort.

But nothing could comfort Riva. Her mother had cursed her, and now her mother was dead. There was no going back, no changing her mind, no explanation or plea that could alter what had happened. For the truth was and the truth would always be that Esther had died unforgiving.

Riva dropped to her knees. "Why?" She was pleading with her mother. "Why did you reject me? Couldn't you understand that I have no choice?"

Riva blinked and stood up again. She could no longer see

properly: The room had become almost misty—shrouded in a thin film of grayness. Esther had only just died, she thought, and already the stove was acting up.

She blinked again, and the mist cleared. She looked around her. She saw her father, Berl, standing to one side, his eyes focused on a spot somewhere in the distance. He looked so solitary, she thought, so utterly alone.

She walked up to him, and placing one hand gently on his shoulder, she spoke his name.

He turned his head and looked at her. With an effort, he smiled at his only daughter. "It is better this way," he said. "She did not deserve to suffer anymore."

Riva nodded, for what else was there to do? Her hand lost its determination and began to slip off Berl's shoulder.

He turned suddenly and, catching at it, gripped it firmly.

"She thought she was doing the right thing," he said.

Riva glanced down as tears stung at her long black eyelashes.

"Esther loved you," Berl continued. "That is why she did not want you to leave."

Still Riva could find no words.

Berl let go of her hand. "Go outside," he urged, "and breathe in the fresh air of our country. Look at our world, the one you will soon be leaving." He patted her head, letting his hand rest for a moment on her long brown hair. "You are doing the right thing," he whispered. "You deserve a better life."

And then he pushed her away, gently and yet determinedly. He could not bring himself to watch as she stumbled blindly out of the room.

The *shtetl* looked different under the snow, under that smooth white blanket that covered the essential poverty of the place. It looked, thought Riva, almost peaceful.

The snow had a cleansing power, as it hid from view the thick black mud that the children constantly trod in and out of the houses. It covered the thatches on the closely packed houses, and filled in the holes in the roofs. It hung over the picket fences that separated the houses from the central pathway. And the snow was democratic: so thickly had it fallen that it had even covered the cross on the distant church that dominated the valley—a symbol of an alien culture in their midst.

As Riva stood there, she could almost pretend that she was

on her own in a fairy-tale wasteland. Only when someone briefly opened a front door would a staccato burst of conversation suggest that three families shared one home and four people one bed.

Riva pulled her brown shawl over her head and began to walk. She was a tall woman and a graceful one. She strode through the narrow streets, her head held high, her piercing blue eyes flashing in her olive face. She walked past women dressed as their forebears had, in long dowdy skirts, heavy shawls and scarves, past children swaddled in huge overcoats, their feet covered by calf-length boots, past even the *Shabbes klapper*, who had begun knocking on shutters, warning of the onset of Sabbath.

She acknowledged none of these sights. Instead, she walked beyond them, up the snow-covered slopes. She walked without thinking, out of the depths of the *shtetl*, through the first layer of pine trees, until she was surrounded by the tall, still forest.

Only then did she stop. She put one hand on her cheek and felt the warmth that her flight had engendered. I am alive, she thought, and my mother is dead.

She looked up at the spiky branches, covered in snow, which stretched above her as if they wanted to reach the very peak of the blue sky. In their midst, among soft cluster of powdery white, she thought she saw her mother's face.

And she remembered.

She remembered Esther's last words.

"Go," Esther had said. "Build your life. Take your children to suffer in a world apart from us. Go—but go without my blessing."

One lone tear fell from Riva's eye. It was followed by no others. I will not cry for my mother, she thought.

Neither would she listen to Esther. She was determined: She would leave this country, this place that delivered nothing but pain to her people. Her children would have a better life—that was her resolve.

A breeze rustled at the branches: A piece of snow dropped to Riva's feet. She looked up and saw that the image, that face that was almost as familiar as her own, was beginning to waver, was disappearing already.

"Mama," she whispered. There was no reply.

She left the forest, left it without a backward glance. She had no need to fix it in her memory. It was already part of her, and she would never forget it.

Riva walked fast and had reached the *shtetl* by the time she caught sight of her small family. They were walking closely together, her husband, Zelig, leading Haim by one arm, while he held Toleleah in the other. Zelig's face was white, his thin black hair that hung down the sides making him appear even paler. His shoulders were hunched, a habitual pose gleaned from years as a tailor. He was walking slowly, joylessly.

When he caught sight of Riva, he smiled tentatively, as if he did not know how best to react.

"Zelig is weak": Riva heard Esther's judgment of her husband ringing in her head.

Deliberately she brushed the echo away. As far as Esther was concerned, nothing Riva had done had been right: Of course her mother would reject the man she had chosen as a husband. Zelig was not weak. True, he had suffered much after his parents were killed in a pogrom, yet he had survived. That, surely, was a sign of strength. He knew what it was to be uprooted: He would be a good companion in their new life.

She smiled back at him and saw the relief in his eyes. She took one further step forward.

Toleleah stretched out two arms and jumped out of her father's arms. She nuzzled into Riva's breasts.

"My little dove," Riva murmured, and the tears that she would not cry for Esther came unbidden to her eyes. She clasped fiercely at her three-year-old daughter.

Toleleah struggled against the constraint: She wriggled and arched her back. She stared with round black eyes into her mother's face. "*Bobbe* died today," she stated.

Riva nodded.

"Hannah said she's gone far away," Toleleah continued. "Has she gone to South Africa?"

"Don't be silly," came Haim's shrill riposte.

Riva bent down, and depositing Toleleah on the ground, she put her arms around her son. His thin lips, she noticed, were blue with cold. His cheeks were red, but it would be unwise to attribute this to a result of youthful exertion. For the red was an angry one, a red of protest. It spoke of the effort that it cost Haim to walk, to run, and sometimes even to speak.

Riva looked up at Zelig. "He should be indoors," she said.

Zelig shrugged. "He wanted to be with you at this time. We all did."

And for the first time since Esther had died, Riva felt a connection to another human being. She put one arm around each of her children and looked up at Zelig.

"We will build a new life together," she promised, and found that she was smiling. She heard the rasp of Haim's breath as he sighed, almost in relief. She kissed him gently on the cheek. "I will guard you well," she said.

1

South Africa: 1906

"Dumi," Riva called, "don't forget the windows."

"Yes, missus."

"And the table must be polished."

Dumi was already halfway out the yard. He turned to look at Riva. There was a short delay. "Yes, missus," was his final, distant reply.

Riva stepped back into her kitchen. Her mood was so elevated that she would not be put off, not even by her houseboy's apparent rudeness. Actually it was no wonder that he was so anxious to get out of her way. She'd already told him about the windows and the polishing—told him twice, in fact.

Not that it mattered, she told herself: Kaffirs, she judged, were odd, one never could tell whether they heard one's instructions. Better to be safe and repeat herself than have one thing out of place for tonight.

For tonight was an important occasion. It was the Cyns' second anniversary in their Ferreirastown boardinghouse, and they had invited their closest friends to mark it. Riva was determined that it was going to be a celebration to end all celebrations.

She deserved it, after all. None of it had been easy: not the journey across Europe and down Africa, or the arrival in this war-torn country, or the trying to make ends meet in an alien society. Imported clothes were so cheap these days that Zelig's beautifully wrought suits found few buyers. His contribution to their daily income had become increasingly negligible.

It was Riva who had become the family wage earner. She had

worked a regular fifteen-hour day—baking, sewing, washing, cleaning, keeping livestock—and still there was never enough money or enough time. For four years she had known what it was like to be bone-tired every second of the day. On several occasions she had been at the brink of total despair. Her past life had haunted her. During her darkest hours she had thought that Esther was right: They should never have left Lithuania.

But the acquisition of the boardinghouse had been a turning point. Soon after arriving, Riva had realized that the only way they would ever be secure was to buy property. She had scrimped and saved, depriving herself of even the smallest luxury, in order to put a small deposit down on this particular house. Zelig had protested that the place was too run-down and their payments too large to be manageable, but Riva persisted. She'd got the measure of Jo'burg, even if she was convinced that she would never learn its languages. She knew how many single immigrants there were who would pay good money for a clean bed and a wholesome daily meal.

"Oy," she said out loud, "speaking of wholesome—it's time to get them out."

She pulled her long white apron over her head, and then carefully withdrew a tray of cheese *rugela* from her large stove. She prodded one of the pastries with a fork and nodded her head in satisfaction. Perfect, she thought. Her regulars would be well pleased. Putting the tray on the counter, she went to get the next.

"Can I come, Mama? Can I?"

Riva turned to find seven-year-old Toleleah standing by the door. The child was a mess—her face smeared with a thin layer of dust, her knee-length pinafore torn on one side and muddy on the other.

"What have you been doing?" Riva asked. She clucked her teeth.

Toleleah tossed her head in a kind of dismissal. "Playing," she said. "Can I come?"

Toleleah, Riva knew, was not being rude—just behaving as usual, direct, energetic, and to the point. Look at her now, as a childish voice called to her from the street. She didn't bother to go out: She just turned her head and yelled back. "Not now," she replied.

"Julia," repeated the voice.

"For godsake!" Toleleah shouted. "Can't you see I'm talking to my mother?"

Riva struggled to conceal the smile that came to her lips. She didn't really approve of the casual way her daughter negotiated street life, and yet sometimes she couldn't hide her admiration. The child was so knowing, attuned to the ways of the city in a way that Riva would never be. While Riva's days were centered on the home, her daughter lived a kind of double life: Indoors she spoke Yiddish and answered to the name of Toleleah, while in the streets English was her language and she was called Julia— the name that an ignorant customs official had given her.

"So can I?" Toleleah asked.

"If you change right now," Riva said. "And tell your brother to come along. He needs some fresh air."

By the time Riva had packed the *rugela* into separate containers, both her children were waiting patiently by the yard gate. They made a contrasting couple, Riva thought, as she hurriedly wiped the kitchen surfaces. Toleleah was so vigorous, her skin a tanned and healthy brown. Haim, on the other hand, was still pale and white, thin like his father and with a furrowed brow.

South Africa had cleared his health a little—better the dryness of Jo'burg's climate than the cold of their motherland—but Riva had long given up hoping that Haim would ever be entirely healthy. For the most part he was stable, but many were the nights when she had extra cause to worry, when she sat by his bed breathing with him in the vain hope that she could ease his pain.

Still, he looked well enough today, she thought, as she watched him listening to his ebullient sister, his head cocked on one side in an attempt to catch the flow of Toleleah's undisciplined chatter.

She took off her apron and flung her shawl over her shoulders. They were so different, her children, she thought once more, and yet they complemented each other. Haim brought Toleleah down to earth, and at the same time only Toleleah could make the serious Haim giggle and play like a youngster should.

Yes, she thought, I am well satisfied with them. She picked up her many boxes and walked toward them.

"Hurry now," she said. "We have much to do."

* * *

Supper was a grand affair. Riva had made sure that the table groaned under the weight of her excellently cooked food, and Zelig kept the wine flowing freely. Each guest brought a bottle or two, placing it beside the man of the house as they congratulated him on his family's success in this their new country.

They were all Jews, all immigrants. There were the least successful of them—the lodgers, who could not be excluded anyway, since their meals were paid for, and their other friends. The lodgers, too, were all old friends by now (Riva's boardinghouse was among the best, and only increasing wealth could motivate a person to move from it).

Danny Rabinowitch was one of the lodgers, and as he toasted her health, Riva thought fondly that no celebration would ever be complete without him. He was an argumentative man, agreed, but he knew how to enjoy himself and spent endless hours entertaining the children.

And then there was Fanny Woolf—not the most jovial of women, but she minded her manners. She'd been their first lodger, so for her this evening must also be tinged with memory. Beside her was ranged the Forman family—parents and two teenagers all equally taciturn. Jo'burg had not blessed them, and they were about to move to Oudsthoorn to try their hand at a bit of farming.

Their friends were there also—Hymie and Mitzie Cohen, their next-door neighbors, and Solomon Levine, the man who had met them off the train when they arrived, who had guided them through their first, confusing days in Jo'burg. And after supper there would be more people coming into the house, using this party as a way to assert their sense of belonging in South Africa, or just a way to forget the hardship of their everyday life.

By ten o'clock the dishes had been cleared away. A silence descended as the company digested their food. Haim yawned. Riva knew that he should be in bed, but she did not have the heart to send him off. Left to his own devices, he would fall asleep, and then Zelig would carry him up to his room. It was late, after all: Riva glanced at the clock—their pride and joy placed on top of the mantelpiece.

Toleleah saw the danger in that glance. If she wasn't careful, Mama would pack them off to bed, and then the evening would be over. Toleleah was not having that: She was determined to stay awake until midnight. She cast around in her mind for something to get the company going again and remembered something Mitzie had said earlier that evening. She turned to her. "*Muma* Mitzie," she piped up, "what is it you were going to show us?"

Hymie groaned theatrically. "You didn't tell them?" he asked.

"Of course I did," Mitzie replied. "We should keep all our efforts secret?" Ignoring Hymie's protestations, she got up, pushed her chair away from her, and stood in the center of the room, her arms outstretched. "Come on," she called.

Hymie appealed to the assembled company. "This woman will be the death of me," he complained. "My bones are old. But will she let me rest? Never."

"Never," Mitzie echoed. "Up you get. Hymie and I have been taking dancing lessons," she explained. "Tonight we will demonstrate."

Hymie pretended to grumble as he went up to his wife. He placed his arms around her. He fooled no one. Hymie, they all knew, loved being the center of attention: He would keep them all spellbound with his stories, and he was always inventing new and more bizarre forms of entertainment.

"Only one dance," he told his wife. "After all, we have no music."

But before they could begin, Danny leaped to his feet. "Wait," he cried. "I will be back."

Mitzie and Hymie, poised in the center of the big carpet, their arms held stiffly, each large and round, made a fantastic sight. "What is he getting now?" Hymie wondered out loud.

Nobody could hazard a guess. Danny was, after all, unpredictable. It was quite possible that, once out of the room, he would completely forget to return.

But Danny did come back. In his hand was a battered case.

"Don't tell me," Solomon shouted as Danny opened it, "that playing the violin is one of your accomplishments?"

Danny nodded. "I learned it once," he said. "Not well, but adequately. What tune would you like?" he asked of the Cohens.

"A waltz," Mitzie proudly replied.

Danny launched off into his own version of "The Blue Danube." It was a proficient, if eccentric, performance. The tune became almost raucous.

But Danny's rendering fitted in perfectly with the Cohens. They bent into a waltz that had little in common with the established drawing-room steps. The watching company roared with laughter as Hymie whirled Mitzie round the room, her layer of petticoats swirling around her. Up and down the two huffed and puffed, their faces growing red as they concentrated on their steps, giving full rein to their energy.

In the end it was Hymie who gave in. He collapsed, laughing, as he tried to regain his breath. He attempted to rise and bow when the others clapped, but he only succeeded in burying himself further in the deep armchair.

"I am too old for this," he huffed.

"Let us have some real dancing." Danny jumped to his feet. He began bellowing out one of the folk songs from the Old Country. He stood in the center of the room, held his arms out wide, and began to make wild circles.

Solomon, as Danny had expected, could not resist joining in. Soon the two of them were moving together, their arms waving, their heads spinning, their legs going up and down as they danced, always on the point of falling and yet always saving themselves. The rest of the company gathered round, clapping, singing, shouting encouragement, their numbers swelled by others who had dropped in to drink the Cyns' health.

The dancing continued for some time, as each adult demonstrated the specialty of his home district. Many were the disputations about which part of Russia and Poland had first created a particular step, but all were concluded good-naturedly enough.

Riva presided over the company, over the different conversations that ebbed and swelled in her living room, with a growing confidence. With one eye, she kept a watch on Haim's slowly drooping eyelids, and with the other she looked out for empty glasses, filling them from the splendid array of slivovitz and schnapps that Danny had produced.

Riva suspected that this party marked her own coming of age. She was established here—established six thousand miles from her birthplace with people who honored the memory of home and who, in their daily life, continued its traditions.

She had broken with the past, yet it still surrounded her, embraced her. The fear that she had betrayed her family was at last beginning to fade. The yoke of her mother's accusations might, she now hoped, drop from her shoulders. She was convinced Esther had been wrong. It was not a betrayal to leave the poverty and persecution of Lithuania: It was a liberation for both herself and her children.

She wiped a tear hurriedly from her eye. She laughed when Zelig, sensing his wife's precarious mood, pulled her to her feet. They danced, the two of them, danced to the sound of Danny's violin, to the accompaniment of their friends' urging, to the feeling of their own togetherness. They danced until they could dance no more, until midnight had come and gone, until it was time for the party to end.

"Do you think the boy is all right?" Hymie asked as they walked through the yard to their house. "He seems so frail."

Mitzie linked her arm to his. She, too, had noticed Haim's pallor, but now was not the time to speak of it. She knew how much Hymie valued his contacts with the two children. They were like grandchildren to him—replacements for those he would never get to know, the ones who were left at home. God knows how they would fare in the coming years.

She pushed the thought out of her mind.

"We are old," she whispered to Hymie as they strolled through their ever-open back door.

"Speak for yourself, woman," he answered, pinching her bottom.

Danny Rabinowitch was also worrying about Haim. As he lay in his hard single bed, he could hear the boy coughing. It was a harsh, racking sound, and Danny found himself breathing in rhythm to it, as if by doing so, he could encourage Haim to sleep more peacefully. Danny thought of going next door and seeing whether the child was covered up but decided against it. Toleleah, he knew, would still be awake, and his entrance would be sure to worry her. She had enough responsibility on her young shoulders already: He should leave her in peace. He would instead go fetch a glass of water. Perhaps it would still his nerves and help him to sleep.

Zelig was still sitting downstairs in their most comfortable of chairs, a look of contentment on his face.

The evening had been everything he desired. He had reveled in the gathering of their friends—all in his honor. It was these simple things that made life worthwhile.

He watched his wife as she trod slowly round the room, clearing the dishes and extinguishing the gas lights. She was a fine figure of a woman, his Riva—thickening a bit now, but still in her prime. He loved to see her move this way, her body in tune with its surroundings. He would imagine what lay beneath her stiff clothes. Soon they would be in bed together, and then he could explore her to his fill.

Riva turned around to see Zelig looking at her. She pushed a wisp of hair away from her forehead and went up to him. Delicately she sat down in his lap, put her arms around his neck, and kissed him slowly on the mouth.

"It was a lovely evening," she said. "Let's go upstairs."

2

Julia woke with a start.

She peered into the darkness, searching for the cause of her disruption, but everything was as it should be. She could hear Haim's breathing, the tread of the night-soil carriers as they went about their work outside, the distant clanging of the mine shaft: nothing unusual, nothing that might have broken into her dreams.

She was wide awake, but that didn't bother her. She smiled to herself as she stared straight at the tinsel stars that Danny had stuck on the ceiling.

Julia loved those stars. They made her feel safe, reminding her of the decorated fir trees that stood in the front parlors of the rich *goyim*. And, more important, they formed a special link between herself and Haim. Many were the evenings when her brother talked about those stars, weaving stories around them, fantastical, involved stories, in which Julia was always featured.

"That one is millions of light-years away," Haim would say as he pointed to the smallest. "No one else has ever seen it. But you, you get there in a second."

"How?" Julia would ask, prompting him to retell his fables.

She loved it when Haim played so with words. He was an expert, a wonderful constructor of fables. And best of all, when he wove his stories, he was the equal—no, not the equal, the master—of everybody. At these times Julia could forget that he was not as strong as other children.

"Saturn, Jupiter, Julianus," she whispered to herself.

Suddenly she jumped. A sound had filled the room, a horrible sound. It was eerie: a high-pitched whine followed by a sort of whistle.

It had come from Haim's bed.

Only when it was over did Julia find the courage to investigate. For protection, she wrapped a sheet around herself. Tiptoeing over to her brother, she looked down at him. She was, by now, accustomed to the dark: She could see that his eyes were closed.

"Haim," she whispered.

He gave no sign that he had heard. She stood for a long while, waiting in dread for the sound to recur. All she could hear was his quiet inhalation. Reassured, she turned away.

She had already taken a few steps when something occurred to her. Turning back, she placed a hand on Haim's forehead.

And then, abruptly, she removed it. For, expecting a slight clamminess, she had found instead that where her hand had touched his skin, it was even now burning.

Something was wrong, badly wrong.

"Haim," she said loudly.

Still he did not stir.

Julia dropped the sheet and fled from the room. She ran across the landing, and flinging open the door to her parents' bedroom, she opened her mouth. But no words came out of it. For she felt suddenly embarrassed at the sight of Riva and Zelig, who had thrown off their bedclothes and were lying entwined together in the middle of their bed. Julia could not bring herself to disturb them.

Julia left the room and went instead to Danny's.

There was nothing threatening about the way he slept. He was lying flat on his back, snoring. When Julia shook him, he grumbled and turned. She shook him again—more roughly this time. He opened one eye.

"You're snoring," she said.

"For that you wake me up?" Danny growled. "If I wanted such information, I would have married."

Julia's mouth turned down, and her lips trembled. "D-Danny," she stuttered.

He reacted immediately. He swung his legs onto the floor and, putting his arms around her, pulled her onto his lap.

"What's the matter, my little dove?" he asked.

"It's Haim."

"Another bad night?"

"I don't know," Julia whispered. "He feels hot."

"Let's go see then." Danny deposited Julia on the floor and grabbed for his flannel dressing gown.

Riva was praying silently. She had started doing so almost the minute that Danny woke her. She didn't know how she had guessed (even before she had seen her son) that something was worse than usual, but she had. As soon as she'd opened her eyes, the fear had gripped her.

She'd turned to Zelig. "What are we going to do?" she'd whispered.

He had looked away from her. "At least let's see Haim before predicting the worst," he'd said. He seemed angry.

At that moment she'd felt so alone that she had started to pray. She was not a religious woman. She went to *shul* only sporadically, and yet talking to God was what she needed: It was her way of stopping herself from falling into the pit of her own terror.

As she watched Dr. Levy bend over Haim, Riva stared fixedly at his face, trying desperately to read his expression. She could find no comfort in what she saw.

He had finished now. Gently he pulled the sheet up to Haim's chin. He glanced at her before nodding to himself as if confirming something.

"Let's talk outside," he said.

But once outside he did not talk. "I think I should discuss this with your husband," was all he said.

And with that, Riva knew that her worst fears were confirmed. She walked beside the doctor, down the stairs, into the kitchen, her lips still moving in prayer.

At long last Julia heard the front door slam. She did not budge. She was completely still as she watched her father come back into the kitchen, his face a deathly white. She watched as he stood beside his wife, as his hand rested on her shoulder. She saw that there were tears in his eyes.

"Will Haim be all right?" she asked plaintively.

"God willing," Zelig replied. He did not look at her. "Your brother is very ill," he said to the air. "He has a disease called pneumonia. The hospital can't do anything for him, so we will keep him at home. You must move out of his room."

"But Haim wants me there," Julia protested.

"Haim needs rest," Zelig replied firmly. "Get dressed now. Go play."

"Go and play, go and play": Those were the words that echoed in Julia's head. Her parents had not time for her: Every time she stepped into the house, she would be ordered out again.

Riva sat by Haim's bed and gazed at her son. He was so pale, she thought, so devoid of life. It made her feel so powerless. Desperately she wished she could breathe into him, that she could give to him her own strength.

I love you so, she thought. She picked up one of his hands and lifted it to her lips. He responded with a slight smile and a squeeze, but soon his hand was limp again, as if even that small gesture had been too much for him.

Her eyes filled with tears, and she looked away. No matter how bad she felt, she would not show her fear to Haim. She must be his strength, his rock onto which he could grip.

She watched the door as it opened to admit Zelig. She saw that he smiled cursorily at her before walking over to feel Haim's brow.

"Not so hot," he told her.

She nodded.

"He's getting better," Zelig said.

This time she couldn't bring herself to nod.

She knew that Zelig was doing his best, that he had taken on, as his role, the act of reassuring her. But the problem was that he wasn't very convincing; even Haim smiled at his predictions of early recovery. And Riva knew that nobody could reassure her, that nobody could help her throw off the feeling of doom that haunted her.

It had become part of her daily life, this feeling, something that she could transmit to no one but that nevertheless possessed her totally. She realized she had always carried it, since the day that Esther had died. She'd managed in the last four years to push it to the back of her mind, to lose it amid the hope of the new life. But Haim's illness had brought it flooding back with a vengeance. She felt now as though it would never leave her.

She looked down at her hands and smiled sourly. What hope, she thought, what new life? Her hands were symbols of her defeat. She had left her home, her family, her friends, and come looking for a better life: the cuts, the ravages, the harshness of her skin, showed how futile the search had been. South Africa had disappointed her: She knew with a finality that the gold that lay beneath its earth would never be hers.

And yet she had still remained optimistic. After all, her children were better off than she had been. They were getting an education, they could read already—surely their lives would be easier?

"If they live," she muttered. "Only if they live."

"Of course he'll live," Zelig said brusquely. Deliberately he softened his voice. "You must not give in to despair," he concluded.

Riva got up and walked to the window. She stared outside, stared at her daughter, who was getting off the yard gate. At that moment, Julia looked up. Riva shrank back into the room.

And worse than that, Julia hardly saw Haim. She was no longer allowed to sleep in the same room, and her daily visits were both restricted in time and closely monitored by her parents. They asked her continuously to keep clear of them. They had, they said, enough to worry about without her getting underfoot. "Go and play," they would repeat. As if she could play when she never stopped thinking, dreading, worrying, about what might happen.

"Toleleah," Fanny Woolf called. "Come wash your hands."

Julia jumped off the fence.

The meal was a joyless occasion. The Cyn table, formerly so laden, was now less than a shadow of its former self. Fanny had taken over the running of the household, and as a consequence, their standard of living had undergone a severe drop. Fanny, always suspicious of being taken advantage of, mercilessly hounded Dumi, who in turn responded by doing the very minimum required of him. Not that anybody really noticed. Meals were now grim affairs. Food was there to be consumed as quickly as possible.

Julia spooned the thin gruel into her mouth as fast as she could. She needed urgently to leave this place of silence.

And then, just as she was about to get up, Danny's voice cut through the air. "Toleleah is not happy," he announced.

Riva and Zelig exchanged one mutual guilty glance before Riva looked away.

"Zelig?" Danny prompted.

"I am sorry we have so little time for you," Zelig's voice ate at Julia. "I hope you understand."

"Yes," she said. She put down her spoon.

Fanny cleared her throat. "Prices," she said. "They go up continually. I think the shopkeepers are doing it deliberately: It's a conspiracy. . . ."

"The child must be allowed to spend time with Haim," Danny interrupted.

"He's too ill," Riva protested. "It would be bad for both of them, and besides . . ."

"I feel for you and your troubles," Danny gently answered.

"Danny," Fanny said, "is this your business? Shouldn't you—"

He silenced her with a glare. "I have to be honest," he told Zelig. "You have two children, and they have always been together. It is not right to separate them. Perhaps they can help each other. . . ."

"When Haim is feeling better," Riva said.

"Then, too." Danny looked sadly at her.

Julia could contain herself no longer. Getting up, she pushed her chair away. It hit the floor with a bang, but she didn't bother to pick it up. She ran, instead, outside.

As soon as the door had closed, she came to a stop and stood in the yard, searching for something to do. Her mind was crammed with thoughts, and she was trying to empty it as fast as she could, empty it of Danny's words, of her mother's distance, of her father's false cheer.

Desperately she ranged backward in time. She thought of the games that she and Haim used to play, the games that were theirs alone. She could not remember them.

She put her hands up to her forehead and dug her fingers in. Of course—they played by that jacaranda tree over there, it was their home away from home, their make-believe place in Lithuania.

There, beside the blossom of South Africa's heat, brother and sister had pretended to feel the cold of the winter snow, to hear the banging of the *Shabbes klapper* and the keening of the *shofar*, to smell the fragrance of a score of dishes of *cholent* warming in the baker's oven.

They played this way, lost in the world of make-believe that Haim was so good at creating. Julia was too young to remember their mother country, but when Haim talked of it, it became real.

Well, she decided, she would keep it going for him. She stood, and she remembered.

She was still at it when Zelig joined her.

"Your mother and I have agreed that you should spend more time with Haim," he said. "Would you like that?"

Julia kept her face down as she nodded. Against her bidding, tears began to course down her cheeks. She was blind to anything but her own sense of relief. She felt rather than saw her father kneel beside her, she felt his tears as they mingled with hers.

"It will be all right," he insisted, and Julia knew he was trying to convince himself. "It will be all right."

Haim rallied soon after Julia first visited him alone. He smiled at his sister's entrance, and squeezed her hand. There they sat, the two of them in silence, as the adults tiptoed out.

Finally Haim spoke. "I missed you," he said simply.

"I missed you, too," Julia answered.

"Don't be afraid," Haim whispered. "I'm not."

He sat up in bed, the first time he had done so in a long while. "I'm hungry," he announced.

Great was the rejoicing in the household when Julia transmitted Haim's message. Riva summarily evicted Fanny from the kitchen and put on a whole chicken to simmer. When it was soft, she strained the carrots and onions, obtained some ice from the fridge of Dr. Levy, used it to lift off the chicken fat, and proudly carried the nourishing broth to Haim.

He ate it all, and everybody remarked on how instantaneous was the transformation. Some color crept back to his thin face. He became animated for a while before falling into a deep sleep that they told each other was restorative. For the first time since Haim had taken ill, smiles were seen about the house.

"You see," Zelig told Riva when they were finally alone. "There is no need to be so pessimistic."

She smiled at him and nodded. "I must stop letting the past haunt me like this," she said, half to herself.

Husband and wife embraced, experiencing a closeness that they thought had gone forever.

But their optimism was short-lived. Haim's recovery didn't last. Dr. Levy was once more a frequent visitor. Always now, he shook his head sadly after seeing the boy.

One day, April 14, 1906, it was, he stayed almost twice as long as usual. Julia had hidden herself in Danny's room, and had left the door ajar so that she could hear what the doctor said. She heard him on the landing.

He was closing his bag as he waited for Riva to finish tucking Haim in. Julia could hear the doctor's heavy breathing and smell his odor of tobacco and methylated spirit.

"I'm sorry, my dear," he said. "It will not be long."

Julia heard a sharp intake of breath and then a sort of sliding noise. She knew that her mother must have fainted, but she did not come out. Instead, she waited while the doctor called for Zelig, and together they took Riva to her bedroom.

Only then did Julia creep out and make straight for Haim's room. Her heart was beating, her head whirling with what she had heard. She paused at the doorway and took a deep breath. When she was ready, she stepped inside, a brittle smile on her face.

Haim was sitting propped up in bed by a pile of feather pillows. He had thrown off the white sheet, and Julia could see, as if for the first time, how thin he had become. His bony legs stuck out of his pajamas, and his frail hand rested limply on the mattress.

She had an impulse to turn and flee, which she sternly resisted. She readjusted her face so that it bore a smile: As if her own life depended on it, she tried to pretend she was happy.

"The doctor has left," she said in a voice of practiced cheer.

Haim looked straight at her. "Am I going to die?" he asked.

"Of course you're not," Julia said. She almost believed herself. When Haim spoke, his voice was weary and somehow timeless. "Tell me the truth," he pleaded. "Somebody tell me."

Julia could not. She could not even speak. The tears welled up, and try as she would, she couldn't stop them. On and on they came, running down her face and onto her neck until her shirt collar was soaking.

All the while Haim just sat there, looking.

When the storm abated, he patted the bed. He seemed completely calm. Julia went and sat beside him.

"I needed to know," Haim said. "Somebody has to listen to me."

He began to talk, slowly and almost inaudibly. As he went on, his voice gained in strength. A torrent of words flowed from his mouth, one jumbled on top of the other, sentences piled helter-skelter but still coherent.

He talked of his fears, of his memories of the country in which they had been born, of their arrival in South Africa, of the games he would never again play, the meals he would never again eat.

At one point Julia had heard more than she thought she could bear. She jumped up.

"You're feverish," she said. "I must get Mama."

Haim gripped hold of her skirt. "Don't go yet," he begged.

So Julia reseated herself, listening, crying inside, enduring. Her whole spirit revolted against the expression of his pain, but something kept her rooted to the spot.

Haim, she knew, needed to talk. No one else would listen to him: She would have to bear it. She fought with her own demons as she sat there—with her own fears of death and darkness and of desertion. It was as if she survived Haim's words by breathing them in and storing them high up in her chest—she did not let them pass, now was not the time for her to collapse.

For twenty minutes Haim talked, until he no longer had the breath. He lay back, exhausted, but Julia saw that his face was calm.

"Thank you," he said simply. "Fetch Mama now."

Haim died that very night. They were all there: his family sitting beside his bed, Danny and Fanny at a distance, and Mitzie Cohen, who had come in to see how he was and stayed until the end.

At first Haim lapsed into a sort of half-waking state. Every now and then he would open his eyes and smile faintly before his eyelids flickered and his face went blank.

There was little conversation as they waited. The lights were turned down low, so that all the occupants of the room were bathed in a soft yellow.

Julia could not bring herself to leave the room. With all her might she held on to a fragile thread of hope. Haim might still recover, she told herself. He had to recover.

At ten minutes past twelve he stopped breathing altogether.

The room was completely silent—the absence of Haim's tentative hold on life spoke volumes. Everybody knew what had happened, but no one wanted to admit it. It was as if they were gripping tight to those last precious seconds, unwilling to move on to an acknowledgment of what had happened.

Even as they sat, the color was already draining from Haim's face.

It was Julia who broke the silence. "Mama," she cried as she flung herself toward Riva.

Riva did not move. Gently Danny disentangled Julia and held her back. Only then did Riva respond.

"Mama," was what she, too, shouted. She shook her head violently as she heard her own words. Her face crumpled, and she fell onto the bed, covering Haim with her own body.

For seven days Riva had sat *shivah* for Haim, sat in a straight-backed chair, her face streaming with tears over which she had no control. The following two nights she had gone to bed only to find herself lying wide awake, unable to think of anything other than death.

The second night Julia crept into their bed. She burrowed into the space between her parents, pulling the sheet over her head to muffle the sound of her sobs. Part of Riva wanted to reach out to her child, to comfort and to hold her, and yet she could not. She could not stretch her hands out again, she was lost herself, she could not help.

She pretended she was still asleep. She lay motionless while she felt Zelig stir. She breathed softly while he stroked at their youngest—their only—child's head.

"I miss Haim," she heard Julia cry.

"There, there," Zelig replied.

"I miss Granny, too," Julia sobbed.

Riva stiffened. How could Julia remember her grandmother? Only Haim could have done that.

"Why did they die?" Julia pleaded.

Riva groaned.

"I think you better go back to your own bed," Zelig said gently. "I will help you."

As the two left the room, Riva began once more to cry.

3

ALL OVER THE UNION LIVED THE AFRICANS OF SOUTH AFRICA: PEOPLE who had once inhabited the whole of the country, people whose land had been gradually taken over by white farmers, by mining companies, or by the government.

Nathaniel Bopape was one of these. The son of a Xhosa chief, Nathaniel had been born into a nation on the brink of defeat. His people had once roamed free in the Transkei: Now, their lands were restricted. They had once owned many head of cattle: Now, their herds were diminished. They had once been a stable community: Now, increasing numbers of men were forced to work on white farms to earn money with which to pay their taxes.

Nathaniel accepted all this, for why should he not? That was what life had always been to him: The stories of the old days were as fairy tales. Besides, he was a young man. He refused to allow his head to be filled with worry.

Since he was the oldest son of his father's principal wife, he would one day be chief. It was not an honor for which he longed. His father, he thought, was a wise ruler, and the chief's duties were many, his life onerous. Nathaniel preferred to roam the veld, to be with the animals, to sit under the wide skies and look up to the heavens, to revel in his youth, to feel his freedom.

Yet one day something happened to change all this. It started when the white man came, as he sometimes did, to the village. Two of them wearing a kind of brownish uniform. They nodded to the chief, pretending to defer to him, but Nathaniel sensed their insincerity. He did not like them, and he was afraid, so he stuck close by and listened to what they had to say.

And when they had gone, he confronted his father. "What did the government agents want?" he asked.

Chief Bopape raised one eyebrow. His son, he thought, had grown overnight: so tall and strong, a warrior in his build, a good boy whom the years would teach sense. He saw that Nathaniel was waiting for a reply. "Why do you ask?" he said.

"Please, Father," Nathaniel begged, "tell me what they wanted."

The eyebrow went up again. "While the agents talked to me," the chief began, "I chanced to look up to the roof. Through the grass I thought I saw a dark shadow, a shape in human form."

Nathaniel swallowed.

"Since I am a Christian, I do not believe in witchcraft," the chief continued. "I assumed that the shape was a man. And that man, I further assumed, was you. Was it?"

Nathaniel nodded.

"Then you know what the agents wanted." The chief took one step away.

Nathaniel paralleled and blocked the move. "What do you plan to do?" he asked.

"Let us test your English." The chief was prepared to be patient with his eldest son. "What exactly was it that the agents told me?"

"They said that every boy over the age of eighteen must pay a two-pound tax," Nathaniel mumbled. "Either that or work in the mines for three months a year."

"And did you hear what they said would happen if I refused to allow my people to pay?"

"They will dethrone you," Nathaniel said. "They will put a policeman in your place."

"Well done, my son," the chief said. Again he tried to walk away.

"But what will you do?" Nathaniel's demand pursued him.

"What would you have me do?" The first hint of exasperation showed on Chief Bopape's face.

"Resist," Nathaniel urged. "Resist as others have done."

"The others have been quickly punished," Chief Bopape replied.

Nathaniel was ready for that. "Our people cannot pay," he said. "They will be forced to go to the mines. Fathers will lose the labor of their sons, and their cattle will be further diminished. Is that not punishment?"

"I will not allow our people to be divided," Chief Bopape countered. "Unity is everything."

Nathaniel frowned. "What does unity signify when you accept the white man's pay?" he asked.

"What do you mean?" The chief was furious now, his brows like thunder.

Well, Nathaniel would not be intimidated. "I know they pay you," he said.

The chief shrugged. "That is the way of the world."

It was Nathaniel's turn to be angry. "That is the way of greed," he said. "You do as they demand because you have become their servant. You profit from the oppression of your people."

Chief Bopape took one step forward. He pushed his face so close to his son's that their breath intermingled. "Honor your father," he growled. And with that, he turned on his heel and marched resolutely away.

Two weeks went by. Nathaniel fumed, while his father pointedly ignored him. Even so, Nathaniel did not give up hope entirely: He convinced himself that the chief would see the truth in his forebodings: that when the chief finally told them all about the tax, he would urge nonpayment.

But Chief Bopape did not. When finally he called his people together to explain the poll tax, he took trouble over his presentation. He used the full force of his lifelong authority to get his own way.

He made the poll tax sound like a mere administrative detail: He spoke of the opportunity opening up for the young men to travel to the white cities and share in the wealth of the mines. He twisted the situation, presenting it as a victory—a personally arranged truce with the authorities with only a few minor drawbacks.

Nathaniel watched as the people swallowed their chief's explanations. Not all of them were fooled. There were dissidents, who gathered together to voice their disquiet. But when Nathaniel tried to talk to them, they turned their backs on him. He was Bopape's son. They did not trust him.

Nathaniel decided to leave home. He told nobody about his plans. The night after the meeting he went to bed. He did not sleep, he waited until only the jackals cried out around them. Then he got up and tiptoed out of the hut.

He worked slowly and methodically. He made a hole on each side of a tin can, and he attached a string between them. He took a long swig of water before filling the tin from the gourd in his hand. He put the tin to one side. Then he got out a piece of material that he had saved, placed a few items of food on it, and knotted three corners together. Satisfied with his arrangements, he hoisted the tin over his shoulder, grabbed the cloth and a long stick, and set out.

He was about to descend the hill that led away from his village when he heard a shout. He looked back to see his father running toward him. He stood stock-still.

"Where are you going, my son?" The chief's breath came out in gasps.

"I am leaving." Nathaniel's voice was deliberately firm.

"Don't go, my son," Chief Bopape said. He stretched out a hand and gripped Nathaniel's arm.

"I must." Nathaniel hoped that the chief could not hear the doubt in his voice.

"You are young and thick-blooded," Chief Bopape said. "I understand your impatience—I even applaud it. But"—he tightened his grip—"courage is not enough: One needs an old head to make decisions. All my life I have worked for my people. I have learned how to be wily. And the most important thing my advanced years have taught me is when to fight and when to bide my time."

Nathaniel shook his head. "Don't you see it's over?" he asked. "If we don't fight now, we may never have another chance."

"My boy," the chief continued, "you are young and you are arrogant. I know—and this is not something that makes me happy—how harsh is the world outside our small domain. Your journey will humble you. You will find out how right I am. But why should you be humbled? Stay with us—one day you will be chief."

Nathaniel pulled his arm away. "I will not rule over a beaten people," he replied.

The chief frowned, and by the light of a full moon, Nathaniel saw tears in his father's face. He averted his gaze.

"I can see that nothing will dissuade you from this foolish course," Chief Bopape said. "But I will not curse your going. I

wish you good fortune on your journey. I pray that you will
return a wiser and a healthy man."

Nathaniel turned his back on his father. "I will not return"
were the last words he said to his father.

During the long journey to the city Nathaniel learned what
real hunger meant: He learned what it was to have feet bleeding
and raw and yet have no choice but to continue. He learned
what it was to shiver at night, desperately tired but too scared
to sleep in case wild animals crept up on him.

He was forced to harden himself—not only physically but
emotionally as well. He trained himself to ignore the pain in
his body; he learned to suppress the distress that many of his
encounters engendered. He refused resolutely to give in to
despair.

He resisted despair for one reason and one reason only. For
it wasn't that Nathaniel had particular reservoirs of courage—
although he was a brave enough young man. It wasn't that he
could foresee the future—although he knew enough to understand that the white man had won. It wasn't even that he was
more than usually fit—although he had spent most of his life
working in the open. No, what kept him going was pride. He
would not, he resolved, return to the Transkei a beaten man.
He would not allow his father to smile as he limped his way
home. This he knew with a deathly certitude.

But by the time he arrived in Johannesburg, Nathaniel also
knew that unless he got money quickly, he would be too weak
for anything other than death. He had to find a job.

And that was when Nathaniel learned something about irony.
For if he was to avoid the humiliation of domestic service, there
was only one other course of action left to him: to get a job in
the mines, to work in the very place that had caused the irrevocable break between himself and his people.

Never a humorous man, Nathaniel did not laugh at this twist
of fate. Neither did he hesitate. If he must work in the mines,
he decided, then he would do so. He chose a particular site, and
then he waited.

"Hey, *kaffir*, get away from the gate, dammit."

The shout startled Nathaniel. He turned to find himself facing two furious white men, men of the type he knew only too well: two touts for mine labor.

Behind them stretched a long line of weary Africans.

"Move, I say," shouted one of the men, "or I'll kick you to hell and back again."

Just then the gates to the mine compound were opened. Nathaniel inched to one side. He ignored the continued curses; he ignored everything. He disregarded the look of defeat in the faces of the exhausted new recruits: He had no time for pity, he must put his plan into action before he was summarily ejected.

As the gates began to close, Nathaniel slipped inside. Purposefully he separated himself from the line of new arrivals. He walked toward the man he had already targeted.

He passed a series of low shacks, windowless and dark—these must be the sleeping places for the miners. Their doors were open, and smoke issued from each of them.

The ground outside these shacks, a kind of communal meeting area, was uneven and desolate, broken only by the waste products of everyday life. To one side were huge concrete baths, around which miners jostled for places.

It was worse, this place, far worse than he had expected. It was so dirty and so confined: Look at the way the men were caged into their living places, eating, working, sleeping in the same dusty place. It was inhuman, the way they were treated. Nathaniel's courage almost deserted him.

"Hey you, boy," came a shout. "*Voetsak*."

Nathaniel glanced over his shoulder. He saw one of the mine policemen, the kind that had stood guard by the tall gate, running toward him, baton at the ready. Nathaniel forced himself to increase his pace. He was tired, and he only managed to reach his target, a redheaded man, at the same time as the policeman.

The white frowned as these two natives wheeled to a stop in front of him.

The policeman spoke first. "I'm sorry, *baas*," he said. "I'll see to this."

The redheaded one nodded impatiently. But when he turned to go, he found that Nathaniel was blocking his exit.

"I'm looking for work," Nathaniel said.

"Then return to your reservation and contact a labor recruiter," the white man said. Over his shoulder he inclined his head at the policeman.

The policeman put one hand on Nathaniel's shoulder. Nathaniel shrugged it off.

"I will not go back," he said.

The white man was perplexed. "Look here," he argued. "You must know it's against the rules to hire labor on the spot."

Nathaniel did not reply. He stood there, his eyes on the white man, his gaze steady.

The white man was unused to so close a scrutiny from blacks. It made him uneasy. He shifted from side to side: Finally he put his callused hands into his trouser pocket and came out with some coins. He thrust them at Nathaniel.

"Take these, boy," he said, "and buy yourself some food."

Nathaniel did not move. "I am looking for work," he insisted.

The policeman breathed in sharply.

Nathaniel guessed that he had gone too far, but there was no backing out now. If he took the money, if he turned on his heel and left the compound, then he would be admitting defeat. And he could not do that: He would not return home.

He opened his mouth to say something, anything, as he saw that the white man was looking ready to shout. He did not know what he could do to change the situation: He just knew that he had to try.

But before the words could form in his mouth, another man, a fourth party to this discussion, stepped forward. "We're one short today," said this man. "Elias was just now taken to hospital. We could do with a young man on our squad."

"Pick somebody from the new arrivals," the white man replied.

"Ag, but have you seen them?" said the stranger. "Not one of them is even half as strong as this man. This one will make all the difference to our output."

"But the compound manager . . ." the redhead began.

"You could tell the compound manager it's a special case," the black man suggested.

The white man scratched his head.

"Tell the manager that this one can read," the man continued. He turned to Nathaniel. "You can read, can't you?" he asked.

Nathaniel nodded sullenly.

The white man looked relieved. He nodded his head in what Nathaniel took to be consent, and then briskly walked away.

Nathaniel should have been grateful, he knew he should. He glanced sideways at the stranger, a tall man, a big man whose hair was already beginning to gray and whose eyes were bloodshot and lined.

"Tiny Zuma," the man said. He held out one large, callused hand.

Reluctantly Nathaniel proffered his own hand. He was feeling less than grateful. He needed no one's help: His decision to come here was his own, and no old man, especially a Zulu, was going to bail him out. "Nathaniel Bopape," he said sullenly. He turned to go.

"You know what to do then?" Tiny called after him.

Embarrassed, Nathaniel stopped in his tracks. He turned and shook his head.

Tiny was grinning, Nathaniel's antipathy deepened. "You're on my team," Tiny said. "We're going under soon. Come, I will find you something to eat."

"I'm not hungry," Nathaniel said, ignoring the lurching of his stomach.

"You were lucky," Tiny said as he led Nathaniel around the compound. "That man is better than most. If you'd approached most of the other foremen, they would have broken your black back for the cheek."

"I know," Nathaniel said. "I've been watching. I chose him deliberately."

"You would have got nowhere without my interference," Tiny insisted.

"There are other mines," Nathaniel answered. "I would have found something."

Tiny snorted, but he did not reply. He had no need to puncture the boy's arrogance: The mines would see to that. For the mines humbled all men—even arrogant puppies like this one.

They went beyond the compound, past ugly slag heaps, past the red-hot smelting works, the noisy processing plant, and onward to the mine shaft. When they reached it, Tiny showed Nathaniel where to take his place in line.

Nathaniel picked up the tools Tiny handed him, and he endured the long journey underground. Tiny saw in Nathaniel's face the same look of panic that he had once experienced—the same look that newcomers always had and that some could never lose.

"Stick close to me," Tiny said.

Nathaniel acted as if he hadn't heard, or as if he couldn't care less. But, Tiny noticed, he did stay close.

For fifteen hours they labored side by side. Nathaniel was hungry, tired, unused to the endless noise, the heat, or the danger. He was allocated the simplest and the most strenuous of jobs—lashing. For fifteen hours he must dig for pieces of ore and rock.

As he lifted his pick in the air, an image came to Nathaniel: an image of his last glimpse of his father. He launched the pick viciously into the ground.

"Slow down," Tiny advised, "or else you will tire yourself out."

The pick went up again: Down it hit, up and down, up and down, until the sweat poured off Nathaniel's brow. And yet when he looked about him, he saw that his pile was smaller than the other miners', that the wagon stood waiting by him for much longer. The observation only increased his frenzy. Viciously he struck again at the earth.

And after half an hour he collapsed, panting, to the ground.

Tiny let him lie awhile before handing him a mug of water. "Now slow down," he said. He hauled the boy up to his feet.

For what seemed like eternity, they labored side by side. Only at the end of fifteen hours were they hauled back into the daylight. Nathaniel was beyond the point of total exhaustion. He took one step into the fresh air and his feet went from under him. He lay sprawled in the dust, uncaring.

He might have lain there forever. But through his half-closed eyes he could detect a shape blocking the light. It irritated him: He had had enough of darkness, he craved the bright. He reached out a hand to swat at the form, but it merely moved back and continued to cast its shadow.

Nathaniel opened one eye wide. He saw that Tiny was standing there, two tin plates in his hand. As soon as Nathaniel looked up, Tiny passed him one of the plates.

Nathaniel nodded a curt thanks. His stomach lurched again as he looked down at his plate. He took in the pulp of mealie-meal, the lumps and the mush. He spat on it, and threw it to the ground.

The gesture provoked laughter from the miners who were squatting all around.

"Ayiee, Tiny," called one of the miners. "Your new protégé does not eat *mageu*."

"He prefers the dirt of pride," said another.

Ignoring these jeers, Tiny scraped the food out of the dust. When he had finished, he handed the plate to Nathaniel.

Again Nathaniel discarded it. "I will not eat rubbish," he said.

"Then you will starve," Tiny replied. "When you become too weak, they will eject you from the mine."

"There are worse fates," Nathaniel answered.

"And who will pay your tax?"

"I care nothing for taxes," Nathaniel snapped, before dragging himself upright and walking away.

For two days Nathaniel ate only an occasional crust of bread, which he washed down with large gulps of water. The other miners glanced at him askance. They had seen it happen before— a boy wasting away before their eyes. They told Tiny that he was onto a loser.

But Tiny didn't give up on the boy: Tiny was a stubborn man. He watched as Nathaniel grew daily weaker. He did not speak out, because he had got the measure of the boy: He knew it would do no good. Instead, he stuck close by Nathaniel, doing all he could to decrease the boy's work-load, knowing full well that the other miners mocked him for his foolish generosity.

Finally, on the third day, Tiny set his own food aside. "If you will not eat," he said, "then neither will I."

He placed his full plate on the ground and squatted down beside it. He gazed into the distance and whistled through the gap in his teeth.

Nathaniel pretended that he had not heard, but out of the corner of his eye he looked at Tiny. This man, he knew, this man who forced himself upon Nathaniel, must have earned his nickname on account of his bulk. For Tiny was tall and had once been broad: Even now, he was stronger than most of the other workers. But his body showed signs of illness, his muscles had begun to waste. Tiny had the coughing sickness, Nathaniel heard others say, his life had been shortened.

Well, thought Nathaniel angrily, why should he suffer on my account? I never asked him to. "Eat," he said gruffly. "You need your food."

"Why should I?" Tiny asked. "Since you obviously don't need yours."

They sat together, Tiny whistling, Nathaniel thinking furiously. Against his better judgment, against his vow that he would never again trust anybody, Nathaniel liked Tiny. He saw the respect the others paid this man: He knew he was privileged to have been adopted by him.

And in addition, Tiny was playing one card that was a winner. For Nathaniel was starving. He was a young man, and his body needed sustenance. True, his pride was strong, but his hunger strike had not bolstered it.

The inevitable happened: Nathaniel broke. He picked up his plate. Tiny mirrored his action. Nathaniel spooned some of the mush into his mouth: So did Tiny. Soon they had both finished.

"The food is terrible," Tiny said. "But to starve yourself is a way of signaling defeat."

Nathaniel laughed hollowly. He gestured around him, pointing at the barrenness of their surroundings. "What is this, if not defeat?" he asked.

"While we breathe, while we think, we have the capacity for action," Tiny said. "When we die without a fight, then we are nothing but dead *kaffirs*."

Nathaniel threw his plate away from him. "Why are you telling me this?" he demanded. "Why bother with me? What do I matter to you?"

"I was once young," Tiny replied.

"So was everybody," Nathaniel said. He indicated some miners who were lounging under a tree in the distance. "So were they. And yet they care nothing for others."

Tiny shrugged. "Until our people learn that only by uniting and protecting each other can they win, we will stay in bondage."

Nathaniel narrowed his eyes. "Unity!" he scoffed. "You sound like my father. He betrayed us in the name of unity."

"Your father took the wrong course," Tiny said. "But unity is what we need."

"What is this we you talk of?" Nathaniel scoffed. "You are Zulu, I am from the Xhosa nation."

Tiny moved with lightning speed. He threw himself at Nathaniel.

"We are all people!" Tiny shouted. "The *baas* will tell you that we are Swazi, baSotho, Zulu, Xhosa, Tswana. . . . but all I see are men: Men who live under a common oppressor." His voice began to calm. "The *baas* says that a Zulu such as myself and a Xhosa such as yourself," he said, "can never be friends. But we *can* be friends: We *will* be friends." He got up and moved away. "Never forget that, Nathaniel," he said. "I will teach you many things, but the need for unity is the most important."

4

"KWELA, KWELA," THE *INDUNA* SHOUTED. "GET IN LINE."

Nathaniel bent his back forward and straddled his hands against the long low wall. He looked down the row of men—men of different ages and origins, their skin caked with the mud of the mines, their faces expressionless, men who were humiliated in their nakedness.

The searches were part of their daily routine. The *indunas*—black overseers who did the white man's dirty work, their knobkerries and assegais always at hand—would marshal a group of miners into the main compound and order them to take off their clothes.

There the men would wait, shivering as they cooled off from the heat of their labors underground, while one of the *baases* walked leisurely down the line, probing here, gratuitously insulting there.

"What is the sense of this?" Nathaniel muttered.

Beside him, Tiny snorted. "After all your months in the mines, you ask for sense?" he whispered.

There was uncharacteristic bitterness in Tiny's voice. Puzzled, Nathaniel glanced sideways at him. He saw how heavily his friend leaned against the wall, his body aching to collapse after a shift that he should never have been forced to endure.

"Why don't you report sick?" he asked.

Tiny shook his head in exasperation. "Because I have seen the hospital," he said.

Nathaniel did not argue, for he knew just what Tiny meant. The hospital was a disgrace, a halfway house between the hell of underground and the solitude of the grave. Mine doctors, he reflected, might just as well have been trained as undertakers, for all the good they did.

O my father, he thought sadly. Do you know where you are sending the young men of our village? Do you not listen to the tales that they bring back?

There were so many ways to die in the mines. Daily rockfalls claimed lives; undetonated dynamite, sealed by earth alone, went off regularly, killing outright those unfortunate enough to be closest: malnutrition combined with unhealthy conditions sapped the strength of even the strongest men.

So many ways to die it was better not to think of it.

The white man on inspection duty was a bastard among bastards. He reveled in his duties. There he strolled, slowly, savoring every minute, a sarcastic grin on his face. Even as Nathaniel watched, the man went up to one of the miners and poked him in the back. The miner flinched.

"What's the matter? You got a pain there?" the white man asked.

The worker did not reply. The white man jabbed him once again before continuing down the line.

Nathaniel ground his teeth. I will not stand here like a dumb ox if he tries anything with me, he promised himself.

"Keep calm," Tiny Zuma whispered. He tried to make it sound like an order. Nathaniel had grown up considerably during his sojourn at the mine, but he was still prone to sudden attacks of rage. It was understandable—the boy had been born to rule, not to serve—but it was also very dangerous. "Keep calm," Tiny repeated.

He need not have worried, because the white man had had enough entertainment for one day. He threw a cursory glance at the remaining laborers before nodding to the *induna*, who shouted to the men to get dressed.

Their ordeal was not yet over. They had to queue up outside, waiting to collect the pieces of paper that proved they had worked their shift and were thus entitled to food. The queue was peaceful enough that day. It often wasn't. By this point in the process tempers were frayed, and an inadvertent word or movement could cause trouble that would flare into combat.

That was another way one could die in the mine: being killed waiting for a slip of paper.

The ritual was an unchanging one. Having obtained their meal slips, Tiny and Nathaniel walked side by side to the huge concrete baths. They waited as patiently as they could while others washed themselves or their clothes. When it was their turn, they stripped and splashed on themselves water that was no longer clean, before dressing again.

At last they could collect their food. Metal plates in hand they waited for the mealie-pap, which formed their staple diet, to be ladled in.

A cold wind was blowing through the compound.

"Inside?" Nathaniel asked.

Tiny shivered and nodded wearily.

They entered a long shack constructed from wood and iron. In it, forty-five grown men slept on concrete bunks that were built one above each other, stacked like shelves. There was no other furniture, no cupboards and no lockers: Those clothes that were not kept in the bunks for use as pillows were hanging among an array of bicycles on the ceiling.

The place was not even weatherproof. The walls of the room had been hurriedly constructed, and many were the holes roughly patched by old pieces of material. In the center of the room stood the *imbandla*—a big tin of hot coals that was their only form of heating.

Squatting on the earth floor, Nathaniel began to swallow his food. He stared straight ahead as he did so. He would never get used to the rations, even though he knew better now than to throw them out.

"*Nyula* today," commented Tiny, referring to the watery gravy that qualified as a ration of stew meat. Nathaniel grunted in reply.

Tiny did his best to eat without tasting. It truly was revolting stuff. Today it was said to contain meat, but the only evidence of this that Tiny could see were a couple of weevils that he had pushed to one side. He ate mechanically, suppressing the cough that rose to his throat in reaction to the noxious fumes from the *imbandla*.

He was, he noted with detachment, feeling worse today. Well, that was only to be expected. He had started coughing thirteen months previously, and the racking pain in his chest had not let up since. He had seen this happen to other workers: They had gradually got thinner, until they could move no more. The unlucky ones had been taken to the mine hospital and left to die.

Not me, Tiny thought to himself.

He was determined to avoid this fate. He had saved up enough to go home, and he would make sure he would do so before his time came. The only thing that kept him from going now was his urge to teach Nathaniel.

Tiny had once thought of himself as a modest man. Now, he knew that he was in fact unbearably vain: He had the most ambitious of plans—to nurture another human being so that he might carry out his own self-appointed task of organizing the mine workers.

"I better hurry," he said to himself.

Or at least he had meant to say it to himself. When Nathaniel looked at him, he realized he had uttered the words out loud. He grinned foolishly—playing the uncharacteristic fool. The dissimulation set him off on a coughing fit.

Concern showed on Nathaniel's face. "Let's go outside," he suggested when Tiny was finally still, "where the air is clearer."

As the two men strolled into the open, into a blast of chill wind, Nathaniel saw Tiny gasp. At once he regretted his suggestion. The air inside was polluted, but perhaps Tiny needed to be in the warmth.

"Is it bad?" he asked.

Tiny shrugged off the question. He squatted down. "We were talking of wages," he said. "Let us continue."

Nathaniel took his place beside Tiny.

"In 1898," Tiny lectured, "they paid an unskilled miner forty-seven shillings, one penny. By 1901 this had been reduced to twenty-six shillings eight pennies. The mine owners had used their war to almost halve our income." Tiny stopped to give the cough that had welled up full reign. He spat onto the ground—an action that served the dual purpose of both showing his disgust and of getting rid of the phlegm that clogged his lungs.

Nathaniel tried to close his ears to the noise. He couldn't stand it when Tiny coughed so. It tore at his guts to acknowledge how sick this man who had adopted him was.

Yes, he thought to himself. Adopted is the right word. Tiny is my father.

He glanced sideways and noted just how much Tiny had shrunk as the phthisis ate into him.

Well, he would rather not think of it. "Why did the workers accept the cut?" he asked disingenuously.

Tiny shook his head grimly. "Ah, but they didn't," he said. "They stopped coming to the mines. They refused to work at the new rates. So what did the capitalists do?"

While Tiny paused to take a gulp of air, Nathaniel waited.

"They imported Chinese laborers," Tiny continued, as if there had been no break. "They herded them onto boats and into compounds from which there was no escape. They waited for the taxes to bite hard on our people before they again recruited black labor. The Chinese were pawns in their game of Divide and Rule."

He pointed around the compound. Nathaniel saw that at the mine shaft a gang of laborers was just appearing. The men walked with effort, exhausted from their shift, their bodies covered in grime: The sweat had long since dried on them because of the three hours they had to wait while the skips gave priority to transporting rock.

"We are all men," Tiny said, as his hand moved on. "We all suffer the same fate. And yet we pretend to be different."

Nathaniel followed Tiny's finger. All over the open ground that joined their living quarters sat men on tin drums, talking, sewing their fragile clothes together, using stones to play their complex games. In one corner Nathaniel could see a group of youths, some squatting, some standing, tending to each other's hair and making the ornaments that adorned their otherwise bleak garments. He knew that each group of men would talk the same language: that they would fall silent should a stranger appear in their midst.

How long can we endure this? Nathaniel thought. How long?

There was a group of men, friends of Tiny's, sitting under a sickly tree. They were talking animatedly, disputing, shaking their heads. As Nathaniel watched, one of the group rose. He turned and came straight toward Tiny.

The man had long since finished his shift, and he was ready to go out of the compound: On his shoulder was a brightly colored blanket that proclaimed him a Zulu, his earlobes were long and looped. He nodded to Nathaniel, and then greeted Tiny as a brother. He knelt down. He began talking in Tiny's ear.

Nathaniel watched Tiny's face as the man whispered. He saw a change come over it. Gone was the flush of passion that so recently suffused it, replaced instead by a look of pain. Nathaniel strained to hear what was being said, but all that came his way were Tiny's exclamations that punctuated the other man's speech.

The man got up, nodded at Nathaniel, and walked away.

"What's up?" Nathaniel asked.

"Chief Bambata has been defeated," Tiny said gloomily.

"Who's Bambata?"

"He led an uprising with the help of Chief Dinzulu and fled to the Nkandla forests. He fought for a long time, but finally they tracked him down along with five hundred of his warriors. They captured and murdered him. They are displaying his head at the prison to warn others of the fate that awaits them should they resist."

"Others will follow him." Nathaniel tried to ease Tiny's obvious distress.

But Tiny shook his head. "The change has come," he said. "No longer can we resist the armed might of the white man. Four thousand have died, fighting with spears and shields against machine guns. We have lost too often."

Nathaniel shot a worried glance at Tiny. This defeat must indeed be bitter. Never before had his friend talked with such pessimism, never had he told of something bad without adding something good.

"We will organize again," Nathaniel promised. "We will build anew."

Tiny smiled. "You are saying my lines now, Nathaniel," he said. He turned his head, and his eyes seemed to glaze over. "I have taught you all I know, Nathaniel." His voice was muffled. "And now you have the advantage over me. For you have your youth and your strength. When I am dead, you must go on fighting."

"Don't speak of death," Nathaniel protested.

Tiny clicked his tongue, his voice strengthened. "The one truth we can never escape is death, my son," he said. The coughing came again, and this time it was worse than ever. It gripped him like the mine dust, it took over his energy: So fierce was it that he almost blacked out.

But when it was over, all sign of emotion had disappeared from Tiny's face. "Newspapers," he said, "will distract me from my illness. We have a few hours off. Go to the *kaffetaria* and stock up on our provisions. After that, you will find the papers and bring them back."

"But—" Nathaniel protested.

"Go now," Tiny instructed. He smiled craftily. "If you're lucky, your path may cross with that woman who is so often in your thoughts these days."

"I never . . ." Nathaniel began.

Tiny waved him away. "Go," he said. "And at least I will get some sleep."

As Nathaniel strode out of the compound, he cut a striking figure. Hard work in the mine, and perhaps a belated growth spurt, had hardened him, filled out his physique. He had muscles now where once had been only flesh: His neck, once smooth, was covered in sinews of strain. But that was not the only reason why the eye would be drawn to Nathaniel. For this young man, the miners thought, had something extra: confidence, a certain bearing that made people look twice at him.

He was the focus for much gossip in the mine. The white managers, engine drivers, banksmen, and onsetters didn't know what to make of him. He was educated, fluent in English and acquainted with more than one of the African languages. He could be, they thought, of use to them.

They tried to buy him, offering him gang-leader status, but Nathaniel refused. Having once rejected the leadership that was his by traditional right, he certainly wasn't going to help the white man by disciplining his companions. He even refused the job of *sibonda*—a man elected by his roommates to keep the peace, because he saw how the white *baas* sought information from those who accepted this position.

But he couldn't refuse the demands of the other workers. He was one of the few literate men in the group, so he was kept busy writing their letters home. As a result, his network was larger than was normal among the miners.

But even so, few of the miners felt they understood him. He talked willingly of politics, of oppression, and of fighting back, but never of himself or his home in the Transkei.

To add to the enigma, he rarely left the compound. In truth, the opportunities to do so were fairly limited. The mine owners had no desire to acclimatize their laborers to city life. They had been brought to work. Once their contracts were over, they would be summarily returned to the countryside—allowed to come back only if they renewed.

And yet the men were not entirely slaves. They had to be

allowed some freedom of movement. They were forced to sleep in the compound; they worked crippling hours, but they did have some time off.

The younger of them grabbed at this time: They queued for exit permits, and they rushed outside to lose themselves in an orgy of forgetfulness.

Not so Nathaniel. The bustle of Johannesburg confused him, the shebeens revolted him. He had a large network of contacts, but few friends other than Tiny. He separated himself from the other youths, just as he had been separated at home. He did not do as those who, torn from their homes, sought solace in drink and *dagga*. He treated liquor as if it were poison—avoiding both it and those who were under its influence.

He could not, however, totally ignore the outside world. There were things he needed that could not be obtained within the compound confines, small items that made his diet slightly more acceptable, some needles and thread to keep his clothes together. These could only be bought from the *kaffetaria* that stood just outside the mines' gates.

He might have done without these purchases if not for the fact that Tiny had his own small demands. Every week there was something he needed. He asked, nicely, of course, that Nathaniel buy them for him. Such a trickle of requests were there that sometimes Nathaniel suspected Tiny of manufacturing needs in order to persuade Nathaniel to leave the compound.

Nathaniel had become accustomed to his outings, and he had a routine to which he tried to adhere. He would go straight to the *kaffetaria* and get his acquisitions over with. Then he would walk alone, always alone, as he took in the sights of the city.

"Hey, Nathaniel," someone called. "Come join us."

Nathaniel turned and smiled. He waved his hand casually in the direction of the group of miners, meaning to imply that he might choose to come talk with them in a while. But the gesture never fulfilled its intention, for his arm got stuck halfway. He spotted her amid the group.

She was a woman of about his age, a relatively new arrival in the city. Nathaniel had seen her first some weeks ago, and since then his eyes were always on the lookout. He studied her intently, taking care, all the while, to conceal his interest.

She had an easy manner about her, and yet he could see that she was not a loose woman. She dressed in respectable "white" clothes, to which she added a fillip of her own—a gay scarf around her head, a handkerchief tied to her wrist.

She was the object of much attention from the miners. After all, few African women had been allowed to travel to Jo'burg, and those who did were of a certain type. They were gay, loud, and ready for fun. Not so Evelyn (Nathaniel had gone to some lengths to discover her name). She tended to be quieter, more dignified somehow, but with an undeniable appearance of inner strength. Her whole appearance stated that she took life on her terms alone.

Nathaniel had once caught her looking at him. She had stared straight into his face as if summing him up. And then she had smiled and turned away.

The episode had left him acutely embarrassed—angry, even. What right had she to stare at him so? What did she want from him? He resolved to avoid her.

Nathaniel let his hand fall down to his side. As he watched, he saw the woman peel off from the crowd and begin to walk to the *kaffetaria*.

Nathaniel was in total confusion. She had seen him—he knew she had. If he went in, she would think he was following. Well, he would have his walk and come back later, when she would have finished her business.

He turned around and began to stroll in the opposite direction. As he walked, he felt as though eyes were boring into his back. Something was pulling him back. Determined to resist it, he continued on his way. He didn't appear to notice that he was slowing down.

5

BRISKLY ZELIG CYN WALKED THE LAST HUNDRED YARDS TO THE *kaffetaria*. He was feeling better: Once again, he had successfully managed to use the journey to work to shake off his misery. By the time he arrived, he would be ready to stand behind the counter and think of nothing but handing over the right goods and supplying the right change.

On the face of it, the job was a killer—the conditions cramped, the hours long, the breaks short, and the pay insubstantial. The end of each shift on the mines would bring a crowd of black miners jostling to buy the soap, material, sewing thread, and bits of food that filled out their meager rations. White assistants struggled to serve this mass of black humanity who shouted jovially to each other in languages the whites could never comprehend.

There was, in fact, nothing to recommend it. It was the sort of employment that only the destitute would consider.

And yet it served Zelig's purposes well. For as he stood behind the counter that separated him from the endless stream of black humanity, he could at least count his own blessings. No matter how bad his life, these people were worse off.

At least I have a home, he thought, as he pushed the door open.

He frowned to himself. True, he had a home, but what kind of home was it?

His wife was as businesslike as she had always been; she ran the boardinghouse with admirable efficiency, and yet something was missing. She was cold, absent. She spent her passion at *shul* or in her attempts to control their daughter. To Zelig she displayed little other than a combination of brisk kindness and silent contempt.

Sometimes he suspected that Riva's aloofness sprang more from inner pain than a deliberate disdain for him. He thought, perhaps, that he should talk to her about it. But when he'd once tried, she'd looked at him so fiercely that he'd never dared raise the subject again.

He took another step forward. And found that his way was barred by a woman who was standing motionless, lost in her own thoughts. Zelig was hardly conscious of her presence: He was on automatic pilot and, besides, she would soon move out of the way.

When she didn't, he bumped straight into her.

He glanced at her, amazed. "Did you not see me?" he demanded. "Or was that deliberate cheek?"

The woman did not answer. She was, Zelig observed, a tall, strong woman, her skin a rich reddish brown, her eyes deepset and defiant. Those eyes spoke for her. They seemed to be asking what right he had to expect precedence.

Zelig flushed. "Never mind," he muttered. He walked away.

This, he thought as he lifted the flap of the serving counter, is what South Africa has done to me. I have been reduced to its level.

Zelig had nothing but contempt for whites who regarded contact with blacks as polluting. After all, he still remembered how he was once an outcast in the land of his birth, considered less than human because he had been born a Jew.

And yet he had fallen into the same trap. So accustomed had he become to black people getting out of his way that he felt outrage when one of them failed to.

He sat on a high stool, and resting his elbows on the counter, he put his face in his hands. "Oy, what am I becoming?" he muttered to himself.

He started when he felt a hand on his shoulder.

"You okay, man?" one of the other assistants asked.

Zelig smiled. "Sometimes these *kaffirs* get me down," he replied.

The assistant looked relieved. "*Ja*, I know just what you mean."

Zelig, a traitor to himself, got off the stool. "Next," he said

loudly. Only he could have detected the quivering that under-
lined his shout.

Evelyn had not deliberately barred Zelig's way. She had stood
still because she could not be bothered to move, because she
had been lost in thought. It had been a careless thing to do and
she had been lucky: the man who had bumped into her was not
made from the same stuff as other whites in the *kaffetaria*. They
would have rewarded her "cheekiness" with the flat of their
hands.

Thinking about it, she was surprised at Zelig's reaction. After
all, he usually treated his customers with unswerving politeness.

"Ag, they're all the same, these white men," she told herself.
"I must do my best to ignore them."

She must, in fact, she continued to herself, do her best to
ignore all men: They brought nothing but trouble. She was standing in one spot because of Nathaniel, because she had seen him
on her way in and was wondering whether he would follow.

She didn't know why she bothered with him: The man was
hopeless! So he was strong and brave (the other miners called
him the chief behind his back), but what was the point of strength
when he was so shy that he seemed to disintegrate in front of
women? The only way she could ever get to know him was if
she made the first move.

Well, she would not. She did not need a man. Ever since her
father had announced that he planned to marry her to a man
more than three times her age in exchange for *lobolo*, thus forcing
Evelyn to run away to the mission station, she had resolved to
stay away from men forever.

Not that they stayed away from her. At the mission station it
had been the same old story. The white missionary, an apparently
happily married man whose children Evelyn looked after, attempted to pull her to one side when nobody was around. She
avoided him like the plague, but it hadn't been easy keeping his
lust at bay.

It had taken all her inner reserve to free herself from his
clutches. Eventually she'd resorted to blackmail and got herself
transferred to Jo'burg: housed in one of the church's refuges for
washerwomen.

She knew that she had been lucky, and she had the good sense
to capitalize on her fortune. She was a conscientious worker who

had built up a steady clientele. Soon she would be earning enough to rent a room in Sophiatown: For the first time in her life she would be free.

Marriage did not fit into these plans. It would be a disaster to tie herself to a man who would probably feel he owned her. She must keep away from Nathaniel.

No sooner had she remade her resolution when Evelyn saw through the windows that Nathaniel had not gone away. He was hovering in the distance.

Against her better judgment she stepped out of the *kaffetaria* and walked toward him.

"Good day," she said as she neared him.

"Good day," he replied. He hesitated, as if he wanted to say something. But his nerve failed him at the last minute, and he looked away quickly.

That was what was so infuriating about him, Evelyn thought: Every time she gave up on him, she would catch him trying to make conversation. Trying, she thought, but never succeeding. She smiled to herself.

True to type, he began to turn away. "My friend is ill," he muttered, as if in explanation. "I have to go to him."

Andres van der Merwe flung a shilling onto the scratched wooden counter. He had had extensive practice, and the change landed nicely—just out of the grasp of his customer. Andres nodded in satisfaction: now for the second phase of the game.

He turned his head, as if distracted by more important matters. For want of somewhere else to look, his eyes settled on Zelig, who was standing motionless on top of the stepladder. Andres's bonhomie faded. He clicked his tongue in exasperation. Zelig was at it again, standing silently at his workstation, unaware of the long line of miners waiting to be served.

Andres might not have minded Zelig's continual daydreaming—after all, the nature of the job demanded some form of escape—if not for the fact that Zelig was so damn unfriendly.

Andres had watched Zelig from the first. The more he saw, the less he liked the man. Zelig held himself aloof, as if he were better than the rest of the assistants. Andres could have ignored this, but something about Zelig roused his ire. Serve him right that the longest line of customers always seemed to gravitate toward his section of the counter.

Andres was working on a way to put Zelig in his place. He thought about it often. It gave him great satisfaction to toy with the one-liners that would show Zelig which of them had the brains. All he had to do was bide his time—await the right opportunity.

In the meantime, he remembered, he must deal with the problem in front of him. This customer was going to be a difficult one. He was a real "*kraal* type," with his thick blanket around his shoulders, but he was showing the first signs of resistance.

He hadn't shuffled off as did most of Andres's victims. Instead, he stood there looking at the shilling with one of those dumb expressions that Andres had never been able to fathom. Well, Andres wasn't unduly concerned: He'd had plenty of practice with the black.

"Want anything else, boy?" he snapped.

The man pointed to the shilling.

This was the point that Andres usually enjoyed the most, but thinking about Zelig had cast a blight on his enjoyment. He decided to go on the offensive and secure a quick victory. It was a new ploy he'd planned last night when the snoring of the other occupant of his bunk had kept him awake and at the mercy of the unending whine from the mosquitoes.

"Who put that there?" Andres asked, gesturing at the shilling.

"You did, *baas*," the man said.

Andres smiled. "Then it must be mine," he said. He picked up the shilling and pocketed it. He pointed impatiently to the next man in the queue.

Still the man did not move.

Andres was getting irritated.

"You want trouble?" he asked.

"I gave you half a crown," the man said. "My change was one shilling, two pennies."

Andres lost patience. He leaned over the counter and pushed the man with a force that made him stagger backward.

"If you want trouble, *kaffir*," he said, "I'll give it to you."

The man clenched his fist, but he knew better than to hit a white. He made a visible effort to control himself. He bit his lips together.

Andres felt a tinge of regret. Brute force, that's all they understood. As a result, the game was beginning to lose its edge. There was a time when Andres's wit was truly stretched by the varied responses that his private enterprise provoked. Now, no matter how much he changed the way he did it, it always ended with a shove.

"Hurry up!" he shouted to the next man in the line. "I haven't got all day."

Just then there was a commotion by the entrance to the shop. Andres pushed up on the counter so as to get a better view. He saw arms flailing as a man struggled to free himself from a group of blacks who were attempting to hold him down.

So loud was the commotion that, Andres noticed, even Zelig stirred.

"Trouble," Andres said.

From his position on the ladder Zelig had a better view than Andres. He saw a man fighting savagely—a man whom he had heard called Nathaniel. Two huge miners were trying to restrain him, but he swayed in their grip. He would soon break from them: He seemed driven by a kind of supernatural force.

Zelig had never seen this particular man act with such a lack of control. Something must be badly wrong: Perhaps Nathaniel was sick.

Zelig looked down in time to see Andres in the process of lifting up the top of the counter, on his way to call the manager. Nathaniel, Zelig knew, would be instantly arrested.

Without hesitation, with the memory of his recent betrayal uppermost in his mind, Zelig jumped off the ladder. He barred Andres's exit.

"I'll see to this," he said.

"Sure, man," Andres said, surprised at the unexpected passion in Zelig's voice. He reached up behind him to pull something off the shelf. "But take the *sjambok*. Call me if there's anything you can't handle."

Zelig now had no choice: He would have to act or risk Andres's derision. Keeping a grip on his fast-beating heart, he walked briskly to the door. The crowd that had gathered to watch the spectacle was pressed hard against the door. The people parted only reluctantly when Zelig pushed at them.

By the time he was within touching distance, Nathaniel had all but won the battle. He was restrained now only by a coattail, and Zelig could see that it, too, was about to tear.

Zelig did not stop to ask himself why he was interfering. Instead, using his body as a lever, he managed somehow to shove Nathaniel out the door.

Nathaniel was consumed by rage, bereft of reason. Zelig had prevented him from reaching his destination—he had to buy Tiny's provisions—and so he attacked, throwing Zelig onto the ground. Then he jumped on top, thudding Zelig's head into the dust.

His opponent struggled with all his night to get free. He felt no fear, only the will to overcome. I will win, he resolved. I will win.

Everything went quiet around the two men. All Zelig registered was the sound of their breath, intermingling in their mutual effort for dominance. Zelig's arm felt as if it might break as he strained to break Nathaniel's grip. He heard somebody groaning, and it took him a while to register that it was his own voice.

Nathaniel grappled in silence.

Zelig heaved his body, forcing Nathaniel to shift to the right. Together they both rolled. As they turned, Zelig found himself face-to-face with Nathaniel. He took a gulp of air to get the strength for the final push, and he smelled the home-made beer on Nathaniel's breath. Nathaniel was drunk: Zelig was risking his life for a man who was completely intoxicated.

Suddenly Zelig was filled with his own rage. Everything that had happened to him since arriving in this accursed country came flooding back to him: Haim's death, his estrangement from Riva, the unhappiness of his daughter.

His anger gave Zelig the advantage he needed: He found the strength to overcome Nathaniel. One more push and Nathaniel was lying under him.

Zelig was no longer thinking. He pulled his arm back in preparation to wield the heavy whip. Nathaniel went limp, as if wishing for the punishment Zelig was poised to inflict.

In that instant Zelig looked into Nathaniel's eyes. He saw reflected back at him a look that tore at his heart. For he identified in Nathaniel's face the same pain that he daily struggled to suppress.

And Zelig felt shame. What was he doing brawling with a man who had done nothing to him? How could he act so crazily? Sheepishly he stood up.

Nathaniel lay quiescent on the ground, tears flooding down his cheeks.

"Tiny wanted to go home," he muttered. "He wanted to die at home."

Zelig stood above Nathaniel, unaware of the trickle of blood from his forehead.

"Please don't call the police, *baas*," one of the onlookers whispered in Zelig's ear. "We will see there's no more trouble. His best friend just died."

Zelig wiped the blood from his face. He offered Nathaniel an arm.

"I'm sorry," he muttered. "I understand."

Nathaniel seemed to notice Zelig for the first time.

"How can you understand? You are white."

Zelig turned. He walked back into the shop with his head bent, moving through the crowd that now parted easily to facilitate his exit.

Andres had been busy working during Zelig's encounter. He looked curiously at Zelig's dusty trousers and at the stain on his shirtsleeve.

"I tripped," Zelig said briskly.

Andres looked doubtful.

"It's the monotony of this dump," Zelig said. "Makes me careless."

Andres laughed. He clapped Zelig on the shoulder. "Back to work," he said. He glanced toward the street, where Nathaniel was weaving unsteadily, supported by the men he had been fighting.

"You've got to be on your guard against the *kaffir*," Andres advised Zelig. "Next thing you know, he'll be after your daughter. They're not like us. They have no feelings."

Without a word, Zelig reached for his cap. He put it on his head with a kind of slow determination. He lifted the flap of the counter and passed through it.

"Hey," Andres called.

Zelig turned around briefly. "I'm taking a break," he said. "If you want to report me, go ahead."

Andres's voice followed him. "It's okay, man," he called. "I'll cover for you. Next . . ."

When Zelig walked out into the sunshine, he had first to accustom himself to the brightness of the day. He blinked a few times before scanning the street.

It didn't take him long to spot Nathaniel, who was weaving down the street, brushing off all offers of help. He was followed by a small group—a group that included the woman whom Zelig had earlier confronted.

Zelig saw that he was not the only observer. A policeman on the other side of the road was also following Nathaniel's progress. When Nathaniel shouted and shot one fist up into the air, the policeman screwed up his eyes. At the same time he reached down his trouser leg for his gun.

Zelig sprinted down the road. "Hey, boy," he called as he ran. "Hey, boy."

The policeman hesitated when he heard Zelig's shouts. Gun still drawn, he began to cross the street.

The two men reached Nathaniel at the exact same time.

"Look here, Nathaniel," Zelig shouted, "don't take it so bad!"

Nathaniel was too far gone to respond. As his companions melted into the background—all, that is, except the woman—he slid to the ground—and lay there.

The policeman spat on the sidewalk before turning to Zelig. "Is this your boy?" he asked.

Zelig nodded.

"I'll have to take him in," the policeman said.

No sooner were the words out of the policeman's mouth, than Zelig acted. He leaned down and cuffed Nathaniel on the ear. "See what trouble you've made now," he said.

He straightened up and turned to the policeman. He lowered his voice, put honey in it, even. "It's like this, Officer," he explained. "My boy is usually a good boy. He does his work well—my wife says there's not another one like him in Jo'burg."

"They're all bad," the policeman said.

"*Ja, ja,*" Zelig agreed. "But this one's as good as they come. I would hate to lose him."

"The man's drunk," the policeman said. "Smell his stink."

"Not drunk, Officer," Zelig protested. "I poured some whiskey on his head."

The policeman was first startled, and then amused. He smiled. "Waste of good liquor," he commented.

"I couldn't agree with you more," Zelig answered. "But I was so angry that I acted without thinking. For an hour ago this woman"—he pointed at Evelyn—"came to me and told me that my boy, the one I trusted with even my house keys, had made her pregnant. She said he was refusing to marry her."

As he gabbled on, Zelig watched Evelyn from the corner of his eye. *Don't contradict me*, he prayed. She stood there mute.

"I'm a religious man," Zelig continued. "I will not tolerate loose morals. I had some trouble, but now I've beaten some sense into him. He'll marry her, and she'll go to the countryside to bring up the child. It's for the best."

The policeman hesitated.

"My wife will give me hell if my actions lost us our servant," Zelig said hastily. "You know what women are like."

To Zelig's relief, the policeman returned his gun to his holster. "Okay," he said. "I'll let him go this time." He looked down at Nathaniel and spat again. "Don't let me catch you misbehaving in the street," he warned before strolling off.

Nathaniel's eyes were closed: He seemed unaware of the activity that had taken place around him. Zelig bent down, intending to pull him up, but the woman restrained him.

"I'll take care of him now," she said. She softened her voice as she looked him full in the face. "Thank you," she said. "You saved him from jail."

Zelig nodded in embarrassment before walking, reluctantly, away.

Nathaniel felt as though an army of Boers were marching on his head. Up and down they went, up and down, banging on drums, all of them. He groaned and tried to open his eyes.

But to no avail—the lids were stuck firmly together.

As his thoughts became clearer, Nathaniel grew afraid. Where was he? Why couldn't he see?

He knew that there could be only one possible explanation. He must have been in an accident underground, a rockfall must have landed on his head.

Which meant, he thought, that Tiny was somewhere around.

As soon as the name crossed his mind, Nathaniel felt a terrible sadness. He groaned.

A light hand touched at his brow. "At last," said a voice. "I had given you up for dead."

Ignoring the army, Nathaniel strained his eyes. This time they opened a crack. He saw that Evelyn was sitting beside him and that she was smiling.

He could not understand it. He looked around the room,

taking in the rickety table, on which a Bible stood, the piece of material up at the window, the uneven floor, the badly fitting door. "Where—" he started.

"Shh," Evelyn said quickly. "Not so loud. I had to smuggle you in here."

Nathaniel frowned. Smuggle him in? How could she have done that? Come to think of it, how had he got here?

Thinking was too much to bear. All Nathaniel knew was that he must get out of this place, that he must go back to the mine, find his own bunk, and give himself time to remember. He pushed away the bedclothes and swung his feet to the floor.

And then he saw that he was naked. He jumped back into the bed, and pulled a blanket over him. His cheeks were burning.

She had been watching his every action, and now she laughed out loud. "You have nothing to hide from me," she said, "since I undressed you. Your clothes are dry: They're just behind you."

He did not move.

So she turned her back. She laughed to herself as she heard him fumble to get dressed. She tried to conceal her amusement, but, nevertheless, her shoulders heaved.

When she judged that he had had enough time to dress, she turned again. She saw that he was standing sheepishly by the window. She smiled.

"I must go," he said, and so tangible was his embarrassment that she could almost touch it.

"Let me bathe your eye again," she suggested.

His hand went to his eye, and he felt how puffy it had become. He tried to remember what had happened but drew a blank, a total blank.

"What happened?" he asked.

Evelyn wrung a cloth out in the basin beside her and went up to him. "Sit," she said. "I can't reach."

He followed her bidding because he did not know what else to do. "What happened?" he asked.

"You were drunk," she said briefly. She lifted the cloth and dabbed at the cut beneath his eye.

It stung like hell. Nathaniel flinched. And in that moment he remembered. He remembered the policeman. He remembered Zelig. He remembered the fight. And he remembered something worse than all of those: He remembered that Tiny, his friend, his adopted father, was dead.

He had not cried when he had returned to the compound and heard the news. He had not uttered a single word. He had, instead, gone out and got drunk. As simple as that. He had drunk to drown his memory and his sorrow.

But now he was no longer drunk. He could not ignore the feelings that welled up inside of him. He could not. He swallowed them, but still they burst out. And before he knew it, he was crying hot tears—tears of sorrow and of anger. And all the while Evelyn stood beside him and stroked his head.

6

1917

"WELL, MY DEAR," THE MIDWIFE SAID, "THERE IS NO DOUBT ABOUT it. Your baby is already growing inside you."

Evelyn Bopape looked at the midwife without blinking.

"You have been married how long?"

"Ten years." It came out softly.

The midwife smiled. "And this is your first child," she said. "That is a long time to wait."

Since their homes in Sophiatown abutted the same yard, the midwife already knew Evelyn. She had always regarded her neighbor as a pillar of the community, a woman who was lucky enough to be married to a good man (Nathaniel was always on hand to help those who got into trouble), and a woman with strength. So she was taken by surprise when Evelyn burst into tears.

The midwife frowned. Now she thought about it, she had heard rumors of Evelyn's wrongheaded attitude to the church. She was too independent, went the stories, careful to keep her mouth shut, but one could see that she didn't have enough respect. The gossip must be right, the midwife thought. Evelyn could not be entirely clean before God: How else could one explain such a reaction?

She frowned again and hauled herself to her feet. "You have about seven months to get used to the news," she said. "You will. We all do." And with one last distasteful pat of Evelyn's hand, she nudged her out the room.

If the midwife had bothered to follow her patient's progress down the road, she would have been reassured. Almost as soon as Evelyn stepped into the open air, she began to smile. She walked away from the clinic with a spring in her step, and the smile became a broad grin.

She and Nathaniel had waited ten long years, waited with diminishing certainty until they had given up waiting and learned to pretend that it didn't really matter.

But it did matter, it always had. Now she was pregnant, Evelyn could finally admit to herself just how much she had grieved for her failure to conceive.

She could still hardly believe it was true. Ever since she first suspected the pregnancy, she had been in a kind of agony—anticipating disappointment at any minute. So when the midwife finally made the news official, Evelyn could not contain herself.

Suddenly she stopped in her tracks. What if Nathaniel wasn't pleased? What if he had adjusted to his childless status and regarded a baby as an intrusion in his busy life?

She walked on, but more slowly now. The more she thought about it, the more her fears gained ground. She, who had always regarded Nathaniel's silence on the subject of her infertility as generosity, now convinced herself that it sprang from sheer indifference to the thought of having a child.

I will never recover, she thought, if he does not want this child.

But then another voice spoke to her. She had never doubted Nathaniel's love—why should she now do so?

When Nathaniel came home, she did not greet him with the news. Nathaniel's job as an interpreter meant that he infrequently went underground, but his hours were still long, and his conditions arduous. He returned late, weariness etched into his posture. He kissed her briefly, and then sat down at the table to eat.

She'd watched him in the flickering candlelight, and she'd seen how slowly he revived, how his back straightened and the lines went from his face. He finished his food, and she brought him a mug of water. He drained it down to the last drop, and then he stretched back in satisfaction.

"A good meal," he commented.

Evelyn nodded and removed his plate.

"They're taking the sanitation workers to court," he said. "Tomorrow."

She came back for his glass.

"I worry about the outcome," he continued.

She leaned across the table and wiped a crumb into her hand.

At this point he noticed something. He looked at her quizzically. "Are you ill?" he asked.

"I'm going to have a baby." It came out in a rush, unplanned, unstoppable.

Nathaniel did not immediately reply. Instead, his face lit up, threw off ten years of hard labor, became youthful once more. In a flash Evelyn saw the young man she had once known, the miner who woke embarrassed in her bed and who had flinched in anticipation when their lips first touched. She saw the pride of the former chief's son and the pleasure of the organizer. She saw all these aspects for once integrated. In short, she saw the man she loved.

He hid his sorrow well, she thought to herself. He so wanted to hear me say that—every day of the last ten years, he must have wanted it. She walked toward him, and when he rose, she was enveloped in the welcome of his arms.

"Ma Evelyn," said a childish voice.

Evelyn shook herself: She must concentrate. Only that minute she had been on the point of getting her class to sing, when she caught herself in the process of patting her stomach. Hurriedly she'd converted the action into a kind of brushing motion, pretending instead to be removing a speck of dirt. She knew that she needn't have bothered: Even if she rested her hand on her belly all day long, none of her pupils would have noticed a thing. Nothing showed yet—only she was so conscious of her condition.

The hand moved to her stomach again.

"Ma Evelyn?" the child repeated.

Evelyn smiled. "I'm sorry," she said. "I was miles away. Now who has learned the hymn?"

Thirty pairs of hands shot up into the air. "I have, Ma Evelyn, I have," they called.

"Please, children," interrupted a stern voice, "how many times must I tell you? Miss Bopape is your teacher's name, Miss Bopape."

Evelyn turned to find Miss Carmichael standing by the door. "Good afternoon, Miss Carmichael," she said, before fixing her class with a look. They responded immediately, jumping to their feet. "Good afternoon, ma'am," they chanted.

Maud Carmichael nodded at them. "Carry on, children," she said. She held the door open and inclined her head toward the hall. "Miss Bopape?"

When Evelyn followed Miss Carmichael into the yard, she took care to maintain a slight distance, since she had long ago realized that her bulk intimidated the birdlike headmistress. When Miss Carmichael came to a halt, she stopped a few paces away. Think how much bigger I'll be in a few months, she thought to herself.

She smiled at the prospect. "You wanted me?" she asked.

Miss Carmichael's lips tightened. "I have been concerned about you, Miss Bopape," she said. "You have appeared rather tired of late."

For a reason, thought Evelyn.

This time she made an effort to keep the smile at bay. She had never told Miss Carmichael that she was married, since to do so would disqualify her from a teacher's post. As a result, hearing about the pregnancy was bound to come as an unpleasant shock to the headmistress. A shock that I will save, she thought, until I have no choice.

"I am fully recovered now," she said out loud. "Thank you for your concern."

The corner of Miss Carmichael's mouth twitched as she began her routine lecture about the need for discipline. But suddenly, another distraction descended on the two women, a more pressing problem.

A soft wind was blowing through the yard. Whereas in a normal time it would have carried the scent of cooking, of life, of even the occasional flower, instead it carried an almost unbearable stench. Evelyn swallowed hard.

"This is intolerable," snapped Miss Carmichael.

Evelyn nodded and brought the hem of her apron up to her nose.

Miss Carmichael was made of sterner stuff. She merely dabbed at her nose with a handkerchief. "I do hope those bucket boys realize how utterly selfish they are being," she said. "They have made their point, and should now go back to work."

"They're hardly well paid," Evelyn ventured.

"That's as may be," the headmistress countered. "I am not one of those who argues that the native should be left to starve. However"—she peered at Evelyn, and her spectacles quivered at the end of her nose—"if you people are patient, you will see your patience rewarded by trust and, ultimately, better conditions. Change takes a long time. As we civilize the new generation, it will begin to assume a proper place in our society."

Evelyn swallowed again, this time to repel the words rather than the smell. Miss Carmichael, she knew, was not a bad woman—a Christian who devoted her life to those she considered worse off than herself. Her school was a mark of this: Not only were fees kept to the very minimum and the black staff treated with a modicum of respect, but Miss Carmichael also allowed girls to attend. All in all, she wasn't a bad woman.

Nevertheless, Evelyn's background did not predispose her to the kind of lectures her headmistress delivered. After all, she herself had lived among missionaries—she had fled the lust of one. And she had seen what the "civilized" could do to those weaker than themselves: The unending crowd of men forced into the mines was proof enough of this.

The wind picked up, and brought with it a renewed smell. Miss Carmichael was forced to use her handkerchief again. She held it tightly to her nose. "Let us return inside," she said, "before the stench overwhelms us both."

As Nathaniel stepped across the railway line, he was also inundated by the stink. This came as no surprise: There was scarely a person in Jo'burg who was unaffected. After all, sewage had gone uncollected for more than a week now, and all at a time when the weather had been unseasonably hot. There was no hiding from it, and no easy solution: Even if the strike ended that day, it would take some time before all the cesspits were cleared and the smell stopped lingering in the air.

"And perhaps the courts will not force an end today," he muttered to himself.

A heavy clanking of metal interrupted his chain of thought. He left the railway line and went to stand by the scrub that surrounded it. He was feeling almost lazy, enjoying his walk home. He decided to stop and wait awhile.

He looked past the railway and toward the horizon, concentrating on sight rather than smell, absorbing the gradation of browns and reds, and the dust highlighted by the low rays of the sun. The sweat had dried on his cheap singlet, and he was beginning to feel chilled. He shivered.

And then the sun was blocked by the array of carts that passed before him. One after the other they progressed along the railway line—rocking and clanking, these open cattle trucks, each filled to overflowing with weary men.

It is fitting that they are in cattle trucks, Nathaniel thought. For they are like beasts of burden.

Faced with sights such as this, he always felt a wave of thankfulness that he no longer worked on the mine face. He was nearing thirty, and his years underground had already sapped some of his bodily strength: If he had gone on much longer, he would have ended up like Tiny, he knew he would have. And so he felt relieved.

But the guilt always followed closely on the back of his relief. Others, he knew, were not as lucky as he. They had not had his education: They could not choose to take a better job. What right had he to separate himself from them?

"It is not your fault," he remembered Evelyn saying. "You spend your spare time working for their good: If you worked underground, you would be unable to do this." She'd smiled and pulled him to her. "And you wouldn't ever be home with me," she'd said. "You'd be stuck in a compound, imprisoned behind wire." She'd kissed him gently on the forehead.

Perhaps that was the occasion when the seed of our unborn child was sown, Nathaniel thought with a mixture of embarrassment and pleasure.

A child, he remembered now, a child! He could still see the look on Evelyn's face when she had told him. How she must have suffered for the lack of family he thought. And I believed she had come to terms with it. (He would never, he told himself, entirely understand women).

Smiling at his own foolish misconception, he left the railway behind and walked through the dirt roads of Sophiatown, past shanties and hand-dug wells, stepping over holes filled with dust and children who played in it, deeper and deeper into the labyrinth that was the racial mix of Sophiatown.

Except the whites are moving out, he thought. To suburbs like Vrederdorp and Brixton. There, they can live in comfort without rubbing against black skins.

He carried on walking, recognizing people now, nodding at them, exchanging an occasional greeting.

"Hey brother," called a man from across the road, "come have a drink."

Nathaniel shook his head. "My wife is expecting me," he shouted, and waved his hand.

"Boy," replied the man. "Ten years married, and she still has you running. Must be some woman."

She is, thought Nathaniel. And—he laughed out loud at this point, causing a few heads to turn—she will soon be a mother.

He diverted himself from his main course and crossed over to the shop on the corner. He would buy her something special, he resolved, perhaps some of that Rising Sun malted drink she so favored. She would have time to enjoy that before the match.

"We don't have to go, you know," Nathaniel said.

Evelyn looked at him and smiled. "It will be good to be in the open," she said. "And the field is in the east, whereas the wind blows toward the west." She got up and pulled a cardigan around her shoulders.

They did not have far to walk to the cricket match, and they progressed in a kind of easy silence, not touching deliberately, although they occasionally swayed into each other. There was a peace between them, a gentle comfort. Every now and then, Evelyn caught Nathaniel glancing at her with pride.

He pointed. "Look, they've laid the chairs out, so you won't get tired."

But Evelyn's good mood had begun to evaporate. She looked at the black team, and the black audience.

"Why do they play this game?" she whispered to Nathaniel.

He shrugged. "They want to be accepted," he replied. As the ball came whizzing past their chairs, he put his hands together and clapped softly.

He was right, Evelyn thought, and she was being unnecessarily impatient. These members of the Native Congresses were well-meaning people who tried their hardest to improve the lot of the majority. To this end they petitioned the king, sought interviews with visiting dignitaries, did their utmost to bring the plight of their brothers to the attention of the world. And if in the process they had become like images of their former oppressors, was it their fault?

Nathaniel bent his mouth down to her ear. "Sometimes I'm not surprised they're called the Old Boys Brigade," he said.

"They play cricket while half the city is about to go out on strike."

She glanced up, her depression evaporating. He understood, this man, her husband. He felt as she did.

He squeezed her hand. "Look," he said, pointing in the distance. "There's Harold Arnold, the one I told you about. Let me introduce you."

Nodding to those still seated, Nathaniel and Evelyn strolled away from the center of the field and toward the white man who stood expectantly in the distance.

As she got closer, Evelyn had to work hard to conceal her surprise. Nathaniel had often told her of this young Jew who offered to help them in their struggles. He had collected money and advice, giving to relatives of those who died in mine accidents. Nathaniel had spoken of his generosity and steadfastness, and somehow she had built up a picture of a substantial man, not a scrawny boy with spectacles too big for his face.

She greeted him, and she was taken aback when he put out his hand to shake hers. She trembled at the contact. I'm as bad as the rest, she thought to herself, that a white man's skin could make me so nervous.

Harold apparently noticed nothing. He was already talking to her husband, easily and with a genuine show of friendship.

"What do you think will happen?" he was asking.

"I don't know," Nathaniel replied. For a moment he looked back at the men still watching the match. "They're scared that we'll start something we can't finish," he commented. "They think it would be better to go through the proper channels."

Harold raised one eyebrow. "Petitions?" he asked.

"Afraid so." Nathaniel smiled. "The king must be snowed under with red tape from South Africa."

"The trust in the English is incredible," Harold said. "Look at their record after the Boer War. They promised rights to the blacks in exchange for cooperation, and then what did they do?" His face grew serious, and Evelyn saw a glimmer of a hidden power, an iron determination, perhaps. She knew why Nathaniel liked this man. She listened more closely. "They broke every last promise," he said. "They either broke it then, or are in the process of doing so now.

"And it's happening again," he continued. "Black soldiers going to fight the Germans in the hope of ending racial tyranny in South Africa. Instead, they're getting themselves put in the front line and killed." He lowered his voice. "All so that the imperial powers can play war games," he concluded bitterly. Evelyn saw that his eyes were focused on the distance, unseeingly, she thought.

But she was wrong. "Look." He pointed. "The news must have come, the court case must be over."

Evelyn followed his finger and saw how the knot of spectators had tightened and had turned away from the match. They were facing inward now, talking across each other's heads, disputing something, frowning, shouting, dissecting.

Nathaniel and Evelyn, with Harold following a short distance behind, walked fast toward the crowd. Before they had got far, she stumbled. Nathaniel stopped and looked at her with concern.

His arms went around her waist, and he squeezed it gently. That was one of the things about her man, he was sometimes so present for her, so loving. And yet should politics come his way, he could become immediately absent.

Even as she was thinking it, she saw it happen again. He turned to look at the crowd, and was no longer her protector. Instead, he stared intently ahead, concentrating on the atmosphere, the mood, the tone of the discussion that had ensued. He was a political animal, her Nathaniel, he always would be.

And I don't mind, she realized. I am proud of him. "Go ahead," she said out loud. "I won't be long."

His face changed, and she saw the eagerness within. He strode across the center of the field and was soon in the center of the discussion.

But when she caught up with him, she saw that he was furious. "They sentenced them to three months' labor in their jobs without pay," he said. He was inarticulate with rage.

"General strike," called another member of the crowd. "Let us escalate our demands."

Nathaniel nodded his head. But he did not say anything. He listened instead to the voice of one of the leaders of the Transvaal Native Congress, who had stood himself on a chair and was speaking now in a loud voice.

"Gentlemen," he called. "Order—I beg of you." The crowd began to quiet. "The Congress has anticipated this result," the man continued in an authoritative voice. "We have decided that we are not strong enough to strike. We must be vigilant. If we do not stop the hotheads from talking of strikes, then the whole of Johannesburg will go up in flames. . . ."

"Let it burn!" shouted somebody.

"Let it burn," came an echo. Nathaniel nodded his head in agreement.

The impromptu meeting—to the background, Evelyn noticed, of a continuing cricket match—went on for some time. When it was over, she and Nathaniel walked with Harold to the entrance of the field.

"So will they strike?" Harold asked.

Nathaniel shrugged. "I doubt it," he said. "Even if the Congress is wrong, there is no other organization with the strength to arrange a concerted action. We might have to wait—however hard that is."

"Well, let me know if there's anything I can do to help," Harold said. He shook hands with Nathaniel, inclined his head shyly in Evelyn's direction, and then walked quickly away.

"A good man," Nathaniel commented, as they watched Harold's retreating back.

Evelyn picked up the sadness in his voice. She looked up at him. "You are disappointed?" she asked.

He smiled. "*Ja*—disappointed," he said. "But then maybe I'm wrong. Tiny always told me that I pushed too hard—that it was necessary sometimes to bide one's time. Perhaps I haven't changed. Perhaps I'm too eager to rush into confrontation."

"There were many others who called for action," Evelyn reminded him.

He placed one hand on her cheek. "You are my comfort," he whispered. The hand moved down her face gently. "And soon we will be three," he said. His voice got louder. "I have thought of a name. We will call our son Moses."

"Why do you assume a son?"

Nathaniel laughed. "I feel it in my bones," he said. "Our Moses will be born and he will be a leader—a man who can lead our people from the wilderness."

Evelyn shivered. "That's a lot to bear," she said.

Nathaniel's hand moved away. "We all have a lot to bear," he said somberly.

7

DELIBERATELY JULIA MOVED HER TEETH APART, UNCLENCHED HER

DELIBERATELY JULIA MOVED HER TEETH APART, UNCLENCHED HER
jaw, and straightened her body. She breathed in, exhaled slowly,
and closed her eyes, feigning sleep in the hope that it would
come.

But it didn't. Her night was well and truly over. She could
ignore neither the first trickle of blood between her legs nor the
cramps that came fierce and fast.

"Damn," she muttered. "Damn, damn, damn."

The incantation didn't help at all. There was no point, she
knew, in cursing the regularity of her body—she was wasting
her breath. It was too much to hope that she could escape the
burden of being a woman even on this, her first day in a new
job.

Oh, well, who cares? she thought. They won't expect me to
have a brain, so what does it matter if I'm tired?

She threw her sheet onto the floor, got out of bed, and went
to the window.

The sky was the sort of intermediate color that came just before
daybreak. Here and there could be seen orange tinges in the
blackness. In a moment the darkness would lift completely, and
the first rays of the sun would begin to warm the earth. Then
the whole of Ferreirastown would begin to stir.

But for the present there was no one about in the streets.

No one white, that was. In the darkness Julia could just make
out the forms of the black laborers as they trudged to work.
They were beginning their day, but already they looked tired.
They walked barefoot, or in shoes whose soles were paper thin,
shuffling reluctantly to their daily grind.

Julia yawned and opened the window. She sniffed at the air, and she thought she could smell newly baked bread, the smoke of an oven, the promise of a hot summer's day. She smiled.

She looked more closely at the street, and what had seemed like a uniform parade of human beings was given shape. She saw that weary as they were, the men walked confidently along the road, nodding at each other, exchanging an occasional greeting. It was as if, she thought with surprise, the street belonged to them. Dawn, this time before day, was the only time they could walk so freely.

Two men stopped below her window and vigorously shook each other's hands. They spoke in a language that Julia could not understand.

And I don't even know what language it is, she thought idly.

As if reading her thoughts, the men broke into raucous laughter. Abruptly Julia shut her window.

She remembered that she had been awakened during the night by sounds of shouting. Thinking her parents were arguing again, she'd turned over and forced herself back to sleep.

Now, she matched the noise of the night with the laughter below. She realized that it hadn't stemmed from either anger or resentment. Those, she realized, were jubilant cries—backed by bangs, as if people were letting off firecrackers in the street.

Julia pulled her best dress from the cupboard and dragged a comb through her hair before making her way quietly downstairs. She did not, after all, want to wake anybody: The last thing she wanted to do was to talk.

Somebody coughed behind her. She turned to find her mother staring at her. Riva was by the oven, her long apron wrapped around her, her hands holding two cloths. There was a smear of flour running along one cheek, and a strand of gray hair, an escapee from the restraint of her bun, on the other.

She looks small, thought Julia. For a split second, as the two women regarded each other, Julia's annoyance at finding her mother up was replaced by something much less habitual: by a rush of love for this woman, and a glimmer of understanding.

"So this is how you plan to make an impression on your first day?" Riva's words cut through Julia's thoughts.

"What's wrong with it?" Riva had talked in Yiddish. Julia answered, as was her custom, in English.

"What's wrong?" Riva's voice rose. "What's wrong is that

you're going to work, not a party. As for your hair: It's a disgrace."

Even as she spoke, Riva noticed how Julia's face seemed to withdraw, to shrink, even. She felt a twinge of remorse for the harshness of her words. She had not meant to undermine the child. Come to think of it, she didn't even know why she had begun with an attack. It was something, she thought, in Julia's expression—something that she found hard to tolerate.

She softened her voice. "You know that working for Mr. Felstein will be better than all those shoe stores," she said. "He's a good man. He will give you a real chance." Her eyes traveled the length of Julia's body. "But if you come in looking like that," she said, "what will Mr. Felstein think? He wants a worker, not a debutante."

A debutante, thought Julia, as she looked down at her dress: I should be so lucky. But she saw herself through her mother's eyes, and it made her feel ridiculous. At the same time, she heard the softness in her mother's tone. Riva, she guessed, was only trying to make sure that the day went well.

"I'll go change," she agreed.

But as she climbed the stairs, her resentment returned. What, she thought, did her mother know about the world? Riva had always worked hard, but she'd always worked at home. She did not have to suffer the humiliation of being judged by mere appearance. And she had no experience of the outside world: Why did she think she knew better than Julia?

"Damn her," Julia muttered as she trudged up the stairs. "Damn all of them."

Riva heard Julia muttering behind the closed door. For once Riva did not blame her daughter. She had been too harsh on the child. She knew she had. She wished that she could turn back the clock, that she could greet Julia with a smile and some fresh pastries, as she had intended.

She opened the oven door and looked at the products of her labor. It was far easier to cook, she reflected idly, than to bring up a daughter.

"I must try harder," she promised herself.

When Julia reappeared, she was dressed in her working clothes—a floor-length brown skirt, a matching long-sleeved top, and a pair of stout shoes whose toes only were visible.

Riva nodded her head in satisfaction. Julia, she thought, now looked the part: God willing, the Felsteins would see through her arrogance to find what a good worker she was. Riva was hopeful she would stay at this job longer than the rest.

"Very nice," she commented.

Julia scowled.

Remembering her recently made resolution, Riva did not let her hackles rise. Instead, she walked to the table, pulled out a chair, and seated herself.

"What is it, my daughter," she asked, "that makes you so unwilling to go out to work? You keep telling me how old-fashioned I am. Would you rather I kept you at home?"

Julia did not take the chair. She kept her distance while she shook her head.

"What is it then?" asked Riva. She thought she genuinely wanted to know.

Oh, God, thought Julia. How can she not know?

"Tell me," Riva urged.

"I wanted to stay at school," Julia explained in a small voice. "I wanted to study. I was good at it. I wanted more time there." The words came out in a rush.

And they met the wall of Riva's incomprehension. Her resolve now discarded, she did the worst possible thing. She laughed. She threw back her head and laughed.

"Do you think we're millionaires?" she sputtered when she was able. "Do you come from a family of leisure, that you can afford to study your life away? You're eighteen years old and unmarried. Of course you must work."

Riva's ridicule was like a slap in the face. "You would have let Haim study," Julia said loudly.

The laugh was abruptly cut off. Riva narrowed her eyes. "Haim is dead," she said loudly.

Julia sighed. "So I noticed."

Before she knew what was happening, Julia saw that Riva had risen, that her chair had fallen to the ground, that her mother was staring at her wild-eyed.

"Don't you dare mock Haim's memory," Riva hissed.

Julia took a step backward. "I . . . I . . . didn't mean," she said. On her tongue were forming apologies, excuses, pleas for for-giveness. But as she opened her mouth to express them, it was as if a shutter came down. Haim, she thought, is dead. He's been dead for more than ten years.

She would not apologize. "I'm going," she said. She walked past Riva and out the back door.

When the door closed, Riva realized that Julia had gone, had gone without eating breakfast. She should not have done that: She needed to keep up her strength. Riva thought of calling her daughter back, but did not.

As she walked down the road, the bounce in Julia's gait began to return. She saw how the streets were strewn with brightly colored paper as if a carnival party had only just passed by. She remembered the shouts in the night, and for the second time she wondered about them. Danny would know, she told herself. It was still early; she had time to stop in to see him.

Danny's house was a small place—not much more than two intercommunicating rooms dingily decorated. Danny lived in it as he had found it—dark and shabby—his few possessions strewn amid the ever increasing piles of papers and pamphlets that he collected.

Julia walked through the small entrance hall and into the living room. When she saw Danny was sprawled in an armchair, his eyes red and bleary, an empty bottle of liquor by his side, she frowned. Danny, she thought, was going through one of his bad patches. Her own feelings of energy evaporated: She had so wanted somebody to be nice to her; she really didn't feel like listening to his problems.

But Danny was not, as she had first thought, depressed. He jumped up when he saw her.

"My favorite girl," he bellowed. "Where were you last night?"

"Why, what happened?" she asked. "I heard shouts."

"What happened? What happened?" Danny threw his arms in the air. He turned and spoke as if to an invisible audience. "The world turns upside down, and she asks what happened."

The audience, Julia noticed, was not invisible. It was composed of a young man standing by the door to Danny's only other room: a tall, thin man, bespectacled and handsome enough in a rangy kind of way.

"You've met Harold Arnold, I think?" Danny asked off-handedly.

As Harold inclined his head toward her, Julia, for a reason

she couldn't understand, blushed.

Danny didn't notice. He stamped his foot and clapped his hands together. "So you really haven't heard?" he asked.

Julia smiled and shrugged.

"What joy that I am the one to tell you," Danny said. "Never did I think I would live to enjoy this day." He squeezed Julia on the shoulder. "There's been a revolution in Russia," he said, so loudly that she winced. "The czar is no more."

Julia tried to smile, and yet the news meant little to her. Russia was a long way away—a place for which she had little feeling—a horrible place in some ways, since it was the repository of all Riva's good memories—the ones from which her daughter was excluded.

"They did it!" Caught up in his own excitement, Danny was oblivious to the coolness of her reaction. "They did it. A few crazy revolutionaries who never gave up."

"Not just a few," Harold said. His voice was surprisingly deep for one so young. Julia blushed again. He smiled at her. He, too, seemed slightly embarrassed.

"From what I hear, the whole country came out behind the Bolsheviks," he finished lamely.

"Bolshevik, smolshevik," Danny protested. "Haven't we been telling them for years that the only way was to kill the czar? Meet force with force, terror with terror, that's what we said. And finally those *donderheads* did it. Listen to me," he appealed to Julia, "my mother country is liberated, and I use South African words in the moment of celebration." He picked a bottle from the floor and, seeing it was empty, tossed it across the room, where it landed in a wastebasket. "You know what this means?" he asked. "The war's as good as over. Russia is free."

Harold laughed. "Ag, Danny," he said. "You anarchists are incurably optimistic. The struggle isn't over in a night. The Bolsheviks have a long, hard road ahead of them."

Danny turned to Harold. "That's what you Communist party members don't understand," he said, half-irate, half-joking. "Our people will never submit to another ruler. Do you think they're going to exchange one order for another? Do you think they're going to submit to Bolshevik form-filling now?"

"The Bolsheviks didn't fill forms," Harold said mildly.

"I'll give you that," Danny said, all traces of animosity gone from his voice. "The Bolsheviks did their part. A new age has dawned. I must find something with which to celebrate." He brushed past Harold and entered his second room, humming loudly to himself.

He left behind a silence. Julia looked down at her feet.

"What do you do?" she heard Harold ask.

"I'm about to start somewhere new," Julia replied. Her voice sounded thin. "I'm going to learn accounting."

"Oy, that's right, my darling." Danny, thank God, could never bring himself to let a conversation continue without him. "It's your first day: You've come round for my good wishes, and I waste my time arguing with this relic of history. Here, come have a seat and tell me how you're feeling."

As Julia fitted herself into a small space in Danny's only armchair, her host gestured at his other guest. "This one they say is a genius with figures," he announced. "He could help you. And that's another thing," he told Harold. "What is it you communists think you're doing? Here you are a diehard Bolshevik, and meanwhile working for your brother, Solly, whose only ambition is to sup with other capitalists."

Harold shrugged. "I have to earn a living," he said. He smiled at Julia. "I must be going," he said. "I hope to meet you another time." With his hand on the doorknob, he suddenly turned around. "If you do need any help," he said, "don't hesitate to ask me."

"Help her by all means!" Danny shouted at Harold's retreating back. "Anything as long as you don't try teaching her your brand of what you call politics."

Danny grumbled as he began to pick through the empty bottles. "That's a good boy," he said. "But tenacious. I kept telling him that I am an old anarchist who can't stand committees. Yet does he leave me alone?"

When he saw that Julia did not smile, Danny stopped what he was doing and came over to stand by her. He put one of his broad hands on her shoulder.

"And how is my *meidle*?" he asked. "You are pale."

Julia's eyes filled with tears. She blinked them back and shrugged.

"Just nervous, I guess," she said. She *was* nervous. She realized, for perhaps the first time, that she dreaded this job, because she was scared that she might fail. Riva, in all her ignorance, was right: This job was better than her previous ones, it held out the promise of new opportunity. And what happens if I miss my chance? Julia thought.

"Maybe my mother's right," she said. "Maybe I should get married."

Danny shrugged his shoulders. "I'm hardly the person to talk about that," he said. "But I don't need a wife to make you tea in the traditional way. If that doesn't calm you down, it will at least occupy your stomach with worry about whether it can keep the liquid down."

As always, Danny's magic worked on Julia. By the time she arrived at the Felstein furniture factory, she'd managed to put her doubts to one side. If this doesn't work out, she thought, I can always get another job.

The sight of the first-floor offices was reassuring. The sound of heavy machinery was just a distant hum, and the air was almost completely free of sawdust. A few wooden desks were placed at various points in the room, each piled high with wads of paper.

A woman smiled when she saw Julia standing by the door. She raised herself from her chair and, with her hand on her belly, began to waddle over.

"I'm Rona Felstein," she said. "And you must be Julia."

Julia nodded.

"Well, come in," Rona said. "We don't stand on ceremony here. The place is in chaos after last night."

"The Revolution?" Julia asked. "You've been celebrating?"

Rona gulped. "Hardly," she said. "We had a big order in." She lowered her voice conspiratorially. "Look," she said, "let me give you some advice. Don't talk about what happened in Russia to my father. His blood pressure's high enough." She turned her head and opened her mouth. "Dad!" she bellowed.

Morrie Felstein had a smile all over his fat face when he greeted Julia. He took one of her hands into his and squeezed it.

"Just in time," he said. "I was certain that Rona would have the baby here in the office before you turned up."

Julia looked anxiously at the clock on the wall.

"I'm not late," she stated uncertainly.

"Not at all." Morrie laughed. "But in this business, everything has to be done yesterday." He sat himself down and looked at Julia. "You will be taking over Rona's job," he said. "This is a good business, and do you know why? Because I have kept it in the family. But now my *meshuggeneh* daughter's going to have a baby. I warned her. Children only bring you grief, I told her, but would she listen?" He reached over and patted Rona's stomach affectionately.

"Don't take any notice of him," Rona said. "He talks tough, but he's got a soft heart."

8

1921

FROM THE *JOHANNESBURG EVENING TELEGRAPH*: NOVEMBER 27, 1921:

STORM CLOUDS OVER THE RAND

The possibility of an impending confrontation between miners and their employers was increased last night when talks between the two sides broke down.

Asked to comment on the likelihood of an all-out strike the Chairman of the Chamber of Mines appealed for calm. The Chamber, he said, was doing its utmost to resolve the deadlock. He said that a strike would be to the benefit of no-one. "The wealth of the Union of South Africa," he told the Telegraph, "is built from the gold of the Rand. Anyone who threatens this is doing the whole country a disservice."

The Chairman refused to be drawn on rumours of an enforced pay reduction throughout the Rand. "We are reasonable men," he concluded, "and we are confident that an agreement will soon be reached."

"... *ons sal binnekort saansten.*" Henrik translated the last words of the article into Afrikaans.

Jamie de Groot nodded his head sagely. "What did I tell you?" he said. He ran the back of his hand along his mouth. "The Chamber will back down. They'd never dare do it to us."

"Don't be so certain," Henrik replied. "You can't trust these

Englanders. They say one thing, and then they go and do another." He frowned. "Come on," he said. "Let's get out of this *verdomte* place. I spend enough time underground not to want to smell the furnaces for a moment more than necessary."

The two miners strolled away from the shaft entrance and began to make their way to the gate. Ignoring the line of blacks waiting to descend to the coal face, they moved quickly past the ore-filled trucks that, having been brought to the surface, were being heaved along the rails. They had finished their shift and were ready to forget about the mines, to wash the coal dust from their throats, to go home, eat, and dream of times when they would no longer have to work on the mines.

And yet this day they could not entirely forget, for the talk of strike was pressing on them.

As they were about to go through the gates, Henrik returned to the subject. "Hey, Jamie," he said. "What about your sister: She works at the Chamber, doesn't she? She must have some information."

Jamie glanced from left to right. "*Ja*," he replied in a whisper. "She sees things, all right. As a matter of fact, she's taking some papers to that man—you know, the one that hangs about the union building? That thin Jew—Harold something or other."

"Who—that bolshie?" Henrik's voice rose in surprise. "You trust your sister with a commie?"

"Not so loud," Jamie hissed. He bent his head closer to his friend. "Can't you see she had no other choice? She could lose her job if she's spotted in the union offices. Anyway, what that Harold said the other night makes sense—we workers must stick together."

It was at this point that Nathaniel Bopape rounded the corner. When he saw the two whites, he steered away from them. But so intent was Jamie on justifying his sister's actions that he didn't even see Nathaniel and, by coincidence, mirrored his actions. The two collided.

"For god sake, you *blerry kaffir*," Jamie shouted, "can't you watch where you're going?"

Using his elbows to reinforce his point, he walked past Nathaniel. "Ag, I'm fed up with this place," he said to Henrik.

Henrik nodded. He took one last look at the paper before crumpling it and throwing it onto the ground. He spat on it. "God, I'm parched," he said.

*   *   *

When they were safely out of sight, Nathaniel bent down and picked up the paper. He walked over to the nearest living quarters and sat down on its concrete steps. Carefully he smoothed out the paper, and then began to read.

"So what do you think it means?" asked a miner who had appeared from the block and who had waited patiently until Nathaniel was finished. "Will there be a strike?"

Nathaniel shrugged his shoulders. "The bosses say no, but they're not going to tell the *Telegraph* what's on their mind," he said. "It's obvious that the drop in the price of gold is putting pressure on them. They'll have to do something."

"What about us? Where do we fit in?"

Nathaniel smiled bitterly. "We'll be the last to be consulted," he said. "That's the only thing I can guarantee."

"There'll be a strike," Harold muttered as he refolded his paper.

"Not in my factory, there won't," Solly called. "Unless a certain person forgets to finish the wage slips."

Harold smiled, turned back to his work, and was soon immersed in his books, nodding to himself in satisfaction. He knew his pleasure was difficult to understand—Julia often teased him about this, about how mere figures could engross him so.

What Julia didn't understand was that for Harold, every number contained its own story. From a balance sheet he could judge the past and foresee the future. After half an hour with a strange set of accounts, he could accurately judge whether the employer got on with his laborers, whether the company would prosper or fail, even whether the accountant had just had a fight with his wife.

And there was, he thought, one other advantage to his skill: It was the excuse that enabled him to see Julia. Without it, he suspected, she would not spend time with him. As it was, she consented to sitting beside him as long as he was teaching her. As soon as he attempted to widen their relationship, she would instantly back off.

He wondered why she was so wary. Maybe, he thought, the answer is simple. Maybe she just isn't interested. He sighed heavily.

"Daydreaming again?"

Harold glanced up to find his brother standing by the desk, arms folded in a gesture of mock anger. Solly was a substantial man, his formerly lean frame already turning to fat that his well-pressed gray suit could do little to conceal. Business worries were making their mark on his face: Small lines, Harold noticed, had begun to appear around the eyes. They were accompanied by deep purple bags.

"You work too hard," Harold said.

"And what else should I do," Solly asked, "when I have an accountant who hasn't produced the wage slips?"

Harold smiled. "Have I ever missed payday?"

"And have I ever not reminded you?" Solly countered. "Sometimes I despair of you, Harold. If it's not your crazy politics occupying your mind, it's that *meshuggeneh* Julia Cyn. And visitors, visitors, all the time." Solly pointed into the distance. "You've got one now," he said.

When Harold followed the direction of his brother's finger across the factory floor, he saw the only person that Solly could mean, the only person who looked out of place. She was a young woman dressed in a simple cotton frock, a pretty enough girl who stood uneasily beside a large pile of mattresses, shrinking away as each new item was added to it. She looked vaguely familiar.

"Go on," Solly urged. "Go see to her."

Harold walked toward the woman, wondering again why she seemed familiar. He didn't manage to work it out. "Can I help you?" he asked.

She held out a hand. "I'm Sandra de Groot," she said in a clear, pleasant voice, the Afrikaans accent unmistakable. "We've met before." She paused and waited for Harold to remember. When he didn't, she continued, "My brother, Jamie, is a miner."

Harold's brow cleared. "Oh, yes," he said, "I've seen you waiting for him after our meetings." He paused, and the frown returned. "What can I do for you?"

The woman glanced around her nervously. "Is there somewhere . . . ?"

"You want to speak in private?" Harold asked. She nodded. "Hey, Solly," Harold shouted, "can we use your office?"

"Use it, use it," Solly replied with a dismissive wave. "What for did I start a business, if it wasn't to cater to your numerous interests?"

Once they were safely ensconced in Solly's cubicle of an office, a small enclosure surrounded by glass that allowed constant monitor of the factory floor, Sandra burst into frantic speech.

"I work at the Chamber of Mines," she gushed. "As a junior. I speak good English, you see, and maybe one day I can be a clerk, or even a secretary. My mother's a widow, and Jamie doesn't earn much, so . . ." She stopped herself abruptly. She flushed. Out of her pocket she withdrew a piece of paper. "Here, read this," she said.

Harold took the paper and glanced at it. His eyes widened as he read through once, and then again. When he had finished, he placed it down on Solly's desk. "Where did you get this?" he asked, his voice displaying neutral interest.

Sandra swallowed. "I . . . I . . . copied it," she said.

"And why bring it to me?"

"I thought it might mean something . . ." she began.

"It means something all right." Harold's voice was harsh now. "It means that, despite their denials, the mine owners are set on reducing the wages of people like your brother. It means they plan to attack the standard of living of one of the most significant sectors of the working class. It means all this," he said, and he looked straight at Sandra, "if, and only if, it is genuine. And if it is, why bring it to me?"

Sandra blinked. "I didn't know what else to do," she said in a small voice. "I don't know the union. I don't want to get caught stealing from the Chamber." She blinked again. "My mother needs me: We need my income." She lost her battle: Tears welled up in her eyes.

I see agents provocateurs everywhere, Harold thought. It's this country—so full of divisions. The English patronize the Afrikaners, and in turn the Afrikaners resent them. Both are united in despising the Jew, and what all three have in common is their hatred of the native.

"I'm sorry," he said out loud. "Thanks for bringing this to me. I won't mention your name when I give it to the SAIF." He smiled and pulled out a chair. "Please, take a seat," he said. "Tell me more about your job."

Harold was waiting for Julia when she emerged from the house in a cotton shift drawn in so that it bellowed above the waist, its clean white collar peeking out from underneath a loose beige cardigan. She glanced around her shyly.

When he saw her, Harold breathed in sharply. As she stood there, unaware of his presence, she looked composed and, at the same time, unsure. That was, he thought, what attracted him to Julia: This very combination of strength and vulnerability. That was what kept him persistent despite her every rebuff.

It was a good sign, he thought, to have been invited. He knew that she regarded the Felsteins almost as family.

She looked straight at him. She smiled, and that smile wiped away his day of work. It was his turn to feel shy.

She walked straight over to him. "Come in," she said. "They won't bite: They're nice people, really they are."

Together they turned to go in, but before they entered, Harold happened to glance up. He started in horror. For above him the sky had suddenly seemed to go black and to screech out at him. It was horrible, like a presentiment of doom. He shuddered and closed his eyes.

When he opened them again, he saw that the blackness was nothing more than a couple of ravens that had flown straight above him, blocking out the fading sun. He smiled in embarrassment. Julia, he thought in relief, had not noticed his overreaction.

"Come in," she repeated, as she took Harold through the open front door and into the huge dining room.

They were greeted by Morrie and Esther, who seated the young couple side by side and plied them with a variety of delicious home-cooked food while they left the conversation up to the other guests.

Finally everybody, as Morrie announced, was stuffed. He turned to Harold.

"So, my boy," he said, "I hear you're a genius accountant."

Harold smiled at Julia.

"No, no," Morrie said. "Not from her. She keeps you a dark secret. But it's your brother who sings your praises."

"You know Solly?"

"Know him?" Morrie roared. "Why, when I was younger, I used to coach him in soccer. He wasn't bad, wasn't bad at all. Success has made him fat, thought." He looked Harold up and down. "You're in better shape," he said. "Do you play?"

"Not really."

"So tell me—what is it that occupies your time? Apart from Julia, that is."

"Politics," Harold replied.

A deathly and sudden silence descended on the table.

Julia kicked herself. She should have known this was going to happen—she should have warned Harold. Morrie was an affectionate, warm man, but on one subject a tyrant—he would not allow politics at the table. She tried to interrupt, to change the subject, but Morrie got in first.

"Politics." His voice was deceptively sweet. "And what aspect in particular, may I ask?"

"At the moment," Harold replied, and he hesitated as if he knew that he was getting himself into more hot water, "at the moment, the strike," he finally said.

Morrie put his glass down on the table. "I see," he said. "So you are a man of many talents—an accountant and a miner."

Harold smiled. "You don't have to be a miner to be interested in the strike."

"So tell me, young man," Morrie said. "Why are you interested in the strike?"

"Because I want to live in a society that is free and equal." Harold's eyes shone. "And I believe that only the organized working class can bring it about."

"A communist," Morrie muttered. "And, I assume, an unbeliever?"

"I am not religious," Harold replied, "if that's what you mean."

"A man who has forsaken God."

Harold felt Julia stiffen beside him. Drop it, he told himself.

"A man who spits on our traditions," continued Morrie. "A boy who calls himself a man."

Harold could not stop himself. "I believe in something more precious than God," he said. "I believe in justice for all people."

Morrie thumped the table with his large fist so hard that the paraffin lamp wobbled. Esther reached out to steady it, an uncomfortable expression on her face.

"Now, Morrie," she warned. "Harold is our guest."

"Don't we believe in plain speaking?" Morrie was in full cry now. "Shouldn't we put right a guest, such a young man, too, whose head is filled with so much nonsense? This young man who believes in justice, a justice founded on a dictatorship, no less? Am I right, or am I right?"

"A dictatorship of the proletariat," Harold said softly.

"A dictatorship," Morrie confirmed, "composed primarily of Jew-haters."

The dinner disintegrated after that. Conversation at the Felsteins faltered, until finally it ground to a complete halt. It wasn't Harold's fault: He kept his thoughts to himself. But every time somebody else began to speak, Morrie would chip in with a muttered "A Bolshevik—huh!" and knock the speaker off his stride.

Finally Julia could stand it no longer. "Let's go," she whispered. Within minutes they had thanked their hosts and were on their way.

Harold was depressed. Julia hadn't said a word since they'd left the Felsteins, and neither had he. He had no idea how to break the deadlock, torn as he was between the twin poles of anger and upset.

Morrie Felstein, he thought, is an idiot, a destructive fool. How could one live in South Africa without discussing politics? How could he, a child who had witnessed the defeat of the 1906 revolution in Russia, not feel inspired by the events of 1917?

And yet, if he could have taken back the words he'd uttered so casually, he would have done so now. It wasn't the social isolation he minded, it was Julia's withdrawal from him. For the first time in his adult life he realized that there was something as important as, perhaps more important than, politics. And that something was Julia.

His time was running out. They had already reached the intersection that separated her street from his.

Taking his courage in both hands, he turned to her. "Angry with me?" he asked.

"No," she said quietly, "not angry."

She was speaking the truth; she was not angry. She was, instead, confused. It had all gone wrong, her pathetic attempt to bring her two worlds together. She should never have dreamed of it.

She did not blame Harold. She knew of his interest in politics—his passion for it—and she respected him for it. Moreover, his behavior at the table had made him grow in her eyes. Because of the thinness of his physique, she had assumed he was somehow weak, but he had shown, in the calm way he dealt with the enraged Morrie, that he was strong. That realization set the seal on her attraction to him.

And yet she was disturbed. The world was such a complicated place. Why was it, she thought, that people continually fought? What was the point of all their arguing? As she looked at Harold, she felt an overwhelming sadness.

His heart went out to her. She stood there, her expression mirroring her feeling, her dark hair falling gently around her face. She was open to him. She was showing herself vulnerable, truly vulnerable, for the first time since he'd met her. He itched to console her.

But he wanted to do something more. He couldn't stop himself. He reached over and kissed her lightly on the cheek.

When she didn't push him off, he moved a trifle closer. And still she stayed where she was. He touched her lips gently, and then embraced her.

He got no further than that. A small voice spoke out from the shadows. "Harold," it said.

He started, and turned. Sandra de Groot, he saw, was standing a few paces away, sheltering from sight beneath a small balcony. She must have seen him about to kiss Julia, he thought, and wondered why he felt slightly guilty. He stepped toward her.

"I brought you these," she said abruptly, and she held some sheets of paper at him: It was too dark to decipher them.

"You better come in to my house," he said. "I can't read a thing here."

He turned to find that Julia was walking purposefully away from them. He called out her name.

She neither stopped nor turned around. "I'll see myself home," she replied.

Sighing, Harold escorted Sandra into his house.

When she got in, Julia went straight upstairs. She pulled her dress over her head so hard that she ripped it in the process. She didn't care: she didn't care about anything. She walked up to the basin that was placed on a high stand in the corner of her bedroom. She dipped her fingers into the water and splashed it on her face. Then, viciously, she began to scrub.

It took her a long time to complete her ablutions, and by the time she had, her cheeks were reddened and sore. Her ill-temper remained. She grabbed a nightdress, shoved herself into it, and jumped onto her bed.

And then she heard her mother's voice. "Julia, Julia," Riva called. "A visitor."

She might have ignored Riva's shouts if not for the fact that she would melt in the face of another confrontation. She shoved her arms into her dressing gown and stomped down the stairs.

"What?" she asked.

Riva was waiting at the bottom, a disagreeable expression on her face. "Visitors," she commented sourly, "at this time of night." She put her hands on her hips to emphasize her disapproval.

Harold was standing just inside the door. He threw her a tentative smile.

Julia scowled at him. "You better come into the dining room," she said.

She followed him in and shut the door on Riva's face. Then she faced him.

He was beginning to think the visit was a mistake. He steeled himself. "I wanted to see if you were all right," he began.

"I was in bed," she snapped.

"I'm sorry." Harold faltered. He moved toward the door.

"Who was that woman?" Julia demanded.

Harold stopped and turned.

"Who was she?" Julia repeated.

"Sandra de Groot." Harold's voice was soft. "You met her once," he concluded. He sounded puzzled.

Or guilty, Julia thought. "And what is she to you?" she asked.

"A friend," Harold replied.

"I see," Julia said, "a friend like me."

Harold stared straight at her. "No, not like you," he said. "She's helping me with some work."

"What work?" Julia was relentless.

Harold hesitated. "I can't really talk about it," was what he came up with. "It wouldn't be fair," he said quickly.

"I see," Julia repeated. She thought she did see—only too clearly. This de Groot, this pretty Afrikaner, spent time with Harold *and* had secrets with him. Secrets from which she, Julia, was excluded. Well, she knew where she stood—didn't she?

"I'm tired," she said.

Harold nodded. "Sorry to disturb you," he said. "I just wanted to tell you I had a lovely evening."

Julia made a face.

"Not the argument at the Felsteins," he said quickly. "But I enjoyed the journey back. And when . . ." He took two hurried steps toward her, kissed her passionately on the lips, and then retreated fast. "Good night," he said.

Suddenly he was gone, leaving Julia to stand in the middle of the arid dining room, her confusion multiplied a hundredfold.

Sandra was bone-tired by the time she got home. She had hoped to slip in unnoticed, but when she saw the light shining through the moth-eaten curtains, she knew that Jamie must still be up. She set her face into a deliberately neutral expression and walked in.

Jamie was waiting for her. "I was worried," he said.

She glanced at him in surprise. It was rare that Jamie exhibited even the slightest concern for her. "I went to see Harold," she explained. "He says there's bound to be a strike."

"*Ja*," Jamie agreed, "everybody's talking about it." He clicked his tongue. "It's going to be hard for Ma," he said. "Just when we've got on our feet again." He hardened his voice. "But no *kaffir*'s going to take my job," he concluded.

"It's not the *kaffirs*, though, is it?" Sandra asked. "It's the bosses who are our enemies."

Jamie snorted in derision. "You've been spending too much time with that bolshie. You in love with him or something?"

Sandra shook her head violently. "Why would I be?" she asked loudly. He's got a girlfriend, she thought to herself. I saw them kissing.

"Thank Christ for that," Jamie said. "Bloody interfering commies."

9

1922

> To: All members of the South African Industrial Federation and federated unions:
>
> Following our recent delegate meeting, the SAIF has agreed to ballot all mining and electrical workers. Members will be asked to decide whether to strike with the coal miners in protest at recent wage cuts.
>
> The ballot will be held on January 2, and ballot papers will be issued at all pit heads.
>
> BE SURE TO VOTE. IT'S YOUR JOB ON THE LINE.

They had gathered outside their places of work, the white miners of the Rand. The mine shafts were silent, as if they, too, were waiting. Their human cargo was all outside—those who had just ended their shift, those who had no need to be in that day, those who should even now be winched down in buckets. They stood together, silent, disciplined, expectant.

They were not alone. Among them mingled people who had never been underground but whose jobs neverthless depended on the mines: shopkeepers, outfitters, salesmen—men from every walk of life. The chairman of the Chamber of Mines had been right: The wealth of South Africa was founded on gold—if the miners struck, then everyone would be affected.

All over the curve of the Golden Reef, from Heidelberg in the east to Krugersdorp and Randfontein in the west, similar meetings were occurring. For they were united now, the white miners of the Rand—united in their need to hear the results of the ballot. A strike was in the offing: a strike that would change their lives.

But regardless of how serious a strike might be, there was a holiday atmosphere among the crowd. As they milled together, gossip was exchanged, the sound of laughter rang out, good-tempered banter flew in the air. They had been waiting a long time for this.

Harold was among them, standing beside Jamie de Groot. Harold had come to hear the news firsthand, and he could barely contain his excitement. They would vote for a strike, he thought, they had to.

"Here it comes," muttered Jamie. "About *blerry* time."

The mood grew all at once more serious. The crowd stirred as a man mounted the orange crates that stood in front of them. He was small and timid-looking; his clothes crumpled; he stood for a moment blinking into the sunlight. He should have been an object of ridicule, but the day had given him stature. For this was no longer an ordinary man—this was an SAIF official, and as such he could have stopped the most acrimonious argument, the most intense lovemaking, even, because nothing was more important than the news he brought.

"Brothers," he called.

A sigh went up. A collective intake of breath.

"Brothers," the man continued, "I bring with me the results of the ballot." He reached into his pocket and drew out a piece of paper. His hand trembled as he held it in front of him.

"Get on with it!" shouted a deep voice.

The official cleared his throat. "The vote was taken," he said in a reedy voice, "on the issue of a strike against the recent wage cuts in our industry. The official results of this ballot are as follows: those in favor—fourteen thousand. Those against—one thousand, three hundred, and thirty-six." He refolded the paper, put it back in his pocket, and then looked straight at the crowd. "Brothers," he said, and his voice had gained in strength, "we are now on strike."

For a moment nobody moved. Time was frozen. The official's words hung over the crowd, and the crowd seemed reluctant to let them land.

And then the spell was broken. Jamie's fist shot into the air. "Strike!" he called.

His words were echoed from all around. "Strike!" they shouted. "Strike. Hurrah!"

Harold broke into a huge grin. He wanted to pinch himself, since he could hardly believe he was part of it, that he had been part of it from the first. Look at them, these men of the soil, who had voted so solidly for a strike. It was a turning point in South Africa; their time had come. Now, the working class would show the bosses what it could do!

He turned to Jamie and shook his hand heartily. "Brother," he said, "it has started."

Jamie laughed. "*Ja*," he agreed. "This is the best day of my life. We will win."

The man on the orange box was still talking—telling of arrangements that had been made, of action to be taken, of meeting places and picket points.

"As if we need to picket," Jamie said. "Everybody voted for the strike." But along with the others, he moved closer. They had voted as individuals: Now, the results of the ballot had unified them. They gathered together in a tight knot, and they listened carefully.

Harold turned and looked back at the mine. The black workers were waiting just inside the compound gates. He spotted Nathaniel in the forefront of the watchers.

Harold crossed the road. "Good news!" he shouted.

Nathaniel did not return his smile. It was possible that he had not even seen or heard his friend, because he continued to look past him, concentrating on the crowd. The miner immediately next to him was doing likewise. As Harold came closer, he saw all the blacks were watching the scene in silence and in a kind of fear.

Harold took one step nearer. "Nathaniel?" he asked. "Aren't you pleased? This is an unprecedented show of workers' strength."

"Of white workers' strength," Nathaniel replied.

"You could join them," Harold said.

Finally Nathaniel looked straight at Harold. "Could we?"

Harold blushed. He had, in his excitement, got carried away, he knew he had. For of course the white workers were not about to let the blacks join them.

But then he looked back at the crowd, and his shame evaporated. He felt the energy of those men. Burned on his mind was the time when Jamie's fist had been raised to the sky: That was a worker in action, he thought, that was progress. They were using their true power for the first time, exerting their industrial muscle. Only good could come from this.

"You could hardly expect them to accept a wage cut, could you?" he asked Nathaniel.

"It's not as simple as that," Nathaniel coldly replied. "You know it isn't. They're striking against the abolition of the color bar."

"But that is only because they have no developed sense of class consciousness yet," Harold protested. "At the moment they think that as long as you're at the bottom of the pile, they must be better off. This strike will change things. Wait and see."

Through the wire Nathaniel smiled. "I'll wait, my friend," he said. "I'll wait. What other choice do I have?" And with that, he turned away and walked back across the mine compound.

"Papa!" shouted Moses, as he threw himself into Nathaniel's arms. He laughed as his father tossed him in the air. "Higher," he instructed. "Higher."

Evelyn was at the door, and she was smiling. She loved to see them play like that, she never tired of the sight. Moses was nearing five, and yet sometimes she still caught herself thinking of his birth as a miracle—never more often than when she saw her husband with their son. They were so alike in appearance, those two, and so fond of each other's company. She did not know how she and Nathaniel had ever lived as a couple alone.

"Enough now," Nathaniel said, as he put Moses back onto the ground. "Let me greet your mother."

He went up to Evelyn and kissed her.

"So, my husband?"

Nathaniel frowned. "You heard they voted to strike?"

She nodded. "What about our people?"

"The bosses brought us together as soon as the whites walked out," he replied. "They told us they have to close the mines. People will be fed but are advised to stick close to the compounds. They cannot guarantee protection."

"Why should you need protection?" Moses' small voice piped up.

Nathaniel knelt down until his face was level with the boy's.

"Because the white miners may attack us," he said, "if they think we're still working."

"But aren't you on strike?" Moses asked.

Nathaniel shook his head. He saw the boy's lips move as if he was working at something. He waited patiently.

"If you're not on strike, then you're a scab," is what Moses came up with.

Evelyn took one step forward. "Moses," she began. "Watch your—"

But Nathaniel cut her off. "It's not as simple as that," he gently explained. "The whites haven't asked us to join their strike, since part of the reason they're striking is because of us."

"But why?" Moses asked.

"Because we Africans are made to work for less money, and the mine owners wanted to cut costs. So they decided to offer us Africans more work," Nathaniel said. "The whites didn't want that."

"So the strikers are bad?" Moses frowned.

"It's not as simple as that," Nathaniel said. "They had to refuse a wage cut. They're not bad—they're backward. If they were not so blind, they could ally with us. We would be willing to help them. Do you understand?"

Moses nodded, although his eyes showed that he distinctly didn't understand. Nathaniel pushed him gently in the direction of the house and laughed softly. "Go along now," he said. "I'll tell you more about it later."

As the boy ran away, Nathaniel stood up. He strolled over to Evelyn and put one arm around her waist.

"It's a mess," she commented.

"Harold thinks the process of the strike will make the whites understand that we, too, are part of the working class and therefore their allies."

"Harold is wrong," Evelyn stated.

"I'm afraid so," Nathaniel agreed. "Harold doesn't know the whites like we do."

For two months the white miners struck. Solid to the last man, they refused to go down into the bowels of the earth. For two months the black work force, confined to the mine compounds, buffeted by the dual forces of white anger and the white state, stayed idle. Many of them were forcibly moved out of the compounds and sent back to the country without a penny to their names, so that the Chamber could save on the food bill. They were powerless to intervene in this, the greatest of confrontations between mine owner and worker. No one asked them for their help. No one used their labor.

"Strike" was the word on everybody's lips. It pervaded the very air they breathed. No aspect of life was left untouched by it. People dug out their old lamps, and oil became a rare commodity as electricity faded from the towns. Whole sections of the Rand became no-go areas as the strikers prepared themselves for the battle to come. Stores were strangely empty as women began hoarding food, planning for the day when the whole country came out.

Jamie stood in line, grinning broadly. It was good to be part of the commandos, he thought, really good. At long last the Afrikaner was fighting for himself, fighting against the bosses and against the *kaffir*.

"We will win," he said out loud. "We will win."

"*Ja*, of course we will win," the man next to him agreed.

A drum sounded, and Jamie and his companion fell silent.

"Fellow commandos," came a faint voice from the front. "We are about to move off to Boksburg Gaol, where our brothers have been imprisoned. We will show them that we have not forgotten them, we will give them comfort. Maintain your discipline, stick together, and listen to our instructions. Our band will make our march an easy one."

The drum sounded again, and was joined by another and then another. The march had begun.

Jamie's feet moved one in front of the other, marching to the sound of songs from his childhood. He had never felt so happy or so powerful, as he walked among his fellow Afrikaners. They would win against the industrialists, he thought. For too many years they had been despised. Now their time had come.

When finally the march drew to a halt, Jamie could see the solid outline of the Boksburg Police Station. In there, he knew, were strikers arrested a few days ago. Well, they wouldn't be in there long, he thought.

"Free them!" came a shout.

"Free them," echoed Jamie.

The cry went up and up into the air. The drums began again,

rolling in accompaniment to the sound of voices.

At first the jail was quiet, receiving the cries without apparent reaction. But then, as Jamie watched, a side door opened. A line of police issued from it. They stood against the wall, guns in hand.

"Ag, look at them," cried one of the strikers. "*Blerrry* cowards, you can even see the whites of their eyes."

A derisory laugh went up. Jamie moved with the crowd—one step closer.

"Free them!" he cried.

The line of police, to a man, were like statues: They made no response. The crowd shifted uneasily.

And then the drums banged again, with the other instruments, recorders and trumpets, joining in the melody. From the front, one lone male voice began to sing.

> *"The people's flag is deepest red,*
> *It's shrouded oft our martyred dead."*

The voice seemed lonely, melancholy. But as the verse progressed, it gained in strength and in beauty.

> *"And 'ere their limbs grew stiff and cold,*
> *Their hearts' blood dyed its every fold."*

Jamie stood transfixed by the sound—imagining the days when he was a child, when his father had still been alive, when they'd stood in the midst of an open veld and looked at the land that was once theirs.

"Then raise the scarlet standard high," sang the voice.

"Within its shade we'll live or die," sang Jamie, and he felt, rather than heard, that the whole crowd was singing with him.

"Though cowards flinch and traitors sneer," they sang, "we'll keep the red flag flying here."

Of what happened next there were many versions, none of which were in complete agreement.

After it was over, Police Captain Jock Fulford said that the crowd moved menacingly toward him—about to storm the jail. His only intention, he said, was to maintain law and order: About that he had no choice.

The crowd's view was different. Many had no idea what happened, but of those who claimed to remember, most said a cheer went up among the men, a rousing, good-natured cheer. There was no push forward, they said, no thought of storming the jail.

The only thing that the two sides could agree on was that the song was over by the time Captain Fulford spoke.

The policemen, to a man, crouched down on one knee.

"Fire," ordered the captain.

The policemen were well trained, and they obeyed their orders. Before there was a chance for the crowd to react, shots rang out.

They only fired one round. But when it was over, there were three bodies lying still on the ground. Jamie's was one.

Julia traveled home without really noticing her surroundings: She had made the journey so many times that she traveled it automatically. Only when she found herself walking down her street did she come to consciousness. It had got dirtier, she realized, since the strike began. Well, that wasn't surprising—only the other day, she had caught some children riffling through the rubbish. She had sneaked some bread from the kitchen—Riva would never have approved—and given it to them, but she had seen that look in their eyes as they snatched it from her. They needed more, she knew, than a few stale crusts.

"Julia."

She glanced up and saw Harold. She cursed herself for her inattention: If she had been more on her toes, she might have avoided him—just as he had quite obviously been avoiding her. But it was too late now. She set her mouth in a determined grin. She did not want to show him how much she cared, how angry she had been at the way he'd dropped her after the night he'd kissed her.

She saw how his face lit up, but that was no consolation. All he wants is to revert to the old ways, she thought bitterly. Well, she wouldn't give him the satisfaction of showing that she cared. "Hello, Harold," she said brightly.

"Julia." He put out a hand, but she moved away as if she hadn't noticed it.

"I've been busy lately," she said.

"Oh."

"Well, then," she said. When he gave no indication that he

was going to say anything else, she walked past him. "I've got to go home," she said.

She took a few paces before she heard his voice again. "Julia," he called. She turned and looked at him.

"I'm sorry I've been so absent," he said quickly. "I've missed you. But it's this strike, you see. I've been working at headquarters, and we're so short of manpower I haven't been able to get away."

The strike, thought Julia. Bloody strike. "That's okay," she said.

"I'm going to visit some friends," Harold told her. "Want to come?"

It was in her mind to refuse, to walk on home, to leave Harold Arnold to his strike, his work, his politics. All of that was in her mind.

But her heart had a different strategy, and it seemed to control her mouth. "I'd like to," she said.

When they finally arrived at Harold's friends' house—a journey that took Julia through parts of Jo'burg she'd never seen before—she wished that she'd refused. For contrary to her every expectation, these friends were black—Evelyn and Nathaniel Bopape, Harold called them.

Julia didn't know where to look. She had never visited a native, never been to one's house. She tried to keep her face a careful neutral, to avoid wrinkling her nose at the smell emanating from the open sewage tank at the back of the yard. She smiled to hide her own confusion.

"Julia Cyn," said Evelyn. "Is your father Zelig?"

Julia nodded. Evelyn said something to Nathaniel—in Xhosa, Harold later explained. Julia looked down at the ground. She wished she had gone home, she resented Harold for bringing her here.

"Your father is a good man," Evelyn said. "He once saved my husband from being arrested." She smiled, and her face was suffused with a warmth and comfort it was difficult to resist. "Come," she said, "let me take you to my son, Moses. He's dying to meet you, but he's too shy to venture out."

The relief that Julia had felt on hearing Evelyn's words were somewhat driven away by her shock at the inside of the Bopape house. She could not believe that anything could be quite so small, quite so dark, quite so depressing. It was clean enough, she supposed, although she could not really see. But to think that a couple and their five-year-old lived, ate, slept, in this small space!

"Come now, Moses," Evelyn coaxed. "Let's go outside."

A weight seemed to fall from Julia's shoulders when Moses crawled out from under the only bed and came to stand by his mother. When they all got outside, she breathed in deeply and exhaled in gratitude. She understood now why the adults had been in the open when they had arrived.

She avoided Harold's eyes—for some reason she did not want him to see how strange all this was to her.

But she soon found that she was enjoying herself. Evelyn and Nathaniel were warm and lively company, and she could see how much Harold relaxed with them. Of course, there was a lot of political banter, plenty of exchanges about the strike, but Julia didn't really mind. She kept quiet when that went on, waiting for it to end.

She couldn't get away with silence entirely. "You're not following the strike?" Evelyn asked at one point.

Julia shrugged shyly. "I don't really understand it," she said in a small voice. She hoped she didn't look too foolish.

She needn't have worried. "Well, at least you'll admit it," Nathaniel said. "Unlike this one." He shook his head in Harold's direction. "He pretends to understand, and won't listen when I tell him how wrong he is."

"Ag, Nathaniel . . ." Harold began.

Suddenly a man came rushing into the yard.

Julia shrank back.

The man was young and black, covered with blood dripping down his forehead.

Evelyn exclaimed loudly and, with Nathaniel, went to support the newcomer.

There was a rapid exchange of conversation, all incomprehensible to Julia. But she didn't need words to see that the newcomer was terrified, and she understood that she and Harold were causing his fright.

When he had finished talking, Evelyn began to soothe him. Julia heard her own and Harold's names mentioned. Visibly the man began to calm.

Having achieved her goal, Evelyn went inside, only to return with a basin and cloth. She pointed to a seat, and as soon as the man had taken it, she began to clean his head.

"What happened?" Harold asked.

Evelyn shrugged and continued with her work.

Harold turned to Nathaniel. "What happened?" he repeated.

Julia, whose eyes had followed Harold's, was shocked by the look in Nathaniel's face. For Nathaniel was no longer the genial host, the kind stranger. Instead, his forehead was set in a grim frown, his mouth in a tight line.

"What happened, you ask me?" he said slowly. "Your friends, those glorious members of the working class, attacked this man."

"Why? What did he do?" Harold asked.

Nathaniel jumped to his feet, and for the first time Julia saw how big a man he was. She felt suddenly afraid.

But Nathaniel's wrath was aimed at Harold, not at her. "Why did he need to do anything?" he snarled. "It's enough that he sprang from his mother's womb, that she was black and that he is, too. You don't need a reason to attack a *kaffir* in this country."

"Oh, come on, Nathaniel," Harold protested.

"No, Harold," said Nathaniel slowly. "I have tolerated your foolishness long enough. You are well-meaning, but your blindness has become intolerable. Don't you see what's happening around you? Can't you see?"

With each word, Nathaniel took one further step toward Harold. His fists, Julia saw, were clenched and big as hammers. Her face went white.

"Can't you see?" Nathaniel repeated.

Julia let out a small cry, but Nathaniel did not hear. He took one further step.

"Nathaniel." Evelyn's voice was authoritative. "You're terrifying the girl."

Nathaniel stopped in his tracks. He shook himself as if emerging from a trance. He smiled, apologetically, in Julia's direction. "These are terrible times," he said. He reseated himself.

In the awkward silences that followed, before their white guests departed, Evelyn glanced surreptitiously at her husband. He had cooled down, she saw, but he had not forgotten. Nor had he forgiven Harold. She felt a shiver of fear. She knew how much Harold meant to Nathaniel, how close was the two men's friendship. And she knew, without being able to justify it, that if Nathaniel gave up on Harold, then he personally would be much depleted. Thank God, the girl was here, she thought. It would have been much worse without her.

When Harold finally got up to go, after a concerted effort on everyone's part to keep the conversation going, even Evelyn was relieved. She did not rise: She was cradling a sleeping Moses in her arms. She smiled at Julia. "We will see you again," she stated.

Julia nodded and turned to Harold. But he wasn't finished yet. He put his hands into his pocket and drew up what could only have been a wad of money. This he thrust at Nathaniel.

"I know you cannot work," he said, "and have no strike pay."

Nathaniel glowered as he waved the money away. "We manage to look after ourselves," he said. "My wife takes in washing. Save your charity for your white friends."

Again Evelyn interfered. "Nathaniel," was all she said, but her voice spoke legions.

Reluctantly Nathaniel held out his hand. "There are many in need," he admitted. "I will take this on their behalf."

"We thank you, Harold," Evelyn said.

When they had finally disappeared from sight, Evelyn tried to talk to Nathaniel about his reactions. "Harold is young," she began.

"He's old enough to know better." The tone said it all: It defied her to continue with the conversation.

Carefully she laid the sleeping Moses on the ground. She got up and went to stand by her husband. In silence they looked toward the horizon, to where pink streaks were announcing the end of the day.

And in another part of the Rand, Sandra de Groot, Jamie's sister, was also looking at the sky. She had come out for some air, she'd said, but in reality she had wanted to leave the house, to get away from the racking sounds of her mother's grief, the half-begun sentences of condolence, the awkward way the others looked at her. They're relieved it wasn't their brother, she thought. And already they're worrying about what tomorrow will bring.

As the sky became suffused with pink, softening the outline of the harsh earth, the bitterness fell, for a moment, from Sandra's mind. She was wrong, she knew, to criticize their friends and neighbors. The strike had hit them all badly, they were all hollow-cheeked, their children whimpering in continual hunger, and yet they had dug deep into their purses and brought something, every last one of them, as tribute to the grieving household. For the first time since she'd heard the news, two solitary tears rolled down Sandra's cheeks.

But the moment was lost all too soon when the door opened and Sandra once more heard her mother cry. The bitterness returned.

"Someone will be punished for Jamie's death," she vowed.

10

1922

NOT ONE OF THE CROWD STIRRED: THEY STOOD TO ATTENTION, FIVE thousand of them stood in Jo'burg's Union Grounds, completely still as one lonely trumpet sounded the Last Post.

And even when it was over, when the last note had died away, the crowd was reluctant to move. The people continued to stand motionless, staring straight ahead, waiting perhaps for a focus for their concentration and their energy.

A man climbed onto the platform, and the crowd responded by moving a step closer. The man held up his hand as if to hold off the encroaching wave.

"Brothers!" he shouted. "We came to remember our fellow strikers, felled by police guns. They are martyrs to our cause, and we will never forget them. And we are not alone when we vow to keep up the struggle in the name of those who fell at Boksburg. All over the country, not only in the Rand but in the Cape, the OFS, Natal, memorial services are being held. In meetings such as ours, resolve is being redoubled. In Jo'burg we will march in protest: In our capital, Pretoria, work will stop at noon while our brothers stand to attention in front of red flags hung at half-mast." He paused and looked around the crowd, smiling at the murmurs of appreciation that greeted his words. Then he took a deep breath.

"And what," he asked, and his voice rose, "does our prime minister, General Smuts, say while South Africa mourns its brave sons?" He looked around him. "I tell you what he says!" he shouted. "He says nothing."

"Shame!" came the cry.

The man waited until the noise had abated. "And what," he finally asked, "does Smuts do?" A pause. "I tell you what he does—he organizes for our defeat. We know that troops are being mobilized, and we know what that means: They will soon be in our streets, our mines, our homes."

"Never," shouted the crowd. "Never."

Again the man held up his hand. "Ja," he said. "You are right. We will not let them crush us. We are not alone, neither are we powerless. General Barry Hertzog, leader of our Nationalist party, spoke the truth when he said that the country is ninety percent behind the strikers. We have only to ask, and the Platteland commandos will join us in our fight."

This time when the crowd surged forward, the man did not hold up his hand to stop it. Instead, he waved it onward. Go out, he seemed to be saying, although his voice could no longer be heard, go out and fight.

And the crowd obeyed him; it surged toward the Union Ground exit. Everybody was pushed in its sway, those who wanted to go and those who did not. The crowd was on the move.

"You see?" repeated Harold when he and Danny had finally managed to detach themselves from the melee. "You see how militant they are?"

"I see!" Danny shouted above the din. "And I also am not deaf. What good will come from having allies like Hertzog? Haven't you heard the way he speaks of communists and of natives? Your friend Nathaniel is right. No good can come of this."

"Look!" Harold shouted. In the distance the crowd was forming into a procession. A band began to play. And there, right in the front, was a flag—a huge red flag.

"How can we not be involved in this?" Harold asked. "It's a revolution, I tell you."

"Some revolution," Danny commented bitterly. "Can't you see the slogan, right behind the flag?"

Harold stood on tiptoe and craned his head. "Workers of the world unite," he read.

"For a white South Africa," Danny finished. "A white South

Africa," he repeated. Harold didn't hear. He was pushing his way toward the marchers.

Morrie was waiting for Julia when she arrived at work. Beside him stood Gert Prinsloo.

"You have not changed your mind?" Morrie asked Julia.

"Why should I?" she answered briskly. She averted her eyes to avoid the look that Gert shot at her.

But Morrie did not ignore it. He turned to Gert. "You want to find a job elsewhere?" he asked.

Gert looked down at the ground.

Morrie paused, but when no reply was forthcoming, he softened his voice. "Look here," he said. "I don't like this any more than you do. But I am a businessman, not a director of a charity. Would you work for me if I didn't pay you?"

Morrie smiled when he saw how Gert's eyes remained focused on his shoes. "Of course you wouldn't," he said. "So how can they expect to keep my furniture when they haven't paid for it? I understand that you need to keep on friendly terms with them for the future, and that is why I have asked Julia to make each decision. All you have to do is to remove my goods when she so instructs."

He turned to Julia. "If they don't pay," he said, "I want that furniture back. And I want it today," he concluded loudly.

"Come on," Gert muttered. "Let's go."

Julia sat next to Gert, perched high above the ground, as he headed the horse-drawn car westward. Their journey through Burgherdorp, Fordsburg, and finally to Langlaagte was a familiar one, this time conducted in almost total silence. The lack of conversation wasn't the result of any choice on Julia's part. In fact, she tried, initially, to talk, but when Gert responded only with monosyllabic grunts, she gave up. Gert was being childish, she told herself. It's not my fault, she thought. I'm only doing my job.

And after all, there was no real reason to talk. Johannesburg was in turmoil that day, and there were plenty of things to see. Ranks of mounted police passed this way and that, their faces under their round helmets looking grim and resolute. Crowds that gathered at every street corner grew silent at the police's approach, but broke again into frantic chatter as soon as they had ridden by. There was a tension in the air, and an excitement, too. The commitment of the strikers had risen to fever pitch, and yet those who opposed them had not wavered. Things had to change, and change dramatically—everybody knew that.

Julia's eyes widened as she took in the sights and the sounds of Jo'burg. She felt somewhat shocked, as if the strike had finally broken into her consciousness. At Morrie's nobody spoke of strikes, and so she had been protected from the enormity of what was happening. But now she saw by the battle lines being drawn up, by the determination in the faces of strikers and police alike, that there was no avoiding what was happening. And in realizing this, she felt her own ignorance.

I'll ask Harold, she resolved to herself. He'll explain it.

She smiled to herself. She and Harold were closer these days: Ever since they had gone to visit Evelyn and Nathaniel, ever since she had comforted him about Nathaniel's inexplicable behavior, the bond between them had been strengthened. And the strike had even benefited her: for with Harold so occupied, there was no question of her having to choose whether to take their relationship a step further. He was her friend, her good, brave friend.

"Nearly there," muttered Gert—his first voluntary statement in a long while.

Julia looked up in surprise. They had left the city, she saw, and the bustle had been replaced by peace. The sky was an undisturbed blue, the veld shimmered in front of them. The cart moved slowly, making its way down the dirt track, throwing up red dust in its wake.

At first Julia could hear only the clip-clop of the horse, but as they progressed, she became accustomed to the sounds of the countryside: the clatter of the cicadas and the buzzing of the bees as they set to work on the wildflowers that struggled for light among the tall, pink-tipped grass. In the distance she could see a small *kopje*—a hillock—crowned by one lonely wild pear tree. It was all so peaceful and so spacious—Julia loved this countryside with its colors of reds and faded browns.

"I wouldn't mind living here," she said.

Gert gave a short laugh. "You think so?" was all he said.

They were approaching the town. Julia saw the yellow of the mine dumps in the near distance and the settlement of small houses that surrounded them. It was a familiar sight, and she would not have given it a second look except there was something changed about it, something . . . She realized what it was. She turned to Gert.

"It's so quiet," she said.

Gert glanced at her once before hurrying on the horse with a flick of his whip.

Julia blushed. Of course it would be quiet—how could she have forgotten that the metallic clanging of the mine shaft would be stilled?

"Idiot," she whispered to herself. She looked down at her list of families to be visited as she attempted to conceal her embarrassment.

Harold was no longer thinking, driven as he was by the momentum of the crowd. They must have walked for miles, and yet he felt no fatigue. Instead, his head was buzzing with the sounds and the sights that he had just experienced.

There seemed no limit to the crowd's capacity, no brake on its actions. Their numbers had swelled as they progressed, and so had their daring. At first they had been singing and shouting slogans, taunting the display of police strength from afar. But when the police did not react, when it became plain that they were under orders to remain at a distance and so avoid a repetition of Boksburg, the crowd grew bolder, making forays into the police lines to spit at the feet of those who had killed their comrades.

At Fordsburg they went one further. Harold was at the back of the march and did not see the actual event, but word spread like wildfire. The group at the front, it was said, had stormed the police station. When the men in uniform turned tail and ran, the crowd liberated the weapons left behind. That done, they razed the station to the ground. Harold would not have believed the tale except for the evidence before his eyes, for the police station was still burning as he passed it, and the number of guns among the crowd was growing visibly.

And still the crowd pressed on, onward toward the mine. A shiver ran down Harold's back. The workers were on the move: Nothing could stop them. Rumors were no longer unbelievable: Fiction had been turned into fact.

"Nothing will get in our way," Harold muttered.

"Scab," came a shrill voice in the front. "Let's get the scabs."

Harold stopped in his tracks. He recognized that voice, he was sure he did. He frowned—he could not pin it down. Where had he heard it before?

"Scab," called the voice.

Harold managed to catch a fleeting glimpse of the woman in the front.

It was Sandra de Groot—sister of the slain Jamie—shy, serious Sandra, now in command. Unbelievable, Harold thought. That she should change so.

He pushed his way forward, as the crowd, reacting to Sandra's call, moved inexorably toward the mine compound.

And then, all of a sudden, Harold stopped. The ranks behind pushed into him, but he held his ground. He stared straight ahead of him, transfixed by his sight of the crowd's target.

They were about thirty in number, Africans, all of them, poorly dressed, undernourished, rigid in fear behind the wire fence.

"Scabs," called the crowd, and it spread out to push against the fence, propelling Harold with it. The wire vibrated: The Africans moved back.

With a force that he didn't even know he possessed, Harold fought his way free of those around him. He pushed and shoved sideways, without a thought of the damage that he might be causing. He had only one objective. He must reach Sandra, he must get her to listen to reason.

He succeeded. A gap opened up and he exploited it, hurtling forward until he found himself next to her. She was still shouting, brandishing, at the same time, something that looked like an iron bar.

"Kill the scabs!" she screamed.

Harold reached up and pulled the bar from her hands. "Sandra!" he shouted. "Sandra!"

While the crowed pushed forward, Sandra turned to look at him. She was so much changed. Her face was suffused with a passion that drove out the faded prettiness, the reticence, the fatigue. She was a vibrant, angry, militant woman—not a girl any longer. And she was intent on murdering innocent bystanders.

"Stop it!" Harold shouted. "These men are not your enemies."

Sandra's eyes flashed over his face, and she seemed, for a moment, to still herself.

"Tell them to stop it," Harold pleaded.

But once again Sandra's face hardened. She grimaced, and shook her head slowly.

It took all of Harold's concentration to hear her above the noise. "What do you know of our lives, you and your *kaffirboetie* friends? Have you suffered as we have?"

She did not wait for him to answer. Instead, she shoved her face closer to his. "During the Boer War my father was imprisoned in a concentration camp," she said. "He came out a beaten man, and he died defeated. We lost everything, *everything*—can you understand that?"

She laughed hollowly. "But then, how could you? Your brother owns a factory, while mine is buried underground." She spat on the ground. "Jamie is dead," she said, "and someone must pay."

With one ferocious tug, she freed her arm. "Kill them," she called.

Harold had held his breath while Sandra spoke, and now he didn't feel able to release it. The crowd buffeted him from all sides, and he felt a heavy weight on his chest, a tension as if his lungs might be about to burst. When he forced himself to breathe out, there came not air, but a deep hopeless sob. His cheeks were streaming with involuntary tears.

He could never remember how he found the strength to free himself. But manage he did, for he suddenly found himself on his knees, in the middle of an empty section of the street. Behind him, the crowd still shouted as it battered at the wire.

Harold could not look back. He ran—driven by his own guilt, his confusion, his anguish. He had to get away, to shut out the noise of the crowd. He was like an animal, with only escape on his mind.

Panting, he turned the corner. He came to an abrupt halt: There in front of him, strung across the road so that there were no gaps, was a line of mounted police.

Relief washed over him. He waved his arms frantically, pointed toward the mine. "Do something," he shouted.

But the police made no sign that they had heard. Nor did they move.

Harold ran toward them, stood in front of their horses, felt the hot breath of those huge nostrils, and shouted again. Still no response.

He saw an officer, standing to one side. He directed his shouts at this man. "Please do something," he pleaded. "They're going to commit murder."

The officer was chewing a stick, and Harold saw how his jaw worked—round and round, up and down, impassively he sat and chewed.

In desperation Harold reached up to the horse's bridle. But the officer was quicker than Harold was: His whip stung at Harold's hand, forcing him to detach it.

"If I were you, sir," the officer said quietly, "I would run along home. We have the situation under control."

Gert stopped the cart in the middle of the village and jumped down. He pointed to one of the houses.

"You tell them," he said. "I'll do the carrying." He made no attempt to help her out.

Julia smiled brightly. "That's what Mr. Felstein wants." She clambered down from her perch and, clipboard in hand, walked toward the nearest house.

Her first two visits were tolerable enough. The miners and their families seemed dazed by what Julia told them. They shook their heads when she asked them if they could keep up their installments, and they stood aside while Gert humped their possessions into the cart.

They were completely passive, but their appearance spoke for them. With an effort, Julia averted her eyes from them: She did not want to see how hollow their cheeks had become, how white their skin, how dark the rings under their eyes.

It's not my fault, she told herself. There's nothing I can do to stop this happening.

But even so, she hesitated before knocking on Adele Smit's door. Usually she enjoyed the prospect of seeing her friend, for this was not, by any means, her first visit. She had got on with Adele from the very beginning. While other miners' wives made her feel ill at ease, an interloper in their closed community, Adele accepted her, made an effort to get to know her.

In return, it was Julia who had persuaded Adele that she could afford, with judicious budgeting, to acquire the sideboard for which she yearned.

And now Julia was here to divest Adele of her few worldly possessions.

"Julia?" The word was framed as a question.

Julia tried to smile. She thought of Morrie and how he was relying on her. She thought of how grateful he had been when she said she would go, of how much he had helped her and made his home her own, of how burdened he had looked of late.

"I need to talk to you, Adele," she said, and her voice was strong.

Adele nodded and stepped out of the way.

When Julia got inside, her resolve began to weaken. She looked around the shack. She saw the tin can with a single protea flower standing in it. She saw the scrubbed rush matting that kept the sand from rising from the ground. And then she saw Adele's youngest child sitting silently on a chair, his white face bloated from malnutrition.

A host of stories she thought she'd long since forgotten came rushing into Julia's mind. She remembered Zelig's description of the *shtetl*, of the cleanliness amid abject poverty. She remembered Harold talking about the long hours his mother had worked, pounding the Gentiles' washing against the river stones in order to survive, unwanted, among them. And superimposed on these memories came a picture of Evelyn: Evelyn, stoic, uncomplaining, and strong.

She did not understand why this montage of images crowded in on her. She tried to banish them with speech.

"Mr. Felstein can't afford to wait any longer," she said. It's not my decision, she told herself.

There was no anger in Adele's face, only resignation. "Someone has to do it, I suppose," was all she said.

Julia flushed. "Gert," she called.

While they waited, the women avoided each other's eyes. Julia started to count. By the time I reach a hundred, she thought, Gert will have finished and I'll be able to leave.

Gert was at the door. He took off his hat, and holding it in both hands, he nodded at Adele. Then he looked at Julia, his face a careful blank.

"Over there," Julia said, as she pointed at the table. Twenty-four, she thought. Twenty-five.

"My family trekked out here." Adele's voice broke into Julia's counting. "All they wanted was some land they could call their own. We didn't ask for much—just a roof over our heads and shoes for our children."

She gestured to her few sticks of furniture. "This is all I have left," she said. "And what does it mean? My children are starving." She turned her back. "I cannot watch," she said. "Take what you want."

With two hands, Gert gripped at the table. He lifted it into the air.

Forty, counted Julia. Forty-one. Forty-two . . . But no matter how hard she counted, she could not stop herself from hearing what Adele had said. Forty-nine, she thought. There was a kind of buzzing in her head, a scrambling of thoughts. "Someone has to do it." She heard the words as if they had only just been spoken.

And then her head cleared. Someone has to do it, she thought. But that someone does not have to be me.

"Put it back, Gert," she said loudly.

Gert looked at her, astonished, his callused hands gripping the table still poised in midair. "Put it back," she repeated.

A calm assuredness descended on her. Ever since the strike had started, she had felt foolish and confused. Now, she no longer felt that way. She knew what she should do, and the knowledge strengthened her.

Morrie was wrong, absolutely wrong. Even when he talked of money problems, he still did not contemplate a future without a chicken on his table, some candles to light on the Sabbath. These people had nothing.

"Let's go," she told Gert.

Gert's face was transformed. He stared at her in relief, she thought, relief combined with something stronger.

"Let's get out of here," she repeated, and then she understood his look. Respect, that was what it was.

Together the two climbed back into the car. Gert clicked his tongue, and the horse stepped forward. Slowly they moved off up the road, out of the dip in which the mining village stood.

Just as they were about to turn the corner, Julia looked back. Adele was still standing by her doorway, a child beside her. She did not wave, but Julia thought that she must have smiled, because the child said something, and Adele ruffled its hair.

Nathaniel's face, while he listened to Harold, was a neutral blank. It had been that way ever since Harold had come stumbling into their house, dirty and tearful, and had burst into an account of what he had witnessed.

Harold assumed that Nathaniel was concentrating, but Evelyn, who knew him better, knew also how dangerous that look was. She held her breath, hoping that Nathaniel would speak, would move, would by some small indication shed part of the anger that he hid behind this wall of neutrality.

But Nathaniel refrained both from comment, and expression. He was like a panther, Evelyn thought, ready to pounce and to destroy.

"And the police," Harold said, "did nothing. They laughed at me as I left."

At last Nathaniel stirred. "Why should they not laugh?" he asked coldly.

"What d-do you m-mean?" Harold stuttered.

Nathaniel, who had been squatting on the ground, jumped lightly to his feet. "Where have you been?" he asked. "Why do you think it's been so easy for the strikers to obtain arms? Why do you think the police have made no attempt to collect the weapons—many of which are theirs?"

"I don't know." Harold frowned.

"Ayiee," Nathaniel said, "I can't believe this. Is it because we're black that you refuse to understand?" He put his hand under Harold's chin and jerked Harold's face upward. "Can you not see the parallel?" he asked. "Weren't you the one who told me how the czar's police let the peasants arm themselves against the Jews?" The hand let go.

"They *wanted* the strikers to attack the natives," Harold said dully.

"Control the *kaffir* is how they would put it," Nathaniel replied. Now, there was no escaping the contempt, the ridicule, the ferocity, in his voice. "Your precious vanguard and your so-called enemy, the police of South Africa, will always be united on that one principle."

Before Harold looked away, Evelyn saw how his eyes had filled with tears. The panther need not spring, she thought, for the victim is already dying. She wished she could do something to help.

And yet she could not intervene. This was her husband's territory. Harold was her husband's friend, her husband's comrade. An interjection by her would get neither of them anywhere.

Harold had risen. He looked straight at Nathaniel. "I was

wrong," he said. "I know I was wrong."

Nathaniel did not reply.

"Please forgive me."

Nathaniel spat on the floor before turning away.

Moses tugged at Evelyn's sleeve, but she silenced him with a wave. The child was scared: He was frightened by his father's aggressive stance. She knew she should comfort him, but she could not. She needed instead to concentrate, as if by doing so, she could will Nathaniel to change.

For what mattered was his response. If he made no move, no gesture, no hint of forgiveness, then Harold would walk out and never return. As a result, both men would lose a friend.

But, thought Evelyn, Nathaniel will lose more than that.

She, who knew her husband so well, had watched him develop from an awkward youth into a confident leader. He had let her into his most secret thoughts: She had heard his fears, his hopes, his passions. And yet there was one part of his innermost territory to which she had no access—the part that reacted when he felt he had been betrayed.

Never so clearly had Evelyn seen this in action. Harold thought Nathaniel looked like a judge, and Moses thought he looked like a fury, but to her he looked like the child he must have been when he turned his back on his father.

He could not forgive Chief Bopape, she thought. And he has carried the pain ever since. For his sake, I pray that he can forgive Harold.

But it was too late: Harold was on the move. He was halfway out of the yard, his shoulders hunched in a kind of defeat. Evelyn sighed.

And then, only then, did Nathaniel speak. "We all make mistakes," he said. "At least you can acknowledge yours."

As Harold turned back, Evelyn found that, in her relief, she was crying.

Julia and Gert drove back into a Johannesburg that was dramatically altered. Whereas they had left a city in turmoil, now they returned to one that looked like it was on the brink of war. Even the sky had changed: The blue had gone, replaced by dark clouds that hung low above the city.

MARTIAL LAW, proclaimed the newspaper headlines, but they didn't need to read on to see what was happening. For troops, not policemen, patrolled the streets, and they did not stop at mere observation. They carried their guns at the ready, they charged those who had the temerity to be out in their territory, they worked in tandem to dig trenches that they occupied with grim resolve.

Their actions were echoed by the strikers. They, too, were in the midst of new preparations; they cleaned their arms, patrolled the areas over which they had control, dug trenches of occupation.

The battle lines had been well and truly laid. There was now no going back.

At first Julia was too elated by her own action to take much notice. But as they drove through the city, as the normally sedate horse began to shy occasionally and to twitch its tail in agitation, she grew increasingly worried. She looked to Gert for reassurance.

"What's that?" he muttered.

A low droning sound was coming from above, getting louder as she listened. Julia looked at the sky, but there was nothing to see.

She shrugged and smiled at him. "Sound travels in strange ways," she said.

No sooner had she finished speaking when an airplane appeared through the clouds. Straight toward them it flew, far too low for comfort, and the noise was deafening.

Julia ducked: Gert's reaction was even more extreme. He threw himself on the floor of the cart.

That, along with the roar of mechanical engines, was more than the horse could take. It reared up and began to canter forward, heading straight for one of the newly constructed trenches. A piece of furniture flew out the back and crashed to the ground. Julia was tossed against the side of the cart, landing heavily on one shoulder. She struggled upright, but once again the cart swerved: Only by dint of extreme effort did she manage to hold on.

"Gert!" she screamed.

He was no longer frozen. He stretched across and grabbed the reins. Then, with all his might, he pulled, his muscles straining in his neck as he did so.

He had acted just in time. The horse stopped a few yards before the trench.

"Are you all right?" he asked.

Julia nodded.

Gert smiled shamefacedly. "I overreacted," he said. "For a moment it was like the war. I thought we were going to be bombed. Silly, really."

"Not so silly," Julia said. "Look!"

She pointed to the empty place in the sky so recently occupied by the plane. But it wasn't entirely empty. For the airplane had done its own kind of bombing—it had left a mass of paper that even now was floating to the ground.

Julia stretched out her arm and grabbed one of the pieces. She read through it briefly before handing it to Gert.

"Women and children of Fordsburg," it said. "The time has come to evacuate the district. Leave your homes. Make your way to Milner Park, where government troops will protect you."

"Drop me off here," Julia said.

"But—"

"No buts. I know you live in Fordsburg. You must go to your family."

"Where have you been?" Riva cried. "I've been driven half-mad with worry."

Julia heard the anguish in Riva's voice. "It took a long time to come home," she said. Then she noticed the clock in the hall. Perplexed, she gazed at her mother. "I'm not even late," she said. "Why were you so worried?"

"Mr. Felstein came around," Riva replied.

"Oh."

"He wasn't angry," Riva said quickly. "He said he understands, and that he forgives you. You can go back to work tomorrow."

"He forgives me," Julia muttered. She began to walk away.

But Riva's voice followed her. "Don't do anything rash," she pleaded.

"Mr. Felstein's been good to you. You might never find such a responsible job again."

For once Julia did not respond with anger to her mother. Instead of hearing criticism in her mother's voice, she heard the doubt and the uncertainty.

I've grown up at last, she thought in suprise. She remembered how Riva had once said that she was lucky to be able to go out to work. Now, she knew how right Riva had been. She had escaped her mother's fate—she had a chance to be part of the world, to be active in it, while Riva's only role was to watch from afar.

And as she thought this, she knew something else. She knew how much she cared for Harold. It had been fear, not doubt, that had made her push him away: fear that if they got too close, she would become like her mother, a woman dependent on a man she had grown to despise.

It need not happen to me, she thought to herself. She pulled her shawl back around her shoulders.

"I have to go out, Mama," she said, and it was the first time in ages that she had called her mother so. "Please understand," she said. "I do it not to defy you, but because I need to find Harold."

She had passed her mother again when she suddenly turned back. Impulsively she kissed Riva on the cheek.

"Don't worry," she said. "I'll be fine." She reached the door and opened it. When she took one last glance back, she saw that her mother had not moved, was standing motionless. Gently she closed the door.

After Julia had left, it was a long time before Riva moved again. She was lost in thought. What did I do, she was asking herself, that my only child has become so much a stranger?

Julia never found Harold that night. When she knocked on Harold's door, it was Solly who answered.

"Harold's been arrested," he said. "One of his friends came to tell me. He was distributing party leaflets telling the strikers not to attack the natives, when they pulled him out and took him to jail."

It took two weeks for the government forces to vanquish the strikers. Two weeks of death and destruction. At the end, the dead numbered 214. Thousands had been hurt, and thousands were in prison.

The miners had been outgunned. The strike was over. It ended formally on March 16. The Chamber of Mines had won. Life was to return to normal—but South Africa would never be the same.

Julia was waiting for Harold when he stumbled from the jail. He had been lucky—there was little evidence against him, and he had eventually been released without charge. Others were not so fortunate. Indeed, eighteen of their number were charged with murder, and four would later be hanged.

But Harold did not act as if he were lucky. He stood blinking on the steps, completely passive, as Julia rushed up to him and kissed him on both cheeks. Then she led him home.

On the doorstep Harold broke down. He cried, his sobs racking a body that had grown thinner than ever.

"There will be another time," Julia said.

Harold shook his head violently.

"You should have seen how they brought in the blacks. People who weren't even involved in the strike—who had been picked off the streets because they were in the way. They arrived all bleeding and battered. They treated us bad, but this was inhuman."

"You didn't do it," Julia said, comprehending his pain.

But Harold was not to be consoled. "Nathaniel was right. I was wrong . . . stupid . . . blind.

"What hurts," he cried, "is that I was wrong: that the party was wrong. Nathaniel and Danny spoke the truth. The strike was racist to its core. Of course a man deserves a living wage, but not at another's expense."

She took Harold in her arms and hugged him as his tears wet her shirt.

11

1924

IN 1924 THE DEFEATED STRIKERS GOT THEIR REVENGE: THEY THREW General Smuts and his South African party out. The Nationalist party, which had gone to the polls on the twin slogans of "Segregate the Black" and "Save the Poor White," formed a coalition with the Labour party. Together they came into office dedicated to fighting the "black peril."

Within months one of the principles for which the strikers had starved and died—the retention of the color bar—was in the process of being legitimized. Blacks were to be kept in their place: Job reservation ensured that whites began to congregate closer to management.

"And so," said Nathaniel bitterly, "no matter how hard we work, we can never rise above certain grades. People are angry, but what can we do?"

Evelyn, who was kneeling by a basin of water, shrugged. She frowned as she restrained her son with one hand while attempting to wash his face with the other. "Come on," she cajoled. "The sooner we do it, the sooner it's over."

But Moses continued to struggle. "Let me go," he insisted. "Let me go. I don't care if I'm dirty."

Evelyn tightened her grip. "Mrs. Thoka came to see me yesterday," she told Nathaniel. "She couldn't stop talking about where's she going to go when they proclaim Jo'burg a white area. And what could I tell her?"

Nathaniel was about to reply, but Moses got in first. "She could go and live in the country," he said. He glowered when he saw his parents exchange a fond smile. "She could," he squeaked. "They all could. What's so funny about that?"

Nathaniel knelt beside Moses and, taking the cloth from Evelyn's hand, began gently to dab at his face. "There's nothing left in the country for our people," he explained. "The whites have taken our land, our livestock has perished. If all those who live in the city were to return to the country, they would be starving in a matter of weeks."

"Not us," said Moses. "We're chiefs."

Nathaniel frowned. "We are not chiefs," he said. His hand still held the cloth, but he made no attempt to move it.

"We could be."

"By whose right?" Nathaniel asked, and still he knelt there motionless.

"It's the law," Moses insisted. "The Xhosa law. You could still be chief."

"I will never be a chief," Nathaniel said softly. He looked straight into his son's eyes. "I no longer believe that any one person should inherit the right to be ruler," he said. "Governments must be a result of the consent of the people—all the people." He shook himself, as if waking from a trance. Briskly he finished with Moses' chin, and then threw the cloth into the basin. He leaned his head back a fraction and inspected his son. "That's better," he said. "At least we can see what you look like."

"If I was chief," Moses muttered, "nobody would be able to make me wash my face."

But his parents' attention was concentrated elsewhere. Nathaniel stood up, pulled on his jacket, while Evelyn went indoors. She came out holding a package of food, which she handed to her husband. Together they strolled to the yard entrance.

"See you in two days." Nathaniel kissed Evelyn.

She nodded and turned her head. "Moses," she called, "come say good-bye to your father."

With Moses in tow, Evelyn emerged from the house.

"I'll just take the washing down," she said. "And then we can be off. Wait over there like a good boy, will you?"

Humming to herself, she laid down her basket and began to remove the items that were hanging on the line. She worked deftly and efficiently, dropping the pegs into a tin, folding the clothes and neatly placing them in a growing pile. The sun was already high in the sky, and the clothes were soft and hot to the touch. Evelyn smiled to herself.

It was at this point that Moses came into vision. He was lost in a world of his own, walking on painstaking tiptoe. In his hand he held a long stick, at the end of which was a can overflowing with something that looked like brackish water. His tongue was stuck out in concentration. As the can tipped slightly, he adjusted his arm and moved it to one side. He took another step, and changed course, heading straight toward a wooden stool.

"Moses," Evelyn warned.

But she was too late. Moses tripped on the stool and sprawled forward onto the ground. His can went flying up in the air, only to choose Evelyn's clean washing as its landing place.

And just as the sun passed behind a cloud, a dark stain began to spread on the piece that had been uppermost on the pile—Nathaniel's white shirt. As Evelyn watched the dark spot grow, she shivered.

Against her will, she was transfixed by the sight, somehow unable to move.

"Mama," Moses said nervously.

She whipped around on him. "I told you to keep out of the way," she snapped.

His lips quivered, poised on the brink of sobbing. And then the sun came out again, and the liquid stopped spreading.

Evelyn softened her voice. "Up you get," she said. She whipped the shirt from the pile and looked at the clothing below. "It's not too bad," she continued. "Only one shirt to redo." She picked up the rest of the pile and took it indoors. "Come on," she said when she reemerged, "let's get going." They walked toward the street.

"Good day, Mrs. Bopape."

Evelyn turned and saw her next-door neighbor beckoning to her. "Good day," she replied.

"And how's the little one?" said the woman, as she chucked Moses under the chin. When he flinched, she laughed.

"What can I do for you?" Evelyn asked.

"I was wondering," the woman said, "whether you or your husband could write me a letter. My son's having trouble with his pass, and every time we go to the office the queues are too long, so they send us away empty-handed."

"Certainly," Evelyn replied. "I have a few things to buy, and then I'll be only too pleased to help you."

"Many thanks, Mrs. Bopape," said the woman.

"Think nothing of it." Evelyn reached down for Moses' hand, and they began to walk.

Her mood elevated as she progressed along the road. She loved this home, this her Sophiatown. She was, she thought, strolling among friends: making her way through the crowded alleyways, the mix of people who shouted greetings, sold their wares, gathered on street corners to exchange the local gossip. On the doorsteps sat musicians of different disciplines: men playing guitar and kazoo, the more traditional sound of *foco* as a concertina and home-made drum joined together to create their own kind of disorder and, from inside a two-story building, a band making *tickey draai* from strings, guitar, and concertina.

"What a racket," she said to Moses.

"*Ja,*" he happily agreed.

Nathaniel's ears were assailed by a different, and far less pleasing, kind of noise—the din of the mine workings. He stood with a group of new recruits and raised his voice so that he could be heard above the whine issuing from the shaft head, the trolleys banging their way past him, the hammering and swearing of men at the end of their shift, the muttering of those nearing the beginning.

". . . if you're fast," he concluded. He looked inquiringly at the foreman.

"Ag, let's take a break," the white man said. "I'm dying for a cup of coffee." He wandered away.

Nathaniel leaned lazily against a post. He ignored the noise—it was second nature to him—and basked under the hot glow of the sun. He glanced around, and his eyes came to rest on his friend Steven Mkula, who was among those queueing to go underground.

Haven't seen him for a long time, he thought. "Steven!" he shouted.

But Steven did not respond: He stood as Nathaniel had first seen him, motionless, his eyes focused on the ground, a look of blank grimness on his face.

Nathaniel frowned. After telling the new men to stay put, he hurried over to Steven. Already the line of miners was beginning to move: Twelve men climbed into the waiting bucket, while two others stood on its edge and pulled on the suspending chains. The bucket began to descend, another appeared. Steve shuffled forward, his face still focused downward.

He looked up only when Nathaniel placed a hand on his shoulder. For a second his face cleared, and he gave a brief smile. But then his mouth turned down again, and his eyes clouded over. "Hello Nathaniel," he said glumly.

"What's up?"

Steven glanced nervously around him. "I left my work scarf at home," he muttered.

That was all Nathaniel needed to hear in order to understand his friend's grim expression. He flicked his eyes, first at Steven, and then toward the exit.

"I can't not work the shift," Steven said. "I can't. My wife's expecting, and I need the money. I have to go down."

The line moved again. Steven was next. "Then you'll be all right," Nathaniel said as confidently as he was able. "Anyway, it's about time that old scarf takes a rest. It's so filthy, it's going to get up and walk away from you one day."

Steven smiled. He put one foot in the bucket and hoisted himself in. "And if anything happens," he shouted, "I know you'll come and get me out."

Nathaniel waited until his friend's head had disappeared down the shaft before returning to his novices. "Miners' superstition," he explained in answer to their puzzled glances.

Evelyn was at home unpacking her shopping. She lifted the top of her storage box and placed two tins inside it. The mealie-meal sack she pushed into the driest corner, covering it with a further layer of sacking. Then she began to get up.

But she forgot how cramped her room was, and she misjudged her movements. As her head came up, it hit hard on the corner of the table.

She felt the blow as a piercing pain in her head: Momentarily the world went black. She reached out an arm to steady herself, and closed her eyes. When she opened them again, she could see all right. And yet, she thought, I can't be properly conscious. Her senses were not working properly: Everything had gone quiet. There was no music, no shouting, no laughter or tears, not even the sounds of children playing.

And then she did hear something: a single footstep. Relieved, she looked toward the doorway. A dark, indistinguishable form was standing there, blocking out the sun.

"Hello?" she said.

"Mrs. Bopape."

At the sound of her neighbor's voice Evelyn smiled to herself. She got up and rubbed her head. "You've come so that I can write the letter," she said. She took one step toward the door.

And then for the first time she looked into her neighbor's eyes. And she understood immediately why there was no sound in the street, why her neighbor had come over.

"The mine," she said.

"There's been an explosion," the woman confirmed.

Evelyn did not stop to think. "Moses!" she shouted. "Go play with the Tsele children," she ordered, when he, startled by the urgency in her voice, came running to the door.

She took off, half-running, half-walking, in the general direction of the mine.

As she hurried along, her heart was pounding. Nathaniel, she told herself, would be all right, she was sure he would. He was, after all, an interpreter, not a miner. There was no reason for him to go underground. She kept moving forward.

Evelyn was right. When the explosion happened, Nathaniel had been above, still translating instructions to the new recruits. It was a routine job, and his mind was elsewhere. In the background the drilling and banging, the whine of the mine shaft, the clatter of newly emerged wagons, were so familiar that he no longer heard them.

And then it happened. A blast—a huge rending blast so powerful that for a fraction of a second the ground seemed to rumble and sway. A cloud of dust issued from beneath the earth.

The new recruits, buffeted on all sides by unfamiliar noises, laughed nervously. But around them the other men stopped immediately, no matter what it was that had previously occupied them. They had heard this sound before: Too many times they had heard it.

A single whistle blew. A few of the men muttered something unintelligible, here and there a cross was drawn, a breath held. Nathaniel wheeled around, and with others ran toward the mine shaft.

When they arrived, there were two foremen standing by an empty bucket, looking down in somber silence.

"Where's the rescue team?" Nathaniel asked.

One of the men turned. "It's no use, man," he said. "It was too far underground. Nobody could have survived."

"Where's the rescue squad?" Nathaniel repeated.

The others behind him pressed at his back, and they, too, were asking the same question.

"There isn't one," the foreman replied. "They've gone off shift, and the next lot aren't due for an hour."

A miner, one of the old school, a man who had been there many a year, pushed his way to the front. "Then we must organize our own," he said. He looked at the crowd. "Who's coming with me?" he asked.

The men (and among them, to his shame, was Nathaniel) looked away, focused their eyes on a spot in the ground or in the sky—anywhere but at the shaft or the man who stood at their head. He understood, this miner did. He nodded to himself and slowly walked toward the bucket. He swung one leg over.

Nathaniel looked up just in time to see the movement. He blinked: For as the miner hoisted himself into the bucket, he saw another man, a man engaged in the selfsame motion. He saw, in his mind's eye, Steven descending. And he heard Steven's voice: "You'll come and get me," he heard.

He took a step forward. "I'll come," he said. He got into the bucket. The chain began to roll.

By the time Evelyn arrived at the mine, a crowd had already gathered by the gates. It was comprised, in the main, of women, although the fact that they were made of flesh and blood was not easy to discern. For each one stood completely still, her face like granite, fists clenched tightly. Not one lip moved, not even in prayer. They were waiting, merely waiting to hear the worst.

For a long time, nothing happened. No one complained: This was part of the agony, this waiting for the procession of the living before one could begin to count the dead.

And gradually it arrived. As each man turned up, to stand motionless in front of the crowd, his wife, his sister, his mother, his friend, his lover, breathed a sigh of relief. Just a sigh—no more than that. They suppressed their feelings of jubilation: How could they show it while others suffered so? Nathaniel was not among these men.

Evelyn waited, a woman turned to stone.

She lost all track of time. Night fell suddenly, like a black curtain of foreboding. The compound was lit by flares. And still nothing happened: Nothing appeared from the mouth of the deadly mine shaft. The people waited.

"It's too late," someone moaned.

"It's never too late to hope," replied a priest who had come to attend the vigil.

Just as he finished speaking, there was a movement from the shaft head. They all saw it, almost immediately. The waiting silence grew in intensity. The wheel turned, slowly, agonizingly: A bucket limped to the surface.

The crowd drew a collective intake of breath. For the bucket contained live men—blackened by smoke, coughing, some only giving the faintest of movements to show that they still breathed, but they were alive.

A miner detached himself from the crowd and rushed inside. When he returned, he read out a list of names.

Nathaniel's was not among them. The bucket went down again.

The next consignment was a different kind of cargo—in it was one man standing: The rest of his companions were dead.

Slowly the cage was unloaded. Black miners laid the bodies gently on the ground. In blackened rows.

Evelyn had once seen a field after it had been caught in a brushfire. She'd gone to look at the stubble that remained, and in it she'd found carcasses of birds, trapped in the fire, their wings first singed, their bodies finally burned to death. They had lain in awkward positions, as if the fire had bent their bones, had set out to make their elegance look ungainly.

Through the gates she could see that the same had happened to these men, that they, too, had been caught in midflight.

Except these men had never possessed wings: Those had been clipped so many years ago, when the white man had devastated their country.

The wheel stopped turning. There was no longer any point. Nobody stood below ground, waiting for them to come.

The flares were extinguished.

The women turned to go. In unison they turned. They had made no sign to each other. They were still stone: ambulatory stone. Not one wail of anguish was heard that night, not one curse: These things would follow. For the moment they must return to the homes that would never be the same.

As Evelyn trudged down the road, she heard a persistent footstep behind her. She shook her head and stopped. So did the sound. Without looking around (for she did not want to speak), she started up again: Again she heard the tread of her pursuer. She didn't care, she kept on walking. The footsteps persisted, heavily they followed her.

They will not go away, she thought, until I face them.

She turned. She saw that it was a man who was following her, a man blackened by smoke, a man who hesitated when he saw her face.

"Mrs. Bopape?" he asked.

She nodded.

"My name is Ntemi," he said. "I knew your husband."

Again she nodded.

"Nathaniel saved my life," he said. He hesitated and gulped.

"He pulled me out," he suddenly continued. "He pushed me in that bucket without giving one thought to his own safety. There are ten of us, and we all owe our lives to your husband."

The man fell to his knees. His head in his hands, he began to sob.

Evelyn walked a few steps back before bending down to pat his head.

"Why do you cry?" she asked.

"I'm alive," sobbed the man. "And he is dead."

Evelyn removed her hand. "You need feel no guilt," she said softly. "Nathaniel lived his life for others. It is right that he should die saving them."

And with that, she went home to tell Moses.

In the long days and the endless nights that followed, Evelyn renounced often the words of comfort that she had spoken to the miner.

It was not right, she told herself, that Nathaniel should die saving others, that he should give his life to them.

You had no need to be underground, she silently screamed to her dead husband. Why have you deserted me? she thought more softly.

She found herself coming across his clothes and wanting to rip them apart; catching sight of his picture and wanting to spit at it; seeing his son and wanting to deny the resemblance. Her whole being rejected his memory, his life, his death.

No one would have guessed that this was what she thought.

To the women who descended on her household, who arrived bearing gifts of sugar, candles, soap, and food, who stayed to cook and clean and brew endless drinks, Evelyn was a picture of strength. Too strong, said some among them, it would be better if she allowed herself to collapse.

And her pretense went further. To Moses, she was patience exemplified. She tolerated his sudden fits of temper, his endless questions, his tears, his demand for an explanation.

"Your father was a good man," she kept repeating. "A leader of men. He will be remembered for the good he did. And you must follow in his footsteps," she continued. "We named you Moses because that was what he wanted."

But inside, she continued to rage at Nathaniel. His absence was an unbearable void for which she blamed him. Her mind began to wander. If he had been there, she thought, she could have coped with his death, she would not have wanted to scream when a succession of women came up to her and pronounced the age-old words: "Misfortune walks in a queue."

They meant, of course, that tomorrow they could be the ones bereaved, that her loss was bad luck, a bad cast of the dice.

But she denied the words. She had not been merely unlucky. It was Nathaniel himself who had cast the die. He had thought himself strong enough to play with fate, and in so doing he had allowed death to win.

She could not say those words aloud, she could not so betray him. But she believed them, oh, yes, she did believe them. She acted the part of the grieving widow, while inside she was learning, for the first time, how to hate her husband.

Harold came to visit her on the fourth day—the minute he heard the news. He rushed into her house and hugged her fiercely.

Perhaps because he was a man or (more likely) because he was white, the women who had occupied her house began to make excuses. They left the room, saying that they needed to fetch something, that they would soon be back. They took Moses with them and they left Evelyn, almost alone, for the first time since Nathaniel died.

It was a tremendous relief to her, to look around their room, her room, and to see a space where people had been. She smiled at Harold.

"Thank you for coming," she said formally.

Harold nodded.

"Julia is well, I hope?" Evelyn continued.

"She's not feeling so good," Harold said. "That's why she hasn't come. She sends her love and will visit you soon."

"Nothing too bad, I hope?"

"No," said Harold. "She's pregnant and gets rather tired at the moment."

He had not meant to say the words, to bring into this house of death the news of a life in the making, but Evelyn's small talk had unnerved him. He glanced at her nervously.

She did not seem to mind. Her face lit up, she smiled a warm, generous smile. "I'm glad," she said. "A child will bless your recent marriage."

The smile faded. "We would have wanted more," she said reflectively, "Nathaniel and I. But it didn't happen. We worried about it sometimes. But now," she continued in a stronger voice, "I realize that it was for the best. How could I have supported more than one?"

She gave a short laugh: Her mouth turned down. "Do you know that I have to leave this house?" she said. "I have to go, because since I do not have a husband in work, I no longer have a right to live here." She nodded. "Another child would have made my burden worse."

"Oh, Evelyn." Harold took a step toward her.

She flinched. She looked at him dry-eyed. "Why did he die, Harold?" she asked in a small voice. "Why did he die?"

"He died as he lived," Harold replied, "helping others."

As Harold said those words, a pain, the same she thought as the one she had experienced just before she heard the news, flashed through her mind. When it had gone, she felt clear, lightheaded, even.

She looked him straight in the eye. "That is not the reason," she said.

Harold glanced at her, confused.

"Do you want to know why he died?" she asked. "He died

because he was black. Oh, I know what you're thinking," she burst out quickly, as though afraid she might be interrupted (although Harold had given no sign that he was about to speak). "You're thinking that many whites have died underground." She looked away. "But don't you see how the odds are stacked against us?" she said in a distant voice. "*Kaffirs* are not people; if one dies, another will take his place."

She paused, unmoving, as if she were holding her breath. "Except nobody could ever take Nathaniel's place," she said.

These, she knew, were not the words she had suppressed ever since she had heard the news, but they were words that nevertheless rang true. A weight seemed to lift from her brain.

She had been wrong: This she realized. Nathaniel had not caused his own death—forces beyond his control had done that. And it was to his credit that, during his short life, he had fought against those very forces, against those pressures, those humans who were forcing South Africa into such a brutal straitjacket.

"He was a good man," she said. "I loved him so."

Tears fell down her cheeks, but she did nothing to stanch their flow. Neither did she move away when Harold put his arms around her. She continued to cry, wetting his shirt with her grief.

And then, abruptly, she stopped. She moved away, dried her eyes with a handkerchief, and sat down on a chair. "I should have done that when I first heard," she said. She looked past him and through the open door. "I really thank you for coming, Harold," she said, "but I think you should go now. Your presence is making my neighbors uncomfortable." She smiled again at him, and this time he saw that there was nothing forced in her expression.

Yet he was not ready to go. There was something he wanted to say. He hesitated, on the verge of leaving. "Evelyn . . ." he began.

She looked at him inquiringly, but he felt suddenly embarrassed and was unable to continue. She smiled again. "You were going to invite me to come and stay with you," she stated.

"How did you know?"

She clicked her tongue. "You and Nathaniel," she said. "No wonder you were friends—both so idealistic, both so willing to flaunt convention."

She got up and walked over to him. "This is one convention we cannot flaunt," she said. "I wouldn't last a week as your guest. Someone would make sure I moved away, would hurt my child, if necessary."

Harold nodded in a dubious kind of agreement. "We could try it," he said.

"No," Evelyn replied. "It would not work." She pushed him gently. "Thanks for coming."

Harold walked to the door. He opened it. He did not know what else to say, how else to help. He felt defeated, privileged and defeated.

"There is something you can do for me," he heard.

He turned around quickly. "Anything."

Her words came out slowly, hesitating. "You could employ me," she suggested. "I could come and work for you and Julia as a housekeeper."

When Harold looked as though he was about to reply—to refuse, she knew—she interrupted him.

"Don't say no," she said. "I understand it goes against everything you believe. But this country does not let us keep our ideals intact. I do not shirk from hard work. Being in your kitchen will be far less demeaning than washing some strangers' dirty clothes or starving in the countryside. You think about it and let me know."

12

1925

HAROLD TIPTOED INTO THE ROOM. LEANING OVER JULIA, HE KISSED her on the forehead before brushing aside a wisp of damp hair. Julia was pale and still, her normally strong features somehow flattened by the last few hours. Harold kissed her again.

She opened her eyes and smiled. "We have a daughter," she said.

Harold had begun to laugh, but when he noticed how Julia winced, he swallowed the sound. He took a step forward and pulled the sheet up to her chin.

"I will look after you," he promised.

Just then the nurse arrived. She was carrying a white bundle, which she placed in Harold's arms.

"A bouncing baby," she said. "Fit and well."

He looked down, and his eyes filled with tears. There she was, his tiny baby, her head covered in a shock of downy black hair. She was beautiful.

"Rosa," he whispered.

Nervously Julia glanced sideways at the baby. Its eyes were closed, its face relaxed: It looked so new and so innocent. And yet Julia was not deceived. She'd learned how selfish a child was (hadn't Riva always told her that?), how this one had pushed its way out, uncaring of the pain it caused. She almost hated it for that. Not it, Julia mentally corrected herself. Her.

She had seen the look that suffused Harold's face when he had held the baby—that look of joy and of love. She'd envied him that look, and at the same time she'd resented it. It was all very well for him—he'd got a daughter without the slightest effort. He hadn't had to brace his legs against ugly stirrups, he hadn't become a lump of flesh, a mere recipient for endless waves of agony.

The baby opened its eyes and, as if seeing her mother for the first time, let out a yell. Julia started and tried to move away.

"Now, now," clucked the nurse, who seemed to have been watching Julia, who seemed to read her inner thoughts. "You're a mother, and when Baby calls, Mother responds."

Evelyn sat by the sleeping Moses, her face set firm. Only when she heard the sound of the gate closing did it unfreeze. She felt an immense relief as the tears began to flow.

She was proud of herself: She'd pulled it off, fooled Harold into thinking she shared his joy over the baby. He couldn't possibly have guessed what she truly felt.

It wasn't that she begrudged him his happiness. He was a good man, and he deserved to have a family; he was the kind who would mature under fatherhood.

And yet, when he told her the news, part of her had gone dead. She had wanted desperately to turn away, to shut his eagerness out. She'd pushed that part of herself away: She'd imitated his jubilation, she congratulated him unreservedly.

And so she'd held on until she heard the gate close: Only then did she begin to cry. At that point there was nothing she could do to stop herself: No matter how much she berated herself for being irrational, the tears continued to fall. She was in their grip, totally, completely, awash with them and with the feelings that came pouring out alongside.

It wasn't about having another baby—she didn't think so, anyway. Although Moses had become rather difficult since Nathaniel died, she would not have wished for any different child. He was a good boy, and given time, she was convinced he would become his former carefree self.

She reached over and touched him gently on the cheek. "It isn't you," she whispered.

She removed her hand quickly when he stirred, and held it to her cheek, feeling the warmth of another human being. That's what it's about, she thought. This very warmth.

The tears began to fall again. She was crying, she knew, for her husband, for his death and for what might once have been.

It wasn't often she felt this way—in fact, she went through her daily routine without much feeling at all. But the thought of the birth, of new life that would soon invade this household, was almost too much for her. Her head dropped into her arms, and her body shook as she sobbed.

And Moses, who had been awakened by the sound of his mother crying, lay completely still. He watched her shaking with unblinking eyes.

The door to the Cyn house was open, and the sound of revelry issued from the dining room. Harold hesitated: He had been looking forward to telling them the news, but suddenly he felt the need to delay. This was something that could be diluted in the telling: Even Evelyn's pleasure had made him slightly uneasy.

He looked into the oval mirror that hung above the umbrella stand, and his mood lifted again. He grinned at his reflection: He liked what he saw; he felt as if he had matured overnight. His face seemed to have lost part of its boyish quality: The strains of his vigil had thinned it out, and the brightness in his eyes helped to diminish the prominence of his spectacles.

I'm a father, he muttered to himself before turning reluctantly away. He walked toward the laughter.

The Cyns' dining room was comfortable, but it bore none of the marks of modern South Africa since Riva stubbornly rejected the new styles of art-deco furnishing, and chose instead to stick to the symbols of the Old World. Everything was on a grand scale—the feather cushions with their intricate embroidered covers, the wall hangings depicting scenes of the countryside around Vilna, and the heavy carpets in their somber colors of purple and ocher.

There was a great crowd sitting around the table, their conversation coming thick and fast. Fanny Woolf, the Cyns' oldest lodger, was there, squashed between two men of portly build who were talking loudly over her. Zelig sat at one end of the table, smiling benignly. Riva was at the other, ladling out servings of *tsimmes* to the protesting company. And to her right was Harold's brother, Solly, jovial and loud beside his wife, Molly.

For a moment Harold was taken aback. He could not understand why these people were collected together, why Solly was there. Had they heard, already, about his baby?

But when he noticed the seven-pronged candelabra on the

table and the sideboard groaning with traditional food, he remembered. Of course—they were celebrating the start of the new year! Harold and Julia had been invited some time ago, but they had used the imminent birth as a reason for refusal.

It's ironic, he thought. Julia didn't want to come to eat with her family, while Solly seizes every opportunity. He smiled to himself. He was enjoying the fact that nobody had noticed him, that they were all so occupied with their celebration that they hadn't even turned around yet. It was like being a ghost, a phantom observing an age-old ritual.

As he watched, he saw Molly shiver. She must have felt his eyes on her, for she turned and called his name. She said it during a lull in the conversation, and so her soft voice penetrated. The assembled company looked at Harold in surprise.

"A girl," he blurted out.

Solly, a young man whose muscle was already turning to fat, was on his feet with surprising agility. He ran over to Harold and shook his hand.

"*Mazel tov,*" he said.

He was followed closely by Zelig, who was on the edge of tears. He hugged Harold to his chest, slapping his back delightedly.

"Thanks be to God," he kept repeating against the background of a babble of frantic congratulations and conversation.

And then, over the head of the two men, Harold caught a glimpse of Riva. She had stayed where she was, her hand holding the ladle, frozen in midair, a peculiar look on her face. It was not distaste he saw, but something more intangible. It was as if her relief that her daughter was safe was mixed with something akin to disappointment

In that instant Harold intuitively understood Julia's hostility toward her mother. He had never thought their relationship quite natural, something that he couldn't understand, since Julia point-blank refused to talk about Riva. "She never loved me," was all Julia would say. For the first time Harold understood what she meant.

But the understanding was only fleeting. As he looked at Riva, her face changed. She was beaming. She was laughing. She waved toward Harold, calling him into the family fold.

"A toast," trilled Fanny Woolf.

"And then four more," said the man next to her, pinching her on the forearm.

After about an hour, Harold made an excuse and left. Everybody forgave him his early exit: After all, he had been up all night. He needed his rest, they told each other.

But Harold did not go home to rest. He walked instead toward the outskirts of Ferreirastown.

It had just finished raining; the streets were deserted, and there was no sound other than the slush of his footsteps as he trod through the sandy surfaces. Harold looked up at the sky. The clouds had cleared, and he marveled at the heavens above him, the bright twinkling of a mass of stars so far away and so immutable. It was quiet. Elsewhere in the world others were being born, others were dying, but for once in his life, Harold gave them only a momentary thought. He reveled, instead, in his solitude, in this unexpected sense of his own smallness contrasted with the immensity of the universe around him.

When he reached 41a Fox Street, he climbed down the rickety steps that led to the basement. He got to the bottom and opened the door.

As he registered the fact that the room was in total darkness, a lump rose to Harold's throat; a sense of bitter disappointment intruded into his calm. Evelyn had been ostensibly delighted, but Harold had thought that some ambiguity lurked below the surface of her reaction. And although the family celebration had been gratifying, he had felt out of place there. Even as he had drunk Julia's health, he had been planning his escape into the place he truly counted as his. On this day he wanted to be with his real friends, to share the news with the people he loved most in the world.

And now there was no light to welcome him. Harold could not understand it. Something must have happened while he had been isolated in the nursing home: a police raid, perhaps. Whatever the reason, Harold felt cheated. He turned to go.

But suddenly he heard a soft click, and then the room was flooded with light. Harold blinked, his eyes dazzled by the uncovered bulb at the center of the ceiling. A hand slapped him on the back. His heart thumped. Was this a trap? He turned to face the worst.

He found himself staring into the laughing face of Xuma. And that wasn't all: The room was far from empty. From behind the rickety benches pushed the students—men from all walks of life, their skins the varied colors of the South African racial mix.

"A toast to our comrade." Xuma held up a mug. "Even for you, we could not break the liquor ban," he said in a mock whisper, "but we do have condensed milk tonight." The men in the room laughed and clinked their mugs.

"How did you know?" Harold was bewildered.

"Haven't you heard we infiltrate everywhere?" someone called. "We communists have our spies in the most unlikely places."

Harold blinked again into the fierce light. For the second time that evening his eyes filled with tears of joy. He saw the room and its occupants anew. His habitual irritation at the poor furnishings, the makeshift study area, the peeling walls, was absent. Instead, he saw what this room represented to him—a haven that blocked out the cruelty of the world they inhabited. It cast a glow and a warmth that came not from the wealth of its furnishings but from the feelings of fraternity that seemed to penetrate the very heart of the room.

"Another comrade for the struggle," called Strini Mabiletsa from the back rows, "and one who is truly equal, since she, too, cannot read."

Xuma handed Harold a piece of broken chalk. "Your reward for producing another person for the struggle," he said, "is to teach. Always to teach," and he sat in the front rows, aping the posture of a recalcitrant schoolchild. "Give it to us, Dad."

Harold laughed. "Don't try that one with me. I've discovered to my cost how well-read you are. But the one advantage in my becoming a father is that this night you will be forced to listen."

Harold went to the wall. In the absence of a blackboard the walls had been blackened so that chalk would show up on them. Harold wrote one word: *Rosa*.

"Rosa," he said "will be her name. After a friend of my mother-in-law who lived in Russia before the Revolution. But it also puts us in mind of Rosa Luxemburg—a German revolutionary assassinated in 1919. Tonight we will talk of her."

The session went on for another hour. The atmosphere was light—in deference to Harold's new baby—but it was serious as well. The men gathered in the room had come to learn, and they were dedicated in their striving. Harold marveled, as he often did, at their persistence. In the days, they held down the menial jobs that were open to them. And yet at night, they were always there concentrating on learning to read, to write, and to understand.

The evening ended, as it always had to, with a pass-signing ritual. These men were grown, many of them past their prime, and yet they were not allowed to tread the streets at night without the consent of a white *baas*. So Harold would play the *baas*, solemnly signing their permissions to be out. The process always filled him with embarrassment, but the recipients of his crudely forged passes did not seem to mind. That was part of what he had learned in this dismal room: These people retained their dignity regardless of the humiliation that was heaped their way.

When it was over, Harold watched Xuma locking the door before bidding him good night. He walked back alone to his small house in Yeoville.

When he arrived, Evelyn's light was out, the house was still. He was relieved: He needed at the end of this day to be alone. He went straight to the bedroom.

He looked around him with fresh eyes. Beside Julia's bed were two pictures—one of her, and one of her mother. He examined them both. Riva's eyes dominated, with a hint of what he had seen in them this evening. He picked up Julia's picture and kissed it.

He was about to climb into bed when he changed his mind. He went instead to the small nursery that he had only just finished decorating. A raffia crib stood against the wall, its headboard covered in frilly white lace. To the side of it was a rocking chair. He sat down on it and put his hand gently in the crib.

"Now we are three," he told the room.

13

1936

"GET ALONG NOW," EVELYN ORDERED. SHE WAVED HER HAND IN the general direction of the garden. "Go and play," she said.

But nine-year-old Rosa took no notice. Or, to be more accurate, she pretended to be carrying out Evelyn's instructions while having no real intention of doing so. She stepped back, placing herself at an angle so that Evelyn would need to twist around in order to see her. Then she firmly closed her mouth.

If she could keep quiet for a few minutes (and this in itself required some concentration), then she knew that Evelyn would forget her impatience, would smile when she finally spoke, would answer her questions and, if she was very lucky, would take her to the kitchen and pour her a glass of homemade lemonade.

She bided her time by looking around her. In the distance her brother Nicholas, two years her junior, had teamed up with some of the neighborhood kids and was involved in a furious game of soccer. She could, she supposed, have joined in (she had long ago established that to call soccer a boy's game in an attempt to exclude her was to invite a smack in the mouth), but she didn't feel like it. Far better, she thought, to stay by Evelyn and talk. She gave a little skip in the air.

Evelyn, who saw the skip out of the corner of her eye, chose to ignore it. She unclipped one of Rosa's dresses from the line and began to fold it.

"Ugh," said Rosa.

Evelyn's lips twitched. She bent down and dropped the dress into a basket.

"I hate that dress," came Rosa's voice.

Evelyn turned and looked at Rosa. "Let me give you some advice," she said. "Don't start complaining. This is the dress that your mother has said you will wear to the bar mitzvah, and therefore this is the dress you will wear."

"But it itches me," Rosa said. "And I don't even want to go to the *blerry* bar mitzvah."

"Don't swear," Evelyn chided, before concentrating again on her work.

She managed to continue without interruption for at least five minutes, and during that time Rosa remained completely quiet.

Although Evelyn took care not to glance her way (for that would start her off again), she could imagine full well how the child must be looking. She would be standing, Evelyn knew, straight-backed, a tall, graceful girl, her brows set in a frown of concentration.

Evelyn did not need to be a mind reader to know that Rosa would be frowning. The girl was so often lost in thought that she might have been in danger of appearing dull if not for her mass of unruly black curls, the mischievous smile that was never far away, and her olive skin burned a deep brown by the South African sun, all of which gave her a special kind of vibrancy. Hers was not a conventional face, but nevertheless it had beauty in it.

Or perhaps I'm just being partial, Evelyn thought, because I know her so well.

"Evelyn." Rosa's plaintive voice broke into her thoughts.

Evelyn sighed. "Yes, what is it?" She turned, and the smile that she threw at Rosa belied her pretense of exasperation.

Rosa's brow cleared. "Tell me more about Nathaniel," she said.

Evelyn clicked her tongue. "You'll be the death of me," she said. "Always asking the same questions." Nevertheless, she threw the last of the clothespins into their receptacle, and went to sit on the wooden chair that was supporting one half of the line.

"Thanks a million, Evelyn," Rosa gushed.

Evelyn watched the child run toward her, and wondered anew at Rosa's eagerness to listen to stories about a man she had never met. It was one of the things they did together—reliving Nathaniel's life—one of the many things.

Evelyn never fully understood how it was that she and Rosa had grown so close. True, she had seen the child almost every day of her life, but the same applied to Rosa's brother Nicholas, and that bond was only one of loose affection. But between Rosa and Evelyn was a fierce and loving connection: so fierce that it sometimes felt to Evelyn as if she were the child's mother and the child were hers.

She pushed any such notion out of her consciousness—she was black, Rosa was white, and besides, Rosa already possessed a family.

And yet she couldn't help thinking about the cause of their bond. Perhaps, she thought, it was she who had manufactured the closeness—manufactured it in compensation for the extremity of her reaction when she heard of Rosa's birth. She could still remember her first sight of the baby, how her misery had been transformed into a kind of fascination, of awe at this new life. Perhaps this reaction was nothing more than an attempt to hide her ill-feeling at the happiness of others.

But Evelyn knew that it would be dishonest to place the blame entirely at her door, for Julia had something to do with it. Julia had been an anxious new mother, one who found it difficult to recover from the shock of childbirth, and she had looked to Evelyn for help with the baby. Both women assumed that as Julia grew more proficient, Evelyn's role would diminish.

And yet, as her baby grew into a person in her own right, Julia had seemed to retreat further. It was hard to pinpoint exactly what caused this withdrawal—perhaps the fact that she had fallen pregnant with Nicholas too early—but it was as if Julia were frightened of Rosa, as if she were pushing her into Evelyn's arms.

"And after we've talked about Nathaniel," Rosa said, as she sat on the ground beside Evelyn and put her head in Evelyn's lap, "after that, you can tell me about Moses as a little boy."

Moses, thought Evelyn grimly. He's the real reason. For Moses had never wanted to talk of Nathaniel as Rosa did: He had never sat at his mother's knee and listened with shining eyes to the exploits of his father. On the contrary, should Evelyn mention Nathaniel, then that would inevitably be the excuse for Moses to pick a fight, to walk out, to return to the outskirts of Sophiatown where he had chosen to squat and not return until his temper had abated.

"Ayiee, Moses," she said. Her hand dropped to Rosa's hair and began to stroke it.

Julia, who had been standing on the veranda that nestled in the house's flat roof, stepped back into the shadow. She felt like a spy, even though she hadn't been spying on them. On the contrary, she had gone out to look at the sunset, but because it wasn't a particularly splendid one, her eyes had strayed downward. She had been smiling, enjoying the cool breeze that was blowing away the worst of the day's heat, when she happened to glance to the corner, to the place where Evelyn and Rosa were sitting.

Her move backward was purely involuntary, as was the way her smile evaporated. If she had thought about it, she would have judged herself silly: Neither of them would have minded if they had seen her watching.

But for some reason it didn't feel right: It was as if she had become a voyeur, an observer in her own house.

"I've got to get dressed anyway," she told herself. She walked back into the house.

As she made her way through the living room and to the master bedroom, Julia couldn't help marveling at her surroundings. It hit her like this sometimes—the sudden realization of how far she had come, of how different her home was from her parents'.

The contrast could not have been greater. While Riva's preferences still ran to heavy furniture, velvet drapes, dark wallpaper, Julia had chosen only light and airy shapes and colors. While Riva and Zelig still lived in their sprawling Ferreirastown house (in an area growing ever more decrepit as the better-off moved to the more prosperous suburbs), Julia had taken up Harold's offer of a new house in Yeoville. She had chosen the latest in fashions: a two-story, light, bright, smooth-angled house.

It was a question of money, Julia supposed. Although Riva and Zelig were not in need (thanks to Harold's continuing generosity), they could not have afforded a new house, a new car, a separate gardener and cook. Harold, on the other hand, was doing very well. He was much in demand as an accountant, and his share in Solly's business had increased tenfold in value. No wonder, then, that the two lifestyles were so different.

But it wasn't, Julia thought, as she reached into her wardrobe, only a question of money: It was a question of attitude. Riva still dwelt in the Old World, still kept pieces of thread, old newspapers, tin cans, against the day when disaster would strike. She could never move forward.

Julia bent down and slipped her high heels on. She draped her foxtail over her shoulders and then put on her hat. She looked in the mirror and smiled, well satisfied with the smartness of her image.

From the garden came the sound of Rosa's laughter. Julia looked quickly at her watch before leaving the room.

Julia was not the only person to hear the laughter. For at the same time as Julia made her way downstairs, Moses reached the top of the drive and was about to go straight toward Evelyn's quarters. When he heard Rosa's shrieks, he changed his mind. Turning away from Evelyn's room, he rounded the corner, a broad smile on his face.

He saw them almost immediately: Rosa and his mother. They were running down the garden, Rosa in front, still bellowing with laughter, while Evelyn followed as she playfully flicked a handkerchief in Rosa's direction.

"You can't get me!" Rosa shouted. She swerved to the right, and tripped. She landed sprawling, on the ground. As she raised her head, on the brink perhaps of bursting into tears, she spotted Moses. In an instant her face cleared and she was on her feet.

"Moses!" She ran up to him and flung her arms around his neck, hanging on so that his head was pulled downward.

He gently resisted. "Hold it," he said. "You'll break my neck." Laughingly he pushed his head up, when he suddenly spotted his mother. She was stopped in midaction, her hand holding the handkerchief still outstretched, as if she had suddenly frozen. There was an expression on her face, an indecipherable expression—could it be guilt? he thought.

"Hello," he said.

The expression had gone: In its place was a smile. She dropped her hand and walked over to him.

"It's been a long time," she said.

"Well," he said awkwardly, as he detached Rosa from his neck, "I've been busy."

His mother nodded. "Come," she said, "I will make you some tea."

"Can I have some, too?" Rosa asked.

Evelyn shook her head. "Look there, your mother's coming

out of the house," she said. "Go and talk to her, because soon she will be out for the evening."

Rosa thought her mother was the picture of elegance. Her heels clicked as she walked, her skirt with its hem just above the ankle swayed in time, her hat was perched jauntily at just the right angle to be truly fashionable. I'll look like that when I grow up, she thought. She ran up to Julia.

"You look gorgeous," she said. "Where are you going?"

"Daddy's picking me up for a social at the bookshop," Julia replied.

Rosa jumped in the air. "Oh, can I come?" In her eagerness she pulled on Julia's jacket.

Her mother inched away. "Careful, darling," she said. "You'll get me all dirty."

"Can I? Can I?" Rosa pleaded. "They like me at the bookshop."

But Julia was peering past the driveway toward the hill in the distance. "Is that your father's car?" she asked.

Rosa scowled. "Yes," she said in a low voice.

"I'll meet him at the bottom of the drive," Julia decided. "Otherwise we'll be late." She patted Rosa on the head. "Go call your brother," she said, "and tell him to come say good-bye."

Moses was sitting on Evelyn's one chair, while she perched on the bed. They each had a mug of tea by their side, and they were both feeling rather awkward. They had managed to exchange basic information—the kind about state of health that meant very little to either of them—and now it felt as if there were nothing left to say.

Or too much left unsaid, thought Evelyn. She cleared her throat. "Are you still squatting?" she asked.

Moses nodded.

"And work?"

Moses shrugged. "It isn't easy," he said.

"So you will need some money," Evelyn stated. She got up and pulled the trunk from under her bed. She opened it, found the money box where it had been hidden under a pile of old clothes, and counted out some notes. Then she pushed herself to her feet and handed the money to Moses.

He neither looked at it nor counted it. "Thanks," he said roughly. He shifted in his seat.

Evelyn's eyes were drawn to the picture above Moses' head. When he sat like that, proud and withdrawn, ineffectually concealing his discomfort, he reminded her so much of his father. She looked at Nathaniel's picture, the one taken just before he died when he had sat formal and stiff posing at a meeting of the ICU, and she smiled to herself. In that picture Nathaniel appeared so grown up, so strong. And yet for some reason (perhaps because she had aged while her husband had remained frozen in time), it was not like this that she remembered him. Instead, she thought of him as the awkward youth he had once been, the man who had needed to be coaxed and gentled into her bed.

"Your father . . ." she began.

Moses did not let her finish her sentence. He had seen her eyes go up to the picture, and he thought he knew exactly what she was about to say. She was going to tell him about his father the hero, about the way Nathaniel had worked every waking hour of his life, had sacrificed his life for others.

Moses had no doubt that he was right: She was bound to be going to say all that, since that's what she always said about Nathaniel. For what seemed like the whole of his life Moses had had to live in his father's shadow. He couldn't even borrow money—and why shouldn't his mother give him some?—without having to listen to lectures about how his father would never have done likewise.

Well, this time, he resolved, he wasn't going to stick around to be humiliated.

He jumped to his feet. "I must be on my way," he said harshly. He left the room without so much as a backward glance.

When he reached the bottom of the drive, he was still muttering under his breath. He heard his name called, and he reluctantly looked up. He saw Harold and Julia sitting in the Ford while their children talked to them through the open passenger window.

Harold waved. "Want a lift?"

Moses smiled and shook his head. "I'll make my own way," he called. He did not stop to talk, he began instead to walk down the road. The further he got away from his mother, the freer his movements became. He felt good, he thought, with money in his pocket.

He stopped and pulled it out. It was quite a thick wad, he saw—Evelyn had been generous. He felt a moment's contrition: Perhaps he had been too harsh on her. But then he frowned. He would never be able to live up to his father, no son could live up to a saint. It was her fault, her continually harping on Nathaniel's rectitude that had driven him away. She had only herself to blame, and if she chose to save her money for him, then that was her business.

He stuffed the money back and continued to walk.

"But who'll put me to bed?" Rosa was asking.

"Evelyn will." Julia's voice was slow and deliberately patient. "I've asked her to do it as a special favor."

"And what happens if I have a nightmare?"

"Darling," Julia said, and this time it was impatience that suffused her voice, "Evelyn will be there. And we will be back later. You can't come because you need your sleep. Tomorrow is your cousin's bar mitzvah."

"I'd rather come now," Rosa said.

Julia did not deign to reply. She pushed Rosa's hands away from the window. "Give Evelyn a hoot," she told Harold.

As Harold obliged, Julia rolled up the window. "Go on now, darling," she said. "Evelyn will look after you." She tapped Harold on the knee. "Let's go."

As he drove away, Harold happened to glance in his mirror and catch a glimpse of his daughter. Nicholas had already run off, anxious to rejoin his game, but Rosa was standing as if rooted to the spot. Harold's heart went out to her: She looked so pathetic, her face drawn and, in the dwindling light, an uncharacteristic pale color.

"Do you think we should be doing this?" he asked. "She does seem upset by our leaving."

Julia sighed. "You know this is important for me," she said. "I've worked so hard to get the bookshop operating properly, and tonight's the celebration."

Harold smiled. He reached over and touched her hair. "And you've done a good job," he said.

They continued to drive, each lost in thought. For his part, Harold was concentrating on a particularly knotty problem he was having at work. He'd managed to push his concern for Rosa out of the way—after all, she was an ebullient child who would soon bounce back.

Julia was not so lucky. She was determined, more than determined, to go to the function—nothing could hold her back. And yet that didn't stop her from feeling guilty, from feeling that she had somehow betrayed Rosa. Motherhood was just so difficult, she reflected, no wonder her own mother been oppressed by it.

And yet, said another voice, from deep inside her, I cannot afford to think that way. It had taken her so long to break the confines of the home, to dare to involve herself in the setting up of the left book club and the bookshop, that she still worried she might be pulled back into domesticity. That was why she had insisted on going tonight: That was why she wouldn't take Rosa.

I have a right, she told herself as she looked straight ahead.

Moses weaved his way through the streets of Sophiatown, through the buildings constructed from a myriad of materials— tin, wood, zinc, sacking, mud bricks—a jumble of streets that sprang up seemingly overnight, overcrowded, unsanitary, and yet full of energy.

As soon as he had left the white areas, a spring had begun to return to his walk. He felt at home in Sophiatown—Kofifi, as it was affectionately known—it was his kind of place. He liked the healthy chaos that permeated it (it wasn't sterile, like the white areas), the unexpected (it wasn't predictable, like the white areas), and the mix of colors (it wasn't white, like the white areas).

And he liked the night life, the singing, the dancing, the drinking that took place in the home of the *skokian* queens.

"Except not tonight," he told himself. "I must spend this money frugally."

He was passing Mama Mina's establishment when he thought that, just at the point when it was getting going, for the first blare of music hit the street. He smiled and kept on walking.

But the music followed him, beckoning, calling him back. He felt in his pocket where Evelyn's money was safely nestling. He removed his hand as if it were burning: That money was to set him up, to help him find a safer kind of housing, not to be drunk. He progressed a few more paces.

The music called again. Evelyn wouldn't like it, Moses thought.

Hasn't she always boasted how little my father drank? A cymbal clashed.

Abruptly Moses stopped. "Ag, what's wrong with a few drinks?" he said out loud.

"That's right, brother," came a voice from deep in a dark ally-way.

Moses laughed. He turned on his heels and, without hesitation, walked back to Mina's.

"Attention," called a voice, and there was a bang. "Attention, everybody."

The flurry of conversation died down almost immediately. Julia, who had been involved in a rather boring conversation with one of the oldest (and, she had to admit, the more pompous) comrades, was relieved to be able to end it. She looked to the center of the room, where Sonya Kodesh was standing, a tin plate in one hand and a fork in the other.

Sonya bashed the two together. "Attention," she repeated.

"All right, Sonya," someone called. "We're listening."

Sonya handed her implements to the person standing next to her. "Fill your glasses," she instructed.

As bottles were passed from hand to hand, Julia felt a presence beside her. She looked up to see that Harold had come to join her. She smiled at him, and he put one arm around her shoulder.

"You're looking wonderful," he whispered, as the conversation began to swell again.

"Ss'sh," Julia reproved. "Or Sonya will start with the plate again." She covered her already full glass with a hand.

"Comrades and friends," Sonya called. "A moment's silence, please."

She smiled when the room went completely quiet. "On behalf of the book-club committee," she continued, "I would like to thank all those who contributed to the success of tonight's event." She held up her hand to halt the smattering of applause that greeted her statement. "We are very grateful to them," she said, "but it is to someone else that we owe our main thanks. Without her, this club, these premises, would still be no more than a distant idea. She organized us, goaded us, raised funds for us, licked stamps on envelopes, found sponsorship from places we would never dare approach. And all of this she did as a relative new-comer—as one who had until recently devoted her time to child-raising. It all goes to show"—Sonya's voice became louder—"that looking after the home must be hard work, since she did all this for us with apparent ease."

Sonya ignored the groans that issued from various points (occupied, mainly, by men). She raised her glass. "I will not take any more of your time," she said. "I would just ask you to join with me in a toast to our comrade Julia Arnold."

Julia's cheeks were burning. She did not know where to look. As those around her muttered their congratulations, as glasses were raised in the air and summarily downed, she stared down at the floor. Tears came flooding into her eyes, and she blinked. It would be the limit, she thought, if she cried now. She bit her lip.

Harold's arm tightened around her. "Congratulations," he whispered.

The occupants of Mina's one-room shack were united in a frenzied dance. The air was rent by a cacophony of sounds—by the banging of drums and the clang of stones against tin, by the ululating of women giving strength to the sound of the male soloist who sang of the lives of those around him. In the center people danced, deaf to the music and yet moving in time to it, women and men entwined in sexual poses that held no love—only a dark and vibrant despair.

Moses was at the focus of the dance. Around him swirled a group of women, their dresses flying up around them as they twisted and turned to follow his movements. He was insensible to their taunts—to the way they egged him on. He danced as if alone, driving his body in time to some inner frustration that pounded through his whole being. There was a fury about the way he moved, the way he swayed: a fury that was reflected in the tiny dots that his pupils had become and in the flash of their vast white surrounds.

Mina stood on the sidelines and frowned. Moses was a frequent patron, and the signs he was displaying were ominous ones. Mina knew that men like Moses, men who had not yet fully habituated themselves to the most potent of her liquor, were the worst. They lost control suddenly, and then there was no holding them back.

If Moses went on like this, Mina thought, she would be forced to intervene. There was a narrow line over which she could not let her customers tread. It was safe for them to express the life force that they daily held in check (that was, after all, why they came to drink), but if she lost her hold on them, things would deteriorate rapidly. It only needed one person to cross over the narrow line from make-believe into boundless rage and the assembled company would explode. If that happened, people would surely be hurt, and Mina herself would no longer be able to operate.

"Come on!" Moses shouted. "Get up, everybody. Let's go! Let's *go*!" He took the last swig from the jam jar that he'd been holding, throwing his head back so as to get the last drop, and then hurled the jar away from him. It hit the tin wall with a resounding crash, and shattered into a thousand smithereens.

Mina took a deep breath. She stepped into the melee, parting couples as she went. No one resisted her progress: The stories of what happened to those who did were legend.

Only Moses did not seem to notice when the musicians expectantly skipped a beat. He moved to his own inner rhythm, his eyes now closed.

"Come with me." Mina gripped him by the shoulder.

Moses' eyes remained closed. He shrugged. "*Voetsak*," he said. "I'm having fun."

The music faltered, made one attempt to revive, and then died altogether. Moses did not care. He danced on, desperate now in his need to feign enjoyment.

Mina gripped tighter. "I am taking you outside."

"Are you?" Moses stopped. He opened his eyes.

The room was deadly silent. Young as he was, Moses Bopape was a person to be feared. He was unpredictable—at one moment shy and presentable, at the next a veritable fury. Even with all her experience, Mina's ability to control him was by no means assured, for Moses represented a new breed of youth springing up in the townships. They were wild, these *tsotsis*—untamable, respecting no authority but their own.

"Mina has taken on too much this time," one of the clients whispered to his nearest neighbor. "Moses will walk all over her." He began to join the rest of the crowd, who were edging their way toward the small opening that led to the street.

Moses felt the silence, and he felt the fear encased in it. He smiled and looked around him. He saw that he and Mina were alone in the center of the room. Through half-closed eyes he saw cow dung on the floor (now scuffed into a tawdry mess), the shattered remains of the jar he had thrown, men in *modianyeo* hats, their trousers hanging loose above their layer of vests, almost

comical in their fear as they crowded in the doorway, a prized concertina laying on its end where it had been hastily discarded.

His smile faded. "Ag, what's all the fuss about?" he muttered.

With the sixth sense that enabled her to keep her livelihood
against the twin evils of competition and police interference, Mina
felt, rather than saw, Moses' shame.

"Come now," she coaxed. "See what you have done."

Moses' head dropped. "I only wanted to dance," he said. "That
is my mission in life."

"And you have succeeded. Now it's time to rest."

The company breathed a collective sigh of relief as Mina led
Moses away from the center of the room and toward the backyard. Those who were still interested enough to observe what
happened next would have seen Moses drop to the ground in the
section of the room where a pile of blankets delineated Mina's
sleeping space. They would have seen Mina draw the rough curtain around him and leave him where he lay.

But not many did watch. The music started up again, tentatively
at first but soon gathering pace as a lone male soloist was joined by
a chorus and the chorus accompanied by the bang of stone on tins.
The music pounded out into the dark night. The drama was over.
Moses was forgotten. What he had just done was not unusual.
After all, each of them knew by experience the troubles that beset
the black man in South Africa.

"Now now," Evelyn said gently. "Wake up, and you'll see it's
only me."

But Rosa continued to flail against Evelyn, calling out in horror
at some mysterious force that still bound her in sleep.

Evelyn leaned over the bed and gripped onto Rosa's arms. She
shook the girl.

"Wake up, Rosa," she said. "Wake up."

It was at this point that Julia came to the door. She and Harold
had only just returned, and she had been looking in on the children while he parked the car. She hadn't expected trouble; she'd
heard nothing while she walked down the corridor, but then perhaps her senses had been slightly diminished by her slight inebria-
tion. She had gone first to Nicholas's room, picked up his sheet,
and recovered him. Then she'd crossed the corridor and opened
the door of Rosa's room.

What she saw was a dark form bending over a bed. What she

heard was a voice calling for someone to wake up. A kind of terror gripped her heart.

She put her hand up to her head, for she suddenly felt dizzy. Her recent success fled from her mind, everything fled. She was pulled backward toward another time—she was no longer a married woman with two children, she was a mere child. She had seen such a sight before, she had heard such a cry. It was Haim lying there, Haim who would never come back, Haim whose death had taken her mother away.

She wanted to cry out, but she could not. She gripped at the doorframe for support. She shut her eyes.

And then she felt Harold behind her, and she came back to her senses. How ridiculous she was being: Evelyn was black—she could not be Riva. And Rosa was a girl of nine, nothing, either in temperament or in appearance, like Haim had been.

She let go of the doorframe.

And at that point Rosa opened her eyes. She looked past Evelyn, toward the door. Her eyes brushed over Julia's form and went past her.

"Daddy," she called as she stretched out her arms toward him.

14

JULIA OPENED HER EYES WIDE. THE TRANSITION TO CONSCIOUSNESS had been sudden and complete: One minute she was fast asleep, the next she was not only awake but also absolutely alert. Adrenaline pumped through her veins; she could hear the sound of her heart pounding.

She sat up and looked around her. Through a chink in the curtain she could see that the sky was only just beginning to lighten. The house was completely still: Soft snores emanated from Harold's bed. Since he wasn't ordinarily a heavy sleeper, Julia knew that no noise had awakened her.

"I must have been dreaming," she told herself. She lay back again and, closing her eyes, waited for sleep to overcome her.

But no matter how hard she tried, she could not clear her head of thoughts, disturbing thoughts, which kept flitting across it. She saw her daughter again, quite still in Evelyn's arms: She saw how Rosa had stretched out her hands to Harold, how she had bypassed her mother.

I'm like Riva, Julia thought bitterly. I can't get on with my own daughter.

It was a self-judgment too cruel for her to totally accept. She remembered how they had toasted her last night, how they had all turned and thanked her for her work. That would never have happened to Riva—the woman who couldn't leave the home, who couldn't even learn to speak properly the language of her new country.

I'm not like her, Julia thought. I'm not.

And neither, she thought, was Rosa like the person she had once been. Rosa's brother hadn't died, Rosa would never have to struggle as Julia did, would never have to go to work against her will.

And Rosa's nightmares are her own imaginings, Julia thought. She will be as right as rain in the morning.

With that, Julia drifted back to sleep.

Moses felt a rough hand shaking at his shoulder. He curled himself further into a ball, shifting away from the interference. But the owner of the hand was persistent. It carried on worrying at him, becoming more frantic as he pretended to ignore it.

"Get up, get up."

The words pierced through his skull. Moses felt terrible. The shouting in his ear was bad enough, but what was worse was the monotonous thumping that pressured on his brain, causing him to wince with pain. He was itching all over, his body ached.

Gingerly he opened one eye. He saw immediately that he was lying on the floor. He must have fallen there, dead drunk, the previous night, and someone had covered him with a horse blanket. Around him were the remains of last night's festivities—the half-empty plates of food and the formerly full bottles of *bojaloa* now drained to the last drop.

A shaft of pain shot through Moses' head, forcing him to close his eyes again. He lay there puzzling: Why did he feel so bad? Many was the night he spent drinking in the homes of the *skokian* queens and never had a hangover such as this.

And then he remembered. Last night, in a fit of ill-temper, he had partaken of the deadly *mbamba*, a drink brewed from yeast, so vicious that it could waste a man within the space of one short year. Moses had always avoided the worst of the home-brewed alcohol, but last night the devil had seized him by the throat and he had downed a whole skinful, cursing the echoes of past warnings that tried to hold him back.

Ayiee, he was truly suffering for his foolishness now. Groaning, he got first onto his knees, and then, with effort, to his feet.

"About time," Mina said.

Moses stretched. His whole body was full of aches and twinges.

Experimentally he explored his mouth with his tongue. It was all furred up in there, as if he had eaten some unripe passion fruit. He grinned lopsidedly at Mina.

"You couldn't give me something to take the pain from my body?" he asked.

Mina threw down her broom in exasperation. These men, she thought, what did they expect? Foolishly they drank and danced the night away, and then in the morning they expected an instant cure for their hangovers.

Well, she had no patience for them: Her usual practice was to turf them out on their ear and warn them to leave it a few days before they returned.

But Mina had a soft spot for Moses. Eighteen years old and with a strong young body, he was attractive to behold. Sure, he swanked around, as did all the lazy youths, but there was no real malice in him. Mina had observed how Moses kept on the fringes of outlaw society—indulging himself, yes, in some of the easy pickings that came his way, but never getting involved in the nasty business of violence by blade.

Mina knew of his family: She had met Nathaniel and Evelyn when they had a house together, and so, in memory of his father, she kept a benevolent eye on him. She could not stop him drinking—after all, she earned her living from people like him—and yet it pained her to see a youth floating toward a life that would inevitably be cut short by dissolution.

Mina had long been a *skokian* queen. She was famed for her hospitality and the cleanliness of her home, but that didn't mean she was proud of where life had led her. She knew she had no choice—after all, who else would employ her? But on the mornings after a big night, when the sounds of drumming and dancing were just a memory in the back of her brain, she felt a melancholy for the fate that had befallen her and her people. The dancing was adapted from home, but it had a new ferocity that spoke of the humiliations and bitterness of the conditions in the cities.

Seeing Mina distracted, Moses took the opportunity to slump down into a chair. He stared outside. In the yard he could see an old man—the source of the thumping sound—bashing at the hard earth.

"What's going on?" he asked.

Mina shook herself out of her reverie. "He's burying the beer," she said. "We have been warned that the police will be out in force today. Our only salvation is that they're lazy *skelm* who don't like to get their hands dirty before midday."

She picked up the broom and swished it noisily over the floor-mat of cow dung. "I have to clean up here before they arrive," she said. "There's a pot on the stove. Help yourself."

* * *

Fifteen miles away, in the gracious northern suburbs of Emmerentia, Molly Arnold had work to do. She came into the garden just in time to stop one of the natives from spoiling her careful work.

"Not there," she snapped, as she caught her maid placing a plate of canapés too near the alcohol. "And make sure you cover them."

She stood back to examine her efforts: the result of weeks of meticulous planning. She had to admit to herself—it did all look lovely. The long trestle tables that lined the walls of the marquee were covered in the finest white linen on top of which rested trays of delicacies in silver platters. The stands that held the seven-pronged candelabra had been polished until they gleamed even in the darkened light of the tent, their shine complimenting that of Molly's best cutlery.

There was an air of brisk efficiency about the place as the staff bustled to and from putting the final touches under Molly's ever-critical eye. Solly had said she should go and rest, but Molly didn't dare. One never knew what would happen when one's back was turned.

She did not believe in being soft on the native: "Give them a chance and they'll take advantage of you," was her motto. She liked her servants to be polite and clean and to follow her instructions to the letter. That was the best way, she thought. True, the method had its problems—the black was naturally subservient and seemed to lose his common sense when under instructions. But, on balance, Molly felt it was better to have them stupefied than to have to put up with the kind of curt treatment that her sister-in-law Julia took from her girl.

Evelyn, Molly reminded herself, was due to arrive soon. Molly transitorily regretted having asked Solly to book Evelyn for this afternoon, but then the feeling passed. Molly had discerned in the past that Evelyn was, despite her evil looks, a good worker. Why else should Julia Arnold's house look so spotless? Julia herself could hardly find the time to worry about domestic matters.

Yes, Molly thought, for one afternoon I'll make an exception and ignore Evelyn's lack of manners. A feeling of goodwill at her magnanimity flowed through Molly.

"It's going to be all right," she muttered.

"All right?" her husband bellowed. "Why shouldn't it be?"

Molly shifted herself so that she was no longer in his grasp. Men! They never understood anything. They thought these events just happened. They never knew the extent of the planning and worrying that went into them.

"I hope our guests behave," she said.

"You mean mine, don't you?" Solly asked in a friendly enough manner.

Molly allowed herself a brief smile. "I mean anyone's," she said.

Solly guffawed. "Come off it, Mol," he said. "Your friends wouldn't fart in a gale for fear that somebody would smell it twenty miles away."

Molly stiffened. Why did he have to be so crude? And calling her Mol! The times she had asked him not to. "I suppose you forgot to ask Evelyn," she said stiffly.

"I asked her. How many times have I told you so? She'll come: Don't fret about it. You better go powder your face, or whatever it is you get up to. It's almost time for *shul*."

In the dark corridor that served as Mina's kitchen, Moses found a tureen simmering. His mouth watered. He grabbed a tin plate from a shelf and sloshed some of the stew onto it. Then, leaning against the door, he began to spoon it into his mouth.

The hot substance landed heavily in his stomach. He chewed methodically, concentrating on keeping the food down. Eating, he knew, was the only way to prevent more suffering later.

He bit into a piece of fat, turned and spat it out on the floor.

"Are you an animal, then?" Mina scolded, "that you use my floor as a dustbin and you stand to eat?"

She dropped her broom, and grabbing Moses' plate from his hands, she hustled him out of the kitchen and into the yard. She set the plate down on the small table that stood under the wilting vines. She kicked a chair toward him.

"Eat properly," she said. "And mind yourself. If you're not careful, the table will fall over."

Moses ate more slowly now, savoring each mouthful. The stew was made of the cheapest ingredients—*kaffir-vleis* they called it—but Mina had flavored it well. As the nausea abated, he began to enjoy this meal. It reminded him of Evelyn's cooking. I should go and see her, he berated himself, and make it up with her.

But then he forgot Evelyn and looked up. In the distance was the sound he knew only too well, the sound of metal hitting metal. The noise got louder and louder, until his ears were assailed by a terrific clanging. The whole neighborhood erupted, the din was deafening. It swelled into the air, gaining the momentum of a people possessed.

Moses did not have to look out to know what was happening. Beyond the yard, on street corners, in other yards, stood the inhabitants of Sophiatown, banging at the very fabric of their tin houses, warning those ahead of them that the police were in sight.

Mina came running out of the house. "I suppose you've had another drink," she said.

Moses nodded.

"They'll arrest you if they smell liquor on your breath," Mina said.

"Can I hide here?"

Mina pushed at him. "How would that be safe? They know all about me. Mine is the first house they search. Quick, go out the back way. And be careful. They're in a ferocious mood today."

The bar mitzvah was in full swing, and Rosa was in seventh heaven. All her expectations had been fulfilled. She had not been cowed by the huge crowd already assembled when they arrived. She had caught Evelyn's eye where she stood looking starched and proper behind an overladen table, and Evelyn had winked at her. That gave Rosa the courage to fill her plate and go sit and eat before searching out her cousin.

Terence acted very self-important: That was the only annoying aspect of the afternoon. He nodded gravely when Rosa congratulated him, and then promptly refused to tell her anything about his preparations for his coming of age.

"It's a matter between men," he said.

Men! Rosa thought. Who did they think they were? Terence might be a year older than she was, but he knew nothing. Nothing of importance. He even cried on the one night he'd spent away from home.

With that thought for consolation, Rosa soon recovered her poise. She wafted in and out of the adults' enclosure, pretending to be a grand lady, her head high in the air, in blissful ignorance of the food stains that now littered her lacy dress. She inclined her head toward her parents' friends, but was too occupied in her own world to stop and talk to them.

Moses' breath came thick and fast as he dodged amid the narrow lanes that jutted through the outskirts of Sophiatown. He knew the place as well as the oldest of its inhabitants, but he also knew that no one could properly predict what changes the night had brought. What once had been an empty field would overnight become another section of the sprawling mud city. What was once an easy escape route would suddenly be crowded with dwellings hastily erected from the first materials that came to hand.

Moses was not overworried. The police, he knew, would be having the same problem. They, too, would find themselves boxed in on all sides at a place that only last week had been open space. And they had the added burden of having to maneuver their vans through places that might have been constructed to stanch the progress of the strongest of vehicles.

Boy, they were out in force today. Moses had never seen so many *kwela-kwelas* placed at various intersections like jackals waiting to feed off the kill. The panic in the streets was tangible. Moses had passed some roads where there was not a man in sight. Only women and children dared show their faces, and even they trembled when they heard his footsteps. This was a raid to end all raids.

There was a kind of unspoken solidarity among the inhabitants of this shantytown. Twice already Moses had thought himself boxed in by the approaching forces, only to find someone quietly pointing out an escape route to him. Soon he would be out of the environs. Then he would be safe.

Moses jumped nimbly down from a wooden fence. One more twist and he would be free. He would, he resolved, stay clear of the place until the police left. He thought of taking a trip to the city center and picking up a few bob by shining shoes. With luck, he might also be able to pick a few pockets.

But all Moses' plans evaporated when he landed. There was a policeman waiting under that fence: one of those large, red-faced ugly bastards, his hand on his holster.

"Where are you going, *kaffir*?" the policeman asked.

Moses' heart sank, but he did not run. With his own eyes, he had seen what happened to those who tried that route. Instead, he stood still, his eyes on the ground in a subservient pose.

The policeman swaggered over, standing so close that Moses could smell the stink of black tobacco on his breath.

"You've been drinking," the policeman accused. "Where do you live?"

Moses did not reply. There was no point, for he was a squatter and squatting was an offense.

The policeman smiled and beckoned behind him. "You're under arrest," he said.

Harold pointed to the distance where Rosa was sitting under one of the long trestled tables, her eyes focused dreamily on the middle distance.

"She's recovered from last night," he commented.

Julia sighed. "I knew she would," she said. "She always does."

"I suppose so," Harold agreed doubtfully. "But she's so sensitive, our daughter."

"She's fine," Julia replied. "But look at her, the way she sits with her head in the clouds."

"Is that so bad?" Harold asked. There was something uncharacteristically sharp in the tone of his voice.

"What do you mean?" Julia asked.

Harold glanced away. "I . . . I think you might be a bit harsh on her," he said quickly.

"Why do you think that?" Julia asked.

There was menace in her voice. What right had Harold to criticize, she thought, what *blerry* right? It was okay for him, waltzing in at the dead of night and being embraced in Rosa's arms, but he didn't have to put up daily with Rosa's peculiarities, her tempers, her endless, endless questions. "Why do you think that?" she repeated.

Harold's mind was working overtime—searching out an escape route. He'd chosen a bad time to bring this subject up, he knew he had. Julia had always been sensitive about Rosa—much more sensitive than about her son—and Harold had made it a principle not to interfere. But recently he had decided that he should say something, that he should perhaps try to get his wife to talk about the difficulties she so patently had with their daughter.

It was hard to find the right words, and he knew that if he phrased it wrongly, she would be the first to leap down his throat.

The trouble was that she seemed so guilty about it, so ready to assume that he was saying she did not love Rosa. And he knew that was not the case. On the contrary, she seemed caught in a circle of love, a circle so tight that it was seemingly impossible to break.

"I only think . . ." he slowly began.

He never got to finish his sentence, for just then a pile of plates shattered loudly on the floor. They turned together and both saw Evelyn standing behind one of the trestle tables, a peculiar look on her face. Harold left Julia's side and hurried over to the table.

But Molly got there first. "You clumsy *kaffir*!" she shouted. "My finest dinner service, and you broke the presentation plate."

Evelyn, the woman who always had a reply to every situation, did not react.

"What have you got to say for yourself?" Molly demanded.

Still Evelyn stood silent.

Harold placed a restraining hand on Molly's arm. "Leave her," he said.

Molly looked around as if suddenly aware of the spectacle she was making. She turned and stalked off. "Somebody always protects that girl," she muttered. "She'll get her comeuppance one day."

"What is it?" Harold asked Evelyn.

"It's Moses. He's been arrested. I must go to him."

15

no longer wishing to
assume that he was saying

"I MUST GO TO HIM," EVELYN REPEATED IN A LOUD VOICE. METHOD-
ically, with fingers that seemed to have suddenly become stiffened with age, she began to remove her white starched apron.
When she had succeeded, she carefully folded the apron and laid
it on a chair. Then she slowly began to walk.

Harold met her at the entrance to the big tent. "I'm coming
with you," he said.

"There is no need," Evelyn replied. "You have your family
here."

"I'm coming with you."

They got into Harold's car and drove the three miles to Johannesburg's central magistrate court in silence.

When they arrived, the place was buzzing. People crammed
into the palatial buildings, jostling with each other for space and
attention. In every nook and cranny hurried consultations, whispered bartering, low sobs, were taking place.

It was impossible to know where to begin. One look at Evelyn's
face told Harold that she was relying on him totally. So he was
relieved when he caught sight of Mannie Kahn—a lawyer friend
known for his sympathy for Africans. Mannie, a large, untidy-
looking man, was moving down the corridor at a great pace,
papers crammed into his brown leather suitcase, his white wig
askew on his head. Harold intercepted him.

"What are you doing here?" Mannie asked. "I wouldn't choose
to spend my spare time in this hellhole."

"I don't believe a word of it," Harold said. "You thrive on
all this."

"I used to," Manny corrected. "But this tumult is too much,

even for me. What brings you here?"

"I've come to find Evelyn's son. He was picked up in Sophiatown."

"He and three hundred others," Manny said. "The police made a meal of it today. The place is mobbed with people either charged with contravention of the liquor laws or with trespass."

"Where do you advise I start looking?"

Mannie looked at his watch. "I can give you two minutes," he said. "That's all. But you'll have to keep up with me. I've lost half my clients already in this chaos."

As Mannie proceeded down the hall, Harold glanced back at Evelyn. She shook her head. "I'll be in your way," she said. "I'll wait outside."

She found herself a bench, and she waited. She could not understand what was happening to her. She was filled with an irrational kind of panic, she was going to pieces. She had no reason to fear the worst, and yet she could not get it out of her mind. All her life Evelyn had been prey to premonitions that she'd firmly ignored. But now, no matter how she tried to calm herself, she could not rid herself of the dreadful certainty that her son was in bad trouble.

To an onlooker Evelyn appeared as a stereotype of African patience: a heavyset woman sitting dumbly on a bench, waiting without hope, her mouth occasionally moving as she muttered incoherently to herself. And yet the appearance belied the reality. For Evelyn sat only by sheer force of will. Many were the occasions when she was tempted to leave the bench and enter the courts to call loudly for her son. She did not do so. To draw attention to herself in such a manner, she knew, would end in her certain arrest. What good could come of that?

She sat for hours while Harold, with Mannie's help, made the rounds. White privilege operated in South African courts just as surely as it did in all other areas of life. As a result, the two men had little difficulty in gaining access to even the inner sanctums of the police stations.

But no amount of inquiring, cajoling, or threatening yielded any result. Moses, it appeared, had disappeared into thin air. He was not among those who stood in line, waiting to be seen by a magistrate. He was not, said the police, in a holding cell, held under one of a variety of charges—disrupting the peace, assault, selling illegal liquor—that prolonged the legal finagling.

And neither, according to the court records, had he already been processed and released.

Eventually Mannie admitted defeat. "Maybe they let him go without charge," he suggested. He looked at his wristwatch. "I'm afraid I have to go."

Harold thanked his friend for his trouble and then went to find Evelyn. He spotted her as soon as he emerged. She was seated on the same bench, still unmoving. As he stood for a moment beneath the huge white pillars of the courthouse, Harold felt a tremor of fear. Evelyn looked so small, so defeated. He had never seen her like that—not even after Nathaniel's death. Then she had been in agony, but she had also been angry: Now, she just looked collapsed.

He took a deep breath and went to stand in front of her. He held his arms open, palms up, and he shook his head.

Evelyn rose. "We must go to Sophiatown," she said.

When they reached the shantytown, they began to work their way through the streets, searching for anyone who might know of Moses' fate. They made an odd couple—a white man in a business suit holding on to a black woman whose face was a miserable blank. They looked everywhere, even eventually approaching strangers in their effort to glean information, however sketchy.

But Sophiatown had little time for them, and not many of its inhabitants gave the two so much as a second glance. In every narrow street someone had been arrested, and in every extended family there was worry about money for fines.

"What do they want from us?" one old woman wailed. "Every day they come. Even those who are merely returning from work are arrested for being drunk and disorderly. They drove us from our homes in the country. Now, they make our lives in Jo'burg a misery."

Harold shook his head in sympathy. South Africa, he reflected, was a bitter land. Harold prided himself on being well informed: He knew from hearsay how the pickup vans ventured out with increasing ferocity these days. But to see Sophiatown after one of these raids was to really understand what the *kwela-kwela* signified. For this shantytown, this land of almost gothic appearance, where makeshift buildings paid tribute to the imagination of those who assembled them, was a place in deep mourning. Usually so lively, this day Sophiatown was completely subdued. Everywhere on street corners people gathered to recount their stories; every second person had a tale of the brutality of the police against defenseless men.

Harold and Evelyn made their way to Mina's establishment. It was like visiting a bomb site. The police, as part of their tactics to terrorize the location, let nothing—no wall, no dwelling, no person—stand in their way. They raided without mercy. If fences stood in the way, they smashed them down: If children played in their path, they walked right over them.

Mina's had been reserved for especially brutal treatment. The tin and wood shack no longer even existed—it had been totally annihilated. The ground on which it had stood was pitted with deep holes, the very fabric of the former building littered among them. The police had been persistent. They had dug deep into the earth, pulled up the casks of home-brewed beer, and smashed them open: The fermenting liquid seeped into the earth, polluting the air around it with a foul, yeasty stench.

Mina herself had disappeared. Only an old man, the one that Moses had observed early that morning covering the gaps in the earth that were now exposed and bare, sat amid the rubble. His eyes were a rheumy red, and his hands trembled when Harold approached.

"She's gone," he said in answer to Harold's question. "She was good to me."

"Gone where?"

"Where do people go when they can no longer live?" was all the man replied. They got no more from him.

"Let's ask Raymond Siponja," Harold suggested in desperation. "He's a party member, and perhaps he has heard something."

Evelyn was by now fully convinced that something terrible had happened to Moses. She sat in the car throughout the journey to Raymond Siponja's house without really registering anything.

But for Harold this was a time for observation. He took in the subtle changes in the landscape. Sophiatown had formerly seemed like a seething mass of unsanitary conditions, but he began to realize that in the township, just as in the white suburbs, there were subtle gradations in status.

Mina had lived in one of the poorest areas: in a dip in the land where pools of brackish water collected and piles of rubbish were discarded to rot. But Raymond had more money. His house was constructed on a small hill, and it had a look of permanence about it. One wall was even made of brick, giving the tin roof a more solid foundation on which to rest.

Raymond came to the door wearing a dressing gown of tattered wool, only its shining silk collar indicating the former glory of the garment. He stuttered, apologizing for the state of the place, as he invited Harold and Evelyn in.

The two rooms were spick-and-span, and although poorly furnished, there were a few items—a large radio on the sideboard, a broken-down fridge—that spoke of some, albeit small, income.

"You keep the place nice," Harold commented.

Raymond smiled shyly. "I do my best," he said.

Harold introduced Evelyn to Raymond. "We're looking for her son," he explained. "We thought you might have heard something through the grapevine."

"I was asleep," Raymond said.

"But you must know someone who saw something," Evelyn said. Her voice was beginning to crack under the strain.

Raymond thought hard. "Thomas Ngubo was also picked up," he said, and then he shook his head. "But that's no good. They let him go."

"Because his housing was in order?" Harold asked.

"Ach, no." Raymond laughed. "Because he's too educated. Started demanding his rights. The police don't want that sort of trouble. They dropped him off like a hot potato."

"Perhaps my son was as lucky," Evelyn said.

"Perhaps," Raymond said. "Although there are not many like Thomas. He could talk his way out of the mortuary, that one. I tell you what. I'll go and ask him if he knows of Moses."

While they waited for Raymond to return, Harold had time to reflect. The room showed no visible clues to Raymond's personality. There was not a single indication that the man had any kind of social life—in the kitchen was one cup, one plate, and one spoon—or any outside interests. If he kept the literature that the party distributed, he hid it well. I don't really know the man, Harold thought to himself. All these years I have sat in meetings, and I don't even know whether he has ever been married.

Raymond returned within ten minutes. He shook his head. "Thomas saw Moses in the *kwela-kwela*. Moses shouted your brother's address out the window. But after Thomas was dropped from the van, he took off like a shot. He didn't want to stick around for them to change their minds."

There was nothing for it but to return to Yeoville. "We'll probably find Moses on the doorstep when we return," Harold said, mustering up an optimism that he no longer felt.

There was no Moses when they returned, only Julia, who came running out of the house when she heard the car. There was no need for her to ask any questions. The answers were already inscribed on Evelyn's face. When she stepped out of the car, Julia walked up to her, intending to embrace her. But she stopped herself. Evelyn did not look as if she wanted to be hugged. She looked, instead, impenetrable, isolated in her own thoughts. Julia took an inadvertent step back.

Evelyn did not appear to notice. She walked slowly to her room and shut the door.

When Evelyn did not appear the next day, Rosa asked if she could accompany Harold on his continuing search. For eight long hours she trudged behind her father as he visited law offices, courtrooms, and police stations, a picture of Moses in his hand.

For Rosa, it was an eye-opening experience. It was the first time in her short life that she understood that the politics that always seemed so glamorous was not a game. She saw the bruises on the faces of the newly released, the joy of their families, the uncertainty writ large on their future. She saw all this, and through new eyes interpreted it.

For Moses was a person to Rosa. He wasn't the poor black masses—the people who occupied much of her parents' concern—he was . . . well, he was Moses. An elder brother almost: a tangible presence in her small world. Not a principle, but a friend. And he had just disappeared; vanished without a trace despite the considerable lengths to which her father, the man Rosa secretly thought could achieve anything he set his mind to, went to find him.

"Should I go talk to Evelyn?" she asked Julia when they returned weary and without so much as one scrap of useful information.

Julia remembered the way Evelyn had shrunk away. "Leave her alone," she said. "She has enough on her plate without looking after you."

* * *

But in the end Rosa did not heed her mother's advice.

She waited until it was night and the whole household was asleep. Then, slipping on her dressing gown, she tiptoed her way out of the house and made her way to Evelyn's dwelling. She knocked softly on the door.

When there was no reply, Rosa went in anyway. She saw that Evelyn was lying fully clothed on her single bed, her eyes open and focused on some point in the ceiling.

Rosa stood there, ill at ease. She waited for Evelyn to say something—to turn her from the room, even—as long as she somehow acted. But Evelyn did not speak and she did not move.

Rosa nearly turned away, nearly went back to her own room and her own bed. But something inside of her made her persist. Instead of feeling the rebuff and reacting to it (as her mother had done), she went up to Evelyn's bed and climbed in. She threw her arms around Evelyn and hugged her close.

At first Evelyn did not respond: She lay there stiff and unyielding. Then, gradually, Rosa felt some of the rigidity leave Evelyn's body. Emboldened, Rosa nestled in further. She stroked Evelyn's tight-knit hair.

"We will find him," she whispered.

Moses woke with a start. His sleep had been uneasy, and some small sound, perhaps the dim sensation of his nearest neighbor stirring, had been enough to nudge him out of it. He opened his eyes quickly. He smiled to himself, convinced that it had all been a bad dream induced by overconsumption of Mina's alcohol. Any minute now Mina would berate him for his foolishness and send him on his way.

But the smile faded quickly. As he looked around him, he took in the awful familiarity of his surroundings. He was lying where he had fallen the previous night—among a jumble of other bodies. He was shivering. The night was cold, and with only a brown sack to cover his nakedness, damp seemed to have penetrated through the dirt floor to the very core of his bones.

Through holes in the rafters he could see stars twinkling in the heavens. Dawn had not yet come, but even so, Moses knew they would soon be roused by the angry clanging of the morning bell. He lay still, listening to the rise and fall of the men's breathing, the coughing that sporadically broke out among the crowd, and the rustling of hens who reluctantly shared their one-room barn with the workers.

Moses was tempted to rise and pick his way through the sleeping bodies toward an atmosphere that did not stink of stale sweat and of urine. But he forced himself to lie quietly. He was engaged in a battle to survive, and part of that battle, the most important part, was always to preserve his strength.

So he lay still, reviewing the occurrences of the last few days.

From the moment he was picked up, things had gone from bad to worse. He had been pushed into an overcrowded *kwela-kwela*, and the first thing he noticed was the stench of fear—a stench so strong that he could almost touch it.

He had tried to remain calm, to repress the panic welling up inside of him. He gripped onto the iron bars of the small window in the back door to at least prevent himself being pushed further into the dark interior. Then he began to take stock.

He spent the journey to the police station working it all out. The moment that every black man dreaded had finally come to him. Until the time when he had landed right in front of the white policeman, Moses had been lucky. He had survived on his wits, the profits of petty crime, and handouts from his mother. He had skirted the edges of the law, squatting being a way to live cheaply and without ties.

This existence, outside of the rest of society, had not bothered him. In fact, he had laughed at Evelyn's warnings about it. He had almost begun to believe his own boasts that he would be successful in completely dodging the system.

But there's nothing like contact with the South African police to clear your thoughts. As soon as he was picked up, Moses realized that he had been living in a fool's paradise. The predictions of his mother's friends and employers, warnings that he had formerly treated with contempt, came flooding back. Nineteen thirty-six, they all insisted, would go down in the annals as a bad year. General Hertzog's new acts, the first of which abolished any remaining African voting rights, and the second of which limited the Native Reserves to 12 percent of the country, was a foretaste of things to come: It encouraged the police in their raids.

With his arrest, Moses became one of the victims of the new order. He had been stupid to assume that he was untouchable;

that he could evade the tightening noose around the necks of black people.

But then Moses calmed himself. Ever since he had stopped living with Evelyn, he had been trained in a hard school. Getting caught breaking into the white man's home (something that had almost happened a number of times) was surely a bigger offense than mere squatting?

He would be fined, he told himself—at worst sent out of the city. He would be all right.

The reality of what followed was in strong contrast to his imaginings. Through the barred windows he saw buildings pass in a blur as the van hurtled toward the center of Jo'burg. It finally lurched to a stop, throwing its occupants onto each other in a swearing jumble.

The doors were flung open. A black policeman—bastard, Moses thought, although he had sense enough not to utter the word out loud—jumped into the van, and with a *sjambok* whipped the prisoners out. Then the men (the women having been separated from the main group and led off) were forced to line up on a rough piece of ground that was encircled by barbed wire.

Moses did not panic. He had heard others talk lightly of their own arrests. According to these experiences, the prisoners would be herded into a holding cell to await their visit to the magistrate. They would be cursorily dealt with—seen in batches of ten— and summarily sentenced. It could not be as bad as all that.

And yet, what was this that was happening? Instead of being herded toward the police station, the men were made to stand in line for over half an hour. If any of them moved, they were roughly ordered back. Questions were met with barked instructions to remain quiet.

At long last a white inspector swaggered out of the police station. He paused to wipe his face with a dirty handkerchief. He slowly ambled over to the line and surveyed it, a grim smile on his face. He made no attempt to speak—either to his constables, or to his prisoners. He was obviously waiting for somebody.

He was soon joined by another white—this one in civilian dress—a man in his early forties, whose hands were grimy from hard work: a tall man who had to bend down low in order to reach the inspector's ear.

The officer continued to smile and stare straight ahead, as if he were unaccompanied. Only when the civilian shoved a handful of bills toward him did he show emotion. He looked quickly from side to side before grabbing the money, which he stowed inside the flap of his shirt pocket. Then he walked away, whistling.

Alone now, except for a couple of black policemen who kept a respectful distance, the civilian began to stroll down the line of prisoners. He did so slowly, as if looking for some kind of sign. As he passed each man, he concentrated on his eyes. Every now and then he would pause for a long time before nodding to himself in satisfaction. Then he lightly tapped the shoulder of the man in front of him.

The chosen ones seemed to know what was expected of them: They left the line and stood to one side, their small group growing larger as the strange inspection continued.

Moses had no idea what was going on. What was this oddity doing? he thought to himself: What fate was in store for the men so selected?

But even through his confusion, something, some sixth sense, told Moses that he needed all his wits about him. He noted that the civilian was only choosing the youngest and fittest-looking of the lineup. It would not, he decided, be healthy to be among the chosen. He sagged his shoulders and breathed in so that his chest hollowed.

His tactic seemed to work. The civilian passed him without so much as a second glance. Moses relaxed.

The white man had apparently finished. He gestured toward his collection of twenty or so youths, pointing to an open truck that stood at the entrance of the jail's enclosure. The group began to move as one—reluctantly but knowing better than to resist the shouts of the police who prodded them on their way. Moses breathed a sigh of relief. He had escaped whatever fate awaited those unlucky youngsters.

But his ordeal was not over. Out of the corner of his eye Moses saw one of the black constables approach the white man and say something to him. The white man looked back: straight into Moses' eyes.

"Ag, I can't be bothered." His voice floated over to Moses.

The constable said something else. He gestured to the white officer, who had reappeared on the jail steps. The farmer—Moses now realized with a sinking heart that that is what the man was—looked as if he was going to argue. But the white policeman intervened.

"Get on with it, for Christ sake, or the deal's off," he shouted.

The farmer nodded ill-temperedly. He waved his stick at Moses.

"Get in the truck, boy," he said.

Moses stood stubbornly in line. "I have been arrested," he whispered to himself. "I have a right to be tried."

The man in the line beside him nudged him hard. "You better get going. It will be worse for you if you don't."

Moses ignored this advice. He planted his feet firmly on the ground and stared stubbornly ahead of him.

It was an action he would regret often in the coming weeks. Two constables marched up to him. They lifted him up into the air and carried him to the waiting truck. When he tried to resist, one of them slapped him hard. They threw him in the truck so he landed with a bang on the wooden floor. The other men scrambled out of his way, cramming themselves into one corner so that Moses lay alone.

When the white farmer climbed into the truck, Moses understood why his companions had given him such a wide berth. For the farmer stood above Moses, his legs straddling Moses' body. He raised his whip.

"A cheeky *kaffir*, hey?" he shouted as he began to beat Moses about the head. "I'll soon see to that."

The first blow landed on Moses' ear. Moses put up his arms to protect himself.

This seemed to enrage the farmer further. "There is no escape," he said. He shot a look at the other men, who were cowering in the truck. "Pay attention," he sneered, "to what will happen to you if you are insubordinate."

Thick and fast the farmer hit out at Moses, his lithe body concentrating on the application of maximum force.

After a while Moses' resistance left him. He felt only pain and the need to escape that pain. He accepted the blows numbly.

So long and hard did the man beat him that Moses lost consciousness. When he awoke, he found himself on the floor of the truck, buffeted by its motion as it sped along a dirt track. The man beside him handed him a ladle of foul-tasting water.

"Don't antagonize him further," he advised. "It'll only be the worse for you."

"But where are we going?" Moses asked.

"To a farm. We are penal labor."

"But we haven't been tried," Moses protested.

His neighbor giggled. "I suppose you were going to plead 'not guilty'?"

"But still . . ."

"Where have you been all your life?" his newfound friend interrupted. "True, there is a court system for farm labor. But this farmer is too impatient to tolerate the red tape. He's greased the right palms. He comes into town once a month to restock his provisions. If he waits for the courts to sit, he would be held up an extra few hours, doing all the paper work. So he goes to the back door: It's quicker, simpler, and he nabs the young ones."

"And how long do they keep us?"

"That depends," another of the truck's occupants said ominously, "on how we behave."

"Shuddup back there," the farmer called from the front. "Save your breath for the work."

They arrived at the dead of night. Roughly the farmer ordered them out of the truck. Moses saw they were standing in a farmyard, which was surrounded on all sides by picket fencing. On one extreme of the yard stood a small whitewashed building. To its left was a barn newly constructed, with a huge iron lock securing its door. The only other building was the largest of the three—another barn, this time dilapidated with age, its door standing crookedly on its hinges. The farmer gestured to this third building.

"That is your new home," he said.

The man in front of their group began to move toward the barn. The farmer stopped him with one stroke of his whip.

"What's your hurry, boy?" he shouted. "You have not received your welcome speech." He stood in the center of the yard and clicked his fingers. From the house came a timid-looking woman, who handed the farmer a shotgun. He pointed it at the men. "This," he said, "is the law around here. I am its agent. I am not a hard man. Behave yourselves and we'll have no trouble. But step out of line and . . ." He pointed the gun toward them, looking along the barrel as he pretended to take aim.

They were stripped of their clothes and given hessian sacks to wear. Then they were shown into the big barn that was to serve as their sleeping place.

There were echoes in Moses' memory of this treatment: echoes of the time when Evelyn would talk of the conditions his father, Nathaniel, had suffered. Moses wished now that he had paid more heed to Evelyn's words. When he was young, he closed his ears to her stories: He had fought against the memory of his father, the hero. He had not wanted to hear of the life of the man who had been foolish enough to get himself killed rather than stay to know his son.

And now, when Moses got an inkling that perhaps Nathaniel had not chosen to die but had instead been chosen by his circumstances, it was too late. Moses was completely unprepared for the fate that had befallen him.

He knew this as soon as the barn door closed. The other men scrambled to find a sleeping area in a place where the roof was not too crossed with holes. They settled down immediately, leaving Moses to negotiate his way through the ranks of snoring bodies. He ended up crammed against a set of farm equipment, the spikes of which stuck into his back no matter which way he turned.

Moses had only just settled down to sleep when he was aroused by a loud clang. The doors were flung open, and a few tin cans thrown in. Again Moses was last in the scramble. By the time he reached the mealie-meal porridge, it was all but gone. He vowed to be more alert in the future.

But try as he would, it took him a long time to get on top of the situation. That first beating, his first in his life, had knocked the stuffing out of him. When they began to pull potatoes out of the hard ground, Moses' body ached almost immediately. He was faint with hunger and fatigue. If only they would slow down, if only he could rest for a while, he would be all right.

But the lines of men moved inexorably, ever onward. To the accompaniment of their own mournful chanting, they bent down low, picking potatoes with one hand while they placed them in the bags around their necks with the other. Only when they got to one end of the long field could they pause for a minute to empty their sacks and grab a sip of water. Then they started off again.

A whip awaited those who fell behind. Often, on those first days, Moses felt the lash from the overseer: Frequently he wished to be dead. It wasn't just that he was slow and unfit or that his delicate hands, unaccustomed to physical labor, wept blood until he believed that they could bleed no longer; it was that the farmer picked on him incessantly. He was used as an example. He was the archetypical "cheeky boy," now due for a final comedown.

On the first night the farmer ripped Moses' coveted suit into small pieces.

"See that!" he shouted as he whipped himself into a frenzy of outrage at the fine material from which the suit had been tailored. "You think you can wear clothes like that? Never again, my boy. You are here for life. For life. And unless you start working better, it won't be a long life."

For life, for life—the words echoed in Moses' brain. He got to the point where he thought he was beyond caring—let them kill him, as long as they left him alone. And yet he never did lie down, motionless, under the lash. Despite his inner protestations, he was not ready to surrender his hold on his existence. He was so young. He had had so many plans. He would not lie down now. He summoned energy from a glorious fantasy of revenge. He would leap at the farmer, he thought, and choke the very life from him before burning his property to the ground. Moses realized that such a thing would never come to pass, but he used the thought to comfort himself.

16

Gradually Moses' body hardened, slowly he found himself able to keep up with the pace of work. He was helped in this by the arrival of a new lot of "recruits." With their arrival, the farmer seemed to forget about Moses—concentrating instead on breaking the spirit of another youth.

Moses learned to pace himself. He fell asleep the minute his head hit the layer of straw he had managed to bundle together for a pillow. He was well in front of the crowd when food was thrust at them, and without scruple, he grabbed for the lion's share of it. During the day he placed himself on the picking line between two of the strongest men so that they could cover the ground without leaving the occasional potato that would earn them another savage beating. He had two preoccupations: to get through each day without attracting attention to himself, and to procure for himself what comfort he could from this hell on earth.

It wasn't only Moses' body that hardened. His whole inner being turned to stone. When the farmer attacked one of his compatriots, Moses felt no sympathy for the victim—all he experienced was relief that he was not on the receiving end of such savagery. When one of the men got sick, chilled by the strong winds that whipped right through their narrow coverings, Moses was unmoved—he felt only resentment against this disturbance to his coveted rest. He was a loner who cared nothing for the others: a legend in the barn—a ferocious fighter only to be approached with care.

So did this young city man turn into a farm animal. By day he toiled: by night he slept. As his flesh withered under the dual impact of hard physical labor and inadequate nourishment, he lost the charm that had formerly been his trademark. He was becoming a brute: a man whose eyes one would choose to avoid. He was disliked by all.

All, that was, except one. For on the farm there was a young black woman by the name of Peggy Zungu. She alone felt for Moses. She alone kept watch as he suffered and changed.

Peggy was the sixteen-year-old daughter of the farm cook, and her life expectations were limited in the extreme. Her future was clearly laid out before her: When her mother died or became too fragile to continue, Peggy would take over supplying the laborers with food. In the meantime she helped out in the kitchen, waiting on the *baas* in a pristine white apron that concealed her tattered clothes. When the farmer required her to, she also labored on the land.

Peggy had been born on this farm and had never traveled more than ten miles from it. She was not penal labor like Moses, but more surely than he, she was a prisoner.

Her family had once farmed the land on which they were now so poorly employed. When the white man took over, he had boasted long and loud about his generosity in not throwing them off. Peggy's parents were initially grateful, and by the time they'd realized how things really stood, it was too late. They had become dependent on him, reduced to the status of half-slaves. They lived in a half-constructed house on the white man's land; they worked for the white man; they were paid in food; and their children were destined to follow in their footsteps.

That Peggy still had wishes, ambitions, and an inquiring mind was a result of one of the many contradictions in South Africa. For no matter how much the subjugation of the black people increased, the new conditions in themselves created new hopes. If Peggy's family had continued to work for the farmer as his sole laborers, they would have found it difficult even to believe that there was a world outside the farm. But once the farmer seized on prison labor to fuel his expansion plans, Peggy's horizons broadened.

All sorts of men turned up at the farm. Young and middle-aged, educated and illiterate, anything as long as they were fit. They came from a variety of backgrounds; from Jo'burg, from parts of the country where until recently black farmers worked their own land; from factories where some of them had even come into contact with the black union—the ICU.

Peggy sought out these men and encouraged them to talk. She listened to their stories with rapt attention, and all the while she dreamed: She would one day leave this farm.

Peggy's family customs were firmly rooted in a Christian tradition. On Sundays they would all traipse up to the farmhouse, where the farmer's wife would read a weekly sermon before doling out the staples of mealie-meal and four eggs that made up the bulk of their provisions. The farmer's wife had a penchant for those parts of the Bible that dealt with the darker side of her religion, with the endless pain of fire and brimstone, but she was also accustomed to stressing the Lord's injunction to turn the other cheek. Peggy saw the hypocrisy in this, but that did not prevent her from becoming a devout Christian herself. Whatever others did to her, she vowed, she would not do to them.

Perhaps it was this part of Peggy's personality that made her see the good, now so heavily concealed, in Moses' personality. Peggy's mother, a woman made bitter by overwork, was accustomed to scoffing at what she saw as Peggy's weakness. She laughed her head off when Peggy defended Moses.

"Child," she said clutching her sides, "that one's as bad an apple as ever came our way. You're wasting your time with him."

"He has been ill-treated," Peggy answered.

"And which of us hasn't? Have you looked in his eyes? You will see wildness therein. Soon he will go crazy, mark my words. And then where will your contrariness have led you?"

But Mrs. Zungu did not realize how wrong she was. She did not know that her daughter's peculiar interest in Moses was not fueled by contrariness. It fed instead by something much more dangerous—by sexual attraction. For the first time in her life, and without realizing what it was she was experiencing, Peggy felt the stirrings of desire. When she passed Moses, she could feel a tug so physical that she wanted to go and hug him: It was only with the most extreme effort that she managed to carry on walking.

But she was nothing if not discreet. No one, looking at this stolid young woman, could have guessed at the tremblings of her heart, at the way her thoughts kept returning to Moses.

But it wasn't only Peggy's discretion that ensured her privacy, it was Moses himself. Mrs. Zungu never guessed at the truth because, when she looked at him, she saw a man made ugly by his experience. No one, she thought, could be attracted to that.

What she didn't realize was that Peggy, who had little to mark the passing of the days, had a strong visual memory. She remembered clearly the look of Moses when he first arrived. Because the farmer always picked on one of the men, she habitually kept an eye out for that one. And she saw that although Moses had obviously been beaten, he was still very handsome. He had such style as he came down off the truck, stumbling at first but then gathering himself together to stand erect and unafraid.

She kept in her mind's eye this first image of him, disregarding, at the same time, the deterioration in his physical appearance, the way his face had hardened and tightened. And she was not put off, either, by his behavior. She went out of her way to pass him delicacies—a piece of fruit picked from under a tree, a lick of honey from the farmer's kitchen—anything that might help him preserve his strength.

He never acknowledged her gifts. He would nod at her curtly when they passed, too lost in his own degradation to recognize kindness from the hands of another human being. Peggy did not mind: Charity, her religion taught her, would be rewarded in heaven. She continued to smile widely at Moses and to watch over him from afar. She kept herself alert to his needs and to the farmer's plans for him.

One night as she waited on the white family's table, Peggy overheard the farmer boasting to his wife.

"I could tell those government people a thing or two," he said.

"Yes, dear," his wife said absentmindedly, as she piled his plate with roast potatoes and then covered the huge slab of roast beef with dark brown gravy. She passed the plate over.

Her husband's knife and fork were poised in the air. "No matter how stubborn the *kaffirs* I get," he said, and then dug into the meat, "I know how to tame them." He began to chew. "Take that Bopape boy," he said. "You should have seen the cheek on his face when I first got him."

"Yes, dear."

"Now, he's a good worker," the farmer said, as his head went down again. "So good that I'm going to make him a charge hand."

"Yes, dear."

Peggy's heart sank. She knew what the farmer intended. He himself was hated by his laborers, but with a rifle at his side he was seemingly invulnerable. But the men he chose out of the prisoners' ranks, the ones who were seemingly promoted, were easier targets. Not one of them had escaped some kind of injury—a pick in the back, a hit on the head in the darkness, a failure to get up one morning.

Peggy had worshiped Moses in silence: Now, she set out to warn him. Made bold by her own fears, she accosted him as he trudged back from the fields. She drew him to one side.

"The farmer plans to make you an overseer," she whispered.

"So?" Moses snapped. He resented this obstacle in his way to the rest that he craved more than life itself. He tried to move around her.

"Don't do it," she pleaded.

"What does it matter to you?"

When she did not reply, Moses looked for an instant into her face. He saw the glimmering of something he had long stopped expecting—kindness from another human being; kindness offered without any strings. He was oddly touched: He almost reached out his hand toward her and told her that she should stop bothering about him. He no longer cared—why, then, should she?

But he was too far gone to make even that gesture. The numbness descended on him. He walked off without a word, leaving Peggy standing, helpless, on that dusty farm track.

In fact, Moses enjoyed his newfound status. His elevated rank qualified him for double rations and the only mattress in the barn. During the day he was able to rest from his labor by stepping out of line and pretending to survey the work of the rest of the men.

True, Peggy's warning did have some foundation. Even Moses, so desensitized to the regard of others, noticed how his compatriots avoided him, how they went silent when he approached. He felt, rather than heard, the mutterings behind his back. But the crushing of Moses' spirit had correspondingly enlivened his physical reflexes. He was always alert, even in his sleep. He would be able, he told himself, to prevent anyone doing harm to him.

So the days passed, and Moses became a man avoided by all. Even the farmer, although he ostentatiously clapped Moses on the back in front of the others, felt contempt for him. The farmer's attitude, though seemingly contradictory, was easily explained. Here was encapsulated another of the oddities and distortions of South African life. Moses seemed the living proof of the theories under which the farmer lived: that he could mold and break the *kaffir* at will. Moses was unaffected by his new-found unpopularity. The farmer found himself less easy in his sleep. He, who had formerly laid his head to rest secure in the knowledge that his farm was growing with the times, found himself waking up at odd hours and worrying about Moses. "I'll get that *kaffir*," he muttered to himself. "He will not escape me."

One day the farmer's opportunity came in the form of a new batch of prisoners. In the bottom of the truck was a young man. He couldn't have been more than fifteen years of age, and yet he had been badly beaten. Somehow or other he had provoked the farmer's ire and had become the target of the *sjambok*.

The man was carried from the truck, and for three days he lay in the barn crying with pain. On the fourth day he ran away.

It was a futile gesture for a boy born and bred in the city. He didn't get more than two miles before the farmer brought him back. He was dragged in front of the barn and tied to a piece of wood.

The farmer called all the workers together. "Now," he shouted, "I will show you what happens to boys who turn on me."

He marched into his house and finally emerged carrying a long-handled whip made of horsehair. He took a few steps toward the frightened youngster. And then, before he could hit out, a glimmer of an idea, a smile of pure sadism, crossed his face. He beckoned to Moses.

Without speaking, he handed the whip to Moses.

Moses knew what was required of him, and he didn't particularly care. In this place it was kill or be killed. Ignoring the muttered protests of the other workers, he took the whip and walked toward the boy. He raised his arm high, intent on striking.

The farmer smiled. *Ja*, he thought to himself, this is the right way to do it. I'll kill two birds with one stone. For the farmer knew that once Moses beat the boy, his goose would be well and truly cooked. The other workers would ensure that he didn't last another week.

The farmer closed his eyes, anticipating his victory in the sound of the lash as it hit down on human flesh.

So the farmer missed what happened: He didn't see how Moses

seemed to have been turned to stone, how he stood there like a statue, frozen in midaction.

To those who kept their eyes open, Moses' arm hovered in midair for what seemed like an eternity. Then the whip hit the ground with a dull thud.

The boy winced and then looked around wildly. Was he already dead that he had heard the whip but felt no pain?

Moses just stood there. He could never explain what stopped him from hitting the boy. It was the first blow that was so difficult to achieve. If he'd managed that one, he would have had no trouble continuing. He would have been driven on by his own self-hatred, hitting and hitting until he no longer had any strength in his body.

And yet something stopped him from striking out. Perhaps it was the sight of Peggy, standing on the outskirts of the muttering group of laborers, tears streaming down her face; perhaps it was the look of terror in the boy's face, a look that reminded Moses of the child he had once been.

Whatever the motivation, Moses could not do it. He kicked the whip away and turned his back on the boy. The crowd of waiting men parted silently to let him through. One of them clapped him on the back as he passed.

The farmer, who had finally opened his eyes, went red, his mouth turned downward. He picked up the whip, and he started to beat the boy. But when he looked back, he saw that his laborers were deliberately flouting him—that they had, to a man, turned away. Apoplectic with anger, the farmer marched back home and slammed the door.

And after that day, there was no respite for Moses. In the farmer's eyes, to tolerate insubordination was to lose face forever. He resolved to break Moses: to break him until death itself would seem like a merciful release.

Within a week Moses was reduced to a cowering pulp. No matter what he did, the farmer was always before him—berating him, berating him, snatching his plate of food (the others now brought the food to Moses when he could no longer fetch it himself) from his hands. It looked like the end had come.

At that point Peggy showed a determination that nobody could ever have guessed she possessed. She became like an acquisitive squirrel, stealing food without thought or conscience. Some of the products of her crime she gave to Moses, but the bulk she kept to herself. She hid it in the room she shared with her parents—under the bed, inside her Sunday shoes, stuffing it even between the leaves of their large family Bible. She, who had never dreamed of flouting the authority of her parents or her white employers, almost reveled in her newfound furtiveness.

She sidled up to the farmer's wife one day when they were both stirring huge pots of plum conserve.

"Missus," she said softly. "Can I ask you a question?"

The farmer's wife did not look up. She swept a strand of hair away from her sweating face. It was as hot as hell in the kitchen, and she was dying to get away. She didn't like this work, at such close quarters with the natives, but she certainly wouldn't have dreamed of leaving them to their own devices. Heaven knew what a mess they would make of her kitchen!

"What do you want?" she said briskly. "Is it your time of the month again? I told you I have no more rags to spare."

"Tell me, missus," Peggy wheedled. "How far is the town?"

"Town? Which town? You mean Boons?"

"Johannesburg, missus."

The farmer's wife looked up and smiled. Really, the girl was the limit, with her stupid questions. How could a person keep sane, with types like this for company?

"A long, long way," she said. "Why do you want to know?"

"Just asking, missus."

"Well, you are not here to ask. Stir the jam. Can't you see it's burning?"

Peggy did not give up. She went to the laborers and asked them, instead. They were much more amenable: Always ready to talk about a place other than the one to which they had been abducted, they got involved in lengthy disputations as to the actual distance from Jo'burg and the best way of getting there.

A week after Moses' final fall from grace, Peggy was ready. She did not close her eyes that night. At two she rose. There was no need for her to dress; she had gone to bed fully clothed. Quietly she removed the food from its hiding places and wrapped it in an old piece of cloth that she knotted around her back. She stood for a while in front of her best shoes—patent leather, and her pride and joy. She could not take them with her. They had been given to her by the farmer's wife, and to remove them would feel like stealing.

She crept out of the room and went toward the barn. Moses was lying by the door—the others had put him there because the air was purer. He did not stir when Peggy bent over him. She kissed him on the forehead, the first time she had ever dared to come so close to a man, and she felt how feverish his brow was. If she had been thinking of turning back, his condition gave her courage. Peggy knew that without hope of rescue, Moses would soon be dead.

"Good luck, sister," a soft voice said from within the barn. Peggy did not reply.

She took one look back at the farm when she was halfway down the dirt track. The moon was full that night, and Peggy saw the big farmhouse gleaming white in the darkness. She did not need to see the other details: The layout of this land was as familiar to her as her own body. She could imagine, without looking, the rolling fields of brown and rust, the splendid vista of emptiness broken only by the occasional tree that greeted one when one rounded the corner, the small stream that sparkled on the edges of the farm. With a sigh poignant with the sorrow of leave-taking, she began her journey.

For Evelyn Bopape, life was nothing other than routine. She no longer expected to see her son alive, and she no longer consciously thought about further avenues to explore. They had done everything they could: They found nothing, absolutely nothing.

Moses, Evelyn was convinced, was dead, lying in some unmarked grave in Sophiatown. Well, she would not think about it. She buried herself in her daily duties: washing, cleaning, looking after the children, mending, cooking—anything to keep her mind away from his rotting body.

Washday was the worst. It required no thought, and yet it took up so much time. When she was pounding clothes against the stone sink, she could lose herself in the noise and the action. But when she came to hang up the washing, she felt trapped within the limitations of a mind that refused to accept the inevitable. Try as she would, she could not keep images of her son from crowding in on her.

"Only two more basketfuls," she told herself as she pegged a pair of socks together. It was then that she felt a presence beside her. She turned to see a young girl standing there.

Evelyn took in the girl's appearance. She saw the battered

shoes, the graying, formerly white bobby socks, the tattered red A-line skirt that hung above the knee, and the crumpled yellow short-sleeved shirt. The girl's hands were roughened by hard work, and her arms and legs scratched as if she had just forced herself through a hedge of tearing brambles. Her face was round, almost moonlike, as she stared beseechingly up at Evelyn.

Evelyn's heart went out to the girl. She, who these days spoke only in harsh tones, made a supreme effort to soften her voice.

"Who are you, my child?" she asked.

"Peggy Zungu."

"And what can I do for you?"

Peggy's eyes closed, and for a moment it looked as though she were about to faint. But when Evelyn dropped her washing and reached out to give support, Peggy moved away.

"Are you Evelyn Bopape?" she asked.

"I am. Do I know of you?"

Peggy shook her head. "It's about your son, Moses," she said.

At the sound of his name, Evelyn froze. She stood stock-still in the Arnolds' garden, her senses vibrating with the pain of what she knew she was about to hear. She would never forget that moment. She saw it all—the bright red of the flame-tree bloom, the piercing blue of a cloudless sky, the green of the immaculately watered lawn—as if this were her last moment on earth.

"He is dead," she stated. She could hardly believe her eyes when the newcomer shook her head.

"Not yet. But you must act now before the farmer kills him."

As her first wave of panic receded, Evelyn came to her senses. The experience of the last month seemed to wash away from her. It was as if her whole character stiffened, as if the Evelyn Bopape of old suddenly returned to her body. She half-led, half-carried the protesting girl to the kitchen, where she plied her with food and drink before allowing her to continue her story.

Evelyn wanted to leave immediately, to go to fetch Moses back by herself, but Harold and Julia prevented her from embarking on such a rash course. Harold flung himself into action. With his daughter once more at his side, he contacted a lawyer who, armed with a writ of *habeas corpus*, battered on the doors of the local police.

The embarrassment of those in charge was tangible. They would have denied Moses' existence; after all, he had not even been processed through the holding cells, if not for the number of unquestionable facts in Peggy's tale.

Peggy's ever-watchful eye had taken it all in. She, whom the farmer treated as a dumb receptacle of his orders, had overheard all the details—the name of the policeman, the place of collection, even the increasing amount of the bribe, about which the farmer had so often complained.

Armed with the facts, Harold got his legal documents. He was ready to drive to the countryside. In this, too, he was accompanied by his daughter, Rosa. Evelyn stayed in Johannesburg with Peggy.

The journey, which had taken Peggy a full three days to negotiate, took Harold ten hours. With Rosa beside him, he sped down roads that turned from tarmac to dirt within miles. It was a difficult journey, but Harold did not appear to notice. He was hell-bent on getting to Moses without delay.

Father and daughter spoke little throughout the journey. Harold concentrated on the road: Rosa dozed and dreamed, keeping her mind away from the awful possibility that they might arrive too late.

Rosa was shocked by the appearance of the farm. Peggy had described a large estate, numerous outbuildings (including the infamous barn), and a palatial white house. But to Rosa's city-tuned eyes, it appeared tawdry and dilapidated. She could see no signs of what she considered a farm to be—no neat fields with cows grazing peaceably, as shown in the pictures in her books. Instead, there was empty land as far as the eyes could see—field upon field, brown upon red—and very little else.

"It's breathtaking," Harold muttered.

Rosa could not agree. She thought it all rather tacky.

The farmer's wife was also a terrible disappointment. An aged-looking woman dressed in the most rudimentary of clothes, she was quite obviously thrown into total confusion by her visitors.

"My Piet isn't here, *meneer*. My Piet isn't here," was what she kept repeating, glancing around wildly as if they might steal the broken-down furniture that filled her dingy house. She served them each a cup of tea sweetened with condensed milk and accompanied by a deliciously light biscuit that Rosa stopped herself eating after she saw Harold push his to one side.

The farmer had obviously been sent for. He arrived on the run, furious at this interruption in his daily toil. He was coated in the dust and grime of the land. He was a tall, weatherbeaten man, his skin leathery and his hands covered in calluses.

"Whoever you are," he blustered, "get on with it."

Harold held out a document.

"I have here a writ," he said.

The farmer waved the paper away.

"You're in the country now, man," he said. "Don't throw your documents at me. I care nothing for city ways."

Harold raised his voice. "A writ for one Moses Bopape, a man of Xhosa extraction, illegally held on your farm. I hereby inform you that, should you fail to deliver the said person to my care, I will send for the police, who will compel you to so do."

The farmer laughed mirthlessly. "The police, as you so grandly call them," he said, "is one constable who happens to be a great friend of mine. What do you think he's going to do for you?"

Harold was unmoved. "Nothing, perhaps. But I would then be forced to bring reinforcements from Johannesburg. I can't imagine they'd be delighted at your obstruction."

The farmer frowned. "Don't threaten me," he said. "I care nothing for you city slickers. What do you know of life in the country? As long as your food reaches your table, you never consider what it takes to dig it from the ground."

Harold paused. He looked into the farmer's face as if weighing his opponent's character. When he spoke again, his voice was softened. "What can Moses mean to you?" he asked. "He's just another laborer. You have plenty."

The farmer blanched. He turned as if to leave. Then, after a moment's hesitation, when Rosa saw his shoulders heave as if he might be weeping, he waved a hand in the general direction of the barn. "Ag, take the *kaffir*," he said. "He's finished anyway."

If the farmer's house had been a disappointment, there were no words to describe the conditions under which Moses was living. The sight of the barn crammed with men was one that would haunt Rosa for the rest of her life. She smelled the dank air of their one-room sleeping place and saw the crusted remains of stale mealie-meal on the battered tin plates. She saw the resignation of men unfairly condemned to a state of bondage. Men clothed in sacks, pitifully thin, with hollow eyes and beseeching faces. She was ashamed of herself, but her only impulse was to get out of that place and never return.

For Moses, the shock was almost as great. He hadn't looked up when the door had opened, although he'd registered in the back of his mind the change in available light. He hadn't looked up for the simple reason that he no longer cared who entered. There'd been a time when even the creaking of the door had struck terror in his heart because it might herald the farmer's appearance. But that time had gone. These days he almost welcomed the farmer, since each visit would bring Moses nearer the point of death, and death, thought Moses, was infinitely preferable to life.

But though he didn't look up, and though he was sunk in a kind of semiconsciousness, Moses could not fail to sense the change in atmosphere. All conversation, muted at the best of times, ground to a halt. In the back of the barn a man coughed and then stopped abruptly: Someone else laughed nervously.

Moses heard a voice call his name, and the voice sounded vaguely familiar. I'm dreaming, he thought. He heard a child's voice repeat his name, and once again he felt, in the back of his mind that he knew the voice.

He did not bother to open his eyes. He was past saving, past caring, past feeling. If he was hallucinating, so be it. Worse things had happened to him, and he had taken them in his stride.

He felt a hand on his shoulder, and he moved to brush it away. He heard the voice again, "Moses," it said.

"Go away," he muttered. "Go away." He tried to turn over, but the hand restrained him.

"Moses," said the voice. "Can you open your eyes?"

He opened his eyes. He saw that the hand was white. He followed it upward, and found himself staring into Harold Arnold's face.

"I've come to take you home," Harold said.

Moses closed his eyes. Secure, once more, in darkness, his only haven, he tried to laugh. But the laugh got stuck in his throat and turned into a cough that bent him in half, racking his body with pain.

When it had subsided, he opened his eyes briefly. "It's too late," he said.

Harold bent down, locked his arms around Moses' neck, and

then hauled him to his feet. Moses had no energy to resist. All he could register was a slight wonderment at the ease with which Harold was carrying him. I must have grown small, he thought to himself before a merciful darkness descended.

17

WHEN EVELYN WALKED INTO THE ROOM, HER EYES WERE DRAWN automatically to the chair by the bed. Moses was sitting on it, staring at the wall. This was no surprise: In fact, so habitual was his position that Evelyn might have reacted with shock if he'd been anywhere else.

She managed to suppress a sigh. She knew from experience that it would only provoke him. But repressing her inner feelings of irritation was harder to accomplish. It was, she couldn't help thinking, all becoming too tiresome. Or to be more accurate, Moses was. She didn't know how much longer she could continue to be tolerant of his incredible passivity.

During those first weeks when he'd been quite obviously ill—racked by fever and tossed in pain—she had felt nothing but love for him. She'd stayed awake long nights, been driven almost to the point of herself falling sick, but she hadn't begrudged him so much as one second of her vigil. All she'd cared about was that he was alive: that her son had come back from the dead.

But when he grew stronger, her feelings began to change. Not in the beginning, for she knew that the brutality to which he'd been subjected was bound to have affected him mentally as well as physically. So when he first flew into one of his unprovoked rages, or sat for hours in sullen silence, she had tried to understand and to bear with him. He would progress, she told herself, he would improve.

But now, a full two months after his return, she was beginning to doubt. She had to face the fact that Moses had made absolutely no effort to truly recover. He was sunk in depression, uninterested in the world, preoccupied exclusively with his own secret thoughts. He ate when food was put in front of him, but he chewed mechanically and did not seem to care about the taste. He moved when asked him to, but he shunned the outdoors and gravitated to the chair as soon as her back was turned. He talked when he was spoken to, but in the whole two months she had never heard him volunteer one single word.

In fact, she thought, he was like a zombie—a graceless, unconcerned ghoul. He didn't even look like himself: His face was hardened and blank, he no longer reminded her of Nathaniel.

This time when she sighed, she sighed aloud.

Moses heard her, and it made him want to hit out. But with an effort, he kept his reaction to himself. It wasn't her fault: He knew she found him frustrating, that she had done her best to make him better, to coax him into his old self.

But he also knew something else, something that she did not seem to understand. The simple truth was that he could not be coaxed, not because he was stubborn, but because he was powerless. There was no way he could return to his former, carefree self.

For he had lost the capacity to care—to feel, even. The one emotion that still remained intact was rage—he found himself flying into unexpected, and even inexplicable, fits of temper, but when they abated, all he felt was a deadening kind of numbness. He saw how his mother suffered, and yet he could do nothing to alleviate her pain: He was adrift in his own kind of aimlessness; nothing mattered, nothing at all.

He had failed her, he knew he had. He had let her down, and at the same time he had done something worse than that: He had failed his dead father. Nathaniel would never have given in as Moses did, Nathaniel would never have been beaten.

He scowled. Who cared, he thought, who cared? He would not put up any longer with being compared with Saint Nathaniel. He concentrated on his point in the wall, that lone blank, useless point.

There was a soft knock, and then the door opened and someone came in. Moses did not turn around. He knew it was Peggy, and he had no desire to acknowledge her. For if Moses found Evelyn annoying, then Peggy was doubly so. He couldn't stand the way she looked at him with those wide, teary eyes: It made him want to reach out and hit her. She thought of him as a victim, as the person she had saved, and he supposed that she was waiting for him to thank her. Little did she know how hard he was, how indifferent he felt, how much he wished that he had been allowed to die.

A choking sensation gripped at his throat. He made an attempt to breathe, and his chest seemed to collapse as the air rushed in. He needed to get out, he was suffocating. He breathed in again. I've got to get away from here, he thought. I've got to go.

Evelyn, who heard Moses gasping, did not rush forward. She'd heard the sound before, and she was no longer devastated by it. When it first occurred, she'd thought he was having a heart attack, and she'd panicked. But after it was over, the doctor told her that Moses was physically well, that his heart was strong, that his lungs were sound. It was some kind of panic reaction, he had said: Moses was creating his own pain.

So now, when he gasped, she did nothing, and when Peggy made as if to run over, she threw the girl such a look that she stopped in her tracks. Evelyn frowned to herself. This attack, she thought, started with Peggy's entrance. And it's not the first time.

She sighed again. Peggy was another problem: She couldn't go home, and she couldn't go on living here. Something would have to be done.

"Peggy's moving out," Julia said. "Evelyn's found her a room in Sophiatown."

Harold nodded. "She's so young," he said, "but she can't stay here." He stretched across the table, picked up the horseradish dish and spooned some over his plate. "Moses can't seem to stand the sight of her," he continued. "I don't understand why—she goes out of her way for him."

Rosa scowled. That's just like adults, she thought. They don't understand anything. Can't they see how Peggy moons over Moses, how she goes soppy every time he comes near her? No wonder he hates her guts. And anyway—she smiled to herself—what do adults know?

"Moses is going, too," she said loudly. "He's leaving tomorrow."

But this piece of information, gleaned by careful eavesdropping at Evelyn's door, did not impress her parents. They were already talking about something else, and so all she got in acknowledgment was a vague nod from Harold.

They were talking politics, of course. God, it was enough to drive a person around the bend the way they kept going on and on about their precious party. Rosa didn't know why they bothered: All they got out of it was boring socials and endless meetings. And they were so proud of themselves—so proud of mixing with Africans. They talked about it (about how the party had recovered after the '22 strike—whatever that was—and begun to actively recruit blacks into its ranks) endlessly, until it made her want to scream.

"Mom, I need you to write me a letter for school," Rosa said quickly. That got her mother's attention.

"Forgot your homework again?"

"No." Rosa's voice was soft.

Julia pushed her chair away from the table. "So what is it?"

"I don't want to go to religious assembly."

Julia stood up. "Fine," she said. "I'll ask if you can read in the quiet room instead."

"No, I don't want that." Rosa paused. When she spoke again, the sentence came out in a quick burst. "I want to go to Christian assembly," she said.

Julia stopped. "That's not religious?" she asked in surprise.

"Well, it isn't. Sarah says . . ."

Oh, God, Julia thought, not another "Sarah says"! It was getting too much the way Rosa never stopped talking about Sarah Lewis, never stopped quoting Sarah's father, the judge, or admiring Sarah's mother, the housewife. She sighed.

Rosa heard the sigh, and she raised her voice. "You don't let me do anything I want. . . ." she began.

Nicholas rolled his eyes upward, while Harold, who had been watching from the sidelines, almost did the same. He knew exactly what was about to happen—Rosa would berate her mother until Julia put her foot down. Then Rosa would flounce off, and for the next few days the house would be soured by her angry sulking.

He knew that this would happen not because he was clairvoyant, but because it was part of a continuing pattern, a pattern that had abated somewhat during Moses' disappearance but that had then returned with a vengeance. Harold did not really understand it, but that didn't bother him: He was a man of action, after all.

"Julia," he suggested, "why not write the letter?"

Julia whipped around and glared at him. "You write it," she snapped before marching out the door.

Later that night Harold reached over and touched Julia's shoulder. He was relieved to find that, although she flinched, she did not entirely move away. "I'm sorry," he whispered. "I didn't mean to undermine you. But it was too unimportant an issue to cause a fight."

Julia turned around—another good sign. "Why unimportant?" she asked.

"Children go through phases about religion," Harold said.

Julia snorted. "I don't give a damn about the religious aspect."

"I know you don't," Harold replied. "But if we refuse to write the letter, Rosa will call us hypocrites. After all, we do tell her she must make her own choices. How can we then tell her which assembly to attend?"

Julia's eyes narrowed. "You and I both know it's not an assembly she's choosing," she said. "It's an identity. She doesn't want to be a Jew anymore. She wants to be like *goyishe* Sarah Lewis in her sparkling white house."

"*Goyishe*, hey?" Harold teased. "It's seldom you use that word."

But Julia was not to be jollied out of her conviction. "The Lewises represent everything we despise," she insisted. "And look at how our daughter embraces them."

"Is that so bad, my Julia?" Harold asked softly. "When you were a child, did you never envy the Christians? Did you never feel ashamed of your mother, walking to *shul* muttering to herself in Yiddish?"

"It was different for me," Julia snapped. "My mother was a fanatic until the day she died."

"Your mother was impossible," Harold agreed.

"Rosa has it easy in comparison."

"Easier, yes," Harold said. "But not that easy. She has a lot to contend with: She's white, but she's brought up to feel her position is unfair; she's a Jew, but her parents don't act like Jews; and if that's not bad enough, she's a daughter of two communists."

Julia laughed and moved closer. "All right, all right," she said. "You win. Let her be bored to death at assembly." And as

Harold's arms closed around her, she pushed her misgivings to one side.

And so Rosa got her letter, and with it came final endorsement of her new position in the school. She was well pleased. She had worked so hard to be accepted into Sarah's crowd, and only the fact of different assemblies had stood in her way. Now, she was no longer separated with the other Jewish kids: She went with the majority, and never once did her new friends so much as mention the switch. They treated her as one of themselves; she was safe.

Gone was the time when she slunk out of school with only a lonely journey ahead of her. These days she walked through the gates arm in arm with Sarah—for Sarah and she were acknowledged best friends—and hung outside the gates, chatting with the boys from the school up the road.

She didn't care that things were gloomy at home, that Evelyn no longer treated her as special, that Julia and Harold were so preoccupied with their own lives. She had chosen for herself, she was different: She reveled in her newfound identity.

"I'm not a freak," she kept reassuring herself. "I fit in."

And yet her newfound confidence was, it seemed, built on a floor of sand. For just when she was feeling secure, it happened: the moment she had most been dreading. She emerged from school, her arm linked with Sarah's, and saw immediately the danger that awaited her—among the gaggle of boys stood a skinny, pale-looking child.

Rosa knew his type, knew it only too well. She did not need to look for confirmation at the yarmulke on his head. He would be defiant in his identity: He would be trouble, she was sure of it. She pointed her hand away from him. "Look, Sarah," she said in a voice full of false cheeriness, "is that your mother's car?"

Sarah threw a cursory glance down the empty street before plunging back into the crowd.

With a sinking heart, Rosa allowed herself to be led into the thick of the gang. She put on her haughtiest air, keeping her face well away from the newcomer, but she was convinced that he was following her progress. He'll know, she thought miserably. He'll be able to tell I'm a Jew.

Sarah headed straight for Thomas Blake, who, as luck would

have it, was standing beside the skinny boy. As she allowed herself to be propelled forward, Rosa prayed for some kind of divine intervention that would save her from the impending disaster. She knew that Sarah wouldn't be able to resist commenting on the stranger's gauche appearance, and she knew where that might lead.

Don't do it, she silently prayed.

"Who's your friend?" Sarah inclined her head cockily in the direction of the boy.

"Jacob Swiece." Thomas blushed. "Newly arrived in the country."

Sarah took one step back and made no attempt to conceal the way she was examining the newcomer from tip to toe. "An unattractive specimen," she drawled. Rosa secretly agreed: She hated that boy—how dare he come here and barge his way in, making things so uncomfortable for her?

"Ag, leave him alone." Thomas's voice broke through Rosa's internal monologue. "He doesn't even speak English."

"Then what's he doing here?" Sarah asked. "My father thinks the whole country is flooded with undesirables these days. He says they come here saying they're running away from Hitler, but really they're just looking for an easy life. He says they carry disease." She thrust her face close to the boy. "Are you ill, my man?" she asked in her haughtiest fashion.

The boy stood his ground. He might not understand the language of Sarah's question, but it was plain that he got the message. And worse than that, he didn't seem to mind. He stared, unblinking, at Sarah, fear or embarrassment strangely absent from his face.

A few snickers issued from the watching crowd. Sarah, a girl who in some ways ruled through fear, was in difficulty. If the boy did not climb down by indicating that he was somehow intimidated, her position in the pack would be shaken. She would not, Rosa knew, tolerate this: She was accustomed to having people jump to her every command, and she upped the stakes when it didn't happen.

Rosa tugged at Sarah's arm. "Let's go," she said. "Don't waste your time on him."

"You're right," Sarah said loudly. "After all, he's only a yid."

She had uttered the one word that would rally the gang. "Yid,

yid," cried the other children, and they walked away with Sarah, leaving Jacob to stand alone.

"The trouble with yids"—Sarah had fully recovered her poise, and she spoke with a kind of world-weary sophistication—"is that they're so utterly without grace. And they're all *blerry* bolshies. Don't you agree?"

"Yes," Rosa answered clearly for all to hear.

When Rosa got home, earlier than was usual, she walked fast up the driveway, as if someone were pursuing her. But when she reached the house, she did not immediately go inside. Instead, she veered away from the door and ran into the garden.

In the middle of the garden stood a jacaranda tree, its branches large and spreading, like gnarled fingers reaching out for her. This tree was hers, and the place where she went when she wanted to be alone.

She made straight for it, and hanging on to the lowest branch, she hauled herself up. She scrambled to the top. Only when she had reached the very pinnacle of the tree and was safely wedged in did she stop moving. She noted with detachment that she had scratched herself, that there was blood on her knee and the beginnings of a bruise on her thigh. She didn't care—she felt no pain.

She looked out across the garden, and at the stretch of empty grassland that stood on the other side of the road. That "*miniveld*" was her domain. She would often sit in the tree for hours as she imagined battles occurring, kings being crowned, damsels rescued.

But this time, no matter how hard she tried, she just kept seeing the face of that boy. He had looked at her curiously when Sarah had spoken—as if he had been wondering why she said nothing to defend him.

She closed her eyes quickly. She wondered what would happen if she lost her balance. She would land on the ground, she thought, with a satisfying splat. But no—that wouldn't help. Knowing her luck, she'd only manage to break something, and then there'd be the humiliation of doctors and sickbeds and no going to school.

At the thought of school, a shiver ran down her spine. She didn't know which was worse, the fact that she had acted that way to a total stranger, or her fear that she might meet him again.

On balance, she decided it was the latter. She hated him, she really did. Why did he have to pick her school to stand outside of? And why did he have to dress like that? Who cared that he was different, that he was a Jew, that he came from another country? There was absolutely no need to proclaim it so.

Miss Brinson, her headmistress, would agree. Only this morning she had told them how they were all equal in the eyes of God. Some people, she thought, could accept the fact without struggling against it—why did Jews and communists have to make such a big deal out of their differences?

She shut her eyes again. She wouldn't think about it, she really wouldn't. She'd think instead of Miss Brinson, of the wonderful stories she told during morning assembly.

Her favorite, she thought, was about Peter—the man who had denied Jesus thrice. She liked it especially because they never said anything boring like three times—it was twice and thrice and it sounded special.

But then, in the middle of that thought, she had another. She was like Peter, she thought, she had done it, too. Hadn't she denied her upbringing by pretending she was not a Jew? And then today she had done it again, she had first denied Jews and then communists. She was like Peter, she was lost, and she didn't have even his excuse—she had been under no threat.

She was lost—she would go to hell. Tears welled up in her eyes.

But wait a minute—maybe she was still safe. Peter had denied Jesus on three separate occasions, but hers had only been on two. Today couldn't count as twice, she told herself, it just couldn't. She was safe.

She made a promise to herself. She would not, she resolved, follow in Peter's shoes any longer. She would be careful—there would be no third betrayal.

"That's it," she said, and she jumped from the tree.

She landed neatly, and it was a carefree Rosa who ran once more across the lawn and toward the house. The number three kept recurring in her mind, and she played tricks with it. "Thrice three is nine, twice three is six," she muttered. This magic chant, given supernatural powers because of the Bible, drove away the remnants of her worry. She was safe, she knew she was, the Bible had kept her pure.

Rosa and Sarah were sitting, their feet up, in the back of Mrs. Lewis's Rolls-Royce. They had been shopping, and now, they told each other, they thoroughly deserved a rest. They stared out of the window, pressing their faces to the glass and making awful grimaces, when someone came near.

The car was making slow progress. Central Johannesburg, a booming area with gleaming shops and new office buildings, was jammed with traffic.

"I don't understand," Mrs. Lewis muttered in exasperation. "It's not usually so crowded."

Sarah and Rosa continued to chat. They talked about Sarah's impending birthday party, and who should be included in the invitation list.

"Mary sniffs," Sarah said.

"Ja," Rosa agreed. "But she always gives good presents."

"Stop them," came a distant cry. "Stop them."

The two girls turned around together. They stared out of the back window. Both girls turned back to see what was happening. Both saw the same thing: a group of black men running down the middle of the road toward the car.

"My father says the *kaffir* is slow." Sarah giggled. "He should be here. Look at them go."

The men came closer, and as they did so, they separated a bit, preparing to divide so they could negotiate the line of traffic ahead. When they parted, the girls caught a glimpse into the far distance. They saw a number of whites, all dressed in uniforms, also running, obviously in hot pursuit.

"Who are those funny-looking people?" Sarah asked.

"Grayshirts," said Mrs. Lewis with distaste.

"What's a Grayshirt?" Sarah asked. Rosa's heart sank.

"Don't concern yourself about it, darling. We'll soon be off." Mrs. Lewis used her fingers to drum nervously on the steering wheel. "The traffic is a scandal," she muttered.

"Look, they're catching up with us," Sarah said. "How exciting."

As the small bunch of Africans came abreast with them, Rosa felt an agonizing sense of foreboding. She rarely listened to her parents' conversations these days, but she remembered clearly them discussing the Ossewa Brandwag—a nationalist organization whose language grew increasingly close to that of Hitler's. These Grayshirts were part of them, she knew they were: She wished that she could disappear. What if they were after her?

"They're getting closer," Sarah shouted. "Look, Rosa!"

The glee in Sarah's voice forced Rosa to snap out of her imaginings. God, she thought, I'm being stupid. Why should they be after me?

She knelt beside Sarah and looked. And at that moment her relief was turned to horror, for she caught a glimpse of the leader of the first pack. She could hardly believe her eyes. Moses, their Moses, was in front.

No, it couldn't be. Nobody's luck could be that bad. Rosa blinked and looked again. But there was no escaping the truth. It *was* Moses. Worst of all, she knew that he had recognized her.

Rosa shrank down as Moses banged on the car window.

"Rosa," he shouted, and his voice was muffled by the thick glass. "Let me in. They'll kill me."

Mrs. Lewis turned to Rosa. "Do you know that boy?"

Rosa shrank down still further. "No," she whispered.

The traffic in front of them began to move. Mrs. Lewis gunned the engine. In a trice they were off. Rosa looked back only once. She saw Moses fall to the ground as the car swished past without him.

There was a short silence in the car. Rosa saw Mrs. Lewis glance at her in the rearview mirror. If she says anything, Rosa thought, I'll tell her to go back.

But Mrs. Lewis kept her suspicions to herself, and Rosa kept quiet.

18

WHILE MOSES LAY SPRAWLED IN THE MIDDLE OF THE ROAD, HE experienced a moment's blissful peace. At last, he thought, I am at rest. For the first time in ages, he felt as though he were making a choice.

When the Grayshirts had first started to abuse, and then to chase, he had run automatically. It had been an unthinking action, a habitual one: He felt as if he'd been running ever since he had been rescued from the farmer: running from the farmer, who would not leave his mind, from his mother whom he had so disappointed, from the fear and the anger within himself.

But now he felt completely calm—let the Grayshirts finish what the farmer had started. He had seen the hatred in their faces: He had heard the blood in their cries. He had learned enough about hatred and violence to recognize it in its purest form. Well, let them do their worst: He did not care.

He closed his eyes. As if from a great distance, he heard shouts as they approached. He was at peace. At last he would be allowed to give up.

But the blow that he expected—welcomed, even—never came. He heard the sound of footsteps going away—those were his friends—and of more coming toward him—those were his enemies. But after that he didn't hear anything out of the ordinary, only the horn of a car behind him. Confused, he opened his eyes.

He saw immediately what had happened. The car was stopped in the road, and its driver was gesticulating at Moses, shouting at him to get out the way. The Grayshirts had moved out of the road and were standing on the pavement, awkwardly talking among themselves. Opposite them stood a policeman, his stick hanging by his side.

Moses almost laughed out loud. How pathetic, he thought, how scared were these whites! His gang in Sophiatown would never have reacted like that—would never have been stopped in their tracks by a single policeman. They would have acted with decision and taken the consequences—the police were slow-witted and the odds were that they would have been gone before the policeman even moved.

"Ag, shit," he said to himself in disgust as he stood up. He spat on the ground. To the driver of the car who was still shouting insults at him, he directed an exaggerated bow before strolling over to the pavement.

He looked at the triangle of which he made one corner (the others being the policeman and the group of Grayshirts) and he almost laughed again. They were deadlocked, all of them. The policeman knew what was going on and wanted to prevent it without directly interfering: The Grayshirts hadn't given up on their goal, but they weren't going to risk arrests. And as for Moses . . . well . . .

He frowned. He was not, he realized, ready to give up. That moment had passed. They had lost his respect. He would not make it easy for them, he would not let them spill any *kaffir* blood today. He took a deep breath, and then quickly he began to walk away.

What happened next was entirely as he had expected. The policeman was released by Moses' actions—as long as he didn't have to see the confrontation, he didn't care. So he, too, walked away—but in the opposite direction. And as for the Grayshirts, they jostled each other, bounced up and down on their feet in expectation, took deep breaths while they watched the policeman near the corner. As soon as he had turned it, they would be off.

The policeman rounded the corner, and both Moses and his pursuers broke into a run. They were in deadly earnest, all of them and the uninvolved knew it. People stepped into the road to let them go—not one voice was raised in protest.

Moses was running for his life. His legs pumped up and down, his arms made rapid circles in the air, and the sounds around him, those ordinary street sounds, dwindled into nothingness. All he could hear was his own breath, coming fast and furious and despairingly: his own breath, that is, along with the panting of his pursuers. He was concentrating on one thing, and one thing only—the way to escape. His brain was focused, sharpened, precise: His eyes acted with it, registering side alleys, roads, buildings, all with only one aim in mind—escape.

They were coming close now, too close. He turned to the right, swerving and almost falling to the ground. He stretched his arm out to balance himself, and scraped his elbow hard against a lamppost.

But he felt no pain, only panic. For the road he had entered was a dead end—a high brick wall blocked his way. He turned his head and registered a flash of gray. He turned back and ran, using all his strength to pick up speed. His lungs, he felt, were going to burst, his feet almost burned the pavement when they touched it. With incredible speed, he approached the wall and, at the last moment, leaped.

He almost made it—he really did. He got high enough to grip the top of the wall with his fingers. But the grip was only tangential, and he slipped down the wall, scrabbling until he landed in a heap at the bottom.

The Grayshirts were almost upon him—he could see that. A flash, like lightning almost, tore at his head. He would not, he could not, be defeated. He focused on the building to his left. "Nutt's," it said. Moses got to his feet and made for it.

Arnold Nutt's Hardware Store served a small but faithful clientele. Many of its regulars had moved out the area, but they still returned to Nutt's. They had always shopped at Nutt's: They would continue to do so as long as they could. True, the shop had its disadvantages. It was inconvenient, tucked away in a side street. In addition, one had to tolerate interminable delays in getting served, but the quality of his goods was reliable, and the unexpected never occurred—not like in those new-fangled stores that were springing up around Jo'burg.

"I'll have two pounds," a customer in the front of the queue said.

At this point, Moses came flying through the doorway. The effect on Nutt's was immediate: Heads turned, conversation ceased. All that could be heard was Moses' heavy breathing, punctuated by tiny gasps of outrage.

From behind the counter Arnold Nutt glowered. This was incredible! Was nowhere safe these days? He lifted the detachable part of the counter that separated him from his customers. Menacingly he advanced toward the intruder.

"Hey, *kaffir*," he said as he made his way toward Moses. "What the hell do you think you're doing here?"

When the man made no move, just stood there staring, Arnold hesitated. "I'll call the police," he warned. They stood and faced each other: stringy sixty-year-old Arnold Nutt and the gasping Moses, whose arm was by now bleeding copiously.

One of the customers looked through the windows of the shopfront and saw the group of Grayshirts who had congregated outside the shop.

She moved quickly. "Let him be," she told Nutt. "The Grayshirts are chasing him."

Arnold Nutt stopped in his tracks while he tried to figure out his next move. He didn't like the Grayshirts, and he had no wish to further their cause. On the other hand, it wasn't his business to intervene in a fight between them and the blacks. He had only one impulse—to get them all away from his store so that he could return to measuring rice.

He was in a quandary. He knew he must choose from a number of tricky options.

The woman who'd spoken had stated her preference: Well, he'd always suspected her of being a liberal. He glanced at the other two. They seemed frightened.

He made up his mind.

"This way," he said to Moses. "You can leave by the back."

Rosa was waiting for Harold when he stepped out of his car. Absentmindedly he fondled her hair. "Not at Sarah's today?" he asked.

"I'm due there later," Rosa replied.

"Oh, good," Harold said. He lifted his briefcase from the front seat and registered how heavy it was. He would, he realized with a sinking heart, have to work late again.

"Daddy, can I ask you something?"

"Fire away." Harold began to walk toward the front door.

"What do the Grayshirts want?"

Rosa looked so small and so vulnerable, her forehead crisscrossed with worry lines. She's still a child, Harold thought, despite the rate at which she grows. He went back to her and bent down until he was on her level.

"Has something happened?" he asked gently.

"No," Rosa said loudly. "I just want to know what the Gray-shirts want."

Harold frowned. "It's a difficult question," he said. "I'm not sure even they know the answer."

"But you do," Rosa insisted.

Harold smiled. "I think they want their lives to be different," he said. "They're mostly Afrikaners who've had a hard struggle to make ends meet. They're full of anger, and they want to be in charge."

"And who do they hate?" Rosa asked.

Harold was at a loss. This was where children confused him: when they asked questions like this. The honest reply was, of course, Africans, Jews, and communists—after all, that was who the Grayshirts hated.

He looked at her standing there so serious, so small, he thought again. He didn't think she'd understand. "They hate people who don't agree with them," he said vaguely.

"And would they kill?" Rosa was persistent.

"Kill who?"

"Anybody. Just somebody they saw in the street."

Harold hugged Rosa to him. "Don't worry, my darling, you're safe. We'll protect you."

Rosa shrugged off her father's embrace. She began to walk off down the driveway.

"Rosa!" Harold called.

She looked back. "It's all right," she said. "I was only asking. I need to tell Sarah something."

Moses had worked himself into a frenzy by the time he returned to Sophiatown. He went to the street corner that had become his gang's unofficial resting place. His only greeting to the others was a sullen nod.

They maintained a respectful distance. Each of them had long ago learned that Moses was a man with whom one must be extra vigilant. There was something wild about him, something out of control. He showed no fear, and for that he was a true asset to the group. The disadvantage, however, was that he would occasionally turn on them, directing at his own gang the full force of his rage. And so they had learned to judge his moods, and to tread carefully when he was angry.

Moses took a switchblade from his trouser pocket and began whittling at a piece of wood that he'd found lying on the sidewalk. He whistled through his teeth as he did so.

"We're in the wrong league," he said.

The group heaved a sigh of relief. At least Moses was speaking.

"What do you mean?" Pretty Boy asked eagerly. The scar that ran the length of his face puckered up as he grinned.

"We need to expand," Moses answered.

"We do okay," Pretty Boy said.

"It's all small beer compared to the true pickings. I'm sick and tired of working my backside off for a few bob. We need to go where the real *geld* is."

"So what's on your mind?" Bloke asked.

"The Belsen Foundry Works pay out on Friday. That means the safe is full on Thursday. We could get a real haul if we went in there. We only have to cut the fence and get in through a downstairs window. It'll be easy after that."

"And what if we're caught?" Pretty Boy's voice was full of wonder. The prospect of breaking into Belsen's thrilled him. He shifted from foot to foot, hoping that Moses would lay his worries to rest.

"That's a risk we take. But think what we could gain." Moses was growing convinced that this new idea was one of the best he'd ever had. He spoke with conviction. "We'd get enough to lie low for months."

Pretty Boy hopped up and down excitedly. "Now you're talking, man. We could do it. We could get enough to retire."

Bloke's voice cut through Pretty Boy's voice. "You think they're gonna just let us stroll in and take their money? They'll have guards."

Moses turned to Bloke and narrowed his eyes. "Are you in or out?" he asked casually.

Bloke gulped. "I'm in," he said quickly. "But we better have the right equipment."

Moses nodded. "Agreed."

"He's hanging out with *tsotsis* now," Peggy said. She was sitting beside Evelyn, and when she turned, Evelyn could see that there were tears in her eyes.

Evelyn kept her face a careful blank. There was no reason, she thought, why Peggy should notice her irritation. After all, Peggy assumed that she was doing Evelyn a favor when she came and reported on Moses. She had no inkling that Evelyn just did not want to know.

In this way the two women, tied together because of their feeling for Moses, were very different.

Peggy had chosen to preserve her love by watching over Moses—despite the fact that he continued to reject her. Her life consisted of working in a clothing factory, and sleeping in a small room in Sophiatown. But she did not experience the true drudgery, and the loneliness, of her position, because her thoughts and even her dreams were concentrated on Moses. He exerted an almost physical pull on her: She felt it when she caught a glimpse of him—her Moses—dressed in swanky American clothes, his hat with its wide brim set at a jaunty angle, his pockets stuffed with money.

Despite the fact that she knew his opulence was a result of crime, she could not condemn him. She loved him, she would continue to love him—no matter what he did.

Evelyn couldn't do likewise. Since he had returned from the farm, he'd rejected her so persistently that she had grown first impatient and then angry. Who did the boy think he was? He was not the first black to suffer in South Africa: She knew with certainty that he wouldn't be the last.

She dealt with her anger by keeping her love for Moses in a compartment: a compartment with a date on it. The date started in the year of his birth, and it ended in 1935. In this way she didn't have to face what Moses had become, or to spend her time wondering, as she had been doing, how she could help, where she had gone wrong.

Not that it was easy. For not only did Peggy's reports keep coming in, but Rosa, too, had got into the act. She seemed to spend her whole time talking about Moses these days—pressing Evelyn for information. Evelyn couldn't understand it—for some time Rosa had avoided altogether the subject of her son, and she had assumed that this was because Rosa was disappointed in him. But then all of a sudden Rosa had started asking questions, questions that Evelyn could not answer, since she never saw her son.

Come to think of it, there was Rosa now—skulking round

the corner and quite obviously listening to Peggy. It was definitely strange: Rosa didn't even like Peggy. Evelyn thought; in fact, she had also suspected that Rosa was jealous of her.

I'll never understand the younger generation, Evelyn said to herself. She leaned back in her chair and, closing her eyes, let Peggy's conversation wash over her alongside the warmth of the sun.

The first emotion that came over Rosa as she listened to Peggy was one of relief. Peggy was definitely talking in the present—describing Moses' actions only the day before. That meant that Moses was still alive, that he had somehow managed to escape the Grayshirts.

But she soon realized that the fact of Moses' survival did not let her off the hook. She had betrayed him—she truly had. And she had been caught at it—he'd seen her, all right.

She didn't know what she would do when she next saw him again. He must hate her, he really must, and he would tell them all about it. Thank God, she thought, that was unlikely—he hardly ever visited Evelyn these days.

But again, this knowledge did not console her. She had committed the sin of betrayal, and she had done it more than once. She had forsaken her people, her parents, her lifelong friend. She would never forgive herself, she never could.

She kicked at a stone and watched as it flew into the air.

Thursday night Mrs. Radistebe crossed the street on her way back to the suburb in which she worked. She had spent the afternoon with her six-year-old son, who lived with relatives in Sophiatown. For a few hours she had played with the boy, forgetting the needs of the white family that employed her. Now she was late. Madam would be angry. Mrs. Radistebe rehearsed her excuses as she walked to the bus stop.

Out of the corner of her eye she saw four youths. It was a warm night, and so Mrs. Radistebe noticed how they were dressed in clothes thick enough to ward off the severest frost. They even had on overcoats, whose collars were turned up, concealing their faces.

As she walked toward them, one of them glanced at her. Seeing a harassed woman old before her time, he turned away, uninterested.

They were standing close to each other in a circle, muttering so softly that Mrs. Radistebe could not distinguish a word of their conversation. But she knew one thing: The youths were up to no good.

She crossed herself. She was glad she wasn't going to be around when they got into action. She hurried on, breathing a sigh of relief when they were no longer in sight.

Pretty Boy had "borrowed" the overcoats from a clothing store up the road, and had been in such a hurry that he hadn't chosen well. The others were all right, but, man, was Bloke drowning in his. It enveloped him, trailing on the dirt behind him, and hanging limply off his arms.

Bloke took their teasing in good measure, but he was itching to go. He shrugged off Pretty Boy, who was making an exaggerated attempt to find his hands.

"Watch it," he said. "They who fish must know what they will catch." From deep within the folds of the coats, he pulled something out. Pretty Boy gasped as he saw what lay in Bloke's open palm. It was a revolver.

When Moses saw the weapon, he himself had to suppress a momentary feeling of terror. His heart sank: So that's what Bloke meant by being properly equipped. No wonder he was looking so satisfied: He'd certainly managed to up the stakes.

And yet, thought Moses, when his first reaction had dwindled in intensity, Bloke was right. If they were serious about breaking into the works, then they had to be prepared for anything. Everybody knew Belsen employed security guards, and they were sure to be armed.

"Good," he said nonchalantly.

"That's one for four," Bloke said. "Who's holding it?"

It was a challenge—Moses rose to it. "I will," he said. He lifted the gun from Bloke's hand and casually put it into his pocket. "Let's go."

It had been easy getting in. They had cut the wire and prized it apart until there was just enough space for a man to squeeze through. Bloke, who because of his size should have had the easiest time of it, got tangled up when he, but not his coat, slid through. He had sworn foully when they laughed at him.

"For Christ sake, let's get on with it," he whispered.

Moses agreed with Bloke. The adrenaline that had rushed through him when they cut the fence was fast evaporating. He felt in his coat pocket, searching out the cold metal in a bid to reassure himself. It was no consolation: It only made him all the more frightened.

"Let's go," he said, even though the others were ahead of him and moving fast. He hoped that they were too far away to notice the tremor in his voice.

They had not even had to break a window. They found an opening in the ground floor that was easy to negotiate. Moses climbed through last. He was in such a hurry that he landed on top of Pretty Boy, who had only just preceded him.

When they managed to disentangle themselves, they found that they were standing in a room so vast that it dwarfed them. In center was a huge foundry, its blackened chimney stretching up to the ceiling and beyond. It was almost alive, that foundry— glowing red in the darkness. Huge, dark shapes, the instruments that fed the fire, lay abandoned by its side.

"Where to now?" Pretty Boy asked.

"Upstairs," Moses replied with a certainty that he did not feel. "The offices must be there."

The place was like a desert—a long corridor painted a murky green, with small rooms leading off it. They worked their way through each of these: Most of the offices were barely furnished and devoid of anything that could hold money.

They hurried down the corridor until they came to a door labeled MANAGER. It wasn't locked. As Pretty Boy opened it, a creak resounded through the factory.

There were three desks in the place, and it didn't take long to search them, because they were almost empty. All they contained were pens, old invoices, and a calendar adorned with naked women. There was no money, and nothing that looked as if it could conceal any.

Bloke looked at Moses. "What now, big boy?" he asked.

And then, before Moses had a chance to reply, they heard it: a soft footstep followed by another and then another.

"Who's that?" Bloke whispered.

"How the hell should I know?"

"Sssh," Pretty Boy said, making them all jump. His voice had reverberated loudly in their ears.

The footsteps came closer.

With one thought in their minds, they crouched down low. Their only chance was to keep out of sight of the glass window that was embedded in the door. Perhaps the footsteps would pass by.

They held their breath as they saw a light shine on the door. Behind the light was the distorted shape of an ominous shadow. The knob began to turn.

Bloke nudged Moses. "Do something," he hissed.

Moses had no choice. There was nowhere to hide; if the watchman came in, he would be sure to see one of them and, with the flashlight on his side, would have the initiative.

With a decisiveness that he did not feel, Moses rose, pulled the door to him, and then jumped out. He was no longer thinking: His body was acting for him. Before he knew what he was doing, he had the man by his throat and was pointing the revolver at his temple.

"*Moenie skit nie, man, moenie skit nie*—don't shoot me, I beg you."

Moses found himself looking down into the whites of the eyes of an aged man who was trembling with terror. The man's neck, Moses observed with detachment, was very skinny: It would be so easy to break.

"Be silent, *oom*," he commanded, "and nothing will happen to you. Otherwise . . ." He moved the revolver up the man's skull.

Bloke stepped forward. He stared unblinking at the terrified specter of Abraham Masemola. "Where's the money?" he demanded.

"What money?" Abraham's voice squeaked.

"The payroll. Where is it?"

"They don't keep it here," he said. "Do you think they would leave an old man such as me in charge of such riches?" Abraham pleaded. Tears welled up in his eyes.

"He's speaking sense," Pretty Boy said uneasily. "Let's get out of here."

Moses slackened his grip on Abraham, who fell to the ground and lay there unmoving.

"Who's for going?" Moses asked.

"Sure, man," Pretty Boy said quickly. Bloke grunted in the background.

Moses stepped over the prone body of Abraham Masemola. He was followed by the others in the gang.

They had gone a few steps down the corridor when Bloke wheeled to a halt.

"He can identify us," he said, pointing at Abraham.

"I won't say anything," Abraham said. "I promise. I won't even say you were here. No harm done," he pleaded.

Bloke walked back to him and stood above him, his legs straddling the old man.

"You've lived a long time, old man. What more have you to look forward to?" he said. Bloke turned to Moses. "I say he can't be trusted."

"Leave him," Moses replied.

Bloke merely stood. To Abraham, he stood there for what seemed like forever. Then he began to bend down.

"Leave him," Moses ordered.

Bloke straightened up. He stared into Moses' eyes. "You are responsible," he said. Moses nodded. Bloke walked down the corridor quickly.

The rest of the gang followed.

Abraham Masemola lay on the floor for a long time, his mind a blank. He felt nothing. He merely lay, waiting, for the energy to flow back into his body. It took some time before he felt anything. When he did, it was a kind of stickiness down below. Gingerly he felt with his hands along the floor. He was, he discovered, lying in a pool of urine. Without even realizing it, he had wet his pants.

Tears sprang into his eyes. He, who had suffered so much in life, found this final humiliation the worst to bear. It was the last proof of his inability to act in the world. Slowly he raised himself onto his knees and then to his feet. He began to limp back to his cubbyhole. He would have to take his pants off and wash them somehow. He would wait while they dried. He would not sit down: His chair must not know what had happened to him.

Outside, the group parted without speaking. There were no words to use, and there never would be any. Something had happened between them; something that could not be undone.

They had failed each other in some undefinable way. Never again would they operate as a gang.

Moses hardly even registered the fact that he was alone. He walked fast, too fast. He was running away, running from his own complicity, from the person he had become, but no matter the distance he went, he could not get far enough. Despite the bulk of his overcoat and the warmth of the evening, he was shivering. I almost killed a man, he thought, I almost shot dead someone who had done me no harm.

As he crossed over a railway line, he felt in his pocket. The gun lay there. He picked it out and flung it out. His hand made a wide arc, but when he looked at it again, he saw that he was still gripping the gun. It would not leave him: He would have it forever.

Trembling, Moses used his left hand to prize open the right. The gun dropped down. A spray of dirt rose as it hit the ground. Moses left it where it lay and ran from it, fearful that it might somehow follow him.

He arrived in Sophiatown in record time. The streets were deserted; the eerie light of the night sky giving the makeshift buildings a ghostly air. As Moses walked, he passed the shebeens that dotted the township. He heard the sounds of revelry and of drunkenness. He passed them by.

He didn't know where he was headed, he just kept walking, trying to escape his own thoughts, yet pursued by them. He arrived at the street where Peggy lived. He didn't pause for thought. He walked through the tumble-down yard and knocked on a back window.

Peggy was a light sleeper. She heard a soft knock on her window, and immediately she was alert. She hugged her bed-clothes tightly as the knock was repeated. Sophiatown was a dangerous place: She had listened to many stories of how unwary women had let strangers into their place and had been found dead in the morning.

The knock came again.

"Go away," she said timorously.

"Peggy."

Peggy jumped up. That was Moses' voice. She, who had never been unclothed in front of a man, did not hesitate. She ran to the window and wrenched it open.

Sure enough, Moses was standing outside. On his face was a look that Peggy had never seen: a look of desolate desperation.

"What has happened?" she asked.

"Can I come in?"

Again Peggy acted without thought. Pulling a cotton jacket over her nightie, she went to the back door and opened it. Moses slid through it. She led him to her room. When they got there, Moses stood like a zombie in the center of the small space.

"What has happened?" Peggy asked.

"I am so cold."

Peggy persisted. "What happened?"

She saw how his whole body shook. He looked longingly at her bed.

The first hint of doubt insinuated itself in Peggy's mind. Her mother had warned her about the lengths men would go to in order to defile a woman. Was this a trick by Moses—an act of revenge against her for her interference in his life?

She looked directly at him. She saw that she did not have much time. Already he was turning, making as if to leave.

"Yes," she said.

Her word was not enough. Moses just stood. He regarded her with eyes that seemed to go right through and beyond her. Peggy took a deep breath. She removed her jacket and climbed into bed. She held the sheet open.

"Come," she said simply.

When he had got in beside her, Peggy's courage almost deserted her. She lay there rigid. She could not even pray to God for guidance: He, she knew, would not approve what she was doing. So she lay there.

And then she felt Moses' body. It was trembling—shaking uncontrollably. She reached over and pulled him to her.

He stopped shaking, and for a long time he lay so still that her fear began to leave. She felt as though she had watched over Moses forever, watched him from afar until she knew him intimately. She had dreamed of this, without even acknowledging that fact to herself. There would never be another man in her bed: Moses was the only one for her. She relaxed herself, she lay next to his body, reveling in the fact of his closeness, of the rise and fall of his manly chest, and she felt no shame at all.

"I will always be here for you," she said.

That was all Moses needed. The words that had been dammed up inside him for so long came pouring out, mixed with his grief, his confusion, his anger. He talked and talked, his words piled helter-skelter on top of each other—words about his father, his experiences on the farm, his utter desolation at what life had delivered to him. And all the time Peggy held him. She was smiling.

From that day on, Moses began to heal. Peggy knew, as if by instinct, what to do. She did not react as his mother would have. She did not argue, plead, give advice. She merely stayed with Moses.

He was not ill in any physical sense of the word, but he mended as surely as if he had been. In the long nights he faced what had happened to him at the farm: He looked anew at the person he had become and at the reasons for his transformation.

He did not rail at the brutality of the farmer: The whips and cudgels that had burned his flesh were no longer of any concern to him. Instead, he did something much more difficult: He admitted to himself for the first time that he had slipped into a kind of savagery with very little provocation. Others withstood the ill-treatment that was daily dealt to them: Moses had faltered, and in so doing had slipped to the very edge of degradation and despair.

The turning point came when Moses was able to admit the thing that haunted him most: that he had enjoyed his power over the other farm laborers. When he had faced a frail Abraham Masemola below him, he had felt a recurrence of those sentiments—the enjoyment that someone else's life was in the balance and that Moses could pass judgment. It was that which had driven him to a kind of madness, and it was a repeat of that sensation that frightened him into sanity.

Peggy reported weekly to Evelyn. She informed her of Moses' progress, and the two women would sit together companionably, happy in the knowledge that the one they both loved would recover. By mutual consent, Evelyn kept away from her son. She did not visit Moses: She sent a message that she would always welcome him, but she waited until he was ready to take the first step.

And then one day Moses was ready to face his mother again. He came alone. He walked into her room.

Evelyn smiled and held out her arms to him. For a while they embraced, feeling once more the love that they had for each other. It was Evelyn who eventually pulled herself away. She held her son at arm's distance so that she could look at him. This was a different boy she was seeing. No, even that wasn't correct—this was a man.

Evelyn played with the idea of putting her realization into words, but she stopped herself. Moses, she understood, did not need his mother to validate his triumph against his own misery.

"No Peggy?" was all she said.

Moses shook his head. "We thought it best that I come alone. We have news for you. We will be married."

"I'm glad."

Moses smiled, and his eyes strayed to Nathaniel's portrait on the wall. "Do you think he would have approved?" he asked.

Evelyn shrugged. "I'm sure he would have wanted you to be happy."

"That's as may be," Moses replied. "But he's been a hard man to live up to."

When Moses left the house, he stopped to smell the frangipani vine that grew up the back door. He bent his head down to the fragrant blooms and breathed in their scent.

As he did so, he saw out of the corner of his eye that there was somebody near. He turned to find Rosa standing a few yards away. She wasn't looking at him. She was just standing, her head bent down as she examined her feet.

Moses left the frangipani to its own short life. "Sometimes the hardest thing to do is to forgive yourself," he said to the air.

He began to walk, passing Rosa on his way. He touched her head lightly.

"Better start saving up," he said. "Peggy and I are getting married."

When he was in the street, Moses glanced over the garden fence. He saw that Rosa was still rooted to the spot. He hoped she was smiling, but he didn't stay long enough to check.

19

1948

"How's your thesis going?" Julia asked.

Rosa, who had been staring moodily out into the garden, pulled a face. She had been thinking of something else, something private, and her one-word reply came out without premeditation.

"Boring," she said.

She regretted the word almost immediately. She didn't have to look at her mother to know that Julia would be nodding her head, would be smiling, would be pleased. "You should never have . . ." she whispered to herself.

"You should never have studied geology," Julia said. "I told you so at the time."

Rosa nodded.

"You write so well," Julia continued. "You should have been a journalist."

"No, Mom," Rosa muttered. "You should have been a journalist." It was a statement made to the ether rather than to her mother, and her voice was pitched so low that Julia couldn't possibly have heard. Not that she needed to—the conversation was a familiar one: Sometimes Rosa thought she and Julia only had it because they had nothing else to say to each other.

Except this time, she thought, I do have something to say. She cleared her throat.

"Are you going canvassing again?" Julia asked quickly.

"Yes." Rosa got up. She smoothed the creases from her skirt. While they stood at arm's length from each other, Julia couldn't help experiencing a moment of sheer admiration. Rosa was so attractive, she thought: The quirky child had grown into an elegant young woman. Julia noticed now she had pulled her curly hair away from her face: It was the right decision—her strong features, her tanned skin, made a striking combination that the soft frizz both softened and highlighted.

She had good clothes sense as well, thought Julia, as her eyes traveled downward. She took in the broad-shouldered, tight-waisted red jacket that Rosa had contrasted with a straight black skirt, its hem a foot from the ankle. She nodded in satisfaction.

But when she came to Rosa's shoes—a pair of high heels, Julia's admiration turned to irritation. The fact that Rosa couldn't do anything about her height didn't mean she should accentuate it.

"Mom," Rosa said.

"You prefer canvassing to manning the office, don't you?" Julia tried.

This time Rosa did not even bother to nod. Julia, she thought, must know that she was trying to say something, and was doing her utmost to prevent it. Well, she wouldn't, she couldn't allow that: She was not going to be intimidated into silence.

"Mom," she said loudly. "I've got something to tell you."

"So tell me," Julia said. "Am I stopping you?"

Rosa smiled. That tone of voice, the way the sentence ended in a querulous interrogation, always surprised her. It seemed to come not from her mother, but from her grandmother—not from the sophisticated suburbs of Jo'burg but from the *shtetl*. It was the voice that showed that although Julia hardly ever referred to Riva (now long dead), she still carried her inside.

"I'm waiting." Julia's voice was sharp.

Rosa took a deep breath. "I want to move out," she said.

"To where?"

Rosa blinked. "I've found a room in a house," she said quickly.

Julia did not immediately reply. Instead, she stood and looked at Rosa, and her face was both bland and at the same time hard. She's thinking of a way to stop me, Rosa thought.

"How will you pay the rent?" Julia asked.

"From my inheritance." Rosa's voice trembled as she said it. "Is that all right?" she anxiously concluded.

Julia just shrugged. "As you yourself keep telling me, you're a grown woman," she said, "with your own money. There's nothing more I can say." She closed her lips tightly, as if to signal that the conversation had indeed come to an end.

Rosa blinked. In comparison to her expectation, Julia's response had been mild. Be grateful for small mercies, she told herself.

But she wasn't entirely pleased. She realized that, without even knowing, she'd been nursing a faint hope that not only would Julia react with equanimity, but that she would go further—that she would actually be pleased.

It was stupid to think that way, she told herself: Julia would never stop judging her, nothing she did would ever be good enough.

"I'll go see Evelyn," she said. She opened the glass doors that led into the garden and walked briskly down the paved path.

As Julia watched Rosa's retreating back, her eyes filled with tears. She couldn't understand why: It wasn't as if Rosa's news had come as a surprise, since she had already overheard her telling Harold about it. And she certainly wasn't crying, as other mothers might, because her baby was about to leave. After all, Rosa had long made her own decisions (her choice of career was proof enough of that), and anyway it was time Rosa had her own home. Just because she wasn't married, that didn't mean she should be penalized.

"So why, then, am I crying?" she asked herself.

She heard a door close and footsteps come toward the living room. Quickly she wiped her tears away.

"How did she take it?" Evelyn asked.

"She was all right," Rosa said. She attempted a smile.

It didn't fool Evelyn. She knew Rosa too well, she could always tell when she was confused or disappointed. And one didn't have to be clairvoyant to guess that the encounter was bound to be a sticky one, that each of the Arnold women would make it difficult for the other.

"I know your mother supports you in your choices," she said.

Rosa frowned. "Sure she does. That's why she criticizes my every move."

Evelyn clicked her tongue. It annoyed her the way Rosa refused to acknowledge that Julia, despite her brisk exterior, loved and approved of her. Admired her as well, Evelyn thought—

which was probably half the problem.

"You're as stubborn as your mother," was what Evelyn wanted to say. But then, she thought, I shouldn't judge her too harshly. After all, it's easy enough to sort out another family's problems: not so easy to understand one's own. She covered her irritation with a cough.

"How are Moses and Peggy?" Rosa might have been reading Evelyn's mind.

It was Evelyn's turn for pretense. "Fine," she said brightly. She had prepared this line, deciding not to speak of her doubts to Rosa since she knew that Rosa and Peggy did not get on so well. And in a way, she reflected, to say that they were fine wasn't an outright lie—it was certainly what they would have said. Any underlying tension was probably her own imagination. After all, Peggy had never been a political animal: She was bound to find Moses' involvement in an increasingly more militant African National Congress difficult to countenance. But this didn't mean that their marriage was in trouble.

"And the children?"

Evelyn beamed. "Lindiwe's full of spark," she said. "Five-year-olds have so much energy. As for George, he's quieter, but he always has been." She shrugged. "They're good children, and Peggy's a good mother."

Rosa nodded distractedly. "Are you going there soon?" she asked.

Evelyn held out her hand. "I'll take it," she said. She put the envelope that Rosa handed her into her apron pocket. "Moses was saying that they haven't seen a lot of you recently. Been busy with your rocks?"

Rosa shook her head in mock anger. "Anyone would think geology was the weirdest subject in the world the way this household speaks of it," she said. "As a matter of fact, I've been canvassing." She glanced hurriedly at her watch. "Which reminds me," she said. "I better go. Dad said he'd give me a lift." She came closer to Evelyn and hugged her warmly.

Julia, who'd been by the window ever since Rosa left, saw the embrace, and it brought back her melancholy. She stood there and wished that she and her daughter could hug in that uninhibited manner, that they could be so close. But wishing, she reflected, was not enough—no matter how hard she tried, something always went wrong.

Take today: She had meant to listen to Rosa's news quietly and to react with pleasure. She'd planned to respond this way ever since she had got over her pique that Rosa had told everybody but her. She would forget that minor hurt, she decided: She would send Rosa on her way with her blessing.

That, at least, was what the rational part of her brain told her. It ordered her to be generous to Rosa, to wish her well in her new life, to respond with warmth.

But her unconscious was less accommodating. It railed in anger, and perhaps in envy, at Rosa's behavior. How dare Rosa wait so long to inform Julia of what was effectively a *fait accompli*—how dare she?

I'm treated, thought Julia, like a villain. And Rosa has no idea how lucky she is.

While she watched Rosa walk back toward the house, Julia warmed to her theme. Her daughter, she thought, had been allowed undreamed-of freedom. She had been given the most elite of educations, had gone to Witwatersrand University not only to do a first degree but now to do a second, had funds of her own (it never stopped rankling that Riva had willed her money to Rosa rather than to her). One would have thought that all this would have made Rosa grateful—or at least more generous toward her mother. But instead of that, she treated Julia almost like an enemy.

And why did she behave like that? The answer was beyond Julia. The only clue she had was that Rosa had said, in the midst of their most ferocious argument, that she was scared of Julia.

Well, thought Julia, that was laughable—Rosa had all the confidence that came from her privileged position. While Julia's most effective contribution would probably remain the left book club, which didn't even operate anymore, Rosa was destined for greater things. She was young at a time of change: She was at university among the likes of Mandela, Sisulu, Tambo—men who Julia knew would make history.

Not for Rosa the struggle to earn a living, to educate herself: not for her the necessity to get married young in order to escape home. She was unrestricted by either children, convention, or family. She could even join the Party and get approval for that:

not like Julia, who'd had to struggle so against the yoke of Riva's disapproval.

And yet she still wants more from me, Julia thought bitterly.

She turned away as Rosa came into the room.

"Your father's waiting in his study," was all she said.

"You're quiet today," Harold commented.

Rosa shrugged. "Not really," she said. "Just resting." She was in fact enjoying the drive, and she didn't particularly want to talk.

She stared out of the car window. There was a time, she reflected, when she would have taken her own car, or a bus, even, rather than let her father drive her to the party offices. She would have felt that she was nothing more than her parent's appendage.

But gradually that feeling had gone. It was partly, she thought, due to her experience at Wits. The university had served as a place of learning not only about rocks, as Evelyn insisted on calling them, but also about politics.

And in the end it had been inevitable that she would join the Party. It was ironic, really. When she was younger, and especially during what she now thought fondly of as her evangelical phase, it had seemed so important to be the same as others. But now, when she had finally decided to be herself, to act regardless of the judgments from parents or peer group, she had gone full circle. She was part of a movement of people who cared about injustice; blacks and whites together, they were filled with the same goals and same inspiration. She had come home.

"We're here," Harold said. He smiled at her as he reached behind and pulled his briefcase from the backseat. "By the way," he said, "how was it, telling your mother?"

"All right." Rosa opened the door.

"There, you see?" Harold said. "I told you she wouldn't mind."

Entering the party offices was like falling into the center of a whirlwind. For a start, the noise was incredible: Telephones rang, duplicators churned, and staples clicked. But it was the occupants who raised the level to an all-time high as they shouted down phones, at each other, to the air. And as for the mess—well, its proportions were mythic: Piles of leaflets teetered precariously on desks, banners jostled with collection boxes, old clothes collected for rummage sales spilled from their boxes.

But none of that made the office either unfriendly or difficult to negotiate. For the place was buzzing with a kind of exhilaration, an excitement that had been building up ever since the election was first announced. Everybody inside the shabby building moved at double speed, shouting, laughing, heckling, swapping anecdotes with bagels and advice with old pamphlets. They were all caught up in what they knew was a hopeless cause but nevertheless an intoxicating one.

Not that canvassing for Michael Harmel, one of only three communist candidates, was easy. This was an election that was being fiercely fought and whose main protagonists were, on the one side, the establishment in the shape of Smuts's United Party and on the other real contenders: Malan's Nationalists.

The Nats had risen in popularity to the point that there was a chance they could get into office, and this is what had raised the stakes. For while Smuts engaged in double-talk, the Nats had easily comprehensible aims: They promised to the country that they would save the whites from the threefold threat of colored blood, the black peril, and the red menace.

No wonder, then, that standing on a doorstep holding a leaflet on which the slogan "Votes for All" was written provoked some interesting reactions. In her time Rosa had been shouted at, spat on, and kicked only once. Her experience was not unusual: So nasty had things become that the Party had decided its canvassers should venture out only in pairs. That's what Rosa was doing here: She'd come to pick up her partner.

"See you later," Harold said.

Rosa nodded briskly. She walked over to Max Freeman's desk.

"So who've you got for me today?" she asked.

Max smiled at her. "You're a glutton for punishment, Rosa," he said. "Most people find that either their shoes or their courage have given out by this point."

"I like it," Rosa said. "Keeps me on my mettle to—"

"Argue with fascists," said a strange voice from behind her.

Rosa turned and found that she was looking at a man she had never seen before. He was about her age, and taller than she. No matter how hard she tried to stop herself, height was the first thing she always noticed about men. He was attractive, she thought, with his broad chest and confident way of standing—

the look of the army about him. But he was, she decided, a difficult man: A hint of steel about his blue eyes and a certain wary alertness in his stance showed her that.

He withstood her inspection without blinking. He smiled at her sardonically.

"They're not fascists," she told him. "They're just confused people, and the Nats are the only ones who seem to be addressing their problems."

The man shrugged. "Some problems," he said. "Hatred of anybody different is what I'd call it."

"That's an ingredient," Rosa conceded. "But you have to remember that many of these people come from the poorest sections of white society."

As she spoke, she couldn't avoid noticing the way the new-comer allowed his eyes to run the full length of her body, letting them linger, even, at various points. She glared at him. But he was shameless: When he caught her gaze, he just smiled lazily at her.

Max Freeman cut through the line that seemed to be joining Rosa's eyes to the man's. "Rosa Arnold, meet Jacob Swiece," he said. "You'll be canvassing together today."

Rosa mentally shook herself. She didn't know what had been happening just then, why she had felt so peculiar when she looked at Jacob.

"Have we met before?" she asked.

Jacob shrugged. "Shall we go?" He turned away.

As he eased the car into the traffic, Jacob couldn't help feeling that he had been wrong-footed. He knew a lot about Rosa Arnold: She was the source of much gossip. He knew about her parents, her friendship with Moses Bopape (now a rising star), that she was considered to be bright and difficult, and that her name was never attached to any particular man. And he remembered clearly what she had obviously forgotten. He remembered that day in 1936, when he had seen her in an agony of indecision, when she had turned her back on him and, he thought, on herself.

He remembered her so well partly because at seventeen he'd identified with her—he could see himself acting the same way, given half the chance—and partly because she hadn't really changed. Oh, she was taller, for sure, and more beautiful— certainly she was more self-assured—but there was something about her features, the strength of them, perhaps, that was instantly recognizable.

"Are you a student?" Rosa's voice cut through his reverie.

He nodded. "Medic," he said. That was the best thing about the army, he thought, it had qualified him for an assisted place at a university. Education, the one method by which he could pull himself out of the poverty of his childhood, was finally in his grasp.

They worked the houses from one end of the street to the other. They had bad luck that day: Three doors slammed on them, a number of faces at the window, and a few vicarious insults.

Rosa seemed to be taking the rejection in her stride, but Jacob was beginning to grow annoyed. He saw no reason why these Boers should be allowed to utter their racist remarks without challenge. Next time it happens, he thought, I'm going to argue back.

His chance came at the very next house. The door was opened by a red-faced man in his mid-forties. He glanced at the leaflet Rosa handed to him, and then thrust it back at Jacob. When Jacob made no move to take it, the man scowled. He held the leaflet between two large, callused hands, and then he ripped it into a score of little pieces, which he scattered in front of him.

Jacob felt Rosa backing away, but he did not budge. "Is anything the matter, sir?" he asked.

"The matter," the man spluttered. "The matter? You *blerry kaffirboeties* come round interfering, and then you ask me what the matter is?"

"Would you mind telling me why you find our literature so offensive?" Jacob asked.

"Jacob," Rosa warned.

"I'll tell you, all right, you arrogant young oaf," the man said. He thrust his face closer to Jacob. "I come from the country," he said. "Forced off my own land during the Depression. Now, things are slightly better, but my father tells me that the countryside's dying for lack of labor: You can't get a *kaffir* to work for you for love or money. And you know why? Because they've all come here. They've come here, and are taking our jobs and our homes away from us."

"I hardly think . . ." Jacob began.

"Well, I don't give a damn what you think!" the man shouted, his face by now an apoplectic red. "Smuts let them all in, and Malan will chuck them out." His face was very close, and he was spluttering with rage.

Jacob felt the spittle touch his cheek. He backed away. In response the man clenched his fist and shook it just in front of Jacob. "Chuck 'em out," he repeated, "every last one of them, and you commies with them as well. Now get the hell off my property before I set the dogs on you." And with that, he slammed the door.

Jacob found that he was shaking. He took a deep breath and walked down the path to where Rosa was waiting. He could hardly bear to look into her eyes. If she's smiling, he thought, I'll kill her.

But she wasn't smiling. She just shrugged. "Win some, lose some," she said.

It didn't make him feel any better. "We could have argued with him," he said.

Rosa's eyes twinkled. "What were we supposed to say?" she asked. "We all know the real reason that Smuts hasn't restricted Africans to the country—after all, he's got all the legislation to do so. But he hasn't acted recently because when he did, he met with such tremendous resistance, revolt even. That's the truth of it, but if we'd said that to Mr. Average Voter, it would have been like showing a red rag to a bull."

She was right, Jacob thought, he hadn't been thinking properly. He should never have got so annoyed: He should have been like her, calm and collected.

But then he had another thought: You're a cold fish, he wanted to say. The impulse to puncture her self-esteem proved irresistible.

He smiled at her. "We have met before, you know," he said.

That smile, though seemingly innocuous, left Rosa feeling uneasy. "Have we?" she asked in as neutral a tone as she could muster.

"Jeppe," he said.

"Yes, I went to Jeppe." She frowned, trying to remember. "Did your sister go there?" she asked.

"Nineteen thirty-six. Outside the gates," was his reply.

Rosa blushed. How could she have forgotten: How could she not have recognized him? The smile on the face of that scrawny young boy with a yarmulke on his head was embedded in her

memory. She saw it all as if it were happening in front of her:
herself and Sarah, arm in arm, insulting the stranger in their
midst.

"I d-don't," she stuttered.

Jacob was enjoying himself. "You chose to disown me," he
said.

Rosa swallowed hard. She breathed in once and out again.
She looked straight into Jacob's face.

"I remember," she said, and this time she enunciated her
words slowly and clearly. "And I'd like to apologize."

"It's okay," Jacob said. He felt suddenly ashamed.

"Well, if that's all? Perhaps we should call it a day." Her eyes
flashed a challenge at him.

When he didn't reply, she led the way to the car.

They did not speak on the way back, for there was nothing to
say. Rosa, for her part, was fuming. She knew exactly what had
gone through his mind—he'd felt humiliated, and so he'd turned
the tables on her, expecting her to crumble in front of him. Well,
she would not give him the satisfaction. She bit her lip.

As for Jacob, he was mainly embarrassed, and perhaps a touch
regretful. He didn't know what had got into him—why he'd felt
so momentarily vengeful.

He tried to make it up to her, to make small talk as if it had
not happened.

"Not much more canvassing to do, thank God," he commented. "With the election so close."

"Mmm," Rosa said. She was staring straight ahead.

Oh, well, Jacob thought. I tried. He did not talk again.

20

1948

ROSA COULD NOT BEAR TO LOOK AT HER PARENTS. SHE STARED UP into space and listened.

"And so the Nationalist party," the announcer was saying, "will end up with a majority, which, although it is unlikely to reach double figures, is enough to enable it to form a government. Dr. Malan's dream of white supremacy has finally been given a tentative endorsement by the South African electorate."

"Oh, God," Harold muttered.

"Sssh," said Julia.

"The Nationalist party's most spectacular gains," the disembodied voice went on, "were in the country districts of the Transvaal and the Cape. Among its preelection promises are the dissolution of the Communist party, the deportation of Indians, segregation of coloreds, abolition of parliamentary representation for Africans, and exclusion of redundant blacks from town. Speaking immediately after confirmation of this surprising victory, a spokesman for the newly formed government said . . ."

"Turn it off," Julia snapped.

Rosa reached over and flicked the switch of the wireless. The voice died out.

"It's only a small majority." Harold's voice sounded loud in the descending silence.

Julia nodded. "They'll throw them out at the next election," she said. "The Nats are all talk and no action."

I wonder, Rosa thought. She did not say the words aloud. The night was depressing enough without them.

* * *

Jacob, for his part, was in no doubt as to what the election meant. He, too, had been glued to his wireless during the initial stages, but when a shape in the voting pattern had become discernible, he felt a need to move, to act in some way.

What he had done was to travel to Bloemfontein—an area that was a Nats stronghold, filled as it was with poor whites, many of whom had only recently come to the city. He had gone there, he realized, because he needed to see for himself. He could not bear to sit at home and listen to self-satisfied voices droning incomprehensible results. He needed to see.

He had wandered through the area, listening with half an ear to the sounds of celebration that seemed to issue from every single house. Without human contact, he had begun to feel like a man from outer space, like a freak intruding on a kind of insane normality. He was beginning to curse himself for his useless journey. Better to stay home and get drunk, he thought: No hangover could produce as sour a taste as this election.

Just then he heard some shouts coming from around the corner. He could not initially make them out, although he vaguely thought he heard the name of Malan rise to the air. Intrigued, for this was the first public display he'd come across, he walked down the road. There they were again, the cries, and this time he could hear them clearly.

"*Vrystat! Vrystat!*"—the Nats' rallying cry.

Impelled by a kind of dreadful fascination, Jacob turned the corner. He found himself facing a group of about twenty, all men, all apparently filled with a kind of vicious euphoria. They had linked their arms around each other as they joined in a boisterous celebration of their long-awaited victory. They were oblivious to their surroundings. They ran over everything, trampling through the flower beds, jumping over benches, separating only occasionally to punch the air with their fists.

"We won! We won!" they shouted. "*Vrystat.*"

The leader of the pack stopped and turned to his companions.

"Who do we want?" he shouted.

"Malan," came the reply.

"Louder, louder," he exhorted. "Who have we got?"

"Malan! Malan!"

"*Kaffir* out, *kaffir* out," came a voice. It was joined by others. "*Kaffir* out!" they shouted.

Their strong voices joined together resounded against the surrounding buildings, filling the air. Jacob swallowed hard and shrank back against the wall. He observed that doors in the street had started to open, that men and women were sticking their heads out and that they were smiling.

Jacob suddenly felt very alone. He had a feeling about this, a bad feeling. He had seen such a demonstration of vicious joy, seen it in the war by men already half-crazed with killing who dealt with the horror by anticipating more killing. But that had been during a time of much stress: This was different—this was taking place in an ordinary street, and ordinary people were greeting it with approval.

Things were bad, he thought, very bad.

He turned on his heel and left that place behind him.

21

1949

Jacob was late for the meeting. He'd been in such a hurry, coming straight from the hospital, that he hadn't the time to shake off the smell of disinfectant and that special kind of concentration his learning demanded. He took a few long breaths and looked around him. He felt, for the first time in ages, that sense of belonging to a crowd.

He was in the middle of Johannesburg, among a group of people who milled around the town hall steps. The meeting was already in full swing, and many were listening intently, but there was still a kind of carnival atmosphere to the gathering, a sense of warmth and relaxation even in the chill evening air.

The city hall steps were a traditional venue: There, people would gather to listen to the variety of speakers, to exchange views, to plan strategy. The size of the crowd, and its racial composition, were, Jacob knew, an indicator of the Party's fluctuating fortunes. Tonight, he saw, there were a few hundred gathered—black and white mixing together in a way unprecedented in the rest of South Africa.

Jacob smiled to himself. It felt good to be part of it.

"So, stranger." Someone clapped him on the back.

He turned and smiled into the beaming face of Norman Bloom. "Hi, Norman," he said.

"*Nu*, you finally made it. Can we hang out the red flag in celebration?"

"Save the flag," Jacob replied, "for something more important."

The smile faded from Norman's face. "Every single comrade is important," he said, "since the Nats are gunning for us. There are bad times coming, and we need as many as we can muster." He smiled, and his round face lit up. He hugged Jacob. "I'm pleased to see you," he said simply.

Jacob couldn't understand why he felt tears rising in his eyes. He blinked them back. He nudged Norman, breaking the man's grip on him. "At least let me listen to the speeches, now I'm here," he said gruffly. He turned toward the steps.

Sam Kahn, who had recently been elected as "native representative" to Parliament, was in full swing. Sam was a good talker, a constant thorn in the side of the ruling Nats with his jibes and taunts. Only the other day he had created a furor in Parliament when, speaking against the newly planned Immorality Act, which would make intermarriage illegal, he had been asked whether he would marry a colored woman. "Why?" he shot back. "Are you a marriage broker? Do you have a prospective client in mind?" The embarrassment of the Nats had been so acute, it was almost tangible.

The smile died on Jacob's face. Embarrassment was just a pinprick against the Nats, against the overwhelming picture of discrimination they were building up. Soon everything would be segregated: buses, benches, waiting rooms, the whole country.

Sam stepped down, and the audience started to break up into smaller groups, chatting among themselves, making dates, disputing past history. Jacob found himself in the middle of a fierce debate between a young and an older African. He listened intently as two strategies were opened to the African National Congress: talk or defiance.

Jacob got so caught up in the debate that he didn't notice the second speaker mount the steps. It was only when he felt a hush descend on the crowd that he looked up.

Rosa Arnold was standing on the top rung, her height accentuated by her position. Her curly black hair, the breeze trifling with it, framed her face.

She had started tentatively enough, but gradually her voice gained in assurance until it rang out into the night. She had a different style from Sam's: Where he had been playful, she was serious; where he ad-libbed, she read her speech. And yet her words were not dry: They were words of passion, strung together with a fluency that clutched at the audience, demanding complete silence and concentration from them.

Jacob was mesmerized as Rosa spoke with a knowledge that seemed unassailable about the conditions of African workers in the country. She talked as if she had met the workers, she spoke as if she had felt their pain. But her speech was not one of defeat. It was a message of defiance. It was a tribute to those who suffered, and it was an exhortation to action.

When she finished, there was a long silence. And then someone coughed and the spell was broken. The crowd burst into rapturous applause. Rosa did not seem to hear them: She stood motionless, staring into the far distance.

As Jacob watched her, he saw the flush fade from her face. She shook herself, smiled, and began to descend. Jacob felt an ache of loss: He wanted to recapture that flurry of passion he had seen come flooding from her. And he wanted more than that: He wanted to wipe away the memory of their encounter (he'd kept her at a safe distance since then). He wanted to start again, and he didn't know how.

He wasn't given a chance to do anything.

Out of the corner of his eye he saw the beginning of the police action. He watched as two officers sauntered up to a group of Africans who were standing on the edge of the crowd. He could not hear what they were saying, but he could guess with certainty at their words. *"Waar is jou dompas?"*—that had to be it.

It was a routine occurrence with a routine reply. The men should produce their documents, should stutter explanations if they were out of order, should be harshly told to continue on their way, or alternatively be handcuffed and pushed to one side. That was what ought to have happened.

Yet there was something in the crowd that evening that made it different. Onlookers could feel it; like Jacob, they watched the encounter. They saw that, as one of the group reached into his shabby coat pocket, a trio of youths swaggered up. A stillness, an expectation, hung in the air.

It happened quickly, as these things always do. Jacob saw a streak of blue uniforms descend on the square. They swept in formation through the crowd, arms raised and lowered as they whipped their *sjamboks* down indiscriminately. As one woman bent to pick up her child, another fell on top of her. The crowd pushed forward, and the bodies became jumbled.

Within minutes people were piled up over each other, scrambling desperately in their attempt to right themselves. When one of the organizers went to try to help out, he was felled with a stunning blow. He lay on the ground, fetuslike, holding his head in an attempt to offset the worst of the assault that descended on him from every direction.

A shoe flew into the air as if propelled by a supernatural force. Jacob heard the sounds of material ripping, of people screaming, of a dog barking somewhere off in the distance.

The crowd began to run—some toward the action, some, in terror, away from it. And Jacob ran with them. He was no longer an individual: He was pushed and pulled through the melee: tugged by the unseen force of the crowd, lost in the suddenness and sheer brutality of the attack.

As he was propelled forward, Jacob took one last look back at the city hall steps. He saw that the police had brought out the horses. Their slow trot soon turned into a canter, scattering all in their wake. Their riders had reins in one hand, whips in the other.

Without thinking, Jacob tugged at the side of his trousers, expecting to find a gun there. Of course, there was nothing. He was not at war. That he had even expected one to be there frightened him. He had become, he realized, a creature of the crowd, moving with its mind, and with its fear.

He found himself running down a side street, away from the police, away from the whips and cudgels. And yet there was no longer any threat. The police had made no attempt to follow those who managed to escape their immediate encirclement. The sounds were distant: Things had quieted.

The crowd thinned, as individuals slipped off into side roads after only the most cursory of good-byes. Jacob stayed with the main bulk: He did not know where he was headed, but he felt the need of company. The group in front of him stopped abruptly. They stood in a circle as if examining something.

"It looks bad," somebody muttered.

Jacob craned his neck and saw that a man was lying in the center of the crowd: a man completely still, with blood on his head.

"Make way," Jacob said decisively, "I'm a doctor."

The words had come easily to him, but when he reached the prone body, he was assailed with doubts. What did he know about tending the injured? After all, he wasn't a doctor—only a medical student with the minimum of practice. He felt the expectation in the onlookers—relief that with a doctor on the scene, the situation was now in hand. He felt a fool as he knelt beside the man, unsure what to do, and this made him clumsy. He fumbled at a coat sleeve, searching for a pulse.

"He's fainted," an imperious voice rang out. "Loosen his shirt." Rosa had arrived. She pulled a scarf from around her neck, and in one fluid motion handed it to the person beside her.

"Go wet this," she instructed.

The man was beginning to revive. He blinked and moaned. Rosa knelt down and helped him to sit up. When the wet scarf arrived, she used it to rub the blood gently from his face. As she did so, Jacob saw that the blood looked more serious than the wound that had caused it.

"How are you feeling?" Rosa asked softly.

"Okay." The man tottered to his feet.

"You should go to the hospital in case you have a concussion," Rosa said.

"I can't do that," the man said simply.

"No, how stupid of me," Rosa answered. "The police will be checking the hospitals." She thought briefly before speaking again. "I know a doctor who'll look at you, no questions asked," she said decisively. She turned to Jacob. "Give me a hand to get him in the car," she ordered.

The man was able to walk, although he was unsteady on his feet, and so it wasn't too difficult to get him into Rosa's Ford. That accomplished, Jacob stood to the side as Rosa climbed into the driver's seat. She glanced at him briefly.

"Get in," she said.

He hesitated, uncertain as to his role.

"I might need help," she said. "I'll give you a lift back to your digs when it's over."

Rosa, Jacob observed, did everything with efficiency. She manipulated the car with a deft hand. She briefed the doctor with a minimum of words, waiting quietly while he treated their companion. She gave their patient a lift back to his home. She didn't hesitate as she drove through the winding alleyways of the sprawl that was Sophiatown. She dropped the man off, dismissing his thanks with a friendly if dispassionate nod. Then she turned to Jacob.

"Do you mind if I stop briefly at a friend's?" she asked.

He shook his head. "Of course not," he said. He was glad there was some reason to prolong the journey. Ever since he'd got into the car, he'd been trying to find the words to apologize to her, and he'd used the presence of the other man as an excuse to delay. Now that they were alone, it was proving more difficult than he'd expected.

"It's not far," Rosa said.

She drove down the road, turning first right and then left, braving the potholes rather than negotiating around them, so that the ride grew increasingly bumpy. When she finally stopped, she glanced at him, and said she wouldn't be long. She hooted her horn twice and got out of the car.

Jacob watched as she crossed the road. He saw a man come out to meet her—Moses Bopape, it was—Jacob knew him by sight. He saw the two hug. They know each other well, he thought, and he experienced a moment's irrational jealousy.

"Rosa." Moses held her at arm's length and looked at her fondly. "Long time, no see," he said at last.

She shrugged. "The election kept me busy," she replied.

Moses reached over, and picking a stray hair from her forehead, he pushed it gently to one side. "I'm not reproaching you," he said. "Although it's always nice to get a visit. I hear you've turned into quite an orator."

"Well, I had the best teacher, didn't I?" Rosa replied. "That tip you gave me about focusing on one person in the audience and directing the talk at him really helped."

"*Ja*, well, everything's learned in this life," Moses said.

"You coming in?"

"I can't." Rosa inclined her head in the direction of the car.

Moses followed the gesture. "Boyfriend?" he asked.

Rosa found herself blushing. "Hardly," she said.

Moses smiled, opened his mouth as if he were about to say something, and then shut it.

"I was passing by," Rosa said quickly, both to fill the awkward silence and to prevent him from changing his mind and saying whatever it was he had so rapidly suppressed, "so I came to tell you that Yusuf is speaking at Wits tomorrow, early evening. I thought you might like to hear him."

"I'll be there," Moses said.

"Well, then," Rosa said. She was feeling Jacob's eyes on her, and something else as well. For Peggy had come to the door, and was standing framed against it, looking toward her and Moses. Rosa gave a quick wave. Peggy did not reciprocate. She probably didn't see it, Rosa thought. She has the sun in her eyes. "I better go," she said.

"See you tomorrow," Moses replied. He kissed her on both cheeks, squeezed her arm, and then strode off, back to his home.

When Jacob entered the meeting room, Rosa was already there, seated beside Moses, smiling and chatting with him. She was wearing a simple print cotton dress, cut in a V at the neck, and a gold chain sparkled against her tanned skin. She looked gorgeous.

An empty seat was to her left, and Jacob made his way toward it. He would talk to her today, he told himself, he definitely would. He would not countenance a rerun of the previous night.

It had been a total washout. During the journey back into white Johannesburg, they'd exchanged hardly a word (Jacob's resolve to apologize got lost somehow), and once at his digs, Rosa politely refused his offer of coffee. She had driven off almost as soon as he was out of the car, and Jacob had been convinced that she was laughing at him. He'd gone to bed in a bad mood, and woken up in a worse one. It had taken him all day to throw off his temper, to realize that he was being unnecessarily paranoid, and that it was he who'd been at fault.

"I'll try harder today," he told himself. He sat down and cleared his throat.

"Jacob." Rosa turned to him as if she had only just noticed his arrival. "Have you met Moses?"

Jacob smiled, and Moses held out a hand.

The hubbub in the room subsided. Norman stood up. "We are honored," he said, "to have as our main speaker, Comrade Yusuf Dadoo from the Indian Congress. As I'm sure you are all aware, the Indian community has a proud record of passive resistance to racist laws that began with Gandhi many years ago and continues today. Comrade Yusuf kindly agreed to delay his return to Durban in order to brief us on the implications of Proclamation 1890."

Dadoo was a good speaker, Jacob thought. He cut a dashing figure, his strong, handsome features enlivened by the passion with which he spoke. He clearly explained the implications of the proclamation, which made it illegal for anybody to collect money from Africans without the permission of either the native commissioner or a magistrate. Aimed ostensibly at protecting Africans from swindlers and racketeers, the law was in fact drafted to prevent any organization of whom the Nats disapproved from raising funds. As such, it would influence them all: the CP, trade unions, the ANC.

The speech came to an end with a passionate appeal for unity among the progressive forces of South Africa. The debate that followed was confused. Unity, everybody agreed, was the correct strategy. But unity with whom? The Soviet Union was no longer regarded as a glorious ally. Instead, the word "communism" was beginning to be used as a bugbear throughout the world. Norman held up his hand to halt the tide of protestations. "Yes, I know we still have our enemies within the broad movement, and that many of our allies are suspicious of us. We must not underestimate these problems. But we must also remember that those people are as concerned as we are, and that they also know that it's time to act. Always remember that without faith in the people, we have nothing."

He looked around him, satisfied that he had restored calm. "Our next item on the agenda," he said, "is more mundane but still the lifeblood of our organization. It concerns our annual fund-raising bazaar."

"Bazaars," Rosa joked as she left the room with Moses and Jacob at her side, "will be the death of me. If one more person asks me to bake a cake, I'll throttle him. Or maybe I could find a better form of revenge. I'll bake a cake and force him to eat the whole mess up."

Moses laughed and put his arm around Rosa. "You don't mean that you can't bake?" he asked in mock horror. "Whatever would Evelyn say?"

"She'd say what she always does," Rosa answered, "that I burn things on purpose as a form of not-so-subtle protest. She'd say that just because you can cook doesn't mean you have to take a backseat."

"And she's right," Moses said. "Evelyn doesn't know where the backseat is."

Rosa smiled. "She's amazing, your mother," she said. The smile faded as she saw that Moses' eyes had become distant, that he nodded as if in agreement but that he wasn't really listening. "Is anything the matter?" she asked.

He shook his head, and his eyes refocused. "You know me so well," he said. "I'm worried about something. In fact, if you don't mind, I'd like to talk about it."

"Sure," Rosa said. "Let's go outside."

Jacob, who had stood aside to let someone through the doorway, watched the two friends walk down the road. They were deep in conversation, their heads close together, their bodies not touching but somehow linked. He felt rather foolish. He'd been congratulating himself on his own proximity to blacks, but now he saw that Rosa had gone a step further. She and Moses had a different kind of relationship, a strong and binding one. He wondered for a moment whether there wasn't more than friendship involved. No, there couldn't be, he told himself; Moses was a married man with two growing children.

"So what do you think?" Moses asked.

"Sounds right to me," Rosa replied. "Although it's going to be tough."

Moses smiled. "Don't I know it. And—" He did not finish the sentence. Instead, he frowned as he caught sight of Rosa's watch. "Shit, is that the time?" he said. "I better go and do it now, before I change my mind. Thanks for listening, hey?" He kissed Rosa on both cheeks and then was off.

Rosa watched him walk away, observing the way his arms swung by his sides, the way he occupied his own space with so much ease. He's a man, she thought. Just that—a man.

She knew that she was a bit in love with him, had been ever since she was ten years old. He had been so exotic, then, so confident, so different. A childish crush, it had been, made stronger when he had, by just a couple of sentences, helped pull her out of the depths of her own confusion. And yet, although it was childish, it had never entirely gone away. Even now, when she knew how settled he was, how much he loved Peggy, how impossible a relationship between them would ever have been, she sometimes caught herself yearning for him.

She shrugged the thought away and began to walk.

"Rosa," came a shout.

She turned her head and frowned when she saw that Jacob was waving at her. She waited impatiently till he came nearer.

He ran toward her and started speaking as soon as he reached her. "Look, I'd like to apologize," he gushed. "The last time we met, no, I don't mean last night, I mean when we were electioneering, you know that time, you must remember. . . ." He stopped when he saw that she was looking at him intently, her face composed but her eyes twinkling. He smiled, and with his hand brushed his hair from his forehead. "What I'm trying to say," he said more slowly, "is that I behaved badly. I don't know what got into me."

Rosa stood and looked at him, and no one would have guessed at the turmoil in her mind. But turmoil there was. The night before she had taken him to Sophiatown not only because she might have needed his help, but also because there was something about him that she liked, that she wanted to know better. It had even crossed her mind that she had dropped by Moses' house in order to get his approval.

Whatever her motive had been, the result was disastrous— just like the first time, in fact. For Jacob sat beside her and said nothing; he allowed his silence to deepen the gulf between them. She found herself growing sullen and angry. She resented the fact that she had even flirted with the idea of knowing him better. She'd obviously bullied him into getting into the car—he'd never wanted to come—and he was sitting out the journey with bad grace.

He's an arrogant pig, she thought. She resolved to one day get her own back.

But when she heard his apology, and she saw that he meant it, the impulse for revenge died on her lips. "It's okay," she said.

He smiled as he brushed his hair from his forehead. "Would you like a drink?" he asked.

George, Moses' eldest, was in the middle of lecturing his sister when his father walked into the yard. "And then," he was saying excitedly, "they drove the savages into the sea, breaking their assegais into a thousand pieces."

Moses walked up behind the two. "Who told you that?" he boomed. He saw George start, and he regretted the ferocity of his tone. He kissed Lindiwe on the forehead, tousled George's hair, and sat down beside the two. "Who told you that?" he repeated, gently this time.

"Our teacher," George said.

"Don't listen to her."

"But . . ." George began.

He was interrupted by his mother. "Why are you teaching the child to be disrespectful?" she asked.

George backed away. He went to stand by the edge of the run-down yard, close by the gate, looking first at Peggy, who came to stand by the table, and then at Moses, still seated under the tree.

"What has respect to do with it?" Moses asked. "They're not teaching history: They're filling the children's heads with propaganda."

"That's as may be," Peggy replied, "but George has to dwell in the real world. If you teach him to contradict his teacher, he will face nothing but trouble."

"As if he doesn't face trouble enough," Moses said, "just by being black in South Africa."

Peggy sighed. "It's true," she conceded. She picked up the heavy knife that lay on the scuffed wooden table and began to methodically slice a round loaf of bread.

"Sandwiches?" Moses asked.

"For George's lunch tomorrow," Peggy replied. "The school informed us that they will no longer be providing as much food. Our government has lowered the subsidy."

Moses cursed. "Our government," he said bitterly, "the one elected by whites only. They haven't let a minute pass before launching their attack. They've lowered the subsidy for African pupils, not for white." He looked up at Peggy. "Do you know," he said, "that they've started a group of eminent academics on an investigation of nutritional requirements of different population groups? Of course, they're going to come up with the conclusion that Africans need less than whites, and so justify their decision to stop feeding our children altogether."

Peggy nodded, while she continued to divide the bread.

When he saw his mother's nod, George breathed a sigh of relief. He was glad that a confrontation between her and Moses, something that seemed to happen more and more often these days, had been averted. So pleased was he that he agreed to Lindiwe's demands to swing her back and forth on the yard gate.

Moses rested against the tree. He closed his eyes, shutting out the setting sun, and listened absentmindedly to the noises around him. In the background was the hum of Sophiatown: the street hawkers proclaiming the quality of their wares, scores of different conversations over closely packed yard gates, the laughter of children as they played in the derelict areas that littered the suburb. He could hear the rhythmic swish of Peggy's knife, the creaking of their gate, Lindiwe's giggles and her squeals of protest when George stopped swinging her. Moses smiled to himself. Lazily he got to his feet and approached Peggy. He put an arm around her waist.

"I'll help you with that later," he said. "Let's all go out to eat."

Peggy smiled. "That would have been nice," she said.

"So let's go."

Her smile faded. "We have not the money."

For answer Moses reached into his pocket and pulled out a bundle of notes. But instead of responding with pleasure, as he had expected her to, Peggy moved away from his grasp. "Where did you get so much in the middle of the week?" she asked.

Moses smiled at the look of suspicion on his wife's face. "Don't worry," he said. "I haven't returned to my life of crime. This is my severance pay. One week's money that they'd held back."

"Ayiee," Peggy said. "They sacked you."

Moses nodded.

Peggy took the news philosophically enough. After all, it wasn't the first time this had happened. Moses' mouth frequently led him into trouble. One week in a job and he was labeled a "cheeky *kaffir*." As soon as he got to know the work force, he began organizing, and that was usually the signal for his summary ejection from work. "Ah, well," she said. "Back to the labor office."

Moses shook his head. "I have a different plan."

"What do you mean?"

When he heard the sharp edge in Peggy's tone, Moses regretted that he had begun to tell her so casually. She wouldn't like it; that he should have known. He had been too carried away by his own enthusiasm to think of her response. He knew he should have planned the telling better. He should have taken her to the meal first, and then informed her after the children had gone to bed.

But it was too late for regrets. Having started, he would have to continue. "I'm planning to work full time for Congress," he said slowly. "They need people like me."

"And how will we live?"

"We'll manage somehow," Moses replied. He moved closer to her, trying to pull her back into his embrace, but she took evasive action.

"I suppose Rosa Arnold put you up to this," she said.

Moses narrowed his eyes. "She was in favor, but it's my decision."

"And since when do you discuss things first with that woman before even asking your own wife?" Peggy snapped.

"It came up," Moses said, "at the meeting. You could have been there."

"I have work to do," Peggy said angrily. "I have children to look after." She wheeled around and marched toward their small house. With her hand on the door, she glowered at Moses. "If Rosa Arnold acted more like other women and found herself her own man, instead of encouraging mine to all kinds of foolishness, she, too, would know what it's like." With her parting words ringing in the air, Peggy entered the house and slammed the door behind her.

"It's my contention," Norman Bloom said loudly, "that women are the stronger sex. Look what they have to go through. Could we men endure it?"

Jacob smiled. Norman was drunk, and he had been holding forth for some time on the question of the differences between the sexes. There was no stopping Norman when he was in full cry: He would go on regardless, enunciating his points, chewing at them and at the opposition, filling the air with his words.

They were all, come to think of it, slightly drunk, even Rosa, which surprised him.

"So the suffragettes came from the bourgeoisie," Norman continued, "but look what they achieved. Look what they suffered."

"It's nothing to what Africans suffer in this country," someone chipped in.

"And if you ask me . . ." Rosa began.

Norman waggled a finger in front of her face. "History, my dear, history," he said. "Never forget it. One cannot compare one person's struggle to another's. I tell you, and you'll forgive me if I digress from my central point, women are wonderful."

Rosa let Norman's voice fade into the background. She was feeling quite tipsy, an unusual state of affairs for her. It was that first glass of brandy, she thought. She'd drunk it too fast. When she'd taken it from Jacob, their hands had inadvertently touched. For a reason she could not have put into words, she was thrown into a flurry of confusion. She'd drunk the brandy in one gulp to mask her embarrassment. Only to find that somebody brought her another. And another after that, she thought, without her needing to ask. She wondered why they kept doing it, and who "they" were.

Not that she minded being drunk—it was quite pleasant, in fact. Everything went slightly out of focus, their faces, their voices, even, and it came as quite a relief. I live in a world of efficiency, she told herself in surprise. And I'm not sure I like it. Well, she could change all that; she could relax, she'd show them.

She reached over to pick up her glass. She mistimed her gesture, and it slipped away from her. If Jacob hadn't acted fast, it would have gone crashing to the floor.

"Thanks," she told Jacob, except that it came out more like "shanks." She giggled.

"Would you like to leave?" he asked softly.

She nodded her head. Better not to talk, she thought, in case she messed up the words again.

Jacob held the chair for her so she could get past, and when she was ready, walked beside her. His arm lightly touching her elbow, he guided her from the restaurant. He must know how drunk I am, she thought. She would not let that bother her. Tonight, she resolved, I'm going to let my hair down.

No sooner had the thought crossed her mind than she was instantly sober. It was something to do with the night air, she thought, which hit them as they walked outside, but then it wasn't that really. It was her damned moralistic background, she thought, her inheritance that probably stretched back as far as the *shtetl*. Why could she never do anything by impulse?

Well, she suddenly thought, I'll pretend I'm still drunk. I won't have my fun spoiled. She smiled at Jacob and leaned toward him.

Jacob registered her closeness, and the devil in him almost won out.

He'd been wrestling with it ever since he'd noticed how drunk Rosa was getting. This is my chance, part of him said; how lucky can you get? She did not seem so terrifying when she was like this. He did not have to fear a sharp comment, a sudden verbal bombardment. It would be easy, he thought, to seduce her.

So when she leaned on him, he nearly acted, pressed home his advantage.

But immediately he felt ashamed of the thought. He liked Rosa too much, he thought, much too much. He could not take advantage of her.

"I'll call you a taxi," he said.

Rosa was relieved. She did not have to pretend to be drunk anymore, she could get in the taxi, go home, and this evening would be behind her. She smiled at Jacob. "Thanks," she said. Her pronunciation was perfect.

He stretched out an arm, and a taxi drew up beside them. He opened the door, and she began to enter. Then she stopped herself. She looked straight at him. "Come with me," she said. She saw a look of uncertainty cross his face, and she smiled. "I'm neither drunk nor confused," she said. "If you want to, come with me."

Their lovemaking was unlike any Jacob had experienced. For a start he was nervous—actually nervous. It wasn't like his first time—when he'd fumbled through the whole performance praying that he wouldn't let his partner down. It was a more deep-seated fear that he would be unable to transmit his feelings for Rosa.

In comparison, Rosa seemed completely at ease. Very slowly she leaned over toward him and undid the tight knot of his blue tie. He shivered. Rosa opened his shirt, button by button, slipping her hands over his chest, gently, lightly, but with an intimation of passion unlike any Jacob had previously experienced.

He tilted her head toward him and attempted to kiss her. She shifted, slipping out of his grasp. Jacob smiled.

Rosa touched his lips with hers, a touch so feathery that it was barely perceptible. He tried to respond; again she shifted away.

She pulled his shirt down so that it slipped over his arms. She discarded it on the floor. Then she returned to his lips. This time he stayed still, reveling in her touch, her skill, his own passivity.

Rosa lifted her arms up and ran her fingers through his hair.

Jacob stopped worrying, he stopped monitoring his own technique, and he began to join with her, to experience her body as she was experiencing his.

Clumsily at first, his hands moved over her dress. She moved closer, pressing herself against him. He gained confidence and caressed her breasts. She arched backward, away from him, and yet still joined to him.

Jacob's reticence was transformed into certainty. As their arms locked behind each other's back, Jacob's passion rose up to meet and to mingle with the longing of this woman.

22

1950

"Happy New Year."

Peggy Bopape squinted toward the bright rays of the summer sunshine and saw two figures framed in silhouette against the light. She had no need to look further. Even as she knelt, scrubbing with vigor at the worn linoleum, she registered the sound of dogs barking and the creak of a rickety gate. There was a momentary shutdown in her neighbor's gossiping; so imperceptible that no stranger would have noticed it. But the brief silence spoke volumes to the habitués of Sophiatown: It warned of the presence of whites.

Who else could it be but Rosa and Jacob? Peggy hauled herself wearily to her feet.

Rosa, who was leaning against the door, observed how Peggy had aged. Her figure had thickened at the waist, and expanded around the bottom. Her once open face was creased into a habitual frown, the lines of worry making her look older than her thirty years.

"How are you?" Rosa asked.

Peggy lifted her shoulders and shrugged the question away. "Moses is not yet back," she said.

"Oh, well." Rosa tried to smile. "It's been ages since we've had a chance to talk."

In one corner of the room, against the mud wall, was a rudimentary desk propped up by an overstuffed easy chair. Peggy got a piece of wood, slotted it under the desk to prevent it from falling, and then placed the chair in the center of the room.

"Come sit," she told Rosa.

With a grateful sigh, Rosa lowered herself into the chair. As she did so, she placed one hand in the small of her back to counteract the sharp stabbing pain that made her flinch. She looked toward the door where Jacob stood, and in answer to the fleeting expression of concern that crossed his face, she shot him a reassuring smile.

Peggy flicked an imaginary speck of dust from the back of Rosa's chair.

Rosa turned her head. "How are the children?" she asked.

Before Peggy had a chance to reply, seven-year-old Lindiwe pushed Jacob to one side and came hurtling through the door.

"Lindiwe!"

She ignored Peggy's shout and planted her small frame in front of Rosa.

"Did you bring it?" she demanded.

Rosa smiled. From the pocket of her flowered maternity dress she withdrew two lengths of ribbon: one black, one green. She placed them in the child's outstretched hands.

A look of disappointment crossed Lindiwe's urchin face.

"Hold on," Rosa said. "Where's the third?" She dug in further, and this time withdrew a gold-colored ribbon.

Lindiwe beamed. She reached on tiptoe and, stretching over Rosa's belly, kissed her roundly on both cheeks.

"Thanks a million," she cried. She held the ribbons up toward Peggy. "Look," she said excitedly. "I'm going to put them in my hair, and then everybody will know I'm ANC."

Peggy grimaced. She nodded curtly at her daughter, and then glanced toward the door, where her son, George, stood.

"Say hello to our guests," Peggy instructed.

"Hello," George said sullenly.

"How's school?" Rosa asked.

"Okay."

Jacob unfastened his bulging briefcase. From it he pulled a large book, a coloring book with a glossy cover. He held it out to George.

"This is for you," he said.

George took the book, keeping it at a distance from his body, as if disowning it.

"Say thank you," Peggy ordered.

"Thank you." George's face displayed no emotion of gratitude, no emotion at all. He walked over to the table and carefully placed the book, facedown, on it. "I'm going out," he said. And with that, he left the room.

Peggy glanced apologetically at her visitors. "Children," she said. "Nothing but problems."

It was at this point that Moses arrived. He strode into the small room, a broad smile on his face.

"It's been a long time," he said, as he shook Jacob heartily by the hand. He kissed Rosa on both cheeks. "And by the looks of you, if you leave it much longer, you'll never be able to get out of this place."

Rosa laughed. From her seat she surveyed him. He had grown, she thought, ever since he had started working full time for the Congress. When she remembered how he had been as a youth, he now seemed a different person—more assured, so much more expansive, so much more his own man. Even his body seemed to have flourished. He was handsome, broad-shouldered, and exuded an easy kind of confidence. True, he, too, had aged, that was only to be expected, but the lines on his face spoke of character rather than of exhaustion.

Jacob's voice interrupted her thoughts. "How's the youth?" he asked Moses.

"Ag, man, things are really moving," Moses replied. "There's a new mood inside Congress—a new militancy. People of the caliber of Mandela, Sisulu, Tambo—they know where they're going. They're finally dragging our organization into the modern world."

"It's been promised before," Jacob said.

"But this is different. The youth are no longer prepared to sit quietly and accept the Nats' attacks. We have learned that being good *kaffirs* gets us nowhere. We have to demand our rights. We have to—"

Lindiwe, who had crept up to Moses while he was talking, tugged insistently at his trousers. "Daddy, why does Jacob call you the youth when you're a grown-up?" she said.

Moses stopped in midsentence. He picked his daughter up and held her in front of him. "In our country," he explained, "we cannot choose when to have our childhoods. They have taken even this away from us." He kissed her on the head and then turned back to Jacob. "We have to act," he finished.

"In the bioscope?" Lindiwe asked.

Moses shook her playfully. "Sometimes I think," he said, "that your whole role in life is to puncture my self-esteem." He lowered her gently onto the floor and patted her on the bottom. "Go see what your brother's up to," he said.

With Lindiwe safely out the house, Moses addressed Jacob again.

"How's it going in your neck of the woods?" he asked.

Rosa felt a momentary sensation of pique. Why was it, she thought, that everybody assumed that pregnant women forgot how to have opinions?

Jacob shrugged. "Difficult," he answered briefly.

A look of irritation crossed Moses' face. "I could have told you that," he said. "But I was after something more specific."

"Like what?" Jacob's face was studiedly noncommittal.

"Jesus, Jacob, you're full of *kak* today. What do you think I want to know? Have you decided?"

Jacob nodded his head uncomfortably. "It went to the vote at the central committee," he answered.

"And?"

"Dissolution."

"Ag, *sies*," Moses said in exasperation. "Don't they know they're playing into the government's hands? What sort of an example is this? The Nats bring in an unlawful-organizations bill, and how does the Party respond? Instead of telling the government to *voetsak*, they roll over and concede without a fight. They dissolve even before the bill becomes law."

"We feel we have no choice," Jacob explained. The tension in his voice was unmistakable. Rosa shifted uncomfortably in her seat.

"You know that is never the case," Moses argued.

"We have been a public organization." Jacob spoke slowly, as if instructing a child. "Our membership lists are in the hands of the police. Our offices have been raided so many times that nothing is secret."

"So what? It's not as if we Africans have any right to privacy," Moses interjected.

"Oh, Moses," Jacob said angrily. "This isn't a game of one-upmanship. We will be banned—there's no doubt about that. You must realize that if we don't dissolve voluntarily, then every member, every sympathizer, will be a sitting duck. The police can pick them off, charge them with belonging to an illegal organization and imprison them without a second thought. And what good would that serve?"

"As a stand on principle, perhaps," Moses replied.

"Come off it," Jacob scoffed. "We're in the real world here. Our object is a just and equal society, not a long list of martyrs."

"That's true," Moses conceded. "But it's not the point. Ever since the forty-six strike, communists have been on the hit list. So why didn't you act sooner? Why didn't you prepare for this? Why didn't you destroy your membership lists? Why don't you go underground?" He hammered out the whys one after the other, insistent, demanding, impatient.

Jacob had gone to stand by the window as Moses talked. "That's all hindsight," he said in a faraway voice. "It's always easy to say what should have been done. It's much more difficult to do it at the time."

"Well, I suppose that's true," Moses said.

Jacob turned back. He smiled. "Anyway, for once in our lives we didn't come to discuss politics," he said. "We came to invite you to our wedding."

In a flash the serious expression on Moses' face was transformed. He went over to Rosa and patted her stomach. "About time," he joked, "that you joined the world of the ordinary. I hadn't mentioned it, but people are beginning to notice something's cooking inside here."

Jacob and Rosa left soon afterward.

Peggy returned to the center of the floor. Kneeling down, she applied herself to her cleaning. Moses stood watching her.

"How are you?" he asked.

"I'm managing."

There was a moment's quiet: a quiet broken only by the swish of the scrubbing brush against the scratched floor. Moses moved the easy chair out of Peggy's way and returned it to its place beside the desk. He sat down on it.

"You're angry." It was a statement of fact.

"I'm busy." She did not look up. "There's plenty of work to running a house," she said.

"I know that," Moses said, "but surely when we have guests, you should relax. Join in the general conversation. Rosa notices your silence."

Peggy shook her head violently. My husband, she thought,

cares more for Rosa Arnold than for his own family. "Rosa wouldn't notice," she snapped. "That one does what she wants. Look at her, eight months pregnant and not yet married. It's hardly respectable."

Moses swallowed. He stared at his roughened hands, at the red dirt that was ingrained in his fingernails. "Does it matter?" he asked quietly.

"It matters to me," Peggy said. "I run a decent house here." She glared at her husband. "And what gives you the right to criticize my behavior?" she asked. "What about the way you treat our guests? You invite them into our house and then you argue with them."

Moses grinned. "A political difference, not an argument," he said.

Peggy pushed the tin bucket away from her. The dirty water splashed from its sides, spilling over onto the floor. "I may not be educated," she said, and her voice was thick with tears, "not like all your fancy friends. But that doesn't give you the right to tell me how to think."

Moses frowned. "I wasn't . . ." he started.

Squeezing the rag into the bucket, Peggy swiped at the spilled water. Moses left his chair and went to kneel by her. He put out a hand to cover hers, to stop her from her obsessive scrubbing. "What's the matter?" he asked gently.

"Matter? What should be the matter?"

"You tell me," Moses said. "I've been away a week, and still you haven't greeted me."

Peggy averted her face from this man she loved, from this man who caused her so much pain. "You truly cannot guess?" she asked.

"Tell me," he urged.

Peggy looked at Moses with an expression close to supplication. She was silently pleading with him, that he could see. But he was unable to decipher her request: He truly did not know what she wanted.

When she finally spoke, her voice was suffused with anger. "I'll tell you," she hissed, "since you insist on feigning stupidity. . . ." She looked him straight in the eye. "It's simple," she said. "I have a home and two children. I do my best for them. When they ask where their father is, what do I reply? He is out at work? No! I must say he is at a meeting, he is organizing, he is spreading the word of the black, green, and gold that Lindiwe so foolishly wears on her hair. So what could the matter be?"

"Oh, Peggy," Moses answered sadly. "Do you think your concerns are so different from those of others? Whose fault is the disintegration of families we see around us? Is it Congress that prevents the mass of people from living where they want, from achieving some small place in the world?"

"Stop worrying about the masses. Worry about your family, instead. Can't you see how wild George grows?"

A look of concern crossed Moses' face. "Has something happened?" he asked.

Peggy sighed. He would never understand, she thought, never. He did not know what it was like to sit at home and worry about him, about the children, about something as basic as where the next meal was coming from. He did not know what it was like to go to church and have to pretend to the community that she knew full well where her husband was, or how it felt to have to defend his actions to those who thought he was leading them into further trouble.

He did not know any of this because he lived within his own world, a world she did not understand. Perhaps if he explained it to her, if he even asked her permission occasionally (for when had she ever refused him anything?), she might have felt less bitter. But, no, he wouldn't do that, his politics were more important than she was.

"What's happened?" he said, louder this time.

She got up. "Nothing," she replied. "I suppose you're hungry?"

"Yes," Moses replied, "I'm hungry." He did not look up when she left the room.

Jacob drove back to Jo'burg. He always did drive these days. That, thought Rosa, was yet another of the changes wrought by pregnancy. She grimaced.

"You were quiet in there," Jacob remarked.

"It's Peggy," Rosa answered. "She always makes me feel unwanted."

"That's just her way."

"Maybe." Rosa bit back a more abrasive retort. "She's not happy, that much is obvious. But I think there's more than that going on. It's me—she doesn't like me. She doesn't like me visiting."

"You're imagining it," Jacob said. "I'm sure she's got nothing against you. Why should she?"

"Oh, Jacob," Rosa teased. "You're such a rationalist. Cause and effect—that's your way. Maybe I just represent something that Peggy dislikes. Maybe it's as simple as the fact that she doesn't go for my wardrobe. Or my unmarried status."

"Don't be silly," Jacob said. "That certainly wouldn't bother her."

Rosa flinched. In a flash she remembered the Jacob of old, the one who had put her down because he felt inadequate. He hadn't changed, she thought, he was the same man. He had tricked her into trusting him; now, he was setting out to undermine her. Already he had taken things away from her: Moses had once been her friend, now he was Jacob's.

Tears welled in her eyes. "Is that what you think of me?" she asked. "I'm stupid. Is that why you and Moses talk as if I don't exist?"

Jacob looked with astonishment at her. What was eating her? What was causing the venom in her voice? She was so touchy these days, always ready to jump down his throat.

He saw that she was staring at him, daring him to reply, ready to pick on whatever he might answer. "Oh, Rosa," he said softly, "what's up with you? You've never needed permission to talk before."

Rosa smiled. He was right, of course—she was being silly. Bloody hormones, she thought, they're responsible for all this. Look at me, all blown up and tongue-tied. Eight months of pregnancy's enough. I'm ready to get it over with: to return to my body.

She squeezed Jacob's hand. "I'm out of line," she agreed.

He smiled at her. "It's understandable," he said. "Don't worry, it'll soon be over."

They drove in silence as the scenery began to change. The disorder of Sophiatown way gave way to the sanitized slopes of white suburbia, with its luscious gardens, all neatly partitioned, sprinklers spurting softly in the afternoon sun. Dirt roads became tarmac, pavements started to appear. Whereas in Sophiatown the daytime streets belonged to children who played in dirty puddles, in white Jo'burg the children ran in and out of soft streams under the watchful eyes of their African nannies. In Sophiatown, happiness was an old tire rolled along with the aid of a stick; in white suburbia, it was a polished bike or a new pair of roller skates.

"Two worlds," Jacob commented, "tied together in blood."

Rosa nodded. "Why didn't you tell Moses that you agreed with his criticisms of the Party's decision?" she asked curiously.

Jacob shrugged. "I don't know. Loyalty, I suppose."

"Loyalty!" Rosa said. "He's on our side."

"And anticommunism is everywhere. Look at what's happening in America, in Britain. How could Congress not be affected by it? The Soviet Union is enemy number one, and we indigenous communists the threat. Things are going to get tough."

23

ROSA AND JACOB WERE MARRIED FROM HER PARENTS' HOME. As Molly Arnold later remarked to her husband, Solly, it was the most unconventional of weddings. For a start, the bride was a full nine months pregnant. And then the groom, whose father had insisted on the religious part of the ceremony, patently took the whole thing as a joke. He arrived late and had no time to change from his casual clothes.

The couple's distant relatives, invited as if they were an afterthought, stood to one side, unable to hide their disapproval of the bizarre mixture of guests. Blacks and whites mingled freely, greeting each other as if they were brothers, drinking from the same glasses when everybody knew that the consumption of alcohol at "mixed" gatherings had recently been declared illegal.

The rabbi vented his disapproval by mispronouncing Jacob's surname and leaving the house soon after the conclusion of the ceremony. With him went any pretense of solemnity.

"Thank God that's over," Jacob told Rosa. "Now, we can enjoy ourselves." He leaned back and turned up the volume on the gramophone. He watched in satisfaction as the first set of guests walked to the middle of the room and took the first tentative dance steps. He picked up his drink, took a long swig of it, and began to tap his foot in time to the music.

After a while he turned to Rosa. "You wouldn't . . . ?" he began. Then he frowned. Of course she wouldn't feel like dancing—the day must have been tiring enough already without that.

He saw that she was gazing about her with a smile on her face, and she didn't appear to have heard him. He was glad of that;

it gave him an opportunity to look at her, to drink in the sight of her. She looked beautiful, he thought, ravishing in the last stages of pregnancy, softened and made more human by it. To think that he had once been terrified of her, that he had labeled her cold and withdrawn. He knew better now; he had seen her vulnerability and her passion.

He put his head close to her and nibbled her ear. "I love you," he said. "Come on, let's slip away—nobody will notice."

She laughed and shrugged him off. "Get on with you, Jacob," she said. "Go mingle."

Jacob held up both hands in a gesture of mock surrender. "Okay," he said. "I get the message." He took another swig of whiskey and looked around the room. "Hey, Max," he suddenly shouted, "isn't this a great wedding?" With that, he left Rosa's side and danced his way across to the window.

Rosa was actually finding the whole event rather peculiar. She was enjoying it, it was good to see all their friends gathered together, but she also felt a trifle off-balance. She had wanted to laugh during the most formal part of the ceremony, but she had wanted to cry as well. Bloody hormones, she thought to herself. She looked down at her belly with a kind of affectionate desperation. Nine months, she thought, could be a long, long time. "It's enough already," she told it.

For reply, she experienced a cramping sensation. She gritted her teeth. "Bloody false labor," she said.

"Swearing at the child before it's even come out," Evelyn commented. "Tut-tut."

Rosa turned, and linking her arm into Evelyn's more substantial one, moved close to her. "What do you think of my wedding?" she asked.

"Not bad," Evelyn replied. "If I say so myself."

Rosa kissed her on the cheek. "Thanks for everything," she said. Then her face became more serious. "And I don't mean the wedding," she said softly. "I truly mean thanks for everything, for being around for me, for putting up with me."

Evelyn nodded. "It wasn't so hard," she said.

The two looked into each other's eyes, and they saw their own tears reflected there. Then Rosa broke the moment by throwing her arms around Evelyn's neck and hugging her.

Julia saw their embrace from across the room, and felt a habitual twinge of jealousy. She was about to move off and make herself useful, when she stopped, took a deep breath, and walked over to Rosa. She forced herself to smile. "Everything's going well," she said.

Rosa nodded. "It is, isn't it?"

"More water for me," said Evelyn, and she left them by themselves.

Julia thought she saw the glimmer go out of Rosa's eyes. She shrank away a fraction: She nearly uttered another nicety, made her excuses, and left. But something prevented her—"A time for choice," she heard her inner voice say. She turned to Rosa.

"Darling," she said, and she was shocked to hear how nervous she sounded. "Darling, I want to wish you all the luck in the world. Jacob is a good man—you've chosen well. I wish you everything in life, children, happiness, and success in work as well. I hope you have it all. You deserve it."

Rosa was astounded. When she was a child, she had imagined moments like this, ached for them, even, but they had never happened. As an adult, she had made herself give up hoping, and she'd even got to the point that she'd forgotten she wanted them. She couldn't remember, ever in her life, when Julia had said something so clearly out of love. She wasn't trying to create distance, or to get away. Unexpectedly Julia had broken the mold of their mutual diffidence.

The tears that had welled in her eyes when she had hugged Evelyn spilled over. "Oh, Mom," she whispered. "Thanks." She buried her head in Julia's shoulder.

Julia found that she, too, was crying. She swallowed hard. "This is a wedding," she said. "Not a wake." She stroked Rosa's hair briefly and pushed her forehead gently away. She smiled. When she had felt Rosa's head on her shoulder, the room had gone quiet. Now, she registered that the volume was up high, that people had begun to dance and to shout over the music at each other. "Your guests must be missing you," she said. She blinked a stray tear away. "Oh, my God," she added. "Molly's heading for us."

When both Julia and Rosa suddenly moved away, Molly gripped her handbag close to her waist. "Circulate," she told herself grimly, "circulate." She saw Solly whispering intently into Nicholas Arnold's ear, and decided against joining them. After all, she knew better than to interrupt the men at work.

She began to push her way through the crush.

"These Nats," someone beside her said drunkenly. "There's no stopping them."

"Ag, no, man, we'll manage." A second man turned to Molly. "Won't we?" he asked pleasantly.

Molly moved on.

She smiled at a couple who were leaning against the wall, balancing their overflowing plates and glasses of champagne precariously on their knees.

"Cribbage? You're talking cribbage? Well, let me tell you, Danny Rabinowitch was the best."

"In Yeoville perhaps. But I'm talking Doornfontein, 1936."

"What are you saying? That's sacrilege. Danny, God rest his soul, would never have been seen dead in Yeoville."

Molly moved on.

"Music, more music," called a drunken Jacob Swiece.

"*Nu*, so it's music you want," said the man next to Jacob. "But you still haven't answered my question. Where are the Jews to go?"

"That's a different matter," Jacob responded. "All I know is that they have no right to take land from the Palestinians."

Molly moved on.

Molly saw Rosa was now seated in the far corner of the room.

"Congratulations, darling," she said, as she lowered her perfumed cheek down to Rosa's level.

"Thanks, Molly." Rosa turned back to the man beside her. "You know Moses, don't you?" she asked. "Evelyn's son."

Molly smiled distantly, but when Moses held out his hand toward her, she had no option but to shake it.

"P-pleased to meet you," she said.

Moses nodded and put his arm around Rosa.

Molly moved on.

She lifted her hand to her hair and patted the wave back into shape. In so doing, she lost momentary concentration. She walked slap into a man standing alone in one corner of the room.

"I do apologize," she said.

The man opened his eyes, stared at her, closed them again, and then, in front of Molly's horrified gaze, slowly sank in a drunken stupor down to the floor.

"Oh, my God," she said.

It was at that point that chaos ensued. As Molly stepped away from the man, a tremendous crash echoed around the room. She looked up and saw that the floor near her was covered by splinters of glass. In the wreckage that he had created stood a uniformed policeman, his gun drawn, his face a startled red.

"Nobody move!" he shouted.

Molly froze.

She was the only one who did so. Every single other person in the room swung into frantic action. Even her husband, Solly, was moving.

She couldn't understand it: What on earth were they up to? They were running about like chickens with their heads cut off, dashing to and fro, glasses in one hand, bottles in the other, throwing the contents into vases, soup tureens, wastebaskets, anything in sight.

There was a loud breaking sound. The front door burst open. Molly twisted her head around and watched as a score of policemen rushed into the room.

"Nobody move," ordered the man in front.

The room stilled immediately.

"Turn that *blerry* racket off," said the policeman.

A hand reached for the gramophone. The music halted abruptly as the needle screeched against the record.

Harold Arnold pushed his way through the silent throng.

"What is the meaning of this?" he shouted.

"You're all under arrest."

"For what offense?"

"Consumption of alcohol during a mixed gathering. And for breaking the Immorality Act."

"And where is the alcohol?" Harold asked. "As for the other, I can't see anybody making love amid the wreckage you created."

The officer looked at his second in command. The man shook his head.

"You've hidden the drink," the officer shouted. "Bet you think you're clever. My man here"—he pointed to the policeman who stood in the circle of glass—"saw everything. He'll testify in court."

"Your man," Harold sneered, "as you call him, will certainly be called on to testify. He illegally broke into my house, smashing a window on his way. Unless he can produce a search warrant, I demand that you charge him with housebreaking and malicious damage. There are plenty of witnesses."

His words were interrupted by a loud shout of astonishment. Guests and intruders alike stared at the middle of the room. They all saw Rosa Swiece, née Arnold, standing stock-still, a shocked expression on her face, a puddle of liquid spreading around her.

"What's happening?" Jacob shouted drunkenly from the sidelines. "Is she hurt?"

"That, my friend," the person nearest to him, a fellow medical student, said pompously, "is what our teachers call the onset of labor. I don't know if you knew this, but you are about to have a baby."

"Oh," Jacob said. He turned away blithely. Then he stopped in his tracks. "Oh, my God," he exclaimed. "We have to get her to hospital. Clear the way. Clear the way."

Martha Swiece was born on February 16, 1950. She was a big baby, weighing eight pounds twelve ounces, with lungs to match. On her head was a shock of black hair. Her eyes were a deep brown.

Her mother stayed in the maternity hospital seven days. She was attended by a succession of visitors the likes of whom the nurses had never before encountered. Over the head of this new baby raged political arguments, friendly heckling that could turn into sudden shouting matches and then unpredictably revert to long sessions of joke-telling, and many fond tears.

Throughout all this, Martha slept serene. She woke only to let out a bellow that continued unabated until she was suckling at her mother's breast. She slumbered through the newspaper reporters who came to ask Rosa about the police apologies for their illegal entrance at the wedding.

Jacob was in seventh heaven. He loved babies, this he realized as soon as he had laid eyes on Martha. He had been hopeless during the birth. In deference to his status as an almost-qualified doctor, he had been allowed to stay during the labor, something he'd regretted immediately. He could not abide to stand by, useless, as his wife suffered wave upon wave of pain that rendered her speechless, and oh so vulnerable. He feared for her. "Let the baby die," he whispered to himself over and over again. "Just let my Rosa survive."

But as soon as it was over, he forgot his fears. He held the bawling, white-wrapped bundle of his daughter gently in his arms, and he beamed at Rosa.

"This is the best thing we've ever done," he said. "Let's do it again."

Rosa groaned and threw a wet towel straight at him. "We're communists," she said. "Everybody's equal. Next time, *you* do it."

And yet Rosa did not really mind. She surprised even herself. For it was only when she finally held her young baby that she could admit to herself how fearful she had been. She loved Martha with a passion as strong as she had ever felt for anybody. All the bad temper of her last few months of pregnancy, the fears of the changes that the baby would force on her, evaporated when she held that small body close, this small miracle that she and Jacob had brought into the world.

"Hey, what's the matter with you, girl!"

Peggy Bopape shook herself. "I'm sorry, madam," she said.

"Well, so you should be." Peggy's white boss gave a sigh of exasperation. "I asked you three times whether you can work late tonight."

"Well, madam," Peggy said. "My children . . ."

"If you can't, I suppose I'll have to find somebody else at this short notice. I did tell you when I hired you that your duties would include some evening work. That is why I was looking for a girl who could live here."

"Don't worry, madam," Peggy said hastily. "I can do it."

The matter was closed. Mrs. Adams went away satisfied that she had properly drawn the line. Peggy returned to her washing. And yet her mind was many miles away—in Sophiatown. It was always like this. As she labored in the white woman's kitchen, she was beset with worry about her children, especially her difficult son.

She washed the white child's face, and she thought of George. Had he gone to school today, or was he walking the streets alone? She spooned food into the white child's open mouth, and still more did she think of her son. Was he getting into trouble? He was so rude, so untamable: It would be just like him to cheek a policeman and end up in jail. She tucked the white child into bed between crisp cotton sheets, and she thought of her own son, falling exhausted onto an unmade bed.

As Peggy fretted, powerless to change her circumstances, the bitterness in her heart against her husband grew stronger.

Never a woman to close her eyes to adversity, Evelyn knew what was happening to her son's marriage. She did not try to intervene directly. It was her policy never to come between husband and wife. The young, she thought, must make their own way. No mother, no mother-in-law, could change the dynamics of such a relationship as Peggy and Moses'.

But Evelyn did make sure that she was around for Peggy and the children. She visited them as often as she could. She helped them financially. At first she tried to save a little each week and give it directly to Peggy. When Peggy started, out of pride, to refuse, Evelyn accepted the situation. But she was not a woman to take such obstacles lightly. Instead, she spent the money herself—on books for the grandchildren, on clothes for the two of them that she would deliberately dirty so as to pass them off as secondhand goods.

She arrived at Peggy's house, her arms laden with items for the children. So high were they piled that they obscured her vision. It was only when she set them carefully down on the mattress in the corner of the room that she caught sight of Peggy.

Peggy was motionless on the floor. That was enough to alert Evelyn. Peggy never sat. She even ate on her feet. Her excuse was that there were not enough chairs in the house, but Evelyn suspected that Peggy just couldn't stand to be inactive—not even for a minute.

"What's the matter?" Evelyn asked.

"George," Peggy replied.

"Has something happened to him?" Fear gripped Evelyn like a vise around her heart.

Peggy slowly shook her head. "I cannot get through to him," she replied. "Every time I try, he runs out of the house and doesn't return until after dark. I am so worried about him."

An irrational surge of irritation went through Evelyn. She knew she was being unkind, but for a moment she felt an impulse to shake Peggy. George was a boy: It was natural he wanted to be out in the streets. What reason was that to worry a person half out of her mind?

Evelyn controlled herself. Perhaps, she thought, Peggy's responses were so hard to bear because her own had been quite different. She had suppressed the worry for her son: She had decided there was nothing she could do, and so she had let matters run their course. She knew that such inaction had almost ruined Moses.

"Do you want me to speak to him?" she asked quietly.

Again Peggy shook her head. "It will do no good. His father is the only one who could make a difference."

"Taking my name in vain again?" said a voice from the doorway.

Moses was standing there. He had a genial look on his face, but Evelyn knew him well enough to understand what the look concealed. Her son, she realized, had given up any attempt to reconcile the differences between himself and his wife. He pretended to take her complaints seriously—but in no way did that ever change his actions.

Not for the first time, Evelyn experienced a shiver of fear. How long could things go on like this before their differences became too great, before they led to a final parting? And if that were to happen, she thought, it would be Moses who would suffer most. Peggy was a survivor—she would continue. Moses, however, was more vulnerable. Despite the fact that he spent little time at home, Evelyn knew how much his family mattered to him.

"We were discussing George," she said. "Peggy is—"

"George," Moses interrupted. "I've just met him outside. He's looking healthy, don't you think? He and I are going to kick a ball around in a minute."

Moses' voice was a shade too loud, a shade too hearty. His interruption had been seemingly casual, but Evelyn understood that it was deliberate. He was telling her something: He was telling her not to interfere.

She ignored his warning. "Peggy feels that George—"

"Never mind." This time it was Peggy who interrupted. She had risen from her chair, and she was already moving out of the room.

Evelyn shut her mouth. Peggy did not want her help.

In her innermost heart Evelyn knew that she did not handle Peggy's responses sensitively. Even as she listened to Peggy's growing list of complaints, Evelyn felt proud for her son. He was doing what his father had done. This, she knew, was what she had always wanted for Moses. And Peggy had guessed Evelyn's views.

Moses seemed relieved that his wife had stemmed the conversation. He walked over to Evelyn and embraced her. "How are you?" he asked.

"As usual. And you? Is the campaign getting off the ground?"

This time the smile on Moses' face was genuine. "*Ja*," he said. "The idea is really beginning to grab us. We're still working out the details, and then we'll put it to both Congresses. But I think it's going to come off—and if it does, it'll shake this society to its very foundations."

Evelyn smiled. "You remind me so much of your father," she said. She reached up her hand and ruffled his hair.

Moses moved away a fraction. It was an almost imperceptible shrinking, but Evelyn noticed it. It had happened before: Moses seemed to avoid physical contact these days. Was this another consequence of his difficulties with Peggy?

That thought brought her back to the problems in hand. "Look, my son," she said. "About your family."

Moses warded off her words with a sweep of his hand. "Leave it, Mama," he said. "This is for Peggy and me to solve."

Evelyn heard the warning in his words. She had tried: She could go no further. She nodded and changed the subject. "Rosa and Jacob are doing well with their baby," she said. "I never believed Rosa would take to it so readily."

Moses smiled. "I'm pleased," he said simply. "I nurse a real affection for Rosa."

"And I," said Evelyn. "She is lucky. Jacob . . ."

She had turned to search for something in her bag, and in so doing she glanced outside. What she saw made her freeze in her tracks. For Peggy was standing by the open door, a look of fury writ large on her face. Evelyn was not a woman easily cowed by another's anger, but this was indescribable. Peggy's face was contorted by rage; it was hardened by an inner bitterness.

Evelyn forgot completely what she had been about to do. She turned back to Moses to say something about it, to draw his attention to the extremity of Peggy's reaction.

He had obviously not noticed a thing. "Tell them I'll visit soon," he said, before Evelyn could utter a word.

When Evelyn looked out again, Peggy had vanished. She did not reappear the whole afternoon, and eventually Evelyn left, deeply disturbed by what she had seen and by the realization that there was nothing she could do to help.

24

1952

"Mummy," shouted Martha, "look at me, look at me!"

Martha was quite happily skipping in and out of the sprinkler. But every now and then she stopped what she was doing so that she could check that her mother was paying attention.

Rosa was trying to read the newspaper while appearing to Martha as if she were watching wholeheartedly.

This, reflected Rosa, was the worst thing about having a child—the fact that she could never entirely devote herself to anything because of Martha. She'd recently started doing some part-time research, and would catch herself worrying about trivial things such as diapers, or the right brand of apple juice. When she went out at night, she could not stop herself from holding her breath every time a telephone rang. And when she was with Martha and she only wanted to read the headlines, even that was difficult.

Not, she thought hastily to herself, that she had any regrets. Martha was a continuing joy, and raising her, watching her grow and develop, had brought undreamed-of pleasure. When Martha was born, Rosa thought that she could not love a person more than she loved that tiny baby, but she knew now that she had been wrong. Her love for Martha, her fascination, kept growing stronger.

But is it enough? she thought.

"Mummy!" Martha shouted.

Rosa looked up just in time to see Jacob enter the garden. His striped brown suit was somewhat the worse for wear, his hat looked as though he had sat on it, and the knot of his tie was loose.

Rosa glanced down at her watch, and saw that it was already midday. It had been a long meeting, she thought, heavy going on top of a night's work. She stood up. "How was it?" she called.

He smiled and stretched his arms above his head. "Good," he replied. "But tiring. Is that coffee over there?"

Jacob sat down while Rosa poured out a cup of coffee. "What did you decide?" she asked, as she handed the cup to him.

Jacob took a sip. "Defiance," he said. He yawned.

"Jacob," Rosa said sharply.

He put his cup down. "Oh, I'm sorry, darling," he said. "I've never had as many calls as last night—I began to think that my patients were feigning illness to keep me away from that meeting."

Rosa nodded impatiently. "And?"

Jacob shook himself, and seemed to throw off his exhaustion. "It was agreed to start a concerted defiance campaign," he explained, "just as we discussed. The ANC and the Indian Congress will join forces, as will some of us whites. We decided to target a few laws—the pass and curfew ones for a start, of course, but also the Group Areas and Suppression of Communism Acts, and a couple more. We'll organize bands of volunteers to deliberately go and break the laws."

"And they'll go to prison rather than pay their fines?"

Jacob nodded. "We're starting to recruit volunteers from all over the country," he said. He glanced quickly at Rosa. "I volunteered," he said. "Hope that's all right."

She smiled. "Of course it is," she said. "I wouldn't have assumed otherwise."

He put down his cup and, reaching over the table, took her hand in his and squeezed it.

"I'd like to volunteer myself," she said.

Jacob released her hand and picked up his cup again. "They wouldn't let you," he said casually.

"Why?" It came out angrier than she'd planned. She softened her voice. "You mean *you* wouldn't let me?" she suggested.

He glanced at her in surprise. "Surely you know me better than that?" he asked, and his face showed how hurt he felt.

She felt immediately remorseful. "Who wouldn't let me, then?" she asked.

"It's not personal," Jacob said. "It's just that we made a decision that since volunteers will be expected to go to jail, they must be carefully selected. People who can't afford to lose their jobs, for example, or those with young children"—he glanced at Martha—"won't be asked to take part."

Rosa bit her lip. "*You* have a young child," she said.

"But you're her mother." Jacob was perplexed. "She needs you."

If you were around more often, Rosa thought, she might need you, too. She didn't say the words out loud. But after all, he was right, Martha did need her. She must be patient: There would be plenty of time in the future in which to be active. Change the subject, she ordered herself.

"Did Moses volunteer?" she asked.

Jacob smiled. "What do you think?"

"Peggy won't like it."

"Yes, well, Peggy just doesn't understand, does she?" Jacob said as he got to his feet. He yawned and stretched again. "I must get some sleep," he groaned.

"You won't have lunch with us?" Rosa asked. "Martha was looking forward to it." So was I, she thought.

"That's sweet of her," Jacob said. "But I don't think I can keep my eyes open much longer. I tell you what, I'll take her to Zoo Lake, if I wake up in time." He leaned down, kissed Rosa on the forehead, and then began to walk toward the house.

She was, she decided, just being petty. This Defiance Campaign was going to be big, she knew it was, it would rock the country.

"I can hardly wait," she told herself.

On June 26, 1952, the phones at Johannesburg's central police station didn't stop ringing.

"Hey, Captain!" called the desk sergeant. "Looks like we've got another."

Captain du Plessis swore under his breath. What the hell was going on? What was this madness spreading through Jo'burg? The day, he reflected, had started quietly enough. He'd had time for a sweet cup of milky coffee and a real fresh *koeksister*. Rubbing his stomach contentedly, he'd begun to supervise the processing of the previous night's trawl. It was all as usual. There had been no warning that anything was about to break.

And then, at nine o'clock, the phone started, and it hadn't let up since. It was the same story told over and over again. The captain grabbed at the receiver. "What is it?" he snapped.

A weak voice filtered through the other end. "I don't know. I have a gang of *kaffirs*—"

"Squatting in a European facility," du Plessis interrupted. "Well, kick them out of there, and be quick about it."

"I can't, Captain. They won't go. They want to be arrested."

"Jesus Christ, do I have to do everything?" He slammed the telephone down. "Tell the boys in the pickup to leave as soon as they arrive," he shouted down the corridor. "This city is making them cocky," he muttered to himself. "I should have stayed in the country. These bastards wouldn't dare try anything there."

But Captain du Plessis was wrong; it was happening outside of the cities. The Defiance Campaign was taking off. In every small *dorp*, in every sleepy South African hamlet, the Congress was at work. The call was out for volunteers, volunteers who were prepared to go to jail.

Moses was among the organizers. He had traveled the country setting up networks of support, until finally he'd been sent to a location (one of the newly established African housing areas that ensured that blacks and whites could no longer mix socially in the Transkei, a place not far from where his father, Nathaniel, had been born).

When he'd arrived, he'd been met by Dumisani, his local contact. But as they tried to enter through the location gates, a policeman barred their way.

"*Dompas*," he snapped.

Both men's documents were in order, and the policeman gestured Dumisani on. He shook his head at Moses.

"Not you," he said. "We don't want troublemakers here."

Moses had been left to stare through the barbed wire that surrounded the whole location. He swore to himself—had he come all this way for nothing.

Dumisani, however, was unconcerned. He winked at Moses. "If Muhammad can't come to the mountain . . ." he said, before turning on his heels and disappearing into the depths of the location.

Within half an hour Moses understood what he had meant.

For the people came trickling out. At first one by one they came, and then, taking courage, they arrived in groups, in tens, in fifties. They made their way single-mindedly to the open veld, and stood there patiently beneath the blazing sun.

A small *kopje* served as a natural platform in the center of the veld. From it Moses could see the heads of the people dotted around as they waited patiently under the sun, the women's *doekies* bobbing up and down as they gossiped. Beyond them a cloud of reddish dust rose into the air, churned up by a passing truck, and then sank back to merge again amid the dry land. A few *kraals* in their final stages of disintegration dotted the veld— a testimony to an abandoned lifestyle. They would not even be allowed to return to the ground from which they came, Moses reflected: Already the white town showed signs of encroaching on them.

Dumisani waited until the last stragglers has had arrived. Then he climbed up onto the *kopje*.

"You all know why you're here," he said. "So I won't waste any further time. I introduce a friend, Moses Bopape, who comes from the African National Congress."

Moses took the platform. He explained the rationale behind the Defiance Campaign: He spoke of the Indian passive resisters who had shown the way so many years before, by protesting against the abolition of their rights. He told the crowd how the African and Indian Congresses had joined together to revive this form of protest—to tell the government strongly but peaceably that the people would not take the flurry of new restrictions lying down.

He spoke eloquently, and his audience listened attentively enough. But after he had finished, their reaction was muted. There were a few raised hands, and some basic questions. That was all: There was no display of enthusiasm, no ready agreement.

A feeling of unease fluttered around the congregation until it settled on Moses. He knew that they were slipping away from him, that they had had enough excitement for one day. They had defied the glares of their masters to attend this meeting. Now, it looked as if they might be satisfied with this, as if they must just turn and go home.

Moses had an impulse to exhort them further to action. Instead, he thought back to his training. He had learned, he remembered, that people must make their own decisions, that an outsider could go only so far. After that, it was for the people to decide.

He knew all this, and yet he railed against it. If nothing came of this meeting, he would have to accept the fact. He would move on, start again, find a more receptive audience. But a sense of failure would dog him. What had he done wrong? He frowned, and his heart felt heavy.

It was at this point that Dumisani stepped onto the platform. He had a strange look in his eyes, a look that Moses did not entirely trust. He scowled at Moses, and then he shivered. He held out his hands to Moses, wrists together as if they were bound.

"Oh, thank you, *baas*," he whined. "For arresting me, I thank you."

Moses narrowed his eyes. Dumisani was ridiculing him: He was caricaturing a volunteer. Was he then a spy? Had he worked so hard before the meeting only so that he could turn its participants over to the Boers? Moses felt his own sense of unease spread through the audience. There was silence—an uncomfortable, drawn-out silence.

And then somebody broke the spell: Somebody laughed.

The laughter was infectious. It swelled into the air, drowning the clacking of cicadas lurking in the long grass. As the laughter increased, a group of crows took off into the air. The crowd laughed louder, unrestrainedly, riotously, as they reveled in Dumisani's caricature of their own daily behavior.

And then they began to speak. "Go to jail?" one man called. "Are you gone crazy, man? Isn't jail the place we spend our lives avoiding?"

"These radicals need their heads examined!" shouted another. "Volunteers to defy the law, indeed! We have enough *tsotsis*. They break the laws every day. Go ask them to join your foolish campaign."

Moses frowned and glared at Dumisani. But Dumisani was unaffected by Moses' disapproval. He made his way jauntily off the *kopje*, jumping nimbly down the sides to join his compatriots. Before he left, he whispered into Moses' ear.

"Answer them," he said. "For that is what they need. They won't be able to act until their doubts are answered."

A man got up. "We have heard of your leaders. Of Mandela, Sisulu, of all of them," he said. "They describe our lives, and they are eloquent. We respect that. They have struggled to get good jobs. Fine, we need more Africans in their positions. But what do they have to lose? What will they sacrifice?"

There were grunts of assent in the crowd. Moses raised his hand. "Mandela will go to jail," he promised. "Sisulu will go to jail. Dr. Naicker will go to jail. Dadoo will go to jail."

"And you, will you go?"

"But of course," Moses answered. "Am I not *ivolontiya*? Do I not wear the khaki pants and white shirt that mark me out as such? Have I not taken the pledge?"

"It's true!" someone shouted approvingly. "These Congress suffer as we do. The *baas* says they come only to stir up trouble for us, but the *baas* tells many lies."

The meeting was turning. Moses could feel it. Nods, rather than shakes of the head, were becoming commonplace. The people were moving.

It was at that point that a delicate old woman with graying hair and eyes wary from life got up.

"And what of your wife?" she called in a voice that denied her bodily frailty. "What will she do while you languish in jail?"

"A good question," called her neighbor. "Does your wife support your actions? Does she object?"

Moses cursed to himself. If there was one thing he had learned to respect during the campaign, it was the strength of these womenfolk. They held the family together, they protected their children, they observed, with lucid eyes, the behavior of their men. And they were so shrewd. Untutored, illiterate, they knew what was important. They had hit Moses in his sore spot, with an accuracy that was deadly.

For of course Peggy objected: Moses' involvement in the Defiance Campaign had made the gulf between them wider. They no longer even argued: Instead, there was a silence between them, a strained, bitter silence that contained all the hurt, all the resentment, they felt for each other.

"There are women in the campaign. We do not ask just for men," Moses said evasively.

Moses saw Dumisani shake his head anxiously. He seemed to be shooting a message over to Moses, a plea for something.

Dumisani was not the only one who sensed Moses' evasion. The women heard it, and they went straight for the gullet.

"What of your wife?" they shouted, more than one of them this time.

Moses took a deep breath. He appealed for quiet. When he finally got it, he spoke loudly, slowly, deliberately. "It is a good question," he said, "and has an answer that is not a happy one. My wife feels that she suffers because of my actions."

"And is this her imagination?" someone asked.

"It is not her imagination. She does suffer." As he said it, he realized that he was indeed speaking the truth.

Excited exclamations greeted his words. He raised his voice. "I grieve for her suffering, but I cannot give up," he shouted. "For I say that we must take action: We must build a movement that will resist apartheid. Only by doing this can we ensure that my son, who witnesses our arguments, does not have the same problem with his wife: that my daughter does not suffer the same consequences from her husband. I am sorry my wife resents my activities, but I feel I have no other choice."

A flurry of conversation broke out among the audience. Moses waited for it to die down. He had done the right thing—he knew it. He felt an ache for Peggy—for the fact that he could never talk to her like this, for the misunderstandings and for the silences. Maybe I can tell her, he thought. I will try.

A stout woman (Dumisani had already pointed her out as one who ran the biggest shebeen in the area) raised her voice. "This man speaks from the heart," she said, and she cast her eyes around, daring anybody to disagree with her. "Things were bad before the Boers got in, but now they're even worse. No longer can we walk our streets at night, or farm the land our fathers owned."

"And no longer can we run a shebeen without nightly raids," an unseen voice from the back retorted. "Which plays hell with our profits."

The woman wheeled around. "When you learn to hold your liquor, John Malake," she jeered, "when you are ready to wear long trousers, then you can talk of profits." Satisfied by the ululations that greeted this, she faced forward. "Our children go barefoot for want of shoes," she said. "They stay away from school for want of books, they do not eat for want of food. I say that we must do something, that enough is enough. I volunteer."

A man, far removed from the woman, stood up. "I volunteer."

"And I."

"And I."

The offers came fast and furious. Moses set up a table and took down the names one by one, questioning each as to his or her family circumstances, rejecting those who would leave behind children without anybody to care for them. Those who remained he told to gather in the same place the following night.

"I'm back," Jacob called.

Rosa pushed her papers to one side. She walked through her study and into the sitting room. She saw that Jacob was already seated on the soft leather sofa, his legs stretched out in front of him, a heavy cut-glass tumbler of whiskey by his side. She smiled to herself as she approached him. He had only been away a week, and yet she'd missed him badly. She was happy to see him again, to look at those handsome features and notice the rings beneath his eyes, the weatherbeaten look on his face.

"How was it?" she asked, as she sat beside him.

"Wonderful," Jacob replied. "Word's spreading like wildfire. All over the country people are volunteering. They're breaking every one of apartheid's petty laws. God knows how the government's going to react when it gets its breath back." He turned to face his wife and ran a hand gently down her cheek. "And you? You look tired."

Rosa shrugged. "There's been a lot to do around the house," she said. "Including answering Martha's three million questions on where you'd gone, when you'd be back, and would you remember the peaches."

"She's asleep?"

Rosa nodded.

"I'll look in on her later," Jacob said. "I got the peaches, and I brought her some of the best biltong I've ever tasted."

"She'll be pleased. She's got something for you as well—some ropy loquats she saved, but don't tell her I told you. You must be hungry. I'll fix you a bite to eat."

As she walked away, Jacob examined her from head to toe. He liked her in those modern slacks, he thought, they showed her figure without trying to diminish her height. He must tell her so later—later, when they were in bed. In the meantime, he thought, she did look tired.

"Have you been overdoing things?" he called.

Rosa looked back and smiled. "Not really," she said lightly.

She did not add that she was bored and that she suspected her inaction was the thing that was making her tired. She wanted to change the subject. "Tell me your news," she said.

"I'm going to talk at a meeting tomorrow," Jacob said. "You don't mind, do you?"

Rosa breathed in sharply. This was the moment she had been waiting for—when Jacob would tell her that he, not she, was ready to make his act of defiance. Well, she would not let herself down, she would act as she had resolved. "Of course I don't mind," she said loudly. "I'm proud of you. Mustard or mayonnaise on your sandwich?"

Jacob winked at her. "Forget the food and come over here."

Moses stood outside the location gates and gazed in wonder at the people who had assembled around him. Over a hundred of them stood ready for action: people dressed in such a variety of clothes that they made a startling sight. There were those who had managed to scrape together the rudiments of a volunteer's uniform: who were dressed in khaki pants topped by the buttoned-up white shirt. And then there were the others: some in rags that clung to them, some in the black, green, and gold of the ANC.

But it was the small group of women in traditional costume that was most eye-catching. They sat together in a group, straight-backed and proud, some with children sleeping on their backs, their turbans erect on their heads, their long, decorated costumes flowing down their limbs, their faces with the colored makeup around their eyes and cheeks that gave them an eerie, almost threatening look.

Moses shook himself. The time for idle observation was past. "Let us take the volunteers' oath together," he said.

"I am prepared to take up on my shoulders the risks of my life for my people for the liberation struggle," they intoned. "I will do as my leaders tell me. I won't do anything which I have not been instructed to, no matter how the consequences may be."

The die was cast. They were ready to defy.

Moses divided them into groups of twenty, and he put himself in the first batch. Then, having checked that everybody knew what they were supposed to do, he set out with his group.

They walked together into the town, keeping an even pace,

looking neither to the left nor the right. They made straight for the railway station. They did not talk—each, perhaps, was experiencing a moment of self-doubt or anxiety, but they did not speak of it. Their energy was concentrated on what lay ahead.

Once they arrived, Moses hesitated. A member of the group pointed one finger upward.

Moses' face cleared: There indeed was a sign, partly concealed. EUROPEANS ONLY, it said—*SLEGS VIR BLANKES*.

With nineteen others behind him, Moses made straight for it.

When he opened the door, he saw that the place was already occupied by one young white family, two white men of middle age, and one elderly white woman. They had been conversing, the room had an air of pleasant chitchat still about it, but as soon as Moses appeared, they stopped abruptly.

"Yes?" asked one of the men loudly. "What do you want, boy?"

Moses took one step inside and held the door open for the others. "We have come to wait for a train," he explained.

If it hadn't been a serious occasion, Moses might have burst out laughing. For as soon as he had finished his sentence, he saw five jaws drop together as if they had been choreographed. One of the men spluttered, the other turned red, the elderly woman took a handkerchief out of her handbag and held it up to her mouth, and the young couple pulled their toddler protectively to them. And all of this, thought Moses, because a group of Africans had the temerity to say that they planned to wait for a train in the station's only waiting room.

"What the hell," said the second man. "This is a disgrace."

Moses did not laugh.

The volunteers had by now all managed to enter. Several of them sat down on the benches.

"I'm . . . I'm going to c-call the p-police," stuttered one of the men. "Unless you get out immediately, I'm warning you, I'll call them."

"We are part of the Defiance Campaign," answered a woman from the group. "We will sit here until we are either allowed to do so or are carried out of here."

Nods of agreement, murmurs of confirmation, followed her statement.

The white contingent got up. Huddling together for protection, they left the room.

The police were a long time coming. So long, in fact, that the man next to Moses started to complain. "If they don't hurry up," he said, "we'll be done for breaking the curfew rather than the segregation laws."

Everybody burst out laughing, and they were still doing so when the door crashed open. A white policeman stood there, his *sjambok* in hand.

"*Voetsak, kaffirs,*" he said. "This is a whites-only facility, and you know that as well as I do. If you want to catch a train, you must wait outside."

"The only way we'll leave here," came the answer, "is if you arrest us."

The policeman frowned. He prided himself on being a reasonable man. He'd never encountered a rebellion of this kind, and he didn't understand it. He was sure that there must be an easy solution. He scratched his head. "Look here," he said in a mild voice, "you know that if I arrest you, you'll be fined. And very few of you can afford that."

"We won't pay our fine." This from more than one point in the waiting room.

"We will go to jail," an old man explained. "We will go with our heads held high, and we will be remembered for it."

The policeman gave up. He beat a hasty retreat into the railway office. They heard him on the phone. "You better send a van to pick up these *kaffirs,*" he said. "They've lost leave of their senses."

And so Moses and all the other members of his group were carried bodily to the police van. As it drove away, hooting through the narrow streets, they saw the next group heading for the station. They cheered, and those in the back stuck their thumbs through the bars of the black *kwela-kwela.*

"*Afrika!*" they shouted.

"*I'mayibuye,*" came the resounding reply.

One week later, when Moses was led handcuffed from the court, he saw that Rosa was among the crowd. He raised his hand in a salute, bringing another's with it. "Sorry," he said.

"No problem," his neighbor replied.

As they walked forward in a line, Rosa managed to push her way through to the front. "Hope the next three months aren't too rough," she shouted.

Moses smiled. "I'm in good company," he said. "I'm learning a lot from the people here, and they will look after me." The line pulled him forward, and he was glad to see that Rosa, despite the crush around her, was managing to keep up with him.

"How's Jacob?" he called.

"In the same situation," she said. "He got a couple of months under the Suppression of Communism Act for talking in public."

"Are you okay?" Moses asked.

"Of course," Rosa said. "Who wouldn't be, given the success of the campaign? They say more than four thousand have defied so far."

"*Afrika!*" shouted Moses' neighbor.

"Move," ordered a policeman.

Moses was pushed forward toward the waiting van. As he took one last look around him, he saw another face that he knew. It was Peggy, standing at the back of the crowd. She must have come with Rosa, he thought. He jumped up so he could see her better.

"How are the children?" he shouted.

She shrugged, and he thought he could detect tears in her eyes.

"Are they all right?"

This time she nodded, before turning away. She could not bear to see her man pushed into that horrible van, sent to prison for a whole three months.

As for Moses, the fleeting anxiety that something had gone wrong was replaced by irritation. In that moment his resolve to be more tolerant of his wife left him. He felt angry with her—why couldn't she be more like Rosa? he thought. Why couldn't she?

25

AND AS THE JAILS FILLED UP, SOUTH AFRICA WAS IN THE NEWS again. At first a shocked Nationalist party looked on silently.

But the Nats rallied quickly. They rushed an act through Parliament, an act that made such protest an offense punishable by large fines, long sentences, and even whipping.

Nobody could risk such heavy penalties: The end of the campaign was in sight. Rather than watch it disintegrate slowly, the organizers decided to bring it to a definitive close. In 1953 they did just that.

And yet this was not the end of the volunteers. For no sooner had they discarded defiance, a new ambition, a new strategy, was put in motion. Once more the African and Indian Congresses along with the newly formed white Congress of Democrats sat down at the table and began to plan. . . .

The meeting was a long and difficult one, and by the time he arrived home, Moses was exhausted.

"What did you decide?" Peggy asked.

Moses glanced at her in surprise. It had been a long time since she had asked a question, since she had displayed even the slightest interest in his work.

"We closed the Defiance Campaign," he answered tentatively.

"Oh," Peggy commented, feigning lack of interest. But if Moses had been more alert, he would have easily spotted the triumph in her eyes.

He was still half-asleep. "We've come up with a plan," he said, "for the drawing up of a people's charter. It'll use all our volunteers, and more besides. We'll hold a congress in 1955 to ratify it. We're already—" He stopped in midsentence, as if he'd just remembered that Peggy might not share his enthusiasm. He glanced at her.

She was staring into the cast-iron pot. "Two more years," she said, "that you will work on such nonsense."

Moses did not immediately reply. Instead, he stood up and dusted at the debris that had collected on his brown trousers. His eyes focused on some point in the distance. "Two years, twenty-two, two hundred, if I could live that long," he finally said.

"My husband, you're a fool," Peggy said harshly. "What can you hope to achieve? Our people have no chance: They will never be able to change anything."

"I don't believe that," Moses said. "One day we will change things—it's inevitable."

"If it's inevitable," Peggy retorted, "then it will happen with or without you: You are not needed."

"That's not true," Moses replied. "We are all needed. For unless we plan for it, it'll be harder to achieve; unless we dream of it, it'll take longer."

She heard the passion in his voice, she saw the conviction in his eyes. He never looked at her like that, she thought sadly. "I have lost the capacity to dream," she said out loud.

"Then perhaps I have to do it for both of us," Moses softly replied. He began to walk away from her. "I'm going out," he said.

"We're going to ask them, to ask these people who have no vote and no voice, to participate in drafting a new kind of constitution," Jacob told Rosa. His voice strengthened. "It's a brilliant idea," he said. "We'll ask people what they would like to happen, and out of their demands we'll write a Freedom Charter—a constitution ratified not by a sham parliament that sits in Pretoria, but by a congress of the people."

"And the volunteers will collect the demands?" Rosa asked thoughtfully.

"That's right," Jacob said. "We'll use those we've already got, all eight thousand of them, and we'll recruit more. Think of it—thousands of people going into every nook and cranny of our country asking of people: To what do you object? What do you want? What's important? How could it be different?"

He strode over to Rosa, and putting one arm around her shoulder and the other in her right hand, he began to waltz her around the room. "Think of it!" he shouted. "It'll be wonderful!"

"Jacob," Rosa laughed, "stop it at once."

But he didn't, he kept whirling her faster and faster, until they both became dizzy and fell in a heap to the floor. There was a moment's silence, and then Jacob gently placed one hand on Rosa's face and began to stroke it.

"I'm going to bed," he whispered. "Coming?"

They were lying in bed, Rosa's head resting on Jacob's shoulder, when she broached the subject that had been plaguing her since his return. She took a deep breath. "I want to be part of it," she said.

"Of course you do," he replied absentmindedly. "And you shall be." He squeezed her arm.

She shifted slightly away from him. "I want to be a volunteer," she said. "I want to go to the country."

She felt him stiffen.

"I'll ask my mom to come and help with Martha," she said quickly.

"That won't stop her missing you," he said.

His voice was deliberately neutral but Rosa knew him too well to be deceived. He was, she realized, going to put obstacles in her way. He was starting diplomatically, but if she resisted, he would up the stakes—not for nothing had he sat in endless meetings, maneuvered on infinite committees.

Well, let him try—let him realize that she would not give in. "Martha misses you when you're away," she said, and her voice was bitter.

"Calm down," Jacob said soothingly. "No need to get worked up about this."

"I'm not worked up," Rosa insisted, and she hated the fact that her voice had indeed risen and that there was something a trifle unbalanced in it.

"All I'm saying," Jacob said slowly, "is that Martha needs you still."

Rosa pushed his arm away and sat up. She yanked one of the two pillows from under his head and plumped it against the wall before leaning on it. "What about my needs?" she asked. "My need to be more involved." She paused. "I'm going whether you like it or not," she said quickly. She glared down at him.

It was an effort for her to keep her eyes from blinking. His were unwavering as he looked up at her. At that moment she hated him for his self-assuredness, for his confidence and poise. "Don't you see?" she wanted to shout. "That's why I have to go—because you are strong, while I've lost faith in myself." But she was scared the words might sound silly. She bit her lip. I'm going, she told herself, whatever he says.

She was right, those meetings had trained Jacob. And one of the things that he had learned was how to bow to the inevitable. He saw the resolve in her face, and he knew that he was beaten. He didn't like it, he didn't like it at all, but he was not going to waste his energy on such a losing cause.

"Okay," he said. He shrugged and smiled at her.

She felt immediately grateful. "Thanks," she said gushingly. She smothered his face with grateful kisses. "Oh, thanks, Jacob," she kept saying.

When Rosa came into the room, Jacob knew that by conceding he had done the right thing. She looked so radiant, so alive. Her eyes shone, there was a kind of skip to her walk, and when she smiled, there was nothing but genuine happiness there. Looking at her, it dawned on Jacob that there had been something missing, something of herself repressed.

He remembered her speech on the city hall steps and how her face had been enlivened by passion. He had so wanted to preserve that part of her—after all, that was what had attracted him—and yet, when it had begun to evaporate, he hadn't even noticed. Now that it had returned, he felt somewhat guilty. His Rosa was a political animal, not a person to accept passivity easily.

"So don't tell me," he said. "You're off tomorrow."

She laughed. "Not quite. In a few days." The smile faded as she looked him straight in the face. "Will you be all right?" she asked.

"Sure," he said. "We'll miss you, but we'll manage—Martha and I. With a little help from your mom, of course." He was pleased to see that the radiance returned. "Where are they sending you?" he asked.

"Cape Town, initially," she said. "I saved the best news till last. I'm traveling with Moses."

Jacob's smile did not waver. "Great," he said enthusiastically. His lips suddenly felt stiff. Moses is my friend, he told himself firmly. But he was Rosa's friend first, came another voice.

Moses, for his part, didn't mention to Peggy that Rosa was to be his traveling companion. This in itself wasn't so peculiar; it was only one omission among many. But he still felt a bit awkward about it, as if he were hiding something important from her.

He dealt with his guilt by turning the blame her way. It was her fault, he told himself: She'd always been jealous of Rosa, and there'd never been any cause for it. He refused to worry about it.

Nevertheless, he did not break his silence, and for the sake of a peaceful life, he went one step further: He asked Rosa to pick him up not from home, but from a place some distance away.

He was waiting by the side of the road when she arrived. She stopped the car and, reaching over, held the front door open for him. But instead of climbing in, he opened the back door, threw his duffel bag onto the backseat, and began to climb in after it.

Rosa frowned. "Surely you're not getting in the back?" she asked.

He shrugged. "Yeah."

"Oh, no," she said. "Come in front, or I'll get a cricked neck trying to talk to you."

"I don't know . . ."

"Don't be so silly," she interrupted. "Come on, or we're going to be late before we've even set off."

They drove in a kind of companionable silence while Rosa negotiated the Jo'burg traffic. Only when they were on the road proper, when they were no longer stopped every fifty yards by red lights, did they begin to talk.

Their conversation was faltering at first. They were, each privately realized, quite nervous. They had not been alone for years, and it wasn't easy to reclaim a casual friendship outside of the company of husbands, wives, comrades. But as mile followed mile, it became too much of an effort to keep up their mutual diffidence, and they began to relapse into old ways. They talked, they argued, they laughed at each other's jokes, they let silence come between them, not now as a tense presence, but as a comfortable relaxation.

"Do you remember when I pretended I didn't know you?" Rosa asked after one of these periods of quiet. "When the Grayshirts were chasing you?"

"How could I forget?" Moses replied. "My dominant thought at the time was that if they didn't finish me off, I'd come straight round and shoot you."

"You didn't, though," Rosa said in a faraway voice. "You forgave me, instead."

"*Ja*, well, I had just discovered how to forgive myself," Moses said, "so I thought I'd spread it around a bit." His voice was light, but when Rosa happened to look his way, she saw that his face was in deadly earnest. She smiled at him, and he stretched out a hand and placed it lightly on one of hers. "Rosa," he began. But he never finished the sentence. "Oh, shit," he said instead. He pointed down the road.

A police car was parked across it. She slowed down.

"Tell them I'm your servant," Moses muttered.

She glanced at him in surprise. "I'll do no such thing," she said.

"Do it," he ordered, and his voice was harsh.

She had just time to reflect that if Moses commanded his wife like this, he must be a hard man to live with, when the policeman tapped at her window. She rolled it down and smiled at him.

"Yes, Officer?" she asked.

He hoicked one finger in Moses' direction. "Out," he said. He turned his attention back on Rosa. "Is that your boy?" he asked.

"Yes."

"Well, why do you let him ride in the front with you?" the policeman barked.

She swallowed.

"My missus has been driving for a long time," she heard Moses say. "She's frightened that she will run over an animal. She asked me to ride in the front so that I could spot them. God's truth, *baas*."

Moses had in his voice that perfect tone of humility: He was doing it just right. Rosa, even in her panic, was almost impressed. But she was also saddened: How awful, she thought, that somebody of Moses' caliber would have this as part of his repertoire—

that all black activists must have it, too.

"Is he telling the truth?" the policeman snapped.

"He is," she said in a clipped voice. "He's got good eyesight when he bothers to use it." She was just as bad as Moses, she thought—worse, in fact: While he acted the good servant, for her being a missus was second nature.

The policeman strolled all the way around the car before giving up. He nodded at Rosa. "You can go on your way," he said. "But in future, be careful."

This time when Moses got into the backseat, Rosa did not object. And when she got tired and he took over the driving, it was her turn to sit in the rear. We get more rest that way, she told herself, but still she felt as if a tiny bit of the pleasure of the journey had been taken away from her.

One day turned into the next before they arrived on the outskirts of Cape Town. It was still dark, some hours before daybreak. When Rosa glanced back, she saw that Moses was asleep. He looked so peaceful, while she was dog-tired. She stopped the car and settled down in her seat. Within minutes, she was dreaming.

She woke abruptly with the sun already high in the sky—it was boiling inside the car. She reached into the glove compartment and pulled out the Thermos, but when she opened it, she found that it was empty. She licked her lips, they felt so cracked, and ran a hand through her hair. Moses was still sleeping.

"Now you see why I choose the back," came Moses' voice. "More room to sleep in."

They drove into Cape Town, picked up takeaway coffees and a couple of *koeksisters*, and traveled through the clean opulence of the white city. It was beautiful, Rosa thought, a place built on flower-covered hills, dominated by the majesty of Table Mountain, which stood supreme above them.

But gradually the city began to change. They progressed now through winding alleyways rather than straight tarred streets, past dilapidated houses rather than whitewashed mansions, right into the depths of District 6—an area once mixed, but now proclaimed by the Nats to be suitable for "coloreds" only.

Rosa had to concentrate hard to avoid potholes that were big enough to sink the car, corrugated iron that littered the streets, and dead ends that stank of urine. She found it quite difficult, and driving did nothing to improve her temper: It seemed like forever before Moses, who was navigating, announced that they had arrived. Rosa stopped the car and hooted her horn.

Thomas Johannes appeared almost immediately. He was a man known slightly by both Rosa and Moses—a man who was probably known only slightly by everybody, since he did not appear to like talking at all. He was polite, but only just; he never indulged in chitchat, and he hardly ever smiled. His legendary efficiency, however, made up for all.

He looked at his watch. "On time," he said. He just about cracked a smile, shook their hands limply, and then spoke again. "Start now?" he asked.

"Sure," Moses said. Rosa nodded her agreement.

Thomas stepped into the middle of the street. He walked down it a few paces. Rosa, who was watching with a puzzled expression on her face, noticed a group of people in the distance. They had appeared as if from nowhere, coming through entrances in their dwellings that were cleverly concealed. They looked at the VW but made no attempt to come any closer. They watched, instead, with wary eyes.

"Listen, you people!" Thomas shouted. "We're from Congress. We've come to talk to you. Let's do business. Meeting in ten minutes." He walked back toward the car, climbed in beside Moses, and said, "First left." Rosa obeyed.

"Stop," said Thomas. He got out and repeated himself to the apparently empty neighborhood.

But it was not empty. As she became accustomed to her surroundings, Rosa began to notice doors opening, men and women emerging in two's and three's and walking toward a rough piece of ground that served as a rudimentary playing field. By the end of ten minutes a small crowd had gathered.

"Ready," Thomas said. He looked at Moses. "You talk."

Without further ado, Moses got out the traveling table from the back of the car, set it up along with a shooting stick that served as a chair, and gestured Rosa to it. Then he walked to the front of the crowd.

He held up his hand, and there was silence. "Friends," he started, "I thank you for coming to our meeting." He paused and looked around him. "But that is not correct," he said, "for this is not our meeting, but yours. All over the country similar gatherings are taking place: Our organizations have joined hands to call elected representatives to the Congress of the People. At this congress a Freedom Charter will be adopted, and it is for this reason that we have called you together. We want you, and all the peoples of South Africa, black and white, to draw up this charter. We want you to speak of freedom."

From his pocket he withdrew a well-worn document, and he began to read.

"We call the farmers of the reserves and trust lands," he started. "Let us speak of the wide land, and the narrow strips on which we toil. Let us speak of brothers without land, and of children without schooling. Let us speak of taxes and of cattle and of famine. Let us speak of freedom." He paused and looked around before resuming. "We call the miners of coal, gold, and diamonds," he continued. "Let us speak of the dark shafts and the cold compounds far from our families. Let us speak of heavy labor and long hours, and of men sent home to die. Let us speak of rich masters and poor wages. Let us speak of freedom. . . ."

Moses' voice rang out into the clear air, and Rosa was not the only one who could not take her eyes from him. He mesmerized them all as he read on, through the call to the congress. They stayed silent as he went through every section of South African life, through workers of farms and forests, of factories and shops, through students, teachers, preachers, housewives, and mothers. And after each group, after he had given examples of subjects to be covered, he ended with one sentence: "Let us speak of freedom."

When he had finished reading, he put the paper away. He looked straight at his audience. "Let us speak then," he said. And the silence cracked: They shouted, they laughed, they called out their complaints, their solutions, their wishes. When Moses asked those who wanted to list a demand to go to Rosa's table, there was a sudden rush.

Within minutes, she was inundated. "We want our voting rights back!" people shouted at her: She wrote it down. "We want jobs," they said: She wrote it down. "We want to end police raids," they called: She wrote it down. "We want to kill all whites"—this, too, she wrote down.

Their anger was, after all, understandable. For years they had been powerless to prevent the quality of their lives from deteriorating. As Cape coloreds, they had retained the right to vote long after Africans and Indians had been deprived of it. And then the Nats got in and just stole it away from them. There was nothing they could do about it.

Now, at last somebody was asking what they thought of this: what it was that they wanted. From every mouth came a demand, a wish, a hope for a better way of living. Rosa kept writing until she got a cramp. This charter, she thought as she shook her hands to get the feeling back into them, would mean something. It would live on into the future.

"It's great," Rosa told Jacob. "It's always tiring, often aggravating, and sometimes disturbing, but it's great. You know, that time in Cape Town I was in such a bad mood—dirty and exhausted—that the last thing I wanted to do was to go to a meeting, and yet the meeting itself gave me so much energy that Moses had to hold me back afterward."

Did he indeed? Jacob thought. "How is Moses?" he asked.

She threw him a dazzler of a smile. "He's well," she said. "And it's been good to spend protracted time with him. We seemed to have lost touch in the last few years." She picked a peach from the fruit bowl and began to peel it. "How are you?" she asked, as her knife sliced at the skin.

So finally she asks, Jacob thought. "I'm fine," he said loudly. "I'm—"

"Mummy," came a cry.

Rosa dropped the peach and sprang to her feet. "I'll go and see to her," she said. She was halfway out the door before she seemed to register the expression on Jacob's face—an angry glowering, it was. She turned and stopped, and on her face was confusion. "You don't mind, do you?" she asked.

With an effort, he smiled. "Go ahead," he said. "Of course I don't mind."

He used the time while she was out of the room to speak sternly to himself. He was being ridiculous, he knew he was—feeling jealous of his own child. Of course Rosa would need to spend a lot of time with her. Although Martha had been fine while her mother was away, she was acting up a bit since her return. And even if he felt critical at the way Rosa gave in to Martha's every whim, he could sympathize. She was trying to make up for her absence, trying too hard, perhaps, but the effort was perfectly well motivated.

He was imagining everything else—imagining that something

had gone on between her and Moses, and that she was using Martha as an excuse to keep her distance from him.

"I won't let my paranoia affect me," he said.

When she returned, a good half hour later, he had cleared the table, turned the lights down low, and opened a bottle of wine that he had stuck in an ice bucket. He raised it questioningly at Rosa. She nodded, so he poured her a glass, which he took over to her.

"You must be tired," he said. "Come and sit on the sofa."

She shot him a grateful smile and did as he suggested. He followed her to the sofa and sat beside her.

"When do you plan to go again?" he asked casually.

"Couple of months," she said. "I don't want to leave Martha too soon, and anyway there's a lot of collating to be done."

The smile vanished from Jacob's face. She doesn't want to leave Martha, he thought. Nothing to do with me. But then he remembered his earlier resolution, and he forced himself to relax. He put his arm on the back of the sofa and took another sip of wine.

"It's good to be together again," he said softly.

"Mmm."

He moved his arm around her shoulder.

She froze. She didn't know why that happened, but as soon as she felt him touch her, she went rigid. It was a physical shrinking that she experienced, an urge to move away. She had been so enjoying sitting beside him companionably, feeling the pleasure of being clean, of wearing ironed clothes, of relaxing without having to move on. But as soon as he touched her, she felt tense again, on her guard, defensive.

Not that she had anything much to defend. For when Jacob sensed her tension, he took his hand away as if it had been burned. He did not say anything. Neither did she. Instead, they sat side by side, each lost in private thoughts.

Finally Jacob got to his feet. "I'm going to bed," he said.

"I'll join you in a minute," she replied.

26

JACOB SAW MOSES WALKING UP THE DRIVE, AND HE WENT TO MEET him halfway. The two men shook hands and smiled at each other.

"She's just giving Martha a final kiss," Jacob said. "Only the forty-seventh of today."

"Does Martha object to her going?" Moses asked.

Jacob shrugged. "She hates the thought," he said. "And it is hard to say good-bye. On the other hand, Julia spoils her to bits while Rosa's away, and Rosa returns guilty enough to do likewise, so she gets the best of both worlds, really."

Moses nodded absentmindedly. He heard what Jacob was saying, but he was thinking of something else: of his own family, and the way Peggy had turned her cheek to him when he left, expecting a routine kiss to be planted there, expecting to receive, although Moses knew she had no intention of offering him even so much as a smile in response. When that happened, he'd been seized by anger and he'd circled around her—avoiding her cheek as if it were diseased.

And now, as he listened to the squeals of childish delight issuing from the house, he felt a pang of regret. He realized something that he usually avoided, that in his war with Peggy the children were also affected. He remembered Lindiwe's face as he had left the house: that pert, pretty child trying to hide her disappointment and her misery. He sighed.

"So that's how you feel about taking my wife away again," Jacob joked. "I don't know whether to be angry on her behalf or relieved on mine."

Moses laughed and put an arm around Jacob's shoulder. "Your Rosa's a force of her own," he said. "She works me into the ground, that one. Now tell me—how's the collating of the demands going?"

Jacob raised his eyes to heaven. "It's unbelievable," he said. "The amount of work involved. But it's inspiring as well. You wouldn't believe some of the things people say—how poetic it is—and this from men and women who hardly graduated from primary school, whose handwriting is only half-formed."

"*Ja*," Moses replied. "Whatever else this charter achieves, it will have taught us professional activists humility."

Just then Rosa emerged. She sort of stumbled out the door, and when she had finally managed to negotiate the whole of it, Moses saw why: Martha was holding so tightly to her legs that as she walked, she moved the child along with her. She did not seem too concerned: She waved at Moses and progressed awkwardly to the car, where she waited for the men to join her.

"One more kiss," she told Martha.

Martha jumped at Rosa and wrapped her arms around her neck. She squeezed with a desperation that verged on panic. Rosa was finding it impossible to detach her. Only when Jacob physically peeled her off did she let go.

But she did not give up. "Mummy!" she cried, and stretched her arms out.

Rosa looked in panic at Jacob.

"Go on," he said.

She jumped into the car and slammed the door shut.

Jacob saw tears welling up in her eyes. "She'll be all right as soon as you've turned the corner," he said. He bent down and kissed her through the open window. "Look after her," he told Moses, who had got into the back. Then he stood to one side and watched as the VW reversed quickly down the driveway.

Once out of sight, Rosa stopped the car to wipe her eyes. "I'll be okay in a minute," she said. She laughed as if to illustrate her words, and then started up again.

"Jacob's a good man," was Moses' only comment.

Her eyes met his in the mirror, and she nodded.

Moses and Rosa needed to readjust. They were nervous with each other, tentative in their conversation, careful to defer to each other about when to stop, what to eat, which route to take.

As the trip progressed, their unease with each other disappeared, and a kind of teasing jocularity took over. They were friends, thought Rosa happily, real friends.

Not that things were always easy. They were traveling in the countryside, avoiding the main cities this time. People's response to the charter was little different. In fact, their welcome was sometimes even more enthusiastic, but Rosa began to realize how in Jo'burg she'd been cushioned from the mores of everyday South Africa.

She'd had a protected upbringing, she now realized. Of course, she'd been different from conventional white society, but that hadn't mattered so much because there'd been enough people like her or her parents to cushion her from white disapproval. But here, out in the middle of nowhere, she had none of that protection. People—white people, that was—stared at her and Moses with undisguised hostility. The hostility was political, although only political in a racist context: for the objection was not against the Freedom Charter *per se* (of which they probably knew nothing) but instead about a black man and a white woman traveling together.

Even though they now sat separately in the car as a matter of course (and she never got used to this), she still felt as though these country folk could see right through her, that they knew that she was different and that they hated her for it.

When she'd asked Moses about it, about how it made him feel, he'd shrugged the question away. "You get used to it," was all he said.

But Rosa could not get used to it, because she found that she was experiencing a secondary difficulty: She didn't like being hated, she didn't like being excluded. It made her feel awful to think that way. After all, the majority of the country were daily excluded, but that did not mean she could rid herself of a feeling of disturbance, of being in the wrong.

She frowned and tossed her head as if to push the thought away.

Moses misunderstood the gesture. "There's a roadhouse coming up now," he said.

She saw that he was right, and she realized that she was feeling thirsty. She wouldn't mind going to the toilet, either, which was peculiar, since that made it the fifth time in an hour.

"The things you think about when you're on the road," she said to Moses.

She slowed down and maneuvered the car off the dust track and into the small parking area. She got out, and so did Moses, and they stood side by side, stretching the weariness from their limbs.

"I'll wait here," Moses said eventually, and he leaned against the car.

She nodded and walked to the building.

It was a small establishment, the kind that dotted the country roads, with battered Formica counters, a few tarnished chrome tables and chairs, and an all-male clientele. When Rosa entered, she saw that in one corner sat a weedy-looking youth, his tin wireless beside him. Opposite him were two older-looking men, hunched over a desultory game of cards. Three other men sat by the bar counter. They heard her footsteps and swiveled their chairs around to face her.

Rosa drew her cardigan around her. She shivered. The day was cold—in these regions, when the sun disappeared behind a cloud, one could feel the chill seeping into one's bones—but she knew that what she experienced was not the effect of the air temperature, but rather the frigidity of the reception.

All conversation in the place ceased: The only sound was the reedy trill of Boeremusic emanating from the youth's radio. It was altogether a strange experience, like being trapped in an aging photograph, the brown edges defined by the dryness of the earth outside. Except that this picture had menace contained within it, and the knowledge that its occupants did not take kindly to strangers.

Well, she would not allow them to intimidate her. She chose a table isolated from the other clientele, and sat down at it.

A potbellied man whose stomach was covered by a grimy apron pushed up the flap of the bar counter and walked over to her.

"What do you want?"

"Beer, please," she said.

"No beer." There was violence in the way he spoke.

She regretted asking. They must have known that she was buying for Moses, and that was against the law. What the hell's the matter with me today? she thought. "Coffee, then," she suggested to the man.

"No coffee."

"What do you have?" she asked.

"Cool drinks or milkshakes."

"A Pepsi, then," she said.

"No Pepsi. Only cola."

"I'll have a milkshake," Rosa said. "And two colas to take away. Could I use your toilet while you're getting them?"

"No facilities for women," the barman said over his shoulder as he returned to the bar.

The drink, when it eventually emerged, was sickly sweet. Rosa took one sip, and then, when nausea rose to her throat, she hurriedly rejected it. It was completely artificial both in taste and in texture. She wondered at the foolishness of it all. In this land abundant with ripe fruits—with guava, kumquats, papaws, mangoes, and a score of other varieties that hung rotting from the trees—it was almost impossible to buy something fresh to eat.

She got up and walked to the counter. She placed a few shillings on it and then reached for the colas.

"What's the matter?" one of the men at the bar said. "You haven't finished your drink."

"She wouldn't, would she?" the person next to him chipped in. "Not her. She only drinks Hottentot muck."

Rosa backed away. In so doing, she bumped into the table where the youth was seated.

"*Hoer*," he said. He got up abruptly and took one step toward her.

She didn't stop to think: She ran from that place. And then a funny thing happened, for the faster her body moved, the slower her thoughts became. She had time to reassure herself that they were not following, to worry again because she was spilling the drinks, to register the pounding of footsteps behind her, and to see the shock in Moses' eye and the urgency in his mouth, when somebody grabbed her from behind.

"*Kaffir*-lover," hissed a voice. "*Kak. Jy gaan vrek.*"

Desperately she looked at Moses.

And saw him turn away from her.

She had no time to hate him. She ripped instead at the buttons of her cardigan and then pushed her arms apart while she tore it from her shoulders. She didn't know where she got the strength from, but she managed to wrench herself out of her cardigan and thus free herself of the man. Leaving him holding her garment, she began to run.

"Get her," she heard. "Get the English whore."

A car came straight toward her, its door flapping open. I'm

lost, she thought, as she tried to veer away from it. They're going to kill me.

"Rosa!"

It was Moses' voice, she realized. It was her car, as well, and he was driving it, urging her to get inside. She launched herself at it and grabbed the passing handle. When the car kept moving, her arm was nearly wrenched from its socket.

"Hold on," Moses shouted.

"I can't." she screamed. "I can't."

"You can do it," said his voice. "Hold on. You can do it."

Turning the wheel, he reached across and grabbed hold of her and gripped her tightly. Inch by inch, he pulled her in.

"Close the door," he muttered.

She did as she was bid. Slamming it with effort, crying in rage, frustration, and fear.

And Moses drove like the devil himself. He drove straight down the dusty road, his teeth gritted, his eyes ablaze, his hands steady. They were followed for a while; a pickup truck tried to come up behind them, but Moses was inspired. He lengthened the distance between them and their pursuer. He drove until the truck was nothing but a dot in the distance; he drove even after the truck had disappeared.

And only after many miles did he stop. He pulled up abruptly by the side of the road, under a tree, and he turned to Rosa.

"Are you all right?" he asked.

Rosa did not reply. Instead, she got out of the car, walked a few steps, and was suddenly sick.

Moses came up behind her. "Are you all right?" he repeated.

She turned and nodded. And nodded again. And before she knew it, she found that she could not stop nodding. But when Moses put his arms around her, the nodding did change course—it turned into a shiver. She felt his warmth about her, but she was freezing cold. She snuggled into his embrace and trembled.

They stood like that for some time, until Moses sensed that Rosa had calmed. He moved away from her a fraction and smiled at her. They looked into each other's eyes.

Suddenly the memory of what had just happened boomeranged on her. She gripped at his arms and pulled at him, desperately, searchingly. She didn't know what she was doing, she acted by instinct—out of the blue, it seemed then; out of a blue that stretched back to her childhood. She kissed him full on the lips.

She had made the first move, but he was not slow to respond. His lips touched hers, and they did not give way. They moved with hers, they responded, and they made their own initiatives.

For what seemed like an age, they were locked in the embrace.

When they finally separated, it was a smooth action, achieved mutually. They stood and looked at each other, and neither saw embarrassment in the other's face.

Moses broke the silence. "We've been wanting to do that for a long, long time," he said.

She nodded.

"I'm glad we've cleared it out of the way," he continued.

She did not take offense, for she knew exactly what he meant.

There had been affection in their kiss, and a kind of hunger, too, but they both knew that it would never lead to anything more serious, because they would never want it to. Or, she corrected to herself, because to do so would be to break a taboo—like sleeping with your brother, except in this case her brother was black.

These thoughts she kept to herself. "I'm dying of hunger," she said.

He laughed. "Pregnant women are insatiable," he commented.

She was astonished. "How do you know?" she asked. She herself had only begun to suspect it.

He shrugged, and putting his arm around her, he propelled her to the car. "Something to do with the frequency with which you vomit," he said. "And as for the number of times you stop to pee . . ."

Rosa was now sure: She was pregnant, and her only thought was, Thank God Jacob doesn't know yet. He would never have let me come with Moses.

Moses climbed into the driver's seat and waited for her to get into the back. When she did so, he started the car. But before he could drive off, she touched him lightly. He turned and looked at her.

"Thanks for saving me back there," she said.

"Did you think I wouldn't?"

"Not really," she replied. "But thanks anyway."

He nodded and drove back onto the road, this time at a more

leisurely pace. She stared out the window at the flat, dry land around them, and she felt a kind of peace descend on her. In silence they progressed until she spoke again. "Tell me about Peggy," she said.

They headed back three weeks later. Rosa dropped Moses off and drove straight home.

Since they'd kept in constant telephone contact, Jacob knew exactly when she was due back, but when she stepped out of her car, exactly on schedule, he wasn't there. Not that it mattered initially, for Martha came bouncing out of the house, and in the following three hours Rosa did nothing but pay attention to her—occasionally answering one of Julia's many questions.

But after her mother went home and she had put the child to bed, Rosa began to grow angry. Julia had mentioned that Jacob would be late—but not this late. He had done it on purpose, she knew that he had. She remembered the first time she'd returned and how touchy he had been then: He was obviously planning for a rerun.

Well, she was too tired to play his game: She would not sit and wait for him, she would ignore his childishness. He didn't deserve anything more: After all, she never acted this way on the many occasions when he arrived home from a trip.

She switched off the living-room lights and walked down the corridor until she arrived at the bathroom. With an angry flick of her wrist, she turned on the hot tap.

"He's just being childish," she muttered to herself.

In fact, as far as Jacob was concerned, he was being nothing of the kind. True, he had deliberately not come home early, but he'd done so with what he thought was only the best of intentions.

He'd also remembered how he'd behaved on Rosa's first return, and he'd resolved this time to act differently. To this purpose, he decided to allow Martha and Rosa some time alone before he entered the picture. So instead of canceling his afternoon surgery, or asking a colleague to fill in for him, he had sat it out.

What he hadn't foreseen was that the session was overbooked and, in addition, full of patients who needed more than his usual attention. That, combined with two genuine emergencies, served to make him extremely late.

Nevertheless, he was taken aback to find the house in almost total darkness. He knew she'd arrived because her car was parked in his usual slot. He glanced at his watch: It was only nine. She must be very tired, he thought, but his momentary generosity was soon replaced by a feeling of pique. No matter how tired she was, she might have bothered to wait up for him.

He scowled and made his way down the corridor. "Rosa," he called.

She did not deign to reply, but he knew where she was because he saw a shaft of light coming from under the bathroom door. He opened it and went inside.

She was still in the bath, only her head visible, the rest covered by luxurious bubbles. As soon as she turned around and gazed at him with startled eyes, his anger evaporated. He felt such a relief that she was home and such a love for her. He went and kissed her on the head.

"Sorry I'm back so late," he said. "Somebody's ulcer chose seven o'clock to start bleeding." He sat on the side of the bath and smiled at her. "How was it?" he asked.

Rosa tried to return his smile, but hers came out somewhat crooked. She didn't really know why: All she knew was that, contrary to her expectation, she wasn't delighted to see him. Whereas before, she'd been cursing him for his absence, now she wished that he had taken longer. I need to be alone, she thought.

She felt embarrassed lying there naked in the bath, and she was grateful for the covering of foam. He didn't know, she remembered, about her pregnancy.

"How about getting us both a drink?" she said.

When he smiled again and left, she took a deep breath. "I won't tell him now," she muttered to herself. "I'll wait a few days." Having made that decision, she jumped out of the bath and reached for a towel.

Jacob, who'd forgotten to ask whether she wanted ice and lemon, walked back in. She pulled the towel around her, but too late, she thought: His mouth opened wide, and she knew that he knew.

"Yes, okay," she said. "So I'm pregnant."

Jacob shut his mouth, opened it again, and then shut it. He was at a loss for words, but Rosa was in fact wrong: He hadn't seen that she was pregnant (it was still barely noticeable). Instead, he'd opened his mouth in astonishment because he'd been taken aback by the sight of her body. She's so beautiful, was all that he'd been thinking.

And pregnant as well! He took a step toward her.

She backed away. She glared at him. "Aren't you going to say something?"

He frowned. "I'm delighted," he said quietly. "Unless . . ."

"Oh, don't worry," she said. "It's yours all right."

The thought that it might not be his had never entered his head, and he wondered why she'd said that. But he pushed his puzzlement to the back of his mind. She was just tired, he thought. He'd ignore it. She was overwrought, and no wonder. Women got very fatigued in their first months of pregnancy. Running around the countryside must have taken it out of her.

"I'll get the drinks," was all he said.

He did not need to bring them to the bathroom, because Rosa came out while he was still preparing them. She was wearing a toweling robe, and she had a turban on her head and a smile on her face.

"Sorry to be so scratchy," she said.

He returned her smile as he handed her a glass. "You must be tired."

She nodded, took one long sip, and went to stand by the French doors.

"I'm pleased." His voice was low. "About the baby."

She turned. "So am I," she whispered.

He walked over to her and hugged her gently. "I've missed you so much," he said.

She felt so safe inside his arms, so warm and safe. It would be good to give up and rest forever there, she thought, and she moved a little closer.

"It'll be great to have you back," he said.

Abruptly she pulled away from him. "What do you mean?"

He frowned, but he withstood her glare without blanching. "I mean what I said: that it's great to have you back."

"You didn't say that," she answered between gritted teeth. "You said it would be great to have me back."

"What's the difference?"

"Don't pretend you don't know," she said. "You think I'm not going to be a volunteer anymore."

"Well, are you?" he asked. "Are you up to it?"

"And I suppose you mean back in the kitchen," she continued. "Or back with the nappies."

He laughed nastily. "That's hardly been your forte," he said. "Look at the way you left Martha." It was a low blow, but he no longer cared. She had gone too far.

"You bastard," she hissed. "You've got a nurse in your consulting room, a receptionist in your waiting room, and now you want a pregnant wife in your home."

How can she think that of me? he thought. How dare she? "You're just like your bloody mother!" he shouted. "She's also always wingeing on about how she's left out of this and of that."

"And has it ever occurred to you that she could be speaking the truth?" Rosa replied. "You've always blamed her: You never gave her the benefit of the doubt." Neither did I, she thought.

She pushed the thought away. "You bloody men don't understand anything," she shouted. "It's all so easy for you."

She glared at him. "I'm going to bed," she said. She left the room, slamming the door behind her.

She ran down the corridor, threw open the bedroom door, and then propelled herself onto the bed. She began to cry, and she found that she couldn't stop herself. The tears streamed down, regardless. She muffled her head in the pillow, but it was soon completely wet.

She wept because she realized something she'd never previously dared acknowledge. Her own personal freedom had meant as much to her as the fight for political freedom.

It all revolved around the past, and around the present, too. It had happened because she had been changed by motherhood, changed in ways so subtle that she hadn't needed to consciously register them. She'd been softened and sedated: matured and made passive. She'd been turned into something other than herself.

Only when she drove for miles with Moses, when she addressed a meeting, when she endured fatigue and hunger, did her old self start to return. Only then did she realize what it was she'd been missing.

But now there was another baby on the way. She would once more be facing its insatiable demands, living according to its needs and its time schedules. She wanted more than one child, but she didn't know whether she could countenance another step back: She liked that old self too much. She wasn't ready to lose it again. The tears continued to fall.

"Rosa?" Jacob was standing by the bed.

She smiled at him as she wiped her face. "I know I'm being difficult," she said.

"I haven't understood," Jacob said. "But I do want to understand: Please help me to."

She looked at him. "Can you imagine," she started, "how it feels to fit work around child care?"

He frowned. "But you don't have to work," he said. "I earn enough for both of us."

She was suddenly furious. "Don't you understand anything?" she asked. "I want to work. *Want* to."

She saw a look of pain cross his face, and she was immediately repentant. "I didn't mean to shout," she said. "It's just so difficult to explain what it feels like to pull yourself in two—to want to be with Martha and to want to both work and be active. I don't know how to tell you how it feels."

"It's all right," he answered. "I know I'm being dumb. I never thought about it, and it's been wrong of me. I should have."

This time when she cried, he held her close, and she did not push him away.

27

"GOOD AFTERNOON, MRS. BOPAPE."

Peggy looked through the line of washing in front of her. She saw James Thibusi standing hesitantly outside the gate.

"Come in, come in," she said.

James pushed the gate open and stepped inside the yard. He stood shyly there, as he fingered the felt rim of his hat against his well-pressed brown suit.

"Your husband is not home?" he asked.

"No," Peggy said. "Come take a seat while I fetch you a drink. The day is hot."

"*Ja*," James agreed as he walked hesitantly toward the table that stood under a wilting vine. "And it's true I'm thirsty."

When Peggy returned, James had placed his hat on the table and was sitting down. He rose at the sight of her. She gestured him to reseat himself as she poured him a drink.

"I'm sorry it is not cold," she said.

"It is of no concern," James replied. He lifted the mug to his lips and drained it. "Ah, that's better," he said.

There was a short silence while Peggy refilled his glass. James took one small sip and then looked at her. "It doesn't worry me that there's no ice," he said. "But what about the children? Doesn't their food go bad?"

Peggy shrugged. "What meat we have I buy daily," she said.

"But still," James said. "A refrigerator saves time and money. I'll tell you what: I know that my brother's about to buy a new one. I'll see if I can get you the old."

"Don't trouble yourself on my account."

"No trouble," James said. He reached into his jacket pocket

and drew out a small parcel wrapped in newspaper and tied with string. "This is for you," he said.

Peggy blushed. She didn't know where to look. She felt as though she'd already compromised herself, for this was not the first time that James had come around with a gift. In fact, she realized, during his sporadic visits he always produced something. In the beginning his offerings were innocuous enough— some bread baked by his mother, a piece of meat from his brother's butchery, a trinket for Lindiwe—but lately they had become more personal.

She ought to refuse it, she knew that she ought: She should tell him to desist. After all, she was a married woman, a mother of two.

And yet, came a counter voice, his behavior was always scrupulously correct. He never imposed for long, and he never failed to ask after Moses. And after all, it wasn't often that she was given something. Her fingers itched to open it.

She couldn't resist. "Thank you," she said. She undid the string and placed it neatly in front of her. Then she peeled off the newspaper.

She looked at the delicate china shepherdess in front of her, and she felt like crying. She turned it around, noticing how the light shone through it. "It's beautiful," she whispered.

"My neighbor was about to throw it on the rubbish heap," James said. "It never occurs to some people that others have needs. Not like your husband."

Reluctantly Peggy placed the shepherdess on the table. "Yes, Moses thinks of others," she agreed.

"And what is he working on now?"

"The Freedom Charter," Peggy said brusquely.

"I suppose things are going well?"

"I suppose so." Peggy pursed her lips. It was just like Moses to embarrass her, even in his absence. She couldn't shame herself by admitting that she knew little of her husband's activities: that he told her nothing.

James sensed the change in her mood. He got up and put his hat on his head. "I must be on my way," he said. "I will drop in another day."

"Is that them again?" Jacob asked.

Rosa clasped her belly and twisted around so that she could

see through the back windshield of their large Citroen. She peered beyond the bright headlights of the car behind them. She could just make out the forms of the two men sitting in the front seat of the Ford.

She swiveled back again. "It's them," she confirmed.

"What do you think?" Jacob asked. "Shall we risk it?"

It was a purely rhetorical question. Both knew that they couldn't, not this time.

On any normal night they would have ignored the escort, but this time it was different. They were on their way to a special meeting, and they couldn't afford to drag the security forces of Special Branch in their wake.

They were going to a Party cell, a gathering of the reconstituted organization that was forced to operate in conditions of absolute secrecy. Tonight was to be a strategy session, with some of the newest recruits present.

And therein lay the danger. The Swieces and others were already labeled: Their names were on lists confiscated in the days before the Party was banned. If they were raided, the fact that they were old friends would be a perfect excuse for the gathering. They had learned from experience: There would be no incrim--inating documents for the police to confiscate.

But with new members things were different. Their identities were rigorously protected. They could not be exposed: not when even suspicion of association with the party would mean summary imprisonment.

"We can't go," Rosa confirmed. "It's too risky."

"Hell," Jacob said. "I was looking forward to it. So what's next?"

"Home?" Rosa suggested. "We could give the Special Branch an early night."

But Jacob shook his head. "What say we pay a visit to your folks?" he asked. "We haven't seen them in ages."

"Okay," Rosa agreed. "Mom phoned the other day. You know her—she doesn't apply obvious pressure, but she did happen to mention three times that it's been a long time since she saw us."

The Arnolds' house was at the end of the drive, concealed from the road by a circle of maples. After he had stopped the car in the shaded parking area, Jacob sounded his horn.

A light was clicked on, illuminating the porch area with its overhanging luxuriance of bougainvillea. The front door opened. In the shaft of brightness that poured from the house, they could see Harold peering warily out.

"It's okay, Dad, it's us," Rosa called.

Harold beamed, and hurrying over to the car, he opened Rosa's door, helped her out, and hugged her.

Rosa surrendered herself to his embrace. He's such a rock, my father, she thought. And he's improving with age.

Harold did in fact look younger than his sixty years. His gray hair gave dignity to his kind face, and a passion for golf ensured that he was physically fit. His face was heavily lined in a friendly, rather than a worried, manner. He was a man universally liked, universally appreciated: a quiet man whose presence was welcomed everywhere.

He looked down the drive to the place where the now-darkened Ford lurked.

"Still the same?" he asked.

Rosa nodded.

"God, they're persistent." Harold tucked his arm into hers. "If their reaction is anything to go by, the Congress of the People can be already considered a resounding success. Have you heard that they've started serving people with banning orders, so as to stop them from going?"

Rosa nodded. "Max got one the other day."

Harold nodded, and together they strolled toward the front door. "Do me a favor," Harold suddenly said in a low voice. "Don't mention the police inside: You know how it would make Nicholas feel."

Rosa stopped abruptly. "Nicholas is here?"

"Yes—and Jane of course." Harold patted Rosa gently on the arm. "Come on in," he urged. "They'll have guessed it's you. They'll be insulted if you go away."

Rosa, with Jacob behind her, allowed herself to be led into the house. They went to the dining room, a large formal area with a huge oval table, a set of twelve straight-backed chairs, and a huge polished sideboard that had once belonged to Julia's mother.

Rosa nodded at her brother. She pecked her sister-in-law on both cheeks before sitting down. She watched as Nicholas rose to shake Jacob's hand.

They were so different, those two men. Their clothes pointed to the different worlds they inhabited. Jacob was dressed casually in white baggy trousers and a matching open-collar shirt whose sleeves were pulled up to the elbow. In contrast, Nicholas might just have stepped out of a boardroom meeting. He was wearing a gray suit with a formal double-breasted jacket, a striped blue shirt, and a gray tie. Diamond cuff links glittered against his even tan.

"I was going to give you a call," Nicholas told Jacob. "Some of my executives need a checkup, and they're dissatisfied with their current man. I thought I could send the business your way."

"Sure," Jacob said.

An uncomfortable silence ensued, broken only by the clinking of cutlery against china as Julia served them from the wooden trolley that stood beside her.

"Tell me . . ." Jane began, as simultaneously Jacob chipped in with a "You know . . ." The two stopped and smiled at each other.

"After you," Jacob said.

Jane giggled. She turned to Rosa. "Remind me when your baby's due," she said.

"Middle of August."

"You must be getting excited," Jane said.

"Sort of," Rosa replied. "But I'm not as obsessed with this pregnancy as with the first. And there's so much else to occupy my mind."

"The Congress of the People, she means," Julia explained.

Nicholas sighed.

"Is everything under control?" Julia asked.

Nicholas sighed again.

Rosa couldn't stand it any longer. She turned to her brother. "Tell me, Nicholas," she said sweetly. "What do you think about the Freedom Charter?"

Oh, God, Jacob thought. Here we go again.

Nicholas shrugged his well-padded shoulders. "It's okay if you like that kind of thing," he said.

"And what kind of thing is that?"

"A gesture," Nicholas replied. "A piece of showmanship. A flash in the pan that will attract publicity."

"It certainly has all those elements," Harold agreed. "But there's nothing wrong with that, surely?"

Nicholas leaned back in his chair and smiled. "Suppose not," he said briefly. He picked up his cup and pulled it to his lips.

"So what would you suggest instead?" Rosa asked, the sweetness replaced by ill-concealed hostility.

Ding, ding, round two, thought Jacob.

Nicholas put his cup back down. "I know you despise my way of operating," he began.

"Darling, nobody despises you," Julia said.

Nicholas ignored her. His eyes were still on Rosa. "I don't like apartheid any more than you do," he said. "You always make the mistake of thinking that anybody who doesn't agree entirely with you is an enemy. But I'm not a Nat supporter, and neither is Jane, or any of our friends, for that matter."

"Yeah, but then you've got the best of both worlds, haven't you?" Rosa asked. "You don't like what's going on, but you do nothing to stop it, and so you enjoy one of the best standards of living possible—a standard of living that is a direct result of the exploitation of others—and at the same time you manage to keep your conscience clean."

Nicholas flushed. "You're talking off the top of your head," he said. "I pay my workers bloody well. I treat them well, too. And they appreciate it."

"Oh, God, Nicholas," Rosa sneered. "Your benevolence astonishes me. I don't know how your pocket can bear the strain of two homes, three motorcars, four servants, and so much philanthropy."

Round three begins here, thought Jacob. And the gloves are off.

But Nicholas controlled himself. He waited until he was sure that Rosa had finished, and when he spoke, his voice was entirely reasonable. "I'm not putting down what you do," he said. "But you've got to face the fact that you're on the margins."

"Whereas you, of course, are at the center of things," Rosa snapped.

"I know you work hard for a cause in which you believe," Nicholas replied. "I respect you for that. But people like me are more at the center, and that's a fact you'll one day have to face. We have influence, and because we sound reasonable we have more sway." He smiled and visibly relaxed. "Look," he said, "I don't for a moment doubt your motives. It's just that I'm not sure that your tactics will lead you anywhere other than to increasing isolation. People are scared of you, and as the Nats clamp down on you they're going to get more scared. Whereas I believe in working within the system, in changing things at the center, not just worrying at the periphery."

"A lot of good your so-called working in the system has done anybody but yourself," Rosa said. "Open your eyes, won't you? I mean, at least we've been part of the Defiance Campaign, at least we helped organize the Freedom Charter. And what exactly is it that you've done?"

"Uh-uh," Jacob said softly, as he saw Nicholas's fist clench.

"Oh, Rosa, you're so fucking smug," Nicholas snapped. "You don't understand anything, so what gives you the right to lecture others?" He shrugged off Jane's restraining hand and glared at his sister. "It's you who needs to open your eyes, you and your precious banned Party. You say that we should all reject the Nats in favor of communism, but don't you know what Stalin's been doing? You must have heard about it, unless, of course, you're too busy to read the headlines."

That sentence, that sentiment, was Nicholas's mistake. For while he and Rosa argued about South Africa, their parents would not interfere. No matter how much they agreed with Rosa, they wouldn't side with her, because they would see that as being unfair to their son.

Once Nicholas attacked their Party, then that was different. They sprang to its defense.

"The papers," Julia scoffed. "How can anybody believe anything they write?"

"There are witnesses," Nicholas said, "who've managed to escape the terror."

"White Russians. Traitors to the Revolution, the lot of them," Julia said.

As Nicholas's face showed that he was framing a suitable retort, Harold intervened. "Our Party is a separate organization," he said.

"Tell us another," Nicholas interjected.

Harold ignored him. "Whatever is happening in the Soviet Union—and mind you, there is no proof of the allegations—does not undermine our struggle. We have right on our side."

Rosa, pushed to the sidelines by her parents' passion, stopped concentrating. The irony of it all, she thought, was that on this issue, she couldn't help secretly agreeing with Nicholas. Stalin had gone off the rails: They had all heard the rumors of mass trials and secret imprisonments and the echoes of state-sanctioned murder. And even though the South African Party was a separate organization, what happened in the Soviet Union did affect it. Widespread repression there gave credence to the view that communists were undemocratic, that they wanted to eliminate the opposition.

Still, she was the last person prepared to back up her brother's arguments. "I'm going to see Evelyn," she muttered.

Evelyn was in the kitchen, bending over a newspaper with her glasses perched perilously on her nose. She smiled at Rosa.

"I heard you arrive, but I wasn't expecting you so soon," she said. "You didn't last long."

Rosa drew up a stool and perched herself on it. "They're discussing the Soviet Union," she said. "I'll leave the rest to your imagination."

Evelyn sighed as she folded her newspaper. "It is a pity when people cling to hopes rather than facts," she said. "But understandable."

Rosa shook her head. "Well, I don't understand why my parents have to pretend to be blind."

"I think it's because they feel that the world is against them," Evelyn replied. "And the Revolution in Russia brought them so much hope. To reject it now would be like rejecting their own child."

"Well, it won't do any of us any good," Rosa said. "We are made to appear stupid. It gives the people like Nicholas an ax to grind."

"Ag, you and Nicholas," Evelyn said. "It was the same when you were children. Always fighting for your mother's attention." She paused and glanced at Rosa. "It's a battle that you won, you know," she said.

Rosa smiled. "Only because I got involved in politics. Nicholas could have chosen that, too."

"It's harder for a boy."

"*Ja*, well I can't feel sorry for Nicholas. He's made his bed, and a very comfortable one it is, too, even if he does have to share it with that weakling of a wife," Rosa said. She hurried to her next sentence before Evelyn could frame a suitable riposte.

"Julia mentioned you're retiring next year," she said. "What nonsense is this?"

Evelyn removed her glasses and placed them down on the counter. "I am no longer young," she said.

A shiver of fear ran down Rosa's spine. She was at a loss to explain it. Of course, she knew that Evelyn was mortal; just like everyone. And yet, she thought, Evelyn is special. She isn't meant to age: She can't retire into obscurity.

"Where will you go?" she asked brightly.

"To Sophiatown," Evelyn replied. "Your parents are generous, and they'll give me a good pension. I could rent somewhere near the children. Peggy needs my help." A look of discomfort crossed her face.

Moses picked up the china shepherdess. He held it up to the light as Peggy had done, marveling at the delicacy of it.

"Where did you get this dainty item?" he asked Peggy. "I really like it."

Peggy smiled. She was pleased that she hadn't given in to her feelings of disloyalty and hidden the statuette. It made her feel good that Moses had noticed it and that he obviously liked it.

"James Thibusi gave it to me," she said, as she watched him in the act of replacing it.

His hand stopped in midair, and it looked as if he might be about to let go.

"Watch out!" she shouted. She took a step toward the table, but then breathed a sigh of relief. The shepherdess was safely down; she need not have panicked. "Sorry . . ." she started to explain, but Moses' voice cut her off.

"James who?" he asked.

"Thibusi," she replied. She frowned.

Moses picked up the shepherdess. He looked at it and then at her. Then he strode over and grabbed her by the wrist.

"Why are you seeing that man?" he asked.

Now that it had surfaced, Peggy didn't know whether to be pleased or angered by Moses' jealousy. She wrestled with two conflicting feelings: Moses, she thought, is absent so much of the time, he has no right to tell me who I may see. And yet, she thought, the violence of his response shows that he still does care.

"He's a friend," she answered noncommittally.

Moses' grip tightened. "A friend," he grunted. "When did you see him?"

Peggy winced. "You're hurting me."

"When?" Moses snapped.

Peggy knew of the reservoirs of anger within Moses. After all, his inner rage had been the first thing she had noticed about him. But until this day, he had never directed his fury at her.

But now he was, and she reacted in an unexpected way: She wasn't so much afraid as indignant. He had no right, no right at all!

"What business is it of yours who I see?" she asked.

Moses let go of her arm. "Everybody knows Thibusi is a spy," he stated.

"A s-s-spy?" It came out in a stutter.

"Ja, man. He's the SB's latest recruit."

"You're making it up."

Moses glowered. "Are you crazy?" he asked. "Where do you think Thibusi gets his money? Have you ever seen him go to work?" Moses raised the china figure above his head. "Where do you think he gets fancy things like this?"

In one smooth movement he hurled the object across the room. It hit the wall with a crash before landing on the floor, smashed into a myriad of small pieces.

Tears sprang into Peggy's eyes: She could do nothing to stem them. She, who had given up weeping some time back, was crying as she hadn't done for years: crying for a pretty trinket.

"James is a gentleman," she sobbed. "Why would he bother to spy on me?"

"Those jackals want everything," Moses replied, "every crumb they can scavenge. The Freedom Charter has got them rattled. They know the congress is going to be held, and they're scared to death of it. Not one of us has been left alone. They follow us, they harass us, they threaten us with prison."

"People come and go in this place," Peggy said. "How am I supposed to guess who is and isn't a spy?"

Moses came to with a start. He had felt so furious at the way Thibusi had insinuated himself into his life that he hadn't stopped to think. And of course Peggy was speaking the truth. How was she to be expected to know that Thibusi was in the pay of the security services?

"I'm sorry," he muttered.

Peggy wiped the tears from her face. "You should have told me," she said dully.

Moses nodded. "I should have. But I didn't want to worry you."

"Worry me!" Peggy said softly. "You don't want to worry me, but you tell me you're being followed. Where will it all end? What is to become of us?"

"I don't know, Peggy," Moses answered. "I just don't know."

"Is it still bad between them?" Rosa asked.

Evelyn nodded. "This country," she said, "does terrible things to our people. If we're not fleeing the police, we're busy destroying each other."

"But Peggy's so weak," Rosa said.

"Weak?" Evelyn looked straight at Rosa. "You try bringing up two children on her budget."

"That's not what I mean," Rosa argued. "What I was trying to say is that Peggy's too passive. Don't you think that she should try and understand how important Moses is to the movement?"

Evelyn narrowed her eyes. "Sometimes, my girl," she said, "you disappoint me. Have you no idea what it's like for women?"

"What do you mean?" Rosa tried to hide the hurt in her voice.

"Come on, Rosa," Evelyn said. "You talk of uniting people, and yet you won't face the different conditions under which we all live. Peggy has to think of the children."

"But I, too, have a child, and soon will have another."

"It's not the same," Evelyn said. "Your Jacob can afford to be tolerant of your notions of equality between the sexes."

"But I've had to struggle for that," Rosa protested. "Peggy doesn't even try. She doesn't want to change."

"No, Rosa," Evelyn said. "However much I love my son, I am not blind. I know that we cannot just blame Peggy: I know that their marriage is breaking up because Moses will not change."

"Neither will she."

Evelyn sighed. "You have been brought up privileged," she said. "There's no reason why you should understand."

It was a reproof harsher than Evelyn had ever delivered, and Rosa was shaken by it. That's twice in one evening, she thought, that I've been told I don't understand.

She didn't say anything, and neither did Evelyn. The subject, it appeared, was closed. Rosa didn't stay much longer. She said good-bye and went to find the others.

"I'm tired," she said abruptly.

If she hadn't still been feeling disturbed by Evelyn's remarks, she would have laughed at the look of relief that crossed Jacob's face.

As the Swieces reached the bottom of the drive, Rosa turned to Jacob.

"Stop a minute," she said.

"Have you forgotten something?"

Rosa did not bother to reply. Instead, she got out of the car and marched over to the Ford, which was waiting by the side of the road. She tapped on the window.

When the surprised driver rolled down his window, Rosa leaned through it.

"We're going home," she said. "Straight home via the usual route."

The two men stared silently ahead. Feeling oddly dissatisfied, Rosa returned to Jacob.

He smiled fondly at her. "Punishing them?" he asked. "That's not like you."

Rosa leaned back in her seat and sighed. "Stupid, I suppose. It's Nicholas," she said. "He always makes me act crazy."

Rosa saw by the look on Jacob's face that he didn't believe her. She closed her eyes against any further inquiry. "They're getting on my nerves," she muttered.

28

"DID YOU HEAR THEY SERVED BEN WITH BANNING ORDERS?" JACOB asked.

Rosa nodded. "Martha was there at the time and came back with lurid stories of policemen climbing through windows. She was terribly excited. Wherever she goes, so, it appears, do the police. I'm sure she's going to grow up thinking life's one big spy comic."

"Well, at least we made it," Jacob said. "We're free—unbanned, the both of us—and the congress is only a few days away."

"Don't count your chickens," Rosa joked. Jacob looked at her. In her seventh month of pregnancy, Rosa was blossoming.

Suddenly there was a rustling of leaves, followed by a muffled curse. Jacob looked to the end of the garden in time to see two shadows detaching themselves from the bushes. He sighed as the men, obviously police, walked over to them.

"Good evening, *meneer*," one said pleasantly enough.

"Quiet here," commented the other.

"*Ja*, nice," agreed the first.

Jacob stood up. "As you can see, we are neither holding a meeting, kissing a person of another race, or breaking the liquor laws. So what do you want?"

For response, the first man handed Jacob a buff envelope.

"Shit," Jacob said. He glared at the men. "You've done your job," he said, "so kindly leave my property."

They did as they were bid. They left behind them a soured atmosphere.

"What was that you were saying about chickens?" Jacob asked Rosa.

"Open it tomorrow," she suggested.

He shook his head. "Might as well know the worst." He opened the envelope and looked through the sheaf of papers.

"Banning orders?"

Jacob nodded. He crumpled the papers into a tight ball and threw it on the grass. "Strict ones," he said. "I'm allowed to go to work and to talk to you—Martha and the servants, I suppose, don't count. Apart from that, I'm not supposed to be in a room with more than two people at a time."

"When do they expire?"

"A month after the congress. Typical, isn't it? I shouldn't pay them the compliment of getting rattled, but still, I really wanted to be there."

Rosa took his hand in hers.

"Never mind," she whispered. "You will be there."

"In spirit," Jacob replied. "It's not the same."

"And through my eyes."

Jacob nearly tore his hand away. "It's not the same!" he wanted to shout. "It's not the same!" But he knew that he was being unfair. After all, it wasn't her fault.

"There, you see," he said instead. "You might lecture me about the strains of being a woman, but in this one thing you're fortunate."

Rosa frowned. "What do you mean?"

"The Nats haven't caught on to this equality stuff," he replied. "So they served me with a banning rather than you. Don't say there aren't advantages."

Rosa narrowed her eyes, but, "Martha will be cross that she missed the drama," was all she said.

When Rosa arrived in Kliptown, site of the Congress of the People, she found herself wishing that Jacob were with her. Never in her wildest dreams had she imagined this. From every corner of South Africa people kept arriving: women in saris, men in blankets, people barefoot, some wearing a zebra-type uniform, some dressed in suits, women in traditional costume, with head-dresses that put inches on their height.

Despite police roadblocks that had been erected throughout the country, they continued to flood toward the open square in

Kliptown. They arrived by busload or truckload, in cars packed so tight that they hugged the ground, or, in some cases, walking. They came singly and in twos and in deputations, freshly awakened or punch-drunk from lack of sleep, silent or singing. Waves of them kept descending on the place: women in ANC uniforms, their thumbs raised in the Congress salute, men in formal suits, a flag flying above them—black and white, they mixed together in the chaos that they had so lovingly created.

Rosa pushed further into the crowd. She came up against a small group of African boys dressed in short pants and white shirts, with scarves knotted around their necks. They held a banner to the crowds: WELCOME, DELEGATES, read their message: WE WANT FREEDOM OF GOVERNMENT AND TRUE EDUCATION.

She kept moving and managed to get through the fence only after showing her delegate credentials. And there she would have stopped completely if not for the press of people behind her. As it was, she shuffled off to one side, and as soon as she was sure that she was out of the way, she stopped and stared.

She had been part of this, but now she could scarcely believe that out of small planning meetings, of weary miles traveled, of writing and collating and more writing still, had come something quite so monumental.

Above the people who were carefully picking over each other to get to seats, signs jostled. WE WANT OUR LEADERS, said one banner, referring to the absence of the banned organizers. WE WANT BETTER HOUSES; FREEDOM OF SPEECH; DOWN WITH BANTU EDUCATION; EQUAL WORK EQUAL PAY proclaimed others.

The delegates were to sit on planks of wood, which rested on bricks and were separated from the observers by a barrier made of canvas. A platform had been built in the front with a huge flag, its four-spoked design representing the congress alliance, behind it. The platform itself was as yet empty, although every now and then someone would mount it, tap the microphone, and provoke an electronic reverberation through the gathering.

At the back of the square were literature stalls, places where drinks could be fetched, vats of food large enough to serve thousands.

It was all too incredible. She felt suddenly very, very small.

"Rosa."

She turned her head, but all she saw was strangers.

"Rosa, Rosa."

It was Moses' voice, but where was he?

"Rosa. Under the 'Work and Security' banner," he called.

She tried to make her way toward him, but the crowd was too dense. She felt a momentary claustrophobia.

"Let her through," said an old woman loudly. "Can't you see that she's with child?"

The crowd parted, and soon she and Moses were beaming at each other.

He gestured around him. "This is more than we dreamed," he said.

She nodded. "Where've you been?" she asked. "I went to pick you up, but Peggy said she hadn't seen you since yesterday."

"Aiee, it's been chaos," Moses replied. "I spent the night dodging the curfew with a group whose passes were out of date. We only just made it here." He held up an arm and gestured through the crowd. "Hey, man, Raymond!" he shouted. "Over here."

Raymond Siponja came bounding toward them. He slapped Moses on the back and kissed Rosa. "Isn't this something?" he asked.

"*Ja*," Moses agreed. "But what happened to you last night? We waited for hours."

"I didn't think we would make it," Raymond replied. "We got stopped on the road, a whole truckload of us. We'd been drinking, you know, and the police wanted us all out. We were panicked, I can tell you. Those of us who had passes couldn't remember where we'd put them, and we were the legal ones. As for the others . . ."

"So you talked your way out." Rosa smiled.

"Not me," Raymond said. "One of the comrades: a small, quiet type. Man, did he have presence of mind. '*Baas* man,' he whined, 'we going for this wedding.'

"'At this late hour?' says the policeman. 'Come on, sir,' replies our comrade. 'We're getting late for the wedding. My wife will murder me.'" It worked like a dream. 'Okay,' says the Boer, and I tell you this one was more stupid than usual. 'Okay,' he says, 'but please don't make a noise. Decent people are trying to sleep.'"

"So you obliged."

"Sure—we took off like a shot before we pissed in our trousers trying not to laugh."

"Comrades," called a voice from the platform, "please take your seats. We will soon be ready to begin."

Rosa moved to one of the front rows. When they saw her belly, people shifted to give her room. A woman reached out and patted it as she passed.

"This is the best education of all for the new one," she said.

"Welcome, people," a voice called.

The crowd stopped stirring: The band stood up. "Let us sing 'Nkosi Sikelel'i Afrika,'" he said. Within minutes, the crowd had also risen, and was singing as if with one voice.

And after the last note had died down, they stayed on their feet. "Afrika!" called a speaker from the rostrum. "Mayibuye!" came the deafening reply as ten thousand thumbs were raised.

The congress had begun. From the thousands, the hundreds of thousands, of demands collected over the last two years, a proposed Freedom Charter had been drafted. The congress was there to ratify or reject it, to accept or amend it. A man mounted the platform and began to read the draft.

"We, the people of South Africa," he said, "declare for all our country and the world to know: that South Africa belongs to all who live in it, black and white, and that no government can justly claim authority unless it is based on the will of the people."

He paused and looked around him—he had an eye for drama, this man. Then he continued.

And as she listened, Rosa marveled at his words. It never ceased to amaze her—that simple realization that the black majority of South Africa, who suffered daily such terrible indignities, would draw up a charter that gave South Africa not just to themselves, but to all the people who lived in it.

". . . we, the people of South Africa," continued the speaker, "black and white, together equals, countrymen and brothers, adopt this Freedom Charter. And we pledge ourselves to strive together, sparing nothing of our strength and courage, until the democratic changes here set out are won."

At that there was a stirring in the crowd, like a human wind, that rose softly into the air. "Umm-humm," it went, and it was the voice of assent spoken separately by thousands of simultaneous voices.

The speaker waited until it was over, and then began to go through the separate clauses. "The people shall govern," he said, and the noise swept through again. "All national groups shall have equal rights," he called, and again came the wind.

And then finally he came to the end. "Let all who love their people and their country now say, as we say here," he called, "these freedoms we will fight for, side by side, throughout our lives, until we have won our liberty."

And Rosa sat and was amazed not just by the congress, but by herself as well. That time, she thought, on the road with Moses, when she had felt so out of sorts, when she had resented her exclusion from the whites, then she must have been mad. For what a privilege it was to be part of this community, to be part of this history. She'd often speculated why it was she'd chosen to be active. Her parents' involvement did not seem like reason enough, and now, as she sat there, the answer came to her with an unswerving kind of clarity. For nowhere else in South Africa, nowhere else in the world, she thought, could she experience this kind of belonging, of rightness. She was lucky to be part of it.

"I'm back, and there's more than one of me," Rosa shouted.

"The Special Branch is out there," came Jacob's reply. "So I better keep away."

Rosa turned to her guests, people from out of town who had come to stay the night. "Jacob's banned," she explained, "so he can't come out and say hello until we're sure the police won't come crashing in. Help yourself to drinks while I go and see him."

She hurried down the corridor and looked in on Martha, who was sleeping peacefully. She went up to the bed and gently kissed Martha on the forehead: Martha mumbled and turned away.

Closing the door quietly, Rosa walked into her bedroom and saw that Jacob, too, was in bed. He was stretched with the sheet up to his chin, his head propped up by four pillows, a magazine in his hands and a whiskey by his side.

He looked up and nodded casually, and she felt a twinge of resentment. She frowned. "Aren't you going to ask me how it went?" she said.

"How did it go?" he asked in a bored tone.

She tossed her head in the air. "I'll tell you later," she said. "I've got guests to see to."

His voice sounded out. "I thought that the presentation of the heroes' award to Father Huddleston was incredibly moving."

She turned and stared at him. "How . . . ?" She could not finish the sentence.

He smiled at her, and he tossed the sheet off the bed. She saw that he was not in pajamas, as she had expected. He was instead fully dressed, and his clothes were covered with a thin layer of dust.

"I got back just before you," he said.

"But how . . . ?" she asked again.

He jumped out of bed. "After you left this morning," he said, "I thought about it and decided that I'd be damned if I'd let them stop me. So I drove to Kliptown and climbed onto a flat roof near the meeting ground. I probably got a better view than you, although the quality of the sound left something to be desired."

"And nobody saw you?"

"Muller from the SB did—right at the end—and he sent some of his men after me, but there was such a crowd that I managed to get away. Means I can't go back tomorrow, I suppose, but at least when this one"—he patted Rosa's stomach—"asks where I was when the Freedom Charter was signed, I can hold my head up high."

Rosa laughed and looked into his eyes. "It really was something, wasn't it?"

"Yes, honey, it was," Jacob said.

The second day of the congress was just as well attended and just as energetic. Each clause of the charter was discussed and debated before being voted on. The process was continued hour after hour without interruption. But right toward the end a huge sandstorm blew up. It was a ferocious eruption, whistling through hair and clothes in a frenzy of untapped energy. It swept through the audience, drowning out the sounds from the microphone. Even nature, it seemed, was rebelling. Rosa looked down, closing her eyes against the force of the wind.

And then, as suddenly as it had arrived, the storm abated. A silence that was almost deafening settled on the congregation. Rosa raised her head.

She gasped and heard the echo of her breath run through the gathering. For the landscape had changed dramatically. The storm had left something in its wake: an ominous, terrifying sight.

On the horizon, as far as the eye could see, stood police horses in the hundreds. The crowd, crammed into that meeting ground, was completely surrounded. The horses had encircled them, and were standing tall and threatening, not one gap between them. So closely were they packed, they blocked the light, throwing the meeting ground into a pit of artificial darkness.

Rosa gasped. She started to rise, and then forced herself to calm down. She sat down again and gripped the plank as if it might disintegrate beneath her.

"So, finally, the government has sent its delegates," a voice boomed out.

It was a well-timed sentence, and it went some way to breaking the tension in the gathering. But still there was fear, and still there was anger. As the horses began to move in formation, Rosa heard the mutterings that swelled into the air, rising to the sky and out toward this almost medieval invasion.

The crowd was turning. Good-naturedly they had sat as the charter was passed: Now, they would sit no longer.

The row of horses began to pace, down the sloping ground, toward the gathering. Each time they lifted their massive hooves into the air, each time they pranced, the tension tightened. The police felt it, and they shifted their Sten guns from hand to hand. And then Rosa saw behind the horses to the second line of attack—police vans and Saracens. Tanks! To deal with this peaceful gathering!

A policeman climbed onto the podium. He held a megaphone. "You're all under arrest," he shouted. "Nobody move."

Rosa's hand went to her breast. She felt the rage around her, and she knew that if the crowd made a move, there would be a massacre. Nobody could get out. She looked at the platform.

She saw Ida Mntwana, a tall, stately woman, move so as to block the policeman from view. Ida stuck her face close to the microphone. "Comrades, this is the hour," she shouted. "Please do not do a thing. Let's start singing."

"*Nkosi Sikelel'i Afrika*," sang Ida. By the time she had got to the end of the first lyric, the crowd had risen to its feet. Ten thousand voices rang out again. The veld vibrated with the sound of it: The horses trembled, their nostrils flaring in the air.

And when the last words of the anthem faded into the distance, the People's Congress continued. In the midst of this police invasion, the remaining clauses of the charter were debated and passed. The police stood by and waited until the end, until the last clause had been passed.

"Why the hell didn't they stop us?" Rosa asked, as the crowd walked toward the police guard at the exits. It was taking some time to get out, because the police were searching everybody, confiscating everything.

Moses frowned. "I'm sure they had a reason," he said. "My suspicion is that they wanted us to pass the charter so they can use it against us in the future."

And then there was no more time for words because they were abreast with the police.

It was almost ten o'clock by the time Rosa got home. Jacob was waiting at the door. He grabbed her and hugged her tight.

"Thank God," he said. "I heard there was a raid."

Rosa clung to her husband. She was crying.

Gently he stroked her hair. "Was it so bad?"

She disengaged herself and looked up at him. She smiled through her tears. "Bad!" she said. "It was wonderful. I'm so sorry you couldn't have seen it. Today we made history: We really made history."

Jacob smiled. He put his arms around her belly. "You and the people and our unborn child," he said. He frowned as something crackled beneath his touch.

Rosa laughed. She reached down into her smock and pulled out a document. She held it in the air.

"The Freedom Charter," she said. "In Xhosa. I smuggled this one out."

29

THE SWIECES' SECOND BABY ARRIVED EARLY, BUT IT WAS LONG IN coming. Rosa felt the onset of labor in the first week of August, on a Monday. When the cramps started, she and Jacob were full of excited anticipation, but then nothing—nothing, that was, except pain—happened. Monday turned into Tuesday and then Wednesday, and as time began to take its toll, Rosa grew increasingly exhausted.

The surveillance of the police had increased. When Rosa was finally taken to the hospital, they followed so closely that she had to restrain Jacob from reversing straight into them.

Jacob was frantic with worry, which he tried with little success to hide from Rosa. When true labor took hold, she heard his words of comfort and of confidence and then looked into his eyes and saw the doubt and fear there.

It was nothing like her first experience of childbirth. When Martha was born, the pain had seemed unendurable, and yet Rosa had always known that she would survive it. But this time, contrary to her every expectation, it was so much worse. She lost control, she lost her way amid it all.

The sheer number of medical personnel in the room didn't help. The midwife—that harbinger of normal delivery—was pushed to one side as a succession of doctors took turns examining Rosa. Finally the chief obstetrician was called.

"What do you think?" whispered the resident.

The chief shook his head, and the next pain that Rosa experienced was a hundred times harder to bear.

She had to have a cesarean. She'd always been terrified of anesthetics, but by the time the doctors told her of their decision, she didn't give a damn. Her main—her only—wish was to stanch this terrible pain. The baby, Martha, Jacob—all had become irrelevant.

She floundered out of an anesthetic fog to find Jacob hovering above her. She reached out her hand, but something tugged her back. She looked up and saw that it was attached to an IV. Her head ached. Where was she? What had happened to her?

"You're going to be all right," Jacob said, and there were tears in his eyes, tears of relief, Rosa thought.

"I'm thirsty," she mumbled.

Jacob smiled. "You can't drink for a while," he said. "You're getting liquid through the drip. Be patient."

She smiled weakly and looked around her. She was in a big room, shining and antiseptic, surrounded by bleeping monitors and ungainly pieces of ugly medical equipment. In the opposite corner was a bed, and on it a prone body. The bleeps, she realized, were coming from there.

She was so sleepy, the haze threatened to engulf her again, but something, a niggling worry, made her fight to stay conscious. There was something missing: What was it?

Then she got it. The baby!

"Our baby?" she asked of Jacob in a voice that was made tiny by that vast space.

"A girl," Jacob said.

Rosa relaxed. So it was a girl—a sister for Martha. She would be delighted.

But then again the worry returned. She tried to push herself upright, but a sharp pain tore through her guts. She gasped.

Jacob stroked her forehead. "Lie still," he said gently. "You won't be able to move easily for a while."

Mutely she sank back. She stared at Jacob, her eyes pleading.

He took a deep breath. He pulled up a chair, and sitting on it, he held gently on to Rosa's hands. "The baby is fighting for her life," he said. "She's in intensive care."

"Will she live?"

"She's got a greater than fifty percent chance. She'll be okay. We'll soon take her home." Rosa heard optimism in his voice, but she also heard something else. She heard the cost of such false cheeriness. She heard the things he didn't say—the trepidation he stopped himself from expressing.

It was her turn to stroke his hand. It was she who was comforting him now, she who was the strong one.

She was moved out of the post-op ward and into a private room. But when she asked to see her baby, the nurse laughed.

"Don't be silly, dear," she said. "You're in no state to move."

"Bring her here, then."

"Baby is not well enough. You do want us to do the best for you, don't you, dear?"

When Jacob saw fury in Rosa's face, he stepped between the two. He went to work on the nurse—wheedling, coaxing, threatening, until at last a bed from the operating theater was produced, and Rosa was wheeled to intensive care.

Their baby was a tiny thing. She lay motionless in her glass enclosure, a bright light glaring at her, a tube coming out of her mouth. A linen cloth swaddled her body, making her appear even more minute.

Rosa looked at her, and the tears streamed down her face.

"It's my fault," she sobbed. "I did too much."

Jacob leaned over Rosa. He held her face firmly in his hands, and he stared intently at her. "Never say that," he ordered. "Never think that. It isn't your fault. These things happen."

Rosa pretended to agree, and yet the feelings did not go away. She was guilty, she knew it. She should never have pushed herself so hard throughout her pregnancy. She should have put the baby first.

She willed that baby to live, she bent her energy into making it survive. She spent long hours beside the baby, coming away only at Jacob's insistence.

And the baby—Rachel, they named her—came slowly to life. The first good sign was when she was able to breathe unaided. They took the ventilator away, and without the artificial echo of this mechanical aide, she seemed a thousand times improved. She began to open her eyes, to look around her, to take in her mother's presence. She grasped Rosa's hand. She held on to it with persistence.

"She's a fighter," Rosa whispered to Jacob.

"How could she be otherwise," Jacob answered, "with a mother like hers?"

They dwelt on hope—Rosa and Jacob—in those early days. They had eyes for nobody but the baby. For the first time in their adult lives, politics seemed irrelevant. They regarded the policemen who continued to dog the hospital corridors as irrelevant. They concentrated their efforts on wishing the baby better.

And throughout it all they never once discussed the issue on both their minds—their concern about whether the baby would be normal, or whether she had suffered brain damage. By mutual consent, they left such speculation alone.

Evelyn was smiling broadly when she arrived at Moses and Peggy's Sophiatown house.

"Good news," she announced.

Moses looked up from the desk. "Rosa?" he asked, and in his voice was a passion that he usually reserved for politics.

Peggy, who was sitting on the bed patching a pair of George's trousers, glanced up. Her face was a placid blank.

Evelyn smiled again. "She's out of hospital," she said, "and so's the baby. They've done all the tests: Rachel's going to be all right."

"I'm happy for them," Moses said.

Peggy placed her sewing neatly into the wooden box beside her and rose. "Can I make you some tea?" she asked Evelyn.

Evelyn looked at Peggy as if registering her presence for the first time. The smile on her face faded slightly, but then she told herself that she was imagining things. After all, Peggy had only offered tea—what could be hostile about that?

"I'd love some," she said.

But as she sat sipping the hot liquid from a cracked white mug, Evelyn knew that she wasn't imagining the almost tangible tension between Moses and Peggy. They seemed to be circling each other as if contact would prove disastrous. Peggy even went so far as to make a huge detour around the room rather than walk in a straight line to the tea caddy and thus pass close by Moses.

Evelyn's good mood began to fade. How long, she thought, could the two of them live this way? She would have to say something.

As if he had guessed her thoughts, as if to forestall her, Moses jumped in with a question. "Have you decided where to go when you leave the Arnolds'?" he asked.

"I was going to settle in Sophiatown," Evelyn replied. "But now . . ."

He nodded gravely. "It doesn't look good."

Peggy glanced up. "What are you talking about?" she asked.

Evelyn opened her mouth to reply, but Moses got in before

her. "I told you," he said sharply, "that they're threatening to demolish Sophiatown."

Moses was right: He had indeed told her. It was all, he lectured, part of apartheid's grand design. The country was in the process of full-scale segregation, as the whites consolidated their power. They'd managed to chase blacks from their benches, their parks, their bus stops, their shops: Now, they were after their homes.

Sophiatown, the government declared, was no longer suitable for its black residents. Its inhabitants were to be moved and the Africans taken to the new "Bantu location," which was an amalgam of all Jo'burg's black settlements; South Western Townships, it was named, Soweto for short.

"Even you can't have missed the protests, can you?" Moses asked.

She did not deign to answer. He knew that she hadn't missed them; and they had even discussed them last night, so there was no reason to reply. The way he treated her, she thought, was beneath contempt. After all, her only failure was that she'd been on the wrong wavelength, that she hadn't immediately known to which of their many concerns Moses and Evelyn were referring.

"It's been a well-organized campaign," Evelyn said. "But whether it works is another matter."

"*Ja*, I'm afraid so," Moses agreed.

Peggy said, "If you'll excuse me, I must go and fold the children's clothes."

Evelyn asked Moses to accompany her for part of the way home. She squeezed his arm. "My son . . ." she began.

He nodded his head and spoke before she could finish. "It's bad what goes on between Peggy and me," he said. He stopped, and Evelyn saw that his face was resigned. "I don't know what to do about it," he continued. "She just won't tolerate my involvement."

"Have you tried talking to her?"

He smiled, but his eyes did not smile with him. "Yes, I've tried," he said. "But what can I do if she doesn't want to hear?"

Evelyn frowned. "Try again?"

"What's the point?" Moses muttered. "She will not listen."

She did not like the hardness in his voice. "You're a renowned orator," she said, "who has addressed crowds of thousands. How come you can't get your own wife to listen?"

Moses pulled his arm from hers. "If you don't mind, I'll leave you here," he said. "I have work to do."

Evelyn frowned. No wonder Peggy has difficulties, she thought, if he walks away from every confrontation. She kept the thought to herself. "Don't go yet," she said.

He smiled weakly at her. "Honestly," he said. "I do have work to do." He pecked her on the cheek, and then he left.

She watched him go, and she knew that there was no point in calling him back. If he had been listening, he would have understood that Peggy's hostility stemmed not from viciousness, but rather from her isolation. But he was not listening—or he was just like Peggy and did not want to hear.

Peggy awoke with a start. She was alone in the bed—Moses was on one of his frequent trips—and at first she thought that she must have had a bad dream. But then it came again, the sound that had awakened her: a rumbling issuing from the streets, a sound so loud that her bed vibrated with it.

"What's happening?" Twelve-year-old Lindiwe was bolt upright on her mattress on the floor. "Is it an earthquake?"

George's reflexes were quicker than his sister's. He was already halfway out the door when Peggy ordered him back. "Don't run out!" she shouted. "This is not an earthquake."

"Well, what is it?" Lindiwe was terrified.

Peggy softened her voice. "We'll see in a minute," she said. "After you both get dressed."

The rumbling came again.

With trembling hands, Peggy dressed herself; the buttons were in the wrong order, but she took no notice of that. She patted her hair into a rough kind of order; she shivered and pulled a cardigan around her, although it was not cold. And then, with a child on each side of her, she opened the door and looked outside.

It was hard to see at first, for her vision was almost completely obscured by clouds of dust: dust that made her eyes stream with water, that caked her mouth, that spread through the open door like a plague, that darkened the dawn light. But as she grew accustomed to this uneasy, artificial gloom, she began to make out the shape of the disaster that had befallen them.

The rumbling was caused by trucks and bulldozers; scores of

them, hundreds, even. They lined the road, spreading far into the distance. From the clouds of dust that still rose beyond them, Peggy guessed that the vehicles she could see were but few when compared to those that followed behind.

Each vehicle contained a set of uniformed men—army and police together—their guns already cocked in their hands. They stood, these men, and they stared at the newly awakened inhabitants of Sophiatown, and in their unblinking eyes was written a kind of dare. Peggy pulled her children closer to her.

The trucks had stopped moving, except for one. On it stood a man with a megaphone. "You are all being moved!" he shouted. "Stand by."

Peggy saw that the vehicles held other occupants: black men, employees of the city, young men badly dressed, with sullen faces and angry brows. Their heads were bent down low, but when the man with the megaphone spoke, they looked up.

"Okay," shouted the man with the megaphone. "Let's get down to business."

The young men jumped from the trucks and, pushing through the startled crowd, they ran into the houses.

They started further up the street, and Peggy had time to see what was happening. She saw how they reemerged with their arms full of household goods: of beds, of mattresses, documents, cooking utensils, babies' cribs—the very fabric of people's lives, possessions accumulated over generations that looked somehow tawdry when torn so roughly from their resting place.

The men had no respect for their baggage; they flung it, linen and crockery alike, straight into the trucks. Then they hurried back inside, only to return with another load.

As Peggy watched, and as she waited, she forgot to feel afraid. Instead, an anger began to smolder inside of her, and then to burn. How dare they, how could they do this to her? All her life she had struggled to keep a clean home, struggled against the dual odds of third-class citizenship and Moses' neglect. She was proud of what she had achieved: If the white man thought that he could come and blow it all away, then he was wrong. She would not let him.

She pushed the children behind her, and when one of the men reached her door and tried to get past, she blocked him with her body. She stared straight into his face.

"How can you do this to your own people?" she asked.

The man cast his eyes down. "It is my job," he muttered.

"Is this a job of which your mother would be proud?" she said. "These are our homes."

"Please, *'me,*" he begged, "let me through. You cannot stop them. You are lucky they do not bulldoze your home with the possessions still inside."

"Lucky?" Peggy said. "You call this lucky?"

The man's eyes filled with tears. "Look around and see what is happening to those who resist," he pleaded.

Peggy did as she was bid. And she saw her neighbor two doors down, Joyce Nomjana by name, a mother of five, also stand in the way of those who sought to enter.

"*Ashihambi Hare Ilohe!* We shall not move!" Joyce shouted.

The young removal men came nearer, but they stopped when Joyce brandished a frying pan in front of them. When she took a step forward, they beat a hasty retreat.

Peggy began to smile, but not for long. For as she watched, she saw three armed guards advance on Joyce. The man in front said nothing, he gave no warning. Instead, he used his rifle—one blow on the head was all it took—to knock Joyce to the ground. The other two jumped forward and began to kick at her prone body, laughing and jeering as Joyce's children grabbed ineffectively at their sleeves.

Peggy forgot the things that she habitually told Moses; she forgot to think first of her family, she forgot to protect her children, she forgot it all as she started to run toward her neighbor. But the man beside her saw what she intended, and gripping her hand hard, he pulled her back. "It will do no good," he whispered, "they are too strong. They are angry enough to kill her: They have no respect for our womenfolk. Don't put yourself in the path of their rifles, I beg of you."

It was at this point that Moses arrived. How he got through the cordon around Sophiatown, Peggy would never know. It just happened: One minute he wasn't there, and in the next she saw him come running. He saw the man's hand on Peggy's arm and he increased his speed, and there was something in his eyes that Peggy had not seen for a long time. But now was not the time to think of that. She shook her hand free.

"I'm all right," she called. "It's Joyce."

Moses slowed down and looked past Peggy. He saw a policeman kick at Joyce, and he took one step in her direction. But then he stopped and glanced at Peggy, and in his eyes was framed a question.

Peggy was suddenly filled with fear. She could stop him, she knew she could, she could call him to her. She opened her mouth.

And then she closed it again. She, who had prayed for years for Moses to offer her a choice, now found that she did not want to exercise it. She could not, she would not stop him. He was her husband, he was the one man in her life, she would never take another: That she realized. If he died, she would never recover. But still she could not hold him back.

Keeping a firm grip on George and Lindiwe, who were both growing hysterical, she nodded at her husband.

Her nod was all he needed. He leaped into action, leaped over the intervening fences like a man possessed. He grabbed at the police who surrounded Joyce and he pulled them off, one by one. They did not know what had hit them, they had not expected this. They were passive under his assault.

At first, that is. And then reinforcements arrived: Seeing what was happening, a whole troop of police descended on Moses. As Peggy forced herself to watch, they clobbered him to the ground, beating on him, swearing at him, and then finally dragging his unconscious body into a *kwela-kwela*.

"Daddy!" Lindiwe cried. She looked up at Peggy, the tears running like rivers down her dust-streaked face. "Is he all right?" she asked.

"I don't know," Peggy answered in a trembling voice. "But you must be proud of your father. He fights for us and our community. Look now at Auntie Joyce rising. Come, let us fetch her some water."

Numbly Peggy allowed herself to be deposited in her new house. She was, she supposed, one of the lucky ones. At least she was given a dwelling. Many others had nowhere to go, and they were forced to set up camp beneath hastily erected tents made from cardboard and tin.

The authorities had no respect for the community they had so hastily uprooted. They assigned each family a dwelling, zoned into tribal areas, separating neighbor from neighbor, friend from friend. The racial mix of Sophiatown, where Africans, Indians, coloreds, had lived side by side, was no more: Those days would never return.

In its place had been created a prison for the black inhabitants. They were put in tiny spaces, devoid of personality, unlit by electric light, serviced by a few standpipes, with no proper sewerage and no roads on which to walk.

Soweto: only half-formed, and already it had an ominous ring. A vast area of land, thirty-two miles in all when it was completed, a piece of ground, equipped with a few rows of dull gray matchbox houses, planted on the dirt like some kind of science-fiction low-grade production factory. It was a desert, a place of emptiness when compared to the flowering of communities in Sophiatown, Pimville, Western Native Township, and all the other places now to be abolished to satisfy apartheid.

At first Peggy sat in the middle of her small pile of possessions, unmoving. She sat as dark fell. She ignored her children's attempts to talk, she shook Lindiwe's hand from her shoulder. She continued to sit. She sat and sat like stone.

And then, suddenly, she was in motion again. "George," she said briskly. He ran to her side.

"You must go to the city," she told him, "straight to the Swieces. Be careful. If anybody asks what you are doing, tell them the *baas* asked you to deliver a message to his friend. Tell Jacob and Rosa what's happened. Ask them to look for your father."

For once in his life George did not protest. He left the house hurriedly, glancing from left to right.

Peggy had plenty of time to think during the long hours that followed George's departure. She restricted her thoughts quite firmly. She would not allow herself to contemplate what might have happened to Moses; she even refused to cry. Instead, as she automatically imposed some semblance of order over this, her new home, she thought of their life together.

Not of the bad times, but of the good. Of the beginnings in another place of hell and of the young, untamed spirit she had first loved. Her Moses, she realized, had not changed so much. He still had those qualities that had made him so attractive to her. He was a fighter, a free agent.

And he was right. Until that day, she hadn't understood, she had closed her ears when he talked of the people, "I cannot care for a faceless mass," she'd always said.

But today the mass had been given a face, and it was of her neighbor Joyce, a woman who had always been good to Peggy, a Christian woman, a good woman. At long last, Peggy did understand. She knew now the impulse that drove Moses onward, because she, too, had experienced it. Joyce had never harmed another human being. And yet, if Moses had not intervened, her basic impulse to protect her home (an impulse that Peggy had also experienced) might well have ended in her death.

Oh, my husband, Peggy thought. Please survive. Please let me tell you that I was wrong, that you were right.

The car arrived at midnight. She heard it coming, but she did not go outside to greet it. She sat by the doorway, hugging to herself the sleeping form of Lindiwe.

The car stopped. She saw that there were three figures inside it, all crammed into the front seat—her son, George, and Jacob and Rosa, who was clutching the six-month-old Rachel. Their faces were grave.

Rosa was the first to descend. She handed the baby to Jacob, and then gently she helped George down the short step. Peggy watched it all through the film of her own grief. Her face was dry as she looked at her son. He had gone gray, she observed, the brown tinged with a pallor of stress and of grief.

Peggy's thoughts came slowly, but they were powerful nevertheless. Even as she felt her own heart breaking, she knew that she must be strong for her son. Gently she placed Lindiwe on the floor, a pillow supporting her head. She got up. She held her arms out wide to George, welcoming him into her embrace.

And yet what was this? George did not move away from the car. Instead, he looked at Rosa, who was pulling at the front seat, leaning toward the rear of the car. Peggy breathed in sharply, and then, with effort, forced herself to exhale. I must stay calm, she told herself.

Her back erect, she walked slowly to the car. She had no eyes for anybody—no eyes for anything but the back of the car. She leaned over the window and looked inside.

There she saw her husband lying motionless, his face caked with blood.

She scrambled through the front seat, pushing at it in her effort to climb over and join her husband. Rosa restrained her.

"He's all right," she said softly. "We found him in a police station, but he wasn't charged. He's been badly beaten, but Jacob says he'll be all right. He's been asking for you."

"Moses." It came out in a sob.

"He's going to be all right."

And then, and only then, did Peggy allow herself to feel and to cry. Her tears started to flow. They flooded down her face, dripping onto the red dirt of Soweto, watering that barren land.

The Swieces stayed the night, keeping watch over Moses. While Lindiwe slept, Jacob amused George with an endless series of chess games, the two hunched over a grimy board, their faces made garish by the yellowing kerosene light. Outside, Soweto was still, its streets deserted, its small concrete dwellings shining ghoulishly in the moonlight.

Peggy and Rosa sat side by side beside Moses.

As dawn cast a rosy glow in the sky, Rosa looked at Peggy. Rosa's small infant was sucking at her breasts, making tiny satisfied noises that gurgled through the barren room. It had been a long night, thought Rosa, and an unusual one. Never had she and Peggy managed to sit together in such a manner, never had they relaxed like this in each other's company. Perhaps, she thought, I can even go one step further. She took a deep breath.

"When I was a child," she said, "and you first arrived in our household, I resented your presence."

"I didn't notice," Peggy replied. She looked down at her lap.

Rosa laughed. "You're a bad liar, Peggy," she said. "You noticed, all right. It's just that you tolerated my rudeness."

"You were only a child," Peggy said.

"And so were you. But you were so much better behaved than I was. And so much more resourceful."

"I did what I had to."

Rosa looked at Peggy, at the suspicion in her face, at the tentativeness of her replies. They had never got on, but Rosa had always placed the blame for this securely in Peggy's court. Now, she realized that the fault had been hers as well. "I was jealous of you," she said abruptly.

Peggy was shocked into dropping her guard. "Of me? But you had everything."

"And you had Evelyn," Rosa replied, "in a way that I never had her. I used to want her as my mother, and then you got her as your mother-in-law."

Rosa paused and looked down.

Peggy waited.

"Yes," Rosa said softly. "I was always a little in love with Moses."

There was a short silence. For a moment Rosa feared that Peggy would not acknowledge what she had said, that she would leave the sentence to hover forever between them.

And then Peggy sighed. "I feared you," she said. "You were so articulate, so fierce, so much more in tune with my husband's life."

Rosa glanced at Peggy. "I wouldn't be so sure of that," she said. "It's not easy—friendship between blacks and whites in this country. Moses will talk politics to me, that is true, but he withholds something of himself from our conversations. It is you who know the man; it is you he loves."

Peggy didn't have time to reply, because Moses stirred and called her name. She gripped his hand.

"I'm here," she said.

He tried to struggle upright, but she gently pushed him back.

"I'm sorry . . ." he began.

"Hush now."

"But I want you to know . . ."

Peggy placed one finger over his lips. "You did right," she answered. "Today I was proud of you."

Moses smiled.

Soweto began its first awakening. From each house stepped people, their faces drawn from lack of sleep. Cautiously, carefully, they made tentative moves toward each other, introducing themselves, exchanging information, beginning the new life that had been forced on them.

In Sophiatown the bulldozers had already completed their task. Scores of buildings reduced to rubble, remnants of generations of life, abolished in one short day. The rubbish was carted away, dumped so that no one would ever see it again.

The government had plans for this location, and carried them through in record time. Out of Sophiatown's ruins they created a new town, a clean, white, sparkling town. Its name in Afrikaans was Triomf. In English it is not much different. For Sophiatown became the symbol of the "triumph" of the apartheid state against the people of South Africa.

30

EVELYN STOOD AT THE BOTTOM OF THE GARDEN AND SURVEYED THE house from there. It was so familiar to her, she knew every nook and cranny of it, and yet she could still remember her first sight of it. She remembered the day she had moved here with Harold and Julia, and the young Rosa and Nicholas, too. Then the house had been the height of fashion, with its flat roof, its balconies at different levels, its square, light rooms.

It was no longer fashionable, she thought. Fashions had changed—and so, she thought, had everything else.

"Evelyn," came a distant voice.

She shrank back into the bushes. She didn't want them to see her; not yet, she didn't.

She watched Julia come into the garden and stand with her hand at her forehead to shade her eyes. Evelyn smiled to herself, feeling vaguely guilty. This position, she remembered, was a favorite hiding place. Twenty years ago that figure by the house would have been hers, while Rosa would have been where she now stood.

"Evelyn," Julia called again.

Reluctantly Evelyn turned from the bushes and walked up the lawn, making her way to Julia. The childishness, that kind of weightlessness she'd experienced when she'd been hidden, left her. The old familiar pain in her hip, the weariness in her bones, the feeling of fatigue, returned.

"Well, that's not surprising," she muttered to herself. "I'm nearly seventy."

* * *

As Julia watched Evelyn walk slowly toward her, it was almost as if she could feel the twinges herself. I suppose it's hardly surprising, she thought. We've been through so much together.

She thought back over those years, through the times when she had been jealous of Evelyn, through the times when she had relied on her, back to the time when the two had first met. She had, she remembered, been taken to the Bopape house by Harold. It was a visit she would never forget, a visit that was a turning point for her. Evelyn and Nathaniel, she remembered, had been so kind—and yet she had been in awe of them.

She smiled to herself. Not much has changed, she thought. I'm still in awe of her.

She shook herself briskly as Evelyn came closer. "The car's ready," she said. "And they're asking each other once again why you won't let them drive you further than the bus stop." She saw a look in Evelyn's eyes—a look of desperation, was it?— and she regretted her words. "They won't argue any more about it," she said hastily. "They know what you want."

"I hate partings," Evelyn said.

Julia nodded. "Come on."

She turned toward the house, but Evelyn put out a hand and restrained her. Julia turned again. They stood still, these two women, as they looked into each other's eyes. Neither spoke. It was Evelyn who finally broke the silence. "They don't understand why I'm going," she said. "You do, don't you?"

Julia nodded. She wanted to speak, but when she opened her mouth she found that she could not. Her eyes filled with tears. Evelyn reached forward and put her arms around Julia. They hugged, briefly, before Evelyn broke the embrace and walked away.

"Safe journey," came Julia's voice, but so thick that it was barely understandable. Evelyn nodded and continued to walk.

By the time she got inside, Evelyn had recovered her composure. She held out her arms, and the six-year-old Martha came running into them.

"You will write to me?" Martha asked for what must have been the twentieth time.

"Yes, my honey, of course I will," Evelyn said. She bent her head to the child's ear. "I love you," she said. "Don't forget that. Now be a good girl and go and see your grandmother in the garden. I think she might need you."

She patted Martha's bottom and gave her a gentle push. She smiled when Martha ran out. Slowly she straightened herself up.

She saw that Rosa and Harold were waiting by the open door, and that Moses and Lindiwe had already reached the car.

"I'll be out in a minute," she told them. "I just want to have a last look." She turned and stared up at the stairway, as she heard, with relief, the sound of Harold and Rosa walking across the drive. She did not really want to have a last look, the house itself meant little to her, but she needed to be on her own. She needed to conserve her strength before the ordeal that lay ahead, before those final partings.

She felt a moment's relief that Jacob had gone to work and that Peggy had understood the pressures on her and had said her good-byes the day before. George, too, Evelyn thought with a smile, had stayed away, but this was not because he understood. It was because he was at an awkward age—half child and half man—perhaps the most painful stage of all. He shied away from emotions, and the merest hint that his mother wanted to spare Evelyn by saying good-bye on a separate occasion had him jumping to join her.

As for Peggy—well, she had done her best to make Evelyn's farewell easy on them both. She'd kept it quite formal, and Evelyn had understood and even been grateful, for Peggy was not a demonstrative woman. She could not stem, however, a slight irritation at the last when Peggy's composure had remained unruffled.

But then she told herself that she was being unfair. Peggy was unusual in the sense that Evelyn's departure did not come as a surprise to her. Unlike the others, she had suspected that Evelyn would go, had predicted it, in fact, on that day when Evelyn had showed her the letter from the mission station—the one that said that the missionary who had tried to seduce the teenage Evelyn had attempted to atone for his sin by leaving her a small plot of land in the Transkei.

"If it weren't so pathetic, it would be laughable," Evelyn told Peggy. "What does the country mean to me any longer?"

"The country stays in our blood," Peggy replied. "In mine, and in yours as well."

She did not elaborate, and when finally she spoke again, it had been to change the subject.

She did not need to speak, because Evelyn had understood

her words and the look that went with them: It was a look imbued with memory, it was a look that displayed Peggy's continuing sorrow that she could not go home to the land in which she'd been born, to the country, where she felt most at ease. "You have kept your heart in the country," Evelyn told Peggy, "not I."

But even as she said the words, she began to wonder. It was true that she had put the country behind her, that she had pushed all memory of her family to the furthest regions of her mind, that she was adjusted to city life. And yet there was a part of her still in the country, a part that she had deliberately cut away when she was young, but a part that seemed to be staging a comeback now that she was growing old.

For years she had not thought of her family. Now, they began to return to her—their names, their faces, their way of being. Not her father so much—she would never forgive him for driving her from home—but her mother, her aunts, those generations of women who had lived in that land for all their lives.

And as she thought of them, all now long dead, she began to experience the tug of the country. She wanted to walk the veld they'd inhabited, to look at the horizon that had been the boundary of their world, to sit by her mother's grave and remember the person who had once been central to her every breath.

And in the end she'd realized one simple thing: She wanted to go home. The voice that was the rational Evelyn, that knew that she was being overly romantic, that told her of the harshness and the poverty of the Transkei, was drowned. She wanted to go home.

"Evelyn," came Harold's voice.

She shook herself and looked around at this place that had been her home for so long. She smoothed her hand along the banister and automatically looked at it, checking for dust. Then she turned and quickly left the house.

Rosa was waiting by the car. She had on her face an expression that Evelyn knew so well, an expression from her childhood, an expression that was courage fighting with distress. She ran to Evelyn and, bending down a fraction, hugged her fiercely.

"I'm going to miss you so much," she said.

"I will miss you, too," Evelyn answered. She felt Rosa's tears on her shoulder, and her own began to fall.

"You grew into a wonderful woman," Evelyn whispered. "You had promise as a child, and you did not betray it."

"Thanks to you," Rosa sobbed.

"No," Evelyn said, and she pushed Rosa away from her a fraction. "Thanks to you." She turned quickly and got into the car. "Let's go," she said.

When they arrived at the bus station, Harold got out, and opening the trunk, he pulled out her two suitcases. He put them on the ground, and then he looked at her. She was relieved to see Moses pick up the suitcases, and with his daughter by his side begin to walk toward the bus.

"Of course we'll send your pension regularly," Harold said. "But if you need any more money, you must let us know."

"I'm sure that won't be necessary," she replied. "You and Julia have been more than generous."

Harold shook his head as if to deny the fact, but he did not speak.

She looked at him long and hard, as if she were drinking in his image. "You remind me so much of Nathaniel," she said finally. "You always have."

"He was my teacher," Harold replied.

"I know," Evelyn said. "And you have honored his memory. You've been a good friend, Harold." She took a step toward him, touched his cheek briefly, and then turned away because she could not bear to hug him.

He understood. He did not follow her, he let her go.

Lindiwe was looking beautiful, Evelyn reflected, as she put one foot on the first rung of the bus. Like George, she was poised between childhood and adulthood, but in her case the awkwardness was absent, and already one could see the woman she would become. She took after her father, Evelyn thought, both in looks and in character. Her life would not be easy.

Evelyn stretched out her arms to the girl. "You, I know, will write," she said.

Lindiwe nodded. "And you better write back. No excuse—especially not old age—will do."

Evelyn smiled. "You're a hard taskmaster," she said. She hugged her grandchild, her favorite grandchild, to her. "Be happy," she whispered, "and strong." And then, just as she had done with Martha, she gave Lindiwe a little push.

She looked at Moses.

"Well, my son," she said.

He did not smile, neither did he reply. He, out of all of them, she knew, understood the least why she was going. He had spent long hours trying to dissuade her, telling her that the Transkei would be like a foreign country, that she would be a stranger there, that she should stay with her family and her movement. He did not give up easily, her son. They had almost come to blows about it.

She smiled at him. "I must go," she said. "Don't hold it against me."

He blinked. "I'll miss you," he said.

"I will be with you," she answered, "in my thoughts."

"And by your example," Moses said. "I am proud of you, my mother."

She nodded and turned away from him, and she was grateful that the bus driver suddenly started the engine, that a person behind was pushing at her to hurry her along, and that the crowd of people around the bus took one step back as the driver ground the gears into first.

They were standing together as the bus moved out—Harold, Moses, and Lindiwe, not touching, but close enough. She would always remember the sight of them like that, she thought, those three generations still united. And then she smiled, because she had achieved the impossible in South Africa. She forgot they were different colors. And both those families are mine, she thought.

She leaned back in her seat and closed her eyes. She was weary, oh so weary. The partings had been worse than she anticipated.

And yet, she thought, as the bus began to leave Jo'burg, I have done the right thing.

The truth was that Evelyn could not have stayed, she did not have the strength to stay. All her life she had struggled; now, she wanted a rest.

Things were going to get tougher, she knew they were. She hoped that the generations after her would be able to withstand the pressure. As for herself, she needed some time, at the end of her life, to be by herself: She needed, she thought with an ironical smile, to go home.

31

1960

MOSES' FEET WERE BEGINNING TO HURT HIM. IT WAS HARDLY SUR-prising. He'd been up since dawn, and he'd hardly stopped walking.

He'd begun at the Seeiso Street bus station, mingling among the early morning commuters, watching to see what would happen. In effect, nothing did, because no buses arrived. The commuters waited in vain. It was a good start, Moses thought. The Pan African Congress had campaigned well among the drivers, in that they had shown organization.

He'd gone from the bus station to Bophelong location and joined a group of about two thousand who were heading for Vonderbijlpak Police Station. As the march progressed, it swelled until it was almost doubled, as people from the nearby Boipatong location joined in.

It was a good-tempered crowd that day, a friendly crowd with an almost holiday atmosphere about it. At the front walked the PAC leaders, their hands empty, for they had left their passes at home. Their aim, Moses knew, was to present themselves at the police station and get arrested, thus starting a chain reaction that should spread throughout South Africa.

Moses and most of the ANC, from which the PAC had recently broken away, doubted that they would succeed. Their campaign had been too precipitous, and although their leadership was determined, they had not really bothered to organize at grass-roots levels.

"They have not even learned from our mistakes," someone

in the ANC had said, "never mind from their own. They think that one campaign on passes can mushroom into an attack on the state. Did they not see what happened during the Defiance Campaign, how we were forced to retreat when the stakes got higher?"

All of this Moses knew to be true, but he couldn't help reflecting that this action, this call for resistance rather than protest, had found support. Why else should so many be marching, not only here but all around Vereeniging? Why else were they willing to be arrested after so little campaigning?

But when they reached the police station, Moses saw that the crowd had no real cohesion. It did not know what to do when the obvious happened: when the police attacked. It took only one desultory baton charge to send the people running. Moses shrugged and went with them. Better, he thought, that they dispersed—there was always a chance that if they had stayed to face down these nervous police, someone might have got hurt.

"Moses." Raymond Siponja, who'd also come to observe, was walking from the opposite direction. The two men met in the street and shook hands. "What happened?" Raymond asked.

Moses shrugged. "A baton charge and the crowd dispersed."

"Same thing at Everton," Raymond said. "Except they had to buzz the crowd with Sabre jets before it made a move. The numbers were impressive, around twenty thousand, as far as I could guess. And I hear that it's not over yet: In Sharpeville the crowd held its ground when the aircraft flew down low."

"Let's go see, then," Moses suggested, and side by side the two men began to walk.

They arrived at the Sharpeville police station at around one o'clock. The crowd, as Raymond had said, was indeed still there, around five or six thousand of them, Moses guessed, and still good-natured. Moses and Raymond had no trouble walking into the thickest of it. They strolled through groups of gossiping women, of children playing in the dust, of people casually talking in the midst of Saracens. Only the police were silent, as they stood behind a wire fence. They held the ubiquitous Sten guns in their hands, but they made no sign that they would move.

"I guess they're calling headquarters for instructions," Raymond said.

Moses nodded and turned away from his friend, distracted momentarily by a woman who was reaching the climax of a long and involved joke she was telling.

It was then that he heard an unexpected sound—a sharp report coming from the direction of the police station. It was followed by a few cries, nothing really dramatic. Hardly anybody took any notice, caught up as they were in their own communities.

But Moses had come to observe, and he was alert: He turned in the direction of the sound just in time to see that the crowd around the Saracens, formerly a casual, relaxed group, had been jolted into a kind of furious action. Voices and thumbs were raised into the air, the people began to move not toward the police station, but away from it, in a kind of anarchic confusion.

There was a moment when the group of women next to Moses was still blissfully unaware of what had happened, and the women greeted the punch line with a roar of rowdy laughter. But suddenly the woman who had been telling the joke stumbled and fell to the ground.

As one of her group went to pick her up, the sound of firing hit the air. It was rent with noises, with the chattering of Sten guns and the volleys of bullets.

Moses did not know where to look, his eyes swung wildly from one end of the compound to the other. He saw a policeman astride a Saracen, with a machine gun in his hands, and he saw that the man was moving the gun in a wide arc, pointing it at various sections of the crowd as it shuddered out its fire.

He saw the person who had gone to help the woman raise herself to her feet and stare in horror at the blood that stained her hands.

He saw some children come running toward him, their eyes wide, their mouths open with screams that had no voice, and he saw one of them suddenly fall to the ground. The child did not get up.

He saw hats, shoes, shawls, fly in the air.

And he saw the space that the crowd had already vacated, and he saw that it was not completely empty: It was littered with bodies: still, quiet bodies.

"Run!" shouted Raymond. "Run!"

He was not the only one to shout so. From the front came a jumble of fleeing people, of children, men and women, babies crying in arms, old people hobbling, some clutching their arms, their legs, and many falling as they ran.

The machine gun continued to echo through the compound. "Run!" shouted Raymond. Moses ran.

"Ma Evelyn, Ma Evelyn."

The child's cry echoed across the veld. On hearing it, Evelyn left her shack, and with her hand shading her eyes, she squinted into the distance. There he was, that small, grubby little person, running his way toward her dwelling, his head sporadically disappearing under cover of the long brown grass.

Evelyn smiled to herself as she watched eight-year-old Sipho Balintulo making his way toward her with more than his usual haste. He was a cheeky youngster, this Sipho, his bony knees habitually covered with scratches he'd got by scrambling through some farmer's fence or throwing himself too hastily down the stony banks of the river.

He was a habitual visitor, and Evelyn had accepted his presence without comment. She knew how hungry he must be, and how (after the desertion of a husband who had gone to the mines to make ends meet and ended up moving in with another woman) his mother had given up looking after her children. So if Sipho was around, Evelyn prepared a meal and laid out an extra plate.

Her action was not merely one of charity, or because she liked the boy, but also, as she finally convinced him, a *quid pro quo*. For Sipho ran errands for her. He fetched water from the tap some miles away, and he made a halfhearted attempt to patch the fencing around her house. He was young and careless, but Evelyn valued his attempts to ease her life. After all, she was no longer a young woman, and the Transkei was an inhospitable place compared to the luxury of the Arnolds' house in Jo'burg.

Most important of all was the fact that Sipho supplied Evelyn with a link to the outside world. Despite her resolve that in her retirement she would ignore the news and concentrate only on herself, Evelyn experienced a hunger to find out what was happening. Sipho became her main source of information, and for that she valued him highly. He kept his ears open for anything that might interest her, and his eyes ready for discarded newspapers.

He had not visited her for some days, and Evelyn guessed that his mother must have taken a turn for the worse. That was one of Sipho's attractive qualities: He was a boy who had somehow learned to be gentle. Of all the Balintulo children, he was the one most likely to look after their mother when things got bad.

As he came closer, Evelyn was relieved to see that Sipho was grinning. She felt a sense of relief for the boy. Whatever had ailed his mother had not been terminal. And he wasn't only grinning—he was smiling proudly, as if he was really bringing her something of utmost import. In one hand he held a tin water container, which jogged up and down as he ran. In the other he waved a scrap of paper.

"Ma Evelyn!" he shouted as he wheeled to a halt in front of Evelyn.

"My child," she said. "What can be so important that you have spilled every drop of that precious water?"

Crestfallen, Sipho looked down at the empty container in his hand. "I will get some more," he mumbled, and turning his back on Evelyn, he slowly began to walk the way he had arrived.

Evelyn stopped him with a laugh. "I still have water," she said. "Come sit down. Tell me how your mother is."

Sipho turned, and Evelyn saw that a frission of depression crossed over his usually sunny face.

"She is not so well, Ma Evelyn," he said. With an effort, he forced himself to smile. "But she is getting better."

His voice was optimistic, but Evelyn knew him too well to miss his unvoiced fear. She nodded slowly. She patted a place on the ground beside her.

"Now, tell me what is so important that you lost all our water for it," she suggested gently.

In a flash Sipho's face was transformed. A look of excitement suffused it as he dropped the water container on the floor and waved the scrap of newspaper in Evelyn's direction.

"They killed them," he said. "They shot them."

"Who killed who?" Evelyn asked.

"The police shot the protestors," Sipho replied.

Evelyn experienced a flash of fear, and she breathed in sharply. For a moment she lost all cognizance of her surroundings. She stayed on her feet, but for a time it was as if the world turned first gray and then black. She put her hand onto the ground to steady herself.

Her state of semiconsciousness did not last long. The blurring of outline she had just experienced faded as she saw clearly the look of alarm crossing Sipho's face. She forced herself to calm down. She told herself that she was doing this because of the child, but inwardly she was a more severe judge of her own reactions than he. She despised herself for her fears. She, who had always thought of herself as calm in the face of any threat, noticed that these days she was prone to sudden panics and anxieties. It must, she thought, be a result of my isolation. I am too out of touch.

Resisting the impulse to grab the scrap of newspaper out of Sipho's hands, she spoke in a seemingly unconcerned voice.

"Sit down," she said, "and let us see how your reading has progressed."

Sipho crouched beside her, and Evelyn listened while he haltingly deciphered the headline.

"Sixty-seven dead," Sipho read. "In S-S-Shaps . . ."

Evelyn glanced down. "Sharpeville," she said.

She scanned the article quickly, as Sipho continued to spell out the words. By the time she got to the bottom, the fear that had originally overcome her had been replaced by a feeling of numbness. The newspaper article was garbled, and had been written some weeks before, but Evelyn had long ago learned to read between the lines. In broad outline what had happened was this. A crowd of people had gathered outside the Sharpeville police station protesting against the pass laws; the police, for reasons the reporter could not explain, had opened fire, shooting volley after volley of .303 bullets supplemented by Sten gun bursts.

The gunfire had continued until only the dead littered the forecourt. Sixty-seven people—men, women, and children—had been killed: Almost two hundred were said to have been injured.

"My God," Evelyn muttered.

Sipho Balintulo glanced up. "Would my father be dead, Ma Evelyn?" he asked plaintively.

"I doubt it, child," Evelyn replied. "Sharpeville is a long way from the Cape."

Having been reassured as to his father's safety, Sipho's scatty brain was led in another direction. "Ayiee, it's a big place, their South Africa!" he exclaimed in wonder.

"*Our* South Africa," Evelyn corrected.

Sipho was perplexed. "But we live in the Transkei," he protested.

"Which is part of South Africa," Evelyn replied fiercely. "I don't want to hear you talking about their South Africa and our South Africa ever again."

Sipho gulped. He had been so excited when he heard the conversation around him: He knew immediately that this massacre they all spoke of was worthy of Ma Evelyn's attention. He would never have dreamed of repeating such talk to his mother, who expressed a dislike to anything that occurred outside her immediate environment. But Ma Evelyn was different. Not trusting his own powers of retention, he had gone to work to get her the full story. He was proud of the way he'd managed to filch the scrap of newspaper that the adults passed from hand to hand. He had been sure that Evelyn would praise him for his resourcefulness.

Instead, she spoke with uncharacteristic venom. She, who was usually so patient, so willing to listen and to teach, looked at him as if he were a stranger. He wondered what he had done wrong.

Evelyn saw Sipho's discomfort, and she bent down and ruffled his cropped hair. "They deliberately breed ignorance in our children," she said in a meditative tone. "That is what Bantu education is all about. It is not your fault that your head is full of this nonsense. But you must be wary of what you are told. You must be on guard against falsehoods."

Embarrassed by the seriousness of her tone, Sipho shot Evelyn a winning smile. "I will, Ma Evelyn," he said. "But tell me—was your son, Uncle Moses, at this Sharpeville?"

"I doubt it," Evelyn said. "The Pan African Congress called this protest. They are a group of individuals who left the African National Congress to form a separate organization, while people like Moses stayed within the ANC."

"I see," Sipho said, and he nodded his head seriously. "The Pan ones like the whites."

Evelyn smiled. "On the contrary, they feel that the ANC works too much with whites. The Pan Africanists say that only a purely black organization can liberate our people."

"So are these Pan Africans bad?"

Evelyn smiled wryly to herself as she reflected on how easy it was to categorize their world into good and bad, black and white. "No, my son," she answered. "In my opinion, the PAC is misguided. But that does not give the police the right to shoot down unarmed people."

"I see," Sipho repeated. He quite plainly did not see, but Evelyn decided against further explanation. A child was a delicate thing, she thought. With not enough water, he can shrivel and grow into an embittered adult, with little capacity to hope for the future. But too much water, she thought, can drown the young seed: can make him close his eyes because he is overwhelmed by the complications.

Sipho was not one to accept silences easily. He searched around for something to say. Of course! What was he thinking about? He had almost forgotten that other nugget of information that he'd stored up for her.

Perhaps, he thought now, the two events were linked. That had not occurred to him before. "That's who the man is!" he shouted as he jumped up and down in excitement. "He must be a Pannist."

"Pan Africanist," Evelyn corrected. "And what man is this you speak of?"

"He came in the middle of the night," Sipho said. "He is a stranger."

"We are all strangers in this bitter land. You mean he's another poor soul 'endorsed' out of his home?"

"No," Sipho said. "This one is different. He came with the *baas* . . ."

"The white man," Evelyn interrupted.

"The white man," Sipho dutifully continued. "He has an evil look on his face, with scars all over, and as he walks, the chains on his legs and arms clink. They put him in a house on top of that hill in the distance. He's a dangerous man. Do you think he's a murderer?"

Evelyn, who was in the process of dismissing Sipho's story as the product of his overfertile imagination, became more attentive at the mention of chains. "How do you know he's dangerous?" she asked.

"The b—the white man said so. They said we must be careful of him and not go anywhere near him. They said he will harm our children in their beds." Sipho thought awhile and grinned. "But then I'm safe. I sleep on the floor, not in a bed."

Evelyn rose abruptly. "Where is this man's house?" she asked.

Sipho pointed in the distance beyond the veld and toward a rock-covered hill. "A long day's walk away. It is the home of Grandfather Dineka, who disappeared one night and who haunts his old dwelling," he said. "Perhaps that is why the man is not allowed to come near us."

"If he is not allowed here, then I must travel to him," Evelyn decided.

"But it is far," Sipho protested.

Evelyn looked to the west, where already the first rays of the pink evening light were beginning to suffuse the horizon. Soon it would be dark: The sun rose and fell abruptly in these parts. "Tomorrow is soon enough," she decided. "Come, let us eat before you return to your mother."

"In cold blood," Moses said quietly. "They shot them in cold blood."

He looked across at Rosa, and in his face was neither pain nor distress. There was something else written there, she thought, something indecipherable.

She frowned and thought a minute. He had told his story in a neutral voice, a voice that was almost deliberately devoid of emotion. He had come over, she knew, specifically to tell it, despite the fact that it was many days old, that it had already been thrown out into an astounded world, reports and pictures, too, of the violence that rained down on an unarmed crowd.

She wondered why he'd bothered to pay this special visit—on a day when, after his tour of the Cape, he could only have just returned.

She looked at him, and she saw that although his face was blank, his eyes seemed to be pleading with her. He wanted something from her, she knew that. She concentrated hard—she did not want to let him down. What would Evelyn have done? she asked of herself.

And then her brow cleared. "Do you feel guilty?" she said softly. "Guilty that you survived?"

He started, shook his head, opened his mouth to reinforce his denial, and suddenly, unexpectedly, began to weep. He could not stop himself once the tears started; he hung his head down, but they continued to fall. For ten long days he had kept back his pain, his misery, his shock. Now, it came flooding out, and he could do nothing to stanch it. He turned away from Rosa, so she would not see, but the shaking of his shoulders told their own story.

It did eventually stop itself. Gradually the tears grew less frequent, until finally they abated. Only then did he look at Rosa.

"I needed that," he said.

She nodded.

"Thanks for—"

He was interrupted by Jacob, who came storming into the room. In his hand he held an evening paper.

"Look at this!" he shouted, and so caught up was he that he did not notice anything strained in the air, and thus he gave Moses time to recover and to wipe his eyes. "Look at this," Jacob repeated.

There was one word printed in huge black letters on the front page. "Emergency," it said.

"They've given themselves almost unlimited powers," Jacob said. "The right of summary arrest, of curfews, of instant orders. And the next thing they're going to do is to ban the PAC, and the ANC along with it."

"We've been through this before," Rosa said softly.

"And this time we'll be better prepared," said Moses.

At the crack of dawn, with the sky still caught in that uneasy transition between dark and light, Evelyn emerged from her house. She felt the night's stiffness begin to leave her bones as she poured water from her dwindling supply into an old can. She balanced the can on a ring of stones, underneath which she had already laid a bundle of dry twigs. She lit the twigs, and then, holding the small of her back, she blew gently on them until the smoke abated and they began to glow.

She turned to fetch some mealie-meal from the store inside her house, and in so doing, she tripped over the prone body of Sipho Balintulo. She exclaimed in surprise.

Rubbing the sleep from his eyes, Sipho smiled tentatively up at her.

"So you slept here."

Sipho nodded. He eyed her warily.

"Why did you not tell me?" she asked. "You could at least have come into my house and been protected from the cold night air."

This sentence Sipho interpreted as a gesture as friendly as he could hope for. He jumped to his feet.

"I did not want to ask because you would have sent me home," he said.

Evelyn snorted. "Quite right. Just as I am going to now."

"Oh, please, Ma Evelyn, don't," Sipho said. "I want to come with you. I want to see the man."

"And what of your mother?"

"She won't worry."

Evelyn sighed. "And school?" she asked.

"Sometimes Bantu education is worse than no education at all." With a cheeky smile, Sipho was quoting Evelyn back at herself.

She gave in. "All right," she said. "But for once you must stem your endless whys. I am an old woman and have not the breath to answer your questions at the same time as I walk such a great distance."

She turned away and began stirring the mealie pap into the hot water. While it cooled, she began packing a large sack.

"Why . . . ?" Sipho began.

He stopped himself abruptly.

"The journey has not yet begun." Evelyn smiled. "You may finish your question."

"Why are you taking so many provisions?"

"For the man on the hill," Evelyn answered. "If the police dumped him there in the middle of the night, I can guess that he is without food or water. Now let's be off."

Sipho was right: The journey to the desolate house on the hill was an arduous one. Evelyn, who was finding her breath less easy to regulate these days, was forced to take constant rests on the way. She would sit on the ground while Sipho fussed around her, pouring her a drop to drink, bringing her wildflowers to inspect, chatting animatedly, as if the conversation he had stemmed on their march was always there, waiting to burst out anew.

It was during one of these breaks that the full force of what she had read yesterday hit Evelyn. So far her main reaction had been relief in the knowledge that her son, Moses, would not have been among the Sharpeville crowd. Now, as she sat in the quiet heat of the countryside, her eyes welled with tears for the sons of those who would never look at the sun again, for the mothers of children whose lives were ended so certainly and yet so casually. The bitterness ran deep in her heart. How long can our people meet guns with words, she thought. How long can we go on?

She was torn between despair and a desire for vengeance. And yet, there was nothing that she could do.

"I am old," she muttered to her companion, as she put her hand on Sipho's shoulders and levered herself upright.

"*Ja*, Ma Evelyn," he agreed. "You are old."

She smiled to herself. Sipho had not yet learned to dissemble, to deliver to his audience the words it wanted to hear. With him, Evelyn could be herself. She could show her age, and her weariness, and he would accept it without question. Sipho embraced Evelyn's transitional status in his life. She had appeared and made his lot better: When she disappeared again, that would be part of the bargain. He would go on as he had always gone on: facing each fresh obstacle in his life as best he could.

"There it is!" Sipho's shouts cut across Evelyn's thoughts. She saw that they had indeed arrived.

She found herself staring at a one-room dwelling that had formerly boasted two windows and a door. The windows were now completely smashed in, their frames old and rotten. The door was still present, but it hung from its hinges, threatening to fall at any moment. But it was the roof that was most shocking: One only had to give it a cursory glance to see the holes that were now more plentiful than the tin that had once provided sanctuary in this exposed location.

There were two ways of regarding this house: through the eyes of an inhabitant and through those of a tourist. To the latter, it would have had a certain rustic charm: The structure was there— it only needed some work to make it comfortable. And the view, Evelyn could almost hear the visitor cry, made up for the current lack of amenities. For it was magnificent. The house was set on the highest ground for miles and on a clear day the grandeur and scale of the landscape were breathtaking. All around the brown veld dominated: The shimmering heat in the distance sparkled in the air, the soft grass whispered promises to the romantic.

And yet one only had to live a few months in the Transkei to know that vistas like this meant nothing but trouble. For someone living all alone on this hillside, water would be hard to obtain: If seedlings did not die of thirst, they would be eaten at night by the creatures of the veld. And the jackals would be there constantly, with their threatening cries ringing into the night.

What good the knowledge that a small amount of money would ensure a safer dwelling when money was as scarce as water? What good a view that brought with it so much isolation?

"Good day," Evelyn called, and she wondered at the tremor that suffused her voice. Sipho's wild stories have got to me, she thought, I must pull myself together. "Good day," she called again, and this time her voice was firm.

When the man appeared in the doorway, Evelyn saw at once why Sipho had feared him. For the man was covered with bruises, now in the first phase of healing and thus made more ugly as they swelled in purple and black splotches on his face. Over his left eye was a deep cut that was beginning to fester. He walked in a lopsided way, as if each step tore at the gash on his ankles. His trousers were frayed so much so that one more rent would make them completely inoperative. On his shirt was a brown mess of dried-up blood.

Sipho ran behind Evelyn and buried his face in her skirt. She pushed him away. "Get out from there, boy," she said. "Can't you see that this gentleman has been badly beaten? Come now, we must tend to him."

The man smiled, and in a flash his whole appearance was transformed. As his black eyes filled with tears, a sort of gentleness shone through, and a gratefulness. Now, it was a kind of inner dignity that one noticed, a strength and pride on his battered features.

Evelyn walked toward him, her hand outstretched.

"Evelyn Bopape," she said.

"Nathaniel's wife," the man said, as he limped to meet her. "I have heard much good of you."

"And I heard that the police brought you to this place."

The man nodded somberly. As he shook her hand, Evelyn could feel the tremor in his fingers. "Nat Phakasi," he said. "I come from—"

Evelyn cut him off in midsentence. "Later is the time for talk," she said. "First let us tend your wounds. Sipho," she commanded, "fetch some water quickly."

She did the best she could with the inadequate implements she had on her. While the man crouched on the ground she cleaned the cut on his face with an iodine-soaked rag. She tended to his wounds on wrists and ankles alike—deep cuts that had been gashed in part to the very bone.

"They delight in putting on chains too tight," Nat said between gritted teeth.

Evelyn nodded without looking up. She never once regarded him as she worked. If she had seen the pain registering in his face, she would not have been able to continue with her work. She kept her mind concentrated on other things—on the foresight that had prompted her to pack the disinfectant. There was nothing in the room that could have helped this man: nothing clean, no blankets, no mattress, no food.

Nat winced as Evelyn bathed his wounds, but for the most part he remained silent. Only after Evelyn had built a fire and cooked a nourishing meat stew did he let out a small groan.

"Go ahead," she invited. "There is plenty of food."

Sipho giggled as Nat dug his spoon into the plate with so much haste that the gravy spattered on his chest. Evelyn glared at the boy.

"Have you forgotten the times when you had nothing?" she demanded.

Sipho shook his head forlornly.

"It is an easy thing to forget," Evelyn said. "But never allow yourself that luxury."

Nat Phakasi took a second helping and then a third, and washed the lot down with a deep gulp of water. When he had finished, Evelyn began to question him.

"Where is your home?" she asked.

"Jo'burg," he replied.

"And what brought you to this desolate place?"

Nat rubbed his chin and leaned back against the crumbling wall of the house. "The Boers dragged me here," he said. "They forced me from my home. If not for the pleading of my wife, I would be wearing only the pajamas in which they pulled me out of bed."

"But why here?" Evelyn was perplexed.

Nat Phakasi shrugged. "They have banished me," he said simply.

"Banished? What is this?"

Nat looked down at his nails. "Ever since the Emergency . . ." he began. He stopped when he heard Evelyn's exclamation. He looked up at her.

"I have been out of touch," she said. "I have heard of no Emergency."

Nat smiled wryly. "It fell on us like a ton of bricks also," he said. "Did you hear of the massacre in Sharpeville?"

Evelyn nodded. "I have only just received the news," she said. "It tore a pain in my heart. How did our people react to such an outrage?"

"With anger," Nat said proudly. "In Cape Town thousands stopped work. The docks were completely shut down. In Jo'burg they had a day of mourning a week after the slaughter. The police broke that up with tear gas. But our people were undaunted. It looked like nothing could stop them. So many came out in protest that the Boer even suspended the pass laws for a while. But then he got nasty and declared a State of Emergency. They started arresting our people indiscriminately. One after the other they began to pick us off. I was expecting the bangs on the door. I thought I was headed for jail like thousands of others."

"And why didn't you end up there?" Evelyn asked.

Again Nat shrugged. "We have had reports that certain people have gone missing. The last time they were seen was when they were dragged from their houses. Their families were told nothing. They appeared to vanish between their homes and the police station. We could not understand it."

"But now . . ." Evelyn started.

Nat nodded. "*Ja*, now I understand. The constable who arrested me laughed when I demanded to go to jail. 'You are going to disappear,' he said, 'as easily as a puff of smoke.' I thought that was the end for me. I thought I'd had it. But instead of killing me, they transferred me to a police van and carried on driving through the night. They stopped for nothing—I had to urinate in my moving cell—except to place me in the charge of first one police authority and then another. Finally they dumped me here. They served me with an order saying that I cannot leave this place. I have no money, no food, and don't know whether I can walk to town to write to my wife and tell her I am safe. Even last night when I had slept on this cold floor, I was awakened by a flashlight. It was the police coming to check that I was still there."

As he told his story, Nat talked at increasing speed, until by the end, his words scrambled one on top of the other, making them almost incomprehensible. He stopped suddenly, seeming to notice the intense concentration on Evelyn's face. He buried his head in his arms. His shoulders shook.

Evelyn let him cry until the shaking subsided. Only then did she speak.

"I will help you," she said.

"What can you do?" His voice was muffled.

"I will write to your wife," Evelyn said. "And bring you food."

Nat looked up. He wiped his eyes with the tattered shirt that lay beside him. "It's the isolation," he said plaintively. "And the worry for my wife."

"I know," Evelyn said.

Nat smiled. "You are a good woman," he said. "To come all this way to tend to me."

Evelyn shrugged off his thanks. This man, she thought, needed all his strength to face the coming days. He would not survive if he dwelt too much in self-pity. It was her job to distract him. She busied herself memorizing Nat's address and talking to him about the old days. She would also, she told him, write to her friends in Jo'burg to find out what this new law was that allowed men to be banished without recourse to court. Her son, Moses, would know—or Rosa, for sure—and if they didn't, then they would investigate.

All too soon came the time when Evelyn must make her way home. She saw the look of disappointment—of anguish, even—that crossed Nat's face when she rose, but there was nothing she could do about it. She was too old, too frail, to stay in this cold place even for just one night.

Nat accompanied them to the bottom of the hill. He waved, the animation fading from his face as he saw his new friends about to desert him again.

"Is there anything else you want?" Evelyn called.

"Some thread," Nat said, and he pointed to his trousers. "And, if possible . . ." He hesitated.

"Tell me," Evelyn urged.

"Ag, it is too much to ask."

"Nothing is too much between friends," Evelyn replied.

"Well, then," Nat said tentatively. "A saxophone. Or if not, some other kind of wind instrument. It will make my days less lonely."

Evelyn smiled. "You are a musician?"

"*Ja*," Nat said. "In this country even music has become dangerous."

Evelyn patted Sipho's head. "Sipho is the one to get that," she said. "A real scavenger, this boy. He can find anything, if he puts his mind to it."

And with that, she put her hand in Sipho's and gave him a gentle push in the direction of home. Nat watched them until the two figures were so far in the distance that he could hardly see them.

When she got back, Evelyn would not allow herself to surrender to the weariness that threatened to overwhelm her. She instructed Sipho to light the paraffin lamp. Sitting beside it, she began to write. First she sent her greetings and an account of what had happened to Nat Phakasi's wife. She sealed that up in a brown envelope and placed it to one side.

The sound of the cicadas had built to a crescendo around her. From every side she was bombarded by their clacking as they sang of their life and of their own sorrows. Evelyn shivered. Suddenly she felt very cold. She blinked. How dark everything had become. Had the lamp begun to flicker and fade? "Sipho," she called.

The next thing she knew was the sound of Sipho's high voice and the sight of his face peering down at her. "Ma Evelyn, Ma Evelyn!" he shouted.

Evelyn blinked. Why was she lying on the floor? What had happened to her?

"Ma Evelyn," Sipho repeated.

"Hush now, child," she said, and she found that her words were slurred in a way she couldn't control. With the utmost effort, she enunciated her next sentence so slowly that no one would have guessed how much effort it cost. "I was in such a hurry to get to bed that I fell where I lay," she said. "Here, help me up."

With calm words, Evelyn soothed Sipho's anxiety. She gave no sign of the thoughts that were swirling around her own mind. She had blacked out: That she realized. And for the second time.

The event the day before when she momentarily lost consciousness she had ascribed to anxiety. Now, she knew that it had been something else: something her body was trying to tell her.

"Ayiee, I am growing old," she muttered to herself as she leaned on Sipho. Her left side felt stiff, and would not do as she bid it. "I need sleep," she said. But still she was unwilling to face the fact of her collapse. It made her angry. She grabbed hold of the doorframe and pushed Sipho away. "Go find yourself a blanket," she said. "This night, you sleep inside. And tomorrow you must go home."

"But . . ."

"I need you to go to town," Evelyn interrupted. "You have tasks to do for our new friend, and I want you to send the letter I have just completed plus post another two I will write. Apart from that, Bantu education is sometimes better than no education at all."

She was desperately tired: More than anything, she wanted to lay down her head and sink into blessed unconsciousness. But Evelyn was a stubborn woman—more stubborn with herself than with anybody else. In spite of her fatigue, or perhaps because of it, she forced herself to stay up and finish her letters. It cost her a monumental effort. Several times her hand slipped off the page and refused to return to it. She had to lift one hand with the other to start again. Added to that was the fact that the page kept blurring in front of her eyes.

But even so, she persisted. She concentrated on keeping her scrawl between the outlines of the page.

And then, at last, she was finished. She put the two missives into envelopes, covered Sipho gently with a blanket he had restlessly tossed off, and lay down. Within minutes, she was fast asleep.

32

1960

THEY CAME FOR MOSES IN THE MIDDLE OF THE NIGHT. THEY DID NOT bother to knock at the door, they knocked it down with sledge-hammers. When it crashed to the floor, they jumped in after it, five or six of them, with dogs straining on leashes. In their hands they held flashlights, which they pointed ahead of them, so that when Moses got up from bed he was temporarily blinded.

"What the hell's going on?" he mumbled as he held a hand up to his face.

"Moses Bopape, come with us," ordered a rough voice.

"Under what law?"

The flashlight in front wavered as the man in charge laughed. "We don't need laws," he said. "Not since the Emergency. Now come with us."

Two constables moved to either side of Moses, and then, taking his arms, they propelled him out of the house.

The police were more gentle with Jacob, although they made no attempt to keep their actions secret. They walked into his office in broad daylight and demanded to see him without delay.

Jacob was in the middle of a conversation when he heard the unmistakable sound of police voices in his outer office. Their barked orders were followed by the softer voice of his receptionist, who was doing her best to dissuade them from barging in. Jacob looked at Philip Cohen.

"You're a patient," he mouthed.

Philip nodded anxiously. The voices came closer.

"Take off your shirt," Jacob said.

There was a knock on the door, the soft, familiar knock of his receptionist, followed by two equally familiar loud raps.

"Jacob Swiece," called a voice. "Open up."

Philip, now shirtless, climbed onto Jacob's examining table.

"Hold on," called Jacob. "I'm in the middle of examining a patient." He was in fact riffling through his desk, pulling out papers from every corner of it.

"I'm warning you," came the voice.

Jacob bundled the papers together and ran over to Philip. "Shift a minute," he whispered. When Philip turned to one side, Jacob lifted up the sheet and bundled the papers underneath him. Then he smoothed down the sheet again. As the door opened, he bent his head to Philip's chest.

"Looking for this, Doc?" The police sergeant was standing by the door, and in his hand he dangled Jacob's stethoscope.

Jacob looked up. "This is an outrage," he said coldly. "Can't you see that I'm in the middle of an examination?"

The policeman looked at Philip, and he uttered nothing by way of apology.

They know that Philip's a contact, thought Jacob. They'll pick him up, too.

But the policeman's eyes moved on to other points in the room. "Your patients may learn to choose their doctors more carefully in the future," he said in a bored voice. "Now kindly come with us."

Jacob knew that there was no point in protesting. He went to his desk and removed his jacket from the back of the chair. He put it on and walked slowly to the door. He turned before he exited, and looked around the room. The policeman placed a hand on his arm.

Jacob just got the chance for one more look, and the last thing he saw was Philip still prone on the table, his face an unhealthy white. His chest, Jacob observed in a detached kind of way, was also white: If he had been Philip's doctor, he would have prescribed a dose of sun.

"Come on," said the policeman.

As Jacob began to move, concern for Philip's health was replaced by a more somber thought. He knew that once they picked him up, they would also be after Rosa. He prayed that she would evade their net, that she at least would be able to escape as they had planned, to leave the country until this Emergency came to an end.

"Phone my wife, please," he told his receptionist.

She nodded.

She went to the window and watched her employer being led toward a police car. She saw them shove Jacob into the back and slam the door. Then, sirens blaring, the car drove off.

The door to Jacob's examining room opened, and a man came out. He was pulling on his jacket, and the receptionist could see that his hands were trembling. She didn't blame him—it must have come as quite a shock to have your doctor arrested in the middle of a consultation. She smiled sympathetically at the man.

"Is there anything I can do?" she asked.

He jumped, and his eyes flared. He mumbled something, and then, quickening his pace, he left the room.

The receptionist shrugged, picked up the phone and dialed Jacob's home number. She let it ring for what seemed like forever, and then she hung up. She looked at her watch: Three-thirty—she'd try again in an hour.

Four o'clock, and Rosa, having picked up the kids from school, was driving them back. She had been forced to make a number of unscheduled stops—Rachel demanded sweets and Martha a special kind of pen sold only in three shops in the whole of Jo'burg—and she was worrying about the time. She was behind with her work, and had a meeting to go to that night. The children were bickering—probably because they were hungry, and Rosa couldn't remember whether there was enough food in the house. On top of that, she had a vague suspicion that Julia had said she was dropping by that day. Julia would be furious if the kids weren't there when she arrived.

She looked at her watch again.

"That's *very* interesting," Rachel said, stressing the middle word, "there's another."

Since Rachel had recently developed a tendency to start every sentence with "That's very interesting," Rosa ignored her. But Martha didn't.

"What's interesting, little girl?" she asked.

"Shan't tell you." Rachel pouted.

"That's 'cause there's nothing to tell. You're always making things up."

"I don't!" Rachel shouted. "I don't!"

"Children, please," Rosa said in exasperation. "Don't quarrel."

"She started it," Rachel said.

"Enough." Rosa knew that there was little point in interceding, and that her only hope was to distract them. "Tell us what's interesting," she urged Rachel.

"Well," bragged Rachel, "I've counted four police cars, and there's another one."

"So?" Martha asked. "So?"

Martha's voice seemed to fade into the distance as Rosa checked her mirror. The distraction she'd been experiencing was gone: She was suddenly alert, completely alert. She saw that Rachel was indeed right—there was evidence of unusual police activity in the area. Her mind began to work furiously, and she took her foot off the accelerator to give herself more time.

"Hey," called Martha as the car passed slowly by their house.

Rosa did not reply. She had seen what she'd expected: She'd looked down the driveway and seen two strange cars parked there. She put her foot down on the accelerator.

"Hey," Rachel protested.

"Shuddup," Martha said. "Can't you see that something's wrong?"

"Where have you been?" Julia asked. "I've been ringing."

"Not now, Mom." Rosa pushed her way into the house. "I have to make some calls."

She dialed Jacob's office. The receptionist answered on the second ring.

"Oh, Mrs. Swiece," she said, "I've been trying to contact you. The police came and took Dr. Swiece away. The waiting room is full of patients, and I don't know what to do with them."

"Get a locum," Rosa said curtly.

"I have." The receptionist's voice was hurt.

Rosa softened hers. "I'm sorry," she said. "I know you're doing your best. I think you better find somebody to stand in for Jacob. The State of Emergency gives them almost unlimited powers, and they might decide to hold him for some time."

She put the phone down and glanced at her mother, whose angry gaze had been transformed into fearful anticipation. She nodded her head and then resumed dialing.

"Come along," Julia said to the children. "Let's go and see if we can rustle you up some biscuits."

It took a mere half hour to assess the extent of the arrests. Moses had been jailed, as had Raymond Siponja, Max Freeman, and hundreds, if not thousands, of others. And there was no doubt about it, they were after her as well—they'd been asking about her at the university.

"Mom," Rosa called.

Julia came running.

"You remember what we talked about the other day?" she asked.

Julia nodded her head.

"Well, we have to put it into action."

"Harold as well? He's playing golf."

"They're picking up everybody," Rosa answered. "Dad has been doing the Congress of Democrats' accounts, and that places him in jeopardy."

"Then I'm coming, too," Julia said firmly.

"Fine," Rosa answered. "Call Dad and get yourself ready. I don't think you need to hurry too much: They can't arrest everybody at once. But leave before morning, hey?"

She looked at her watch—quarter to five.

She must be off soon: They would eventually guess that she wasn't coming home, and they might go so far as to broadcast her license number over the police radio. "Let's get some food in the children," she said. "And then I'll go."

She started driving at five-thirty, and she forced herself to go slowly. It would never do to get arrested for speeding, she thought; that would be the ultimate stupidity.

She did not have to look at the map, because she had already planned her route some days before. When news of the Emergency had first surfaced, they had discussed the matter in full. They could not, they agreed, afford for the movement to be decimated, and so those who escaped the first trawl would get out of the country fast.

And so Rosa drove, all evening and into the night. She ignored the children's complaints—she chided them when they demanded to get out. She drove through the towns of Benoni and Bethal, and as the traffic dwindled, she forced herself to keep her eyes on the lonely beam in front of her and to keep thinking so that she would not fall asleep. She thought of that other time when she had been so much on the road, that time during the Defiance Campaign. It had been good fun, she thought.

She shivered. This was different now—the stakes had got so much higher. Sharpeville had shown that, and Langa, too. The Nats had been threatened, and now they were acting: Things would never be safe again.

She looked down at her watch—1:00 A.M.—and as she did so, her eyes fell on the gas gauge. She started—what had she been thinking of? It was almost empty.

She peered desperately down the deserted road, but everything was in complete darkness. She slowed down and worked out her options.

And then, just when she had decided that she should stop until daybreak, she saw a sign by the side of the road. ERMELO it said: She breathed a sigh of relief.

She was lucky to find a garage just on the outskirts of town. It wasn't exactly a garage, more a gas pump stuck on a concrete surround, and with a low house in its background. There was nobody in sight.

"What's happening?" Martha mumbled from the back.

"Sssh," Rosa said. "Go back to sleep."

She got out of the car and walked toward the house. She knocked at the door and waited.

She had to wait quite a time before a light was switched on and a mumbled curse uttered. Then the door opened slowly. There was a man in a dressing gown standing there, and in his hand was a shotgun.

"Yes?"

Rosa hid her nervousness and put on her most winning smile. "I've run out of petrol," she said. Her mouth turned down. "My mother's been taken ill," she said. "I have to get to her."

The man looked her up and down.

"I have two children in the car," she said quickly.

"Wait," mumbled the man, and he closed the door on her.

When he reemerged, he was dressed, unarmed, and in a considerably better mood.

"I'm sorry to disturb you," Rosa said.

He waved off her apology. "Ag, I get used to it," he said.

He walked to her car and, and taking the handle from the gas pump, he began to crank it up. He pressed his foot down, but nothing happened. He turned the handle some more, and again he pushed his foot. Still nothing.

"Shit," he said. He turned to Rosa. "I'm sorry, lady," he said, "but this *blerry* thing's playing up. I'll just be a tic."

He turned and began to walk back to the house.

Rosa leaned against the car and felt her fatigue wash over her. She looked up at the points of tiny lights in that immensity of the dark sky, and she wondered what was happening to Jacob. At least he wouldn't be alone, she thought, not the way she was. She suddenly felt very tiny.

And then her head whipped around, for she had heard a noise. It was coming from down the road, it was a car coming toward her.

Don't get paranoid, she told herself.

But in seconds it was not paranoia but fear, and then adrenaline, that rushed through her body. For the car was no ordinary car. It had a flashing blue light on its hood. It was a police car.

She wrenched open the back door and shook Martha roughly. "Wha . . . ?"

"Get up," Rosa said. She stretched across her eldest and did the same to Rachel, but Rachel didn't stir. Running around the back, Rosa opened the other door and lifted Rachel out. She saw with relief that Martha had stumbled from the car and was rubbing her eyes.

The car was coming closer.

"Run," Rosa hissed, and with Rachel in her arms, she began to move.

They didn't get far: The land was too open for that. They reached only a clump of low scrub some twenty yards from the gas-pump area when Rosa dropped to her knees.

"Get down," she hissed at Martha, whose breath was coming out in low sobs. She stretched across and pressed on Martha's shoulders to reinforce her order.

"Mummy," moaned Rachel.

"Ssh." Rosa craned her neck and looked at the police car, which had drawn up near her own. She saw a man in uniform get out, yawn, stretch his arms above him, and then stroll over to her car and peer inside. She put her hand over Rachel's mouth.

"Hey, Piet." The man from the house had returned. Rosa could see his face in the garishness of the blue light, and his voice floated clearly over to her.

The policeman smiled. "I saw you had customers," he said.

"*Ja*. A woman and two children. She was here a moment ago. Funny."

The policeman paused for what seemed to Rosa like an eternity before shrugging nonchalantly. "Probably answering a call of nature." He yawned again and stepped back into his car. "I better get on, I suppose," he said. "Only stopped to check out you were okay."

"Why's your light going, then?"

The policeman closed the door and leaned out of the window. "Ag, sometimes I can't be bothered," he said. "So I put the light on to warn the boys I'm on my way, and if they're sensible, they'll go back to bed and leave me alone."

And then his car moved off.

Rosa waited until the light was just a point in the distance, and then she nudged both the children and stood up. With one arm around each of them, she walked back to the man.

He had finished filling the car and was replacing the pump. He turned to her and smiled. "You could have used the facilities in the house," he said.

"I didn't want to bother you further," Rosa said. "You've been so kind to get up." She pushed Rachel, who was still half-asleep, into the backseat and closed the door on her. "How much do I owe you?" she asked. She handed him a fiver, and when he began to root into his pockets for some change, she shook her head.

She got into the car and switched the engine on.

"Hope your mother gets better," he called, as she began to drive away. She did not even have the energy to reply.

She caught one last sight of him in her mirror: He was standing by the gas pump staring straight at her car, and he was scratching his head. She waved her hand, and she saw him lift his in response. She put her foot down on the accelerator.

Automatically she drove until she was sure that she was out of sight. Then she stopped the car. She took her hands off the steering wheel, and when she held them in front of her, they shook. She shivered.

"Mummy," Martha said.

"Go back to sleep," Rosa said. "It's all right."

She bent her head down on the steering wheel and allowed herself just a few tears before she straightened up again. Then she sniffed, turned the key, and they were on their way again.

She stared straight ahead as she drove, through Ermelo and Piet Retief, too. She took in little of her surroundings, only registering them when she was forced to wait until after dawn for the border post to open.

She handed in their passports, and they were returned without comment. And then she crossed over the bridge and into Swaziland.

33

Swaziland was a tiny country in the midst of South Africa, a small kingdom outside of the jurisdiction of the South African state. It was there that Rosa, her children, her parents, and many others who had managed to escape in time sat out the Emergency.

One week turned into the next, and one month into the following, while the exiles created a semblance of ordinary life. Their children went to school, those who could work did, the others occupied their time as best they were able, walking the hills, playing bridge, or planning for the future. Any amusement in the tiny capital city of Mbabane was fair game.

Even, Rosa thought idly, receptions at the British embassy. She leaned back, and putting her glass of oversweet white wine on a table, she began to walk away. She'd had enough, she thought, of muted and polite conversation. She wasn't in the mood for this; better to go back to the flat and be bored there.

But when she tried to move forward, someone blocked her way. She looked up and found herself staring into the eyes, the startling blue eyes, of a man whose fair hair was streaked with gray.

"I'm so sorry," he said, and she heard from his accent that he was not only English but upper-class English.

She smiled and was about to maneuver around him when he held out his hand.

"Richard Crossbanks," he said.

"Rosa Swiece," she replied, as she shook his hand. She liked the way he clasped her hand firmly, and then released it easily. She liked, she thought, a lot of things about him: his eyes, his height, his handshake. Warning bells sounded in the back of her mind.

"Nice to meet you," she said, and again she started to walk away.

But this time he came with her. He had an easy stride about him, she saw. He was comfortable in himself. She glanced again at him and noticed how elegant his clothes were. They were casual and unostentatious, but a closer inspection revealed not one crease or speck of dust on them. He moved in a way that gave an impression of hidden bodily power but without arrogance.

"Do I pass?" he asked, and his eyes were smiling.

She looked away quickly.

"I've heard of you, Rosa Swiece," he said. "You're one of the South African exiles." He paused, and she found that her eyes were drawn back to him. "I admire you," he continued. She felt at once that he wasn't just complimenting her, but that he meant what he said. "You've got a long, hard battle ahead of you," he finished.

"That's for sure," she said. She was beginning to enjoy herself.

"But you'll win," he said.

She liked his manner, as well, she thought, the directness of it. "And what do you do?" she asked.

"I work for Self-Aid," he said. "A charity."

Rosa nodded. Swaziland, she reflected, was stuffed with charities. Their officials were all running around trying to start projects, tripping over each other in the process.

He saw the skepticism in her eyes, and he smiled. "We're different," he said.

"How, different?"

"We believe in helping people to become self-sufficient," he said. "Rather than in pouring out money, which, when it's removed, leaves people worse off than they were before."

"That's a tall order," Rosa commented, "trying to make tiny Swaziland, marooned as it is among hostile states, self-sufficient."

"True," he said, "but—" He never got the chance to continue, because a man came up behind him and hit him heartily on the back.

"So, Richard," the man drawled. "The grapevine tells me that you're creating your usual moral panic. What would we do without you to keep us honest?"

Richard's face became immediately serious—angry, even. He looked straight at the man. "We don't ask people for money in order to see it spent on bribes," he said.

The man smiled. "You're too naive," he said. "Of course, we would prefer not have to oil the wheels, but when you've been on this continent as long as I have, you will learn that sometimes that's the only way to get things going."

"What I don't like about your methods," Richard said—and although he was smiling, there was something of a warning in his face—"is that they're just a blind for your cynicism."

The man laughed. "Always the outspoken one," he said. "Well, let me tell you . . ."

Rosa had heard enough, and she began to walk away when Richard held out a hand to restrain her. "I'll show you round one of our projects," he offered. "If you'd be interested."

Say no, Rosa told herself. "I'd like that," she said.

And then she did walk off.

She was not, however, spared the punch line. Before she left that place, she heard Richard's companion's loud voice. "That's a new one on etchings," he was saying.

Rosa scowled. "Keep away from him," she lectured herself.

But Rosa did not keep away from him. Mbabane was so small and the circles so interconnected that it was virtually impossible to do so. In addition, Rosa enjoyed Richard's company. He was serious about his work, and good at it, too, but he also knew how to enjoy himself.

He seemed to spend some considerable time inventing exotic cocktails with which to lure her to his luxurious house. She knew that he worked, and worked hard, but whenever she came across him, he assumed a pose of gracious relaxation. He was always comparing himself with her, and casting himself in an unfavorable light: He admired her, he said, for she knew what she wanted from life, while he continued to drift.

But despite the fact that he kept telling her how strong she was, he had an uncanny knack of throwing her into confusion. She didn't understand how it happened, but she found herself growing gauche and tongue-tied in his presence. She was rarely indecisive, and yet with Richard she kept changing her mind.

She kept resolving to keep away from him, and then she'd find herself accepting his invitations.

It was boredom, she kept telling herself, that was what it was.

And she was bored. She had even begun to catch herself wishing that it had been she, not Jacob, who'd been taken into custody.

It was a silly thing to wish, at least on the face of it, but there was some reality in it. For Jacob was in prison surrounded by comrades: Incarcerated as he undoubtedly was, he was still in the thick of things. They would all be there, she knew, and they would be planning.

In some ways the regime had presented them with a perfect opportunity: All those busy people finally thrown together—the chances for unfettered political debate must be enormous! Instead of fitting theoretical discussions into overloaded work and family commitments, they could subject their ideas, their plans, their disagreements, to microscopic examination.

It would be happening in both parts of the prison—in the one that held the whites and the one that held the blacks. And they would all come out with a stronger organization. When the Emergency was finally called off, Rosa knew that a more sophisticated kind of political animal would emerge from behind the heavy gates of Pretoria Jail.

Meanwhile, she languished in the dryness of Swaziland. It was a beautiful country, and it was safe even though surrounded on three sides by South Africa and with Portuguese-controlled Mozambique lining its eastern border, but it was dead. Everything here moved at a snail's pace.

And in addition, Rosa had taken a step backward in time. She wasn't alone with the children; that would have had its difficulties, but it would have been manageable. Instead, her parents shared their flat.

Her father, Harold, was no problem: He was a gentle man whose serene calm made him the easiest of house partners. But the same could not be said for Julia. Her every move annoyed Rosa. Not a day passed without some kind of scene between the two women.

It was inevitable, Rosa supposed. She had left her family home so many years ago that she had forgotten the reasons that had originally impelled her to get away. Yet it only took a few weeks in the same small space to observe the old problems flooding back with a vengeance.

The most annoying thing was that Julia didn't seem capable of holding her tongue. She constantly interfered, seeming to take delight in contradicting her daughter. She was so contrary—worse, in fact, than the children. If Rosa ordered Martha to take a bath, Julia would give the child permission to go to bed dirty. If Rosa let a hysterical Rachel off brushing her teeth for one day, then Julia went around the flat muttering about the perils of plaque.

"It's all so petty," Rosa muttered. She sighed and reached for her glass.

Julia chose that moment to join her. She walked out onto the balcony and lowered herself into the chair next to Rosa's. She grimaced. "It's terrible to be old," she said.

Rosa looked at her mother. Julia made such constant reference to her increasing years that Rosa had learned to ignore the opening gambits. Now, she saw that Julia was indeed no longer in her prime: Her hair was almost totally gray, and although the gaze in her eyes was as firm as ever, the skin around them had begun to wrinkle and bag. On her hands were the telltale signs of age spots.

"Want a drink?" Rosa asked.

Julia shook her head. "It's going to be a nice sunset," she said.

"Yes," Rosa agreed, and she gritted her teeth. That was, she thought, one of Swaziland's specialties—sunsets.

"Going out tonight?"

Julia's voice was one of casual inquiry, but Rosa, perhaps because she was more than usually irritated that evening, heard suspicion in it. "I might," she replied. There was a pause. "Would you mind?" she asked.

"Mind? Why should I mind?"

And Rosa, who had really no intention of going out, who had in fact resolved to ignore Richard's invitation, to put a stop not only to the doubt in her mind but also to the whole silly relationship, found herself getting up. "I'll take my key," she said, "so you don't have to wait up for me."

The elevator was, as usual, slow to arrive. Rosa had to wait for ages before it reached the fifth floor, and in that time she toyed with the idea of turning back. She'd really never intended to accept Richard's invitation. But here she was, stepping into the elevator, pretending that it was a fit of pique at her mother's concealed disapproval that motivated her. It wasn't that, she thought. It was because she wanted to go.

A new thought entered her head. When she'd declined, he'd laughingly said he would wait for her anyway. She'd been flattered to find how much their date mattered to him, and at the same time angry that he should presume so. Now, she found herself worrying about the humiliation if she turned up to find him out—or worse still, entertaining somebody else.

She looked at herself in the small mirror of her compact and primped her lips. "I'm behaving like an adolescent," she muttered as she stepped out of the elevator. "I shouldn't go."

Nevertheless, she kept on walking.

Julia leaned forward and rested her arms on the concrete balcony. From this vantage point she watched Rosa walk purposefully down the road. Rosa looked, from above, as if she didn't have a care in the world. It was strange, seeing her from so far away, seeing the carelessness in her sway, the way she tossed her head, the elegance with which she hailed a taxi.

"I hope you know what you're doing," Julia muttered, as she saw Rosa step in.

The taxi turned around the corner, leaving in its wake a cloud of dust.

Richard's home was on a hill a few miles outside Mbabane. It was a place where the worst of the effects of the blazing sun were conveniently mitigated. A light breeze, some localized freak of geography, ensured that the house was cool and refreshing— a place of refuge from the parched outside. When the breeze dropped, Richard had only to push a button to get the air conditioner to take over.

The house was surrounded by a cultured garden contrasting sharply with the red dust, which, broken only by the occasional tuft of brown grass, stretched as far as the eye could see. On the high fences that protected the house, a variety of fragrant climbers grew, filling the air with their heavy scent. A liberally used sprinkler ensured that the plants continued to flourish in defiance of the prevailing conditions.

When Rosa questioned Richard as to his right to live amid so much luxuriance in this land of drought, Richard shrugged and said that the gardener was included in the rent. How could he, he argued, dispense with the man's services and thus deprive his family of its only form of income?

"And you are an aid person," Rosa protested. "Those kinds of excuses have been used the world over to stop people from changing things."

"I agree," Richard said. "But I don't believe in one-man crusades. I do my job as best I can. I think we offer the people of Swaziland some little productive help, and that's the limit of my ambitions." And he'd smiled at her, secure in his own opinions.

That was one of the things about Richard that simultaneously annoyed and attracted Rosa—life was so easy for him. He was generally sympathetic to their struggle, and yet when she tried to describe it in more detail, she got the impression he was suppressing amusement at the earnestness of it all. When she accused him of doing so, he denied it in that voice of his that left her feeling foolish.

"I can't let him do this to me," she told herself as she stepped out of the taxi. "After all, he's only a friend."

Richard had never expected Rosa to turn up. When he heard the sounds of a car stopping at his gate, a vague expression of annoyance crossed his handsome face. He had determined to spend the evening alone, listening perhaps to one of his large collection of classical records while enjoying the slight *tristesse* of being refused by the fascinating Rosa Swiece.

The irritation changed to delight as soon as he saw that it was Rosa. He watched her pay the driver and turn toward him. The last rays of sun were in her eyes and she couldn't see him, so he had time to drink in the sight of her.

She was wearing a beige suit made of linen and cut severely at the waist, and her matching shoes put the finishing touches on the image. Its elegance spoke of Paris or Rome, not of provincial Mbabane. She was a unique woman, he thought, fiery in her politics and fashionable in her dress. He smiled.

But then deliberately he composed his face: He didn't want to do anything to scare her off. It would not do to show her how pleased—and more important, how surprised—he was by her arrival.

Richard had known many women: Courting and winning them was one of his major pleasures in life. He enjoyed and respected the company of women. With them, he found he could be himself, he could talk naturally and at length, touching on a wide range of topics without experiencing the sharp edge of competition that always seemed to creep in when he was with his men friends.

Richard had never married, a fact that he knew caused many a raised eyebrow. But he felt that the reason was simple: He'd never found the right woman. Once or twice he'd been tempted to set up a more permanent relationship, but something had always prevented this, leaving him with a vague feeling of regret combined with an undefinable sense of relief.

Now, in Rosa Swiece, he'd at last met a woman whom he really wanted to possess. Perhaps, he speculated to himself, it's because I can't have her. But he'd got entangled with married women before—their very unavailability had brought its own advantages.

It was different with Rosa. He was attracted to her—everything about her appealed to his senses—and yet it was more than mere physical attraction. He admired her—for her tenaciousness, for her fierce mind, for her gentleness that showed through almost by default, and for the way she could suddenly switch from intense intellectual engagement to throwing her head back and laughing with abandon at something that caught her fancy.

There was, of course, one major hitch. Rosa's commitment to her husband was undeniable. Richard had never experienced as much as a twinge of jealousy in his life. What others possessed did not attract him—and yet he found himself raging inwardly at the luck of Jacob Swiece.

"Richard?" Rosa's tentative voice pulled him from his reverie. He strode up to her and, taking one of her hands in his, led her through the front door.

"You didn't expect me?" Rosa asked.

On a normal occasion Richard would have laughed off her question in a way that would have set the evening off in an appropriately light manner. But tonight he didn't feel like it. He looked her in the eye.

"I'd given up hope," he confessed.

Rosa threw Richard a jittery smile and pulled away from him. She walked down a couple of steps into the large living room and tossed her handbag onto one of his brown leather sofas. When it dropped to the floor, she let it lie there.

"I got a letter from Jacob," she said abruptly.

Richard strolled over to the elegant drinks cupboard that stood in the corner of the room. He took out a bottle of white wine from a cunningly concealed fridge and held it up inquiringly to Rosa. When she nodded her head, he pulled the cork and poured some of the chilled liquid into two long-stemmed glasses.

"Did you?" he said noncommittally, as he handed her a drink. His hand stayed on the glass a fraction longer than was necessary.

Rosa's hand shook. "He sounds well," she continued. "He..."

Abruptly Richard moved away from her. He went to the window and stared out of it. His voice was grave. "You know what?" he said. "I do wish we could have this one evening without reference to Jacob." He turned to face her, the plea in his eyes unmistakable. "After all, he has you all the time," he lamely concluded.

"Not all the time," Rosa joked. "If he keeps getting jailed."

"You know what I mean," he said simply.

Rosa nodded. She looked down at her hands as if she could no longer bear the intensity of Richard's examination. "It's no good," she said quietly.

Richard sat down next to her. He made no attempt to touch her, but even so she could feel the warmth of his body and the closeness of his breath. "I know," he answered. "I understand. But just for this one evening, let's pretend."

When Richard moved closer, she did not edge away. She sat quietly, expectantly. When he put his hand to her cheek and ran it gently around her jawbone, caressing the outline of her face, she did not flinch. She let herself enjoy the sensation, relishing an experience that had nothing to do with real life, with politics, with children, with the tensions at her temporary home.

He touched the lobe of her left ear, and then removed his hand. He smiled. "Dinner, I think," he said lightly, as he sprang to his feet. Rosa returned his smile—perhaps a trifle sadly.

In no time at all, he had prepared a simple meal. He laid it out on the round marble table that stood on his patio. It all looked so beautiful, Rosa thought.

She sat down with him and tasted the cold meats, the salads, the luscious fruits. She was no longer hungry, and she went through the motions of eating, while sipping constantly at her wine. Richard was the perfect host. He kept her glass filled without appearing to even notice when she had drained it, and he did not press food on her when he saw that she was satisfied.

Deftly he cleared the table, while Rosa stared out into the darkness, up into the skies above, feeling dwarfed by the sheer immensity of the heavens.

"You know," he said when he'd returned, "I envy you." He was surprised at the sentence that came out of his mouth unbidden and unplanned. He'd never been aware that he felt this way, but now he'd confessed it, he knew it to be the truth. He did envy her—her life seemed so complete compared to his.

Rosa was as surprised as he. "Envy me?" she said. "For what? You seem to have everything."

"And you have commitment."

She glanced at him to check whether he was teasing her, and she noticed the gravity of his expression. "It's only a matter of choice," she responded, hating herself for the briskness of her words.

Richard frowned. "Choices are a matter of circumstances," he said. "It's different in England. There, everything seems to be safe, so far away. There is no cause for which I would be prepared to sacrifice so much."

"Poor little rich boy, hey?" Rosa said.

Richard did not take offense. He laughed. "Nicholas is right," he commented. "You can puncture a person's self-esteem."

"Nicholas?" Rosa's voice was sharp.

"Your brother—Nicholas Arnold."

"You never told me you knew him."

"I did," he replied. "My family does business with him. I told you the first time we met."

"I don't believe you," Rosa snapped. "I would have remembered." She got up abruptly, pulling her chair away from the table so that it scraped loudly against the tiling.

Richard did not move. He looked up at her, an inscrutable expression on his face. "You know what you're doing, my Rosa?" he said softly. "You're finding an excuse to draw away from me. You're scared."

He was right, and she knew it. Even so, she felt an impulse to deny his words, to walk away now before it was too late. But the memory of his hand on her face, of the proximity of his body, prevented her. Slowly she sat down again. She reached for her glass, but he covered it with his hand before she could get there. She moved her hand away.

And she saw in his face a look of defeat. Finally she knew that he was going to give up, that he had gone as far as he was able. She sat still, waiting for the relief to hit her. It didn't though: Instead, she was disappointed.

And then Rosa knew what she would do. She reached out her hand again, and placed it gently on top of his. She looked into his gray-blue eyes, which were staring at her with an intensity that made her tremble. She could not hold his gaze.

"I'm not forcing you into anything," he said.

"But I want to," she answered in a small, small voice.

He got up and moved beside her. He stood a few paces away, but to Rosa it felt as if they were already joined together, so strong was the thread of their mutual attraction. She shivered.

"Come inside," he said gently.

He led her to the bedroom, and she allowed herself to be guided as if she were in a trance. She registered nothing of the room save the large bed.

Carefully Richard began to remove her clothes. His hands did not fumble, he undressed her as if he already knew each part of her body intimately. When she was completely naked, he stood back and gazed at her.

"You're so beautiful," he murmured.

Rosa was no longer afraid. This experience, she thought, was hers alone. It had no bearing on her outside life, on her love for Jacob. This was to be savored for itself—caught in timeless Swaziland, she knew that she would never regret what she was doing.

She moved and lay on the bed, her arms clasped behind her head. She watched as Richard undressed. It was her turn to look. She loved the way he removed his clothes, not hurriedly, not coyly, and with no hint of modesty. He was sure of his own body, this man.

He had good reason to be. When he stood in front of her, she thought he looked beautiful.

He came to lie beside her and began to caress her with a gentle hand. She let him do it. She had no inclination to dictate what would happen, she lay still, enjoying the feel of his touch as he ran his hand down her neck, over her breast, down her stomach. Already she felt stirrings of desire stronger than any she had ever before experienced.

When they finally made love, it was as if they had always known each other. It felt so right, so perfect. It was not a fierce lovemaking quickly ended, but rather a gentle passion that glowed more brightly as they continued. They lay in silence when they had finished. It was a long time before Rosa spoke.

"Why did you stop me drinking?" she said.

He turned to her and smiled. "I was selfish, really," he said. "I didn't want you to have an excuse of drunkenness for anything that happened. I wanted you on equal terms. I wanted you to know what you were doing."

Rosa leaned over and kissed him gently on the lips. "Well, you got what you desired," she said.

"Rosa."

Rosa opened one eye. She should have been bleary from lack of sleep, and yet all she felt was a calm and a happiness. She looked toward the door, to the place where her mother was standing. She saw that Julia had a paper in her hand.

Rosa pushed herself upright. "Has something happened?" she asked.

Julia smiled. "The Emergency is over," she said. "We can go back."

Rosa's jaw dropped. The Emergency was over—they could go home! Jacob would be released.

She shook herself and lay back down again.

"Are you all right?" Julia asked.

"Yes, Mom," Rosa replied. "I'm all right." And she knew that she was. She smiled.

34

WHEN THE GOVERNMENT WAS SATISTIED THAT IT HAD EFFECTIVELY subdued the rising tide of protest that followed the Sharpeville massacre, it ended the Emergency. The jail doors opened, as thousands of political prisoners came flooding out.

Jacob was among them. He returned initially to an empty house, but secure in the knowledge that Rosa and the children would soon be coming back, he relished the prospect of his temporary aloneness. He allowed himself a week's holiday— after all, his patients had done without him for several months, and another seven days could make little difference. He occupied himself by pottering in the garden and by cooking himself elaborate meals that he washed down with expensive imported wines. He did not consciously think about why he so coveted this time, but it was as if he were preparing himself for the maelstrom ahead: grabbing his one last chance of solitude and calm.

Jail hadn't been all bad. In fact, it had a lot to recommend it—the feeling of comradeship, for example. Or, more strangely, the return of a trim physique as a side effect of the hunger strikes. But it had begun to get on his nerves. He had shared his cell with twenty others, and although they spent many a wonderful time together, one could get sick of the same faces restricted to a single room for all but two or three hours a day. Now, he reveled in his seclusion.

But he missed his family, and when, at the end of the week, it was considered safe enough for Rosa's return, he felt a thrill of happiness.

And yet his pleasure was tinged by a kind of fear that he could not have put into words. When he heard the car drawing up in the driveway, he experienced a moment of insecurity. He told himself he was being silly.

Rachel came bounding out.

"Daddy, Daddy, Daddy!" she shouted in his ear. "I missed you."

"And I missed you, too, honeybunch," he said, as she covered his face with a hundred sloppy kisses.

"I drew you a trillion pictures, but Mummy said that you wouldn't be allowed them all, so I chose the best. Granny helped."

"She did well," Jacob laughed. "They were wonderful."

"We brought you a present," Rachel continued, hardly pausing for breath. "I'm not allowed to tell you what it is, but I could give you a clue."

"Give me one, then."

"Well . . . it's big and colored and you walk on it."

"Idiot," sneered a voice beside Jacob. He turned.

Martha was standing a few paces away, her mouth pursed so tightly that her bottom lip quivered, her whole face emitting an aura of tense anger. Gently Jacob disentangled Rachel from his neck. He walked over to his eldest. She, for her part, made not one single move toward him.

He bent down and hugged her, but she stayed limp, as if she were suffering, rather than enjoying, his embrace. After a few seconds he let go. He moved away a fraction, and holding her at arm's length, he subjected her to a closer scrutiny. "My, you've grown," he commented.

"How could I? It's only been a few months."

"But it felt like a long time, didn't it?"

Martha nodded. The first beginnings of a thaw showed on her stubborn face. Her lip quivered again, but this time it was tears, rather than anger, she resisted.

"I missed you every minute of the day," Jacob said.

Martha blinked. Jacob hugged her again. This time she didn't seem so passive—she even gave his shoulder a tiny squeeze.

"I'm pleased to see you, Daddy," she whispered.

Rosa, who'd been watching the encounter from a few feet away, experienced a surge of relief. She was worried about Martha. Gradually she'd begun to realize how the child was suffering in Swaziland. It was different for five-year-old Rachel: She was irrepressible. As long as she had her teddy, one of her parents, and a constant supply of food to stoke her overwhelming energy, she remained her usual ebullient self.

But Martha was older, less flexible, and had always been the more sensitive of the two. She refused to ingratiate herself with strangers, and consequently received a less positive response from them than Rachel had. She was a furtive child, prone to eavesdropping on grown-up conversations: Rosa had twice caught her crouching by the door to their living room, her ear pressed against the keyhole. It was a lot to ask of a child, Rosa thought, to subject her to so high a level of anxiety at such an early age. Not for the first time, she wondered whether she and Jacob were being unnecessarily cruel to their children. The usual slick response—that black children suffered much more—did not really hold water. After all, black children were also being badly affected by their suffering.

And then there was the fact of Richard Crossbanks. Surely, Rosa thought, there was no way Martha could have known about him? After that one night she had not seen him again, having neither the time nor the inclination. And yet was it a coincidence that, after that night, Martha was more than usually fractious? Did those sly looks she shot Rosa mean anything? And why had she been so quiet on the journey here—so diffident about meeting with her father?

Rosa mentally shook herself. Of course she was imagining it. There was no possibility that Martha could have guessed, and thinking that she had was just a way for Rosa to punish herself. No, Rosa decided, Martha's anger was just a natural expression of a feeling of abandonment by a sensitive child caught in difficult circumstances.

It crossed Jacob's mind, while he hugged Martha, to wonder what Rosa was thinking. She looked so serious standing there—sad, even. She was everything he remembered and more. Beautiful and strong, her eyes unfocused, her hair fashioned in a new style that gave her face a softer and more vulnerable appearance.

He let go of Martha. He stood up to face his wife.

She had not consciously been dreading this moment, but as Jacob came toward her, Rosa felt an impulse to shrink away from him. In the fraction of a second that it took to recognize it, the impulse retreated, and as Jacob enfolded her in his arms, she experienced the rightness of being with him. Richard, she thought with relief, represented nothing but a vague dream: Jacob was the reality. Jacob was kind, strong, and he was hers.

For his part, Jacob, hyped up as he was for the encounter, felt Rosa's initial reluctance: It came as a tiny arrow that chafed at him. It confirmed his growing suspicion. Try as he would, he hadn't been able to avoid noticing something reserved in her last letters to him. He had wondered what it was that made her seem so far away: It was almost as if, he thought, there was something worrying her, something that she was hiding from him. And now, as he felt her holding back from him, he knew instinctively that the feelings he'd dismissed as the paranoia of the imprisoned were grounded in reality.

But as Rosa melted into his embrace, he put his fears on one side. What she had done during their separation was her affair. If she wanted to tell him about it, she would. The words weren't important: What mattered was that they were together again. Nevertheless, he felt too constrained to express the endearments that were on the tip of his tongue.

"Come on," he said instead. "I've prepared us a delicious meal."

"*You* cooked?" Rosa asked.

"I'm a changed man. Gordon gave regular cordon-bleu lessons. I was his brightest pupil. He made me a certificate testifying to that. I wrote to you about it."

"So you did," Rosa said, but her voice was uncertain, as if she'd dismissed it, as if what he had done didn't rank highly in her regard. Jacob shot her a determined smile.

"How was it living with your mom?" he asked, as, arm in arm, they strolled into the house.

Again that look of uncertainty, of something concealed, appeared on Rosa's face. "Fine," she said briefly. Jacob could think of nothing more to say.

The rest of the afternoon they spent becoming reaccustomed— Jacob to the children and Rosa to the house. Their paths crossed frequently, and they smiled at each other, occasionally touching, each preoccupied by his or her own thoughts.

He knows, worried Rosa. He's guessed.

It's true, thought Jacob. I have to face it. Something's happened.

And yet even when the kids had been reluctantly deposited in their respective beds, they did not talk of it. Instead, they sat down together in their sitting room, and they caught up with what the last few months had brought the other.

"I saw Moses when I came out," Jacob said. "Peggy was there to meet him: quite a reunion."

"It's funny how things have turned out," Rosa commented. "The end of Sophiatown seems to have been the turning point for them: They've got on much better since."

"Although Peggy still doesn't understand Moses' involvement," Jacob replied. Not like you and I do, he thought silently.

She must have caught the thought, because she smiled at him, a secret, special smile. The first of the knots in his shoulders began to relax.

"There's so much to say," she mused. "After all those carefully worded letters. You must all have discussed the situation thoroughly."

Jacob nodded. "I'll tell you later," he whispered.

And so they sat together, exchanging news of the last few months, sharing in the mutual knowledge of their friends, in the legacy of their years together. Not once did they speak of the subject that worried them: of his suspicions, of her desires.

But despite this uncharacteristic silence, they arrived at a solution as surely as if they had written it down. They each inwardly resolved that everything would be all right between them. If not unchanged, still they would stay together and reinforce their deep feeling for each other.

That night, after they had made love, Jacob's voice sounded into the quiet.

"You know," he said softly, "if anything happens to me . . ."

Rosa put a finger over his lips. "Don't talk like that," she said.

Jacob nudged her hand away. "I want to," he replied softly. "If anything happens to me, I don't expect you . . ."

This time he broke off voluntarily, not wanting, not daring, to utter the words that were on the tip of his tongue. "You know what I mean," he said, and there was an appeal in his voice.

"I know what you mean," Rosa softly replied. "Now let's get some sleep."

They turned away from each other, each facing a different side of the room but still connected by the warmth of their bodies. As Jacob drifted into sleep, he reveled in the closeness to his wife. He was almost asleep when he felt her move slightly. The bed shook a bit, and then was still again. She can't be crying, he thought, as he surrendered himself to his dreams.

A new mood was sweeping the South African left: a mood of anger, a mood of defiance. So tangible was it that it permeated every aspect of their daily lives.

Since 1912 the African National Congress had dedicated itself to peaceful protest. It would not, its members vowed, give in to the brutality of a regime that paid no heed to the sanctity of human life. It would be different from its oppressors.

But again and again its people had been gunned down. Sharpeville was the proof of that: Sharpeville was the turning point. And after Sharpeville both the ANC and the PAC were declared proscribed organizations.

When ten years previously the Communist Party was banned, it had dissolved itself voluntarily. As a result, it took years to reestablish its links. Lessons were learned from that experience, and the ANC chose a different path. It did not do as the government ordered. It did not close itself down. Instead, it determined to carry on underground.

And it would carry on differently. Once it was banned, once it was illegal to be caught with a mere membership card, then peaceful negotiations lost all meaning. Something else was required. The ANC determined to make its mark on the regime: It would go on the offensive.

And thus it was that in the same year that South Africa left the Commonwealth and proclaimed itself a republic, the ANC made its own bid for autonomy. It prepared itself to launch *Umkhonto we Sizwe*—the spear of the nation—MK for short. MK was to be its army.

The Swiece children couldn't help noticing the change their return to Jo'burg heralded: They did not know what was going on, but they knew that it was different. In later life they would remember it as a time characterized by hushed voices, by conversations that suddenly ceased when they appeared, by a growing and peculiar tendency on the part of their parents to talk together only in the middle of the garden.

Perhaps because they needed to distance themselves from the unmistakable undertow of tension, Martha and Rachel turned their parents' behavior into a game: They spent their time trying to catch Jacob and Rosa in midfurtiveness.

"There they go again," Martha told Rachel. "Moses is with them, and he's handing Mummy a piece of paper."

"Should we try and creep up behind them?" Rachel asked.

Martha turned away. "Not today," she said. "The weather's disgusting. And anyway, I'm bored with it. They never say anything worth overhearing."

"Well, I'm bored, too," Rachel declared, and she marched away from the window.

In the garden, Rosa looked down at the piece of paper and nodded her head in approval. "It's good," she said. She handed it to Jacob.

"The people's patience is not endless," he read. "The time comes in the life of any nation when there remain only two choices—submit or fight. The time has now come in South Africa."

He, too, nodded before returning the paper to Moses. "It'll be distributed on December 16?"

"*Ja*," Moses said. "When we launch MK."

"And everything else?"

"Under control. Those people we sent out of the country for training managed to get word back to us that they'd arrived. The next contingent will go soon."

"And in the meantime," Jacob said, "we have people like me who've had some army experience."

Rosa shivered.

Moses saw her motion, and he took a step forward and put his arms around her. "You do agree with Jacob's decision?" he asked.

She smiled sadly. "Yes, I agree," she said. "I know that there's no other choice. But that doesn't stop me from feeling scared."

"What, with me beside him?" Moses joked. Then he looked seriously at her. "There's not much physical danger," he said. "Since we're going for sabotage—armed propaganda rather than all-out war. We'll only hit railway lines, electricity pylons, and other installations, so we'll have time to plan our actions carefully. We don't want to harm anybody, and that includes ourselves."

"I know," said Rosa. "But it's not you I'm worried about— it's the police."

She watched as both Jacob and Moses, in a show of united

nonchalance, shrugged and turned away from her. It was a show, she knew it was: They were also scared, they just didn't want to admit it. Well, she thought, perhaps they're right: The die is cast.

She stepped between them, and linking one arm in each of theirs, she took the first step toward the house. "Coming in for a drink?" she asked Moses.

He shook his head. "I better get back home," he answered. He kissed her on the cheek and nodded at Jacob.

"See you next Saturday," he said. Then, quickly, he walked away.

"Next Saturday?" Rosa asked with a sinking feeling in her heart.

"A meeting, nothing more," he said. "Don't worry."

"I'm not worried," she said. She paused and looked at him. "Don't you remember that's the day we're going to Nicholas' for supper?"

"Oh, hell. I forgot."

"Jacob." There was anger in Rosa's voice. "You know how nervous I am about this event. After all, it's Nicholas' peace offering to us—his way of burying the political differences. How could you forget? It's the first time he's invited us in such a long time." And Richard Crossbanks will be there, she nearly added, but she didn't.

Jacob frowned slightly. Then he smiled. "I tell you what," he said. "I'll come for a while and then get somebody to call me. I can pretend it's a patient: It's a perfect excuse, actually—it would be very good security."

Rosa bit her lip. It couldn't be helped, she supposed: These things were bound to happen.

Of course Jacob shouldn't have forgotten, he knew that she was nervous about the date, and to be fair to him he had no idea how nervous because she hadn't told him about Richard. Why would she, after all? Richard had become a name of the past, a distant, albeit pleasant, memory of complete irrelevance to her life.

She never thought about him at all, in fact, not until Nicholas had phoned. And then Nicholas had only told her that Richard would be there after she had accepted his invitation—there was no way she could have backed out without making an issue of it all.

"It's not that important, is it?" Jacob's voice was worried.

Rosa shook her head. "No," she said. "It's not that important."

Dinner was worse, and at the same time, better, than Rosa had imagined it would be. Richard was already there when she and Jacob arrived. Such a flurry of greetings ensued that nobody could possibly have noticed either the slight pressure Richard applied to Rosa's hand or the hurried manner in which she pulled it away from him.

The most difficult thing was that Rosa's heart leaped involuntarily at the sight of Richard. She realized that, in her attempt to rid him from her mind, she had downgraded the physical pull she felt toward him. Now, she saw that he was every bit as handsome as she had once thought.

So what? she argued to herself. What's handsome?

Richard, after the slight pressure on her hand, was the model of decorum. He behaved cordially, and at the same time neutrally, toward both Rosa and Jacob. He acted out the part of a former acquaintance impeccably. Many of his comments he addressed to Jacob, showing an informed and lively interest in the state of health in South Africa.

The role he chose for himself—that of an interested foreigner with a detached concern about the evils of apartheid—suited him perfectly. Or perhaps it wasn't a role: Perhaps, Rosa thought, she was seeing the real Richard for the first time. His attractiveness was not in doubt, but what she hadn't banked on was that he appeared to be slightly dull. While Jacob carried with him always the spark of commitment, Richard's face was bland when at rest, his voice politely interested when engaged.

As the evening drew on Rosa relaxed. Richard's no threat, she thought. I'm over him. She smiled to herself.

"How's business?" Jacob asked Nicholas.

Nicholas gave Jacob a glance, checking out whether he was being serious, Rosa supposed, and was apparently satisfied. He stretched back in his chair and put his hands behind his neck.

"I'm out of the woods now," he said. "Just at the right time, too. The economy's beginning to pick up, and I'm ready and willing."

There were many like her brother, thought Rosa. They saw a boom in the offing, and they were rubbing their hands in glee.

Let's see what they do when the first of MK's bomb explodes, she thought.

These thoughts, all of them, she kept to herself.

"Are you settled in South Africa?" Richard asked Nicholas.

"Sure," Nicholas said. "Why not? It's my country, and it's a good life here, politics apart."

Richard smiled wickedly. "And you didn't therefore put your name down for British citizenship before Republic Day?" he said.

"Oh, but that's different," Nicholas said. "Putting one's name down is only a sensible precaution. You never know what might happen. We might get bored after all and want to move. Or my sister's colleagues"—he turned to Rosa and smiled to show that his intentions were friendly—"might make it too uncomfortable for us." He leaned back again. "I doubt it," he said. "Although it might come to that."

"And would you be sorry?" Rosa asked.

Nicholas shrugged. "Depends what happens," he said. "You know I don't like what goes on in this country. I'd like to see change."

"In Swaziland your wife expressed her skepticism of aid as a progressive force to me," Richard told Jacob. "And I do think she has a point. But on the other hand . . ."

He never got to finish his sentence, for Jane, who had risen from the table in order to answer the phone, held it out to Jacob. "For you," she said. Jacob frowned.

"You can take it in the other room," Nicholas suggested.

"That's okay," Jacob said.

He spoke softly into the receiver before hanging up, and when he did so, Rosa felt admiration at the way his face expressed an almost perfect combination of annoyance and concern.

"I must apologize," he said, "but I have to go. One of my patients has taken a turn for the worse."

As a flurry of regret followed Jacob's announcement, Rosa experienced a momentary panic. "I'll come with you," she blurted out. She saw Richard looking intently at her, and she blushed.

Jacob shook his head. "No need to break up the evening," he firmly replied. "I shouldn't be long. I'll pick you up on the way back."

He kissed her on the cheek and then was gone.

After that, the evening took on a different slant. Richard began to pay more attention to Rosa. Nicholas, delighted that the evening was turning out so well, encouraged his guests' mutual involvement.

As Rosa sipped a vintage cognac, she reflected on how similar Richard and Nicholas were—both rich, successful, and essentially apolitical—and how they were not without their own kind of charm. They lived in a way that Rosa had long ago rejected. And yet for a moment she allowed herself to see its attractions.

It was so simple, she thought, so free from friction, so different from her own way of life. They talked, and there was nothing behind their words; they smiled, and their eyes smiled with them.

She jumped as the telephone's shrill ring broke into her thoughts. She held her breath as Jane went to answer it. She smiled weakly when Jane came to tell her that Jacob would be later than expected, and that she should find her own way home.

She went through the motions of returning to her conversation, but not long afterward she turned to Nicholas.

"It's been lovely," she said, "but I'm feeling rather tired. Could I phone for a cab?"

"Don't be silly," Nicholas gruffly replied. "I'll drop you at home."

"It's really not necessary," Rosa protested.

In a flash Richard was on his feet. "I've got a better idea. I'll drive you back," he volunteered. He smiled graciously at his hostess. "It's been lovely," he said, "but I have to be going."

The determination in his face showed that there was no refusing his offer, so Rosa nodded her silent consent as Richard thanked Nicholas and steered her to the door.

He drove through the Jo'burg streets, a faint smile on his face, breaking the silence only occasionally with small talk.

When they got to her house, Richard stopped the car and turned off the engine. Rosa reached for the door handle.

"I'm not going to bite you," Richard said. "I liked Jacob," he added.

Rosa smiled. "I'm glad." She opened the door.

Richard touched her arm. "You look worried," he said.

"Just an odd situation. You must have felt the same. I really am tired."

"Jacob didn't go to see a patient," Richard guessed.

Rosa flushed. "I don't know what makes you say that," she said curtly.

"I'm sorry," Richard said. He looked tired, too. "Will I see you again?" he asked.

"I don't think so," Rosa replied.

Richard switched on the engine. "If you ever need me, then, phone. Nicholas knows how to get hold of me."

Nicholas climbed into bed beside Jane.

"The evening went well," he commented.

"Could there be anything between them?" Jane asked.

"Between who?"

"Richard and Rosa."

"Don't be silly. She's not his type." Nicholas yawned.

"Suppose not." Jane sat up, reached for a pill, and washed it down with a sip of water. Then she settled back to sleep.

Rosa lay in the dark as she waited for Jacob to return. She was pleased now that she had gone to Nicholas'. She felt purged of any remaining doubts. It had been good to see Richard in the flesh and to realize that her attraction to him was purely physical.

Jacob was, she thought, the man for her: Richard had his advantages, but she could never have settled down with him.

It was past two when Jacob finally arrived. He crept into the room, careful not to disturb her. She switched on the light and blinked at him.

"How was it?" she asked.

He shrugged as he began to remove his clothes. "It's moving," he said. "How was the rest of the evening?"

"Okay," Rosa said.

"I liked Richard."

"He said the same of you."

Jacob nodded and climbed into bed. "I might have to go away," he said.

"You've moved the plan forward?"

"We've had to," he answered. "The rumors are that more and more people are going to be banned soon," he said. "And even placed under house arrest. We have to hurry and get this thing off the ground."

"You will be careful, won't you?" Rosa's voice was timid.

As he got under the sheet, Jacob reached over and pulled her toward him. "Darling. Of course I will," he answered.

35

As Peggy put the finishing touches to the evening's meal, she allowed herself to experience some of the excitement that she'd previously suppressed. It was always like this when Moses was away: She busied herself frantically in church affairs, and if she caught herself brooding on his absence, she would sternly reprimand herself. But when she knew that he was about to return, when one of his comrades came and told her so, she would relax her self-control. Then and only then would she begin to think of him.

She had come to accept that her marriage defied all logic. She and Moses were, on the face of it, fundamentally unsuited. But that didn't seem to matter anymore: Despite their differences, their love had continued to flourish. They had been through the worst together—they had gone to the brink of separation. Peggy was determined that, whatever happened, they would stay together.

This resolve demanded from her a compromise. The one thing that she couldn't ask was that Moses alter his basic way of life. He was essentially a political animal—nothing, Peggy knew, could change that. She, on the other hand, was different: She wished only to focus her energies on her family. She tolerated, admired even, Moses' involvement, and the discipline of secrecy that necessarily sprang from it, but she could not pretend to like it. Fighting for somebody only had meaning for Peggy if she knew the person intimately. Try as she did, she still could not understand Moses' willingness to risk everything for a faceless mass.

Despite this, they had made their peace with each other. Gone were the days when she would greet his entrance with a mixture of recrimination and anger. She bore, in silence, and for the most part ungrudging, resignation, the strain of his activities. They didn't talk of his work, but nevertheless they were a team. They had the children, they had their love, and God willing, they had many more years together.

Automatically Peggy crossed herself, and then inspected the room. It was a homely place, she thought, not luxurious but decent all the same. And it meant so much to her, for each item in it was part of her history: That easy chair, for example, was a result of years of saving—each week she had put aside just a few pennies of Moses' wage (if it could be called a wage, since it was so small) from the ANC until she had been able to buy it.

Objects have more meaning when one has to struggle to get them, she thought. Now what else is there to do? She frowned, and then her face cleared: The eggs, of course—she'd almost forgotten to collect them. That's what happens when I think of Moses, she chided herself.

She left the house and went to the chicken coop in the backyard. It was her pride and joy, this place, one of her ways of supplementing their meager income. But this time, she thought, she wouldn't sell the eggs. Moses could have them tomorrow morning.

She smiled and pushed her hand into the deeper recesses of the coop, flapping one of the hens out of the way in order to do so. She touched one egg and then another. She moved her hand around to find if there was a third.

Suddenly she was frowning, because her hand had touched something in there, something that didn't belong.

She felt around the object. It was rectangular in shape, and hard, some kind of box. She grasped it tightly and pulled it out. She cleared the straw away and saw that it was indeed a box, a box of wood. She lifted the top.

And then she stepped back as if the box had bitten her. She replaced the lid quickly, but not before her eyes confirmed to her that the box was full of strange pieces of wire, and of other things, too.

She shook her head: She did not want to think about it. She pushed the box back into its hiding place, and forgetting about the eggs, she hurried back inside.

Back amid the security of her home, she told herself to calm down. There was a perfectly rational explanation for her discovery—there had to be. Once Moses came home and explained, they would laugh together at her fears.

But if this was so, an insistent inner voice kept repeating, why did she feel so jumpy? Was it merely because she felt hesitant about questioning Moses? Or was it because one question would throw open all the issues she'd thought long gone and buried— would, in fact, put their relationship itself in question? No matter how much she tried, she couldn't shake off her growing sense of unease.

Think about something else, she told herself.

And so she did; she thought about the one thing that occupied her mind as much as Moses—she thought about her children.

George and Lindiwe had grown up and all but left home. George was twenty, and worked as a warehouseman in Jo'burg. He came back to sleep, but other than that he was seldom around. Peggy had no idea what it was he got up to during his waking hours, but she knew better than to question him. George had always been a sullen boy, but these days he was virtually mono- syllabic: Sometimes Peggy thought that what George gained in years he'd lost in vocabulary.

Peggy had once blamed George's essential untouchability on Moses' continuing absences. In hindsight, however, she won- dered whether she herself didn't bear the greater responsibility for her eldest's problems. She had wanted so badly to protect him from the harshness of his life's expectations: Perhaps she had gone to extremes. How else could one explain the severity of George's reaction when he turned sixteen?

She remembered that day as if it were yesterday. Every time she thought of it, she cried inside for her boy.

He had gone to the pass office with reluctance, but without showing any great fear. He was an independent boy, and Peggy had not even thought to accompany him: She was only a little disturbed when he hadn't returned by the afternoon. But when night fell and he was still nowhere to be found, she became frantic. She imagined all kinds of things—had he been arrested, deported, injured? She searched for hours, first at the pass office and then through police stations and hospitals, but to no avail.

In the end it was fourteen-year-old Lindiwe who found her brother.

George had taken refuge in a part of Soweto that was yet to be developed. It had become a kind of dumping ground, a place of rotten food that by day was filled with scavengers. The nights were different. George had chosen that particular location because he knew that he'd be alone since nobody ventured there after dark. When Lindiwe found him, he was shivering under a piece of tin, sheltered from the rain but nevertheless wet. His face and shirt were soaked with tears, which continued to fall unabated while his mother half-carried, half-dragged him home.

Peggy had to use all her skills to coax the full story from him. It came out in stutters, haltingly—as if George could hardly bear to relive the experience.

The boy had been badly shaken up, and yet what had happened to him was nothing unusual. Countless others endured the same humiliation—the same stripping in front of cold eyes, the same dancing in front of white policeman, the same warnings about the penalties of being caught, in the future, without a valid passbook.

What George described was the modern ritual of black South African manhood—the time when every boy was issued a pass. No one found the experience pleasant, but what stunned Peggy was the extremity of George's reaction. It showed how completely unprepared he had been. It was then she'd realized that, in her efforts to keep George away from the path his father had chosen, she had done him a disservice.

She'd pretended, both to herself and to her son, that if George were "good," he could escape the treatment that the system had meted out to Moses. She had pretended even when she knew that it was not true. But when she finally came to that realization, it was too late.

For that night was the last occasion on which Peggy heard George cry. He noticeably hardened after it. For a while Peggy kept up her battle to keep him in school—to at least have him matriculate—but George was adamant. Defiantly he cut lessons. He was beaten regularly for his truancy, but all to no avail— George would not attend.

In the end Peggy reluctantly agreed that the boy should be allowed to leave. Better, she thought, that he try to find a job than that he end up as a member of one of Soweto's infamous *tsotsi* gangs.

The risk was high, for Soweto was a rough place: like a cauldron always on the boil, like a melting pot of rage, energy, and destitution. Sophiatown had been a community, not free of crime but still knowable. People had pride in its appearance: After all, they had made it what it was.

Not so Soweto. Artificially it had sprung up, and daily did it continue to spread. Conditions had ostensibly improved: There was even talk that bathrooms might be the next innovation. But no amount of material comfort could make up for the increasing violence of the township.

The mothers of Soweto had to face reality: They were in danger of raising a lost generation—of youths whose families could either not afford to send them to school or who, like George, refused to go. These boys weren't prepared to calmly take on the mantle of third-class citizenship in a nation of conspicuous consumption. So they turned to crime, to violence, and to eventual degradation.

Peggy worried that this was the path George would choose, but since he had gone to work, he had become even more solitary. If he was mixing with *tsotsis*, Peggy had little evidence of this.

Evidence—the word brought back her fears. Quickly Peggy diverted herself.

At least, she thought, I know I don't have to worry about Lindiwe.

Even as the thought crossed her mind, eighteen-year-old Lindiwe appeared at the door. Peggy's face lit up. Dressed in her starched white uniform, Lindiwe looked so composed—so right, somehow. Peggy relived again the pleasure she experienced from the knowledge that her daughter had chosen to train as a nurse.

"Are you going now?" Peggy asked.

"Yes. Night duty." Lindiwe wrinkled her nose in distaste, but there was no real rancor in her voice. That was typical of her. She rarely complained of the hours she worked, of the tedium of emptying bedpans and folding sheets, and she was always serene. She studied hard, and by all accounts she was doing well. And yet she still managed a social life. She'd recently struck up a friendship with a young man—Johannes Cuba. She'd even gone so far as to bring him home to meet her parents.

Peggy liked Johannes: She hoped that the relationship would develop into something more serious. She realized that Lindiwe was still young, but on the other hand, she herself had married early. Johannes's coveted skill as an accountant meant that if

Lindiwe settled down with him, she would have a relatively easy life.

These thoughts Peggy kept to herself. Lindiwe was a calm girl, but she had inherited a strain of stubbornness from her father. If she thought anyone was pushing her, she would clam up, and then, as often as not, do the opposite of what had been suggested. So Peggy refrained from comment, restricting herself to inquiring about Johannes's health.

"He's fine. I'll see him during one of my breaks," Lindiwe replied.

"That's good," Peggy said. "How about supper?"

"I'll get something later," Lindiwe said. "Bye. See you in the morning."

The house felt strangely silent after Lindiwe left. Peggy tried to keep herself occupied while she waited for Moses, but she had long since completed her housework, and her mind kept going back to that strange parcel she'd found in the henhouse. I won't think about it, she resolved. It means nothing. But still she worried.

Moses turned up half an hour later. The years had altered him little, but his hair was graying, as befitted a man about to celebrate his forty-fifth year. His face, however, seemed as youthful as ever. "Politics," he would say loudly when asked what kept him so young, "nothing but politics."

Peggy knew that was an accurate enough statement—Moses fed on politics. It was his reason for existing, and it gave back to him as much as he put into it. Of course, there were times, like after Sharpeville, when he experienced despair. But after each of these occasions he seemed able to bounce back renewed. He was an eternal optimist (although he preferred to call himself a pragmatist), convinced that the freedom for which he'd struggled all his adult life was just around the corner.

He threw his briefcase carelessly onto the table and sat down wearily. Peggy handed him a cool drink, which he gratefully drank fast.

"Ag, it's hot," he said.

"*Ja*," she agreed. "Come on, get your case off the table. The meal's almost ready." She hated the wheedling tone of her voice, as if she were talking to a child, she thought, but Moses did not appear to notice. He did as he was bid.

She put the food on the table and sat down with him, but she found it almost impossible to eat. As Moses dug in, she maneuvered her fork around the plate, making patterns with the food. Every time she was about to take a mouthful, she changed her mind. This can't go on, she thought. She put the fork down.

"The hens are producing well," she said.

Moses smiled. As he did so, little wrinkles deepened on the side of his eyes, making Peggy's heart leap. Her man, she thought, was aging so gracefully: The years had softened him, but in a strong rather than enfeebling way. Sometimes when she looked at him, she had to catch her breath at the knowledge that he was hers. It was like being a teenager all over again. She still loved him so: That was all that mattered.

Inwardly she fought with herself—the temptation to put her anxiety to one side, to suggest instead that they sit in the open in easy companionship as they gazed into the warm night, was almost too much to resist. But she knew that this urge could only be temporary. If she didn't broach the subject now, when she felt in control, it would only raise its head in the wee hours of the night, making it more unbearable.

So she continued. "I found a parcel in there," she said.

"Mmm." Moses forked some more meat into his mouth. Peggy saw that his eyes were watchful.

"It was full of wires." The sentence came out in a rush.

Moses put down the fork. He frowned.

"What was it?" she pleaded. "Is it yours? It's some discarded hobby of George's, isn't it?"

Deliberately Moses wiped his mouth with a napkin and then folded it up neatly. "How much do you want to know?" he asked. He was careful not to look at her.

"Nothing," Peggy answered. Her eyes filled with tears. "I want to know nothing. I wish I had never seen it."

Moses lowered his head. He had always known that this subject would rear its ugly head. No matter how careful his precautions, it could only be a matter of time before Peggy discovered that he was involved with MK. He wanted to protect her from all this—he would do anything, he told himself, to spare her pain. And yet even as he thought it, he was deceiving himself. The one thing he would not do was to give up his activities for the ANC.

She had just offered him a way out—he could deny all knowledge of the parcel, agreeing that it must have something to do with George. He would be lying, and she would know this. But perhaps she would prefer to live with the lie rather than the reality. He opened his mouth to speak before he had come to a decision.

"The parcel belongs to me," he said.

That was all he had to say—for Peggy knew what those wires meant. They were the stuff from which bombs were sprung— they were the things that, ever since the Sabotage Act, could lead to Moses' execution.

There was a time when Peggy would have reacted to his confession by wringing her hands in despair, by trying to force a retraction from him. But she could no longer do that. She had grown up with Soweto—she was not an innocent. She couldn't waste her energy fighting the inevitable.

"I see," she said softly.

Moses reached for her hand across the table. He was relieved when she offered it to him. "I have to," he said.

"I know," she answered.

That was the end of the conversation. They finished their meal together, and then they went to sit outside, appearing to all as a couple at peace with each other.

And it wasn't mere appearance. There was a closeness between them, accumulated through their years together, that nothing could ever shake. But it was an awkward closeness, grounded as it was in so much secrecy. There was too much forbidden between them, Moses thought, too much unsaid.

He sighed. "I'm going away soon," he said.

"For long?"

"A week or two. I'll drop in on Evelyn and check out Nat Phakasi while I'm there. His wife reports that he's been sounding rather depressed."

"Evelyn will be pleased," was Peggy's only comment.

Evelyn, she remembered, as they lapsed into silence, had lost a husband when she was young, and Evelyn had recovered from the loss. But then, thought Peggy, Evelyn was different from her, was stronger. She could not imagine life without Moses: She could not imagine how she would survive.

She sat still, her features composed as she stared into the night. No one could have guessed at the turmoil in her heart: Never would she even hint of it. But if anything happens to him, she thought, I will never forgive him.

*   *   *

Evelyn woke with a start. She fumbled for the clock that lay beside her bedroll. She held it close to her face, but the room was pitch-black and she couldn't see a thing. She guessed it was about 3:30 A.M., slap in the middle of the predawn period she'd learned to dread.

Evelyn was accustomed to early starts. All her life, while others still slept securely, she was up working in the kitchen in preparation for the day ahead. It was something she'd resigned herself to rather than chosen. As a youngster, she'd fantasized about indulging in luxurious lie-ins when she retired. But now that she was in a position to have them, she found that she could do nothing to influence her biological clock. No matter how hard she tried, she woke with the sun.

Recently, however, there'd been a new development—one that she'd learned to dread. These days she woke up abruptly even before the dawn. When it had first happened, she'd dismissed it as a sporadic inconvenience of old age. But now it had become a regular part of her routine.

She hated those hours before dawn: There was nothing to do. She could not be bothered to light the lamp, she found reading by its faint yellow glow an increasing strain, and it was too cold and dark to venture outside. So she just lay, waiting for the sun to rise and release her from the dark side of her own imaginings.

It wasn't the boredom that made her vigil so difficult: It was the way she felt. She didn't drift out of sleep: Instead, she came to with a start, her heart beating wildly, her brain befuddled as it strained against her memories. During the day she managed successfully to dismiss morbid thoughts from her mind, but while she lay in the dark, she was consumed with a kind of foreboding.

She couldn't throw off the suspicion that her body was trying to tell her something—to tell her that she did not have much time left. Fiercely she resisted this hint. Evelyn had no great fear of death, but she was not ready for it. She would refuse, she told herself, to start behaving as if her days were numbered.

She glanced at the clock again, furious with herself for doing so. Not five minutes had passed since she'd last looked—the result would be exactly the same.

But she was wrong. For this time as she peered into the darkness, a faint beam of light flashed through the window and illuminated the clockface. She had one second in which to confirm to herself that her guess as to the hour was pretty accurate before she felt a twinge of fear. Why would somebody be creeping about her land at this ungodly hour?

In the city such an occurrence would not have been uncommon. A hundred explanations—a lover creeping out before discovery, a thief back from the prowl—would still the anxious heart. But the country was different. Here, people went to bed early, and they stayed in bed until dawn. They respected the conventions of early rising: They did not disturb their neighbors' dreams.

And the explanation could not lie in some unexpected illness or a sudden breaking of the waters by one of the pregnant women. For Evelyn lived some distance from the others. If someone was outside, then the only explanation was that he was after her. She crept out of bed and, keeping her head low, made her way to the door.

There it was—the flashlight again—she had not imagined it.

"Ma," a voice whispered.

It sounded like Moses—it couldn't be, could it?

She opened the door a crack. She saw a dark figure silhouetted just to the left of the spreading acacia tree.

"Moses?"

The figure moved toward her. She heard the click of the flashlight, and then he held it up just under his chin. In that ghostly light she saw that it was indeed her son, Moses.

In a flash she threw off her trepidation. She ran toward him as if she were still a youngster. She hugged him tightly, reveling in the closeness.

"Is it safe?" he whispered in her ear.

"No one's here," she replied. "But noise travels for miles, so speak softly until we get inside."

Moses relaxed. He enveloped her in his bearlike embrace, and she breathed in that old, familiar smell of his body.

"My son," she murmured. "What a surprise."

"A good one, I hope," he teased.

"How could it be otherwise?"

Moses let go of her. "I have another surprise," he said. He vanished behind the tree. When he returned, she saw that he was no longer alone.

The other's face was easier to make out in the darkness—for he was white. Evelyn recognized him immediately. She let out a gasp of surprise. "Jacob." It came out in a joyful shout. She lowered her voice. "Is Rosa with you?"

He shook his head, and regaining her wits, she led both men into the house. She closed the door firmly behind her.

Moses lit the paraffin lamp while Evelyn searched for the half-bottle of brandy Sipho had proudly presented to her. He'd stolen it from the missionary's house, and Evelyn, with her profound distrust of all things religious, hadn't the heart to scold him. She hadn't wanted to hurt Sipho's feelings by telling him she no longer drank alcohol, and so she had secretly stored it away. She'd meant to give to Nat, but now she was pleased that she'd completely forgotten about it.

She poured two generous measures into tin cups and handed them to her visitors. She smiled when they toasted her. She sat on one of her two rickety chairs while Moses seated himself on a log he'd carried in, and then she began to question them.

She steered a careful path: She slipped easily into a way of behaving that had once been habitual. She suppressed the obvious question—why they were visiting—and asked instead about their families. She knew that caution must come naturally to them these days: When they were ready to tell her anything, they would do so. In the meantime she could hardly get over the fact that she was seeing her son for the first time in almost two years.

"I hope you'll stay for a while," she said. That was as far as she dared go in eliciting any information on their movements.

"A few days," Moses answered. "We're expecting a visitor." She nodded.

"Do they watch you?" he asked.

She shook her head. "The police don't. But everybody knows my business here in the country. And they'll spot your number plate immediately."

"Well, I have the perfect excuse for visiting," Moses said. He frowned. "As for Jacob—the fact that he's a doctor means we can get away with things that otherwise we wouldn't. People always suspect that doctors have liberal tendencies, and we can spread it around that you've had a few bad turns."

Evelyn noticed Jacob staring at her. She lowered her eyes quickly. But when she looked up again, she saw that his gaze had not wavered.

"Even here in this backward place," she said, as if she did not understand his look, "we have heard of the exploits of MK."

"*Ja*, it's made a splash," Moses agreed.

"I suppose there was no other choice," Evelyn said. "The Boer made sure of that."

Moses shrugged. "Not only the Boer," he said, "but our people as well. They have had enough—you can sense that wherever you go. There's such an anger in the country that without some organized action, there would have been spontaneous rebellions, leaderless ones, that can only have ended in slaughter and defeat."

"And you think that MK will lead to victory?"

"How can one ever tell in advance?" Jacob asked. "In any prerevolutionary period all moves seem to end in failure—all of them, that is, until the one that brings victory in its wake."

"That's true," Evelyn said. "But it's going to be hard." And I fear for you, she thought to herself. Are you ready for this? Is your security good enough: Is it right that you travel the country black and white together, calling attention to yourselves?

She did not say these words: To do so would be to force a tacit agreement that they were in MK. Instead, she got up. "You must be tired," she said in a tone that would brook no denial.

She settled them on the floor. They looked ridiculous—two grown men sharing her narrow bedroll—as they tussled good-naturedly over the blankets. She left them to it. Smiling, she went outside to wait for the dawn.

As she sat there, she thought about MK—of the things that had been said and of those left unsaid, too. The struggle, she knew, had changed. The next generation was in charge, and it was right that they should be. And yet, she thought, it still felt strange to be so isolated from it: to think only of MK when Moses and Jacob turned up.

Did I make a mistake to come here? Evelyn wondered. I could have stayed with the ones I love. They would have let me take a backseat. It was an unwelcome thought, and she pushed it to one side.

It was growing light now—the beginnings of one of those long, hot days in the Transkei. Sipho would soon be with them. Evelyn emptied her mind and sat.

Sure enough, Sipho followed the dawn by a mere half hour. He had stretched out recently in one of those spurts that precede adolescence, and she watched his lanky body as he weaved his way through the grass. She toyed with the idea of sending him away. She rejected it almost immediately. She suspected her own motives in wanting to exclude him. For the first time she wondered whether Sipho had not become a substitute son—with the real thing in residence, she no longer needed him.

"TG 1971," he shouted. It was Jacob's license plate.

She threw him a welcoming smile as she simultaneously placed a warning finger on her lips. "My son arrived late last night," she said. "We must not wake him."

Sipho, despite the changes in his body, was still a child at heart. He could barely contain himself. He jumped up and down excitedly. "Uncle Moses is here?" he shouted, his voice trapped between the squeak of childhood and the gruffness of a man.

His cries must have penetrated the house, for within minutes Evelyn, who was trying to calm the boy, saw a look of incredulity cross his face. She turned to find Jacob rubbing his tousled hair as he came toward them.

Evelyn would have laughed if she hadn't known what dangers the situation contained. For she could read Sipho's expressions like a book. They changed from amazement, to disbelief, to confusion, to fear: all within a fraction of a second. It was as if he could hardly bear to tear his eyes away from Jacob, but at the same time was confused beyond all explanation. White men did not visit his friends—not unless they were up to something no good.

Evelyn got up. "Jacob," she said solemnly, "come meet my friend Sipho Balintulo. Sipho, this is Dr. Jacob Swiece, the son-in-law of my ex-employer."

Jacob offered his hand to Sipho. After a short pause and an appealing glance at Evelyn for consent, Sipho proffered his. When it was over, Evelyn saw that Sipho stared at his own hand in disbelief.

"Extra water, Sipho," she said briskly. "We'll need plenty of it."

"I will b-be quick, M-Ma Evelyn," Sipho stuttered, and then turning away, he ran off in the direction from which he'd first come. But even at that speed he could not resist looking back sporadically, savoring the fact that he had not been dreaming.

"And don't stop to talk to anybody," Evelyn called after him. She turned to Jacob. "If I'd had warning, I would have stocked up with provisions," she said. "I'm afraid I have no coffee."

"But we do," Jacob answered. "We couldn't break our journey without drawing attention to ourselves so we carried our own refreshments. And you know your son—he can't even breathe without coffee, never mind drive. I'll go and get it."

By the time he returned, Evelyn had put a pot of water on the stove and was busying herself by cutting thick slices of the bread she daily baked in her makeshift oven.

Jacob watched her exaggerated movements, a curious smile on his face. There was no way he couldn't have noticed her difficulties: He was a doctor, after all. Nevertheless, she picked up speed—furiously cutting at the bread. She told herself that she was being foolish, and yet she could not slow down.

Jacob frowned. He must say it, get it over with, before it clung like a poison between then. "You've had a stroke," he stated.

Still Evelyn didn't stop. "Is that what it is?" she said noncommittally. Her knife cut again into the bread.

She heard him laugh softly. "What did you think it was—indigestion?" he asked. "Are you playing the country bumpkin now?"

At last she put down the knife. "It doesn't bother me," she said. "It's not so bad."

"Not so good, either," he commented. "By the looks of the way you're holding yourself. Is the left side partially paralyzed?"

Evelyn nodded.

"Have you seen a doctor?" he asked.

Evelyn shook her head. "No point. They can just about spare the time to pronounce you dead—that is, if you manage to survive the walk to the hospital."

"I'd like to take a look," Jacob said.

"Some other time," Evelyn brusquely replied.

Jacob was one of the few people among Evelyn's intimates who hadn't known her most of his life. Because of this, he was able to see things that the others missed. He was able to guess at an aspect of Evelyn that she kept determinedly hidden from view. He wasn't cowed by her vulnerability.

"It's not the end, a stroke," he said. "If you look after yourself and get proper medical care, you'll be able to live, if not for another seventy years, then at least for a good many more."

"What makes you think I want to?" Evelyn snapped. And yet she felt relieved. She softened her tone. "Don't tell Moses," she said.

Sipho returned in time to find Moses emerging from the house. He seemed to have recovered from his shock, and he greeted Moses with none of the reticence he'd displayed when he met Jacob. He shook his hand enthusiastically and began talking nineteen to the dozen: about what he did for Ma Evelyn; about how much he admired Moses; about how he, too, would one day live in Jo'burg; about how his father was making money in the big city.

Moses heard him out with the utmost of patience. Only Evelyn noticed when his eyes began to shift sideways.

"Sipho," she gently interrupted, "stop before you talk my son into the grave. I want you to do something. I want you to take a message to Nat, and this is a message that must be said and not written. Can you do that?"

"I can remember the whole of the Bible," Sipho said proudly.

"Well, it won't be as long as that." Evelyn smiled. "But you must not tell it to anyone. If you do, Uncle Nat will get into a lot of trouble."

"I will say nothing," Sipho promised. "And I will be back like the wind."

Without thinking, he began running. Evelyn called him back. "I haven't given you the message yet," she said.

Sipho looked with embarrassment at Evelyn's visitors. Both remained solemn—as if they had not noticed his childish enthusiasm. He grinned engagingly.

"Dr. Jacob, Dr. Jacob," Sipho shouted, "Uncle Nat says—" He stopped abruptly and stared in amazement at Jacob's hands. "W-what's happened?" he asked.

Sheepishly Jacob followed Sipho's gaze to his hands. He blushed. "I've been washing lettuce," he said clumsily. If he had not been cursing himself at his own carelessness, he would have laughed out loud at the spectacle he must have made. "Does Evelyn know you're back?" he said instead.

"No, I came straight here," Sipho explained. "I saw your coat over on that tree and I wanted to tell you Uncle Nat says come anytime but be careful. . . ."

"Well, run along now, in case she wants something," Jacob instructed. He saw a look of disappointment cross Sipho's face. "We'll join you soon," he added hastily.

* * *

"You did run like the wind," Evelyn commented admiringly as Sipho ground to a halt in front of her.

Sipho smiled. "Uncle Nat says they can come anytime."

"That's good. Now come help me with the lunch."

Sipho crouched down beside Evelyn. Preparing food was one of the things that Evelyn often demanded of him. "All men should cook," she told him, and he held her in too much esteem to tell her that this was not true. So he did as he was bid without argument.

He took the spoon from her hand and began mashing into the bowl that lay at her feet. It was hard work grinding the mealie-meal into a consistency that would suit Evelyn's high standards. He looked around him. "What's happened to the mortar?" he asked.

"I mislaid it somewhere," Evelyn said, hoping that the child would notice nothing out of the ordinary in her tone.

"You know what, Ma Evelyn?" he continued as he ground the spoon into the mealie-meal. "Those Jo'burg people wash their letters blue."

"Not letters, lettuce," Evelyn corrected. "And it doesn't go blue. It's just a way of getting all the grit out."

"Well, Jacob's hands were blue," Sipho said.

"Watch what you're doing with that bowl," Evelyn snapped. "You must pay more attention, or there'll be nothing left by the time it comes to eat."

When the boy was out of sight, Jacob waited another three minutes before crouching down. He pushed his way through a gap into the undergrowth, crawling on all fours until he came to a natural break in the scrub. There, he found Moses, who was sitting motionless as he gazed intently first at his watch and then at the glass bottle in front of him.

Jacob pulled his coat from the tree and threw it on the ground. "Sipho saw my hands," he said. "I must be out of my mind."

Moses nodded, but he did not look up. Instead, he glanced once more at his watch, and then at the bottle that he was holding upside down some distance away from himself. "It's been twenty minutes so far," he said.

"That's good," Jacob commented. "Did you log the thickness?"

When Moses nodded again, Jacob sat on the ground and

reached for the bowl. Inside were the telltale blue crystals of permanganate of potash. They were nicely ground now, and he added the gray aluminum powder to them.

"That's it. Twenty-three!" Moses exclaimed.

Jacob looked in his friend's direction, and confirmed for himself that the viscous liquid was indeed eating through its cardboard cover. It started to drip onto the ground. "Careful," he said. "That hydrochloric acid burns like nobody's business."

Moses turned the bottle and gently placed it upright on the ground. He glanced ruefully down at a hole in his trousers. "Don't I know it," he said.

"Oy, I'm not cut out for this," Jacob commented. "My stupid coat almost gave us away. I don't know why I brought it: and it's too hot to wear it, anyway."

Moses laughed. "Don't worry. These are rehearsal nerves. When the time comes, you'll be okay."

"I hope so," Jacob said doubtfully. "But first we have to try it out. What are we going to do about the noise?"

"I've thought of that," Moses answered. "You can drive the car at the same time, and we'll say it's a backfire."

Jacob looked skeptically at his friend, but for want of a better scheme, kept his thoughts to himself. "Let's go eat," he said.

That night the two friends, guided by Sipho, walked to Nat's home. When they arrived, Jacob suppressed an expression of shock at the state of the house. He wasn't to know that Nat would have laughed if Jacob had told him of his first impressions. For, in truth, the dwelling was much improved. Evelyn had donated all her spare utensils, and Nat had patched the roof and even begun work on fencing around the place. But it was Sipho who had made it a true home for a man whose passion was music.

For Sipho had lived up to his reputation: He had brought Nat a saxophone. No questions were asked as to its source: No money ever changed hands. There it stood in pride of place in the center of the room—almost perfect, with only a few of its pads roughly patched, gleaming from the loving polishings that Nat devoted to it.

Jacob had brought his medical kit, which was just as well. Many of Nat's wounds had healed, but there was one that continued to fester. Jacob grimaced when he saw it. Without saying anything, he got out a hypodermic and injected Nat with it. Then he took some pills, which he labeled carefully before giving them to Nat.

"One three times a day," he said, "until the whole course is finished. And if it flares up again, you must persuade them to let you see a doctor."

Nat smiled. "*Ja*, but I'll live, won't I?"

"To fight again," Jacob answered.

Instead of returning his smile, Nat's face started to crumple. Silently Jacob scolded himself for his own insensitivity.

People, he knew, could endure many things. One only had to open one's eyes to the way most black people lived to know that. But isolation such as Nat's was especially difficult: It ate away at a man's confidence. Despite a few minor medical problems, Nat managed, with help from Evelyn and his family at home, to adequately feed and clothe himself. And yet he was suffering: suffering from the separation from a wife who could not leave their children, from his inability to listen to any music except the sort that he could make on his own, from his total abandonment to the desert of the Transkei.

"We haven't forgotten you," Jacob said lamely. It was not, he knew, enough consolation. It would never be enough.

Nat smiled. "You and all my friends have already done plenty. . . ." he said, and then he stopped, as if he couldn't find a way to go on.

"Sipho," Moses suddenly said. "Could you just go out a minute—to the bottom of the hill there? I thought I saw something."

As soon as Sipho was out of earshot, Moses turned to Nat. "We have come to ask a favor of you, my friend," he said.

"Anything."

"We have certain goods we'd like you to store. Every now and then someone will pass by and perhaps pick them up, or perhaps drop something more off. You'd have to be careful, very careful. Think about it: If you want to refuse, we would perfectly—"

Nat held up his hand. "Anything," he said.

"There was nothing there," Sipho called from just outside the door.

Quickly Moses went up to Nat and embraced him, and then he moved away. By the time Sipho appeared, he was some yards distant and bending down. When he got up, he had Nat's sax in his hand. "I hear you're hot," he said. "Play us a tune."

Nat picked up the instrument. And in that lonely house on the hill, the air was filled with the most glorious of sounds— sounds that swelled out from Nat's mouth and flowed through his body, through the saxophone and into the hearts of his visitors: sounds that spoke of pain, but of a pain mixed with the sheer joy of being alive, of creativity.

They didn't stay long: They couldn't risk being caught by the police, who visited infrequently these days (even they, Jacob reflected, seemed to have forgotten Nat), but who could always be counted on to turn up at the worst moment. They drank the last of the brandy Evelyn had urged them to take. There was not enough to intoxicate, but they felt almost drunk as they joked of the old days.

As they walked back, Jacob turned to take one last look at Nat's solitary place of exile. "I don't know whether I could stand it," he commented to Moses.

"Me either," Moses agreed. "But we may have to stand more than that before the end."

36

1963

ROSA SAT AT HER DESK, REGISTERING IN THE DISTANCE THE SOUND OF
childish squabbles. She did her best to block out the voices. Just
a few more minutes of peace, she silently prayed. Give me that.
She glanced down at the pages of rock analyses she'd spread out
in front of her.

She resisted the impulse to shuffle them again, to prolong the
feeling of satisfaction that they always gave her. She smiled to
herself. Her friends would shake their heads in wonder if they
could see her now—like a kid in a candy store as she prepared
to work. Jacob was the worst—he teased her mercilessly about
what he called her obsession with dead rocks. She didn't mind.
She never tried to explain away her fascination with geology, for
to do so would make the whole thing less precious.

The best part was that her work was hers alone. When she
was out doing fieldwork, her attention focused on the stuff of
ages past, she was not bothered by the current storms brewing
above them all. And when she got her results, or the results of
her colleagues, she worked with her mind alone: No uneasy
emotion came to break into her concentration.

She picked up a pencil and bent her head. She began to write,
waiting for the time when intense concentration would make the
children's raised voices a mere background murmur. But this
time it didn't happen. No matter how hard she tried to concentrate, other thoughts kept intruding.

In exasperation she threw the pencil across the desk. The days
when she could lose herself in her data were gone. They had

been chased away, perhaps forever.

After Sharpeville, after the launching of the Sabotage Campaign, the government reacted as if it were fighting for its life: reacted as only it could. The stories of people being exiled without trial were increasing. Banning orders and house arrests were landed indiscriminately on the heads of Rosa's friends. The ninety-day law that was used to dump suspects into solitary confinement for months on end was in full swing.

And still there was worse. Looksmart Ngudle and Suliman Saloojee were taken for interrogation and killed. They were the first.

The phone rang. Jacob had promised to call today, and she'd been looking forward to hearing his voice. His trip had lasted longer than predicted, and she was missing him badly.

There was a man on the other end, but it wasn't Jacob. She recognized the voice immediately, even though he didn't give his name.

"Trouble," he said briefly.

"Bad?" she asked. Carefully she braced herself against the side table.

"Could be. They picked up our friend from the gutters."

Rosa thought quickly. Our friend from the gutters? She frowned. Of course, that must be Philip Cohen, an architect who'd made his name by inventing a revolutionary kind of sanitation system for high-rise buildings. "He'll be all right," she said.

The man on the other end hesitated. When he finally spoke, Rosa could hear the doubt in his voice. "He's got ninety days," he said. "Someone caught a glimpse of him being taken into Marshall Square, but he avoided our colleague's eyes." The voice strengthened. "Probably doesn't mean anything," he said. "Anyway, there's no point in speculating. I just wanted to warn you that you should expect visitors. I hope they don't find too many people at home."

"I understand."

"Good luck." The man rang off.

As she replaced the receiver, Rosa tried to remember when she'd last seen Philip. She didn't know him well; he was Jacob's contact rather than hers and they'd rarely talked about him. But she did remember when Jacob had described how Philip looked that day in the office when he'd pretended to be a patient. "He's full of fear, that man," Jacob had said.

She pushed the echo to the back of her mind. If Philip was talking, and that was the implication of him not exchanging a glance with one of the comrades, then how much would he be giving away?

And then she remembered. Jacob had said something else about Philip. He'd mentioned casually that he'd been in on their latest actions, that he had even completed a few with Jacob.

If Philip was talking, then that could be very bad for them all.

She shook her head. Her friend was right—there was no point in speculating. There could have been a hundred reasons why Philip wouldn't look at a comrade. After all, Marshall Square was infamous—it was the place of interrogation, the place where threats were made, the place from which Looksmart and Suliman had never returned. Philip might have just been preparing himself for the ordeal to come, caught up in his own terror and anticipation. He might even have been trying to preserve the other man's security.

She hoped against hope that Jacob would phone soon, that he would not be so foolish as to arrive without first checking. But Jacob had neither rung nor returned by the time the police arrived. Forewarned by the phone call, Rosa should not have been surprised. But nothing could have prepared her for the ferocity of their entrance.

Police raids were such a regular part of the Swieces' way of life that the children had taken to acting them out when they got bored. The police dropped in for the most trivial of reasons: Sporadically they looked for illegal literature, routinely they broke in during parties to check that black and white were not drinking alcohol together. Sometimes they just walked about the grounds, displaying a detached interest in the household.

But this time was different. They had lost their air of everyday harassment. They banged on the door with unprecedented force. The man in charge started speaking the minute Rosa opened it.

"Where's Jacob?" he snapped. He was a new man, and by the look of the stripes on his lapel, a senior one. He was blond in coloring, with one of those bull-like necks that seemed to be a specialty of South Africa's political police. A large scar ran down one cheek, giving his reddened face a sinister appearance. He pushed his way into the house. "Where's Jacob?" he repeated.

"My husband," Rosa replied, as she forced the quiver of fear out of her voice, "is not here."

"We know that. You think we're stupid? Where is he?"

"He's taking a holiday," she answered.

The policeman took a step toward the living room. He turned and looked at her, his eyes traveling the length of her body in deliberate calculation. He saw a woman whom he knew to be thirty-nine but who looked somewhat younger than that. She was striking, he thought, if you liked that kind of thing, which, happily, he didn't. As for the way she dressed: Well, despite her politics, she obviously had no difficulty spending money on herself. After last Saturday, when his wife had dragged him round the shops, he'd seen enough cotton frocks to know that the one Rosa was wearing had not come cheap.

Behind him, one of his juniors snickered. The officer narrowed his eyes, and his scar wrinkled as he did so. "Taking a break without his wife, hey?" he said. "And what am I supposed to make of that?"

"My marriage is none of your business," Rosa answered between gritted teeth.

"Ah, Rosa," he said, slurring the *r* as he pronounced her name, "that's where you're wrong. From now on, everything you do is our business."

Rosa straightened herself up. "What is this in aid of?" she asked.

He was sick of being nice to her. "Don't play *stum* with me. Your terrorist friends," he spat out, rolling his *r*s again, "blew up another electricity pylon last night. Just outside Jo'burg—in your husband's patch, so I'm sure you were one of the first to hear about it."

"I haven't had time to listen to the radio," Rosa answered, as her heart sank. She did not want the policeman to know that his hint had hit home. For he had plainly told her that they knew which was Jacob's "patch"—where he had been operating. There was only one possible explanation—Philip must be talking, and he had implicated her husband. "I have the children to care for," she concluded lamely.

Again the narrowing of the eyes, again the slow inspection. And then the man smiled. "Ah, the children," he said. "Doesn't your type ever think of them?"

Rosa held her tongue.

"Because I'm warning you, lady," he growled, "that things are getting serious. You've graduated from the kindergarten. And here's your certificate." His callused hand thrust an envelope into hers. "Read it," he barked. "And make sure you understand it. Among its various attractions are the fact that you are restricted to Johannesburg, and banned from various other locations inside the city."

As Rosa glanced through the three-page document, her eyes began to water. It was a small thing they were doing to her compared to the measures they took against others, but still it hurt. Hurriedly she bit back her tears. She would not show this man how much the message he'd brought affected her.

She looked him straight in the eye. "You've banned me from the university," she said. "You've banned me from practicing geology. How petty can you get?"

He smiled. "Can't have you wandering around the countryside anymore, can we? From now on, you're going to be watched—every second of the day. You play with fire, you get burned. Didn't anybody ever tell you that?"

"If you've quite finished," Rosa said softly, "you can go."

Again he smiled. He took a step toward her. Unprepared for his next move, she stood her ground as he ran one lingering finger across her neck. She shivered, and took one hasty step backward.

"I'll never really go," he answered. "From now on, you're mine. One wrong move"—he opened his hand right in front of her face, held it there for a minute, and then snapped it shut as if he had just squashed an insect—"one wrong move," he repeated, "and I'll have you." He opened his hand and showed her his empty palm. He laughed. There was no hint of frivolity in his face.

Rosa resisted the impulse to look away, to look anywhere but at this man.

Abruptly he frowned. "Ag, you bore me," he said. He wheeled around and, walking fast to the door, threw his parting comment over his shoulder. "Tell your husband there's worse in store for him," he said. "His time is up."

The visit was over. Rosa was left standing by the open front door, watching as the police car reversed rapidly down her driveway.

She was shaking. She let the banning orders fall to the ground, resisting the temptation to slide down after them. She could not collapse now, she could not afford it. She needed all her wits about her when Jacob called. She needed to warn him. The only safe assumption was that Philip had cracked, which meant that Jacob, and all the others, were in danger.

She did not judge Philip Cohen. How could she, after all? They had always known that things would get worse, they had always anticipated that some of them would not be able to withstand the accelerating police pressure. Ninety days was one of the most vicious kinds of laws. It allowed for the solitary imprisonment of political prisoners for months on end: It imposed a kind of isolation that could shake the strongest of them.

But if only it hadn't been Philip—a comparative newcomer to the movement. A more seasoned activist might have been able to store away the most damning pieces of evidence and give them time to cover their tracks. But Philip would be in no position to weigh one piece of information against the other. Once he spilled the beans, they would come out uncensored.

Names, faces, venues, came crowding into her mind. I must warn them all, she thought. And then she told herself to snap out of it. She was behindhand—she had other things to do— and the phone call she'd received showed that everybody was already alerted. Jacob was the only one—and Jacob should soon be phoning.

At that moment the telephone began to ring. Rosa walked toward it, but she was not yet ready to pick it up. She had to think—she had to find the best way to tell him.

She was halfway there when Martha came darting into the room, flew to the phone, and grabbed for the receiver.

"Don't pick it up," Rosa shouted with an irrational terror that welled up inside her and turned to venom in her mouth. She saw the girl hesitate and then drop her hand. She saw Martha's open mouth, and the look of astonishment on her face. She saw it all as if it were in slow motion. And she could do nothing about it. She ran to the phone and, flipping it up, spoke urgently into it.

"Jacob!" she shouted. "You musn't—"

"I wish I were," a polished voice murmured.

Shit, Rosa thought to herself what's happened to me? I must pull myself together. She reached over to touch Martha's head and felt a stab of regret as her daughter moved sharply away.

"Hello, Richard," she said dully into the receiver. "What brings you here?"

"More business, I'm afraid," Richard continued. "My family seems to think that one visit makes me the South African expert. But there are some consolations. I thought we could meet for a drink."

"I'm very busy," Rosa answered, as Martha stalked out of the room.

"Next week, perhaps?"

"I don't know." Rosa watched Martha cross the garden and disappear from sight.

"Are you all right?" Richard asked.

"I'm fine," she said. I must go after Martha, she thought. The girl is suffering.

There was a pause at the other end, as if Richard were weighing up the tone in her voice. "I'm coming over," he finally said. "You sound terrible."

"No . . . don't," she started, but it was too late, for she was met only by the sound of the dial tone.

Automatically she put down the receiver. She had no time to worry about Richard. She would deal with him later. In the meantime she'd better take precautions—she must hide any incriminating materials.

And there was something else she had to do—what was it? Then she remembered.

"Martha," she called. There was no response. All she could hear was Rachel's delighted squeaks as she sat like a queen in her perch on the first branch of the spreading maple tree.

Rosa went to the French doors. "Rachel," she called. "Where's Martha?"

"Ag, she's a bore," Rachel replied. "Always crying."

"I didn't ask you what she was doing, I asked if you'd seen her," Rosa snapped.

She was doing it all wrong. She saw her youngest's lips begin to quiver. "I'm sorry, honey," she said quickly. "I didn't mean to snap. It's just that I need to talk to Martha."

Rachel beamed at her mother. "It's okay," she said knowingly, "I get bad moods, too. Celia says—"

"Yes, darling. But Martha?"

Rachel waved her arms airily in the direction of the drive. "She ran that way," she said. "You'll never find her. She's got a secret hiding place, and she's too *blerry* mean to tell me where it is."

Martha's hiding place was only effective against her slapdash sister. Rosa found it easily—in the garage behind some crates that were piled up in one dusty corner. The girl was sobbing her eyes out.

"Go away," she said as her mother approached.

"I'm sorry, darling," Rosa said.

"Sorry? Sorry?" Martha's voice broke as she indignantly pronounced the words. "You're always fucking sorry." Biting back her tears, she stared defiantly at her mother—waiting for the inevitable reproof for the swear word.

Rosa pushed one of the boxes aside and gingerly sat down next to Martha. "I'm sorry I stopped you answering," she said. "I know how much you wanted to talk to Daddy."

"Well, you're bloody well wrong!" Martha shouted. "As a matter of fact, I couldn't care less who answers the phone."

"Oh, darling," Rosa said helplessly. She pulled the girl to her and held her close. She hugged Martha to her breast, rocking her gently as she felt her resistance going, as Martha's tears wet them both.

"It's n-not you," Martha stuttered when she was finally able to talk again, "it's Susan. She's being beastly to me."

Rosa knew intuitively that Martha was inventing an excuse on the spot. She recognized the lie for what it was, but nevertheless she let it settle between them. "Susan will soon get bored and pick on something else," she suggested.

Even as she said it, she despised the way she was colluding with Martha. And yet it was so much easier to give advice on the vagaries of a social life than to explain why Jacob kept going away, why Rosa snapped at the most trivial of occurrences, why conversations were inevitably held out of earshot of the children.

In principle, Rosa and Jacob had agreed, it was better to be honest with the children. And yet the kind of honesty they meant, and the kind they were able to supply, were quite different. Since they could not tell the children everything, they did their best to warn them of the dangers without giving away the details. Sometimes Rosa thought that Martha was more scared than she herself was, because Martha knew half and not the whole story.

"It'll all get better," Rosa promised.

* * *

When Jacob finally called, Rosa gave him no time to speak. "We've had visitors," she said.

He knew her so intimately; from the very tone of her voice he understood. "Rough?" he asked.

She nodded into the phone as if he could see her. "They were in a terrifically bad mood," she said in a voice of false cheer.

"Anything special?"

"They didn't give much away, but I suspect somebody's wounds are festering in isolation, and they're holding you responsible."

"Well, that's what happens to patients when their operations go wrong," Jacob answered. "I guess I'll declare a moratorium on house calls for the present."

"I think that would be for the best."

"I'll tell my colleagues they're a bad risk," he said. "That sort of patient should be avoided until they calm down. They complain no matter how you treat them. How are the children?"

"Okay," Rosa said. Her voice broke.

"You sound busy," Jacob said quickly. "I admire you for the number of things you manage to do. You really are a special woman." She heard in the tone of his voice the message that he intended. "Don't break now," he was urging. "You can't afford to."

"They're both swearing like troopers," she said. "Seems to be the fashion in school."

"How aggravating for you."

"And they miss you."

"I miss them, too. Give them both a special hug. And look," he added, "I've just thought that if the patients get angry enough to take me before a medical panel, I'll need to have all my records intact. You will make sure of that, won't you?"

"I'll give them to your receptionist," she answered.

"Good idea," he said. "I'm too busy to come back now—I'm involved in the usual rounds."

"I understand," Rosa replied.

"Bye, my darling."

"Good-bye, Jacob," she said, and for the second time that day found herself speaking into a dead phone. This time she did not replace it. She left it to her ear. She waited until she heard the clicks that came onto the line. She put her hand to her mouth as if keeping her silent screams at bay.

* * *

Richard arrived to an open door and a silent house. He tapped quietly on the knocker and, receiving no response, walked inside. "Rosa," he called.

Eight-year-old Rachel came bounding into the room.

"Oh, hi, Richard," she said casually, as if it had only been yesterday when they had last met.

"How are you?" he asked.

"I'm difficult. That's what my granny says."

Richard smiled. "Oh dear."

"Doesn't matter," Rachel said airily. "Difficult people are the most interesting, that's what I think." She turned, as if about to run off again.

"Is your mother around?" he asked quickly.

Rachel waved her hand in the direction of the garden. "She's digging," she answered.

Rosa was indeed in the garden. She was standing at one end of it leaning on a spade and gazing down into a hole she had just dug.

She was a mess, her hair tousled, her face streaked with dust.

"Nice to see you," she said, and he registered an artificial kind of high in her voice. He had been right to come, he thought, something was upsetting her.

It was an odd kind of hole she'd been digging, one that appeared to be brimming over with documents.

"We're in trouble," she said. "I think you can guess what kind of trouble."

"The headlines give me a pretty good idea," he answered.

"I need to see Jacob, but I'm being watched. That's where you can help."

"You want me to see him?" Richard could not conceal his astonishment.

She smiled and shook her head. "I want you to take me out to dinner. We'll see whether they follow us. I'm not sure how good their scrutiny is, but if we take a long time about the meal, they may get bored and I could give them the slip."

"I see."

"It's a risk. You could get into trouble."

Richard did not think long. What, after all, did trouble mean to him? He was British, the son of a lord, a director in a substantial local company. He was a spectator, a man taking a pretty woman out for a meal. "Where do you want to eat?" he asked.

She looked at him intently. "Are you sure?"

He grinned. "Only if you promise to stop looking at your watch."

They dined at a bistro in the center of town. It was not the best of Jo'burg's restaurants, but it was noisy, cheerful, and as Rosa pointed out, had an easily accessible fire door at the back.

Richard was beginning to enjoy himself. He didn't mind the subterfuge of driving along the road as if this were some kind of normal date, and he'd surprised himself by experiencing a childish kind of thrill when he had been the first one to spot their tail. With Rosa directing him, he felt as if he saw a different side of Johannesburg: He could pretend that he, too, belonged to this seductive society.

He ordered a steak and wondered why Rosa's eyebrows rose a fraction as he did so. When the twelve-ounce portion landed on his plate, he understood. She laughed.

"South Africans like their meat," she commented.

There was a feeling between them that he hadn't experienced since that night in Swaziland—a closeness that did not need words to confirm it. Sternly he told himself to keep his hopes at bay. Rosa was grateful to him—that was all. He was merely providing her with her only opportunity to see her husband.

"Tell me something about yourself." Rosa's voice broke through his reverie.

Richard searched his mind for a story that would hit an appropriate mix of confession and humor. He settled on recounting some of his public-school escapades, which he did with the consummate skill of a practiced raconteur. As he talked, part of him sat back from himself, commenting wryly on the stupidity of it all—on the privileged child he had once been and perhaps still was.

She didn't seem to notice his hint of self-doubt. She laughed and laughed, throwing her head back in the sheer relief of abandonment. He looked at her neck, and he wanted to cover it with kisses.

He leaned across the table. Pushing the candle to one side, he took her hand. "Come away with me," he whispered.

She frowned, and he cursed himself for breaking the spell. "I can't," she said. "It's not only Jacob." She must have seen the look of relief that crossed his face, because she frowned again. "I do love him," she explained. "But it's more than that. Hard times are coming. I can't run away."

He released her hand and sat back in his chair. "I envy you," he said.

"You've said that once before."

"But now I fear you as well."

Surprised at the seriousness in his voice, Rosa looked across the table. The lights were dim in the restaurant, and one side of Richard's face was in shadow. From this angle his face lost its charm—he looked hardened, bitter . . . evil, even. Don't be silly, she told herself. I'm imagining it. It's my own presentiment of doom I see in his face.

Richard shifted in his seat, the light changed, and she forgot what she'd been thinking. She glanced behind her.

"I was right," she said. "Their car's no longer outside."

She rose, and was surprised to see Richard laying some money on the table. "I'm going alone," she said.

He shook his head. "I'm coming, too," he said.

"You can't."

"Because you don't trust me?"

Rosa thought quickly. She was going to meet Jacob at a venue they would never use again. Even if Richard knew about the place, even if he told the police, it could do them no harm. And after all, Richard would not tell the police. Having someone by the car might be useful.

"Okay," she said. "But it's a risk."

"So is knowing you."

Richard wondered whether Rosa took them on a roundabout route in order to confuse him. All he knew was that they seemed to be driving forever—down dark alleyways, across deserted streets, up hills he was positive they'd already climbed. At one point he closed his eyes to show her that he was no longer looking, and was relieved to find that she kept on driving in a seemingly random fashion. Of course, he told himself. It's not me she doesn't trust. She's trying to make sure nobody's following us.

He was right in part: She was checking for pursuers. But there was another reason for the length of the journey, a simple reason: She needed time to think.

Part of her wanted to burst out into hysterical laughter at the situation she'd created. Her husband was on the run, her friends, and possibly herself, were in danger, and here she was driving calmly through the streets of Jo'burg, her ex-lover by her side. It was farcical, she thought, it was ridiculous, it was . . . it was being unfaithful.

Richard looked around him in surprise. This place didn't fit his image of a secretive meeting place. It was an ordinary-looking suburban bungalow, one of a number set in a wide road lined with trees. It had a wide driveway ending in a double garage in which he could just see the shapes of two larger than normal saloon cars. It had a large garden, and through the screen of trees that lined the driveway, he could make out the dark shape of an oval swimming pool.

As Rosa flashed her lights twice, Richard had time to reflect on the contradiction of it all. Unconsciously he expected revolutionaries to be earnest, badly dressed, and overserious. Knowing Rosa had broken those illusions for him. But still he couldn't get over the luxury in which many of her white comrades lived. In his book, radicals would eschew servants and anything that smelled of the exploitation of blacks that was endemic in South Africa. Yet now that his eyes became accustomed to the dark, he could see that to one side of the garage was a concrete block that could only have been the servants' quarters. And Jacob did not come from this direction.

Instead, he stepped out from the main house, looking completely relaxed and at ease, just as he had done the night of Nicholas's dinner party. He gestured toward them.

Eagerly Rosa opened the door. "I won't be long," she told Richard softly. "Anybody suspicious comes by, you drive off."

He nodded.

She ran quickly up the driveway like a teenager on her first date. Richard suppressed a twinge of jealousy. Then he settled back and closed his eyes.

As his wife ran toward him, Jacob was thrown back again to more carefree days. She looked so young, he thought, so vulnerable somehow. Her brown eyes were so intense in their pool of white, white surround. Her face, habitually frowning these days, had uncreased for a moment. I'll always remember her looking like this, he thought. Even if I never see her again.

She was close by now, and he took a step toward her. He held out his arms, and she came into them. They hugged, and the passion in that embrace came from both of them.

But both knew that time was running out, and they soon parted. Jacob threw a questioning glance in the direction of Rosa's car.

"Richard Crossbanks," she said. "He helped me give the cops the slip."

Jacob did not comment. There was too little time left to waste it in anything but themselves. He held Rosa an arm's length away, drinking in the sight of her. He saw the dark rings that lined her eyes, her usually brown face ghostly pale in the moonlight. He knew how much their situation was affecting her. She had so much to bear: the fear, her own involvment, the knowledge of his activities that she could not wipe from her mind, the worry about the children. It was little surprise that her face was showing the strain.

And yet, he thought, as he pulled her toward him, she is still so beautiful. He kissed her longingly, reveling in the soft touch of her lips against his.

"We must hurry," he said. "I've got to move soon." He stroked her hair tenderly.

"Philip Cohen," she began.

"I know," he answered. "Philip's cracked. They picked up some people today that only he could have known about. You better tell your dad to skip the border."

Rosa stifled the gasp that flew to her lips. If her father was in danger, then things had truly deteriorated. For Harold Arnold knew little of the Sabotage Campaign. He was an accountant: He did the movement's books. If he had become a target, then there was no hope for any of them. No hope—especially for Jacob.

"Why don't you get out?" she pleaded.

Jacob let go of her and looked her straight in the face. He smiled sadly. "I wish that I could," he said. "But there are still things to do."

There was one part of Rosa that wanted to protest, to order Jacob out of danger. She wanted to pull on him, to drag him to the car, to take him forcibly across to Swaziland. She wanted to plead with him, to tell him to think of the children, to blackmail him.

She didn't do anything of the sort. She threw her arms around Jacob and hugged him tightly. "When this is over," she said, "we'll laugh about it."

"We will," he answered, and in his voice she heard her own doubts reflected back at her. "I must go soon," he continued. "Just one more thing—somebody should warn the others."

"Me?" she asked.

He shook his head. "Somebody who won't be followed. Why not send your mom?"

The door of the house opened, and a man Rosa had never seen before came out. He frowned at Jacob before he stepped back inside.

"You better go," Rosa said.

"I love you, my darling," Jacob whispered. "I always will."

Richard glanced questioningly at Rosa as she opened the door beside him.

"You drive," she said abruptly.

He got out and saw that her face was stained with tears. He put his hand on one of her shoulders in a clumsy attempt to console her, but she brushed it off.

"Don't," she said. "It won't help. Just drive."

37

"MOM." ROSA'S VOICE WAS CASUAL.

Julia looked up. She saw Rosa standing by the door and making no attempt to come in. Julia sighed. She got up and walked the length of the room. When Rosa turned on her heel and moved further into the garden, Julia followed her.

At last Rosa stopped.

"Is this far enough for you, then?" Julia asked.

"It's not my fault, you know."

"I know it's not," Julia said in a softer tone. "I'm sorry: it's just that I'm under a lot of strain, and all these spy games aren't helping."

Rosa nodded. Julia, she knew, was finding the tension especially hard going: The fact that she was only peripherally involved probably didn't help. And now, thought Rosa, I'm going to subject her to even more strain.

Well, there was no putting it off. She took a deep breath. "Mom," she said, "I'd like you to do us a favor."

"So I gathered. What's it now?"

"I'd like you to go to Rivonia." It came out in a rush.

Julia did not reply, but before she turned her head away, Rosa saw the shock reflected in her eyes. "I wouldn't ask if there was any other option," Rosa pleaded.

There was a prolonged silence while Julia stared at her garden. It needs weeding, she thought irrelevantly. She turned back and looked at Rosa. "All right," she said.

Rosa smiled. "Thanks, Mom." She moved forward to kiss Julia on the cheek, but her mother was too fast for her and had already moved off.

* * *

Arthur Goldreich's farm in Rivonia was about twenty miles from Jo'burg. It should have been an easy trip, it usually was, but this time Julia drove there caught up in a flurry of fear. She spent the whole journey glancing in her mirror to check that she was not being followed. She knew she was being irrational—there was no reason for the police to suspect her—and yet her eyes were drawn irresistibly behind her, so much so that on one occasion she almost crashed into the side of the road.

"Bloody women drivers," shouted someone behind her. She looked in her mirror. With a loud roar and a shake of his fist, the driver overtook her and sped off into the distance.

She continued on her reluctant way.

But no matter how slowly she drove, she did eventually arrive. The gates were open, and there was nobody in sight. She progressed down the short driveway and pulled up outside the house. She got out.

The place looked deserted and somehow innocuous in the midday sun. On her right was the low, architect-designed house, its front door ahead of her, its main rooms all facing inward on a sheltered garden that was concealed from the drive. A few chickens scratched desultorily at the dry dust that covered the back of the land.

Julia turned her head.

On her left was a concrete block—three or four rooms long—with a walkway running its length. She took a step toward it, for it was in this low building that the ANC underground had set up its headquarters. Nelson Mandela, the ANC's president, was already in jail, but here in Rivonia the rest of the leadership had taken shelter.

She hadn't got far when a man came out to meet her. He was young, black, and poorly dressed. He glanced at her inquiringly—not hostile but certainly with no trace of a welcoming smile on his face.

"I'm Julia Arnold," she said. She fumbled in her bag. "Rosa Swiece's mother," she continued nervously. "I've brought a message." She stretched out her hand.

He nodded, took the envelope from her, and, still without smiling, walked back to the concrete dwelling. As he opened the door, she saw that four or five men were seated around a table. The air was thick with smoke. She looked away quickly.

When the door opened again, she glanced up, expecting to see the same man. But it was instead Walter Sisulu who was heading her way. She smiled in relief. Gentle, bespectacled Walter was one of the African leaders with whom she felt most at home. She had met him on several occasions, and he had always managed to put her at her ease.

There were not many of them who could do that, since Julia nursed a secret from everybody but herself. It was a secret of which she was desperately ashamed. It was this: She did not feel comfortable with black South Africans.

Rosa would never have understood the slight shrinking that overcame Julia in their company, but then Rosa had a different background. She had been brought up in a household where blacks were treated as equals: Hadn't she practically grown up with Moses Bopape?

Whereas in Julia's own childhood, blacks had been *kaffirs*—*shvartzers* to be despised and feared. It was a prejudice that Julia found impossible to kick. No matter how hard she tried, no matter how much her political beliefs militated against her reactions, she could not throw off the feeling that somehow it was odd and wrong to get so close to Africans.

But with Walter it was different. He was educated. He was polite. Mandela was more fiery, and therefore more difficult to get to know, but Walter was inevitably courteous, and he never failed to talk kindly to her. She smiled in relief.

He strode over to her and took her hands in his. "We thank you for bringing this message," he said. "It took courage."

She shrugged as if it were nothing. "I must be going," she said.

He nodded.

"Nothing to take back?"

"Just tell our friends that we will be careful," he said.

The journey back was nowhere near as frightening as the one before. Julia was glad she had done it—the fear was worse than the actual deed—but she was also glad it was over.

Until the next time, I suppose, she thought.

But there never was a next time.

For it turned out that Julia must have been one of the last outsiders to see Walter free. The following day the police raided Rivonia. They arrested all its inhabitants. Arthur Goldreich, in one of those twists of fortune that sometimes made the struggle an adventure story, managed to escape from jail. But the others were not so lucky. Along with Nelson Mandela, who was already imprisoned, ten of them were charged with 193 acts of sabotage. The maximum penalty was death.

38

MOSES STEPPED INTO THE CENTER OF THE RAILWAY LINE, AND kneeling down, he placed his bag of tools beside him. He did not start immediately. Instead, he looked around him, his ears alert, his eyes straining into the darkness. Everything was dark and still, everything was in its place. Except me, thought Moses fleetingly.

He reached into his bag and pulled out a wire clipper. He placed it by the side of the railway line gleaming in the moonlight. But as he did so, a shadow seemed to pass in front of him: The gleam vanished, the track became tarnished and dull.

He gazed about him, his heart beating wildly. But all was still dark. He looked up at the sky and saw that the shadow was caused by a lone cloud that was moving away from the moon again. He smiled to himself. "You're imagining things," he whispered. As if to confirm this fact, a soft whistle sounded from a small distance away: It was his comrade giving the all clear.

Moses bent down to his task.

He was almost finished when suddenly he felt in his bones that something had gone wrong. He didn't know what it was that had tipped him off—a crack of a twig in the bushes behind him, an eerie silence that was just too perfect, a muffled gasp from his right—but intuitively he guessed that he was in grave danger. He looked across at the railway line. It was as dark and as still as it had always been—a track in the middle of nowhere some twelve miles from Jo'burg. It was a perfect target, carefully chosen: part of a strategically important route but so isolated that there was no chance that anyone would be hurt by the explosion. But all this made it all the more unlikely that the sound Moses had heard was an innocent bystander passing their way.

He glanced behind him at the low rough scrub. It also seemed unthreatening. Nothing moved, nothing happened to back up his premonition. He must be imagining the danger, he told himself. It's funny, he reflected, how I become more rather than less scared as time goes on.

Out of his pocket he got a lighter, snapped it open, registered the flicker of its flame, and reached for the fuse. Well, he thought to himself, this is it.

At that moment all hell broke loose. A shrill police whistle cut through the air, a dog howled, a bright spotlight all but blinded him. "Run," he heard.

He ran. Across the railway line, heading for the cover he knew lay a hundred impossible yards ahead of him. He tripped on the first bar of metal, but his momentum carried him forward. Pushing himself upright, he jumped over the track as he heard the pandemonium behind him.

"Shoot the bastard," somebody shouted.

Moses ducked as a bullet whined past his ear. He looked back briefly and saw twenty, perhaps thirty, men dressed in railway workers' clothes, all armed with Sten guns and rifles. He ducked as one of the men took aim.

He was too certain a target out there on the track. When the next bullet came, he didn't even hear it. He felt instead something thudding into his leg. He registered no pain. It's just a stone, he thought, pleased by the knowledge that he could still think logically.

But when he tried to keep on running, his body refused the instruction. He put a hand to his leg, and he drew it up again: He was unsurprised to find it wet and sticky. "I will not let it stop me," he said out loud. He lurched forward. He could hear them pounding up behind him with a speed he could no longer match. Still he tried to run.

He had only got a few yards further when he was dragged to the ground. "*Jy sal vrek*," somebody hissed in his ear. "You're going to die." He felt a boot strike at his ribs. A searing pain throbbed through his whole body, starting at his leg and radiating outward to all his extremities. He looked up to see a man standing above him. He was just in time to notice, with something akin to detachment, that the boot was lifted up into the air again. It come crashing down on his head. Moses lost consciousness.

*   *   *

Jacob was eating his breakfast—a couple of slices of whole-wheat toast spread thinly with marmalade and washed down with a cup of coffee. He was enjoying the quiet of his comfortable hiding place. He could hear a bird chirping in the distance.

The police crept in quietly, into this house a few blocks away from the place where he'd last met Rosa. He just had time to register how well they had laid their trap when they pulled him to his feet. A smear of butter dripped onto his shirtsleeve. He brushed at it.

"Jacob Swiece," they said, "you're under arrest."

Carefully Jacob folded his napkin and placed it on the table. "I want to phone my lawyer," he said.

The lieutenant in charge laughed. "You know as well as I that you get no lawyer with ninety days." He put an arm on Jacob's back and pushed him forward. "When we charge you with sabotage, then you can get a lawyer. By that time, it'll be too late."

When Rosa put her key in the door, she heard the phone ringing. There was no point, she thought, in hurrying: In these situations it always stopped just before one could get to answer it. So she opened the door without haste, picked up her shopping bag, and walked over to the table and put it down. Only then did she approach the phone.

Her hand hovered over it. "Go on," she told it, "I know you're going to stop."

But it kept on ringing, so she picked up the receiver.

"Bad news," said a disembodied voice. "They've got Jacob." The connection was severed.

Rosa stared at the phone. She heard an echo: "They've got Jacob," the echo said. She would never know whether that voice was her imagination or a stupid police trick, but it didn't really matter, because it served its purpose—it stirred her into action. She dialed a number, the number of a movement lawyer: She did not need to look it up—recent events had ensured that she knew it by heart.

"I'll get on to it right away," said the lawyer. "You want to meet me at the police station?"

"Not now," Rosa said. "I have to wait for the kids."

"Yes," said the lawyer. "I'm sure you're going to have your hands full there."

Rosa put down the phone and looked longingly at the chair next to it. "There's no time to brood," she told herself sternly.

The chair beckoned. "Just for a minute," she promised herself. She sat down on it.

Nothing, she now realized, could pave the way for the realization that one's husband could soon be on trial for his life. "For his life, for his life": The words kept echoing through her head. She continued to sit.

She was still there when when Julia arrived with the children. As soon as Julia heard the news, she started weeping and wringing her hands, but one look from Rosa was enough to send her into the deeper recesses of the house. And Rosa sat.

She didn't know how long she was going to stay in that kind of suspended animation; she just knew that there no longer seemed any reason to move. And so strong was this feeling that, if not for Martha, she might still be there.

The girl defied her grandmother's warnings and came to stand before Rosa. She'd put her hands on her hips, and when she spoke, her voice dripped contempt.

"Well, what did you expect?" she asked.

"Not now, darling," Rosa replied.

Martha stamped her foot. "Yes, *now*," she insisted. "Isn't there something you should be doing now?"

It's funny, Rosa thought, how sensible my children can be. For of course Martha was right; there was something she should be doing. She should have been clearing the house. Not one piece of evidence would they find should they be looking for something to incriminate Jacob.

Two hours later she was sitting in the middle of the floor, looking numbly at the papers that surrounded her. She wished that she could concentrate better, that she could just get on with the task she had set herself. To waste time at this point was a luxury she couldn't afford.

Wearily she grabbed at the nearest pile. She glanced at it. She saw that it was an innocuous enough bunch of newspaper cuttings all dated around the time of the treason trial that followed the Congress of the People. "There's no reason to destroy this lot," she muttered. She stuffed them all into an old suitcase that she'd rescued from the garage.

The next item she examined more closely. It was a copy of the Freedom Charter written in Xhosa. She smiled nostalgically.

She remembered how she had smuggled the document out of Kliptown. She had been pregnant then, bearing Rachel, and she'd stuffed it down her frock. Those were the days, she reflected, when the police wouldn't search a pregnant woman. Now, she wasn't so sure where they would draw the line.

"One for me?" Rachel asked brightly.

As she came closer, Rosa saw how filthy the child was. A fine soot covered her hands and legs; her small face was practically black. Rachel, Rosa knew, was enjoying herself. She showed no signs of noticing the distress that pervaded the whole house—she was treating it all as a big joke. She'd helped light the fire, and now she'd become insatiable in her urge to fuel it. No sooner did Rosa hand her some documents than she seemed to be back again for more.

Rosa knew she should burn the Freedom Charter. Its very existence could be an excuse for imprisonment these days. That was why she was going through with this task.

"Well, give it to me then," Rachel said impatiently.

Her youngest had one hand on the document and was tugging at it impatiently. Rosa knew that she should play safe and surrender the paper to the flames, but she felt a curious kind of reluctance.

"I'll keep this one, darling," she said.

Avoiding Rachel's disappointed look, Rosa pushed the charter to the middle of the cuttings in the suitcase. She covered the lot with some old photographs. She realized that she was being unduly sentimental. And yet, who knew what the future would bring? One day, perhaps, when this was all over, they would frame the charter and hang it in a museum. One day when they were all free. One day when they were all together.

She shook her head and piled another batch of nostalgia into the suitcase.

"Mom," she called.

Julia appeared instantaneously, as if she'd been waiting outside the door. Her eyes, Rosa noticed, were red, her lips inscribed a tight line.

Rosa had no energy to spend on pitying her mother. "Can we find somewhere to hide this?" she asked.

Julia frowned. "What is it?" She put up a hand before Rosa could answer. "I don't want to know," she said. "I only ask because—" She broke off in midsentence and sighed. "You know what I mean," she said irritably.

"It's okay, it's all fairly innocuous," Rosa said. "But when they come, I don't want them to get it. They never return what they confiscate."

"They're not going to come here again?" Julia was alarmed.

It was Rosa's turn to express irritation. "How do I know what they're going to do?" she asked. "I'm just playing it safe. Now can you find a place or not?"

"There's no need to snap at me," Julia said. "I'm doing my best. It's not easy." As she saw Rosa on the verge of taking the suitcase from her hand, she snatched at it hastily. "I'll ask Nicholas to keep it," she said. She looked at Rosa, and her face softened. "Are you all right, darling?" she asked.

Rosa nodded.

"It's hard on you," Julia said.

"It's hard on all of us," was Rosa's reply. "I wonder how Peggy's doing. The rumors are that Moses has also been picked up.".

Peggy was singing softly to herself as she cleaned the windows of her house. It was a lovely day, bright and yet not too hot, and she had a rare day off. She'd woken up feeling calm and happy. She searched her mind for some task that could help sustain her mood. She'd decided eventually to spring-clean the house. It wasn't that the place was dirty—more that it was about due for its three-monthly turnout. And Peggy always enjoyed this task of bringing order to the nooks and crannies of her domain. Perhaps Moses will come back today, she thought, and everything will look spick-and-span for him.

The first she knew of Lindiwe's presence was when a dark shadow crossed the wall. She shivered and turned around, and then, seeing her daughter in front of her, beamed in delight.

"Lindiwe," she exclaimed. "What a lovely surprise. And how's the little one?"

Without waiting for a reply, she went behind Lindiwe and gently plucked the eight-week-old Nathaniel from his blanketlike cocoon on his mother's back. She held him up admiringly. He was so perfect, this first grandson of hers, this namesake for his paternal grandfather: It was so good to hold him.

Lindiwe's marriage to Johannes Cuba was a happy one, and Nathaniel—the perfect easy baby whose gummy smiles could melt the sternest heart—was the proof of it. Nathaniel was asleep and Peggy loath to wake him, but she longed to see him open his eyes and dazzle her in his recognition of his grandmother. "What a handsome boy," she chuckled. For the first time that day she looked properly at her daughter. She was unprepared for the sight that met her eyes.

Lindiwe did not speak, but there was an expression on her face that Peggy had never seen before. The shiver she'd first experienced when Lindiwe's shadow had blotted out her sun returned with a vengeance. It was as if her whole body were gripped by an icy claw, by a presentiment of doom that came when she was least expecting it.

She glanced away, hoping against hope that she was imagining Lindiwe's solemnity. But all in vain. When she turned back, she saw that Lindiwe was trying her best not to cry.

"Moses?" Peggy asked.

Lindiwe did not move.

"He's been arrested," Peggy stated.

Lindiwe nodded. She did not speak, and from that Peggy knew that there was something else to be told, something even worse than arrest.

"Is he hurt?" she asked.

"Yes," Lindiwe said softly.

"Badly?"

"They shot him in the leg. One of my friends who works in Coronation Hospital came to tell me. She was on night duty when they brought him in. They got the bullet out—he was lucky it missed the bone—but when the doctor tried to keep him for the night, the police refused."

"Where did they take him?"

"Marshall Square, she thinks," Lindiwe answered. "My friend gave one of the constables a cup of tea in her attempt to find out more. But you know the authorities—to them a black policeman is a *kaffir* like the rest of us. He couldn't tell her much. Just that Moses would be interrogated."

"We must go and find out," Peggy said.

But instead of leaving immediately, as her daughter had expected her to, she stepped into the house to fry some meat.

She's in shock, Lindiwe thought. She hoisted the still-sleeping Nathaniel back into place and went up to her mother. Gently she placed an arm around Peggy. "We must go," she said.

Peggy turned from the stove, and Lindiwe saw that her face was clear of tears. A kind of determination, of resolution, that she had never seen before, shone through. "He'll be held under ninety days," Peggy said. "That means we can take him food and clothes. He must not go hungry."

As she watched Peggy prepare a package for Moses, Lindiwe felt a growing respect for her mother. Childhood memories—the most vivid ones, the ones focused on the times when Peggy had ranted and raved and fought with Moses about his political activities—came flooding back. In her mind's eye, she realized, Moses had been the solid one, Peggy the weak link. It was on Moses that Lindiwe had modeled herself.

Now, she understood, as if for the first time, that her mother had reserves of strength she didn't need to display. Peggy knew as well as Lindiwe did that Moses' arrest was many times worse than any of his previous incarcerations, and yet she was not panicking, not berating her fate. Lindiwe felt shame that her first impulse on hearing the news had been resentment that she would have to bolster her mother through this crisis. In contrast to this expectation, it was Peggy who was showing her how to behave.

"Can I help?" she asked tentatively.

"Somebody must tell your brother," Peggy said.

"George," Lindiwe scoffed. "He won't want to know. All he'll care about is that it'll make him seem less respectable."

"Don't speak of your brother like that," Peggy snapped. "He comes from Moses' loins, as do you. He must be told."

Moses fought the darkness that was threatening to overcome him. He blinked and wondered why the room had gone all red. He tried to shift himself, but even the slightest movement jarred at his bones. He turned his head, taking in, as if for the first time, this, his new home.

He was lying on a filthy bedroll that took up a full half of the cell. The walls climbed high above him and were windowless. He was naked: They'd taken his clothes away, as they always did, when they'd pushed him in here. To his shivering body he clutched a thin blanket that stank of others' pain. A solitary light bulb shone down at him.

He heard the sound of footsteps echoing down the corridor outside. He shivered and drew the blanket more closely around him, ignoring the stink of urine that pervaded it. "Don't let them be coming for me," he prayed. "Not so soon."

With relief, he heard the tap of a teak baton on a steel door some few cells away.

"Everything all right?" came the cry.

"All right," was the inevitable response.

They did not bother to ask Moses. He heard the footsteps cease, and then something scraped against his door. A glimmer of light shone through the peephole before the metal grill was roughly clanged down into place. Then the footsteps moved on.

Moses felt a fatuous kind of resentment at his exclusion. He wanted to get up and bang on the door. "Ask me," he wanted to shout, "ask me if I'm all right."

He smiled grimly to himself. "And what good would that have done?" he muttered. For he now understood the first rule of a jailed existence—don't draw attention to yourself. What they planned for him was bad enough without his childishness making it worse.

And after all, their routine of checking on people had only one aim: to ensure that no untidy corpses littered the cells. He knew that to complain would only earn him another beating. The visiting magistrates, along with the doctors employed by the Special Branch, were all a stupid bloody joke designed to further dash the hopes of its victims.

He'd met one of their doctors when he'd been first detained. Not the one at the hospital—he was sympathetic enough, but what could he do?—but a special prison medic called out in the night to see if Moses was fit for interrogation. After they'd dragged him through the underground garage and kicked him into a elevator, he'd been taken into a room devoid of all furniture. In one corner stood a man whose black bag was the only indication of seven years of intense medical training.

The man had not even looked at him. "What's wrong with you?" he'd asked in a bored tone.

"I've been shot."

"Well, what's that to me?" the doctor snapped. "They treated you at the hospital, didn't they, hey?"

Moses did not deign to reply. For this transgression one of the constables guarding him kicked him in the back. "Answer the *moreana*," he ordered.

"I'm in considerable pain," Moses said. "They took my pills away from me."

"For your own good," the doctor said. "We can't have you trying something silly, can we now?" He nodded briskly at the guards and then walked out of the room, almost hugging the walls, as if the slightest bodily contact with Moses might infect him.

"Everything all right?" came the distant shout.

Moses groaned.

"Okay, Jacob," the colonel said patiently. "Try this one for size. Name of Philip Cohen."

Jacob shifted in his seat. He made a halfhearted attempt to look around him, but there was nothing in the small room on which his eyes could fix. There was the chair he was sitting on, the table facing him behind which his interrogator sat, and one other policeman standing by the door. For the rest the walls were a dingy kind of gray, and the window a slit stuck three quarters of the way up one wall.

He gave up and looked the colonel full in the face. "I know him slightly," he said.

"Only slightly?"

"That's what I said."

The colonel got up from behind his desk. He sauntered over to Jacob and stood behind him. Jacob could feel his sour breath on his neck. He did not flinch.

"Well, would it surprise you to hear that Philip Cohen, who you say you know only slightly, has implicated you in twenty-six separate and integral acts of sabotage? Hey? Would it surprise you?"

"Nothing surprises me in this place," Jacob said.

The colonel moved back behind his desk. He sat down heavily. He took a sip of coffee from the mug in front of him. Jacob followed the cup as it was lifted to his captor's mouth. He licked his lips.

"Ah, you want coffee?" The colonel sneered, and then he smiled. "I tell you what," he said. "I'll make you a bargain. You tell me all about Philip Cohen, and I'll treat you to the biggest cup of coffee you've ever had. No charge—on me, you understand. And all for telling me about a man who's already betrayed you."

The colonel lifted the mug to his lips again. He tilted it forward so that Jacob could see the hot brown liquid inside it. No matter how hard he tried, Jacob could not prevent the saliva from rising to his lips.

"I wouldn't drink your coffee," he said.

The colonel's fist came down hard and the coffee spilled out onto the table. "Ag, man. Let's stop playing," he said. "We've got you for sabotage. You have nothing to lose."

"Then charge me," Jacob replied. "And let me see a lawyer."

"Oh, don't worry about that. You'll be charged. We're going to lock you up and throw away the key. All in our own good time."

Peggy and Lindiwe sat on the hard bench that lined one wall of the police station's reception area. Across the room was a high desk behind which policemen stood and worked, for the main ignoring the people who came up to make inquiries. On each side other people waited: There was little exchange of conversation—there was nothing left to say.

They had been in this place for hours. George had long ago come and gone again, muttering something about his garage business. Lindiwe was on the verge of commenting sarcastically about George's concern, but one look from Peggy silenced her.

They had seen Julia Arnold arrive with a basket for Jacob. She had been dealt with immediately. Her basket was taken over the counter and searched in front of her. Yesterday's basket was returned without politeness but with none of the sneers that had greeted Peggy's request about her husband. Julia had left after exchanging sympathetic glances with them.

"Even in prison, whites are treated better," Lindiwe remarked bitterly.

"Shush, child," Peggy chided. "Their family has always been good to us."

"Hey, you, over there."

Peggy jumped to her feet. It pained her daughter to watch her scurry over to the desk, a polite smile on her face. "Why don't you return their insults?" she muttered to herself. "What good does it do to be polite to these pigs?"

And yet she did not interfere. Peggy was behaving in the only way she was able. She was clinging to the hope that if she did not lose her temper, that if she gave them no excuse to throw her out, then she would eventually hear news of her husband.

"Yes, *baas*," she said.

"What is it you wanted?"

Peggy took a deep breath. This was the fifth time she had told her story to the very same man. "My husband, Moses Bopape, is being held under ninety days," she said. "I want to send him some fresh clothes and some food."

"Moses Bopape? Never heard of him. And what do you think we are here—a welfare organization? Stop wasting my time. Next."

"Let's go," Lindiwe urged when Peggy returned.

"We will stay," Peggy said firmly.

Moses was frog-marched to a room on the ninth floor. When they pushed him in, he blinked. Two 150-watt table lamps set closely together shone directly in his eyes, temporarily blinding him.

"On the line!" somebody shouted.

He looked down at the floor and then limped so that he was standing with his toes touching the thin chalk mark they'd drawn there on his first day.

He could not see his interrogators' faces. He didn't need to, because, after three nights with them, he knew their voices intimately. There were three of them in all: The black constables on either side of him didn't count. Their job was to stand to attention, pulling him off the floor if he should give in and slide down, and to run an occasional errand for the white *baas*.

"Hey, *kaffir*, how you feeling now?" the one with the heaviest Afrikaans accent and the adenoidal voice shot at him.

Moses did not reply.

"Lost your tongue, boy?"

Moses looked straight toward the source of the light. He needed all his strength to remain upright. The last few days had taken their toll on him. It was his legs that bothered him the most. They felt like iron, but unlike metal, they hurt like hell. They had swelled up, both of them, and every time he stood in this room, his body screamed its protest to him.

"Maybe that's what we should do," another of the interrogators sneered. "Cut out his tongue." This voice belonged to the thinnest of the men, the one whom Moses had learned to fear the most. He never took part in any violence—he didn't want, Moses guessed, to expose his frail physique to any further comment, but he egged the others on unceasingly. This was the one to be watched. He could kill, this one.

"*Ja*, or something else," the third interrogator said impassively. He was the career policeman, older than the others, who carried out his job with a calm impassivity even when his thick fists were thumping into Moses' body.

"Let's try him again," said the first. "Jacob Swiece."

Moses stayed silent. "Mandela, Sisulu—you met them, or they're too swanky to hang out with the likes of you?" the thin one called.

Moses held his tongue. He knew better than to rise to their taunts.

"Goldberg, Mbeki, Mhlaba, Motsoaledi, Mlangeni, Kathrada, Fischer, Bernstein." The names came flying furiously over his head.

Moses felt his knees give in on him. He sank to the ground.

"*Staan op, kaffir*," they barked. A rough hand pulled him to his feet and pushed him back to the chalk line.

And then they started hitting him. Suddenly, without warning, a hand swung at his ribs. As he doubled over, gasping for breath, they thumped him on the back, pushing him to the floor.

"*Staan op!*" they shouted as they stood in a circle, kicking at him. "*Staan op, kaffir.*"

He was on his feet again. This time they took a truncheon to his head. He saw the swing of it, he felt its first impact, he saw the ground come rushing upward toward him. He blacked out.

The next thing he knew, his face was wet. They must have thrown some water at him to bring him to, but that wouldn't explain the stain that was spreading on his trousers. He thought he had lost all human feeling, but a wave of shame descended on him.

"*Vat hom weg.*" The voice in the distance was pregnant with disgust. "Take him away."

"Bopape!" the voice shouted.

Peggy jerked herself upright. She could hardly believe it, but she knew she must have dozed off. Lindiwe had long since left after Nathaniel woke up and started to cry. Lindiwe had lifted him to her breast, but there was no consoling him. He whimpered, cried, and then began to scream unceasingly. It was as if he knew where they were: as if he had picked up the anxiety that increased with every waiting minute.

In the end Peggy had persuaded Lindiwe to take the child away. She did so for a selfish reason—she could not, she judged, afford to antagonize the counter police still further.

But her decision worsened things for her. With Lindiwe gone, she felt completely alone. She sat on the hard bench, and she, too, cried—silently, inside herself, with not a tear as evidence.

"For Christ sake, woman, hurry up," the constable called. He turned to a colleague who sat beside him. "Ag, these people," he said. "They drive me mad with their slowness. Yes?" he barked at Peggy.

"I am Bopape," she said, with as much dignity as she could muster.

"About time, too. You wanted to send your man clothes?"

Peggy nodded. She lifted the brown parcel onto the counter. "And food," she said.

"What do you think we are? A hotel? Clothes is what it says here. If you wanted to give him food, you should have told me in the first place. It's too late now."

Peggy had not the strength to argue with him. She separated the food from the rest and pushed it toward the constable. He took the parcel and shoved it under his counter. He looked down at the book in front of him. Peggy did not move.

"What the hell do you want now?" he asked.

"His old clothes, *meneer*," Peggy whispered.

"What for?"

"So I can wash them, *meneer*," she said.

"God give me strength," the man sighed. "Wait here."

He turned and walked through a door. It was a long time before he returned. When he did, he was holding what appeared at first sight to be a bundle of rags. He practically threw them at Peggy.

She had no idea why she did it, but Peggy did not walk away with the clothes as was expected of her. Instead, she stood by the counter and spread them out in front of her. She gasped.

"Get them away from me!" the constable shouted. "They stink. Don't you *blerry kaffirs* ever wash?"

"There's blood on them," Peggy said.

"What else do you expect? Your husband was shot resisting arrest."

"He was shot in the leg," Peggy said. "But there's blood on the shirt."

"That's your problem, not mine," the man sneered. "You've got what you came for. Get out before I arrest you for obstructing the police in their rightful duty."

Richard tapped his leg on the ground. He stared down at the grayish carpet. He was bored with it, bored with everything in this dingy side office at police headquarters: bored with the secretary's brassy hair, with her wooden desk and clattering typewriter, with the chocolate-box kitten that hung above her head.

"Mr. Crossbanks?"

Richard glanced up. About time he thought. Who do these people think they are? He stood up, and smoothing the creases from his white trousers, he nodded briskly at the man.

"Come in, please."

He was led into a pleasant enough room, which had windows on two walls. The sun streamed through them, making lazy patterns on the flowered wallpaper.

"Now, sir. What I can do for you?" The man took a seat behind his desk. Without being invited to, Richard chose a low-slung leather-covered chair that placed him at a slight angle to the desk.

"I am acting on behalf of a friend," Richard said.

"Ah."

"I understand," Richard continued, "that Dr. Jacob Swiece was arrested and is being held under the Ninety-Day Act."

"That's correct."

"I want to know what evidence there is against him."

The man frowned. "Your friend is Mrs. Swiece?" he asked.

Richard frowned. "That is my affair."

"Uh-huh," the man said.

"I have no obligation to tell you," Richard said.

The man opposite was unruffled by the rebuff. He beamed at Richard, and his square face lit up as he did so. "Look, Mr. Crossbanks," he said, "we are in a delicate situation in this country. I can't expect you to understand—after all, you in Britain have centuries of civilization behind you." He stretched backward. "We are not as lucky," he continued. "However well-meaning our blacks might be—and some of them intend nothing but good—they are still not ready for power. After all, it's not long ago that they fought with assegais."

"I didn't come here for a history lesson," Richard said.

"What I am trying to say," the man continued, "is that you cannot expect me to help you unless you are honest with me." He paused and stared intently at Richard. "Now perhaps you better start again," he suggested.

"My friend is Mrs. Swiece," Richard conceded.

"And would I be right in assuming that Rosa Swiece knows nothing of your visit?" He patently did not expect Richard to reply. He smiled. "You see, Mr. Crossbanks, we understand your friend Rosa better than you do yourself. It's understandable, really: We play by the same rules, Rosa and I. You, on the other hand, are a stranger. Don't get me wrong: We appreciate the business your father's company brings our economy, but we are not a poor country."

"You mean I cannot threaten you?"

"Threaten? Threaten?" The man raised his eyebrows. "Surely it won't come to that. After all, we are having a conversation between friends. You came here of your own free will, and you're free to go at any time."

"You're telling me there's nothing you can do?"

The man looked down at his nails. "I have no power to do anything," he said. He reached across the desk and removed a pair of scissors from the front of it. He began to prod at his fingers with it. Then he looked up suddenly and smiled. "But you, Mr. Crossbanks, you could help your friend Rosa."

"What do you mean?" Richard was beginning to feel that it had been a terrible mistake to come here. He should walk out now, before he got further entangled with this man.

And yet he couldn't. He was like a fly in a spider's web, frozen by the man's smiles, and by his words. He sat still and listened.

"It's like this," the man continued. "Rosa Swiece is in what we call a delicate position. She is guilty as hell, we know that. But we are civilized people. We are reluctant to imprison a woman who has two young children, and, perhaps," he admitted, "the good sense to have friends such as the son of the eminent Lord Crossbanks."

"And? For godsake, man, spit it out."

Abruptly the man put the scissors down. He looked straight across at Richard. "Like I say, you can help her. You know things that would not harm anybody, but could save her perhaps. The choice is yours."

Richard got up and turned away.

"Think about it, Mr. Crossbanks," came the man's voice. "And if I might be so bold as to give you some advice—I wouldn't go on any more of those late-night trips with your friends if I were you."

Jacob was back in the same room, and this time he didn't even bother to look around. He was standing—they'd stopped him from sitting down—and he was staring straight ahead. He held his breath.

"Jacob Swiece," the officer said, "you are hereby charged on five different counts under the Sabotage Act of 1962. It is my duty to warn you that anything you say will be taken down and may be used in evidence against you. Do you have anything to say?"

"I want to see my lawyer."

"In good time. All in good time."

Moses gripped the sides of his chair. The light was a blinding flash in his eyes, but he did not even feel it. He was relishing the relief of being off his feet, of being seated for the first time in this room. Not even the waves of cigarette smoke they blew his way could dent the luxuriousness of it all.

"Richard Crossbanks," they said.

"No."

"Philip Cohen."

"No."

"Nelson Mandela."

"Everybody knows Mandela."

"James Thibusi."

Moses looked up in surprise. He smiled, but only to himself: He was careful to keep his expression neutral. For the first time since he had been in this room, he sensed a ray of hope: He felt as though he might have the upper hand. They were getting desperate—so desperate that they were even trying to make him implicate a man well known as one of their spies.

"I know of Thibusi," he said.

He heard a sharp inhalation of somebody's breath. "Hey, Colonel," the old one said, "this *kaffir* has found his tongue.

Finally he admits to knowing someone."

"You know him well?" the broad one snapped.

"I wouldn't want to know him," Moses answered. "To know a hyena who stinks of his master's leftovers."

A chair scraped abruptly against the floor. "*Ag, hy praat net kak. Vat hom weg*," an angry voice called.

With relief, Moses felt the two arms grasp at him and begin hauling him toward the door. Then his heart sank as the thin one's voice halted his guard in their tracks.

"Hold on!" the policeman shouted. "It's time for the hook."

39

HE WAS HANGING FROM A HOOK IN THE CENTER OF THE ROOM, HIS hands bound together by a leather thong. If he had been able to look up, he would have seen that they had gone a kind of pallid gray. But he did not look up. His head lolled on his chest.

They did not appear to notice. They were like savages as they punched at him, pushing his body first one way and then the next. They grunted as they hit in rhythm, like convicts on a chain gang, as if their lives depended on it. All three of them worked on what was left of Moses Bopape, the thin one included. Sweat poured from their brows.

Peggy was back in Marshall Square, back in front of the high desk, back trying to attract the sergeant's attention. She cleared her throat nervously.

He continued to concentrate on the book in front of him, but he frowned to show that he'd registered her presence. "Yes?"

"Bopape," she said. "My name is Peggy Bopape."

"What do you want?"

"I have come to change my husband's clothes," she answered. For the first time the man looked up. "What name?"

"Bopape."

He pulled the large red book from the shelf beside him, and opening it, he thumbed through it impatiently. "No one of that name here," he finally said.

"But yesterday . . ."

"Look here, my girl," he said. "There is no one of that name here. That is the last time I'm going to tell you." He shut the book with a bang.

* * *

Rosa watched Julia reverse the car down the driveway. Rachel's nose, she saw, was pressed against the back window.

"Give Daddy my love," she shouted.

She lifted her hand in response to Rachel's cheerful wave. "See you later, honey," she called. "Bye, Martha."

But Martha did not turn around, and Rosa regretted once more that she hadn't made a second effort to kiss her eldest through the open window. She shouldn't have been put off like that, she should have defied Martha's angry glare.

It was all so difficult, so much harder than she might have imagined. The trouble was that she found herself dealing with problems on so many different levels: She had to hide from the kids how hurt she felt at the fact that she was forbidden from visiting Jacob while they were allowed to go; she had to put up a show of cheerfulness when all she wanted to do was cry; and, finally, she had to pretend, even to herself, that she was not scared of Martha.

Ever since Rosa had told the children about Jacob's forthcoming trial, Martha had retreated into herself. She barely spoke to her mother these days: It was almost as if she held Rosa responsible for her father's fate.

Eight-year-old Rachel was putting up a brave front. She appeared her usual jolly self, but the nighttimes gave her away. It was after dark when her fears surfaced. For one whole week Rosa was jolted out of a dreamless sleep by the sounds of Rachel's screams. The child had been impossible to wake, and therefore inconsolable. It was as if she refused to face the reality of Jacob's impending trial at the same time as she was tortured by her dreams. On several occasions Rosa had been forced to hold Rachel's head under the shower in order to rouse her.

They eventually solved the problem by persuading Rachel to share a bed with Julia. The mere fact of bodily contact with another human being seemed enough to drive the horrors away.

But no matter how frightening Rachel's nocturnal fits had been, they were easier to deal with than Martha's tight-lipped silence. Nothing Rosa attempted was any good. If she acted normal, she would find Martha gazing at her, a look of contempt on her face. If she tried to talk to the adolescent about what was happening, Martha would as likely as not stalk straight out and lock herself in her bedroom.

"Oh, Jacob," Rosa said to herself as she faced the empty driveway. "What is to become of us?"

She turned and began to walk toward the front door, but a movement in the bushes distracted her. Shit, not again, she thought. She stamped her foot in exasperation. "Come out of there," she ordered, "before I drag you out."

When the figure of a woman emerged, Rosa smiled apologetically. "Lindiwe," she said. "I thought you were a policeman. They've taken to skulking about, checking, I suppose, that I'm not about to stage a jailbreak."

Lindiwe did not return Rosa's smile. She stood, tight-lipped and sullen, beside the bushes. Rosa inspected her. Lindiwe would have been a handsome woman, she thought, if only she occasionally smiled. She was so much like her father in appearance, and yet it was as if, behaviorally, she had been molded from a different block. Peggy talked of the young woman as a quiet, polite, loving daughter, and Rosa could remember her as such, but recently she hadn't caught even so much as a glimpse of this aspect. Instead, emanating from Lindiwe was a smoldering resentment—a dislike that seemed to have no foundation.

"What brings you here?" Rosa asked.

"My mother." Lindiwe glared.

"She is not well?"

"How could she be?"

"And Moses. What of him?"

Lindiwe frowned. "That is why I've come." She looked down at the ground. "They deny all knowledge of him at the jail," she said dully. "They meet our every question with anger. They threaten to arrest us if we ask again."

As Rosa took in the implications of what Lindiwe was saying, she felt her stomach lurch. She had considered herself numbed to any further developments, but now she knew how wrong that assumption was.

Her life had been turned upside down in the last few months. Her husband was in jail, charged with a crime that carried a capital sentence. She'd lost touch with her oldest daughter, and didn't know what to do about it. She was no longer permitted to work. She could no longer even travel. She had to report to the local police station three times every day. She'd thought that things could not get worse.

Now, she knew she had been deceiving herself. Things could,

and would, get worse. But it would not be whites like the Swieces who would suffer the maximum penalty; it would be people like Moses. And she hadn't given him more than a passing thought in the previous weeks. *How could I have been so callous?* she berated herself. *I should have known.*

Even now, she didn't want to face what it was that she should have known. Even now, it felt too painful. For it was apartheid in its most brutal manifestation. It was what could happen to a black man who walked on the wrong side of the street, who looked the wrong way at his *baas*, and who, worst of all, was taken into jail as a political.

Pull yourself together, she muttered internally. *Regrets won't help. We've no evidence anything's happened to him.*

"I'll get onto it right away," she said out loud. "Come in and wait."

"I'll be at home," Lindiwe answered.

"Oh, don't be like that. Come in," she urged.

"My family needs me. I'll be at home."

Rosa set the wheels in motion. She phoned her contacts, and together they chose the best lawyers. Radical practices were overwhelmed these days, but for Moses Bopape most of them would pull out all the stops.

For Moses was universally known and universally appreciated. He was of the generation of Mandela, and he was molded from the same block. He had been instrumental in changing the ANC from a dead organization into a living one: He had been part of all the Congress's many achievements in the thirteen years that had led to the establishment of MK.

His fate and that of the movement were inextricably linked. The telephone wires began to buzz.

Peggy heard the car draw up. She made no attempt to move. She glanced at her children. Lindiwe was sitting with a sleeping Nathaniel on her knees. Beside her, Johannes accompanied them in their vigil. *He's a good man,* Peggy thought. *He is with his wife in times of trouble.*

George had no one next to him. He was still a loner, although that was the only thing about him that remained unchanged. For George could no longer be regarded as a failure. He had started a garage business, and was now in the unprecedented position of employing three mechanics. He looked ill at ease in this small

Sowetan house. He had moved into a larger abode, a place with three bedrooms and a bathroom. He stared in anger at Lindiwe when she scoffed at his pretensions. He looked right through her when she asked him if he rotated his sleeping place each night.

Peggy heard the sounds of a car door opening, but still she did not budge. She was remembering a time, so many ages ago, when she had sat this way. At that time it had been she who nursed a sleeping child. She remembered her fear that turned to joy when Rosa and George had stepped out of the car.

And she remembered something else: On that night Jacob had also been present. Not so tonight. Jacob was in jail. And this time Moses would not return—she knew it in her heart.

The door opened. Rosa came in alone. She looked disheveled—something, Peggy vaguely thought, she had never expected from Rosa. Her eyes were red, her face somehow collapsed.

"Moses is dead," she said. "They killed him."

Rosa had not had time to think how Moses' family would react to her news. She had been too caught up in her own grief as she drove to Soweto. She had been too preoccupied to wonder whether the police would stop and jail her for breaking the curfew they'd imposed on her. She had been too lost in her own memories and in the rage that fueled her forward.

Now, she was at a loss. For none of the Bopapes moved. On George's face was an indecipherable expression: It was, Rosa thought, almost as if he were practicing an appropriate visage of grief and didn't want to talk until he had perfected it. Lindiwe stared straight ahead, her hands over her sleeping child's face as if she were trying to shelter him from the dim light. Her husband, Johannes, touched her lightly, but she shrugged him off.

And Peggy—her face was the worst. It was blank, stolid and unfeeling. It was set in an expression of stone. She could have been a statue if she had not just then given one deep sigh—a sigh of realization and of acceptance.

The sound broke the spell. George jumped to his feet.

"Thank you for taking the trouble to tell us," he said to Rosa. "Please, take a seat."

"Your father has been killed in a white man's jail, and you worry about seating a white woman." The words came slowly out of Lindiwe's mouth, but her face did not appear to move as she spoke them.

Peggy raised herself wearily to her feet. She said, "We thank you, Rosa."

Tears rolled down Rosa's cheeks, and she was ashamed of them. For not one of the others in the room showed any emotion. They acted like people caught in a dream, like puppets who had never known the capacity for grief. She knew that it was not so. She knew how much Peggy loved Moses, how much Lindiwe loved him. But they could not cry. What would be the point? They had always known that it would end like this.

They buried Moses three weeks later—that was how long it took to get his body released. A coroner's court had been convened and rushed through its farcical proceedings. Death by misadventure was the verdict, despite the fact that a doctor recounted in detail the numerous marks he found on Moses' body.

Rosa wanted to raise an outcry to inform the world press, but Peggy stopped her. "What would be the point?" she said. "Would it bring Moses back?"

So they buried him without an inquiry. They buried him as the movement to which he'd given his life lay in splinters; as its leaders waited in jail; as hundreds of whites fled the country and thousands of blacks waited in fear for the bang on their door.

Four thousand people attended his funeral: an individual act of courage by every last one of them.

The police gathered outside Peggy's house early in the morning. They lined the route to the ceremony, they all but surrounded the grave. They jeered at the mourners, daring a reaction from them. Nobody looked their way. The people walked together, behind the hearse, in silence and in pain, as they supported, by their bodily presence, Moses Bopape's family.

Rosa was not among the mourners. She was specifically forbidden to go. She would have disobeyed the edict and slipped out at dawn, but the police were well prepared. They put an armed guard around her house two days before and two days after the funeral. She had no other choice but to send her mother in her stead.

There was a dignity in Moses' funeral procession that no amount of Saracens, of police sneers, could affect. The people walked behind the black car without once faltering. They lined up around the grave and not one of them coughed, not one baby in its mother's arms cried out.

The priest held his Bible in front of him. "Our of ashes..." he began. There was silence around him.

When he had finished the prayer, he closed the Bible and gazed at Peggy.

"I am a man of God," he said. "Moses Bopape was a man of the people. He died for the people."

And now a sound came from the crowd, from far back but still distinct. "He was murdered!" shouted the voice.

The priest nodded his head. "He was murdered," he agreed, "and may God forgive those who performed that evil deed." The crowd stood motionless. "I say may God forgive," he continued, "because for we mere mortals this is a hard sin to forgive. We ask ourselves: What did Moses Bopape ever do to those who took his life? Did he harm a single one of them? Did he ever kill?" The priest looked up. His voice was stronger now. "No," he said, "for that was not Moses' way. He struggled in peace for the rights of his people, and he always remembered how precious is each and every life." The voice dropped. "Moses was a man of the people, and the people will remember him. He is dead, but in our hearts he will live forever."

The priest nodded, and the simple wooden coffin was lowered into the ground. Peggy moved forward, Evelyn beside her. A few paces behind them came George, Lindiwe, and Johannes. They stood on the edge of the grave, looking down at Moses' last resting place. And then, following Peggy's lead, they took a step backward.

Only then did the crowd move. They did not surge forward, they came in an orderly fashion, men from deep inside that group. They stood in two lines, the person at the head of each line picking up a spade. And then, as the crowd sang, their voices swelling first mournfully and then in defiance, the men began to throw dirt onto the grave.

They worked in sequence, they worked together, the spades passed from hand to hand as each man took his place at the top of the line. The dirt flowed like water, high into the air and covering Moses' coffin. It piled up until the hole was no longer there, until it made a mound.

It was at that point that the police took action. From on top of one of the Saracens came the squawk of a loudspeaker. "Disperse in an orderly manner," shouted a policeman, "or you will be arrested and charged under the Riotous Assembly Act. This is your final warning."

The crowd moved, not hastily but still together. They walked back the way they had come.

It was to Moses' mother, Evelyn, that condolences were expressed. For Peggy was completely unapproachable. She had withstood the coroner's court phlegmatically. That was only right, her neighbors commented, what would be the good of showing grief to the white man? They had predicted that she would break down by the graveside—only then would she show the love that she held for her husband.

But they were wrong. Peggy did not wail, she did not cry, she showed nothing of her agony.

"She feels but she cannot express it," her neighbors consoled each other.

They couldn't know how wrong they were. They couldn't know that far from hiding her feelings, Peggy felt very little. It was as if she had died with Moses. She went through the motions of living, she ate when food was placed in front of her, but her spirit was absent. Without Moses, she was nothing.

But it would not be entirely true to say that Peggy felt nothing. Deep inside she nursed an emotion that was more powerful than grief. It was a fierce anger, and it was not directed at Moses' killers. It was an anger at Moses, at him alone, at him for leaving her. What she had once told herself had now come true. She would never forgive him.

"Jacob Swiece, you are charged under the Sabotage Act with committing five separate acts of violence. How do you plead?"

"Not guilty."

As the man in the dock next to Jacob stood up to answer the clerk of the court, Jacob glanced around him. This, he thought, was the one place in South Africa where concessions were made to the stringent laws of apartheid. Nowhere else would he, a white man, be sitting next to two Indians and one African— equals in the dock.

He looked beyond the bench, beyond the battery of defense staff and the lone prosecutor, toward the rows of spectator galleries. They were, at least, divided black from white. He saw his Rosa, who'd been given special permission to attend, sitting on the edge of her seat, her mother beside her. She was dressed in green and black, colors of the ANC woman's league, and he was proud of her. He smiled and nodded in her direction. Then his eyes moved upward.

The crowd at the very top section of the gallery was all black and crammed in together. People stood patiently in the back, as he knew they would stand for the whole of his trial. They were backed by many behind them, and by those who stood outside the court, unable to push their way in because of lack of space. He had seen them when the Black Maria had driven up. He had seen the pride in their faces, the clenched fists: the ANC banners. He had heard the cries of *Amandla* that rang out when he descended from the van.

He smiled and focused his attention back on the proceedings. His comrades had finished their pleas. The prosecutor was on his feet.

"My lord," he was saying, "the state's case is a simple and a clear-cut one. It is this—that between the years of 1962 and 1963 the accused did perpetrate acts of sabotage. We will bring testimony which will inform the court of the aims and intentions of the so-called Sabotage Campaign. We will show written evidence as to the complicity of the accused. But so sure are we of our case that we will only call one state witness." He looked at the clerk. "Call Philip Cohen," he said.

"Call Philip Cohen!" came the shout.

Philip entered from a side door to a silence that was almost deafening. The judge stirred uneasily, as if somebody had shouted out. He gripped his gavel in readiness.

Philip looked neither to left nor right. He mounted the witness stand and raised his hand before being asked. He repeated the oath in a muffled voice.

"Please state your name for the record," the prosecutor said.

"Philip Archibald Cohen." The voice was clear now. He stared straight ahead.

And in the three days of questioning and cross-examining he never once looked at the men whom he condemned. He gave his testimony in a blank, neutral voice. He spoke the truth, and he lied when it was not good enough, without evincing a single emotion. Throughout it all, Rosa Swiece's accusing eyes bored straight through him.

Rosa had crossed swords with Richard Crossbanks over the

extent of Philip's betrayal. "How could he do it?" she said. "To give away a comrade in detention is understandable. But to single-handedly condemn so many in open court—to turn police witness—that is unforgivable."

Richard had looked at her oddly. "You don't know why he did it," he said. "You don't know what pressure was put on him."

"Pressure," Rosa scoffed. "Real pressure is what the Special Branch did to Moses. Philip is unmarked. He's just a weakling, a despicable weakling."

"But then," said Richard sadly, "you are so much stronger than the rest of us."

There was no time to argue with him. The court was in the process of being reconvened. And what good would it do? What good would it do to let Richard know how alone Rosa felt, how her anger at Philip was the blind she used to mask her own desperation, how she cried at night, how she ached for Jacob's arms around her? Richard had, after all, proved himself a good friend. He had stood by her and run the risk of jeopardizing his own position by doing so. He had worked wonders. He had produced money out of air so as not to worry Rosa. He had argued fiercely with the authorities about the date of Rosa's exit visa. He alone had made it possible for her to stay and watch Jacob's trial before she had to leave.

She was no longer scared for Jacob's life. It had become increasingly clear that the state balked at imposing the death sentence on those charged with sabotage. And even if they did so, a white man would not be the one to suffer it. So it was only a question of how long Jacob would be given.

Peggy was packing. Into the simple wooden crates her neighbors had provided, she stashed her worldly goods. It didn't look like much when all was said and done: some blankets, a few pots and pans, her small wardrobe. She put nothing of Moses' into the trunks. His clothes had long since been removed: His books she had given to Lindiwe.

She heard somebody stir in the yard outside, but she did not look up. Ever since she had heard of Moses' death, and even after the funeral, her house had been packed by friends and neighbors. They had come to sit with her, to be with her, in her hour of need, and that she showed them neither gratitude nor simple acknowledgment did not deter them. They brought food, which she numbly spooned into her mouth, and fuel to light her stove.

She felt rather than saw her daughter approach her.

"Why are you going?" Lindiwe demanded. "Without even a fight."

Peggy looked at her daughter without showing a hint of animosity. But neither, Lindiwe reflected grimly, does she show any affection.

"Your father was the one who wanted to fight," Peggy said, "and look what happened to him." She stared past Lindiwe to where Johannes was standing awkwardly in the doorway. "I bid you welcome," she said, "for the last time in my house. But you should not have come. It will put your job in jeopardy."

Lindiwe snorted, and Peggy glanced at her inquiringly. "Johannes lost his job the day he took off four hours to come to Moses' funeral," Lindiwe said bitterly.

"I'm sorry to hear it," Peggy said. She bent down again to her packing. There was not much time left: The buses departed at noon, and she had no space to worry about Johannes. The younger generation must find their own way now: She was finished with life and with living. She had given up.

She had felt no rancor when the authorities had ordered her out of Soweto. She had accepted their judgment without demur. What they said to her made sense in their own terms—and it was on their terms that she had always been forced to live. They told her that she had to leave, to go live in a place that she had never seen.

Well, so be it. If that was what they ordered, then she would comply. What difference did it make to her where she lived?

But then another thought struck her. For the first time she stopped packing and looked at Johannes.

"If you have lost your job," she said, "you, too, will lose your right to stay. Where will you go?"

Johannes let his wife reply. He always did, thought Peggy, a trifle bitterly. She wouldn't have minded if Johannes had occasionally protected her from this whirlwind of a daughter.

"We will squat," Lindiwe said. "No white man tells me where to live."

Peggy nodded. "George will help you out," she vaguely suggested.

Lindiwe snorted. "George. He's putting as much distance between himself and the family as he possibly can. I wouldn't be surprised to find that he changes his surname. He has betrayed the Bopapes."

Peggy glared at her daughter. It's funny, she thought as she did so, how anger is the only real feeling that remains. "George has taken the right decision," she said firmly. "History will prove him right. The struggle is over, but when he marries, his children will be secure. What can you offer your Nathaniel that is equivalent?"

"The legacy of the family," Lindiwe replied.

"Ah," Peggy said slowly. "A legacy of death and defeat. I pity my grandson. It is not much to give."

"It is my only inheritance, and I am proud of it," Lindiwe said.

Peggy narrowed her eyes. "Yes, you always were your father's daughter," she said. "When he was around, you clung to him like a leech. I should have stopped that a long time ago. I should have left him."

"How can you say that?" Lindiwe gasped.

"If you make me talk, you will not like the things I say," Peggy answered.

"Leave me in peace. The bus goes in only one hour."

She picked up a pot and examined it, concentrating as she heard Lindiwe walk out the door. Only when she heard the sound of the garden gate swing shut did she look up. There were tears in her eyes. "At least let me say good-bye to Nathaniel," she whispered. She went to the window. But it was too late. Lindiwe had gone.

She wiped the tears from her face. George would soon be here to carry the boxes. It would not be right for him to see her crying.

40

JACOB WAS TRYING NOT TO COUNT THE HOURS.

They had taken his watch away as soon as he'd been marched through the fourfold gates that separated the inmates of Pretoria Local from the outside. They had taken it away along with his clothes, his pen, his diary (they'd laughed at him for even possessing that), and his first name. They were trying to strip him bare, he knew, strip him not only of his possessions but also of himself.

Well, he would not let them: He would survive. He would find other ways of functioning, other ways of being. Already he didn't need a watch: He had learned how easy it was to tell the time by the way the light slanted through the high window and shone on the walls.

And yet, he thought, as his spirits fell again, what good did it do, taking pride in the accuracy with which he could predict the hour? He had, after all, only a short exercise break, the period for mail-bag sewing, and three monotonous meals to look forward to.

He had been here two weeks, and he had another eleven years and fifty weeks to serve—every last second of it, since politicals would not be given remission. In that two weeks he had been subject to huge swings of mood—elation that the anticipation was over, acceptance of his fate, fury at his incarceration, heartache at the thought of his family, relief at the knowledge that they were leaving.

None of this, he knew, was any good: He must develop a different attitude to the outside and to the progress of time. That was the trick of surviving prison—you couldn't afford to rail against your fate, you must accept it and work with it.

He must develop it, he thought, and he would start tomorrow, for today was special: Today was the day when Rosa and the kids would be arriving in London. He wanted to think of them, no matter how hard it was—he wanted to wish them well.

As Rosa and the girls stepped off the plane, lights went off in their eyes. The lights were accompanied by noise: "Mrs. Swiece, Mrs. Swiece"—it came from the bottom of the stairs. Rosa put an arm around Rachel and glanced back to smile reassuringly at Martha. She got an angry glare in return, but there was no time to worry about that. There were the steps to negotiate, and the journalists, too, followed by immigration, and then . . . and then twelve years without Jacob.

Don't think about it, she told herself sternly. She walked down the steps.

"How are you feeling, Mrs. Swiece?"

She smiled faintly. "Cold," she said. A microphone was stuck in front of her face.

"Could you tell us why you left South Africa?" a man asked.

"I had no other choice," Rosa said. "First they stopped me working, then they put me under house arrest. They wouldn't even let me drive the children to school. Life was becoming untenable: They even persecuted my parents: by banning them, by making their visits impossible. That's why we have come here—my parents will also arrive soon. We felt we had no other choice."

"And how do you feel about your husband, Jacob?"

"I feel," said Rosa, and no matter how she tried, she couldn't stop her voice from breaking. "I feel . . ." she began again, and she wiped a tear from her eye. "I feel enormously proud of him. He and people like him have shown the world that the voice of justice, and of freedom, will never be stilled."

"And what do you say to those who call him a terrorist?" This from a woman in the back of the group. Her accent, Rosa heard, was South African.

Rosa looked straight at the woman. "Those people who call him a terrorist are the real perpetrators of violence," she said. "They're not fussy: They kill by the gun, or the bludgeon. They shoot unarmed people in the back like in Sharpeville, or they murder them in prison as they did to Moses Bopape. And if they can't do that, they kill thousands of children every year—they do that through malnutrition."

There was a brief silence. Then the man in front of Rosa cleared his throat. "What are your plans?" he asked.

Rosa shrugged. "It's too early for plans. In the short term I'll look for a job and settle here."

"And in the long term—will you go back?"

"I'm cold." It was Martha's voice, loud behind her.

Rosa smiled at her interviewer. "The South African regime has confiscated my passport and issued me only an exit permit," she said, "but the regime will not last forever, and you can be sure I will go back when it falls. In the meantime I must get the children inside." She began to walk.

"Rosa, Rosa, here."

She stopped, looked up, and saw, standing behind a barrier of the first-floor balcony, a group of people, all waving frantically in her direction, all joined together in one big blur. She narrowed her eyes, and they became individuals. Richard, she saw, was among them: That was kind of him. And there was somebody else that she knew—it was Max Freeman, waving in the distance. Max Freeman, she remembered, who'd introduced Jacob to her so many years ago. She blinked and picked up speed.

As they sat in Max's car, all three Swieces experienced a moment of bitter disappointment. They had (Rosa included, although she had been here once before) imagined a certain kind of London: a London that was depicted in magazines, a London of cobbled streets, snow-covered lamps, and quaint houses.

And yet the first thing they noticed was how dull the sky was, how muted the light: "*blerry* dim" was how Rachel put it. And although it was snowing, this was not what they had expected, these little drops of white that floated out of the sky and melted as soon as they hit the dirty pavements. It wasn't half as impressive as the hailstones that used to cover their Jo'burg garden.

As for the houses—they were far from quaint. There were rows and rows of them in red brick: no *stoeps*, only a few mingy stairs; no space, only a few enclosed patches; no grass, only dirty wet earth.

"Yech and double yech," Rachel said.

"Shuddup," Martha hissed. "Imagine how Daddy feels."

Rachel's face lengthened, and she stopped staring out so intently.

Six months of incarceration and Jacob was still a D-category prisoner—the lowest of the low. They did that to all the politicals: common-law convicts, thieves, forgers, murderers, even, rose fast in the prison hierarchy, but the politicals were held back. They were allowed only one visit (with no contact permitted) and one letter (maximum five hundred words) every six months, and worst of all . . . no tobacco.

Jacob was no smoker: He'd never liked the taste. But he quickly learned that, in prison, tobacco was the stuff of life. It was the only currency, the only valid form of exchange—the thing that was used to buy some extra food, a dab of toothpaste, and most precious of all, some news of the outside world. Tobacco was an obsession with the inmates of Pretoria Local, and it wasn't long before Jacob joined them in it. He'd even found himself glancing with envy at a prison guard who, having inhaled slowly on the end of his Lucky Strike, ground the thing out and carefully placed the butt in his pocket so as to deprive the politicals of its last valuable shred.

The sun was getting lower now, it would soon be dark. Jacob picked up the book from his bunk and opened it carefully. It was his second of the week, and that meant there were three whole days before he could get another. He must make this one last—he must read it slowly.

As he turned over the pages, searching for the point at which he had left it, he saw the scratches and dents on his fingers. Mailbag sewing was an unskilled job, and Jacob was surprisingly good at it, but nevertheless, if you lost attention for a minute, it was all too easy to poke the heavy needle into your flesh.

Still, he was not complaining. He was grateful for the work—at least it made the time go faster, at least it could be done in company. When they sat together in the open air, he relished the contact with his comrades. They were not allowed to speak—one infraction could earn the offenders the deprivation of three meals—but that did not stop them looking at each other, using their eyes as an increasingly vocal form of communication.

He found his place and settled back as comfortably as he was able on the hard bed. But before he knew what was happening, his mind wandered to that place, so many thousands of miles away, where his family were. Rachel and Martha, he thought, must be getting on the plane soon, on their way for their first visit.

He shook himself abruptly. He would not think of it, for the expectation would grow unbearable. He forced his eyes to refocus on the page.

Rosa parked her VW outside her Swiss Cottage apartment and removed the key from the ignition. She did not immediately step out. Instead, she put her arms on the steering wheel and nestled her head in them. Her shoulders shook.

Julia had been right, she thought, as she wiped the tears from her eyes, she should never have gone on her own. That was the worst thing about her life—she had lost touch with herself, with her expectations and her emotions. She had decided to take the children to Heathrow alone because she wanted them to have her to themselves before they boarded their flight to Jo'burg. She knew that they were nervous: They were, after all, traveling a long distance on their own to a destination that they had learned to fear. At the other end they would be met by her brother, Nicholas, whom they hardly knew and who in all likelihood would be accompanied by a battery of news reporters. And at the end of this ordeal would be one short, unsatisfactory meeting with their father.

She knew she had made the right decision as far as they were concerned. For, Rosa had noticed, the more Julia worried, the more she denied its expression in others. Without Julia's negations, the children had shown her their feelings. Rachel had been excited, focusing exclusively on the flight attendant's blond beehive, and only crying at the last. Martha, on the other hand, had wept all the way to Heathrow and kept on doing so until the gate. Then she had stopped abruptly, wiped her face with the sleeve of her shirt, and smiled bravely at her mother. Rosa had hugged her fiercely and then pushed her forward.

And yet what was good for them, Rosa reflected, has been awful for me. I wish there were someone I could talk to. I wish Jacob were here.

She gripped her keys tightly and stepped out of the car. It was so blatantly cruel, this system that had jailed her husband. How else could one explain their refusal to allow her a few days' entry—or come to that, even to refuse Julia? They took the children's father away, and then they rubbed their noses in it: They made them go out there on their own.

She opened the door to their first-floor maisonette and stepped inside. A scarf of Rachel's was lying by the stairs: Rosa picked it up and hung it on the coatstand. She went into the kitchen, and although she wasn't hungry, she fixed herself a salami sandwich that she ate while standing up. She walked through the narrow arch that separated the kitchen from the living room and slumped down into their own sofa. She looked at her surroundings as if she had only just arrived.

And she saw them as if for the first time. She sat there and looked with the critical eye that she had previously denied herself. She didn't like what she saw: It was all so utilitarian—so bright, brisk, and soulless somehow. It was nothing like her home in South Africa, which, although sparsely furnished, had been carefully crafted to please her.

But then, she reflected, this is not a home. It's a halfway house—halfway between the ruins of yesterday and the fear of tomorrow.

Abruptly she got up, switched off the light, and went upstairs to bed. She lay for a long time in the darkness, wondering about the children. She needed to sleep—she was to deliver a lecture at the university at nine the next morning—but sleep would not come. She reached for the bottle of pills—the ones that Dr. Rastin had given her on the day that Jacob had been sentenced—opened it, and extracted two. But as she was reaching for the glass of water, she changed her mind and put them back. She would not give in: She would show them that she was tougher than that.

Nicholas Arnold climbed wearily into bed beside his wife. The day had been a frenetic one. He'd picked up his nieces from Jan Smuts early in the morning and whisked them away from the press. Their meeting with Jacob was scheduled for the next day, and so he had drawn up a list of activities he thought they might enjoy.

Jane groaned in her sleep and flung an arm over his face. Gently he removed it. He knew he was being unfair to Rosa's kids. Christ, it was a difficult thing that they were undergoing—why shouldn't they be sullen? It wasn't their fault that Jacob was in prison, that Rosa was in exile.

It wasn't even, Nicholas thought, their parents' fault. It was the damned system in this country—a system that split families in two, that allowed some to prosper while it forced others to live in conditions of abject poverty. No surprise then that some chose to fight and to suffer the consequences rather than let the food stick in their gullets as they thought about the conditions under which it had been grown.

Nicholas could not count himself among those resisters. He had always kept himself remote from his parents' politics, and he had married a woman who did not even see anything wrong in the way she lived. Rosa didn't understand: She accused him of selling out, of choosing wealth over commitment, but she was wrong. For the simple truth was that he was weaker than she— he was afraid.

He had never had her courage—he realized that now. Even at school, he had desperately pretended to be one of the boys, pretended while he lived in dread that they would discover that his parents were communists. Rosa had flaunted her background, but then Rosa was a girl. She could have no conception of what it was like to have your friends turn around and jeer at you for something over which you had absolutely no control.

And yet that was not even the entire truth, he reflected. For what he most hated about politics was all the talk that went with it. Nicholas knew that, unlike his sister, he was no intellectual. He was a doer, a child who liked to create things, a man who wanted to get them done. All he asked was that he be allowed to live his life in peace; that he be left to provide for his family in the best way possible.

Nicholas was not an overly modest man. He knew that he had done well—even by white South African standards. He was good at business, and he'd worked hard at it. Why, then, should he be prevented from enjoying the fruits of his labor? He paid his work force well: It wasn't his fault that a thousand petty laws restricted their lives. After all, he didn't even vote in the elections—what would be the point, when there was nothing to choose?

And yet at the back of his mind was always this other voice— his parents' voice, his sister's voice, the clamor that said he was wrong to profit from the poverty of others. He straddled the two worlds in his head: Not even Jane knew the full extent of his dilemma. It was no easy thing to feel a fraud—to act with decisiveness while indecision lurked inside him.

Jane opened her eyes. "Are you ill?" she asked in a faraway voice.

Nicholas turned over. "No, of course not," he said. "Why should I be?"

Jacob had been up since five. He hadn't slept a wink all night, but only at five had he allowed himself to swing his legs off his bunk and to start pacing the cell. He knew he was disturbing the others, to whom this day was another one in the endless monotony of prison life, but he also knew that they wouldn't complain. They understood how he was feeling: They, too, had had their half-hour rations with their loved ones.

So much anticipation, and so little time, he thought, I have to make it all right for them.

Somehow the time passed, somehow he got through the hours that separated him from them. And then, all of a sudden, the warder was at the door and beckoning him.

"Swiece," he said. "*Trek aan. Kom.*"

Jacob scrambled out the door, his heart pounding. He walked behind the warder, and he saw the long corridor as if for the first time. He smelled that prison smell, that unique combination of polish and shit, and although his nose had long grown accustomed to it, he wrinkled it now. He walked past lines of prisoners, knees on the floor, working at the clear polish, working hard although the end of the process was to rub it off, and he felt amazement at the futility of it all. He heard the clanging of a distant door, and he shivered.

And then he was waiting outside the visiting room as the warder turned the key with what must have been deliberate slowness. The door finally opened, and he found himself in a small, dingy room—more like a box, it was, with a narrow piece of Plexiglas at one end. He tried to rush up to it, but the warder held his arm.

"No news—remember that."

Jacob nodded impatiently, and with the warder mirroring his every step, he went to the Plexiglas.

Martha and Rachel were already there: seated, side by side, with a warder next to them. They looked scrubbed, cleaned, and completely unlike themselves. Their feet dangled from their scratched metal chairs, their white socks shining a contrast to the dinginess of their surroundings.

He fitted into the room much better—what with his baggy khaki outfit, with only a frayed red handkerchief for color. He smiled at them to give them courage, and they did their best to respond, but Rachel looked as though she might imminently burst into tears.

"How are you both?" he asked gently.

"Okay," said Martha, while simultaneously Rachel answered, "Miserable."

"And your new schools?"

"Mine's okay," said Rachel. "We don't have to sit on our own, and we get plenty of painting and, best of all, no Afrikaans. But Martha says she hates hers, and the boys all laugh at her."

"You'll get used to it." Jacob hated the platitude even as it came out of his mouth, but what else could he say? What could he do?

"What about you?" Martha asked politely.

He smiled to give himself courage. "I'm doing fine," he said. "But I've had to learn to sew, and I'm all thumbs and fingers. Now I understand your moaning about needlework."

"It wasn't so bad," Martha said.

"Yes, it *blerry* well was," Rachel protested.

"Well, anyway," Jacob said quickly, "I'm fit and healthy and missing you all so much."

Martha bit her lip. Rachel looked blankly at the high window.

"How's your mother?"

Before they had a chance to even open their mouths to reply, the prison guard intervened. "Hey, now, you know the rules. No discussion of the activities of banned persons. One more trick like that and I'll end your visit."

Jacob swallowed hard. He looked away quickly.

"Aunt Rosa is doing fine," Martha said.

"Which aunt—?" Rachel began, but Martha nudged her hard.

"Oh, I get it," Rachel said. She giggled.

Jacob looked at his eldest. That was what always surprised him, he thought: the sheer reserves of his children. Martha understood the rules better than he, and she was showing him how to break them. He smiled at her: the first genuine smile of the visit.

"That's good," he said. "Has she got a job?"

"Yeah, at the university," Rachel said loudly. She winked.

"And she does a lot of talks," Martha said. "All over the country. She's famous, you know. So are you."

"No news," snapped the guard.

And so it went on: for thirty long minutes that dragged their feet, and yet that, once over, were like a mere second's flash. And then the warder spoke again. "Time," he said. "Thank you." That was it. Jacob blew the children desperate but insubstantial kisses through the glass before he was hustled back to his cell.

Rosa was waiting by the barrier in Terminal 3 when the children were escorted out. She waved at them wildly and then rushed into the enclosed area to hug them to her.

"Oh, Mummy." Rachel squirmed. "Don't be so soppy. It's only been a week."

"And how's Daddy?" Rosa asked.

"He's learned to sew," said Rachel.

"He doesn't look good," Martha replied. "He's all thin."

Rosa picked up their bags and began to lead them toward the exit.

"Hey," Rachel said. "You look different."

Rosa smiled. "I finally found a good hairdresser," she said.

When they were traveling down the Euston Road and just about to turn off into Regents Park, she interrupted the flow of Rachel's enthusiastic description of Nicholas's sulky children.

"I've also found us somewhere else to live," she said.

"Where?" said Rachel.

"Why?" said Martha.

"It's a house with a garden in an area called Crouch End," she said. "I think you'll like it."

"Why?" repeated Martha.

Rosa was taken aback. She'd been so excited about the impending change, so full of a new store of energy she'd tapped while they were gone, she'd assumed that both children would have been carried along with her enthusiasm. Now, she realized that it might have been better to delay telling them until they had settled back into their London life. They must feel buffeted by all this change—especially Martha, who was old enough to understand what was going on.

"None of us like the flat." Rosa's voice almost pleaded with her daughter. "And in the new place you can each have your own room."

"What about my school?"

"But, darling, I thought you hated your school."

"I do. But how's a different one going to be any better? It just means I'll have to explain to a whole new set of morons that South Africa doesn't have tigers and elephants roaming the streets."

"Let's talk about it later," Rosa said quickly. "Now, tell me all about Jacob."

As they lay together in their bedroom, Rachel's dreamy voice came wafting over to Martha. "Mummy's changed," she commented.

"No, she hasn't," Martha answered.

"She has, too," Rachel protested. "Her hair's all straight."

Martha clicked her tongue in a kind of grown-up contempt. "Ag, hair—that's nothing."

"Suppose so." Rachel yawned, and a silence descended on the darkened room. It was a good five minutes before Rachel spoke again. "Do you think she has a lover?" she asked.

Rachel had no concept of "lover." Her question was the repeat of an overheard conversation between her uncle Nicholas and aunt Jane. A pillow landed on her head. It was followed by an angry fist, which banged insistently at her.

"She hasn't, she hasn't," shouted the hysterical owner of the fist. "Don't you ever dare say that."

"You're hurting me." Rachel began to cry. She made no attempt to push Martha off: That, she knew, would only make the attack worse.

"I don't care, you stupid little snot." Martha was kicking now as well as hitting.

"Mummy," wailed Rachel.

The light clicked on. Rosa stood in the doorway. "What the hell's going on?" she asked.

Martha jumped off Rachel and stood by the side of the bed. "Nothing," she said sullenly.

"It's not nothing. She hit me. She hit me." Rachel was working herself up into an orgy of recrimination when Martha shot her one fierce look. Rachel knew that look too well. It said that should she continue, she would really get it later. It just wasn't worth it. "It's okay now," she said in a small voice.

"Martha, get back into bed this minute," Rosa instructed. "I'm surprised at you. I thought you were more grown up." With that, she switched off the light and left the room.

41

1968

"WELL," ROSA SAID. "UNTIL NEXT WEEK."

She got up, and walking over to the door, she held it open until the group of four had filed out. "Don't forget your assignments," she said, and then she closed the door.

She returned to her desk, cleared it of tutorial notes, and sat down. Her office was a smallish space, just large enough to fit her desk and five straight-back chairs. The colors were all muted: An outsider, Rosa reflected, might consider it a gloomy room. Its high walls were wood-paneled, its carpet was a dark green, and the leading on the window prevented much of the light from entering. It was so solid, so stuffy, and so unlike South Africa.

It's funny, Rosa thought, how at home I am in this place. She smiled to herself, and when the phone rang, she picked it up still smiling.

"Mrs. Swiece?"

Rosa knew that voice, and it drove her smile away.

"This is the school secretary. Miss Bradley would like to see you."

"Today?" Rosa was already looking at her watch.

"Yes, if that's convenient."

"Your headmistress says you're being obstructive," Rosa told Martha.

"She's an idiot," Martha snapped.

"That may be true," Rosa conceded. "But she has power over you. Maybe you should try and restrain yourself for a while."

"Why should I?" Tears welled in Martha's eyes, and she blinked hard. "Why should I?" she repeated.

Rosa put one hand on her daughter's shoulder. "Look, darling," she said. "You must learn to live in the real world. You have the measure of your headmistress: You know her limits. Why push her beyond them? It only makes trouble for yourself."

Martha brushed the hand away. She put her hands on her hips, and her scowl deepened. "Hypocrite," she said.

"What do you mean?"

"I should think that's obvious," said Martha airily. She could see that she was annoying her mother, and the knowledge seemed to give her pleasure. She dug the knife in deeper. "Daddy's languishing in jail for a useless cause, and you tell me not to make trouble for you."

"The struggle for liberation in South Africa is not a useless cause," Rosa said between gritted teeth.

"Maybe not," Martha jeered. "But it's not going to be won by whiteys. Only the blacks can free their own country, and I don't know whether you've noticed recently, but you're not one of them."

Rosa kept silent.

"You know the trouble with you?" Martha's voice rose. "You call yourself a revolutionary, but you're so fucking conventional that even when the Russians walk all over Czechoslovakia, you don't lift a fucking finger."

"Don't swear so much," Rosa said.

"Oh, fuck you—you and your Turkish carpets and partridges in applesauce. You're prepared to ruin our lives for your principles, and then it's a big fucking deal if I use a four-letter word." And with that, Martha left the room and ran up the stairs, slamming doors on her way.

The kettle had boiled, but things had progressed too far for tea. Rosa went into the sitting room and poured herself a large Black Label. She sat down on the sofa and looked around her. She felt shaken up. Martha could always get to her, because she had studied her mother well and she knew that Rosa was full of misgivings.

Rosa felt as if the struggle were passing her by, as if England had indeed changed her consciousness. Take, for example, this room—it was not a waiting room like the one in Swiss Cottage, but more a part of a home. It was tastefully furnished and pleasing to the eye, and she'd spent money on it to get it so. She had told herself that she was doing it for the children, but she knew that this was not the truth. For she had spent hours shopping to make it look right—hours that she previously spent in meetings, in planning, in debating. Consumerism, she sometimes thought, had taken the place of action in her life.

It wasn't that she was inactive. She went to meetings, she worked in the anti-apartheid movement, she worked with the exiled ANC. But sometimes she thought it was all like spitting in the wind: plenty of talk, plenty of good intentions, and not much progress. It wasn't the fault of anybody in particular—it was just that it was so impossible to conduct a struggle thousands of miles away from a country that was itself politically calcified.

And then came the explosions of '68. The time when workers and students in Paris threw caution to the wind and said, Enough. When 10 million workers went on strike, and the whole of France started to close down. When night after night young people fought the CRS police on the barricades. When the antiwar movement in the United States had already begun to swing the majority of Americans against the Vietnam War; when Johnson had announced that he would not run again.

Into all of this, where did Rosa fit? She was a radical and a political activist. She worked at London University, and so the struggle of the students was central to her thoughts. She was buffeted on all sides by an outpouring of ideas: of Maoism, of a regenerated Trotskyism, of a refusal to dwell in the tired old world of realpolitik. She watched the Vietnamese struggle and saw a nation refuse to bow down after thirty years of war: a nation that was organized to fight and that had the political understanding to combat the might of the American armed forces.

And she saw herself. Stuck in Crouch End. Unable to see her husband. Struggling alone with their eldest child over swear words. Hearing her own words come out of her mouth and wondering whether she still believed them. Identifying with the New Left and suppressing the feeling that what she and Jacob had once been involved in was now dead. Hating the Russian invasion of Czechoslovakia but holding on to her Party membership for old times' sake. It was pathetic. A new generation was taking over, and, at almost forty-four, she no longer belonged to it.

Rosa heard Martha thump heavily along the landing before she bellowed down the stairs. "And don't think," she shouted, "that I'm going to Pretoria again. Because I'm not." A door slammed.

Wearily Rosa made her way to Martha's attic room. She knocked once on the door. She didn't wait for an answer but opened it immediately. She saw Martha sitting on her unmade bed in the midst of a pile of jumbled clothes.

"You don't want to go and see Daddy?" she asked. "Is this what your moods are all about?"

"Why call him Daddy?" Martha demanded. "I hardly know the man."

Silently Rosa counted to ten. "Do you not want to see Jacob?" She paused after each word.

"Why should I? He doesn't care about me. All he wants is to know what's happening to you. I'm sick of it all. I'm sick of flying all that way for a half-hour visit. I'm sick of staying with Nicholas and his wimpy wife. I'm sick of walking through those fucking gates and staring into the eyes of those fucking guards. I'm sick—"

"If *you're* so sick of it all," Rosa interrupted, "just imagine how Jacob feels."

"Why should I?" Martha shouted. "Why the hell should I?"

"Because he's your father," Rosa snapped. "I'm not prepared to tolerate this any longer. I'm going out."

As she closed the door, Martha's voice pursued her. "Don't pretend to me!" she shouted. "You're going out because you've got a date. Probably with your tame member of the ruling class who thinks he's so trendy."

When she knew that her mother was safely downstairs, Martha buried her head in her pillows. She began to cry, softly at first. Gradually her attempts at concealment dwindled, her sobs increased in volume until she was practically shouting out her pain. Perhaps she secretly hoped that Rosa would come back to console her. But her mother did not return: At one point she thought she heard a car draw up and the sound of the front door closing. She wet the pillow with her tears until she could cry no longer. After that she lay still.

Richard was waiting outside the hall when Rosa appeared. He'd been waiting for a while, but he was used to that. It always happened after she had spoken: She was immediately button-holed by a line of people wanting to talk to her, to hear her opinions or to have her listen to theirs.

Rosa was a compelling speaker, glamorous, sure, articulate. No matter how many times Richard heard her (and he went quite often to the anti-apartheid meetings that she addressed) he always found something fresh in her words. And yet she was not as strident as she once had been, or as unapproachable. Teaching, he thought, had been good for her—it had made her more tolerant of others' difficulties.

He smiled as she came out, (alone, thank God—they wouldn't have to make excuses to get rid of an overpersistent admirer this time). She was looking tired, he thought, and a trifle pale. Although her clothes were as fashionable and as well fitted as ever, there was something in the way she walked that seemed at odds with her image, something slightly crumpled, perhaps. She's too much alone, he thought.

He smiled, and walking up to her, he linked his arm in hers. "Dinner?" he said.

She breathed out heavily. "That would be great."

They began to walk away from the meeting hall, at first in companionable silence, but after Rosa had sighed a number of times, Richard turned to her.

"Tired?"

She nodded.

"Depressed?"

"I don't know," she said as she shrugged her shoulders. "Sometimes I find it hard: I get up and talk about the brutality of the regime, the bravery of the people, and about the way the struggle continues, and my heart's not in it."

"Because you've done it too often?"

"No," Rosa said, "because I don't believe the last bit. The struggle isn't continuing: Nothing's happening in South Africa. The movement's been squashed, its leaders are in jail, those in exile are isolated, and the people themselves are just plain scared."

Richard looked at her. "What's this?" he asked. "Post-meeting *tristesse*?"

She glanced sideways at him, and her face was serious. He's another one, she thought, who doesn't really want to hear the truth. It's too painful to think that we might be losing.

This thought she kept to herself. "Jacob always said that struggles had their peaks and their troughs," she said in a more cheerful voice.

"Will Greek do you?" Richard asked.

The room was already dark. Martha turned over and glanced at the clock above her bed. It was eight-thirty—time to get moving. Rosa would have left some food for her—Mrs. Fucking Efficiency, Martha thought. Well, she wouldn't give her the satisfaction of eating it. Rachel was staying at one of her numerous friends', and so there was no one in the house to demand why Martha was going out and where she was going to. She got up and looked in the mirror. Her eyes were red, her face washed pale by tears.

She went to the bathroom, filled the sink with cold water, and immersed her head in it. Gasping for breath, she pulled out the plug, flung a towel over her hair, and began to work on her face. She smeared some pancake onto her cheeks and rubbed it in evenly. On her eyelashes went black mascara, and she used Rosa's eyeliner to mark the rims. Carefully she covered her lips with white lipstick. Her hair was drying already: She removed the towel and used a spray to give it body. She teased it until it stood away from her face.

She looked at the mirror and smiled. She left the bathroom and, going to her room, pulled a long gray sweater from beneath the pile on her bed. She put it on, along with a pair of black fishnet tights. She topped these with a tight leather skirt that barely covered her thighs. She was ready. She glanced at the clock. Nine-thirty: just right for her evening.

Rosa smiled at Richard, who was seated opposite her. "That's better," she said. "My pessimism must have been due to hunger."

Richard raised an eyebrow. "And Martha, perhaps?"

"Who else?"

"Thought so," Richard said. He took a sip of indifferent Beaujolais and frowned. "That child needs a father," he concluded.

Rosa smiled. "Watch it, Richard," she said. "This is the new age: You're supposed to be breaking the bounds of convention, not embracing them."

Richard returned the smile with something akin to self-mockery. He looked down at his broad tie with its wild, flowered design. He had changed of late—along with half of Europe. He, too, had been affected by the turmoil of the sixties and by the political movements that were springing up everywhere. He no longer conformed in dress to the mores of his father's world. He'd grown a beard—not exactly Che Guevara, but close enough—and his hair was longer than it had ever been. His clothes he no longer acquired from Regent Street tailors—instead, he bought off the rack as he nudged away the suspicion that he looked faintly ridiculous.

"Old habits die hard," he said.

She raised her glass in a kind of salute.

"Do you think I should give up my job?" he asked.

"Oh, Richard." She laughed.

He raised an eyebrow. "Oh, Richard, yes? Or oh, Richard, no?" he asked.

"Oh, Richard, we've been through this before," she answered. "If you stop working, you'll end up living on your inheritance and feel even worse about yourself."

"I could go and live in a hippie commune."

"You wouldn't be able to stand the lack of privacy," she said.

Richard lifted his glass. He gazed at Rosa speculatively. "I've got an idea," he said.

She sighed. "Don't," she said. "Don't start."

"You know Jacob would understand," he insisted. "Twelve years is a long time."

"I can't do it," Rosa said. "Not yet. Not with Martha as she is."

Richard threw his head back and tossed the rest of his wine down his throat. "Martha," he said to the ceiling. "Do you have to come everywhere with us?"

She frowned at him, but he didn't appear to notice. "Silly," he continued. "I do believe I'm jealous of Martha. She knows how to make you come running."

Rosa's frown deepened, but Richard, who was staring moodily into his glass, didn't notice. "In fact," he said, "I'm more jealous of an eighteen-year-old than of your husband."

Rosa narrowed her eyes. "Bit difficult to be jealous of Jacob, isn't it?"

On another occasion, if he had not overindulged in cheap wine, Richard would have immediately backed away. But he didn't feel like it this time. He told himself he had to face facts: He had to acknowledge that Rosa's iron wall—the one she erected between them—was driving him insane. The wall was not uniform—there was a small chink in it—but what was the use when only she was allowed to look through it? Well, he'd been "good" for years: He, too, had served his time. Now, he'd had enough of pussyfooting.

"Jacob," he said loudly, "might be in prison, but he has something I don't have—your love." He poured himself some more wine. "Or if not your love, then at least your allegiance." He had some trouble with the word. Maybe he was drunker than he thought; maybe he ought to stop now. But he didn't feel like it. The wine had loosened him up. "Allegiance," he said, admiring the way the word tripped off his tongue, "is, I suspect, stronger than love, as far as you're concerned."

"Don't be cruel." Rosa looked him straight in the face.

"Don't you think it's about time you made your mind up, *Mrs*."—he stressed the word—"Swiece?"

"Oh, you mean you noticed I'm married?" Rosa said.

"And how could I avoid noticing?" Richard replied. "Jacob's not in prison. He comes with you everywhere. He sits on your shoulder, and if I'm not careful, he's going to start sitting on mine. Okay—so that's fair enough. What I don't understand is why you keep me on a string if you want to stay so goddamned faithful to your husband. Why do you?"

He looked fiercely at her, in time to see her eyes water. "What am I supposed to do?" she whispered. Her voice dropped until it was almost indistinct. "You're my friend," she said. She blinked.

Richard flushed. He put down his glass. He no longer felt drunk—merely ashamed. What right had he to push this woman? She had suffered enough. "I'm sorry," he said quietly.

Rosa nodded. Tears were flowing down her cheeks, but she didn't mind. She had come to a crossroads, and crying was the proof of it. For four years she'd immersed herself in an orgy of work, commitment, children. For four years she had run away from the truth in its entirety—the fact that she had lost her country, her husband, and her cause.

For four long years she had felt desperately alone, and had denied this feeling in herself.

And then recently her boundaries had begun to crack. Perhaps she was a creature of fashion just like everyone else. Perhaps it was the spreading ideology of free love that had begun to affect her. Of perhaps there was just so much loneliness a person could bear.

Whatever the cause, she had begun to feel the stirrings of sexual desire that were increasingly difficult to resist. Only the other day she'd almost accepted an invitation to go to bed with one of her students—an American draft dodger and student leader. At the last minute she'd panicked and refused with grace. She had the feeling that he'd been somewhat relieved. Maybe he'd only asked her because he guessed at her need.

And yet here in front of her was Richard—her friend, her companion, in many ways her only confidant. She had always found him attractive—the years had not changed that. He was sympathetic, and she needed sympathy so badly: He loved her, and she needed love.

An image of Jacob in the dock came to her, and she banished it.

She took Richard's hand in hers and, lifting it to her lips, kissed it.

He looked at her eyes, seeking confirmation. He saw it in her smile, in the faint inclination of her head. "Really?" he asked.

She nodded and placed his hand back on the table. She ran a finger along the length of it.

"Shall we go?" he whispered. When she nodded, he got up. He had never felt soberer in his life.

It was five in the morning when Rosa went to sleep in her own bed. It was nine o'clock when she awoke. The house was strangely silent. Rosa got up stiffly. She would have a bath, she resolved, and then she would go wake Martha. She would take the child shopping—that would cheer her up.

She was smiling to herself when she knocked on Martha's door. There was no reply, so she knocked again. When Martha still didn't stir, she opened the door and peered around it. She froze.

Martha was not in bed. By the look of the clothes piled high on the duvet, she had obviously not been to bed, had not, in fact, been home all night. Rosa leaned against the door. She searched her memory for something that might explain this occurrence, something that she might have forgotten. Had Martha told her she would stay with a friend? Was there some easy explanation for her absence?

It didn't come—the explanation—only a silent kind of panic. Rosa felt as if she were being punished for her own transgressions. Why hadn't she come back earlier? Why hadn't she checked on Martha when she returned? And what had happened to the girl? A hundred questions flooded into her brain, a hundred unanswered, panicked questions.

"Pull yourself together," she told herself. "Do something."

She went to the phone and picked it up. She dialed a number without thinking. When it began to ring, she realized that she was phoning Richard. She put the receiver down abruptly. It was her fault that Martha was gone. She would not compound her wrongdoing.

She hurried back into Martha's room and searched through her desk. It was as messy as the rest of Martha's room, and she grew increasingly frantic as she threw the layers onto the floor one after the other. Finally she found what she was looking for— Martha's small red address book, the one that had been her going-away present from her South African schoolfriends.

Rosa looked through it, hurriedly searching for the names that seemed most familiar. For the first time she realized how few English friends Martha had. But there was no time to worry about that. There must be something in there that could help.

Finally she had in front of her a small list. She ran to the phone.

By the third call, her desperation was growing. She'd spoken to three of Martha's schoolmates, and each denied knowledge of her whereabouts. Rosa no longer even believed their innocent English voices—it was a conspiracy, she thought; they were hiding her daughter from her.

She turned the book over and picked up the phone again. She put her finger on the 9. There was no other choice—she must call the police.

It was at this point that Martha entered the house. She looked a mess, disheveled and crumpled in her going-out clothes. Rosa's first impulse was to hug her tightly, but before she could do so, her relief turned to anger.

"Where the hell have you been?" she asked.

Martha pushed past her and went into the kitchen.

"Where have you been?" Rosa followed her.

"What do you care?" Martha stopped and turned back to stare at Rosa.

"What do you mean, what do I care?" she said. "I've been frantic with worry."

Martha cut herself a thick slice of bread on which she smeared a blob of apricot jam. She took a bite before she spoke again. "If you'd been frantic enough to get back home last night," she said, "you would know where I was. I phoned—at twelve, one, and two. You weren't here."

"So what?" Rosa demanded. "What if I got back after that?"

"Then I'd ask you where the hell you'd been," Martha said. She threw the bread and jam into the sink before leaving the room. The door slammed behind her.

42

Richard looked quizzically at Rosa. "Going already?" he asked.

Rosa was seated on the side of the bed, concentrating on rolling one stocking up to her garter belt. She didn't reply.

Richard sat up and swung his legs onto the floor. "Yes, Richard," he said loudly. "I am going." He sprang to his feet. He pulled on a pair of jeans and made his way to the door.

"Want some coffee before you leave?" he asked.

Still Rosa didn't speak.

"No thanks, Richard," he said. "Thanks for asking." He jerked the door open and marched out of the room.

Martha sat cross-legged on the floor and took a long toke of the joint. She breathed the smoke out through her nose, watching it as it flowed from her nostrils and spiraled into the air before disappearing. She waited for that slowing down of sensation, that sinking into a semiconscious state that often overtook her when she was stoned, but it didn't come.

Instead, an image floated into her mind, an image of her father. Or, to be more accurate—two images. She saw him as he must have once been—standing in the middle of their garden, a ball in his hand, his arm stretched out to throw it, a smile on his face. Catch, he called, and he looked so big to her: This must be a memory, she thought, a memory from when she was a small child.

But before she could grab on to it and hold it tightly, the image wavered and was gone. In its place was another picture of Jacob—a more realistic one. This face, she saw, was thin and stressed and it was elongated by the narrow window through which she watched it—it was the face she had been forced to visit once a year for the past four years.

She couldn't stand it: She had to do something. She jumped to her feet.

"Strong dope," commented David.

Martha whirled around. "Where are the others?" she asked.

David stretched and leaned back on his mattress. "Cool it," he said. "Don't panic. There are no others." He giggled. "Wouldn't it be a trip if that were true?" he asked. "If the bomb had gone off, and somehow the two of us were the only ones left in the world?" He sat up excitedly. "What would we do?"

Martha smiled. "Close the doors," she said.

"Lock the windows," David answered.

Martha's stomach rumbled. "Open a can of beans," she suggested.

"Make delicious love."

Martha shook herself. "What the hell are you talking about?" she asked.

David stretched back again. Martha noticed with distaste that his sheets were grimy and crumpled. She frowned.

"I don't know," said David. "Who cares? What happened to the joint?"

When Rosa emerged, Richard was sitting on a high stool by the counter that separated his large living room from the kitchen. He was gazing moodily into his steaming mug. As she passed by, she made an attempt to bend and kiss him, but he jerked his face away so fast that all she got was air. She moved away and, lifting her coat from the back of the sofa, began to put it on.

Richard scowled. "One fuck and you're out the door?" he asked.

"Don't be crude," Rosa said.

He laughed, a hollow, mirthless laugh. "How would you rather I phrased it?" he said. "How about—we made dignified love and then, at precisely nine-thirty P.M., you reluctantly had to go. Is that delicate enough for you?"

"I have to get back to the children," she said. "You know that."

"Go on, then," he replied. He didn't bother to conceal the

resentment in his voice. "Go on back to your precious children."

Rosa shrugged. In an abstract kind of way she could sympathize with his anger: She knew that her commitment to her family was bound to cause him difficulties. But she saw no point in dwelling on it further. She was in no mood to repeat the same old explanations—to hear from his mouth the same objections.

She walked toward the door.

Richard's voice pursued her. "What brilliant excuse are you going to dazzle them with this time?" he asked. "Not the one about a meeting again?" His voice was tinged with bitterness.

She stopped abruptly and turned to face him. "What's got into you tonight?" she asked.

"What do you think?" This time he sounded melancholy.

Rosa sighed impatiently. "Put yourself in my shoes," she said. "What am I supposed to do? I'm torn between them and you—between their jealousy and yours, between their needs and yours."

Richard gazed at her speculatively. She thought she knew him so well, and yet she couldn't decipher the meaning behind the almost-neutral expression on his face. It made her slightly uneasy. She glanced away.

His words when they came were no clearer than his expression. "I admire you," he said. "You've got it taped."

"What on earth do you mean?" she asked in surprise.

Richard got off his stool and made his way toward her. He stopped a few paces away and looked her full in the face. "The way I see it," he said slowly, "is that you are caught on the horns of a dilemma. You're trapped by your feelings for me, which conflict with your feelings for your family."

Rosa smiled. "It doesn't take a genius to know that," she said.

She was surprised to find that Richard made no attempt to return her smile. He stared at her seriously—forbiddingly, even.

"You're lonely and you like me," he continued. "You want to sleep with me, and you want me around to love you. And yet, because of Jacob, you feel guilty. You probably think you have no right to my love."

"So?" Rosa asked impatiently. "We've discussed this endlessly. There's nothing new in it."

"Nothing's new," Richard agreed, "except the way I'm beginning to look at it. I've been a fool to be so patient. It's taken me all this time to work out what your game is."

"I'm not playing any games," Rosa said. "And if you don't mind, I'm tired now. I want to go home." She turned away from him, intending to walk out.

But for once Richard did not let her go. He grabbed at her, and keeping a tight hold on her shoulders, he turned her around to face him.

She set her face into one of those fierce looks that no longer really scared Richard. He had gone too far to be intimidated by her sudden withdrawals, by her impenetrability. He had gone too far, he thought, and yet she would never let him go far enough.

He gripped her tighter. "Martha's your perfect excuse," he said.

Rosa winced. "Martha is going through a hard time," she said.

"She's the reason you give for never committing yourself to me," Richard continued. "You never have to face our involvement, you never have to take any decisions, you never have to spend the night here pursued by images of Jacob's lonely existence, because Martha"—he spat out the name—"would kick up such a fuss."

Rosa blinked. "You're hurting me," she said.

He let go of her and took a few paces back. "You do it deliberately," he said. "You have turned Martha into your watchdog. It can't be good for her."

"Don't be silly," Rosa protested.

"The only hitch," Richard said pensively, as if she hadn't spoken, "is if I get pissed off with it all: if I decide to call it a day."

Rosa closed the top button of her coat. "That's up to you," she said. She opened the front door and stepped out without as much as a backward glance.

Martha found that she was lying on the bed beside David. She couldn't remember how she'd got there. I'm stoned, she thought, too stoned.

It wasn't a new sensation. David smoked pot continuously, and so did Martha when she was with him. As a result, she'd grown accustomed to constant highs in his presence. For the most part she enjoyed the feeling of artificial bliss—being stoned was the only way she ever really felt happy—but sometimes it would all go wrong. Sometimes her mind would jitter out of control; sometimes she would think of the things that she'd rather forget—of Jacob and of her mother—and then she would begin to panic.

She'd never told David about these episodes. The first time she'd tried to describe her feelings, he'd responded by dismissing them with a laugh. This flippant denial had made her panic further. So these days she dealt with the sudden breaks in her consciousness by taking a tight grip on herself, by downing the occasional Valium that she stole from David's large stash, or by walking out of his studio apartment and roaming the streets of London until normality returned.

She got up and breathed deeply. "I'm off," she said.

David did not reply. He was lying on the bed, his eyes closed, a dreamy smile on his face.

Richard stood motionless for a while after Rosa left. Then he shook himself and gently shut the door. He walked over to the pile of large cushions in the corner of the room and plunked himself down on them. He stretched out his arm, and pulling the sleeping tabby from its favorite nest among the cushions, he placed her gently on his lap. The cat purred loudly as Richard stroked her. She gazed up with her sleepy yellow eyes.

"The trouble is," he told the cat, "she knows I won't finish with her. She's got me on a hook."

The cat stood up, stretched, and then jumped off his lap. She shot him one contemptuous look before padding lightly away.

Martha glanced at her watch in surprise. She had no idea how long she had been walking, but she'd thought it would be later than 9:45. She realized with relief that her mind was no longer buzzing in a hundred different directions: The worst of her stoned confusion had worn itself off. That was one advantage of the English cold, she thought, it cleared the brain in record time.

She peered down the road and saw the bus coming toward her. This was her lucky day—she'd be home in good time to put her plan into action.

Julia and Rachel were sitting in front of the television when Rosa arrived in Crouch End.

Julia glanced up. "Good meeting?" she asked. Rachel gave a

faint nod of acknowledgment before concentrating on the screen again.

Rosa went and planted herself right in front of Rachel. "How come you're still up?" she asked, as the girl twisted her neck in an effort to see the TV.

"I told her she could watch until the end of the program," Julia replied. "It's her favorite."

"What isn't?" Rosa commented. She clapped her hands together. "Come on," she ordered, "it's almost over. Quickly, to bed." She turned around and clicked the television off.

"Oh, Mumm-ee," Rachel began, but something in Rosa's face told her that this was a battle she wasn't going to win. She got up slowly. She kissed Julia on the cheek. "Bye, Gran," she said. She walked toward the hall. "Night, Mum." She shot Rosa a sullen, accusing glance.

Once she could hear Rachel's footsteps in the bathroom, Rosa took possession of the sofa. "Martha in her room?" she asked.

"No, she's out," Julia said. "She went before I could stop her."

Rosa sighed. "Jesus," she muttered to herself, "that girl's the limit." She smiled at Julia, yawned, and stretched. "I'm tired of talking about South Africa," she said, as if in explanation.

Her mother did not reply—she threw Rosa a look, instead. It was a curious look, thought Rosa, a knowing look. She's guessed about Richard, thought Rosa. Is she going to say something?

But Julia left the room without commenting, and when she returned she had on her camel-hair coat. "Harold will be waiting up for me," she said.

"Send him my love," Rosa replied.

Julia nodded, and again she looked at Rosa. She does know, Rosa thought. "I'll walk you to the door," she said quickly.

Martha was watching when Julia emerged from the house. She breathed a sigh of relief at the knowledge that her vigil was almost over. She was freezing out there in the cold, her teeth chattering loudly. She'd been waiting for half an hour, and in that time had begun to thoroughly regret wearing her fashionable red oilskin. Her duffel coat would have been warmer, but David said that the oilskin made her look sophisticated, and so she had chosen it. It wasn't much good at keeping the cold out—that damp, monotonous cold that was England's hallmark.

As Julia drove off, Martha shrank against the wall. Julia mustn't discover that she'd been standing there, waiting for Rosa to arrive and her to leave. If Julia knew, that would spoil her revenge.

Martha's scrutiny was a result of a resolution she had made some weeks ago. She knew what her mother was doing with Richard, and she'd decided that if Rosa left for a liaison with her lover, then she would also go out. She wouldn't return until after Rosa came back.

It was easy enough to guess which days Rosa reserved for Richard. The meetings she genuinely had she wrote in her bold scrawl across her diary. But her dates with Richard she seemed to be trying to conceal even from herself. They were in tiny writing—sometimes with his name, sometimes his initial, sometimes only a faint question mark.

Occasionally Martha wished that Rosa knew she knew, but she was damned if she was going to give her mother the satisfaction of telling her. She'd rather watch Rosa suffering, knowing that every time she returned to find her daughter out, she must experience a turn in the screw of her endless guilt.

Still, it was lonely watching. A few days ago Martha had tried to tell her friend Caroline about her deception, but Caroline had looked at her with an expression of such amazement that Martha had immediately changed the subject. Caroline couldn't understand: Nobody could. Nobody knew what it was like to have your father in prison—to have forgotten what he was like, to see him behind bars only once a year.

Caroline thought it was all highly exotic. Martha had heard her telling the others—she was using one of her stage whispers— and she had seen the admiring glances that the story provoked. She had to admit to herself that it did have some advantages— the boys tended to defer slightly to her when they discussed politics—but apart from that, she found their reactions insufferable.

It was time to put Part B of her plan into action. For that purpose she set her teeth into a happy grin and marched into the house. She looked casually through the hall and into the living room. She saw her mother slumped on the sofa.

"Oh, you're back," she said in mock surprise.

Rosa sat upright. "And where have you been?" she asked.

"Out," Martha replied. She yawned and stretched her arms

lazily above her head. "I'm going to bed."

"Come back in here," Rosa ordered.

"Ag, don't nag," Martha said.

Doggedly she continued to climb the stairs. She hummed a defiant chorus of "We shall not be moved" as she progressed to her room.

Rosa let her be. She was too tired to face the teenager, and besides that, she was loath to interrupt what sounded like one of Martha's rare good moods.

If Rosa had caught sight of Martha at that very instant, she would have been thoroughly shocked. For on the girl's face was a look of sheer despondency. Fully clothed, she threw herself onto her bed and fell asleep immediately.

Richard was in the shower when the telephone began to ring. He made no move to answer. Instead, he picked up the soap and lathered his body all over, rubbing the suds in energetically. He almost began to sing but decided against it: That would be too much like parody.

The sound of the telephone continued. Richard turned the jets of water up, enjoying the sensation as the hot water coursed over his body. He smiled bitterly to himself. It was Rosa on the other end—he knew it. It had been four days since they parted, and she always tried to phone on the third after a tiff. The day before, he'd deliberately stayed out of the flat so that he wouldn't be tempted to answer it. It had taken some effort, but he'd managed it. He was determined not to give in now.

He stepped out of the shower and pulled a dressing gown over his wet body. Stepping into the living room, he rubbed a towel vigorously over his wet hair. He saw that his cat was sitting by the telephone. It gazed at him when he emerged.

"Not this time," he said.

The cat continued to look at him. The ringing stopped.

Rosa replaced the receiver and frowned. This was the fifth time she had rung Richard that morning. The day before, when she'd tried him, she'd got no reply. She hadn't been unduly concerned. She'd resolved to try again the next day. Now, she was beginning to worry. She wondered what had happened to break his routine. She hoped it wasn't anything too serious. For a brief moment the thought entered her head that he was deliberately not answering the phone. She shook it off. Richard wouldn't do that: He couldn't.

Through a crack in the door, Martha watched her mother move away from the telephone. She smiled to herself, but there was no real joy in her expression. She knew that Rosa had been phoning Richard—that was the only time that Rosa ever went into her bedroom specifically to make a call—and she knew that Richard had failed to reply. Well, she thought, what difference did it make? He was temporarily out, that was all. Sooner or later, Rosa would get hold of him.

She moved away from the door, and tripped over a pair of shoes Rachel had left in the hallway. She cursed out loud as Rosa came out of her bedroom.

"I thought you were ill," Rosa said.

"Even ill people have to piss," Martha replied, as she turned toward the toilet.

Rosa watched her child's retreating back. She nursed a slight suspicion that Martha had been listening at her door.

"I'm getting paranoid," she whispered to herself. "She wouldn't do that."

By seven o'clock Richard had still not answered, and Rosa was growing increasingly concerned. She could not rid herself of the feeling that something had happened to him. He must have known that she would phone: He must have guessed that she would want to see him. If he'd been called away, he would have told her. He would have—wouldn't he?

"Something on your mind?" Martha asked.

Rosa picked up her fork and speared a piece of veal.

"Just work," she said, as she chewed at the meat. It wasn't a successful recipe, she thought, not worth repeating.

"Going out?" Martha asked.

"I wasn't thinking of it," Rosa replied.

She saw Rachel glance down at her plate. Martha, on the other hand, was looking straight at her, an expression akin to triumph on her face. It annoyed Rosa, it made her edgy. Abruptly she put her fork to one side and pushed her plate away.

"I think I might go out," she said.

She saw Martha mirror her action. "You and Rachel will be all right together, won't you?" Rosa continued.

"And what happens if I want to go out?" Martha muttered.

Rosa got up. "Not when you're ill, darling," she said sweetly.

It was half past eight when Rosa arrived at Richard's flat. His car, she had noticed, was parked in its usual space—he must be in. She was pleased she had come: Their relationship had been sinking into a kind of routine—it was about time that one of them broke the predictability of appointments only by mutual agreement.

She had a key to his flat, but she had never used it. This time she decided she would. She slipped it into the lock and opened the door.

Richard's flat was a simple one-bedroom affair. The front door led straight into the luxurious living room, in one corner of which was placed a dining-room table. So Rosa had no time to give any warning of her presence: She stepped straight in.

She took in all the details immediately. She saw the single rose in the glass vase, the wine cooling in the ice bucket, the candle upon the table, the food already dished out onto the plates. Only then did she take in the personnel. Richard was seated on one end, and a glamorous fair-haired woman on the other. Both glanced around at her: Both looked guilty.

"I'm s-sorry," Rosa stuttered.

She sounded like a teenager, she thought to herself. Well, she wasn't one. She was a mother—and she reminded herself, a married woman. She had no claim on Richard, because she would give him no permanent purchase on her own time. If he chose to entertain other women in the comfort of his own home, then he was well within his rights.

She was only sorry that she had disturbed his evening. In a way she was pleased with what had happened: Richard's demands were growing very insistent. Perhaps it was better that he face reality and try to find another kind of relationship.

As he watched Rosa stumble toward the door, the smile on Richard's face faded. He had planned it this way, planned it without even knowing he was doing so. He had invited Susan, a longtime acquaintance, in the full knowledge that this was the night he usually reserved for Rosa. He hadn't expected Rosa to turn up, but he had anticipated an enjoyable evening—Susan was an expert at a light kind of intimacy—made better by a slight tinge of revenge.

Now, as he noticed the look of faint relief on Rosa's face, he cursed himself for his childishness. When they argued about her commitment to him, he always reassured himself by presuming that Rosa cared deeply about him but could go no further because she was in an impossible situation. For the first time he doubted if this was so: Perhaps Rosa had been playing with him—using him as a kind of glorified security blanket.

The thought made him angry. He would not let her get away with it. He would make her exit as difficult as she made his life.

"Why don't you stay for a drink?" he asked.

"Yes, do," Susan gushed.

Rosa stopped. She resented the coldness in Richard's tone. If he had not wanted her to turn up unexpectedly, why had he given her a key? She was damned if she was going to make it easier for him. If he had only answered the telephone—or even phoned himself—none of this would have happened. Well, she would stay.

"The wine looks good," she said. She sat down at the end of the soft white leather couch.

As Susan later told her friends, it was one of the most excruciatingly embarrassing evenings she'd ever spent. Neither Richard nor Rosa made the slightest effort to ease the situation. They glowered at each other, forcing Susan to keep the conversation running and answering her bright inquiries in monosyllables. She stayed for as short a time as was decently polite, and then she made a few quick excuses that they barely heard. She breathed a sigh of relief when she was safely out the door.

Martha watched as a blonde in a fur coat emerged from Richard's building. She had no reason to suppose that the woman came from Richard's, but somehow she believed it implicitly. The woman looked just the type Richard would go for—confident, rich, sophisticated. For the first time a tinge of doubt penetrated Martha's stubborn frame. Perhaps she was imagining Richard's involvement with her mother—perhaps they were just good friends. The idea made her uneasy. She didn't want to believe that the reality by which she'd been operating—that her mother was betraying her father—was a mere product of her own fantasy life.

"I have to know," she whispered to herself. "I have to find out."

* * *

They faced each other in the room, and the silence was made more poignant by the ticking of Richard's kitchen clock. Susan had long since departed, and not a word had been uttered in the intervening period. There was no point in recrimination—they both knew that. Yet neither knew how to proceed. Instead, they embraced the silence.

When they finally decided to speak, they did so simultaneously. "I don't . . ." Rosa began, while Richard started with "Susan is . . ."

"An old friend," Rosa completed for him. "I could see that." Richard smiled. "You took it very coolly," he said.

Rosa glanced away from him. "I don't own you," she said. "You have the right to do as you choose."

"Ah, yes," Richard replied softly.

Rosa blinked. They were at a crossroads, she and Richard, she knew that now. For many months he had made his dissatisfactions clear: His invitation to Susan, his refusal to answer her calls, were a sign of a heightened campaign on his part. Or maybe it was more than that: Maybe she had already gone too far, maybe he was bidding her good-bye.

She felt numbed at the prospect. If a severing of their link was what he wanted, she would do nothing to influence him. She had always valued Richard for his clarity of purpose. She had no right to pull him into her own confusion, into the mess of her life. Perhaps he was right, they had no future together, there was no need for him to struggle with her in her past. She rose abruptly.

"I'm sorry I interrupted your evening," she said formally.

With dulled eyes, Richard watched Rosa walk toward the door. He noted, as if from some great height, that Rosa, normally so efficient in all her actions, was moving slowly. He was surprised at the observation. His Rosa, the one he held close to his heart, was a woman of decisiveness. He couldn't believe what his eyes were telling him—that she was waiting for him to make a move, for him to call her back.

He toyed with the idea of letting her walk out. It would signal the end for them both, but would that be so bad an idea? He would be heartbroken, he knew that, but his heart had been broken before. Time would heal it: Time would help him forget.

He snorted derisively to himself. How could he, a grown man, be deceiving himself like that? He would never forget Rosa: He would never find a replacement for her. Anything she offered him was better than nothing. It was, wasn't it?

He sprang to his feet and ran so that he was standing in front of her, barring her exit.

"Don't go," he said.

Rosa sighed. There was relief in that outlet of breath, relief mixed with something else—fear perhaps, Richard thought. She made no attempt to maneuver around him. She stood there, passive, as he took her in his arms.

And Martha, who had climbed up until she was standing on the narrow balcony outside Richard's kitchen, saw them embrace. She couldn't stand the sight, she couldn't. She closed her eyes but then opened them again. She had to look.

They were still enfolded in each other's arms, and she could no longer look. She glanced away.

And suddenly she was afraid. She was scared of heights, she thought, she was too far up. The balcony, which was a few feet wide, had seemed perfectly safe from the ground: Now, it was too narrow, she knew it was, she was going to fall. She moved one foot closer in, and somehow it caught on a geranium pot, which went skidding off the side. Oh, shit, she thought, me next. She turned the handle on the French doors, but it did not yield. "Mummy," she called.

They heard her, they heard a muffled cry followed by a sharp rap on the glass. They sprang apart guiltily and looked toward the source of the sound. They both saw Martha's panic-stricken face pressed against the glass door.

Richard ran into the kitchen and flung it open. When Martha made as if to move away, he grabbed at her. Swearing, he heaved mightily, and as Rosa watched, he pulled her into the room.

She was crying and rubbing furiously at her arm.

"Let me go," she shouted. "Can't you see you're hurting me?"

Richard did as he was bid, and the girl crumpled to a heap on the floor. She stared defiantly up at her mother. "Did you see what he did to me?" she demanded.

"Better then falling from the second floor," Rosa replied. She was surprised at how calm her voice was. "What on earth did you think you were doing?"

"Nothing," Martha said.

"Long way to climb for nothing."

Martha glared at her. "Don't pretend with me," she snarled.

"Pretend what?" Rosa asked.

"That you weren't kissing," Martha said. "I saw you. I saw you do it. I know you've been betraying Daddy."

Betraying Daddy. The echo hit Rosa.

"I know that you're weak," Martha continued.

Yes, weak, Rosa thought.

"When the shit hits the fan, you put yourself first. He's in prison, and you got out. He eats porridge, and you dine out. He's alone, and you can't be by yourself for a second."

As Rosa listened to the words, they stopped hitting at her. They were, she realized, a reflection of her own thoughts, of her own fears. For years now, she had heard these voices inside her and done nothing, had not even stopped to listen to them, let alone speak them. And now here was her own daughter giving them voice, spinning a web out of fear and loneliness and trying to hold her mother in that web, trying to freeze time, trying to magic them all back to the sunny, happy days before Jacob went inside.

And as these thoughts raced through her mind, she realized that she didn't have to accept Martha's web. She didn't have to sink into it. Martha was young: These were things that she would resolve in later life. But as for herself, it was about time that she grew up and started to live as an adult, not as a guilty teenager.

Guilt, she reflected, how it carried through the family. Her grandmother, Riva, had never forgiven herself for leaving Lithuania; her mother, Julia, had never got over the death of her brother; and as for Rosa, could she forgive herself? Could she forgive herself for surviving, for being free?

She looked at Martha. "Since you think so badly of me," she said, "I might as well tell you it all. Richard's moving in with us."

Of the three in the room it was difficult to guess who was the most surprised. Martha's shock was mitigated by a sense of satisfaction. Her mother, she thought, had shown her true colors at last. Instead of consoling her, she had announced that that man was going to live with them.

The lying was over: She knew that her mother had forgotten

Jacob. Well, she did not care. She would live with this stranger without giving him the satisfaction of knowing how he hurt her. She would leave as soon as she was able.

"I knew it," she said.

Richard hardly heard her words. He was staring at Rosa with a kind of stupefaction. He had pulled Martha through the door as his heart sank. He thought it was the end: He thought the child had finally wrecked any hope for them. And instead Rosa had announced that this was a beginning: the beginning for which he'd argued throughout the long months.

And as for Rosa, she felt a mixture of relief and trepidation. The words had come out, and as soon as she'd uttered them, she knew that they were right. Martha had gone too far: She could no longer give in to her. For years she had lived for others. Now she would live for herself.

"And now it's time to go home," she said to Martha. She kissed Richard on the cheek. "Speak to you later," she said.

"Sit down, darling," Rosa told Rachel, "I've got something to tell you."

Rachel threw Rosa a cheeky smile and did as she was bid. She looked at her mother expectantly. Rosa, who had spent the whole night planning how she was to tell her, felt a momentary loss of courage. She pursed her lips.

"You're going to live with Richard," Rachel said.

Rosa's jaw dropped. "How did y-you know?" she stuttered. She was sure that Martha wouldn't have told Rachel: Martha never told Rachel anything.

"Oh, Mummy, it's obvious," Rachel said.

"And you don't mind?"

Rachel frowned. She didn't know whether she minded: Actually she thought it was none of her business. She didn't like the way grown-ups behaved, though. They presented you with a *fait accompli* and then they asked for your permission. Honestly, sometimes she thought adults were stupid.

"I'll still have you," she answered.

She saw Rosa's eyes fill with tears. She couldn't stand it if her mother was going to cry now. "Daddy wouldn't mind, either," she said.

Rosa started. "How do you know?"

"Oh, because of the things he says," Rachel replied. "Every

time we visit him, he goes on about how you have your own life to live and how every decision you make will be the right one. Daddy loves you, you know."

Rosa could do nothing to stop the tears from flooding out of her eyes. "I know," she wept, "I know."

43

South Africa: 1970

LINDIWE SMILED DOWN AS THE YOUNGSTER BESIDE HER LIFTED HIS fist into the air and shook it. *"Amandla!"* he said in a shrill voice.

She leaned down and pinched his cheek. "That's very good," she said, "but slogans without action are nothing. Go on now, go help your mother."

Her eyes followed the boy as he skipped through the clinic. She was proud of what she saw, of the benches built by local carpenters, of the cupboards donated by local manufacturers and filled with much-needed medical supplies, of the play area stocked from local shops—and all of this for free. She knew that to an outsider the place might seem tawdry, but she had watched it grow from nothing, and she knew just how much work had gone into it. It's not much, she thought, but it's a beginning. We will build on it.

She turned away and concentrated again on writing up her notes, her ears attuned, as they always were, to the background noise. That was one of the things she'd had to learn—how to finish her work without cutting herself off from her surroundings: She never knew when she might be needed to patch a bleeding knee, to arbitrate in a dispute, to dispense sympathy or advice.

Except the day was almost over and she would probably not be needed, she thought. And then she heard somebody call her name. "A visitor," they said.

She frowned and turned to the door. What kind of visitor would not announce himself personally? And then she understood, for she saw that the visitor was no ordinary person, that it was her mother.

Lindiwe knew that she was going to see Peggy soon, but would never have expected her to come to the clinic. She felt a moment's excited pleasure that Peggy had bothered. She got up slowly and smoothed down her apron. Then she walked to the door. When she reached Peggy, she kissed her on both cheeks.

"When did you arrive?" she asked formally.

"George picked me up from the bus depot at four," Peggy said. "George has been very good to me, you know."

The excitement waned. That's right, Lindiwe thought: Tell me about George, why don't you, the first time that we meet after so long an absence. She pushed the thought aside. "Evelyn will be coming soon," she said.

"Yes—George will also fetch her," Peggy replied. "Do you not want to be there?"

"No. I've got a meeting, I'm afraid."

A meeting, Peggy thought: just like your father. You look like him, too, she wanted to say. But that wouldn't have been right: She never mentioned Moses, she couldn't do so now.

She craned her neck instead, so that she was looking at the dark interior. She took in the sight of a largish room with benches running one side of it, a ramshackle partitioned section that contained a few old toys, and an unpainted door headed "Dr.," which stood on one wall. "So this is your clinic," she said.

Lindiwe smiled. "Yes," she replied. "It's not much, but it means plenty to this community. Not only can people come here for their medical problems, but we also run a crèche, a basketball team, a mothers' group, and a series of lessons on black pride. And we'll soon be expanding. We plan to . . ."

Peggy let Lindiwe's words wash over her. She's got Moses' enthusiasm as well, she thought. She could not help, as she stood there, remembering the times when Moses had come and told her excitedly of the recent developments. It's all turned to dust, Peggy thought, along with him.

She could not bear the thought. "I must be going," she said abruptly.

Lindiwe stopped in midsentence and tried to hide her hurt. It was her fault, she thought, she had hoped for too much. She should have known that Peggy would never understand, would never see how much the Black People's Convention meant to her: how an individual rage at the unfairness of the system had been turned into something more creative, to being part of an organization that was finally stirring a scared people to action.

No, she thought, Peggy wouldn't understand. "I'll see you later," was all she said.

Both Peggy's and Evelyn's journeys to Jo'burg were the result of one event: Evelyn's eightieth birthday. It was, the whole family agreed, quite a cause for celebration. It was also a day beset by the looming shadow of a potential explosion. For it was the first time since Moses' funeral that the Bopapes had come together.

They sat uneasily around George's splendid dining table. Evelyn, the matriarch, was at its head, looking old but nowhere near eighty. She had shrunk somewhat in the preceding years, and she relied heavily on a wooden stick to get around, but when seated, her back was as straight as it had ever been, her eyes as alert.

Peggy was seated opposite her. She was fifty now, and she showed it. Her hair was completely gray, but it was the look on her face, that look of defeat and despondency, that aged her. Her mouth was frozen in a permanent scowl, the wrinkles around her eyes went down rather than up.

She had made few concessions to the occasion. She had refused George's offer of a new outfit and was, instead, wearing a housecoat that was clean enough but faded. She hardly looked up throughout the meal. Instead, she concentrated her energies on her food: concentrated on cutting the meat into small pieces, on raising it to her mouth, on chewing at it as if it were her duty rather than her pleasure to eat. Looking at her you'd never have guessed that she made a special effort to get here—an effort that involved days of indecision and of planning as well as three long bus journeys to George's home in Orlando East.

Lindiwe was seated on Evelyn's right—opposite George. She was doing all she could to contain the resentment that threatened to bubble up from deep inside her.

Lindiwe worshiped her grandmother: She had been delighted when Evelyn had agreed to come. But Peggy's earlier visit had spoiled the occasion. Her resentment had worked on her after her mother had left the clinic; it had eaten away at her pleasurable anticipation of seeing Evelyn again. Peggy, she thought, makes no attempt to understand: She sides with George, she always has.

Lindiwe was proud of the Bopapes' tradition of resistance. She hoped that her own activities were a continuation of the involvement that stretched back to Evelyn's husband, Nathaniel. But Peggy—who had never cried for her husband—had also never forgiven him for dying. Lindiwe could not understand it: Neither could she tolerate it. She hated her mother for the repudiation of Moses' life. She saw no reason to sit around the same table as Peggy.

And she had an added problem. This was the first time she had ever been to George's house. Many years ago she had resolved to refuse his sporadic invitations—to do everything in her power to reject what she saw as her brother's Uncle Tom ways. Only the recognition of how important this occasion was, persuaded her to change her mind.

She did not like George: Neither did she approve of his success. It was types like him, she thought, types who thought only of themselves, who grabbed morsels from the white man's table and then called themselves self-made men, who were undermining the struggle.

The fact that George was her brother had little relevance anymore: It was his membership in the Urban Bantu Council, his usurping of a position of power that he had not earned, that she condemned. She glowered across the table.

Her husband, Johannes, caught the glare, and he tried to contain it. He was seated on George's side of the table, separated from his brother-in-law by five-year-old Bertha and seven-year-old Nathaniel Cuba. For him, the meal had degenerated into a trial of endurance.

He was hypersensitive to every gesture. He worried as he saw his wife frown: He hoped that she would have the sense to keep her mouth shut. He knew what an effort it had cost her to enter this house, and he knew she had come for Evelyn's sake alone. She would do her utmost to avoid clashing with George, but Johannes feared that even this wouldn't be enough.

Johannes glanced past his children and looked at George, who was just then lifting a glass to his mouth. When he sat so, the tight line of his lips concealed by the wine, he looked so much like Lindiwe. It was the strong features of Moses that were echoed by both brother and sister, a resemblance that they did their utmost to negate. Take, for example, the way they were dressed. George was attired as the solid respectable businessman he had become. Even in the stifling heat, he was wearing a striped gray suit, replete with waistcoat and gold timepiece. His starched white shirt shone on his broad chest: his black tie was knotted fiercely beneath his pointed collar. I'm an honorary European, he seemed to be implying.

In contrast, Lindiwe had eschewed Western clothes. She was wearing a brightly colored caftan, which she had topped with a yellow turban. She looked magnificent, Johannes reflected, strong and proud—a true daughter of Africa.

Johannes shifted his gaze away from Lindiwe. He took in the rest of the room and thought how much it reflected George's status. To the inhabitants of white suburbia, it would have looked tawdry, but it was like a palace to the township dwellers.

The whole house contrasted strongly with the Cubas' almost barren dwelling, where a few wall hangings were the only decorations. Here, there was space—George's privileged position meant he had a three-bedroom house despite his childless circumstances—but it had been filled to the hilt with possessions. A large three-piece suite jostled with some easy chairs for prominence; every side table was covered with an embroidered doily on which had been placed silver ashtrays, fringe-laden lamps, small trinkets, paper flowers. It made Johannes nervous to be surrounded by so much ostentation.

But then he wondered whether the contempt he felt for the clutter was not tinged with envy. No matter how hard he and Lindiwe worked, they would never be able to give their children this kind of comfort. The sixties had been a time of economic boom for South Africa, and yet few blacks had seen its benefits. All they got was a widening tide of repression, a tightening of influx controls, a step up in mass evictions. Only a few, like George, had profited.

There was no point in dwelling on it, Johannes thought. To distract himself, he looked back at the table. There was one empty place, and it had been vacant for at least half the meal. It belonged to Dottie, George's wife, a quiet, retiring woman who used any excuse to escape to the kitchen, away from the buildup of suppressed tension.

Dottie, Johannes thought, complemented George perfectly. She seemed to wholeheartedly believe his view that men negotiate the world, while women act as their support. She always did the right thing: Take today—she had given her servant the day off because she knew that Lindiwe would have exploded if a black woman had waited table on her. Johannes suspected that Dottie was wilier than she appeared: She had a way of talking to George that was half-cajoling, half-hectoring, and it always seemed to work. Behind the appearance of docility, he suspected, there lurked a will of iron.

She came in now with a tray of sweets, each individually wrapped and arranged decoratively on the small side plates. Everybody got one—even Lindiwe, who seldom touched sweet things. Johannes watched in relief as Lindiwe unwrapped one and took a small bite before putting it unobtrusively to one side. Lindiwe was really trying, he thought.

And yet, he realized, the conversation had come to an almost dead stop. Evelyn, he saw, was looking vaguely uncomfortable. He picked up his glass. "I propose a toast to Evelyn," he said, "on this, her eightieth birthday."

Around him the assembled company looked relieved as they echoed his actions. "To Evelyn," they said in unison. Even Peggy drank.

Evelyn smiled a faint acknowledgment around the table. When they had finished, she stood up with effort. She nudged George's helping hand away.

"I have seldom made a speech in my life," she said. "But today, this last day when we shall all be together, I will try." She looked around her. "I will not survive much longer," she said, and her voice was surprisingly strong. "But I want you all to know that I consider myself lucky to have seen eighty years." She smiled. "Some might judge my life as one filled with pain," she said. "But I am fortunate to have known two men who are no longer with us. The first is Nathaniel, my husband, a man who I have never forgotten, a brave man who saw hope in the future."

She paused. When she spoke again, her voice was softer, filled with a kind of gentle sadness. "The second," she said, "is Moses, my son, Peggy's husband, the father of George and Lindiwe, the grandfather of Bertha and Nathaniel." She raised her glass. "Moses died for all of us," she said. "We must live for him."

As Evelyn drank, Johannes watched the reaction of the assembled company. This time he noticed how mixed their different responses were. Peggy, he saw, lifted her glass grudgingly, and sipped her wine as if it were a bitter brew. Lindiwe, on the other hand, turned her drinking of the toast into a demonstration. "*Amandla*," she said, as she swilled the whole lot down.

And as for George, he behaved like the businessman he was. He held the glass to his lips, he wet the rim with his tongue, he did not drink but made no demonstration of the fact. Johannes hoped he was the only person who noticed George's silent refusal.

But with a sinking heart, Johannes realized that Lindiwe had also been watching her brother. "Your wine is poisoned?" she asked George loudly.

George took a sip. "Not at all," he said suavely.

"Or perhaps you haven't gone so far as to embrace hypocrisy wholeheartedly?" Lindiwe continued.

George narrowed his eyes. He brushed Dottie's restraining hand away from him. "And what do you mean by that?" he asked.

"I'd think it was obvious," Lindiwe said. "Since you profit by your father's defeat."

George's face stiffened. "Everything I have is the product of my own effort," he said sharply.

"And everything you produce makes the struggle of our people harder," Lindiwe shot back.

Peggy stirred. "Don't talk to your brother like that," she snapped.

Lindiwe turned to glare at her mother. "You have done all you can to disown the memory of my father," she said. "I will talk as I please."

George, Johannes saw, had closed his hands until they formed tight fists. Johannes did not trust George's temper. He tensed himself—ready to spring to his wife's defense even though he knew that she would not thank him for such action.

But he had reckoned without Evelyn, who was still standing at the head of the table, one arm leaning on the back of her chair for support.

She spoke up in a voice that denied her eighty years, that came from deep inside her, from a lifetime of struggle and of arguments, from a well of strength that was still only partly tapped.

"I expected political discussion," she said. "But what is the good of discussion if it is held at the level of the gutter? You, my granddaughter"—she nodded her head in Lindiwe's direction—"have done much of value. You carry the spirit of your father's struggle with you. And yet there is a bitterness in your heart. You condemn others too easily. Your grandfather Nathaniel's first lesson was that our only hope is unity—we cannot afford to dismiss our brothers because their thoughts lag behind ours."

Lindiwe smiled at her grandmother, but her voice was not friendly. "I value the memory of my grandfather," she said. "But we must learn from history. The ANC were wrong: They never realized that only blacks can dictate their own destiny. They did not see how pernicious was the fact of privilege for the few. They were too interested in winning the approval of whites."

Evelyn narrowed her eyes. "You have not learned from history," she said. "You merely use hindsight to justify yourself. Every phase has its time: Your grandfather laid the ground for your current struggle. Men such as Jacob Swiece, such as Bram Fischer, made a great contribution."

"Jacob Swiece is irrelevant," Lindiwe answered. "Power is in our hands. We need to conscientize the black masses: We need to get them to dictate their own destiny. Black consciousness is an idea whose time has truly arrived."

"What is this *conscientize* I keep hearing about?" George said in a mocking tone.

Lindiwe glared at him. "It is a word framed by Steve Biko," she said. "I think even you have heard of him?" She smiled when George did not reply, but it was to Evelyn that she addressed her words. "It is a way of talking about what we blacks of South Africa need to do for each other," she continued. "We need to realize what crimes have been perpetrated against us: not only economically but personally as well. We need to understand how even our own self-images have been handed to us by the whites, and we need to build ourselves anew, build ourselves in our own image."

"Rhetoric," George said. "What good will that do?"

"And you? What good do you do?" Lindiwe shot back.

George narrowed his eyes. "I work in the real world," he said, "to improve the lot of our people. It's people like me, who choose to participate in the system, who will make the difference. You scorn the Bantustans, but they give us independence. You despise the urban councils, but they have the power to fix rents."

"To line their own pockets, you mean," Lindiwe retorted.

George leaned forward. "If you're suggesting," he hissed, "that I'm involved in anything corrupt, then I must ask you to leave my house."

But before Lindiwe could reply, Evelyn rapped her cane on the floor. "Words, all words," she muttered. She sat down heavily in her chair, as if she were exhausted. "When I observe the bitterness in my own family," she said, "I fear for our future."

The celebration, if it could be called that, fizzled out soon afterward. With only the flimsiest of excuses, Peggy retired to her room. She was leaving the next day, despite George's promise to use his influence to extend her permit. She had no time for the city, she said; she should never have left the country—that had proved her undoing. She was happy for George's success, she said, but all she wanted was to be left in peace. And so she went to bed, as silently as she had endured the meal.

Evelyn, for her part, was in a rage. She was at pains to conceal the fact, because she thought that she might well be being unfair. For although she despised the path George had chosen, it was toward Lindiwe that her anger was directed. The child, she thought, was too impetuous. She pretended to be carrying on the struggle in her father's name, and yet she rejected her father's great achievement: the allying of all participants in the movement, of blacks and whites alike.

Evelyn could not sleep for thinking of it, and the more she thought, the more she needed to talk. "I must talk to somebody who understands," she told herself.

The idea took hold, and she couldn't stave it off. In the end she asked George to call her a taxi, and when he refused, she made him drive her into Soweto. She told him where to go, and when they arrived, she told him to wait outside. She went up to the small house and she knocked.

There was a lone saxophone sounding from inside, and Evelyn smiled to herself. She had heard that music before, heard it not in this urban center but in the veld of the Transkei, when the sound carried over miles of empty space and triumphed over it. She knocked again. The music ceased.

When he opened the door, Evelyn saw that Nat had changed little. He'd filled out, perhaps, since leaving the Transkei, and his eyes were not so ringed by sadness, but otherwise he was pretty much identical. At least Nat stays the same, she thought with relief.

"Aren't you going to ask me in?" she said.

Nat closed his mouth, and springing forward, he took both of her hands in his. "My friend Evelyn," he said, and there were tears in his eyes. "Come in, by all means, come in. This is a great day for me: Does it mean you've left the Transkei?"

"I'm visiting my grandchildren," she said. She did not tell him of her birthday, since anniversaries, she thought, were of little relevance.

Nat fussed over her as he led her to a chair. He insisted on making her tea, on asking her a hundred questions about the Transkei, on telling her all about his return to Jo'burg. And then, abruptly, he stopped.

"There's something worrying you," he said.

Evelyn nodded. "I need to talk," she said. "And I thought you might understand, since we have lived through the same times."

"What is it?" Nat asked.

So simply did he give her permission to speak, so intently did he look at her, that Evelyn knew that she had come to the right place. He would listen, and he would understand. "It's my granddaughter," she began. "I'm worried about her."

And having said that, she poured out her thoughts to Nat. She spoke of how hurt she felt that the one political member of her family was rejecting the ways of the ANC—was rejecting the ANC itself, and its basis, the Freedom Charter. She spoke, and as she did so, she realized how much she minded.

And all the while Nat listened.

But when she had finished, he did not immediately reply. He sat still, staring down at the floor. It was a good five minutes before he spoke, and when he did, his voice came from somewhere far away. "While I was in exile," he said, "I dreamed of returning to Jo'burg. I dreamed of the political discussions which I would hold, of the spirit of defiance that I so missed."

"And did that happen when you came back?"

Nat smiled sadly. "No," he said, "I learned instead that it was all a dream: I learned that something happened after our leaders were jailed or exiled, that our people grew afraid."

"They had good reason," Evelyn said.

Nat shook his head. "The state launched an offensive that was extreme," he said, "I wouldn't deny that. But something else happened. Evelyn, we have to face the fact and take responsibility for it. Our people turned away. State censorship became less important, because the people censored themselves. They wouldn't even talk of politics—ayiee, they wouldn't even do that."

He got up and went to stand by the window. "Your granddaughter grew into an adult during that time," he said. "Her father was killed, and nothing came of his death. She saw how blacks suffered and how easy life is for the whites, and she grew bitter. Who can blame her?"

Nat turned and faced Evelyn. "And then," he said, "Steve Biko came onto the scene, and his words shook things up. I've listened to him, and I know that he's talking to the next generation and he's talking sense. After years of defeat, he's giving people like Lindiwe, and those younger than she, the opportunity to find their own sense of pride, the one that their parents had buried. He's telling them to walk tall again."

"There is no place in this movement for people like Jacob Swiece," Evelyn said. "How can that be?"

"Perhaps it is necessary," Nat said. "Perhaps we Africans must stand on our own feet before we can truly consider ourselves equals."

"But Biko's movement is cultural," Evelyn countered. "It will never change anything fundamental."

"Not in itself," Nat agreed. "But if it changes what people think they can do, then it will have an effect. One day this new generation will organize again, and it will uncover our history that currently lies buried under defeat. And when these youngsters act, South Africa will begin to shake."

"You're an optimist, Nat," Evelyn said.

Nat smiled. "Is there another way of being?" he asked.

Evelyn did not reply. She looked him straight in the face, and he couldn't guess what she was thinking. And then she pulled herself to her feet, and hobbling over to Nat, she embraced him. "You've done me good," she said. "I must go—my grandson is waiting all this time." She walked, straighter now, toward the door.

"See you again," Nat almost called, but he didn't. "You've been a good friend to me, Evelyn Bopape," he said instead.

Evelyn nodded, and then she was gone. And for a long time

Nat stared into the space she had vacated, stared and felt the sadness of her absence.

"Do you think I was wrong?" Lindiwe asked her husband. "Do you think I should have kept my mouth shut?"

They were lying together in bed, and Johannes reached over and tried to pull her to him. "What, you?" he joked. "Keep your mouth shut?"

She did not smile, and neither did she yield. Johannes turned on his side and looked at her. "It really hurts," he said softly.

She nodded. "Evelyn carries our family with her," she said. "And she disapproves of me. That hurts."

Johannes reached out a hand and slowly stroked Lindiwe's cheek.

"You are doing what you think right," he said. "That is all anybody can ask of you." And then together they lay in silence, each lost in private thoughts, until the day began anew.

And in another part of town Evelyn was also lying awake, and her head was spinning. It was long time, she thought, since she had subjected her ideas to such a close examination. Her mind, she thought, had grown sluggish: She had been isolated in the Transkei.

But if Nat was right, all their minds had gone a similar way. If Nat was right, they were only just beginning to awaken.

Perhaps, she thought, I find it so hard to believe Nat because I want the people I know to be in charge. I want Moses and Jacob Swiece, too, and the ideas they represent, to be at the forefront. I am just a vain old woman.

And with that in mind, she went to sleep.

Jacob was doing calisthenics. He ran on the spot, up and down, up and down, five hundred times, a short pause and then another five hundred. This was the second time in twelve hours that he had gone through this routine, and on any other day he might have stopped himself. You had to watch that in jail, he thought, self-motivation was essential. One could set oneself unreachable targets and then experience a crushing disappointment at the failure to attain them.

And yet Jacob continued to run. His breath was coming in sharp gasps, but he ignored it. It was better this way, he thought, gathering speed even at the end of his session. When he'd started, he'd chosen a slow rhythm that matched the refrain in his brain. *Van der* went his left foot, *Merwe* replied his right; *van der Merwe, van der Merwe*, it echoed through his brain as he jogged on the spot.

By the time he was moving automatically, he found that his fist were clenched and his body so tense that his muscles hurt every time his feet hit the floor. He realized that the exercise was reinforcing the rage he'd been trying to negate: He broke his rhythm to rid himself of the deadly chorus.

He knew that, in the surrounding cells, his comrades were going through the same process—each choosing his own method of blowing off steam.

Prison Officer van der Merwe was the cause of Jacob's—of all their—rage. Van der Merwe was a past master of pettiness. He used the prison rule book to punish and proscribe, and he especially delighted in finding new ways to torment the politicals. The fact that he was loathed by prisoners and prison officers alike had no affect on him—or perhaps that was wrong, Jacob thought, it probably goaded him to greater excesses.

A slow-thinking man, van der Merwe let nothing divert him from his vendetta. When prisoners were allowed special food in celebration of a religious festival, he forced them to gorge themselves alone in their cells rather than allow them to share the food with their comrades. When a man said he was sick, he was sent out to the cold yard if he so much as stepped out of his bed to urinate in the cell pot. When letters were one word over the allocated five hundred, they were kept back until it was judged too late to rewrite them. And worst of all, when one of the comrades' father died, he was isolated "for his own good" rather than being allowed to share his grief with his fellow prisoners.

It was all so unremitting, and yet so difficult to ignore. Jacob smiled wryly to himself as he thought how, if not for the past four years, he would not have been able to believe the passion that each setback could provoke. Take, for example, van de Merwe's latest injunction. It was, on the face of it, an insignificant disappointment—the banning of a small Christmas play.

And yet its impact had been deadening. Nothing changed in prison: day in, day out, month after month, time was parceled into a series of meaningless tasks. So the time leading up to their first Christmas play had been like a breath of fresh air. At last they had a focus: They spent hours, weeks, months, even, working to fashion from nowhere costumes, scenery, scripts. Every ounce of imagination, every piece of past experience, was brought into the process.

The play itself was a disappointment compared to the excitement that its preparations generated, but it gave the prisoners hope. They had done something together—out of the barrenness of their lives they had created something. They talked about it long after it was over: They began planning for the next play as early as August.

And then, like a bolt out of the blue, van der Merwe had put his foot down. With a satisfied smirk, he'd produced some age-old prison regulation that he used to justify a prohibition on any repeat this year.

Jacob had felt a fury when he heard this—it was all he could do to restrain himself from leaping at van der Merwe's throat. Around him, he heard the muffled gasps of outrage—quickly stifled since it did no good to give van de Merwe even one hint that his prohibitions affected them.

It was funny, Jacob thought, as he began on a third round of push-ups (nothing seemed to tire him out) how everything had taken on an equal value in prison. No, that was wrong—some things, like the Christmas play, had become of overwhelming importance.

In contrast, his life outside had retreated into the shadows. When Rosa wrote to tell him that she and Richard Crossbanks would be living together, he had been saddened but not devastated—not furious, as he was about the play. He supposed that the ease at which he'd accepted the news was due in part to forewarning from the children. Not that they had ever said anything, but he, so hyped up for their visits, had seen the reticence in their eyes when he'd asked about Rosa's social life.

So the news when it came had been almost like an old friend—an anticipated fear come true, rather than an experience that would throw him off keel.

He ached for his Rosa—oh, yes, he still did that. Nothing she decided would ever stop him from remembering her as a young woman, a passionate lover, a new mother, an old friend, and a stolid comrade. She was the love of his life—the only woman he had ever truly cherished. She was the person he wanted waiting for him outside the prison gates when he finally emerged.

Yet he believed that Rosa had a right to her own life. He understood how tough it must have been: moving countries, having full responsibility for the kids (and Martha, he thought, looked as if she could really be a handful), worrying about money. If he had been in her position, he told himself, he might have done likewise. Richard Crossbanks seemed a decent enough type: His Rosa was a young woman—she had a right to happiness. Life was for living—only prison was for memories.

Jacob blinked. He told himself that Rosa's actions were all right, but a part of him wept constantly for the loss of her. There was no point in dwelling on it—in driving himself mad with conjecture. His release was many years ahead—there was no chance of remission for the politicals. What happened when he came through the doors of Pretoria Central (they'd been moved here some years back) was not something he could afford to worry about.

"Twenty-nine, thirty," he muttered, before collapsing on the ground. He was bathed in sweat and would have no opportunity to wash off the stale smell until long after the weekend. But at least his thoughts of van der Merwe had grown less virulent.

He realized vaguely that he had been thinking about something else toward the end of the push-ups: For the life of him he couldn't recall what it was.

The soft sweep of the mops as they swished down the long corridor distracted him. Van der Merwe must have been pleased by this morning's demonstration, for he was shouting less violently at the black cleaning detail. That was something, Jacob supposed.

These black common-law prisoners were the recipients of unbelievable indignities. Excluded from the whites, given food that was even worse, thinner mattresses and threadbare blankets, they were the butt of every white officer's little whim. Jacob's heart would cry out in anger when he caught sight of them, shuffling through the prisons in shoes either too big or too small. It was the details of neglect, the deliberate attempt at humiliation, that angered him the most. No wonder, he thought, that there were reports that the ideas of black consciousness, imported from America, were taking root in the country.

The judas hole on Jacob's cell door was quickly opened, and then just as quickly shut. Something plopped to the floor. Jacob waited expectantly, giving his friend time to move off. Then he dashed to the door and, in a flash, removed the objects from the concrete ground. By the time van der Merwe opened the grill and stared through, Jacob was lying on his bed, feigning dejection. Only after he heard van der Merwe at the cell next door did he look at his windfall.

He smiled. In his hand was a small piece of wax, a makeshift lighting thread running through it. And better than that were the two matches accompanied by a tiny scrap of match box. This was a treasure house indeed. Jacob was still no smoker, but fire was a precious commodity in Pretoria Central. He would use the candle well—he would study that night and catch up on his sociology course.

There was one other thing among his booty—a minuscule piece of paper. Jacob unfolded it. There was one word inscribed— ACTION, it said. Jacob nodded. It was about time, he thought, the edict must not go unchallenged. He put the piece of paper in his mouth and chewed it into a ball, which he swallowed. Then he set about finding a hiding place for his candle—if they followed their plans, they could expect summary cell searches in reply. After that, there was nothing more to do. He lay on his bed—he had earned a rest.

A Red Cross visit to the prison was kept to a bare minimum. The politicals would be lined up in a row, and then the embarrassed official would come into the yard with a few boxes. He would distribute the goods as he attempted to talk to the politicals and van der Merwe tried just as hard to stop him.

The politicals had learned to use this, their only outlet of complaint, apart from the very occasional visit by an MP, sparingly. If there were too many gripes, the official would retreat in confusion, leaving the prisoners to face van der Merwe's wrath. If an individual spoke out without checking with the others, then he laid himself open to van der Merwe's special treatment that could mean days in solitary.

So the politicals had worked out a system. They resolved to complain only after preplanning, and only when they each could play an equal role in the risky business of arguing for their rights. Van der Merwe, always alert to rebellion, had cottoned onto their scheme fast. He'd requested Red Cross visits for first thing Monday morning, and he made sure that the politicals were locked up separately the weekend before.

That's where van der Merwe could never win, Jacob thought. He was an individual who, judging by his general ill-temper, had few personal friendships. He was also accustomed to a brutalized white prison population who informed on their cellmates in exchange for merit points. There was no way he could understand the sense of solidarity among the political inmates: There was no way he could come to grips with the fact that organizing was one of their passions and their skills.

They had found a way to circumvent him. They used the informal network inside the prison to pass notes. In snatches of stolen conversation they discussed strategy. They even had a fluctuating order of action that would expose no individual to greater attention. They were ready to act together when the time was right.

As the politicals stood in line, exchanging not even a single glance, van der Merwe sensed something was brewing. "No talking!" he shouted uneasily.

"Mr. Swiece?" called the official.

"Step forward, Swiece," snapped van der Merwe.

The official courteously handed Jacob his parcel. "Thank you," said Jacob, and then immediately followed on with his complaint; he knew from the other times van der Merwe would try to rush each prisoner back before he had time to say anything. "The commanding officer had given us permission to stage a Christmas play," he said.

"That's good," said the puzzled man.

"And now we've been told that it's forbidden," Jacob said.

"I'll see what I can do," said the official.

"That's enough, Swiece!" shouted van der Merwe.

One after the other, as the men collected their parcels, they registered their complaints. "Not enough toilet paper," said one. "We want to spend our two rand on fruit, not sweets," said another. "We are not allowed to use the new washbasins," said a third. Everybody had his role, and everybody performed it without a tremor, without risking a glance at the beet-red face of van de Merwe.

And then the visit was over, and the fun began. Van der Merwe looked as though he were going to have apoplexy.

"*Verdomte kommies!*" he shouted. "What are you trying to do? Get me in trouble?"

Jacob suppressed a giggle. It was farcical, this situation. Van der Merwe was their tyrant, the controller of all aspects in their lives. And yet, when exposed to outside scrutiny, he degenerated into a small child; a child who could not believe that the playthings he tortured could turn against him.

"Swiece," shouted van der Merwe, "you're on punishment—three meals."

Jacob's stomach immediately began to rumble. Prison food was sparse enough without having to lose a whole day of it.

"I request a visit to the O.C.," he said.

"You can't," Van der Merwe said. "You're on punishment."

Another from the line stepped forward. "I request a visit to the O.C."

"Punishment for you," snapped van der Merwe. "Retroactive." They all lost three meals, but in the end they won. Their right to have a Christmas play was restored to them. A petty triumph, but a triumph nevertheless. That was life in jail—a small reflection on what the mass of the black population must endure every day of their lives.

The Cuba family was seated on the floor and eating their evening meal when there was a knock on the door. Lindiwe sighed in exasperation as Johannes went to answer. This time was precious to her, since it was often the only time in the day when they were all together. She hated it when people interrupted, she wished that Johannes would get rid of the visitor fast.

And then she heard surprise in his voice as he uttered one name—Evelyn—and she was on her feet. She rushed to the door and saw that it was indeed her grandmother standing there. She felt suddenly shy, she did not know what to say.

"I've asked George to wait in the car," Evelyn said. "And I can't be long, because my bus leaves soon. But I wanted to see you again."

"I'm glad you did," Lindiwe said quietly, too quietly. She was scared all of a sudden, scared of what Evelyn might say.

"Come in," said Johannes—he at least had his wits about him.

Evelyn took one step into the room and smiled at Bertha and Nathaniel, who had both jumped to their feet. "I'm pleased you're here," she said, "to listen to what I have to say to your mother." She turned to Lindiwe, and her face seemed to soften. "I have come to apologize for my harshness," she said.

"You don't have to . . ." Lindiwe began, but Evelyn stopped her by holding up a hand.

"It's sometimes hard for the old to face the fact that they will one day die," she said. "And to come to terms with the fact that those younger than they have taken over. Last night I judged you by my history, by my experience. I was wrong to do that. I have come to tell you that I am proud of you, that your father would have been proud of you. You are doing what you can to make things better for all our people, and that is the most that can be asked of anybody."

She looked away, because she saw tears in Lindiwe's eyes and she did not want to break down herself. This was the last time, she knew, that she would see her granddaughter, that she would see any of her family. She ruffled her great-grandson Nathaniel's unruly hair. "Your mother is doing what's right," she whispered almost to herself.

"I know," he said, as he looked up at her with bright eyes. "I will follow her lead."

Evelyn shivered. "I must go," she said brusquely. She turned away from them and began to walk.

And they stood together, side by side, Lindiwe and Johannes and their two children, as they watched this old woman walk toward George's car. She was indeed old, she moved with effort, leaning heavily on her stick. But there was also something timeless about her, something that would never date. It was her spirit, Lindiwe realized, it was her sense of progress. Even at eighty, she still had the ability to think, to change, to admit that she was wrong.

"If I can grow old like that," Lindiwe whispered to Johannes, "I will die happy." He squeezed her arm in response.

44

Britain: 1972

MARTHA WAS WALKING UP THE ROAD, ON HER WAY TO THE LAUNDRO-mat, when she spotted the demonstration. She knew immediately what it was about: She'd been dragged to enough like it when she'd first arrived in England. She could recognize the black-and-white symbol of the anti-apartheid movement from a mile away.

It was taking place outside Barclays Bank: a group of people, around twelve in number, with banners and leaflets, harrying incoming customers, shouting slogans, calling for divestiture.

Martha knew that none of the demonstrators were looking her way (or would think anything of this single woman carrying a black plastic bag if they did happen to see her), but still she quickened her pace. She wanted to get away as soon as she could. She did not want to be reminded of the traumas of the past: She did not want to think about it. Visiting Jacob once a year was bad enough. She did not want to think of South Africa at any other time.

It wasn't something that occupied her mind too much these days, for Martha was a different person away from home: or to be more accurate, she was a series of different people. She had a chameleonlike quality about her: a quality that helped her fit into a diversity of crowds, to change even her basic mannerisms and project a subtly altered image.

To the moneyed students who constituted a significant pro-portion of Bristol University, she was a fun-seeker: to her fellows in the psychology course, she was a sporadic companion at lectures: to the political elements, she was a seasoned agitator.

The only side of her personality she hid from her peers was that sullen, disapproving, resentful product of a difficult past. It peeked through sometimes—in an unexpected tantrum during one-to-one tutorials, in the tone of her voice when she made one of her irregular calls home, but for the most part it was well and truly buried.

Not all newfound characteristics were a product of forced dissimulation. For Martha was genuinely relieved to go to college—and was genuinely altered by the experience. Getting away from home let her out of a trap that had grown increasingly onerous.

Not that life had remained unaltered after Richard moved in. The opportunities for all-out war had been reduced—Richard would not tolerate, he said, the constant state of siege that had greeted his arrival. His edict did bring relief to Martha, who was beginning to find the process of watching her mother and pouncing on her every mistake quite a strain. But she never got used to Richard's presence: She resented his presence in her life, she did so silently, but she did so all the same.

That was why she'd never once contemplated studying in London. She had to get away—to make her own life. She nursed the suspicion that Rosa secretly concurred with her, and it was difficult to tell which of the two was the more relieved when Martha, who had not done well in retaking her A-levels, got into the Bristol department by dint of an exceptional interview. The day before she left home, things had been almost relaxed between them.

When Martha returned to her apartment she found both co-occupants glued to the television.

"It's your mother," said one in a reverent tone.

Martha stood behind the sofa and stared at the image of Rosa. She's had a new hairdo, she thought, as Rosa listened politely to an apologist for the regime who was explaining away the forced removals of Africans to a barren land.

And then, when the man had finished speaking, Rosa launched into him. She piled statistic onto statistic and built a platform from which she exposed his arguments, cast scorn upon them, and called them the lies they were. She did all this in a calm enough manner, but the strength of her arguments was deadly.

She rattled her opponent. "You're nothing but a communist," he shouted at one point.

"And you're a butcher," she coolly replied, before going on with her exposition.

She had him stuttering in embarrassment: Eventually he was phased out from the conversation altogether. The last shot, before the program moved on to something else, was of Rosa, her eyes blazing, her mouth framed in an ironic smile.

"God, she's great," said Martha's roommates, in unison. Martha slammed out of the room.

Martha paid an unexpected and uncharacteristic visit to London. She did not tell Rosa what she was after: She waited instead until the house was empty. Then she climbed the stairs and went up to the attic.

It didn't take long to find her father's letters. They were there, on top of the trunk. Rosa had once told her that they would be there if she ever wanted to read them.

She picked them up and saw how neatly they were bundled, letters not just from this phase of his incarceration but from other times past, and how much they had been thumbed. The place where she sat was dust-free—Rosa must come here often. It made her wonder about her mother: Rosa seemed happy with Richard, yet she obviously spent much time closeted alone with thoughts of her husband.

Martha refused to think about it. She turned the letters over, feeling their flimsy texture, and then, instead of opening them, she delved into the trunk. It was crammed with memories: She dug in once and came up with a myriad of different documents, of photographs, of letters from another age.

She was astonished by the range of it all, some of the stuff was over sixty years old. It wasn't only Rosa's history, but Julia's as well. Of course—she remembered Rosa telling her how, when they left South Africa, Julia had wanted to leave it all behind and how Rosa had rescued it.

Martha flicked casually through the pictures, but against her better judgment she was soon immersed in them. There were photos of her mother as a child, as an adolescent, as a married woman with Jacob by her side. Rosa had looked happier once, Martha thought. She pushed the photos to one side and began to examine those of her grandmother.

These she found more fascinating, or perhaps just easier to take. She enjoyed seeing Julia as a young woman with Harold beside her. Julia, Martha saw, had once been dressed in the height of fashion. Julia and Harold had been together so long now that one could forget what they might once have felt for each other. Now, Martha saw how Harold must have loved her: It showed in the way his arm linked hers, in the way he looked at his wife rather than at the camera.

The pictures stretched even further back in time. In one of them, one so tarnished with brown that it was barely decipherable, there was a picture of a young girl and a boy beside her. This must be Julia and her brother, Haim: the one who died.

Martha turned the picture over to check: 1904, it said. Such a long time ago. And Julia looked so different, so foreign somehow, in her starched clothes, staring seriously at the photographer as if she would never move again. She was a foreigner even then, Martha thought: a Jew fleeing from the pogrom, come to start a new life.

Martha picked up another photo, and this time Julia was in the forefront and there was a woman standing behind her. This must be Riva, Martha thought: Julia's mother. One further glance confirmed it. The family resemblance was very strong: even Rosa, the grandchild, had the look of Riva about her.

And yet the two women were dissimilar, because in the picture Riva looked not full of energy as Rosa was, but somewhat limp. She stared into space, an embittered woman, a woman who had been cruelly disappointed. Riva's mother, Martha remembered, had cursed her once, or cast her out, perhaps—which was it? And she, too, had been a stranger in a strange land: except she had never adjusted to it, she had never learned even one of its languages.

We've all experienced exile, Martha thought. Each one of us.

She shook herself. She could go on like this forever, she thought, and never open Jacob's letters.

With trembling fingers, she undid the string.

And for the next hour she read and she cried alternatively. She realized then how painful it was to think of Jacob—to really think of him. She airily told people that not one day passed without her thinking about her father, and yet now she realized that what she had been doing was remembering a static man— the father of a twelve-year-old (the man she visited in prison was someone else—a no man in a no-man's-land).

She'd never thought to wonder what he had become, how he coped with his long incarceration, what it really meant to him. As she read his five-hundred-word letters, she learned about him. She learned how careful he was to keep always optimistic, and to encourage Rosa. She learned how he cared for his children, for both of them, and how he spoke of their visits with love and with concern. She learned that he was a brave man and that he was suffering.

When she cried, she cried for her father—for Jacob rather than for his fatherless child.

One morning Martha awoke to a phone call. She almost didn't recognize Rachel's voice. The two sisters seldom talked: they had little in common, and although they no longer fought, attempts at conversation tended to lapse into silence. Seventeen-year-old Rachel was doing her A-levels, and Martha found her preoccupations with boys enervating. Since Martha rarely went home, the depth of the gulf between never became too apparent. This was another skeleton in Martha's closet—now active in the women's movement, she talked of sisterhood, while she was a stranger to her own sister.

And so she was surprised, and not a little anxious, to hear a voice that sounded as if it came from a thousand miles away.

"I can hardly hear you," Martha said. "Can't you speak up?"

"No," Rachel's voice grew even fainter. "I don't want Mummy to hear me."

"What's happened?" Martha found that she, too, was whispering.

"I think you should come home for a visit," Rachel said without skipping a beat.

Martha raised her voice. "Why? Has something happened?" she asked. To Jacob, she meant, had something happened to him? It couldn't have, could it? Surely Rachel would have told her immediately, instead of skirting delicately around the subject.

"It's Evelyn," Rachel said in a disapproving voice. "Don't you know? Mummy told me she wrote to you about it."

With a guilty start, Martha realized that she had indeed registered some piece of information about Evelyn in Rosa's latest letter. She could not recall the substance of the line. Cradling the telephone on her shoulder, she reached into the bureau drawer where she habitually stuffed all of Rosa's letters. She unfolded the newest and scanned it.

The sentence about Evelyn was buried in the second paragraph.

"By the way," Rosa had written, "I had some bad news today. I heard that Evelyn Bopape is dead. I don't know whether you remember her. She was Moses' mother, and she once worked for Granny."

After that brief reference Rosa continued to write about her work, her clothes, the stuff of trivia with which she always filled her missives. There was no indication that she was badly upset.

Rachel's voice broke into Martha's thoughts. "You've got to come," she insisted. "We need you."

Martha frowned. Her sister had no right to tell her what to do. "Are you sure it's serious?" she asked. "You're not exaggerating?"

"She won't get out of bed," Rachel replied.

"Can't Richard deal with it?"

"She won't talk to Richard."

Martha suppressed a momentary feeling of pleasure. "What about Julia?" she asked.

"Granny's no help."

Rachel, Martha thought, is deliberately boxing me into a corner.

"What am I expected to do?" she snapped. "She's got you—her favorite."

There was a pause at the other end. When Rachel spoke, her voice sounded strained. "It's you she's always wanted," she said.

Martha sighed impatiently. Rachel had said much the same thing many times before, but her insistence as to Rosa's preference never failed to aggravate her sister. After all, it was patently untrue, wasn't it? Still, she thought, this was not the time to debate the issue. "I suppose I'll come," she said reluctantly.

"I knew you would." Rachel sounded strangely disappointed. Then her voice strengthened. "What train will you catch?"

"How the hell do I know?" Martha snapped. "I hardly keep the timetable in my head."

"Make it soon," Rachel said.

*   *   *

Richard was at Paddington when Martha arrived.

"How did you know which train I was catching?" she asked in amazement.

He was embarrassed. "I didn't," he said. "I would have waited for the next one as well."

Martha looked at him.

Richard paused. "Rosa is very unhappy," he finally blurted out.

Martha looked again at Richard, looked at him as if for the first time. He had been, she realized, nothing but a symbol to her—a symbol of the British upper classes from which she had always felt excluded, a symbol of her mother's betrayal of the family. And yet, as she looked at him, she saw that he was merely a man like any other. Or perhaps not even that—for he was obviously a deeply worried man. His pale skin was almost gray, his forehead was lined with wrinkles. She felt sorry for him—this man whom she had once regarded as her enemy. And she felt more than that—she felt—for him—affection.

She stopped herself from dwelling on this surprising revelation. It was too much to take—all in one morning. "Come on," she said brightly. "Let's go home."

Things were bad at home, Richard thought as he and Martha drove silently. Rosa wouldn't have been human if she hadn't grieved for Evelyn. Yet the severity of her reaction was becoming increasingly incomprehensible. She had taken to her bed on the second day, and hadn't been up for a week. He had moved out of their shared bedroom when she made it obvious that his presence was distressing her. She didn't eat, she didn't appear to sleep, and she talked of nothing that made sense. He would have been less worried if it hadn't been Rosa—strong Rosa—who was giving in so.

It would have been easier if he felt able to help. As it was, he had to admit that there was very little he could do. He had tried, but she cut him out absolutely. He was the foreigner in this situation—he knew now what Rosa meant when she'd laughingly told him how strange she felt in his society. He knew now what it was like to be an exile.

For Rosa had banished him from her mind. She lay in an English bed in her London house, and yet she was not really there. She was elsewhere—she was in South Africa. Her accent, softened by her stay in England, had grown stronger again. She spoke seldom, but when she did, it was of the cruelty of Evelyn's isolated death, of the sufferings of the black South African population, of her guilt at the comfort of her own life, of the way she had turned her back on the struggle.

Rosa's mother, Julia, had been worse than useless. One would have assumed that she, too, would have been affected by the news, but she had greeted it with an equanimity that approached callousness. If Richard had not been so worried, he would have been able to excuse Julia for her inability to express her emotions.

The fact was that Rosa seemed on the brink of a nervous breakdown and that Richard was powerless to intervene. He hoped that her daughter would be able to get through to her.

Rosa knew that Martha was on her way. Rachel had told her as much in one of those gentle voices that people seemed to think was her due these days. They thought she needed comfort and looking after, too. They couldn't know how wrong they were. They didn't understand—none of them. They didn't know that Rosa was culpable. She was responsible for Evelyn's death.

Well, not for Evelyn's death, exactly, but more for the conditions under which she'd met it. Rosa had received scant information, but she knew that Evelyn had died alone in the Transkei. She'd been found lying on the ground outside her house by a young man—his name was Sipho something or other.

That was, thought Rosa, a symptom of her guilt. She couldn't remember the surname of the man who had found Evelyn—she, who had once prided herself on her ability to learn African names, who had worked so hard to respect their traditions.

There was so much she had forgotten. The nine years she had spent in London represented only a sixth of her lifetime, and yet they felt like forever. She had struggled to make her peace with England, and eventually she had succeeded. In so doing, she had rejected her past.

She had settled down with Richard—undoubtedly a good man, but a man to whom Rosa had no right. While Jacob festered in jail Rosa turned her back on him. There was no consolation in the knowledge that Jacob understood: that only helped to turn the screw of her guilt.

For she had prospered while others suffered. Evelyn had been herself exiled. Julia argued that Evelyn had chosen her home in the Transkei, but Rosa knew better. Evelyn had had no choice:

Hardly anybody in South Africa did. Evelyn had been a per-spicacious woman: She had seen into the future. She had known that the time would soon come when she, along with thousands of others considered extraneous to white South Africa, would be forcibly removed from any urban home. She had not stuck around to suffer this final indignity.

If that was choice, then choice was laughable.

And when Evelyn's time came, did she have the luxury of gathering her family around her? Could she pick up a telephone and call Lindiwe to her bedside? Could she summon Moses to hold her hand and be with her at her final gasp? Could she turn up the air conditioning to make herself more comfortable? Would she be offered a variety of exotic foods to tempt her waning appetite?

No—none of that. These things were Rosa's privilege, not Evelyn's. And what had Rosa done to deserve them? Nothing, absolutely nothing. She had been born white, and white she would remain. She had pretended otherwise—she had told her-self that one chose which side to be on and that one suffered accordingly. Now, she saw that it was all an illusion. Her Jacob was imprisoned—not dead. He would come out one day soon, inevitably scarred but essentially whole.

As for herself—she was weak. When the going got rough, she deserted the struggle. It had grown distant, theoretical, a good subject for after-dinner conversation. Oh, she excelled at it—no doubt about that. She was an accomplished raconteur: She made her new friends laugh at the world she'd once been part of. She'd trivialized their activities: It was on the excitement, the glamour, of those days that she'd dwelt—not on the real issues.

And worse than that, she'd been able to make people weep for the people she'd once considered fighters. She spoke of the hardship of their lives, of the way they were abused. Much in demand as a speaker, she knew well how to twist an audience's sympathy. She'd prided herself on her ability to combine a razor-sharp analysis with a true feel of what it was like to be black in South Africa. How many times had people come up to her and told her that she had opened their eyes—changed their lives, forced them into political involvement?

How dared she? She was a traitor. She deserved to suffer.

She heard the door of her bedroom open. She turned to the wall and shut her eyes.

Martha experienced a moment of acute shock. She had spent the journey persuading herself that Richard and Rachel were overreacting, that Rosa could not be so bad. And yet her first glimpse of her mother confirmed the seriousness of the situation.

Rosa looked tired, but it was more than that. She looked ill, but still it was more than that. She looked utterly defeated.

As she stood above her mother's bed, Martha felt a wave of sympathy. Without the makeup and the carefully combed hair, without the fashionable clothes, Rosa was without armor. The pain in her face was obvious.

Tentatively Martha put one hand on Rosa's hair. Rosa made no sign of acknowledgment. Steeling herself, Martha began to stroke the hair, noticing for the first time how gray it had become. Still Rosa did not move.

"Mummy," Martha whispered. "I'm sorry."

She got no response. She kissed Rosa's unreceptive cheek and tiptoed out of the room.

The hope died in Richard's face when Martha emerged. He could see immediately that she was as much at a loss as he. He shouldn't, he told himself, have expected anything else. He knew how badly affected Rosa was at her daughter's rejection of her: Since Martha had gone to college, she had rarely bothered to come home. In fact, now he remembered that the last time he had seen her was when she'd dropped by to pick up Rachel just before their annual visit to Jacob. She hadn't bothered to stop by on her way back: She had instead left Rachel to describe the event.

Martha sent Richard to the shops, and for the next few hours she busied herself tidying up. As far as she could see, Richard and Rachel had been existing off takeouts—in the fridge were plenty of formerly delectable morsels—curling smoked salmon, mushy avocado pears, a few limp shrimps—that Richard had bought in an effort to tempt Rosa, but none of the stuff from which a meal could be built.

When Rachel came home from school to find Martha working in the kitchen, she felt an enormous relief. She had been reluctant to call Martha. She had not believed that the tough, sullen woman her sister had become would have been of the slightest help. And yet Martha was more practical than all the grown-ups put together. She didn't glower like Julia; she didn't sit around like the wet rag Richard had become. And here she was, speaking in tones of ringing confidence about Rosa's imminent recovery. Their mother, she said, would be shocked at the deterioration in the house: They must set it to rights so that they would not feel ashamed when she got up.

Rachel hoped desperately that Martha's confidence was well founded. Rachel had been the first one to notice Rosa's deterioration. She had watched helplessly as her formerly incisive mother had gone to pieces, until finally she had taken to bed. Rosa's self-imposed exile in the bedroom was a relief: At least that way Rachel didn't have to constantly see the agony writ large upon her mother's face. But she couldn't deny it, not like Richard, who muttered a series of meaningless sentences about Rosa needing to rest. Rachel had known from the onset that the problem was more serious than that. She was scared: badly scared. She was only too happy to cling to the wake of Martha's stern assurance.

Martha, meanwhile, was conscious of the fact that she was putting on an act. Although she knew that Rachel was fooled by her appearance of control, she could not lie to herself. Inside she was desperately shaky. She felt so incredibly alone.

In the short time since she'd been home, she had visited Rosa three times. Each time Rosa failed to acknowledge her presence. Martha understood why Richard, who had already endured a full week of this, had grown so ineffectual. She understood why Rachel had assumed a permanently haunted expression. She knew why it was that Julia, by all reports, was useless. They had all grown used to dealing with a woman who was often difficult but always strong: no wonder, then, that they didn't know how to handle this tired, fragile Rosa.

Julia was the next to arrive. She'd heard from Rachel of Martha's visit, and she came, as she sternly said, to get a look at her errant grandchild after all this time. Martha, sensitive to every nuance, noticed how Julia's reserve showed through when she hugged her. Julia pretended to go with the embrace while keeping a part of herself distinct from it. It reminded Martha of the times she and Rosa had come into physical contact. In those days Martha had always assumed that the distance between them, even as they touched, was a result of her own resentment. For the first time she wondered about Rosa's part in it. Everything was odd: everything confused.

She tried to talk to her grandmother, and Julia reacted by denying that anything was wrong.

"Rosa is just overexhausted," Julia said. "I told her to slow down, but she wouldn't listen to me."

"But she won't even talk," Martha insisted. "This isn't fatigue—this is something different."

"Well?" Julia replied. "She'll get over it. Other people have."

And with that curious remark, Julia left: She had plenty to do, she said. Martha should visit more often.

Richard, who'd returned from shopping after diligently buying every item on Martha's list, did not seem surprised by Julia's abrupt departure.

"She can't stand Rosa's pain," he said forgivingly.

Martha smiled at him. This was another first. This was the first time she realized, truly realized, that Richard was part of her life. It was ironic, she thought, that at the point when her mother seemed to have cut him out of her consciousness, she could understand why Rosa had chosen Richard. True, he was unlike Jacob. Jacob's whole being could not be separated from his passionate involvement in political activity, while Richard was more of an onlooker—never a participant. And yet both men had the same gentle aura, the same love of Rosa that permeated their very being, the same offbeat sense of humor.

Richard, even at the depth of his unhappiness, managed to crack a few jokes. Martha observed how close the relationship was between her stepfather and Rachel. They spoke the same language, they understood each other without having to put everything into words. Martha felt very isolated.

Am I keeping by myself for Jacob? Martha thought vaguely. Because my mother wouldn't?

Silently she laughed the thought away from her. She forced herself to go back to the kitchen. She would not, she resolved, be beaten by Rosa's illness: She would think of something.

45

As she went back to scrubbing, polishing, and discarding, Martha racked her brains. All her newfound resources she pulled into the forefront of her thoughts: Her sessions in her consciousness-raising group came flooding back to her. The key was in the understanding, she thought. She must work out why it was that Rosa had been so badly affected before she could hope to help.

Abruptly she put down an encrusted frying pan. She knew what she had to do—or at least she hoped she knew. She left the kitchen and grabbed resolutely for her coat.

"You're not going already?" Richard asked.

"I've just got to visit somebody," she said. "Can I take your car?"

He handed her the keys. "You cook," she said.

When Martha arrived at the Arnolds' Swiss Cottage apartment and rang the bell, it took a long time for her grandfather, Harold, to answer the door. He arrived puffing at the exertion his steps cost him. Martha saw his obvious fragility, and she was afraid. She was depending on Harold: Only he, she thought, could provide the key to Rosa's desperation.

Harold beamed when he saw who it was. From him came no accusation of long absence, no intimation of neglect.

"Your grandmother's out," he said.

"That's okay," Martha said. "It's you I've come to see."

Harold smiled again, and his whole face lit up. Martha's heart filled with love. She seldom thought of Harold these days: She paid him an occasional duty call, and while she was with him she always savored his quiet presence. But once out the door she tended to dismiss his memory. He was a man of habitually few words, and the effort it cost him to breathe these days, combined with Julia's habit of talking over him, made him even more monosyllabic.

And yet he was a man, perhaps the only one, with whom Martha could feel completely comfortable. There was no threat in his manner—he felt no need to prove himself. He had retreated from the world—using his emphysema as an excuse to seldom venture out—but his eyes were as sharp as ever. She hoped his memory and his intellect were also unimpaired.

"Oh, Granddaddy," she said. It came out like a sob.

He took her in his arms—gently, oh so gently. She felt his hands, those hands that used to tickle hers, stroking at her hair. She luxuriated in his embrace—savoring this one retreat from the world. She wanted to stay there forever, protected from the harsh reality, enclosed in the warmth of an adult who expected nothing but love.

With an effort, she gently pried herself away from him. She looked him full in the face.

"I've come to talk to you about Mummy," she said.

He nodded once. "I was hoping somebody would," he replied.

She stayed for only half an hour. It seemed like an age: not because it was an effort, but because she savored every moment of that time. She was almost grateful to Rosa for making this visit a necessity. Her grandfather was in poor health—he would soon be dead. She lived this visit with him as if she were seeing him for the first time. She read his expression closely, she learned from him.

They talked almost exclusively of Rosa. They pondered Rosa's childhood, and what Evelyn had meant to her. For the first time Martha saw her mother through adult eyes—and through eyes that understood, even if they seldom expressed their wisdom.

She felt sad for her grandfather—not that he had not had a good life, he made it abundantly clear that he would do the same again given the opportunity—but because she realized that he had in many ways been trapped in his maleness. In Harold lurked oceans of warmth: He should have had more to do with his family—he understood them so well. And yet he had been the breadwinner: Julia's territory was the home. He had never really been allowed to display his gentle capabilities.

She tried to tell him what she was thinking, but he brushed

her clumsy efforts away. He was a secure man who had no need of praise.

And finally it was time to go: Harold was growing tired. Martha kissed her grandfather on the forehead.

"Thanks," she said. "I think I understand."

Harold nodded. "Thank you," he replied.

When Martha returned, she carried with her a newfound sense of determination. She resisted Richard's questioning look, she packed her sister off to do her homework, and then she climbed the stairs to the attic.

She knew what she was after, and yet she couldn't quite put her finger on it. She began to search again, routing through their common history for the second time in the last six months. And this time she did not discard the things that disturbed her.

She spent instead a good two hours in that place, peering at the remnants of the life they'd once all shared. It was hard going—frequently she found herself staring at an old teddy bear, one of Jacob's favorite ties, a part of her own childish diaries— all of which made her want to cry and to walk away from her exploration. She realized that she was like Rosa. The two of them had that in common—they had boxed the past away: They had pretended that they had no history.

She forced herself to continue. Finally she had covered it all, the letters and the photo albums. She had searched carefully, and it had confirmed her suspicion: There was not a single picture of Evelyn, not one. She nodded to herself.

"Does Rosa talk about *any*thing?" Martha asked casually, after the three of them finished the meal Richard had prepared. "I haven't managed to get a word out of her."

Richard stared at her. He didn't like the way Martha was behaving. She'd come downstairs with a look akin to triumph on her face. Perhaps she was enjoying her mother's agony. It was wrong to have brought her here.

"Well, does she?" Martha asked.

Rachel wrinkled her nose. "She talks about the old days," she said hesitantly. "And about how bad things are for Africans. She's obsessed by that. She says she's as guilty as every other free white South African."

Martha nodded. She shoved her chair away from the table and got up. "I'll go see her again," she said.

Richard opened his mouth, and then closed it again. He watched silently as Martha walked from the room.

Rosa talked about South Africa. She talked without a break, without meaning and without emotion. She flung in statistics, anecdotes, details of laws. She spoke of the great campaigns: of Defiance and the Freedom Charter, of the founding of MK and of the Sabotage Campaign. She spoke of individuals and of movements as if they were one. She spoke about it all: The only thing she left out was her own part in it.

Martha despaired of stemming her mother's flow of desperate verbiage. But finally there was a pause while Rosa took a sip of water. Martha jumped into the silence.

"Did you know that there isn't a single picture of Evelyn anywhere?" she asked.

"What difference does that make?" Rosa's face was already losing its color.

"I went to see Harold today," Martha continued. "We talked about you."

Rosa nodded her head. Well, thought Martha, that at least was progress. At least Rosa hadn't started up again, expelling her grief in a flood of meaningless sentences.

"We talked about the time after you were born," Martha said. "Did you know that Julia suffered a terrible depression after it?"

"So what?"

"It sounds like a postpartum depression," Martha said conversationally. "You know, they're doing a lot of research on it these days. They say it can be very severe."

Rosa glared at her daughter. "You and your research," she muttered. "You young women think you know it all." She stopped herself abruptly. That hadn't been her speaking, had it? It sounded just like Julia.

"And do you know who looked after you at that time?" Martha asked. She skipped a beat. "Evelyn did."

"I let her down when she was old." Rosa said the words numbly. "I always let her—"

"Oh, Mummy, you didn't. Can't you see why you're so upset?" Martha interrupted. She stood up and found that she was shouting: "It's not because you betrayed Evelyn! You didn't let her down. You couldn't have done anything else."

"I had a choice," Rosa said. "Evelyn didn't. I should have stayed."

"You had two children," Martha replied. "You did what you thought was best."

"I deserted Jacob."

Martha refused to allow herself to be sidetracked. Besides, this subject was too close to the bone. "Evelyn was . . ." she began.

"My mother's employee," Rosa said.

Martha raised one hand. "She was your mother—your real mother, your family. Her son, Moses, was more like your brother than Nicholas. Evelyn was the mother you never really had. No wonder you're so sad."

Rosa sat up. "What do you know?" she asked. "Evelyn couldn't have been my mother. She was black."

"I mean that she was the one who nurtured you." Martha paused to allow time for her words to sink in. "And yet you have no picture of her," she concluded.

Rosa's head drooped. "She'd never let me take one. Why was that?"

"Maybe she thought there was no need," Martha suggested. "Or maybe she was just vain and thought she took a terrible picture."

"Evelyn wasn't vain," Rosa muttered.

"Oh, Mummy," Martha pleaded. "Evelyn wasn't a god. She could have been vain—that wouldn't have made her a lesser person. She was a woman, for godsake—not a heroic representative of the African race."

Martha watched as Rosa's eyes clouded over. She had been so close, she thought: She felt as if she had almost got through. And now Rosa was showing signs of retreating again.

Martha wanted to shake her mother. She wanted to throw the bedclothes off, to fling open the windows and let life come back into the room. She got up, instead, and turned to go.

Rosa's voice drew her back.

"Evelyn liked nice clothes," Rosa said softly. "We used to thumb through magazines together, choosing our favorites. She taught me how to dress."

Martha turned back to her mother.

"She was so annoying," Rosa was musing now. "She loved me, I know she loved me, but she refused to put it into words.

She told you once, but why did she never tell me? Why?"

"Perhaps she thought there was no need," Martha said softly, "or perhaps it was just too painful."

And then the dam of Rosa's grief broke. She tensed herself up to prevent the tears from coming, but they were too strong for her. They flooded out, pouring down her cheeks, soaking her pillow, coming first softly and then in huge, racking sobs. She cried like an animal, like a child, like a young baby. She cried for Evelyn and for herself.

The door to the bedroom opened, and Richard came running in. He made a move toward the bed, but Martha, with a strength she would not have believed she possessed, held him back.

"Let her cry," she pleaded. "She needs to. She hasn't cried since Daddy was caught."

When Martha left for Bristol ten days later, Rosa was almost her old self again. Martha's relief at her mother's recovery was tinged with discomfort. Rosa no longer needed her, and although she told herself that this was good, her feelings of exclusion from the family returned with a vengeance.

It was as if the family of three had closed ranks: erecting again the walls to keep her out. Martha returned to Bristol nursing an aching suspicion that nothing of substance had changed.

Rosa didn't show Richard Jacob's latest letter. She had never really done so in the past, but Rachel would tell him what was in it, or he'd overhear Rosa reading it to Martha on the phone. She didn't mind him knowing the contents, she just wouldn't let him read it. They lived together with the memory of Jacob, but Richard was never allowed to get in close.

"What are you doing this evening?" Rosa asked.

Richard's eyes were watchful. "Nothing."

"Let's go out and eat," she suggested. "Just the two of us."

He wanted to say no. "That would be nice," was what came out.

Rosa suggested somewhere fancy, but Richard preferred the local trattoria. He could not be bothered with dressing up, with all the superfluous details that expensive restaraunts demanded from their clientele. He wanted to go somewhere comfortable: someplace to which he'd never have to return.

Throughout the meal he told himself that he was imagining things. Rosa was relaxed and natural, playful, even. It was just like the old days—the real old days in Swaziland. They almost flirted, this couple who knew each other so intimately, they built an air of expectation between them.

Richard pondered their time together as he forked in food he could not taste. They had both matured, he thought; they had changed together. They had lived through the upheavals of the late sixties: They were heading for a time that seemed more dismal. They had shared so much. Whatever happens, Richard thought, I will never be the same.

And then it was time to go home.

They ignored Rachel when they got in. They went upstairs to bed without throwing her more than a cursory good night. Everything moved as if in slow motion for Richard. He took in this place he had considered a home, and he noticed how small an impact he had made on it. It was Rosa's personality that pervaded the bedroom. Richard's money had made it more comfortable, but Rosa's eye had made it unique.

They made love slowly. They savored the touch, the taste, the smell, of each other's skin. There was no awkwardness between them, but neither was there any boredom. It felt, thought Richard, like rediscovering some old, familiar treasure. They were in constant motion, but it was as if they were always at rest. There was passion but no abrasiveness, lust but no compulsion.

They lay together for a long time after they had finished. Only when he felt Rosa stirring did Richard speak.

He put a finger gently over her lips. "I know," he said. He looked straight into her eyes. "I've always known," he continued. "I think I knew it first when I went to plead for you."

He saw Rosa frown. "I went to the police," he explained, "after they picked Jacob up. It was a disaster. The colonel turned the session into an interrogation. I didn't tell him anything—I had nothing to tell—but I knew then."

"I don't understand," Rosa said.

"I realized then that your world was different from mine," he continued. "I realized that you had more in common with Moses' torturers than with me."

"How can you say that?" Rosa's eyes expressed her pain.

"Don't take offense," he said gently. "I don't mean it that way. I mean that I was not brought up like you. However hard

I try, I still think that the rules I was taught are the only rules. But it's not true in South Africa. You all played a deadly game, and you played for keeps. I could never really join in. I've tried to pretend that things would change, but I've always known how it would end."

There was a long, drawn-out silence. Then Rosa reached out and put her hand in his. "I'm sorry," she said.

"I'm not," he replied, and he found that he was crying. "At least I had you—if only for a short time."

46

South Africa: 1976

JACOB CAUGHT HIMSELF WONDERING WHY HE HAD NEVER TRIED yoga. He smiled at the thought: What a thing to ask on this, his last day in Pretoria Central! It was a way, he thought, of distracting himself. He had to contain his excitement, because this wasn't his last day in jail: His sentence was for three days more. But nevertheless he knew that they would soon move him. They always transferred prisoners elsewhere before releasing them: It was part of their system, and nothing, short of revolution, would ever rock that.

The transfer, although disruptive, Jacob thought, was in some ways a mercy. He didn't know how much longer he could have spent with his comrades, repressing his feelings of jubilation so that they would not grow ever more depressed.

Not that they weren't pleased for him. On the contrary, every time one of their number had walked out of his cell door for the last time, a feeling of victory suffused the political section. They had survived, they were surviving, some of them had finally served their time.

But such a victory was always tinged with sadness. After all, they were one big family, enduring their incarceration with a combination of stoicism and love for each other. The clanging of the prison gates signaled a readjustment—a beginning and an end—the time when one of them would be swallowed up in the world outside, would become a distant memory, one of the shadowy free.

So Jacob had tried to keep up an exterior front of calm while, inside, he was boiling over with excitement: Yoga would have helped, he thought, without it he could concentrate on nothing. He began to pace his cell. He thought he knew it intimately, every last bit of it, but suddenly he stopped when he saw a crack in the wall, deep in the corner, that he hadn't catalogued before. He knelt down.

"Not trying to escape now are you, Swiece?"

Jacob jumped. He hadn't heard the door open: He hadn't expected them so soon. But it wasn't that exactly that surprised him: It was the fact that, if his ears were not deceiving him, van der Merwe had just cracked a joke!

It was hard to believe. Van der Merwe had done nothing, during the last twelve years, to improve his reputation. Never once (and van der Merwe, damn him, had no ambitions to leave Pretoria) had he revealed a single aspect of himself that had not proved thoroughly disasteful.

And now, the man joked and smiled! Jacob breathed in hard: Something, he thought, had gone wrong. Van der Merwe had come to tell him that they'd found another way to keep him locked up.

"Ready then?" van der Merwe asked. He stood to one side to let Jacob through.

Outside the prison gates Jacob stood still as he waited to board the car. He was handcuffed, but he did not mind. He was too busy gazing up at the sky—at a huge expanse of blue unrestrained by walls or barbed wire. He felt strangely nervous at the sight of so much space—he'd better take it easy in his first days, he told himself.

Van der Merwe was still beside him and still jovial. Jacob's irritation at his jailer's presence was mitigated somewhat by his growing realization that in his cell his ears had not deceived him. Van der Merwe had indeed cracked a joke—since then, he'd made a feeble attempt to crack three more.

What could it possibly mean? Jacob thought about it. His last month here had seemed unending—longer, in fact, than all the preceeding eleven years—and he had spent them trying to detach himself from the prison routine. Now, he pondered the rumors that he'd only distantly registered. He had not taken it very seriously—soon he would be able to buy newspapers, he had no need to take part in that grubbing around for information that was a major part of the prisoners' daily routine.

He remembered that the recent speculation began after an unprecedented news clampdown. Letters, study books, periodicals suddenly failed to materialize. Nothing got through, no explanation, no justification—just silence. The politicals were at a loss: Even the common-law prisoners, who had better access to the news, were in the dark. Something was happening out there was all they could surmise: something big that frightened the authorities.

Van der Merwe thrust his hand toward Jacob. "No hard feelings." It was almost a question.

Jacob looked the man straight in the eye. He resented that, even at the last, van der Merwe claimed his attention. "You're a bully, Mr. van der Merwe," Jacob said.

Van der Merwe did not take offense. "*Ja*," he conceded. "I do my job well." He paused, and looked down at his feet. "But, hell, we are of the same race," he suddenly appealed. "Us civilizeds have to stick together."

Jacob's wonderment increased. He couldn't believe that van der Merwe was trying to catalog himself in the same department as Jacob. Something was definitely wrong. The man was scared, really scared. It must be big, what had happened outside: big enough to penetrate even van der Merwe's rhinoceros skin.

Well, perhaps Jacob could have his revenge. "When I see men like you," he replied, "I regret being born white."

The car doors opened. Van der Merwe shoved him viciously inside. Jacob smiled to himself.

They drove him—two policeman he'd never seen before—to Johannesburg. These men were different from the warders: They were not hardened by years of prison, and anyway, in their eyes, Jacob had crossed the line. He was no longer a number—he was a man, and they, in the boredom of the journey, tried to fill him in on all the latest developments. Or the developments as they saw them: They talked exclusively of sport, of cars, and of money.

Jacob found their conversation tedious. He nodded as he pretended to partake of it, but his mind was miles away. He devoured the scenery, he breathed in fresh air through the crack in the window. I'm free, he kept saying to himself, I'm free.

But of course he was not free. They delivered him to the Fort, and their attitude changed. In the car they had been in no-man's-land. Once having driven through the gates, they were back in the system. They looked at him anew through surprised eyes. "Why the *blerry* hell were we talking to a commie?" they seemed to be saying as they issued instructions that he should be held in solitary until his release.

But again came the feeling that something strange was happening.

For the Fort was in chaos. Policemen ran everywhere, shouting in irritation at each other. Jacob was handed to first one and then another. They didn't know what to do with him. They had no time, they said. In the end they just flung him into an interview room.

To Jacob's surprise, the room was not empty. It already contained three young men—three young black men. They glanced at him sullenly when he entered. One, a man who was lying on the floor, shied away, pulling himself together only after he'd noticed Jacob's telltale prison garb.

There was silence in the room. Jacob sat down on the floor and looked at the man opposite him. He had been badly beaten, that much was obvious: His right eye was almost completely closed, a line of dried blood trickled from his mouth. He groaned and coughed—fresh blood appeared.

Jacob leaned toward him. "Have you had any medical attention?" he asked.

The man grimaced. He looked as if he were making a feeble attempt to smile.

"I'm a doctor," Jacob said. "I could take a look."

Before he could move, one of the other youths intervened. He stood up and blocked Jacob's access to the one on the floor. "Leave him alone, man," he said. "We look after our own."

Just then the door opened. A policeman's head appeared. "Jeesus Christ, what is going on in here?" he said. The head withdrew. "Who's responsible for this?" they heard him roaring. "Who put that commie in with *kaffirs*?"

When the door was slammed shut, Jacob saw the youth look first at each other and then back at him. The atmosphere in the room was transformed, lightened in an instant. The two healthy youths looked at him with new and eager eyes.

"Are you a political?" one asked.

"Been to the Island?" said the other.

"Do you know Mandela? What's he like?"

They shot their questions out helter-skelter, one after the

other. Jacob had much to ask of them, but no space in which to do it because they couldn't talk fast enough. They asked questions born from considerable excitement and not a little naïveté.

They knew so much and yet so little. They talked of the events twelve years earlier as if they were part of ancient history. When Jacob started to speak, he found that everything he said just increased their queries. They knew little of the history that, for him, was still so vibrant. The Defiance Campaign, the Freedom Charter, the Treason Trial, these were all just words to them.

He did not judge them for their ignorance, because he saw that they were militants, too—young, admittedly, but firm. They were going, they said, to Robben Island: They were three of many; they were proud.

And then, before Jacob could get more from them, the door was flung open. Two hefty policemen shot in. They grabbed Jacob, and swearing viciously, they hustled him out.

He spent the next two nights in solitary, in a cell that was achingly familiar. It was completely bare except for one thin mattress on the floor and one pot in the corner. It was just like Pretoria's jails when Jacob first arrived—before protests from sympathizers had improved conditions marginally. Jacob did not really mind. It wasn't the conditions, it was the slow passage of time, that bothered him. Each second was an hour, each minute a month, each hour an eternity.

And then finally the two nights were over, and the waiting, too. Jacob came awake, his heart pounding. He could hardly bear it, he thought. He could not bear it. He did not want to go—he was scared, he was elated, he could wait no more.

Not that it was up to him: He was still in their hands, and they would decide on the timing. They were merciful, thank God.

They took him, early in the morning, to the commander's office. They read him his banning orders. He did not take them in.

"Any complaints?" asked the commander.

Jacob smiled. Complaints! He had ten for every day he had spent in jail. He could have written a thesis on them. He shook his head. He would not waste even one fraction of his life ahead on useless words.

They made him change his clothes. He wanted to wear prison dress, but that, they said, was against the regulations. They gave him clothes that they said had been brought in for him. He thought that they were having a final joke at his expense: The clothes were ridiculous, flared trousers in a garish red, a frilly white shirt, some shoes ridiculously pointed.

Jacob did not comment. He put them on silently. And then he was ready to go, and the first of the doors was opened. He did not look behind him. He had no need to remember what it was like to be in jail: It was imprinted on his brain forever.

As he walked through the gates, Jacob concentrated on his feet, savoring each step. He'd fantasized this occasion so many times that he almost felt that it had already happened. He was sure somebody would meet him. It wouldn't be Rosa—she would not be allowed in the country, and he'd instructed her to keep the children away. He wanted to see them only when he'd shaken off the dusty remnants of his incarceration.

He'd imagined stepping into a car and driving to Zoo Lake. He would ask, he'd promised himself, to walk alone. To breathe in the scent of a thousand flowers, to swing his arms unrestrained by high walls, to relish his freedom—that was what he wanted. He wanted to do all that, alone.

But it was not to be. For Jacob became conscious of a barrage of noise. He looked up and blinked. Ahead of him, just outside the gates, were scores of people—laughing, shouting, calling people, dressed in garments as weird as his.

He glanced back hurriedly to check what was happening behind him, but there was nobody there. These people had come to meet him. They waved at him, they echoed his name over and over again. He could hardly take it in: their colors clashed, their shouts echoed and fought for prominence, they were a crowd together, and yet each was an individual claiming his attention.

Jacob panicked. He looked back longingly toward the safety of the prison. But the guard nudged him forward.

Jacob took a deep breath. He walked as if in a dream. And then finally he was able to focus. The crowd that at first seemed threatening became a welcoming committee. In the forefront was the familiar face of Martin Buckmann. Martin was jumping up and down like a youngster, waving his arms to attract Jacob's attention.

Jacob came abruptly to his senses. He knew what to do. He stopped. He raised a clenched fist into the air. "*Amandla!*" he shouted.

"*Ngwethu!*" they roared back.

And then he was among them. They surrounded him, clapping him on the back, struggling to shake his hand, laughing, crying, singing. They lifted him bodily into the air. He sat on two hefty shoulders as hands were thrust up to grab his. He smiled: His face was wet with tears.

Eventually Martin managed to detach Jacob from the crowd and escort him to a car. At last they were off—the crowd running fast behind them.

As the crowd peeled off, a peace descended on the car. The two men spoke little. They were using the journey to grow reaccustomed to each other. Both thought how the other had aged: Neither felt the need to put the thought into words. They drove in silent companionship—the one staring wonderingly out the window, the other smiling as he negotiated the busy streets.

"Your brother-in-law, Nicholas, sent his apologies," Martin finally said. "He couldn't make it—business reasons."

"Terror, more likely," Jacob answered. He didn't mind. He felt so out of touch. This freedom he had longed for was a more complicated thing than he had imagined—even without Nicholas' embarrassed presence.

For twelve long years he had been immersed in an unchanging routine. He had studied, talked, grabbed at every scrap of news from the outside. And yet suddenly he felt as if the world had been turned on its head. He had expected a few friends at the gate: not a militant crowd. The blur of the last three days jumbled inside of him: van der Merwe's odd behavior, the three young men in the room, the chaos in the Fort—what did it all mean? He was out, but he no longer knew the rules: It was a strange place to which he had emerged.

He had also to wrestle with his physical surroundings. Everything looked so familiar and yet so strange. He recognized Jo'burg, but it had been transformed. The center bustled with huge, modern buildings; traffic moved faster than he remembered; goods glittered from behind the plate glass of myriad shops.

The two sensations—the wonder at the outward changes, the questioning of the crowd—mixed together and left him speechless. Calm down, he kept telling himself, calm down.

And then, just as they were nearly at Martin's house, they were forced to come to a halt. A makeshift roadblock stood in their path. Jacob forgot his own injunctions: An icy fear choked at him—they weren't going to take him back, they couldn't, could they?

Martin did not appear to notice Jacob's terror, and he certainly wasn't afraid. He took the whole thing in his stride. He waited patiently, he handed over documents without demur, he smiled when the policeman waved them on, and he drove off slowly.

"They're everywhere," he explained. "On all the roads that lead to the townships."

"What the hell's going on?" Jacob asked.

His companion looked surprised—"Haven't you heard?"—and then embarrassed. "No, of course you haven't. Soweto's exploded."

Soweto exploded on June 16, 1976. That day a crowd of school-children took to the streets, protesting the introduction of Af-rikaans in their schools. To strangers, this might seem odd—such passion aroused over mere language, when the children were already taught in tongues that were not their own. And yet it had a deep significance. Afrikaans was the symbol of their oppression, the Nats' mother tongue: the signal of another kind of dominance.

Well, the children would not accept it. They marched to share with the world their refusal to submit.

The authorities responded just as they had once responded to the children's parents. They shot them in cold blood: They killed first thirteen-year-old Hector Peterson, and then more than a hundred others. They fired at random, thinking that bullets would surely stop the children.

But the children did not stop. They ran from the bullets, and then they regrouped. They marched again, in their hundreds, in their thousands, all over South Africa. No matter how many guns were fired at them, they would not give up. They kept on coming. They were cannon fodder, but they were more than that—much more. They were the voice of South Africa's future: a voice that burst out on June 16, 1976.

"And all this," Martin said, as he came to the end of his account, "after years of inaction. We couldn't have believed it was possible. This country has been a desert while you've been in prison. We thought it was over."

Jacob fingered the petals of the rose in front of him. They were sitting in Martin's garden—Jacob had not wanted to be indoors. It felt so strange—not only to be out by choice, but also to be out and at peace when, by all accounts, an insurrection was rocking the whole of the country.

Throughout his stay in prison Jacob had never given up hope. And yet he had matured. He never condemned the actions of his young self, his former self, for partaking in a campaign that ended in personal imprisonment and political defeat, but he pondered their past strategy.

They had been right in their analysis—of this he was positive. They had reached the end of a line in 1960—their conclusions had been wholly correct. The government was not going to change: Only force might make it move.

But they had underestimated the severity of the government's reaction and overestimated their own strength. They had been defeated. The movement was splintered into a thousand isolated pieces. This is what Jacob and his fellow prisoners had come to realize; this was the one hard reality that all the politicals had been forced to accept.

And now Martin was telling him that there was another reality. A new generation had been born: a generation that was every bit as militant as they had once been—and more so, perhaps. A generation that did not carry the baggage of former ANC members. A generation that, instead of dwelling on history, was making it.

"What will you do?" Martin's voice broke through Jacob's wonderment.

"Leave, I suppose."

"They'll never let you back, you know," Martin said.

"They won't let me do anything here. Outside, I may be of use. And there's Rosa . . ." His voice lowered.

Martin looked embarrassed. "She telegraphed to say she'd be in Dar," he gushed. "You never know, miracles can happen."

Jacob smiled. "By the sounds of it, they have already," he said. The smile faded. "How people must be suffering."

Jacob was right: They were suffering—or at least some of them were. For a new divide had opened up inside South Africa. Not a divide between black and white, but an age divide.

The older generation still remembered the fate that greeted those who dared to raise their voices against the government. They remembered all too clearly the names and the faces of those who had not survived. Their ranks had been diminished:

Their leaders were growing old in jail.

But now it was their children who had taken up the banner of resistance. Their children who had never tasted, firsthand, the bitterness of defeat. Their children who were still relatively un-tutored in the ways of the armed forces: who went out into the streets, unarmed, with only their anger, their courage, and their placards to accompany them.

Their parents watched, and they grew afraid.

On June 16 Lindiwe had been in the center of Jo'burg buying up medical supplies. She had timed her journey badly: Stretching the center's limited resources always took longer than she ex-pected. She cursed when she found herself traveling back to Soweto along with the thousands of men and women who spent their days fueling the white city.

To outsiders, Soweto was a jungle—a place without apparent rules. And yet its inhabitants understood well the way the town-ship worked. There was a method for everything—even in the way the trains disgorged their living cargo.

The technique of getting onto the platform at Soweto's In-hlazane Station varied subtly according to one's place in the train. If you were near the doors, you'd have to move fast in order to escape the crush behind. If you were in the middle, you stood poised for motion, bracing yourself backward, so when the first layer disembarked you didn't fall imediately on top of them. And if, finally, you were at the back, then all you could do was wait. No matter how impatient you were—no matter how impossible a route of escape seemed—you had to trust that soon you, too, would be on your way home.

But on June 16 the system was turned on its head.

Lindiwe was at the center of the crush: She braced herself against the inevitable release of pressure when the doors opened. She was thinking of what she'd achieved and where she'd failed. Money didn't stretch as far as it used to: She hadn't been able to afford some of the "must get" items on her list. There was some consolation, though, she thought, in the stack of leaflets that nestled at the bottom of a box of disinfectant.

While she was thinking all this, the doors opened—she'd reg-istered the sound. And yet, she suddenly realized, the train was still full.

"Get a move on!" shouted someone at the back.

"What's the hurry?" came a riposte. "Is your woman warming herself rather than the dinner?"

Nobody laughed: Everybody sensed it now, this whiff of something strange. People glanced about as they steadied themselves for the unknown. Those in the front walked out slowly—their fatigue, their anxiety to slough off the memory of dreary work, forgotten in their anticipation.

When Lindiwe's time came to disembark she saw immediately what it was that had caused the first group of passengers to falter. For Inhlazane Station was occupied. Hundreds of police lined its limits. They said nothing: They gave no explanation. They stood, their guns at the ready.

In South Africa, if one is black, one learns quickly: One has to. The crowd picked up the measure of this strange occurrence. There were police in the stations—well, there must be a reason. They gathered together on the platforms to uncover the events that had unfolded during their daylong absence.

And just as Africans had learned a way of surviving their daily existence, so did the police have their own methods of operating. Admittedly, their way was less subtle. They created a curious crowd or they stumbled upon one: It made no difference. Their solution was identical. They would disperse it—and they would do so by using the maximum force at their disposal.

As individuals in the crowd questioned, discussed, gesticulated, the police began to move. Their batons held aloft, they marched in formation into the center of the crowd. And their weapons preceded them: They threw tear gas into the midst of the commuters, They hit out at random.

Within minutes, the station was a battleground. People ran this way and that—alternatively joining the fray or attempting to escape it, throwing stones, ducking: Chaos reigned.

Lindiwe Bopape eventually managed to get out unharmed. She made her way through a Soweto in which rumors abounded: The shebeens had been raided, and the queens had fought back, said one: A bomb had exploded in the White City Jabavu offices, killing the superintendent, went another; whites were being stoned and buses overturned, said a third. Somewhere among these disparate stories, Lindiwe knew, lurked one truth that could link them all together.

She did not stop to find it out. She acted as if she were driven, driven by the need to go home. She wanted to touch base, she realized, to ground herself. Only then would she investigate fully.

The streets were uncannily quiet after the maelstrom in the station. People scurried into their houses, anxious looks on their faces. Groups gathered in corners only to disperse at the sound of an encroaching footstep. Police vans stood on every street: Out of them stared angry red faces.

The students had vanished. Not only the ones who were lying on mortuary slabs, or the ones who'd been bundled in their hundreds into Jo'burg's jails, but also the others—the able-bodied and the free. They had taken off into the depth of darkness, using a network of communications that sprang up almost instantly.

When Lindiwe got home, the house was in complete darkness. She felt her way to the table and lit the lamp that was always kept there. She shivered when it flared into light. Suddenly she felt cold. Her children, who should have long ago come home, were absent. They had not returned since morning, she saw. The meat was where she had left it: The mealie-meal lay unmixed by the stove.

"Aiyee, what has become of them?" said a voice behind her. Lindiwe turned. She saw one of her neighbors was standing by the door, wringing her hands together.

"What's happened?" Lindiwe asked.

The woman groaned. "They massacred our children," she said. She began to wail. "Where are my babies?" she cried.

"What's happened?" Lindiwe asked again.

"Our children," said the women. "They marched in the streets, and the police opened fire on them. Nobody knows how many have been harmed, nobody knows how many arrested. They are running all over the township, the police and the children as well. And where are mine? Can you find mine?"

Lindiwe had her own children—thirteen-year-old Nathaniel, and her Bertha, who was a mere eleven years—she felt her own terrible fear. But even as her stomach turned over in a kind of awful anticipation, her brain kept working. This was no time for empty conjecture—this was the time for action.

"I will go and try," she said. "You stay here, in case they should return. Let's keep in touch."

She went straight to the community center. If the few reports she'd heard were even half-correct, there would be many people in need that night. The children were inexperienced, but they were far from stupid—they would know better than to go to a hospital, and thus deliver themselves into the arms of the waiting police.

The place was a shambles. Anxious mothers jostled with bustling nurses, calling out the names of their missing children, crying for help, asking endless questions about what had happened, as if to know would be to make it all right. And they were not the only source of the noise, for queues of wounded stretched out the door.

Lindiwe registered her presence with the other workers and then worked her way down the lines, picking out the most severely wounded for preferential treatment. She thought little as she did so. To think would be to concentrate on the fate of her own children, and to do that would be unbearable. She worked methodically, quickly, unfeelingly. She did the job for which she had been trained.

And then she felt a small presence beside her. She looked up, and the first weight lifted from her heart. Nathaniel was standing there a few paces off, his face grubby but unharmed. Lindiwe deftly tied the last of the bandage she'd been working on and then stepped aside.

She grabbed Nathaniel in her arms. "Are you all right?" she asked.

He nodded. "And your sister?"

"We lost her," Nathaniel said in a low voice. "I tried to keep an eye on her, but you don't know what it was like. It was hell. I couldn't do it, I couldn't. I turned round, and she was gone."

Lindiwe's heart sank. "It's not your fault," she said.

"Daddy is looking for Bertha," Nathaniel continued. He was delivering his message with determination, glancing around as if any minute he would be snatched up and vanish. He looked older, thought Lindiwe, older and yet not subdued.

She smiled. "Johannes will find Bertha," she said with a conviction that she did not feel. "Go home now and rest."

Nathaniel shook his head. "I can't," he said. "There is too much to do. I must go to a meeting." He moved away from her, as if he feared that she would somehow dissuade him from his path.

Lindiwe wanted to: She wanted to grab at him, to shout, to plead, to force him into safety. She did none of that. She had known always that this time would come—even through the long, dark years, she had known it. She had dreaded its coming at the same time as she had embraced it. But never had she dreamed that it would be her children in the forefront.

Now, she knew that it could have been no other way. Only the children were brave enough, angry enough, foolhardy enough. They, the thirteen-year-olds, untutored kids, boys in short trousers, had shown the way: Lindiwe only hoped that their parents would have the courage to follow.

47

BERTHA CROUCHED DOWN LOW IN THE BUS SHELTER. SHE DID NOT know what else to do. She had been driven toward it, driven by the weight of a fleeing crowd. She had not meant to settle there, she had just stopped to draw a breath. But then everything changed.

One minute she was part of a panic, she was running from the sound of gunfire and the sight of blood, from her own terrified reactions. And then, within seconds of arriving at the shelter, she found herself completely alone. She had no idea where the others had gone: It was a complete mystery to her. They had vanished into a night that descended without warning. She whimpered softly as she thought about the day's events.

When she'd woken that morning, everything had seemed so normal. The sun was in its familiar position in the sky; her brother was still asleep beside her; her father had long since left; her mother was in the kitchen. She'd roused Nathaniel and got herself ready for school. She had not taken in the details as she went through the performance of those tasks that were habitual: brushing her teeth, knotting her school tie, packing herself something for lunch in case she was delayed. There was no reason to notice it all: It had been a day like any other.

She stopped to gossip on the way to school, and had consequently arrived a few minutes late for assembly. And that was the first indication that something different was happening—even though she had taken no notice of it at the time. Normally their headmaster rewarded those who slipped into the back rows with a fierce glare. But on this morning Mr. Morrison hardly spared Bertha a sideward glance. He was preoccupied by other, more serious matters.

The prayers had been as usual. Bertha sang lustily along with the rest of the assembled company. Her mother disapproved of the school's firm Christian bias, but Bertha never could quite banish the joy she felt when their voices were raised in the singing of hymns. This day was no exception: By the time they were ordered to sit, a warm glow of companionship flowed from within her.

Mr. Morrison's speech did little to chase the glow away. He lectured them in his loud voice, but that was not in itself unusual. Bertha hardly listened to the content. It was something about Afrikaans—Nathaniel, she remembered, had also been talking of the language recently—but other than that, it made no sense to her. She switched off as he warned against the danger of outside agitators, his injunctions to calm and orderly behavior had a familiar, and therefore comforting, ring.

And then her lessons began as she expected them to. Half an hour of arithmetic followed history and English, and then they had a short break. It was all as normal, completely as normal. It was around eleven o'clock that things changed. The first thing Bertha noticed was a distant noise. It was a noise without form— an intriguing noise. She looked up from her exercise book: So, she noticed, did her classmates.

Their teacher tried to distract them. "Remember what Mr. Morrison said," she advised. "Back to your books."

But the noise grew louder, and it structured itself. At first the chants were inaudible jumbles of sound, a bit like the flurry of a thousand different conversations on the commuter trains. But as the procession came closer, Bertha could hear slogans that had long been familiar to her.

"One Anzania, one nation," they shouted. "*Amandla. In-kululeko ngoku.*"

The chants got louder before fading away. But they did not disappear entirely. They were taken up by others in another part of the street. The chanting voices rose to the sky, they changed with time.

"Down with Bantu education," came fresh shouts. "To hell with Afrikaans." Whistles and calls of agreement greeted this. "To hell with Afrikaans!" they yelled.

Bertha could no longer contain her excitement. She ran to the window, barely conscious that her classmates were doing the same. Their teacher flapped uselessly around them, shouting empty injunctions, but she, too, was drawn to watch by the force of her own curiosity.

The sight that greeted them was truly amazing. For in the street strode hundreds—no, thousands, they stretched into the distance—of schoolchildren. They marched resolutely, shouting, their fists in the air, their placards proudly held above them. Rank upon rank passed the classroom window, and still there were more. Wave upon wave turned the corner, and still there were more. Slogan upon slogan drifted upwards, and still there were more.

Bertha grabbed excitedly at the girl beside her. "Look," she shouted, "there's Nathaniel! There's my brother."

And in a flash she was out the door, followed, she guessed, by almost half her class, preceded by a good quarter of the school's other pupils. She caught up with Nathaniel, skipping and jumping, weaving her way through the crowd. He smiled in delight when he saw her. He grabbed hold of her hand.

"Stick close to me," he ordered.

There was no time for conversation or explanation. Brother and sister were swept forward by the tide of children, resolute in their determination to register their protest. It kept swelling in numbers. As the marchers passed schools, hundreds of children ran out to join them. They were part of a huge wave, a wave that walked ever forward. Walked forward, that is, until suddenly it came to a halt. It could move no further, the massed ranks in front prevented it.

Bertha and Nathaniel were in the middle of the street. They were surrounded by their fellows. They wanted to press on. But their way was blocked.

"*Amandla!*" shouted a lone voice. Whispers came back in reply. The police, it was said, were blocking the way.

Bertha glanced around her for reassurance. The crowd shifted on its feet, but there was no panic. This was a celebration, after all—a celebration of protest. If they were turned back now, they would still have won. They would have demonstrated their determination to stick together.

Bertha heard distorted instructions, first in Afrikaans and then in Zulu, ordering them to disperse. She glanced questioningly at Nathaniel. How could they turn back? The ones bringing up the rear had not heard the police orders: They were pushing, jostling at the front of the march.

"Stick by me," Nathaniel repeated.

The crowd was still a jovial one. It began to sing.

"*Asikhathali noma bes'bopha*," they sang, "*izimisel inkulu-leko*"—"We don't give a damn, even if imprisoned, for freedom's our ultimate goal."

Bertha joined in. She was reassured. Her heart soared—not as it had at assembly, at the purity of the sound, but because of the passion and the joy with which the song was sung. The chorus swelled up—over and over again, spreading down the lines of children.

And then it happened. The darkness descended.

No, thought Bertha, as she crouched in the shelter, that wasn't right, that wasn't how it happened. Something else preceded the end of the world: something so ominous that she could not bear to remember.

Oh, yes, that's what it was—the noise. Like thunder from an angry heaven, like hailstones on a tin roof, like a score of cars backfiring. It rang out once, sharply. A pause. And then it rang out again.

Screams rent the air as the crowd began to move, chaotically, frantically, desperately. Bertha tried to keep hold of Nathaniel—she could even now see his fingers straining to grab hers—but the two were torn asunder. That was the last she saw of him.

She was part of the crowd but suddenly curiously separated from it. There was no way she could tell whether the cries came from her mouth alone or from a thousand other mouths. Legs flew, arms flailed, everybody ran.

And even that wasn't how it was. For not everybody ran. Not everybody could run. When Bertha turned back, she saw the fallen. She realized it was better not to look. They lay heaped on the ground, like piles of rags. They were like broken dolls—dolls whose lipstick was beginning to smear and run.

And there were others who did not run. Nathaniel, Bertha thought, was probably among those. They retreated into alley-ways, doorways, cracks in walls. They retreated, but they did not flee. They threw stones and bricks—anything that could come to hand. They shouted—not in triumph but in rage. They made brief forays into the almost-deserted streets to pick up the fallen and drag them from this place of death. They clenched their fragile fists against the mighty machine of war.

Bertha did not join them. She fled with the majority—unthinking, unfeeling, unaware—until she suddenly found herself alone in the bus shelter. She knew that she should leave this place and find her own way home. But her mind was all a jumble. She didn't know where she was. She didn't know what route to take. She seldom ventured out in the township at night. It was considered too dangerous for those her age and sex. In the distance everything seemed magnified. She heard rumblings and claps of thunder, she saw flames streak out into the sky. Visions of the bogeyman, of *tsotsi* gangs, kept crowding in on her.

The worst thing was how alone she felt. She would do anything for company. She was almost relieved when a van screeched to a halt beside the shelter. A couple of men jumped to the ground. She cowered, but she was relieved. At least she did not have to make a decision. They were policemen, this pair, she could smell it. She was in their hands.

Nathaniel Cuba had little time to worry about his sister's fate.

When he left the community center, he had immediately become embroiled in a street discussion. Knots of students gathered everywhere, in the shadows of the night, to talk about what had happened, to wonder what would happen next. Their voices scaled the human register—the high squeaks of boys who yet had to turn into men, the modulated calming of the near-women, the gruffness of those who had attained manhood, the hysteria of the youngest. They talked all at once, little caring whether anyone listened to them. They were pushing their own voices out into the world. They were reassuring themselves that they were still alive.

Only gradually did they calm down. A few individuals detached themselves from the center of the melee, individuals with ideas. They started to assert themselves. Officials of various schools' student representative councils began to gather their members together. There was much to be discussed: There was more to be done.

Already groups were reacting. Small fires sprang up, barricades were erected throughout Soweto. Whites fled the township as a barrage of bricks greeted their every appearance.

The police, they knew, must be regrouping. They had fired to scare the students off. Yet all they had succeeded in doing was to fuel the rage that had simmered from the day the children were born. Well, the police would feel no regret: Their energies would be concentrated on rapidly suppressing this unexpected uprising.

"We must organize," Nathaniel insisted. It felt strange, this echoing of his mother's most recurrent theme. And yet he knew he was doing himself an injustice. He was no longer a cipher for his mother's aspirations. He had seen the fear in her face during his short stay at the community center. He had seen it, and he had pitied it. He had known then that despite her long years of struggle, it was now the youth like himself who had become the vanguard.

"Organize," he repeated.

"Action," came the shout from the back. "We will raze Soweto to the ground."

Excited exclamations greeted this contribution. Individuals peeled off from the group, intent on dispersing into the night to wreak their own havoc.

"Comrades!" Nathaniel was relieved to see that the president of his student council was standing on an orange crate. Joe was a natural organizer, a youth who had earned the respect of others by the way he firmly withstood the school's attempt to scapegoat activists. He held his hand up now to stop them from going, and they listened, tentatively at first.

"We marched together in peace," Joe called. "But the Boers shot us down. They shot at us so that we would run away."

"We will not run!" The cry came from several points in the crowd.

"*Ja*," Joe said. "We will not run."

"We will attack them now," somebody called. "When they are weak. We're wasting time here."

Again people made as if to drift away. But Joe shouted at the top of his lungs. "Stay!" he called. "Stay!"

The sheer ferocity of his voice kept them there, and he capitalized on his advantage. He looked around them, fixing each eye with his. "If we disperse now," he said, "if we go without first planning, if we try to wreak our individual revenge on those who have hurt us directly, then the Boers will hunt us down. Nathaniel is right: We must organize."

Not everybody listened. Some shook their heads and disappeared into the night. But the majority stayed. They formed themselves into smaller groups. They took the first steps toward a plan.

Their fallen comrades were foremost in their minds. Toward their own parents, they might not cast more than a second thought. None went home for fear of being picked up by the police or because they did not want their mothers to bar the door and prevent them from leaving again. But toward the mothers and the fathers of the dead, their thoughts were directed. Groups were dispatched—sent to attend the scores of wakes that were already springing up. They were evenhanded—these children who had grown up in one day. They sent the same number to each bereaved household. Popularity was no longer an issue— all were equal in their eyes.

They flooded into every gathering—talking, explaining, describing, and organizing. In one corner a group issued its first communiqué; in another a handful of youth cajoled money out of drunken shebeen inmates. South Africa had never seen anything like this: organization without known leaders but with a single impetus and a single voice. War had been declared. They would fight.

Few slept in Soweto that night. They were young, these children, they did not grow tired. And as for their parents—how could they sleep? Their fears multiplied as the hours ticked by. If their children had not turned up, they thought them dead. If their children were spotted somewhere, they feared their imminent imprisonment. Trapped by their own anxiety, they were helpless in the face of the children's unstoppable momentum.

By daybreak a group of disorganized schoolchildren had been transformed into a fighting machine. Not a fighting machine in the traditional sense. They had no guns, no ammunition, no tanks or airplanes. But they had one thing that is a basic necessity for any victory: They had anger, the will to win, and, most important of all, they had no fear.

They had posted themselves outside every form of transport. When the first of Jo'burg's human chain began its weary way to work, they were met by collecting tins and leaflets. With one hand, those adults gave to the funeral funds: With the other they held a piece of paper that told them how to act:

"Listen, our parents,
It is us your children,
Who are crying;
It is us your children,
Who are dying.
Amandla!"

The children, the leaflet continued, had declared a national week of mourning. When the adults looked into the eyes of their determined offspring, few had the courage to say that they would defy it.

Jacob was up early. He'd woken at the same time that he'd been forced to wake these last twelve years: In truth, he didn't think he'd ever be able to break that habit.

But this time the experience of waking was completely different. He'd opened his eyes to find himself in a bed, a proper bed, with clean cotton sheets around him. He'd got up, drawn the curtains, and he'd opened, actually opened, the window. He breathed in the fresh air, and he thought about what was to come. He had a day of nothingness ahead of him, but it wasn't prison nothingness, it was a day to himself, which could be filled with his own selfish whims.

The thought almost panicked him. He did not know how to spend his own time, he didn't. He looked around wildly.

And then he told himself to relax. One minute at a time, he thought, that was how he would start—just as he had when he was first imprisoned.

Well, he was hungry—that would occupy some time. He would fix himself breakfast.

He tiptoed to the kitchen: The last thing he wanted to do was to disturb the rest of the household. And then he began to look around, to see what he'd like to eat.

It took ages. I won't have to worry about how to spend my time, he thought, since I'm so slow.

It was the wonder of it all that did it. He picked an orange from the fruit bowl, and instead of immediately peeling and squeezing it, as he had planned to do, he found himself feeling its skin, smelling it, savoring it. He chided himself. He was acting as if the orange were unique, but he knew that he could have another, and another after that. He reached into the drawer and got out a sharp knife: That was another boon, he thought, being able to have an implement that actually cut. He concentrated on the orange, attempting to see if he could peel it in one go.

A knock on the window startled him. He jumped; the orange and knife went clattering to the floor. Not the police already, he thought.

It wasn't the police, it was one lone African, his face pressed against the glass. Jacob stared back at the man, and frowned. This was a face he knew, he thought, that he'd once known. But whose was it?

And then in a flash he got it. "Ray..." he began.

Putting one finger to his lips, Raymond Siponja inclined his head in the direction of the kitchen door. Jacob ran to it and opened it. And then the two men were in each other's arms, slapping each other's backs, calling each other's names.

"God, it's good to see you, Jacob, man," Raymond said. "Let me have a better look."

They parted, and stood and stared into each other's faces.

"You've gone gray," Jacob commented.

"Me?" Raymond replied. "You think I'm gray? Have you looked in a mirror recently?" Then his face became more serious. "I can't stay long," he said. "We're both banned, so if the Boers catch us together, you'd end up back in jail. I took the risk because I thought they might be busy in Soweto this morning."

"That's something, hey?" Jacob said. "An overnight explosion, you think?"

Raymond shook his head. "Maybe it will die down," he said. "But I'm not sure I believe it will. The youth are angry, and they've been brought up tough. They're not going to give in easily—not now the Boer has taken the lid off their anger."

There was the sound of a door opening somewhere in the house. Both men turned and looked in its direction.

"Outside?" Jacob asked.

Raymond nodded, and they walked through the kitchen door.

"I've come to ask your plans," Raymond said, as soon as they were out.

"You mean to tell me them," Jacob replied.

Raymond smiled. "*Ja*," he said. "That's about it."

"So tell me."

"The message is that you'll be of more use outside the country.

If you stay here, they'll stop your every movement: They'll paralyze you. You should apply for an exit permit—you'll have no trouble."

Jacob nodded. "I thought that would be the way," he said. And suddenly he felt a sadness descend on him. He would have to leave his country, leave it perhaps forever. He would have to travel to another place, a foreign place, without even knowing whether he had a family waiting for him. It was almost too frightening to contemplate.

He bit his lip and looked away. "It must be terrible, what's happening in Soweto," he said to hide his tears.

"It's terrible," Raymond agreed somberly. Then his eyes lit up. "But you can practically touch the solidarity among the youth."

Bertha did not feel the solidarity that Raymond spoke of. She didn't know much about what had happened—only the small amount she'd gleaned from others, some of her age, some even younger, who'd been flung into her cell at Protea Police Station. And if the truth be told, Bertha, and many of the other detainees with her, did not give a damn about what was happening. They were too scared for that.

Bertha could count herself among the lucky ones. She was as yet unmarked by fist or cudgel. But she did not feel lucky, for something even more drastic had been done to her: Her spirit had been damaged.

She'd arrived at Protea in a state of trepidation. Her first relief that at least she was not alone had long since worn off. Foremost in her mind was the memory of her grandfather Moses. He, too, had been arrested. He had never come out.

Bertha was not like her brother. While Nathaniel hung on to Lindiwe's every word, Bertha was a child who lived in her own world of make-believe. Nathaniel listened attentively when Lindiwe talked about Moses, while Bertha concentrated instead on the welfare of her large collection of dolls.

Bertha's lack of interest in politics worried Lindiwe, but she did nothing to alter it. Children, she judged, must find their own way in life. Bertha would have to grow up one day: In the meantime perhaps her childishness was a merciful release from the prospects awaiting her.

And so Lindiwe would have been surprised to know that Ber-

tha, when she was ordered to climb down into the forecourt of
Protea Police Station, was thinking of Moses. She, who had never
appeared to concentrate on her grandfather's life, now remembered it vividly. It came to her, flooding back, overcoming her.

But it was more than that. It wasn't the memory that came to
her, it was Moses' very presence. The ghost of Moses walked
beside her, and she was afraid. He came from an underworld,
he came without being called. Surely, Bertha thought, he came
from hell.

And he would not leave her alone. He walked with her as she
crossed to the back door, his icy breath made her shiver. He
looked at police running with guns at the ready, and he laughed.
She feared him greatly: She was in enough trouble—he would
only make more.

The sergeant behind Protea's admission desk did not know
that when this frail eleven-year-old was ushered to stand in front
of him, beside her stood the ghost of her grandfather.

"Stand straight," he ordered, "or there'll be trouble."

The ghost laughed, its eerie voice filling the station.

"Trouble," it intoned. "Then what is this?"

Bertha shivered. She put out a hand to ward the ghost away.

The sergeant had two children of his own. He was a family
man, known for his kindness. And yet he felt no pity for this
trembling child. When she lashed out with her hands, he experienced, instead, a kind of contempt. In his eyes her shivering
was her guilt: rumors of atrocities, of whites killed in Soweto
that night, filled his mind.

"Interrogation room," he snapped.

The ghost cried out.

She was eleven years old. They treated her like a murderer.
They snapped at her, they asked her her name; they repeated
their question as if they did not believe her.

"Come on, *kaffir*, don't lie," they shouted. "What is your
name?"

"Tell them," the ghost urged.

She hated the ghost, but she listened to its instructions. "Bertha Cuba," she mumbled.

"What?" they screamed. "What do you say?"

"Call them *baas*," the ghost advised. "They like that."

"Bertha Cuba, *baas*," she answered quickly.

To learn to call them *baas*, that was easy. And yet they wanted something more from her—something she could not supply.

"Admit it!" they shouted. "You're a member of the SRC."

The SRC, she thought—Students Representative Council—what had she to do with that?" "No, *baas*," she said.

"Of the ANC," they insisted. The ghost beside her shifted uneasily on his long-dead feet.

"No, *baas*," she replied.

Their voices hit out at her, again and again, with unceasing monotony and unfailing vigor. She wanted to give in, she wanted to agree to everything they said, anything as long as they left her alone, but the ghost would not let her. Its hand was around her neck now.

"Let me go," she told it.

"Stand firm," it whispered. "Tell them nothing."

She hated the ghost at that moment. She wanted to sleep, and it was stopping her. She could not see it, it was invisible, as befitted a ghost, but its presence was more tangible to her than the police. It gripped her, hotly now: It kept her rooted to the spot.

"Tell us," they ordered, "or we will never let you go."

"Tell them nothing," the ghost repeated.

Bertha stood still. She was not really there, she told herself. This argument in the room was between a ghost and the police. Her heart thumped, for she did not know which side would win; neither did she know on whose side she really was.

And then, suddenly, everything changed. The door opened, and they dragged another student into the room with her. He could hardly stand upright—he did not look at her. His trousers were torn, and flapped uneasily around his knees. His face was a mass of bruises, his eyes already swelling. He stared straight ahead.

They beat him up, those police, right in front of Bertha. They knocked the student to the ground, they pulled him up, and then they knocked him down again. He made no sound, only Bertha's groans filled the room.

She could not look, but neither could she tear her eyes away. This will happen to me next, she thought, as she watched a human being disintegrate before her very eyes.

And while they beat him up, they spoke only to her. "You're a member of the ANC," they suggested gently. Their words were soft. Their actions now reflected their rage. "Tell us, tell us," they begged.

The ghost grew agitated. Now, it was almost as if she were holding it up. It trembled, it cried out. "The farm, the farm," it kept on whispering. She could not understand it. She did not want to.

In the end she could stand it no longer. She pushed the ghost away from her, using all her strength. It cried, and she covered her ears. It fell, and so did she. She fainted.

She came to consciousness in a dingy cell. She was without thought. She said nothing to the other occupants. She waited: waited for them to fetch her again. The ghost had deserted her, and she felt strangely alone.

In Soweto her parents were also waiting. They had scoured Soweto for her. They had visited all her friends, then police stations, and finally the mortuaries. They inspected the ranks of white-covered corpses—their pain at seeing each small body mitigated by the relief at not recognizing the face. The children had been forced together, but that night their parents were cast asunder. There was little time to console a keening friend: They were driven on by the need to find their daughter.

But all to no avail. Bertha had disappeared.

It was in the early hours of the morning that Johannes finally made up his mind. Determinedly he faced his wife.

"We have no other choice," he said.

He had expected Lindiwe to protest: He had decided to listen to her and then act anyway. His baby had disappeared: This was no time to stand on principle.

"I will come with you," she said.

Johannes breathed a sigh of relief. He pushed a slight feeling of disappointment away from himself.

They walked to George's house. It took a long time. Soweto was in an uproar; many of the streets were blocked, many were already under police siege. But they felt neither fatigue nor wonder. They walked without touching, but they were as one: listening for a child's cry that would lead them to Bertha.

When they reached George's house, they saw that they were not the first. The place was lit up from head to toe. People stood in knots on the *stoep*: well-dressed people and some in nightclothes. Some came, some went, some just stood and stared at the flames of the night.

There was a flurry of agitation here—just as in the rest of Soweto. But this flurry was somewhat different. They had escaped the eye of the storm, they could not escape its consequences. While Soweto had taken its children's actions at face value, had worried about the consequences instead of the reasons, these people were full of unanswered questions. Their brows furrowed, their eyes frowned: Tell us, they seemed to be saying, why has this happened? When will it end?

George mingled among them. While his wife, Dottie, passed out cups of tea, glasses of whiskey, and soothing consolation, George was in his element. He was fully dressed, immaculately so, and he walked amid his guests, dispensing advice, proclaiming his opinion, whispering comments into individuals' ears.

For one moment Johannes's favorite piece of Gilbert and Sullivan flew irrevelantly into his brain: "I am the very model of a modern major general," he thought. He dismissed the tune. He felt his wife edge away, and he pulled her closer.

Dottie was the first to see Lindiwe and Johannes. She froze, and some whiskey fell to the floor. She blinked, and smiling an apology at her nearest guest, she walked over to George. She put one hand on his arm, and from the height of the *stoep* the Bopape couple looked down at the Cubas—their closest relatives.

Anything could have happened next. Relations between the two families had grown increasingly acrimonious. Since Evelyn's death, there had been absolutely no contact. George and Lindiwe had fought desperately over the nature of Evelyn's funeral oration in a battle that Lindiwe lost when Peggy intervened to take George's side.

It was George who felt the most rancor. Lindiwe's every acid comment on his lifestyle struck deep into his heart. Lindiwe's rejection of his wife's overtures was an insult he would not countenance. Lindiwe's continuing involvement in the black-consciousness movement was an example he could not face.

He stood on the *stoep*, and he toyed with the idea of sending them away. He would only have had to make one tiny gesture of rejection, and he knew that Lindiwe would vanish back into the night. If Lindiwe visited him on this night of all nights, she must be in dire need. If he turned her away, he would be doing so forever. He could close the last chapter in a history that he found unbearably painful.

It was tempting, oh so tempting. He cared little for his sister—he had cut her from his heart many years before. And yet, even as he moved toward her, he found that he was smiling gently. He could not understand it. He had resolved to reject her, and he was, instead, welcoming her—making it easy on her.

Dottie would later insist that the ghost of Moses had stood beside George that night. She said this out loud in a moment of uncharacteristic honesty, and she tolerated the derision with which George greeted her statement. But to herself she kept the thought. The ghost had been there, she told herself, she had felt its presence.

Dottie breathed a tangible sigh of relief as George stretched out both arms.

"How can I help?" he asked.

Johannes felt the tension go from Lindiwe. He remained silent while Lindiwe described Bertha's disappearance. He tried to hold his hope at bay while George set to doing what he knew best—organizing. He had contacts in the police, he assured them. There had been many mistakes that night. The police had panicked—they had arrested children at random. He was sure the situation would soon be remedied.

His optimism soon proved justified. In a short space of time he managed where Bertha's parents had completely failed. He found the child in Protea, and he persuaded the authorities to release her.

And so, as a new dawn ended Soweto's long night, one small eleven-year-old emerged from Protea Police Station. She glanced from left to right as if she were accompanied.

48

Lindiwe ran up to her daughter, who was standing on the police station steps. She bent down to hug Bertha, but the child shifted away from her grasp.

"I'm all right," Bertha said.

She did not look all right. She stood on the highest step and her head twitched from side to side. Her eyes were unfocused: Her brow was creased with worry, as if she were trapped in the process of puzzling something out. Apart from her one rebuff she did nothing to acknowledge her parents' presence. When George came up beside her, she jumped nervously.

She turned, saw him, and seemed to relax. She threw him a polite smile. "Thank you for getting me out, Uncle," she said formally. Her head twitched again. She walked down the remaining steps.

Lindiwe made a further move toward her daughter, but Johannes restrained her. He felt as though he'd spent the whole night holding Lindiwe back and he didn't want to do it again, but there was something in Bertha's eyes, some wildness that was not entirely normal. He had felt initial relief at finding her. Suddenly he was afraid, afraid that if they pressed her too hard, they might push her down the precipice that separated the sane from the insane.

And so he stepped between mother and daughter. He linked one arm to Lindiwe. With the other, he gently touched Bertha's shoulder. She shivered uncontrollably—stopping only after he removed his hand.

She sat alone in the front seat while George drove them home. Her head still moved, but she was looking neither to left nor to right. She made no comment as they drove through the debris of the previous night's explosion, past burned-out roadblocks, looted shops, silent schools.

George did not stay: He kissed Lindiwe on both cheeks and drove off to his office, leaving the Cubas alone with Bertha. Since every time they tried to talk to her she began to shake, they could think of nothing else but to cater to her bodily needs. They provided her with food: She ate automatically. They poured some water for her, and she went through the motions of bathing herself. They put her to bed, and she lay there passively, staring with unblinking eyes at the ceiling.

It was a long time before she fell asleep, and all that time her parents sat quietly beside her. Words were no comfort: Any attempt at uncovering the details of what had happened only set off the twitching again. And so to the sounds of shouts from the street, of mysterious explosions, of police sirens, they sat together in silence.

Finally Bertha slept. Not peacefully but fitfully—she tossed and she turned, she groaned out loud, she flung up her arm as if warding something off. But still, to their relief, she slept.

"What can have happened to her?" Johannes asked.

His wife did not reply: She merely looked at him.

Johannes understood. He knew as well as Lindiwe that there were no words to describe the thoughts that ran through both their minds. Bertha was physically intact—that they had seen. But they both knew that physical abuse was not the only device used by the police. Bertha had been terrified: whether by something that had happened or by the fear of what might occur, neither could tell. But they both knew that the fear that strikes at the undefended soul can be more powerful than any form of torture. They looked at their sleeping child, and they were both afraid.

"We must watch over her carefully," Johannes said.

Lindiwe nodded. "Few of us will sleep in the days to come," she said.

Lindiwe was proved right. It was virtually impossible for anybody to sleep. Soweto was, even a few days after the original demonstration, in an uproar. The children refused to go back to school: They were adamant. Black South Africa, they said, had slumbered too long. They would not stand aside and watch their fellow pupils massacred.

They held impromptu meetings in their assembly halls. They occupied or they walked out, there was little difference. The children were giving themselves a different kind of education: They were learning what it was like to take part in an uprising.

They were unpredictable, and yet there was logic in their actions. They were badly educated, and yet they had more knowledge stored up than could have ever been believed.

They, the mass of black children in South Africa, were deprived of a proper education. And yet, when they finally rose up, their minds brimmed over with ideas, theory, the will to learn. They were not unsophisticated, these young black rebels. The ideas that white South Africa thought too dangerous to teach them were foremost in their minds. They talked of dialectical materialism, of black power, of socialism. Because white South Africa had demonstrated how dangerous these notions were, the children sought them out, applied them, developed them.

The school boycott, which was rapidly followed by an enforced closure of all schools, began to spread like wildfire throughout the whole country. All over the Vaal, the Reef, in Pretoria, the Eastern Cape, the Cape Peninsula were townships ablaze with anger. The children were no longer protesting about having to learn in Afrikaans. They had gone a stage further. They demanded the abolition of Bantu education.

Martin pushed an envelope across the table. Jacob did not reach for it. He knew it contained his tickets out of South Africa.

"To Dar?" he said.

Martin nodded. "On Thursday. If you don't go then, they won't let you out."

Jacob pushed his chair away from the table and sighed. "I'm not ready for this," he said.

Martin shrugged. "Who ever is?" he asked.

Jacob knew that Martin was right. None of the people who had left in the sixties could have wanted to go—not Max Freeman, not the leaders of the ANC, not . . . not Rosa, either. He pushed that thought aside.

"Do you think it's the right decision?" he asked.

Martin looked at him without blinking, and for a long time the two men watched each other in silence. Martin broke first: He looked away.

"It's hard," he said in a faraway voice. "The last twelve years have been tough, with so many people gone, and with so much disillusion in the air. You don't know how good it's been to have you stay here, to be able to indulge myself in real political conversations. And now you're going, too."

He turned back to Jacob, and he was smiling in a kind of self-mockery. "That's my selfish reaction over with," he said. "My political head says that you have no other choice. People will be needed in the coming years, people in this country, but you're too well known. You'd be of more use outside."

The boycott organized by the students was only half-successful. Many stayed away that first day. Many were turned away by the student pickets. But even if the state was taken aback by the ferocity of the students' response, it was undaunted. The police moved in, and they patrolled the streets. In the air, helicopters flew over the flimsy structure of Soweto. At railway stations ranks of uniforms beat, arrested, shot at the students.

Many adults showed their solidarity with the students by refusing to cross the station picket lines, but others evaded it by sleeping at their place of work (for once, their employers were sympathetic to their requests). For the rest, they were still confused. They were buffeted by the twin forces of state reaction and student anger. They, like the police, had been totally unprepared for the ferocity of their children's response. As shebeens went up in flames, as government buildings met a similar fate, the adults could only look on. The world was moving on, and they had been, temporarily, left behind.

Lindiwe and Johannes were not among the waverers. They spent little time gathering on Soweto street corners as the parents tried to puzzle out what had happened. They had both known that this day would one day come: not the form of the day, or the age of the rebels, but the inevitability that a section of the African population would one day say "Enough." With a growing respect, they watched the children mobilizing. They helped where they could: with the formation of parent support groups, with advice and information, with medical aid at the clinic.

And yet they had an added problem—what to do with Bertha. On the second day after her release, Lindiwe took her to the clinic. The child had woken after twelve full hours bleary-eyed, as if her long sleep had done nothing to calm her. She volunteered no further information: She volunteered nothing, in fact. She was completely passive, acquiescing to every suggestion as if it mattered little how she spent her time. When night fell, she went back to sleep without a murmur. Her second awakening varied little from her first.

Lindiwe knew well the pressures on the clinic. She could stay away no longer, and so she took Bertha, too. In the back of her mind she thought that contact with the reality of what had happened, of what was continuing to happen, would rouse the child from her apathy.

It turned out that Lindiwe was right—but not in the way she had imagined. It happened when a young boy stumbled in, his eyes red from tear gas, his legs cut by the lash of a score of whips. The occupants of the clinic had become rapidly accustomed to such sights: a few indrawn breaths were all that greeted the boy's arrival.

All the occupants, that is, except for Bertha. She, who had evinced no emotion for over thirty hours, looked at the boy, opened her mouth, and shrieked. She could not seem to stop herself: Out came an unending cry of agony that rent the air. She tore at her hair, she shook her head, she continued to cry out. It was an unbearable sound, it cut through the clinic like a dagger.

Lindiwe panicked. She could think of nothing to stop the crying, of nothing except that she wanted it to end. She stood mute while one of her fellow workers hit out at her child's face, but to no avail. The cries did did not abate until Lindiwe removed Bertha from that place.

And then again she grew silent. She nodded when her mother suggested she stay at home. Nodding was her only form of communication.

Lindiwe had no choice but to leave Bertha alone for long periods of time. She knew that her daughter was in pain, but she did not know how to deal with it. And after all, her daughter was not alone. Throughout Soweto were people who needed nurses, advice, counseling. She had no choice: She could not turn her back on them.

And so it was that Bertha was on her own on the occasion of the police's first visit. They entered without knocking. They kicked the door until it splintered. Four of them, armed, huge, angry, catapulted their way into the Cubas' small dwelling. They started shouting as soon as they saw Bertha.

"Where's your brother?" they demanded.

For the first time since she had stepped out of the police station, Bertha smiled. She nodded her head, again and again. The policemen looked uneasily at each other as the smile turned into a laugh that echoed out in the room, filling it eerily.

One of the policemen took two steps toward her. He picked her up by the scruff of her neck, but she kept on nodding. At least, he thought, she'd stopped laughing.

"Don't play dumb," he shouted. "Where's your brother?" Infuriated by her nodding, he shook her violently.

The laugh returned.

"Ag, let her be," said a voice from behind. Bertha saw that the owner of the voice was twirling his fingers in the air and pointing at his head. She didn't understand what he meant, but the policeman still gripping her obviously did. He dropped her with distaste.

"They're all *blerry* mad," he muttered.

She closed her mouth abruptly.

They ignored Bertha now as they methodically destroyed the house. They put their hands everywhere, and what they touched disintegrated. Sugar, jam, paper, books, piled up on the floor as they worked. It was obvious that Nathaniel wasn't there, but they did not leave until everything had been overturned and wrecked.

When Lindiwe came home, she found Bertha in the same place as she had left her. The child was staring blankly in front of her, apparently unaware of the devastation around her. The nodding had abated, but in its place was an ominous calm. She was completely still—catatonic, almost.

That night the dreams began. Bertha fell asleep where they laid her. She did not move around as she had formerly done, and her parents told themselves that the worst was over. But two hours later they knew that they were wrong.

Bertha sat bolt upright. Her eyes were open. "The ghost," she cried, "the ghost."

When Lindiwe went to comfort her, Bertha made no sign that she registered her mother's presence. "The ghost," she cried, "the ghost."

It took twenty minutes to rouse her to a proper wakefulness. When she finally came to, she stared blankly at her parents. She could not tell them what she had been dreaming; she would not reply. As soon as they laid her down, she fell asleep again.

But the ghost became a constant theme in all their lives. It woke the parents five or six hours a night. It woke them until they, too, were haunted by a phantom that they did not understand. They despaired of ever knowing what to do. Their daughter was unreachable: She was trapped by a mysterious ghost. She stopped eating, she refused to wash. She shrank before their eyes, and there was nothing they could do.

And then, in the midst of all this, Peggy turned up. She never explained why she came: She, who rarely read newspapers, did not tell how she had heard the uproar from her distant exile. She just arrived one day—not at George's, which would have been her natural destination, but at the Cuba home.

"Where is Nathaniel?" were her first words.

Lindiwe bristled. Surely Peggy could see how things were? Her son was on the run, her daughter was present in name alone. She had cleared up the house, but it still showed the effects of the police presence. Half her books—for it was at the books they had directed the brunt of their fury—were so badly marked that she'd had to throw them away. The furniture was propped up in makeshift ways: Their food they shared off two tin plates, since the others had been smashed.

And in the midst of this, Peggy—her mouth set in a thin, disapproving line, the mother who had renounced Lindiwe's father, who had not made one gesture toward understanding Lindiwe—thought she had the right to demand to see her grandson.

"I don't know," Lindiwe curtly replied. "He's on the run."

"And what are you going to do about it?" Peggy demanded.

"What can I do?" Lindiwe picked up her coat.

Peggy's eyes flicked from Lindiwe to Bertha, who was sitting motionless in the corner of the room. "Your children need you."

"There are many children in need," Lindiwe snapped in reply. She kissed the unresponsive Bertha and left the house. Lindiwe was irritated by her mother's presence, but as she walked to the clinic she realized that she was also relieved. As the days passed, she had grown increasingly uneasy about leaving Bertha alone. The police, she knew, were bound to come back, and given what their last visit had done, she worried incessantly about Bertha's reactions. She had even been toying with the idea of sending the child away, but two things had stopped her: where to send her and, more important, how it would feel to lose two children in one week.

For Lindiwe knew that she had lost Nathaniel. He had disappeared into the blaze of resistance, and it would be a long time before he could live with them again. He was dodging the police night and day, protected by a network of households who were not likely to attract as much police attention as the Cubas'.

But Lindiwe's feelings of loss did not relate to his physical absence. It came from something other, it came from the knowledge that Nathaniel was no longer a child. She had seen him briefly two days ago, and although they acted as mother and son, she had known then that he had suddenly and finally grown up.

He smiled when she asked him whether he was eating sufficiently well; he answered politely and with patience. But his eyes gave him away. They had changed irrevocably, unalterably, forever. They were the eyes of a grown man.

The fact was that Nathaniel was gone and Bertha was unreachable.

No, she thought as she walked down the path that led to the clinic, she could not bear it: There must be a way of getting through to Bertha. Perhaps Peggy would manage it.

She laughed to herself. Things were getting desperate if she was relying on her mother. Peggy had proved long ago that she could not face her own life. What, then, could she do for Bertha?

Peggy was wondering the same thing. She didn't know what she was doing in this Soweto house. She hadn't explained to Lindiwe why she'd come for the simple reason that she didn't know.

She had heard of the uprising through a score of different sources—through secondhand tales and through reading the papers, which spoke of terrorists and vandals striking at the heart of Soweto.

No one in the country talked of anything else, and their conversation became increasingly acrimonious. There were those who told the news as they had heard it passed to them. They talked of unarmed children gunned down by ranks of police, of the unprotected being hauled into jail. And there were others who believed the propaganda, who spoke of *tsotsi* gangs running amok, of law and order being gradually restored, of schools being reopened.

Peggy had let it all wash over her. She had not bothered to assess the situation for herself. Well, she had thought, what is it to me? I have given up on that a long time ago. I will no longer sit by and watch as my family suffers and dies. I will keep away from them even if it means that I never again clap eyes on them.

She had thought all this, consciously and deliberately. She had reveled in the harshness of her thought, in the knowledge of how her daughter, Lindiwe, would have judged her for it. And yet even as she thought it, she found herself packing. It was as if she had been split in two. The one side closed its eyes, the second made the dangerous journey to Jo'burg.

For dangerous it was. Peggy had no permission to visit the urban centers—which in normal times would have meant a sharp pickup and deportation back to her Transkei dwelling. And these were not normal times. South Africa's roads were occupied by police and army alike. And not only the roads: the air hummed as a thousand propellers shifted police from one site of unrest to the other.

But despite all this, Peggy got through. Sometimes, during the journey, she toyed with the idea that she was surrounded by a cloak of invisibility. Others were questioned, arrested, beaten, not she. Not once did anybody even ask her for her pass.

And so she arrived at Lindiwe's doorstep. She still could not understand her journey: She still could not comprehend what had driven her here rather than to George's. The only explanation came from deep within her past. God had made her come: He knew that she was needed.

But as she watched her eleven-year-old grandchild swaying back and forth as if on an invisible rocking chair, Peggy wondered whether she was fooling herself. Maybe, she thought in fear, God had deserted her.

She was only fifty-six, and yet she felt as if she was nearer eighty. She had no way of dealing with this world in which she existed.

She looked at the children of Soweto, and they were like aliens to her. They were so fierce, so disrespectful, so convinced of their own rightness. On her way to her daughter's she had been stopped at a number of makeshift roadblocks. The children were holding street collections, and not a person was allowed to pass without giving something. For funerals, they said, as they stared her full in the face. She had wanted to refuse, and yet she dared not. They were a law unto themselves, these youngsters, and they scared her.

Peggy shivered. She would not, she resolved, tempt fate by dwelling on her fears. If she did not know why she had come, then it mattered little. She was here, after all. She might as well make herself useful.

"Come now," she ordered Bertha. "Help me clear up."

Bertha stopped rocking and got obediently to her feet. She waited limply for further instructions, a frail rag doll in child's clothing.

The two had not been working long when they heard the noise. At first came the clip-clop of a horse, a weary sound, as if it were dragging a great burden. That in itself was not unusual. It could have been the local coal merchant going about his normal rounds. But other sounds accompanied it, and these were less easy to distinguish, drowned as they were by the heavy whoosh of helicopters that hovered above.

There was a hum, a buzz of muffled conversation broken only occasionally by a shout of indistinguishable words. And there was a sound of soft treading multiplied: as if an army shod only in slippers was passing by.

Against her better judgment Peggy went to the open door. She saw that the street was flooded with people. In the front was the coal merchant's cart, sheathed now in a different kind of black, and overloaded with wreaths.

Peggy crossed herself. What sacrilege to carry a coffin on an open cart! These children had gone too far: They were making a mockery of burial. And yet she could not tear her eyes away. For there was a dignity about this procession, despite its motley character.

Behind the cart walked the family, dressed in black, heads bowed, arms supporting each other. And behind them came the bulk of the procession—the true procession. They marched in ranks six or seven abreast. They held their heads high, and their fists were clenched in the air. The youth were in the majority, but they were not alone. Accompanying them came people of every age, some dressed in mourning, some walking in ragged clothes, the only garments that they possessed. They did not look up to where the helicopters threatened them from above. They did not look sideways to where police vans and tanks were parked at the ready. They looked only forward.

Not everybody walked. For at the back of the procession came carts, cars, buses, even, each one crammed to the hilt. It was from these vehicles that the shouts came. The others, the ones who were walking, saved their breath for the long journey ahead.

Peggy felt Bertha shiver beside her. She embraced the child, attempting, perhaps, to cover her eyes. But before long they were not alone. Three young girls, children of Bertha's age, detached themselves from the march and came to the Cuba doorway.

"*Amandla!*" said one, as she held her small fist in the air. Peggy frowned in distaste. What right had these youngsters, these girls who had not yet attained the age of puberty, to mouth such grown-up slogans?

She kept her thoughts to herself: She could find no words to rebuke them. As rank upon rank of mourners still passed, she felt a strange lump rising in her throat. She swallowed hard to keep it back.

The children had not come to talk to her, they were staring intently at Bertha, who, by a short gesture of her head, indicated that she knew them.

"Come march with us to Doornkop," suggested the second. Bertha did not move.

"You have been long silent, comrade," commented the third.

Peggy repressed the impulse to laugh. Comrade, indeed! Who did these children think they were?

"We are burying our brothers and our sisters," continued the third girl. "Come with us and show them that they are not forgotten. Come sing *hamba kahle* at the graveside."

Bertha shrank back toward the doorway. "The ghost," she said, "The ghost."

Peggy felt a shiver run down her spine. She, along with the three young visitors, turned to stare at Bertha.

"The ghost," said Bertha. "It will stop me."

There was a brief silence, broken only by the treading of the endless procession. Then one of the girls let loose with a peal of laughter that removed entirely the serious expression from her face. For a moment she was a child again, a young child amused by something trivial.

But her words were not childish. "The Boer is not a ghost," she said. "The Boer will try and stop you with bullets, perhaps, but he is no ghost. With my own eyes, I have seen him bleed when a stone hit his chin. I have seen him run. I have seen the whites of his frightened eyes."

"He is no ghost," another of the girls confirmed with a wise nod of her head.

Bertha shook as if she was warding off their speech. "The ghost," she whispered, her words barely distinguishable.

The first girl took a step toward her. She put a hand on Bertha's arm.

"Come," she said gently. "This is no time for ghosts. This is our time, a time for struggle, a time to remember and to swear our revenge. Come with us."

Haltingly, unwillingly even, Bertha allowed herself to be led toward the procession. Peggy ran in front of the small group, blocking their way with her bulky body.

"Leave her be," she protested. "Can't you see she's not well?"

The first girl looked at her with grave, grown-up eyes. "Mother, we mean you no disrespect," she said, "but we, the children of Soweto, are on the move. We must be together in this, or we will all fail."

Despite herself, despite the objections that crowded to her lips, Peggy allowed them to maneuver around her. She watched as the four girls blended into the funeral procession. She watched until they were mere specks in the distance.

And as she watched, her self-control faltered. The lump that she'd suppressed came welling back. It broke in her mouth, it overcame her eyes. She stood on the dirt street, and she found herself crying. The tears coursed down her cheeks, dripping onto the dust and turning it a browner color. She made no attempt to wipe them away. She cried as the funeral march went on and on. She cried as if her heart was breaking.

And then she could cry no longer. She lifted her apron to her face and wiped it roughly. She turned to go indoors.

"Join us," shouted somebody in the march.

She did not hear the shout. She walked indoors numbed, unthinking, almost. She had no idea what had prompted her to cry. When Moses died, she had not displayed her grief thus. She had stoically borne her pain: She had cut herself off from the sympathy of others. And now she cried for a stranger, for a small body in a makeshift box, drawn by an aged horse, surrounded by others who were too young to be going to a funeral.

It made no sense to her. She could not puzzle it out.

Maybe, she thought as she shut the door, I am crying for myself. For today I learned that the world has passed me by. She dismissed the thought from her mind as she applied herself to cleaning.

When Lindiwe and Johannes returned, rubbing their weary feet—for they, too, had attended one of the many funerals that took place that day—they found Peggy seated in a house that had been transformed. It shone from corner to corner, not one speck of dirt had Peggy left unattended, not one spot of grease displayed itself.

"Thank you, Peggy," Johannes said, as he greeted Peggy with an affectionate kiss. Lindiwe, watching the encounter, felt a stab of jealousy. Peggy, she thought, was prepared to kiss Johannes: How come, then, she kept herself so physically remote from her own daughter?

"Is Bertha in the yard?" Lindiwe asked. "I did not see her there."

"You have all gone mad," she said sharply.

Lindiwe glanced at her in surprise.

"Bertha is eleven," Peggy continued. "And yet you leave her unprotected."

Peggy's voice rose in intensity: She was growing hysterical. Johannes made a move toward her, but she jumped away.

"I always knew it would come to this," she shouted. "Look at the pain you are causing your children."

Lindiwe jumped to her feet. She walked two paces toward her mother. She stopped at a point when their faces were almost touching. "This pain is not of our making," she said loudly. "This is something you never understood. All my life you railed against my father's search for justice. If you had tried to understand, only once if you had tried, it might have made it easier for all of us."

In former times Lindiwe's comment would have led to an inevitable raising of the level of antagonism between the two. Johannes prepared himself to make peace: He was ready for Peggy to leave in protest, and he would try unsuccessfully to dissuade her. He was poised to do it.

But this time Peggy did a strange thing. She looked at her daughter, and she blinked. She took one step backward.

Peggy frowned. "She is out," she said. "She was taken away."

Lindiwe and Johannes both froze.

"Taken how?" Johannes asked weakly.

"By children who called themselves her friends," Peggy said. "They forced her to attend a funeral."

Johannes and Lindiwe exchanged a tentative glance. "I did not see her at Doornkop," Johannes said.

"How could we have, with so many buried today?" Lindiwe replied.

There was a short pause. "Perhaps it is as well," Johannes commented, as if to himself. "She must face reality."

"*Ja*," Lindiwe said, as she flopped down into a chair. "If the children took her, they will look after her."

Peggy had listened to this exchange with a growing amazement. She had expected them to rail at her for letting Bertha go. She had prepared herself to expose the fact that she had no defense worth offering—only her own unbidden grief. And now here they were, taking this development in their stride.

Well, she would not tolerate it.

"Perhaps you are right," was her only comment.

49

Tanzania: 1976

JACOB HESITATED ON THE BOTTOM RUNG OF THE STEPS. HE LOOSENED his tie. Even in the middle of the Tanzanian winter, the air felt stifling to him. He felt an impulse to remove his jacket, but when he looked back he saw that his fellow passengers, who were waiting patiently for him to finish his descent, did not appear at all uncomfortable.

I'm the only one sweating, he thought. Perhaps I have a fever.

He looked forward again, toward the low airport buildings. He saw a group of men coming toward him, the one in front with his arms outstretched. The delegation was solely male, Jacob could see. He set his mouth into an artificial smile. His eyes blurred a fraction. He blinked hard.

And then his disappointment changed to delight, as he recognized the man leading the welcoming committee. It was Marcus Mkize, an old comrade-in-arms, one of the original soldiers of MK. Jacob smiled, genuinely this time. He negotiated the last step and walked briskly toward the men.

The rest of the delegation hung back, as Jacob and Marcus met in the middle of the tarmac.

They shook hands first, not in one curt gesture but using MK's threefold salute, their hands flowing together in a firm greeting. And then, without interruption, without hesitation, they hugged—these two friends, the one whom age had turned to flab, the other spare and wiry from confinement.

"Welcome, comrade," Marcus said, as he slapped Jacob on the back.

"It's good to see you again," Jacob replied. "I thought this day would never come."

"Ah, but we knew it would." Marcus laughed. "We have never forgotten you. We have waited. And," he said, as he turned to gesture the others forward, "the whole of our country celebrates your release. They burn beer halls and government buildings as a tribute to you and our movement."

The others had come close, and Jacob turned and shook hands with each of them. They were all black, and they were all people he vaguely knew: Their faces he had almost forgotten, but at the same time, they were oh so familiar. Exiles all, who had left the country in the dark days of '63, who had stayed on the border of the country hoping for change when that hope had seemed like mere wishful thinking, when every day had brought news of apathy and defeat inside South Africa.

It must have been difficult, he reflected, as they led him into the airport buildings, to hold on to the optimism that had always been a central part of their movement. They had all been through the long years when even tokens of resistance had appeared to wither and die. For him it had been different. He had had no choice but to keep faith and to wait. But for them, with the appearance of freedom, it must have been really grueling. Waiting, trying, and yet achieving little.

"It's been a long time," Jacob commented.

Marcus knew that Jacob wasn't referring to his own incarceration, and he nodded in grave agreement. "*Ja*," he said, "it has been a difficult time." His expression brightened. "But things are really moving now, hey?" He frowned again. "They're children going to the slaughter," he continued. "They are brave but inexperienced. If only their parents would follow the lead that has been thrown up."

"It would be children, though, wouldn't it?" Jacob said. "For they know no fear."

Marcus laughed and clapped Jacob on the back. "Ayiee, you political prisoners, you come from home sounding biblical." He lowered his voice. "The chief sends his greetings," he said. "He was called away at the last moment, or else he would have been here to welcome you back."

Jacob nodded. He looked at Marcus.

"She's waiting for you," Marcus said. "In private."

Jacob had experienced much in the last twelve years. He had

sat through his trial knowing that he might be put away for life. He had heard the judge sentence him, and although it struck to the very core of his being, he had shown little feeling. He had endured all the petty humiliations with stoicism, and cheerfully enough. He had come to terms with the knowledge that his children were growing up as strangers. He had walked out of jail into a world that he no longer truly understood.

And yet, never once had he felt as nervous as he did now. His hands shook, so, he stuffed them in his jacket pocket. His mouth turned down, and he forced it back into neutrality. His legs faltered, and he pushed them onward. But there was nothing, nothing at all, that he could do to still his beating heart.

They took his exit permit from him and said that they would deal with the immigration authorities. They led him, understanding how nervous he was, down a corridor and through a gray-painted door. And then they left him alone.

She was sitting on a hard wooden bench, her back stiff against an ugly green wall. She looked up when he entered.

Time stopped and then reversed itself. Jacob glanced around him, reflecting on how much this room reminded him of jail. He almost expected van der Merwe to come striding in and announce that there'd been a terrible mistake. After all, Rosa Swiece was a banned person: She wasn't permitted visiting rights, van der Merwe would say.

Jacob shook himself. The window, he observed, was unbarred. He was back in the present, conscious of his beating heart. He saw that Rosa was still seated—no, that was not right—she had half-risen from the bench.

She was the Rosa he remembered, and yet she was not that woman. She had aged—well, that was only to be expected. But this fact wasn't what attracted his attention: It was something else—something in her gaze. She was looking at him tentatively, fearfully, even. She was changed. This was not his fierce, sure Rosa. She was somebody else altogether.

He wanted to run up to her and clasp her closely to him. He wanted to use their mingling warmth to erase the years of separation. He wanted to look into her eyes and see, once more, the woman who had raised her fist in that Jo'burg courtroom—raised it despite the grief she must have been feeling. He did none of these things. He stood stock-still and smiled at her.

"I'm sorry about your dad," he said.

Rosa nodded. Harold Arnold had died suddenly a year ago.

"I know how you loved him," Jacob said. "I wanted so much to be with you during that time."

Again Rosa nodded. She told herself that she should speak, that she should make this easier for him, but she could find no words.

"How's your mom taking it?" Jacob continued.

Rosa shrugged. "Who can tell how Julia takes anything?" she said. "She talks sometimes as if he's still alive. She knows he's dead: She's too hard a realist to deny that. But old habits die hard. They were together a long time. I don't know . . ."

She had started speaking, she knew that. And now she had started, she didn't know how to stop. A tiny part of her brain was laughing at her words. How long, it was saying, will you talk about this? Can you spin it out for another ten minutes, half an hour, a lifetime?

She gulped and stopped abruptly.

"Well," Jacob said awkwardly, "I'm sorry."

She lowered her head. "So am I," she said.

He looked at her, not daring to puzzle out what her words might mean. Was she apologizing for the last twelve years or for something else: something that he had not been able to face even during his darkest hours?

"Well," he repeated. It was his turn to stop, since he knew not how to continue.

The silence stretched like a thin thread between them—connecting them at the same time as it served to separate them.

Rosa saw that Jacob could make no further gesture: She saw the fear in his eyes. She would have to do it for the two of them, she thought. She walked toward him slowly. She came right up beside him and looked him straight in the eye.

He took in once more her height, her stature. But he also took in something even better. For as he looked at her, her face changed before his gaze. The tentativeness of her regard was transformed. Her eyes flashed a challenge. They were defiant, and they were so familiar. They were the real Rosa's eyes.

"The girls decided to wait until London," she said.

Jacob smiled. "Wise children," he commented.

"They're grown up now," Rosa reminded him.

She bit her lip, regretting her unthinking reaction. She looked away. But when she turned once more, she saw that he had not minded. He was smiling at her, her husband. She moved one step closer, and then they embraced, each feeling for the first time in so long the body of a spouse that had once been familiar.

The formalities of Jacob's temporary stay in Tanzania having been completed, he and Rosa were driven to a house within the university complex that had been loaned to them. They sat side by side during the journey, not touching, each lost in thought.

Rosa wanted to fill the silence with a thousand words, and yet she could think of none. She wished that these first days were over: She could bear neither the excitement nor the fearful anticipation of what might happen.

When they arrived at the house, they offered their driver a drink, and engaged him in frantic conversation. When he finally made an exit, Jacob and Rosa looked at each other across the empty room.

"Are you hungry?" she asked.

He shook his head. "I wouldn't mind a shower."

"Why don't you have one, then?" she said eagerly.

While he was in the bathroom, Rosa sat down, got up, walked to the door, opened and closed it again without leaving, and stared out the window. She looked at her watch. She opened the door again, and this time she stepped out.

She stood in the yard, beside the small bungalow, and she looked at the sky. It was dusk already, and the blue was in the process of changing to a violent red. Darkness, she remembered, came suddenly in this part of the world. The sky would soon be black and, because it had been a clear day, filled with a mass of twinkling stars.

She stared and stared into the distance. This was a scale of landscape that she had not watched for what seemed like a lifetime.

It was so different from the quaintness of the English countryside—so much grander. Here were no soft, rich greens, only shades of brown and red. Here were no rolling hills, only flat and endless horizons. Here, she thought, was Tanzania, a country that she had only briefly visited, and yet it felt more like home than the England in which she had spent the last twelve years.

She heard the sound of the shower behind her. She looked at her watch. Only five minutes had passed since the last time. She reentered the house and went to stand by the bathroom door.

"Want a drink?" she called.

There was a faint pause, and then Jacob's voice spoke over the sound of running water. "Love one," he said.

Without asking his preference, she fixed him a whiskey and water. After she'd poured it, she wondered whether it was the right choice—it was the drink he used to prefer, perhaps he had changed. Then she smiled to herself: How could he, after all, have changed his choice of drink? He would have had no opportunity to do so.

She poured herself the same, but weaker. She went to the bathroom door and was about to edge it open when she hesitated. And knocked.

The water was abruptly cut off. She heard a fumbling sound before the door opened. Jacob stood there, a white towel knotted around his waist.

"Thanks," he said. He reached for his drink, and his hand inadvertently touched hers. He jumped back, spilling most of his whiskey in the process. He glanced at her sheepishly. "Oh, God, I'm so nervous," he admitted.

She smiled at him. "Maybe we should get it over," she suggested. "It can't be so bad, can it?"

She was proven wrong.

Their lovemaking carried too many emotions with it. They joined together, and yet they were separate, so caught up in their own reactions that they could pay little attention to each other.

Jacob, no matter how hard he tried to push the thought away, was worried about his performance. He wanted to make it good for her. By making it so plain that she must enjoy herself, Rosa felt, Jacob was putting too much pressure on her.

And yet, they thought as they lay side by side afterward, at least they had done it. They told themselves that the first time would be the worst—things could only get easier between them.

Things did get easier but still there was something wrong, something missing. They spent three days together in the house, eating, talking, sleeping together. But neither felt completely at one with the other. They went through the motions of getting to know each other, but there was just so much left unsaid. Neither could find a way of broaching the difficult, potentially explosive subjects.

On the fourth day they decided to go out. They would, they

declared, see the famous Tanzanian coral reefs. They had a car at their disposal, and Rosa had spent the day before Jacob's arrival working out how to get around Dar es Salaam. She drove them both to the beach. They sat under palm trees, sipping beer on the sheer white sand. They waited for the boat to take them to the reefs, and they spoke little. For the first time since they had remet, they were at peace with each other. Each breathed a silent sigh of relief. Perhaps, they thought, the worst was over.

They were the only ones visiting the reef that day. They landed on the small island and said good-bye to the boatman, who promised to return at high tide. They waded out into the water, across the jagged surface, and they donned their snorkling equipment. And then, in the perfect tranquillity of a still sea, they swam, eyes down as they concentrated on the immensity of the ocean floor.

Or at least Jacob did. He felt the water all about him, supporting him, and for the first time he knew, really knew, that he was free. He looked at the reds, the greens, the purples, of those ancient corals, and he gloried in their beauty. He had no need to think, to struggle, to worry: All he had to do was float and gaze in this muffled, timeless space.

Rosa was having a more difficult time. She could not get her snorkle to work properly. She saw her husband floating calmly on the sea, and she felt annoyed as water seeped in, clouding her vision, forcing her to remove her mask and splutter. Suddenly she was angry at Jacob. Everybody, she thought, regarded Jacob's stay in prison as something to be pitied: Nobody knew how difficult it had been for her.

She knew she was being petty, blaming Jacob for something that was completely out of his control, but she could not stop the irritation from rising to her gullet. She thrashed around in the water.

Jacob felt her movement and raised his head. He gestured toward the shore, and she nodded in reply. Together they swam back in. When the water reached their knees, they were forced to walk back to the shore. It was hard going, negotiating the sharp sea floor, and Rosa was in no mood to be careful. She tripped once, and then again.

Jacob stretched out a hand to steady her. Instinctively she moved out of his grasp.

"Come on," he said in a friendly enough manner, "for once

in your life, allow yourself to be helped."

She stiffened and wheeled round. "I have learned to look after myself. I had to," she replied. "I was left on my own."

Rosa's angry riposte cut right through Jacob's sensation of peacefulness. He glared at her. He hated her in that moment— she thought always of herself, of her own precious dignity. "On your own, hey?" he angrily replied. "You certainly replaced me quickly enough."

It was difficult to guess which of the pair was the most astounded. Jacob could have bitten his tongue off. Never once in prison had he allowed himself even to think this way. He had fooled himself pretty well; he knew now that he had. All that time when he had pretended that Rosa's relationship with Richard Crossbanks was of little importance, he must have been nursing his hurt and his resentment. The human brain is a curious thing, he thought idly. It has an endless capacity to deceive.

And as for Rosa—Jacob's condemnation was one that she had been anticipating for more years than she could count. It came down on her like a judgment from on high, like a punishment she well deserved.

And yet she was strangely pleased. The last few days, she thought, had been artificially calm. She had never properly relaxed. She had been waiting for this moment, for Jacob to express what must be uppermost on his mind. Oh, they had ways of evading things, no doubt about it. They talked of the children and said little real. When things got sticky, they spoke of South Africa, of what Jacob should do, of what the future, politically, would bring. It had all been nothing but words. They had been cowardly toward each other.

Well, she was glad it was out in the open. If their relationship was to have even half a chance of surviving, they would have to have it out. Not this, not just her relationship with Richard, but a hundred other matters—important matters, crucial matters to Rosa but matters that Jacob might regard as wholly irrelevant.

For Rosa had changed much in the last decade. She looked back on their old ways, and she knew that she could never return to them. They had had a good marriage, but it had also been a marriage riven through with contradictions. Jacob had never understood how much the fact of her being a mother had held her back. He had never seen them as anything other than equals. He had ignored the special difficulties she had encountered because of her gender. And when times had got rough, they always had politics to divert them.

Jacob's voice broke through her reverie. "Well?" he demanded. "What do you have to say in reply?"

She turned away that he might not see the tears in her eyes. "The boat is back," she observed.

Whites were funny, the boatman thought, as he ferried the tight-lipped couple back to the shore. Take this pair, for example. When he'd dropped them, he had convinced himself that despite their advanced age they were newly married. They had that way about them, that look that was reserved solely for each other.

And now, in the space of four short hours, the atmosphere had completely changed. They were in trouble, he thought to himself, bad, bad trouble. Well, what did he care? It probably meant they would keep him on longer and tip him extra generously in order to put off the time when they were once more alone with each other.

The boatman was right. They both tipped him as if they were proclaiming their individual existence. They walked to the car without speaking, and they drove to their temporary home in silence. When they got in, Rosa went to the bedroom, slamming the door behind her.

Jacob nursed a drink as he waited for his wife to emerge. He didn't feel like alcohol, but sipping at it was something to do as he tried to sort out the confusion in his mind.

He, too, was somewhat relieved by their confrontation. Things had been artificially calm between Rosa and himself. It was inevitable that the unsaid would blow up in their faces. (And Rosa, he'd sensed from the first, was also resentful.) Unless they resolved their resentments, they could never stay together.

He thought, for the first time, that he would not accept Rosa on any terms just to have her. He loved her, he wished to spend his life with her, but not in this quasi-silence where their conflicting needs were buried in the interest of peace. He would fight for her, but if he lost her, then that was that.

He did not wait for her to come out. He put his drink down and marched into the bedroom. She was sitting in a chair, staring straight ahead. Her eyes, he saw with relief, were dry. She looked at him blankly.

He cleared his throat. "I've been thinking about my future," he said.

She did not reply. She heard the telltale words. *My* future, he'd said.

"I've talked to our comrades both in the country and out, and they need me." He looked away. "So I've decided to work full time for Congress," he concluded.

Congress, she thought. How English I have become—I've taken to calling it the ANC. And then she took in the implication of what he'd said. She narrowed her eyes.

"In Britain?" she asked.

He shook his head. "I'll spend some time with Martha and Rachel and then return," he said.

"I see. You're staying in Africa. And what of me?"

"You could get a job here," he said. "Mozambique is crying out for people with your expertise and political experience."

She frowned. "My, you have been busy," she said. "Only one week out, and you already have a rundown on the job situation in the whole of Southern Africa." She hated the harshness in her voice, and yet she felt driven onward by the force not so much of anger but of the knowledge that she must fight for herself, for her own needs. "I've already moved country once," she said. "And now you expect me to pack up again."

"Well, what am I supposed to do? Wait until you're ready?"

"You expected me to wait," Rosa replied.

"No, I didn't," Jacob said softly. "I just hoped you would."

They both paused and stared. They saw their own tears reflected in the other's eyes. They were separated by their differences, separated, they each thought, perhaps forever.

"I'll never be able to explain to you," Rosa said. Because I cannot explain it to myself, she thought.

Jacob nodded, and left the room.

She could not bear to let him go. She could not bear the defeat she read in the slump of his retreating back. She followed him out, demandingly.

"How can I leave the children?" she asked.

He turned. "As you've already reminded me, they're no longer children," he said. He would not weaken now: He would not let her off the hook.

It was the end, Rosa knew it. They were separated by more than twelve years. It was over.

She looked straight at him. And saw him with new eyes. In a flash she realized that she had still not dared to examine him closely. She had been frightened, she realized, to find herself comparing him with Richard and to find Jacob proving less attractive in the comparison.

Now she saw that the two men couldn't have been more different. She almost laughed out loud. Why had she expected similarity? She thought, How could it be possible? Richard was aristocratic English, Jacob a true Jew. Richard's features were fine, Jacob's were strong and craggy. Richard's body was almost effeminate, Jacob's, despite his loss in weight, was firm and manly.

And as she looked, she felt desire for Jacob well up in her. Having decided it was the end, she went straight up to him and kissed him fiercely on the lips. When he resisted a fraction, she did not even notice. She pulled him with her to the bedroom, she led him to the bed, the last thing on her mind was the open door.

This time their lovemaking was transformed. The doubt, the hesitation, was gone. They wrestled with each other on the bed. They made love almost the way strangers might, strangers who had nothing but lust to bind them, who had nothing to lose but their own sense of self.

Not one word did they exchange, and when it was over neither had energy to speak. They lay, entwined, on a crumpled bed.

At this point they had a visitor. He was a young man who gulped when he looked through the open door.

"I've brought your tickets," he said. He dropped an envelope on the floor and fled.

They didn't smile, they didn't speak. They rolled away from each other almost as if by accident. They both knew that they would soon be in London. And once again, the questions, the tangles, the difficulties, would start.

50

England: 1976

MARTHA DID THE STRANGEST THING ON THE DAY OF HER FATHER'S arrival in London: She went to visit Richard Crossbanks. She was deeply ambivalent about her intentions: She made no formal arrangement to see him. She was driven to the act and yet nervous about it. As she drove through the London streets in her Morris Minor, she nursed a faint hope that he wouldn't be home.

When she'd told Rachel of her intentions, her sister had looked at her as if she were mad. Rachel, Martha thought, was probably right. After all, she and Richard had never been close. It made no sense at all, this pilgrimage to a time past.

Nevertheless, Martha drove to his apartment. As she walked up the path, it crossed her mind that Richard might no longer even live there. She had no idea what had happened to him. She didn't even know if her mother had kept in touch with him: She assumed they still maintained some form of contact, but she'd never dared ask.

The fact that she didn't dare was one of the many indications of the extent of the forbidden territory between Martha and Rosa. After Rosa's recovery and her subsequent separation from Richard, Martha hoped she and her mother had surmounted their problems. But life, as Martha continually found, never went according to plan.

For on the occasion of their next meeting, the reserve between them had been almost tangible. Martha thought her mother judged her: She grew sullenly defensive in Rosa's presence. When she tried to describe her life to Rosa, she felt that her mother was sneering at her. She could never, she told herself, live up to her mother's expectations. She could only protect herself by keeping away.

Harold's death had compounded the problem. When Rosa phoned her daughter to tell her that Harold had died, Martha heard the agony in her mother's voice. She felt deep sympathy for Rosa. She knew that Rosa and Julia had never got on, and that Harold was the parent with whom Rosa identified. She remembered her own visit to Harold, and the glimpse she had got of that remarkable man. She understood why her mother grieved.

She took a rushed train to London, all the while resolving to demonstrate her love for her mother, but she was never given the chance. Rosa was so bloody, annoyingly efficient: It made Martha sick. In the flesh Rosa showed not the faintest hint of vulnerability. She dealt with Julia's silent suffering with a dispassionate air that was difficult to credit. She showed herself willing to console the children. The one thing she was not prepared to do was to be comforted herself.

So Martha stopped trying: With an effort, she put away her fantasies of reconciliation. She was polite to Rosa, but no more than that. She got into the habit of communicating with the family through Rachel. She chose to stay and work in Bristol (she had a job as a child psychologist attached to a GP's practice) and when she was offered what would effectively have meant a promotion in London, she refused. Even a metropolis as big as London felt too small when it contained Rosa.

But the trouble was that she couldn't cut Rosa out of her life. She didn't think of her much these days (she told herself that their relationship was irrelevant), but somewhere in the back of her mind she still longed for her mother's approval. One day, she thought, she would have to resolve their difficulties.

Jacob brought that day nearer. His timetable could not wait for Martha and Rosa. His time was up on June 16, and on June 16 he was duly released. Now, Martha had no choice but to come to London, to meet him, and to stay with her parents for as long as was necessary.

She smiled wryly to herself as she rang Richard's bell. June 16—what a day to have been freed!

She wondered whether Jacob had seen anything firsthand. She herself had watched the Soweto uprising, and the subsequent revolt in the rest of the country, on television. She watched these sights in a place to which she no longer related, but they nevertheless filled her with a kind of reluctant excitement.

As she'd watched, she'd thought, anew, that the trouble between herself and her mother did not stem from their clashing personalities alone. It came from this turbulent South Africa that forced choices on whites, that wrung agony from blacks.

That was the trouble, that was why she could neither resolve her difficulties with Rosa nor put them out of her mind forever. For the moment Martha caught herself blaming Rosa for not being a proper mother, a reproving inner voice would scold her for being so self-indulgent. What Martha had suffered was as nothing when compared to the sufferings of black South Africans.

She frowned to herself. She hated to think this way. It was like being trapped in a circle from which there was no escape.

She was still frowning when Richard opened the door.

He blinked in surprise.

"Martha," he said uncertainly.

She felt suddenly shy. He looked different from the man she had once known: different even though she couldn't put her finger on the change. "Hi, Richard," she said. "I was passing, and thought I'd drop in and see how you were."

He did not comment. He moved aside to let her pass, and he followed her up the stairs.

The apartment was, she saw, the same and yet not the same. The color scheme was unaltered. On reflection she could not imagine Richard in any other environment than among these pale beiges and pastel colors.

But there were changes—and significant ones at that. Where there had once been cushions were now plush sofas: where once had hung Navajo blankets were now neatly framed works of art. Richard, she thought, had left his entanglement with the sixties behind. It showed in his dress: She knew now why he'd seemed slightly odd on the doorstep. He was wearing a suit, its elegance and obvious expensiveness far removed from the casual clothes he'd once sported.

"Have you got a new job?" she asked.

Richard, in the act of pouring some water into a filter coffee-pot, looked up. "I'm working for the family firm."

Martha threw her bag onto one of the leather sofas and plunked herself beside it. "Bit of a change," she said, making no attempt to conceal her disapproval.

Richard set the kettle down on the kitchen surface. "Why have you come, Martha?" he asked.

Martha examined her fingernails, buying time. She regretted, now, provoking him.

"I'm not exactly sure," she said. She looked up at him defiantly.

Richard breathed in sharply. When she stared like that, she reminded him so much of her mother that it was almost unbearable. It disturbed him all the more because he'd done his utmost to file away, in the deepest recesses of his brain, his physical memory of Rosa.

After he'd parted from Rosa, he'd refused to see her again. He wasn't trying to punish her—merely to protect himself. He knew that their break was irrevocable: that South Africa, and Jacob, still exerted an unbreakable pull on Rosa. He knew this consciously even as he railed against the knowledge. He had stopped seeing her because he hadn't wanted to find himself pleading for the unobtainable.

As the years passed, his initial pain at the separation lessened. He found ways of diverting himself: He'd flung himself into work, and he'd even indulged in a series of affairs such as had once been an integral part of his life. And yet part of him was deadened—would perhaps be deadened forever.

Martha's presence revived the hurt: Her irony stung him. What she implied was true: Taking on the Crossbank empire wasn't only a change, it was also a defeat. It was a sign that the mature Richard had given up flirting with ideas that had inspired the younger, more hopeful man.

For the most part he'd managed to ignore the change in himself. Being a successful managing director was harder work than he'd imagined. It wasn't all unthinking slog: It required an intellect and an understanding that took up most of his waking hours. And yet, occasionally, in the dead of night, his brain would stop ticking over long enough for him to mourn the past: to remember Rosa and to wonder what would have happened to him if she had chosen him in preference to South Africa.

Abruptly Richard picked up the kettle again. It was not Martha's fault that her presence evoked all these painful longings. Odd as her visit was, he thought he understood her reasons for visiting him on this day when her father was due back.

"Are you nervous?" he asked.

She shot him a grateful smile. "Yes," she said in a small voice. She glanced away and took in the room again. When she looked back, it was on the kitchen door that she focused.

He glanced back, sharing her memory. "You must have been in quite a state to climb that high without anything to hold you," he said.

"I was," she agreed. "I was desperate to know what was going on." She paused. "I gave you a hard time, didn't I?"

"Yup," Richard replied. He smiled, and this time the younger man shone through.

"I did you some good, though," she added. "By my prying, I made up Rosa's mind to live with you."

Richard's mouth turned down. "Some good," he repeated reflectively. "Perhaps it was good."

"You don't regret it, do you?" Martha asked.

Richard shrugged. "Suppose not," he said. He saw the disappointment on her face, and with an effort he pushed his own feelings away.

"How are things between you and Rosa?" he asked.

Martha grimaced. "How do you think?"

Richard hesitated. The stance, that mixture of sullen aggression and insecurity, was so familiar to him. In the old days he had learned not to risk intimacy with her. But she was a grown woman now. A woman who had chosen to visit him: Surely it was worth a try? "You know," he said hesitantly, "I've always wanted to tell you something."

"About Rosa?" The hostility was more tangible now.

"No. About you."

"Go ahead." It was a dare.

"You worship your mother too much," he said. His words came out in a rush.

He had meant to say more. He had known that she would find this statement hard to take: He'd meant to explain that he was not judging her. And yet as soon as the sentence was out of his mouth, he saw by her reaction that she would not listen. She was already rising from her seat, grabbing her bag, which she flung over her shoulder.

"I shouldn't have come," she muttered. She marched to the door. Richard didn't try to stop her.

As Martha drove to Crouch End, swearing at Richard, calling

him all the names under the sun, she knew, somewhere, that she was really angry with herself. She should never have gone and visited Richard—especially on the day of Jacob's arrival. It was her fault that she'd had to listen to his stupidity.

But despite her self-knowledge, her anger kept turning back on him. How dare he? she thought. He, of all people—the man who'd patently suffered so much when Rosa dumped him. He knew nothing about her. He'd never bothered to get through her difficulties at his intrusion.

And for him to suggest that she worshiped Rosa! He was talking of himself, not of her. Hadn't she lived half her life with the dreadful knowledge that she condemned her mother? Condemned rather than worshiped.

She was still angry when she arrived at Rosa's house. She let herself in and called impatiently for Rachel. When her sister protested that they would be too early, she silenced her with one cold look. She tapped her foot while Rachel hurried to put the finishing touches to the table and to check the casserole in the oven.

But gradually as she drove to Heathrow, Martha's anger was converted to shame. What Richard had said was harmless enough. So it was an off-the-mark comment: What did that matter? She had allowed herself to be provoked, she thought. She was just nervous, nervous about meeting Jacob.

She smiled sideways at her sister.

"Look," she told Rachel, "you know how things are between me and Rosa. Could you be a buffer for a while?"

Rachel bit her lip. Why me? she thought. Why is it always me who has to behave?

"I wouldn't normally ask," Martha said. "I know it puts you in a difficult position. But for Jacob's sake . . ."

"All right," Rachel said reluctantly. She stared out the window.

As Rachel predicted, they were ridiculously early. Even if the plane had been on time, they would have had a good hour to spare. As it was, they waited almost two and half hours, cooling their heels in a crowded Terminal 3.

Finally a disembodied voice announced the arrival of the British Airways flight from Dar es Salaam. They knew it would be some time before Jacob emerged: He would have to go through a tedious immigration procedure, since his passport had been confiscated by the South African authorities. He had only an exit permit, his prison-release documents, and his birth certificate (which, given it had been issued by a country that no longer existed, would be of little use) to testify to his existence in the world.

But, even knowing that he would be one of the last to emerge, the two sisters pushed their way to the front of the barrier that cordoned off arriving passengers from the spectators.

It was then that they noticed the delegation: or to be accurate, the two delegations. One was made up of various races: African, Indian, and Caucasian, and in it were people who shot the sisters welcoming smiles. They were from the ANC. Martha knew she was annoyed. The ANC, she thought, has had twelve years of Jacob's life: Can't they give me the first few hours of the next twelve?

She nudged her sister. "Did you know they were going to be here?" she asked.

Rachel waved a hand in the group's direction. "Sure," she said.

"Well, why didn't you tell me?" Martha snapped.

Rachel frowned at her. She didn't reply. Instead, she looked beyond the ANC group, where another group of people was milling. They were all white, and they carried equipment with them: cameras, lights that they were even now setting up, huge-looking tape recorders with mikes wrapped mummylike.

"Lot of press to greet him," she observed.

Martha's annoyance deepened. "Don't be stupid," she said. "Prisoners from South Africa are two a penny. They're waiting for somebody else."

This time, although Rachel still did not reply, she looked at her sister with something approaching pity.

Forty minutes passed, and still Jacob and Rosa did not emerge. Martha stood by the barrier, trying to ignore the crowds around her, the uncomplicated greetings that were taking place.

She didn't, she reflected, like the way she was behaving. First the visit to Richard, and now her surprise at Jacob's welcoming committees. Rachel was right to ignore her reactions. Of course the ANC would meet him: Of course the press would be interested. After all, South Africa was big news these days.

As she stood, she realized that she had blocked off the possibility of sharing her greeting with others purely because she resented it. It was hard enough to meet a father you no longer knew without having to make a spectacle of yourself in front of the world's cameras. She should have stayed at home: She knew that she should. Everything was going wrong: She almost wept.

Jacob told himself that he was well prepared for the first un-fettered view of his daughters, they'd visited him every year. Except for 1975, when Rachel had come alone. Every Christmas they had sent cards with their pictures. In addition, Rosa had taken the precaution of bringing albums to Dar that he had pored over. So he thought that to see them, to touch them, would be the most natural thing in the world.

He was therefore unprepared for what happened. Rosa told him the press would be there, but he hadn't given it a second thought. When he stepped from the immigration hall, he was greeted by a barrage of flashbulbs. He'd looked away, searching for his daughters. He'd seen instead the ANC delegation. He'd walked to the barrier and shaken their hands, smiling, laughing, but still uneasy. And then Rosa nudged him to the left. He saw them—there they were: his girls, standing away from the fuss.

Except that they weren't girls any longer. They were young women.

He realized that even though he'd seen them yearly, he hadn't really seen them at all. In the artificial and strained prison en-vironment, they'd always been ill at ease. He'd spent most of their visits trying to reassure them, to spin out the time so it might last forever.

But now he didn't know how to greet them, what to say. They were like strangers. They stood tall together, composed in this strange madhouse of a place. This was their home, he reminded himself, this was their territory.

Rosa sensed his hesitation. She beckoned the girls toward them. Then she stood back.

He embraced them both together as the cameras flashed again. He felt Martha withdraw, and he tried to pull her closer.

"Don't take any notice," he whispered.

"Why?" she snapped back. "Will I spoil the photo?"

"Martha!" Rosa warned.

And then, luckily perhaps, the press descended on him. He was assailed by questions; microphones were prodded in his di-rection, hands pulled him this way and that. If not for the presence of the ANC's chief representative, who sprang to intervene in the chaos, Jacob felt he might have been pulled to bits.

They led him to an interview room, and he allowed himself to be led. He glanced back only once. He saw his daughters still standing together—Rachel looked as if she wanted to follow, while Martha stood firm.

He walked forward with determination. It would be better, he thought, to get this over with. There would be time later to reacquaint himself with his family.

Rachel's casserole was delicious, or so they kept saying.

In fact, thought Rachel, if they say it once more, I'll scream.

From a distance they must have looked almost like a normal family. They were all on their best behavior, even Martha. Perhaps, thought Rachel, it would have been better if they weren't. It made things so sticky and formal.

There, for example, sat Julia, at the head of the table, picking daintily at her meal and smiling politely. She was the silence-filler. As soon as conversation lapsed, she would stoke it up again—contributing a question here, an observation there.

Jacob was the one who mostly replied. He, too, was working hard. He was evenhanded in his approach—responding to Julia, encouraging her to continue, while taking care to focus his answers on his daughters, to include them in this gathering.

This really is an odd affair, Rachel thought, enforced intimacy between strangers.

"Pass the salt please," Julia requested. Three pairs of hands hurried to comply.

Well, Rachel reflected, what else did I expect? We are all strangers.

Take Jacob. He was an unknown quantity. It was hard to see how he had changed precisely because he was an almost mythical figure in the family—the man who had been present in his absence for twelve years.

Julia, in her own way, was equally strange. Rachel thought that she had softened since Harold's death, and yet that was only a surface impression. It was impossible to understand what was really going on with Julia. She dismissed intimacy gracefully enough, but she dismissed it all the same.

As for Martha—well, none of them knew what she was like. She'd kept away too long, even her everyday life was a secret.

Rachel thought it interesting that not only did she not know whether Martha had a lover, but also that it had never occurred to her to ask. That was an equality between them, Rachel supposed. After all, she had never spoken to Martha about her own involvement with Peter.

At least Jacob and Rosa, she reflected, seemed at ease with each other. They took pains to conceal this fact. They took care not to touch each other, but Rachel knew her mother well enough to see that Rosa was happy. The only explanation, she thought, was that her parents had decided to give it a go. She felt an incredible sense of relief.

Nevertheless, she also felt irritated. They could go on like this forever, her family, making polite conversation—never being able to separate because they had never really come together. She knew that she was being harsh in her judgment—she was feeling particularly fragile at the present—but she could see them sitting endlessly at this table, eating, drinking, trapped in their failure to get close.

"This casserole is delicious," Julia said.

Jacob smiled uneasily.

"Rachel's always been a better cook than any of us," Rosa said.

"Than me, you mean?" Martha asked.

Rosa frowned. "Well . . ." she began.

"It's not like you ever tasted my food," Martha said. "Is that what you're implying?"

"Tell me . . ." Jacob jumped in. He was not allowed to finish his sentence.

"Really delicious," Julia said loudly.

That was the last straw. Rachel took a deep breath.

"I'm pregnant," she announced.

That stopped them in their tracks.

"Darling," Julia said, her fork poised midway between plate and mouth.

"You're what?" This from Martha.

"Is Peter . . . ?" Rosa tried.

"The father?" snapped Rachel. "Of course he is. And before you ask, we did plan it. As a matter of fact, I'm quite pleased about it."

Only Jacob, the man who had been deprived of any real contact for so long, acted as he should. He left his chair, and holding his arms open, he walked up to her. She rose and allowed herself to be folded in his embrace.

"Oh, Daddy," she whispered.

"Congratulations," he whispered into her ear. He raised his voice and looked at the rest of the family. "I better meet this Peter," he said.

There was a short silence. Then Rosa smiled and walked toward her youngest daughter.

Martha's voice followed her. "I better meet him, too," she said.

"Thank God that's over," Rosa said as she climbed into the bed beside Jacob.

"It wasn't easy," Jacob admitted. "But I suppose we shouldn't have expected it to be."

Rosa snuggled up to his waiting arm. "Poor Rachel," she said. "Blurting out her news like that."

"It loosened things up, at least," Jacob commented.

"You mean it got rid of Julia," Rosa replied.

There was a short silence. Rosa leaned over Jacob and switched off the bedside light.

"We'll have to get another," Jacob said. "Now we're two."

Rosa did not reply. They lay together silently. In another part of the house a door was quietly opened.

"I will visit," Jacob said after a long while. "As often as I can."

Rosa pulled away from him. Her eyes now accustomed to the dark, she looked at Jacob. "How did you know?" she asked.

"That you weren't coming with me?"

Rosa nodded.

Jacob sighed. "I suppose I always expected it. You've got a life here. And the girls still need you."

Gently Rosa stroked Jacob's hair. "It's not that I don't . . ." she began.

"Love me?" Jacob said. "Oh, darling, I never thought it was. We'll manage somehow. We won't lose each other again."

"Can I come in?" Martha asked.

"You're in already." Rachel's voice was muffled. She was holding a pillow on her chest, and her head drooped onto it.

Martha hesitated. She had wanted to go sit on Rachel's bed,

but something in her sister's posture stopped her. She walked instead up to the bookshelf. Idly she began thumbing through the childish collection.

"It's weird," she said, "us all being in the same house again."

Rachel threw the cushion off the bed. "What do you want, Martha?" she demanded.

Martha turned. She saw how fierce the glare in her sister's eyes was, and she almost lost courage and returned to her old bedroom. But she took a deep breath. Just because she had begun the day so badly, she told herself, there was no need to end it likewise.

"I came to tell you that I'm happy for you," she said.

Rachel's face softened, but still held a look of suspicion.

"I am happy," Martha insisted. "I think you'll make a wonderful mother. And if you chose Peter, he must be a good one."

She saw her sister's face crumple. She went up to the bed and sat beside Rachel. She took her sister's hands and began to rub them.

"You're cold," she said.

"I feel so stupid," Rachel wept. "I shouldn't have told you all like that. I should have waited."

"Oh, no," Martha replied. "We've done too much waiting in our family. Anyway," she added, "even if your timing was a bit off, I was relieved. At least somebody else was the center of the drama for a change."

"I thought you like it," Rachel said.

"Being the problem one?" Martha shook her head. "No, I never liked it. I just didn't know how else to behave." She leaned over and kissed her sister lightly on the forehead. "Get some sleep," she advised. "After all, you've got somebody else to think about now."

She got up and walked to the door. Just before leaving, she looked back. She saw her sister snuggling down in the bed. She smiled and closed the door softly. And then she stood outside the room. It was like happy families again, she thought. Rosa had Jacob, Rachel had Peter and a baby on the way. And I? she thought. Whom do I have?

She shook herself and went back to her own room.

51

Somewhere in Africa: 1984

"WAIT HERE, COMRADE," ROBERT INSTRUCTED, "WHILE I LOCATE them."

Jacob nodded. He watched as his companion strode into the distance, pushing his way into the undergrowth until he completely disappeared.

Jacob was left alone, surrounded by dark green foliage, embraced by the damp heat, his ears attuned to the sounds of twigs breaking, as somewhere in the distance the new trainees were put through their paces.

He looked around him. He knew that he might be waiting a long time, and so, seeing a tree stump a few paces away, went and sat down on it. He removed a handkerchief from the top pocket of his safari jacket, and slowly wiped the sweat off his brow. He felt a moment's relief, but it was a useless gesture—he knew that. No sooner would his arm drop down again than the beads of perspiration would begin to gather, dripping down onto his collar.

As he replaced the handkerchief, he smiled wryly at the sight of his crumpled khaki shirt. The shirt was part of a suit, a fashion garment that needed daily attention from an iron to stay looking even half-decent. Out here in the bush it lost its arrogance, it simply gave up in defeat. Its inadequacy, he thought, was expressive of the different worlds he inhabited. It showed how his life was split into sections—each containing its own wardrobe, pace, and people.

He had bought the suit during his last visit to London, which had taken place in the depths of an English winter. Rosa and he loved to go shopping together, and they had scoured the West End for lightweight clothes. It was an odd process—searching for summer amid the wreckage of winter sales, but eventually they had found the khaki. They had been so proud of themselves. It would be perfect, they told each other.

There were some lessons, he thought, that one never learned. The sense of humidity, of unending heat, was one of them. It could be remembered, described even, but never experienced unless one was immersed in it.

Jacob wasn't complaining. Although he could have done without certain aspects of his surroundings—his sweat-soaked clothes, for example, or the floods of insects that seemed especially partial to his white skin—he felt more alive when he was sweltering here. There was something about the bush—its proximity to nature, perhaps, or maybe just its isolation—which made his heart soar.

Prison, he thought, must have contributed to his preference for this kind of landscape. For prison had accustomed him to solitude. Even though he had spent his free life in cities, his twelve years in jail had changed him—making him long for peace and quiet, for somewhere without continual bustle.

Not that he often got it. He traveled incessantly these days—flying between Africa and Europe, attending meetings on behalf of the ANC, planning, studying, arguing. It was work that he loved—not the details of it, but his involvement in the movement. He felt privileged to be involved at this time.

For the ANC was no longer the same, would never, in fact, be the same. After June 1976, protests inside the country did not die down. For over a year South Africa was rocked by sporadic youth rebellions. When the government responded with increasingly repressive measures, thousands of children were forced to flee the country. Some settled in exile, and for the most part they joined up with the Congress. They joined the ANC's youth wing, the army; they filled the ANC's school to the bursting point. They brought with them hope for the future and the determination to realize their ambitions for a free South Africa.

The ANC's scope of work multiplied overnight—from each member was demanded an accelerated commitment. But Jacob, like most of them, did not complain. He considered himself a lucky man. In '63, during his darkest hours, he had imagined that the struggle, and his life with it, had ended. Now, he saw that it had only just begun.

And he was doubly lucky. Rosa, now a mature woman, had grown more beautiful, and wiser as well. Together they snatched precious time, managing somehow to dwell in the present. He saw her less than he wished, yet his absence did not sour their relationship. It strengthened it, made it more precious.

Things were more problematic with his daughters. He had missed both their adolescences, the time when they moved into their own unique form of adulthood, and there was no denying that he did not know them well.

It was easier with Rachel, who was now married and the mother of two. Jacob focused his energy on his grandchildren, communicating with their mother through them. He spent many a happy hour on all fours, playing with the youngsters, hearing them screech with laughter. The delight on Rachel's face was enough.

But with Martha he could not bridge the gap. If she had boyfriends, she kept them well in the background. When asked about herself, she would reply monosyllabically. She was not unhappy, Jacob kept reassuring himself, she couldn't look so well if she were. She was just aloof—not only from him but from Rosa, and, he suspected, from her sister as well.

Oh well, thought Jacob. She must live her own life.

He smiled to himself. It was easy to think clearly out here in the bush, easier than when faced with an angry Martha in person.

Sometimes, Jacob thought as he wiped his forehead again, revolutions are simpler than families.

"Found them at last." A triumphant voice broke through his reverie.

He looked up and smiled at the sight of Robert, who emerged from the bush, his arms scratched, his face wet with sweat. Beside him walked a young man whose neatness made a complete contrast—a man whose simple khaki trousers and white shirt were spotlessly clean, who walked on light feet, blending with his surroundings.

"This is Petrus," Robert said.

Jacob nodded. He knew of Petrus, and had long wanted to meet him.

He pushed himself upright and walked toward the two.

He had almost reached them when a slight breeze ruffled the trees above. For an instant the sun shone directly onto Jacob's face, that bright, light African sun, and he was momentarily dazzled. He blinked, the leaves moved back into place, and clear vision returned. But for the first second when he looked at Petrus, it was as though he were looking at somebody else, and that somebody else was agonizingly familiar.

The impression evaporated. He and Petrus were alongside each other. Petrus held out his arm, and his left hand gripped his own forearm in a gesture of respect.

Jacob nodded at Petrus's posture. "It is I who owe you respect," he said with a smile. "We have been hearing of your exploits. Your work is much praised."

The young man scowled, but in an awkward rather than unfriendly manner. To emphasize his point, he shook his head in a kind of rough denial. It was in character, Jacob knew: He remembered somebody telling him how modest Petrus was, how he built up the exploits of his charges and played down his own contribution.

And yet Petrus had not been able to conceal entirely the immensity of the work he had accomplished. He was a legend among the younger comrades. Single-handedly he had built up a military cell within the country: He had been responsible for organizing the transportation networks for weapons; he had found many a reliable recruit inside South Africa. And all of this, they said, for a man rumored to be in his early twenties— for Petrus was a pseudonym, and few knew his history.

"It is important that our leaders visit the comrades," Petrus said quietly. "It gives them a feeling of belonging, a feeling that they need, since many of them have been torn from their families at too young an age."

Jacob glanced sideways at him. Petrus was young, he could see that, and it pained Jacob to hear him talking of youths perhaps only a few years younger than he as if they came from a different generation. And yet it was inevitable. What Petrus must have experienced in his short life was bound to age a person.

"Recent events have turned age upside down," Jacob commented. "The young have made the change because only the young do not fear death."

Petrus smiled briefly, and once again a feeling of familiarity swept over Jacob. It nagged at him: Their connection was just below the surface, but he could not grasp it, it kept eluding him, as if it did not want to be known.

"Have we met?" Jacob asked.

Petrus shook his head.

Jacob felt a growing sense of annoyance with himself. Petrus was familiar, he was not imagining it, he would not rest until he had placed him. He stopped in his tracks and looked at the man—ahead of them Robert was following a barely discernible path in the bush toward a clearing in the distance.

Petrus did not dodge the scrutiny. He let Jacob stare him full in the face; he withstood the examination without blinking. He smiled again.

And then comprehension, along with the memories that it provided, hit Jacob. He could not imagine how it hadn't come to him immediately. "You're a Bopape," he said. "You're Moses' grandson, Lindiwe's son."

"My name was once Nathaniel," Petrus confirmed.

Nathaniel, Jacob thought, was a babe in arms when I was imprisoned, when Moses was killed. He saw that Petrus was looking at him, waiting for him to speak. "How is your mother?" he asked.

Petrus frowned. "I have not seen her for a long time," he said. His face lightened. "But when I was with her, my mother spoke of you often. Even in the times when she was most in favor of separation from whites, she talked of you with respect."

Unbidden, inappropriate, unexpected tears sprang into Jacob's eyes. He blinked, and the man in front of him seemed to melt—in the process he widened, his features broadened, his face aged—and for a fraction of a second he could have been Moses resurrected. Jacob swallowed hard.

This was his past standing in front of him—his past as well as his future. And it was also more than that. It represented the part of him that he thought had been buried forever, that had been lost in prison because he had had too much time to mourn and no heart to do it properly.

He took a step toward his young companion, and he embraced him. "I loved Moses," he whispered. "He was my friend. I have never got over my sorrow that I could not attend his funeral."

"Comrades!" shouted Robert from the distance.

Jacob and Petrus separated. They looked at each other for a brief moment—the white man in his middle fifties, the black youth not yet twenty-one—and they both felt a kind of companionship that came not from contact but from something deeper. Their histories were irrevocably entwined, their futures, too, each separately thought.

"Comrades," Robert repeated.

They nodded at each other and walked toward the group of men and women who squatted expectantly under a rough shelter.

"Comrade Swiece," Robert said, as they approached, "has come to give medical instruction."

Smiling a greeting, Jacob marched to the front of the class. Putting aside all thoughts of Petrus, he began to talk.

Nathaniel (for although he answered exclusively to Petrus, he never could get into the habit of calling himself by his new name) found it hard to sleep that night. His encounter with Jacob, the fact of being recognized by one who had known his family, disturbed him. It threw him off keel, pushing him away from his carefully cultivated neutrality.

Nathaniel rarely considered the past. It was too difficult to do so, a luxury he would not permit himself. That was the way he dealt with a transition in life that had been so abrupt. One moment he was attending school, concerned more with the score of his local soccer team than with anything else, and the next he was part of an uprising, for an instant the hunter and then suddenly the hunted, fleeing from the country.

He'd scrambled over the borders of South Africa along with many of his contemporaries. They had been greenhorns, untutored in the way of the world, aged by battle at the same time they were made more youthful by the sudden separation from their families. Gradually they had sorted themselves out: Some chose to eke out an existence in the front-line states, others to go as refugees to the countries of the West and to try to settle there. But the vast majority, Nathaniel among them, had joined the ANC.

The world he entered was so different from the one he'd left that his new eyes found it difficult to look back at his old life. It was as if his family had been placed on a shelf, a carefully dusted, immaculately looked-after shelf, a shelf with an unforgiving caretaker who forbade access—a shelf without movement in the back of his memory.

His situation involved little real choice on his part. Staying in

South Africa meant imprisonment, and perhaps even death. He carried with him a long list of those childhood friends who had died.

There was no time for brooding these days. There was only time for action. Since joining MK, he had been caught in a whirlwind of activity. He was good at his work; he had a way with people, he knew how to assess them, how to persuade them, how to get the best from them.

The others who looked up to him could not see his sadness; they did not know how he had shoved his image of Lindiwe away from himself because it was too painful to consider. To think of his mother was to raise a whole set of longings that he could no longer afford.

He turned over on the uneven ground. He pulled his bedroll around his shoulders. It was the darkest part of the night. Soon, he knew, he would feel a soft hand shaking him, soon it would be time to go again.

Jacob was awakened by the sound of movement. He lifted himself on his elbows and gazed through the velvety blackness of the night. He saw a shadow move away, and then, as his eyes grew more accustomed to the dark, he saw Nathaniel spring to his feet, immediately alert once roused. He saw the characteristic fighter's stance, that air of readiness, the quick glance of recognition at the surroundings. He watched as Nathaniel walked toward the waiting jeep. He almost let the boy go.

But then he changed his mind. Suddenly he felt an urgent need to bid Nathaniel good-bye—superstitiously afraid not to do so.

He raised himself from the ground, at half the speed of Nathaniel. His back felt stiff: I am no longer young, he thought.

He needed to hurry. Nathaniel was already by the vehicle.

He got there just in time. He put a hand on Nathaniel's back as he was in the process of climbing into the jeep.

"Good luck," Jacob said.

Nathaniel smiled. "I was glad to meet you," he said. "We hear much of you in the movement."

The engine coughed its way into life. The jeep moved off.

Jacob stared after it for a long time. The sadness he'd experienced when he first recognized Nathaniel descended once more.

"What a waste," he said out loud, "that such talent must be

used for fighting. Nathaniel should still be learning, should be experimenting with life."

"*Ja*," came a voice from behind him.

He turned to see that Robert had also risen.

"That is apartheid's worst crime," Robert continued. "It has taken children away from their mothers, and childhood away from the children."

By the time he reached the Swazi border, Nathaniel had put all thoughts of Jacob aside. It had been a long journey, much of it along rough tracks, which meant that the occupants of the jeep were continually buffeted against its doors. That and hunger combined might have been reason enough to forget Jacob, but it wasn't the real reason.

For the lapse in memory was achieved deliberately. Nathaniel needed all his wits about him—he could not let his mind stray for even a minute. His dangerous assignment was only about to begin. He must don the mask of Petrus: The boy Nathaniel was a luxury he could no longer afford.

He shook hands with his driver and stood to one side as the jeep moved slowly away, its lights off even though it was still quite dark. When he could no longer hear its engine, Nathaniel began to walk.

He progressed instinctually. He had made this trip many times before, and he had a feel for the terrain. Only occasionally did he merge into a clearing where he could just make out the orange lights of the border post. He kept away from it—even though he had forged papers that were identical to the real thing, one never knew what whim would motivate the security police to come sniffing around at odd hours.

But he could not afford to keep too far away from it. His contact would be waiting near the border. If Nathaniel did not turn up within a specified time, the man had instructions to drive away. Using the low foliage—cut almost like a hedge—as his guide, Nathaniel hurried forward.

He reached the bank of the muddy stream without too much hesitation. Extracting a piece of string from his pocket, he used it to strap his briefcase securely to his shoulders. Then he scrambled down the steep bank, keeping one hand out to steady himself, splashed into and across the water, climbed up the bank on the other side, and sped his way into the forest that heralded the beginning of South Africa. Dawn had arrived: He had little time to reach his meeting place.

He lost concentration for an instant, made one wrong turn, became temporarily lost, and was late. He was panting from exertion and sweating, probably from fear, when he arrived to find that the the pickup was still there, that its engine was running. Nathaniel tapped sharply on the window. He saw the driver jump and turn. Two wide eyes greeted him.

Nathaniel opened the door to the passenger seat. He stretched out a hand. "Petrus," he said briefly.

The driver beamed at him. "*Got,*" he said, "you gave me a scare. I thought that my time was finally up."

"Sorry," Nathaniel said. Climbing into the seat, he closed the door gently. He appeared calm, but he was actually berating himself for cutting things so finely: He was out of practice, he must concentrate better.

Even as he thought this, his mind kept functioning, weighing, assessing—and his sense, too. He sniffed. There was something odd about this car, he thought, something he couldn't exactly pinpoint.

The driver gunned the engine, and moved off in a cloud of dust. Nathaniel looked at him: He seemed his usual self.

Turning his head, Nathaniel inspected the backseat. There was nothing there, nothing, not even a speck of dirt. And then Nathaniel realized why the car smelled so odd. The car was brand new, its seats stank of fresh plastic. He relaxed.

"Are you getting hold of cars before they even leave the production line?" he asked.

The driver did not look at him. He concentrated instead on the road ahead. "I'll let myself off in Amsterdam," he said. "It's better that way."

Nathaniel smiled to himself. The movement, he thought, could learn a lot from people like this driver. A member of a network of car thieves, the man knew how to keep secret the tricks of his trade. Each time Nathaniel crossed the border, the man was ready with a different car: Sometimes they drove quite a distance together, but never had Nathaniel learned more about his driver than his name—Abraham (which, Nathaniel thought, was probably as false as Petrus).

Aside from that, Abraham was a mystery: Nathaniel sometimes doubted that he even had much of a developed kind of political consciousness. He would be drawn on no subject—not on his trade, his private life, not even on his opinions of apartheid.

And yet he was solid in his own way. He produced cars accompanied by scrupulous paper work: None of their comrades had ever been captured through failures in their transportation.

Abraham did all this for free: He was one of the many who risked imprisonment and even death for the movement. It was, Nathaniel thought, a reflection on how polarized things had become in South Africa. Once upon a time Abraham would have seemed a mere criminal—a grown up *tsotsi* without morals or cares; now, he and other like him gave generously to the movement.

Thinking about it, Nathaniel was once more intrigued. I might as well try again, he thought to himself. He can only rebuff me.

"Tell me, Abraham," he said out loud. "Why do you do this for us?"

Abraham shrugged. He put his foot down on the accelerator, adeptly negotiating a hole in the road.

Nathaniel gave up. He stretched his legs in front of him, and pulling his hat down over his eyes, he shut them. But as he was about to drift off into sleep, he remembered something. He shoved the hat away and leaned forward. Picking up his briefcase, he removed the string and opened it wide. He withdrew a tape cassette and held it up to Abraham.

"Dollar Brand," he said briefly. "The latest."

Abraham smiled in delight. "Ag, man," he said, "I knew you'd come through." He took the cassette from Nathaniel and, flipping away the case with a practiced gesture, slipped it into the tape deck that was set into the dashboard.

"I bought two," Nathaniel said. "One for you."

The sound of a strident row of saxophones cut through the air. Nathaniel settled back to sleep.

But this time it was Abraham's voice that aroused him. It came out of the blue, a non sequitur, a rumination, really, as if Abraham were thinking out loud.

"I used to drive taxis in Soweto," he said.

Nathaniel opened one eye. He knew that he must not overstate his interest: That might put Abraham off. He grunted noncommittally.

"I was making a good living," Abraham said. "I bet you stood at one of our ranks. In those days I could pick and choose my customers, load my car up, stop at points of my choosing."

"*Ja*, and fleece the uninitiated dry," Nathaniel commented.

Abraham ignored him. His voice became distant, almost dreamlike. "And then," he said, "June 16 happened."

Nathaniel heard something in Abraham's voice, something akin to despair, that alerted him. He straightened his posture. "Did you lose a son?" he asked.

Abraham shook his head. "I've never had children," he said. "Me, I'm a bachelor for life." He stopped speaking almost as if they had come to the end, as if their conversation were over. But then his voice sounded above the music. "We taxi drivers saw some sights, I can tell you," he said. "Day after day, they shot at those children." He paused again; the car slowed down.

Nathaniel glanced over at him. he took in a pair of glazed eyes, a forehead set into a deep frown. He kept his mouth shut.

"They were something, those children," Abraham commented. He looked at Nathaniel. "You must have been one of them," he said.

When Nathaniel did not reply, did not, in fact, even move a muscle in his face, Abraham put his foot down on the accelerator. "The children used to stop the taxis," he said, and his voice had got louder. "They needed transportation. They needed to get their friends to hospital, to the mortuary. We, the taxis, were the only non-Boer vehicles left on the roads."

Abraham pushed loudly at his horn, cursed as if something were blocking his way, when in fact the road was empty.

"That's what changed me," he continued. "It happened to all of us taxi drivers. We couldn't ignore the rebellion, we had to take sides. And so we got together and discussed things. We formed an early-warning system for the townships. We were the first to know when troops were on the move, and we sounded our horns to tell the people."

"And now?" Nathaniel asked.

Abraham shrugged. "It still goes on," he said. "The new taxi drivers keep up the custom. But us old ones, the police soon caught on. They used any excuse to endorse us out."

"And so you took up . . ." Nathaniel began.

"My current profession," Abraham completed for him. "A man has to make a living." His voice became harsher. He scowled. "Listen to me," he said. "I've gone soft in the head, talking like a woman. And you, you'd never tell me anything, would you?"

Nathaniel shook his head and smiled.

His smile was not returned. For a brief moment Abraham took his eyes off the road and stared straight at Nathaniel. "Secrecy can become a sickness," he said. "It can separate you from the people."

Nathaniel flicked his eyes away. He stared out the window.

When Abraham spoke again, his voice had softened. "I've been on the road too long," he said. "I'm getting edgy."

He stopped the car abruptly. Behind a tree, Nathaniel saw, lurked another vehicle—Abraham's lift away from this place. The two men got out together. They met in front of the car. Abraham handed Nathaniel the keys.

"The documents are in the glove compartment," he said. "You're safe for a week. After that, abandon the vehicle." He smiled as Nathaniel pressed a tape into his hand. "Thanks, man," he said. "Good luck." He tapped Nathaniel lightly on the shoulder. Then he turned on his heels, climbed into the waiting car, and was driven off without a backward glance.

Nathaniel waited as the car disappeared down the dirt track. He stood in the middle of the dirt track, breathing in the dry air. His head was filled with sounds that were not there: of chanting, of calls of recognition, of cries of togetherness and celebration that turned to anguish as the first of the shots were fired.

He heard it still, that last cry: He heard it fresh in his ears. He looked up in the sky. A buzzard, he saw, was circling above him.

He shook himself, and then climbed into the driver's seat. He needed to free himself from Abraham's comments, from his thoughts of the night before.

He put the key into the ignition and listened, as if from some distance away, as the engine sparked into life.

He put the car in gear. His thoughts turned to his route. The car moved forward. He was on his own.

52

South Africa: 1984

AS SOON AS LINDIWE AWOKE THE PAIN RETURNED SHE SHUT HER EYES tightly in the hope that she could drive it away, but to no avail. It cut at her, it welled up in her throat. It was not a physical pain, but nevertheless it hurt, hurt more, perhaps, because it had no medical remedy.

Leaning on her elbows, she pushed herself into a sitting position. She looked out the window and saw that the sun was low in the sky. It was still early. She lay back again, feigning sleep. She did not want to disturb the others, and anyway, creeping out of bed to busy herself around the house would accomplish nothing. She could not drive this particular hurt away through distraction. It was part of her, had been for a long time; it lurked in the back of her mind, it would never, ever, go away.

Try as she did, she found it impossible to lie still. She tossed and turned, and eventually ended up facing the wall. Wide-eyed, she stared at nothing.

When she felt a light hand touch her hair, she nearly shrugged it off. She forced herself to resist the temptation. It would be wrong to reject Johannes on this particular day. He also carried the pain inside him; he seldom spoke of it, but she knew it was there as surely as she felt her own.

She turned and smiled faintly at him.

He stroked her hair again. "It's Nathaniel's birthday," he said.

She nodded. "He would have been twenty-one."

"He *is* twenty-one," Johannes corrected.

Lindiwe blinked. It had been such a long time since they had last seen Nathaniel—seven years—such a long time. He had been a child when he left. She thought about how he must have changed. She probably wouldn't recognize him, she thought, or he her.

"He's alive, somewhere, and celebrating," Johannes said loudly.

Lindiwe nodded her head in weary agreement. Johannes was probably right. If Nathaniel were dead, she thought, they would have heard by now. Bad news might take a long time to arrive in South Africa, but arrive it did, with a kind of monotonous regularity.

"Sometimes I hate him," she whispered. "Because he has made me so afraid."

Johannes did not reply. He just continued stroking her head.

Lindiwe looked into her husband's eyes. "You have so much courage," she said. "You, and so many others like you, have accepted our children's chosen course. Why is it I, I with my family's history of rebellion, who am on the point of cracking?"

Johannes reached across and gripped her hand. "You are not cracking," he said. Lindiwe thought she detected a kind of desperation in his voice. He's trying to persuade himself, she thought.

He squeezed her hand again. "You are too hard on yourself," he murmured. "You suffer more because of your family's involvement. You are only too aware of the punishments for resistance."

Lindiwe shivered. Ever since they had heard, by a circuitous route, that Nathaniel had joined MK, she had been mutely afraid. It was as if she had never experienced so much trepidation, and yet she knew that she had. This is what it had been like when Moses had been taken into detention.

History, she thought, sometimes seems so circular. In 1963, when Moses was killed, the people of South Africa were organizing, fighting, resisting. And yet, at the very height of their resistance, they had been defeated. The country had become quiescent, each person's energy concentrated on the hardship of everyday life rather than on their dreams for a future, for a free South Africa.

And then, suddenly, the next generation, children like Nathaniel, had gone on the march. Enough, they shouted, we want our rights, we want our dignity, we want freedom! They were indefatigable, those children, they were irrepressible, and they infected their younger brothers and sisters with the same spirit of defiance.

And, no matter what was thrown at them, they were not crushed, they kept on demonstrating, meeting, refusing to go to school. No wonder their parents, who initially lagged behind them, began to join in until whole communities were part of the resistance. The struggle had started up again—but this time the starting point was higher than it had once been.

No, Lindiwe thought, history does not transcribe a circle. It progresses too fast for that: It makes instead a spiral. It is human relationships that are circular. It is I who have become my mother.

For in her darkest nights, an image of Peggy's face by Moses' graveside returned to haunt Lindiwe. Peggy, she remembered, had not reacted. Peggy had refused to display any grief, and instead her sorrow had been transformed into anger not at Moses' murderers, but at their victim himself.

Lindiwe had hated Peggy for her reaction: She had judged her mother for her inability to understand that the struggle was as important as the man. And yet now that she was grown, now that she was a mother, now that her son had chosen to struggle, she wondered if she would act any better.

Will I be able to forgive Nathaniel? she wondered. When they bring the news of his death, will I not want to blame him for choosing the ANC rather than his mother?

"You are stronger than you think," Johannes said, as if he were reading her mind.

"I'm not so sure," Lindiwe said. "Do you know, if Nathaniel were to come now and ask me whether he should continue to fight, I do not know what my answer would be. Me—the daughter of Moses Bopape, the granddaughter of Evelyn and Nathaniel. What has happened to me?"

"You are a mother," Johannes replied.

Lindiwe reached over and touched his cheek. He was, she thought, a good man. The years had solidified the bond between them: They had grown up together, they had seen their children flourish, they had withstood Bertha's troubles and Nathaniel's absence without turning in anger on each other. She, who had once considered Johannes slow, had learned to appreciate his stability, his calm, and his confidence in his family.

"I would do anything to see Nathaniel," she whispered. Johannes nodded.

"Alive," she concluded.

While Lindiwe gave voice to her fears, Nathaniel was beginning to think that his stock of good fortune was running low. The trip had hardly started, and yet already it was faltering. He had encountered one irritation after the other, and he knew only too well that in his line of work even minor problems could lead to major disasters.

The first occurrence was when he'd run straight into a police roadblock only minutes from Ermelo. It must have been hastily erected, for he had no prior warning of its presence. He turned a corner and there it was; there was no avoiding it.

Nathaniel traversed the country often, so he was accustomed to roadblocks. But never before had he been stopped so near the border. Abraham always prewarned him of any police activity and gave directions on how to evade it.

When he saw the barrier in the road, Nathaniel's heart began to pound. He slowed down. It crossed his mind that Abraham might have given him away. Perhaps treachery was the explanation for the break in Abraham's habitual reticence.

He shoved the thought away. He stopped the car and sat quite still, his eyes focused blankly on the road ahead.

A policeman strolled toward him, and when he had almost arrived, he jerked his head in Nathaniel's direction. "Out," he said curtly. His hand went to his holster and rested there.

Nathaniel opened the door. He put one foot on the ground, and smiled, winningly, he hoped, at the policeman. "Should I bring my registration papers, *baas*?" he asked.

"*Ja*," the policeman replied. "Get them. And no funny business, *verstaan*?"

With exaggerated gestures intended to imply innocence, Nathaniel opened the glove compartment. He grinned through the windshield while he felt for his gun. It was on the outside, where he had carelessly left it. There was a mass of papers around it, and his hands tore at them as he pushed the hard object to the back of the compartment.

"Hurry up," the policeman ordered.

"Coming, *baas*," Nathaniel said. Having concealed his weapon, he must now find the car's documents.

He looked down, but to no avail: He couldn't see any registration papers. He found a whole lot of other documents, including a car manual, its unopened cellophane packaging emphasizing the car's newness, but nothing that attributed the car to him.

He cursed himself as his search gathered speed. He should have looked at the compartment before, instead of just shoving the gun inside it. He had slipped up. He'd better watch out.

Then he let out a sigh of relief. There were the documents. He must have overlooked them on his first go-through. As he extracted them, he glanced through them quickly. Abraham had been as good as his word, they were made out in his name, Petrus Kepe. Even his profession, traveling salesman, was there.

Slightly more confident, Nathaniel stepped out beside the car. He looked neither to the left nor the right but took care, at the same time, to keep his eyes level—concentrating on the ground was often read as a sign of guilt.

Nathaniel had perfected a way of dealing with the police and even lectured others on it. One must not, he would say, appear nervous. On the other hand, one had to maintain a fine balance. It could be fatal to exhibit overconfidence. Fatal was, he thought, the correct word. His life, after all, often depended on playing the situation right. He had heard tales of comrades picked up because they raised police suspicion by fumbling with their keys, or because they gave off an air of hostility or tried too hard to please.

So he stood patiently, but not too patient; submissively but not too submissive.

The minutes ticked by. The policeman was in a hurry as long as Nathaniel kept him waiting, but once Nathaniel was ready for inspection, he turned his back and wrote something in his notebook. Only after a protracted time did he shift around again. He stretched out a hand.

Nathaniel placed his pass into the waiting palm. When that was returned to him, he presented the registration documents. They passed muster—Abraham had not betrayed him.

"Open up," the policeman said.

Nathaniel went to the trunk and slipped the key in the lock. It opened easily enough, and he was relieved to see that there were samples inside. He stood away from the car, allowing the policeman access.

He anticipated a summary inspection followed by a sharp order to continue on his way. So he was surprised when the policeman bent his head low and began to riffle through the contents of the trunk. The pounding returned with a vengeance. What had he neglected to do? What did the policeman see that he hadn't?

It seemed like an age before the policeman raised his head. He was holding a striped tie. "Simon," he called.

From the side of the road another policeman sauntered over. "Trouble?" he inquired.

The policeman held up a tie. "What do you think?" he asked. "Doesn't this look too fancy for a *kaffir* to wear?"

The second policeman narrowed his eyes. He felt the material, turning it in his hands, and then he looked at Nathaniel.

"Hey, boy," he said, "what for are you carrying such fancy stuff? You getting ideas above your station?"

"No, *baas*," Nathaniel said quickly. His eyes began to water. Both policeman were watching him now, watching him intently. He must do something, say something, before their suspicions were further aroused. "My *baas* chooses the m-merchandise," he stuttered. "I just take the orders."

The first policeman scowled. He gazed around him. "Expensive vehicle for a *kaffir*," he commented.

Just then a car appeared in the distance. Its muffler was damaged, and as it drove toward them it banged and jolted along the road. Distracted by the noise, the first policeman turned to his colleague.

"Ag, these *kaffirs* are all *dumphkops*," he said. He stuffed the tie into his trouser pocket. "You can go," he told Nathaniel.

"Thank you, *baas*," Nathaniel said quickly. He closed the trunk, climbed into the car, and it was all he could do to restrain himself from speeding off at a hundred miles an hour.

The incident left Nathaniel feeling badly shaken up. He turned it over in his mind, berating himself for his failure to check his papers or inspect his merchandise. Both things were potentially fatal errors. The fact that they passed muster was no real cause for relaxation. They had been assembled by others, who were not as finely attuned to the dangers confronting Nathaniel.

No, there was no doubt about it, he had been remiss. His failure to familiarize himself with the car's contents might have shown in his attitude, and could lead eventually to a kind of questioning that he couldn't evade.

He knew he was being unduly harsh with himself, but that was in a way the cause of his success at his job. He judged himself first: and he accepted nothing short of perfection. That way he could expect it from others.

Only when he thought that he had taken the lesson to heart did he allow himself to relax. There was very little traffic on the road, and he opened the windows wide, turned the volume of the tape up, and drove down the long road. He timed himself well, arriving in the next town in time to satisfy the grumbling in his stomach. He pulled up at a store that stood by the road.

Then he made his second mistake. He was humming to himself, and he walked into the place without thinking. Only when he was standing just inside the cool building, and staring straight into a set of outraged eyes, did he realize what he had done.

"I'm s-so sorry, *m-mevrouw*," he stuttered. "I . . . I wasn't th-thinking."

He left the place quickly and rounded the corner. There it was, the faded sign that pointed to the native entrance. For a moment he stood beneath it. He was amazed at himself. How could he have done that? How could he have walked into a shop without first checking whether there was a separate partition for Africans?

It was incredible, he thought, how soon one could forget the rules that had once been second nature, and that were now at the very essence of his own survival. During his last trip he'd spent only a short time outside South Africa, and yet the basic mechanisms of apartheid had already become foreign to him.

"Well, it's no excuse," he muttered to himself. He walked slowly inside.

He was relieved to find that the man behind the counter was black. He looked around him as he went up to the serving hatch. He saw immediately the difference between the two areas that he'd entered. This one was dingy and unkempt, while the other, although not overly full of products, had been carefully scrubbed, and the cans that lined its shelves were shining and undented. Nathaniel gritted his teeth. This, he thought, was the very basic fact of South Africa. Even money minted in the same bank bought different things, depending on the color of the hand that held it.

"Some cheese," he said brusquely.

He was served quickly and silently. He bought enough for three meals; any more than that might arouse suspicion. He paid with coins, taking care to conceal the wad of notes in his pocket.

The transaction took place with very few words on either side. Only when he was going did the shop assistant catch his eye.

"You're lucky the madam got out of bed the right side today," he said. "She's been known to call the police for less than what you just did."

"*Ja*, I wasn't thinking," Nathaniel acknowledged. "It was stupid of me."

The assistant rolled his eyes. "When it comes to learning about stupidity," he said, "we have the best masters." He shaped his hand into a fist and raised it a fraction. "*Afrika*," he said. The fist was jerked, and then it disappeared under the counter.

"*Mayibuye*," Nathaniel replied. He left the shop quickly.

He thought about why he had made such an obvious mistake. Always before when entering the country, he'd been only too conscious to repress the habits of freedom that one picked up outside South Africa. And yet this time he seemed to be inviting, rather than avoiding, danger.

He couldn't understand why. The only thing that kept recurring was his memory of his meeting with Jacob Swiece. It had affected him, he realized; it had turned his mind to his family.

"Well," he said out loud. "I must think of them no longer." He would not, he knew, contact Lindiwe. That would put him in danger. He did not allow himself the luxury of stopping again, except for gas and to relieve his bladder. He needed time, he thought, to be by himself, to allow the old sense of self-reliance to come surging back, to reaccustom himself to living off his wits.

He needed, in short, to be completely alone, to do as he instructed the younger comrades, to trust no one but themselves, to judge themselves before others. He reiterated his own lectures as he drove to his next rendezvous.

Because he did not stop, he arrived early. He used his time well—sorting through the contents of his car, disposing of articles that might look too fancy to police eyes, checking that his weapon was both well concealed and easily obtainable.

He took all the precautions the textbooks required, the ones that he seldom had the time to indulge in. He checked the area to the left and right. He drove a short distance down the road, and parking his car, he waited to see if anybody should pass by.

By the time a battered kombi made its way slowly toward the clearing in which they'd arranged to rendezvous, he was positive that they were safe. He got out of his car and waited expectantly.

Boy (that was the only name by which Nathaniel knew his contact) stopped the kombi a few yards away. He was not, Nathaniel could see, the only occupant of the vehicle. A woman's head was clearly visible in the passenger seat.

Boy sauntered over to Nathaniel. He must have been in his early twenties, but he did indeed look like a boy—fresh-faced and a sharp dresser who looked slightly incongruous in his grown-up clothes. He grinned at Nathaniel.

"My good friend Petrus," he said, and he shook Nathaniel's hand with gusto.

Nathaniel did not return the greeting. "Who's that in the car?" he asked coldly.

"Don't worry about her," Boy said jauntily. "She's safe. I'll vouch for her."

"Vouch for her," Nathaniel retorted. "You have no right to vouch for anybody. You have no right to bring anybody here."

Boy was taken aback. He had been berated by Nathaniel before, but this time his mentor's words were tinged with something almost vicious. "She's my girlfriend," he protested.

"I wouldn't care if she were your mother," Nathaniel snapped. "You were told from the beginning—no strangers at meeting places, no introducing anybody to the movement without prior consultation."

The grin had frozen on Boy's face. He looked at Nathaniel defiantly, but a slight watering of his eye gave him away. "Ag, man," he began.

"No excuses," Nathaniel said. "If you want to play games, then you must go back and play them with your childhood friends. We cannot afford any slipups. None at all. Do you understand?"

"*Ja.*" Boy nodded sullenly.

"Come on, then, let's load up." Nathaniel made no attempt to soften the tone of his voice.

Together they approached Nathaniel's car. They lifted up the backseat. Beneath it lay two cardboard boxes.

They transferred the boxes into Boy's kombi, Nathaniel taking care to conceal his face from the woman inside. They worked silently, and when they had finished, Boy climbed in.

"Next time," he said briefly. He drove off without another word.

Nathaniel was left standing in the clearing, wondering whether he had not been too harsh with Boy. If he himself had not slipped up that morning, he thought, perhaps he could have forgiven Boy, perhaps he could have found a way to teach the youth rather than to scold him.

He was of two minds about his actions: He knew that Boy had taken his telling off badly and that being upset was not the best way to be to do their kind of work. Part of him was inclined to follow Boy and to make it better. But another side of him resisted this impulse. Boy, he thought, shouldn't have brought the woman. He would have to learn.

Anyway, Nathaniel thought, there would be time to reestablish the bonds of friendship another day. Boy would understand: He was keen to learn, a good comrade whose impetuosity and youth were his major drawbacks. A stiff lesson in discipline, Nathaniel concluded, could only do him good.

And so Nathaniel let the kombi disappear into the distance.

Lindiwe might have spent the whole day thinking about her son if events had not overtaken her. She had gone to the clinic, just as she usually did, and had been met by a queue of patients, some new and some old, which stretched almost around the block. She was not dismayed. She had been doing this job so long, she was accustomed to working at double speed, so she knew that they would see to everybody before the day was over.

But medical duties were not her only tasks. There were a hundred other things to do; the day was never long enough. She had a first-aid class to give, meetings to attend, never mind a mass of administrative duties that she needed to finish before things got out of hand.

The class was easy enough: Lindiwe had held many of them, mainly with local women's groups, and they were always worthwhile. For her students were as well motivated as any. They came neither for qualifications nor to while away bored hours. They came instead to learn how to cope with their wounded children, and those of their neighbors—anything to stop the casualties ending up in the hospital and being arrested from there. As a result, the attention in the room was absolute when Lindiwe spoke. She rarely had to repeat herself, and she ended each session with a feeling of achievement, of a job well done.

There was more scope for complaint during the meetings, but then, Lindiwe thought, there were also more meetings. Sometimes they seemed endless, with one leading straight into another. And it was bound to get worse: As collaborationist organizations were swept aside by the tide of popular protests, local committees took over their tasks, and the meetings began.

Lindiwe, as her street committee representative, had more than her share of them. She'd known it would be like that. She'd accepted the post with a mixture of pleasure and trepidation, and they had both been borne out. It was tremendously exciting. It was also tiring, time-consuming, and often exasperating.

"If I have to spend another hour of my day talking about street cleaning," Lindiwe told a colleague, "I won't be responsible for my actions."

The other nurse smiled. "This democracy is harder work then we originally thought," she said. "But then, the results are better. Have you heard how successful the rent boycott in Soweto is?"

"It's great," Lindiwe agreed. "And so's the queue."

The two began to walk toward the dispensary.

And then it happened. In a street not far from the clinic, they heard the telltale drone of the casspirs moving through the street, heard the bang of trashcan lids warning of their approach, the shouts of children as they gathered themselves together. At first no one in the clinic bothered much about it. Ever since the school boycotts had taken hold, the troops had moved in and the sound of armored vehicles had become part of daily life. If the casspirs came too close, then they would have to act. In the meantime the staff had patients to care for, and the patients their place in the queue to protect.

Nevertheless, the nurses, Lindiwe among them, worked with half an ear concentrated on the events unfolding outside. Things could move so fast these days. What seemed like a casual show of police force could turn ugly within seconds. They prayed it would not happen, but they held themselves ready just in case.

So they all heard how the battle began. A childish voice shouted out in the street and was echoed by another. A dozen stones clattered against the pavement.

The police retaliated. The sound was unmistakable—the dull thud of a tear-gas cannister, followed by a round of shots. Lindiwe looked up. She met the eyes of the other nurse.

"I'll go," she said.

The woman nodded. "Be careful," was her only comment.

Lindiwe had no trouble finding the site of the battle. Even if she had been deaf, she would have located it because, as she got closer, the smell in the air grew stronger, more acrid, a mixture of burning rubber and tear gas. It began to sting her eyes, to insinuate itself up her nose, to make her skin itch.

She turned the corner, and suddenly she was in the midst of it all. The street that ten minutes ago was probably as peaceful as any other had been turned into a battleground.

On one side was the might of the South African Army—a huge casspir rolling toward her. It was moving slowly and it had disbursed many of its occupants. As Lindiwe watched, a group of twelve men in uniforms sank in unison to one knee. They placed their gunsights to their eyes.

They were aiming at a group of youths who stood behind a barrier of burning tires. The youths were in constant motion, as if they were dancing behind their makeshift barricade. They were taunting the uniforms, bending down and throwing bricks, rocks, sticks, in the direction of that solid machine of war. Even when the uniforms kneeled, the youths did not give up.

Lindiwe turned back to the casspir, and she heard the sharp report of rifles going off in sequence.

Everything moved so slowly, and at the same time it all happened too quickly. Lindiwe took it all in. She could not help doing so, her eyes had become a camera that would etch its images in her memory forever. She knew that it was not possible, but she was sure that she could see the fingers flick at the gun, the very bullets leave their casing and trace an arc high in the air. She followed them with her eyes.

The youths had ducked—almost all of them. But one was still upright. He had his arms raised back behind his shoulder as he prepared to launch his missile. He had his mouth open as if he were about to shout. His body was, for a fraction of a second, without contact with the ground. He was high, jubilant, fighting armed might with a stone.

He made no sound when the bullet entered him. His mouth moved slightly, but he made no sound. All that happened was that his arm, instead of launching forward, went limp. The stone in his hand plopped to the ground. His body followed.

Without realizing that she had even resolved to do so, Lindiwe ran until she reached the boy. She pushed his friends out of the way and knelt down beside him.

He was lying, his right leg at a peculiar angle, his shoulder bathed in blood. She gripped hold of the wound at the same time that she reached into her medical bag and pulled out a thick bandage, which she used to tie a torniquet. She was working fast, faster than she ever had before, conscious as she was of the rumbling of the approaching casspir. The boy groaned.

When she had tightened the bandage to her own satisfaction, she glanced at the youths who had inscribed a protective circle around her.

"Carry him out of here," she instructed. "Try not to be too rough. Go to the clinic down the road, you know the one I mean?"

They nodded, their eyes flicking behind her so that she knew that the giant must be close. In a flash she removed a syringe from her bag, and she injected the boy quickly. It was a sign of the times, she thought vaguely, that medical personnel carried morphine already loaded in the needle.

And then she thought no more, for she needs must act by instinct. As the youths sloped off, four of them holding their wounded comrade, as they ran down a narrow street, sheer fear making their bundle a light one, Lindiwe felt the hot breath of the monster on her neck. She moved to one side, scrambling out of its path.

She made it with inches to spare. It was gathering speed now, a thing that might have puzzled her if she had had time to think. But there was no time for anything, no time except to observe. No time except to see the casspir roll forward deliberately on its chains, roll forward into a building in its path, roll through the door, the walls, over the roof. Roll until it had squeezed the small dwelling as one would squeeze a sponge, and crushed it as one would crush an insect.

And then it stopped. Its gears crashed. It reversed. It left a heap of rubble as it moved backward, rubble with odd bits of furniture sticking out of it, rubble that smoked and groaned, rubble that had once been a home.

Lindiwe could not tear her eyes away from it. She strained her ears, hoping against hope that she would not hear a faint cry from beneath the rubble at the same time as she dreaded that the absence of such shouts meant something worse than their presence. The casspir had lost its meaning for her. Even if she had felt its fumes on her neck again, she would not have moved out of its way.

For the first time she understood, really understood, why it was that the children stood unblinking in front of the guns. If they are going to kill me, she thought to herself, let them do it so that they see what they do. Let them see me fall under the wheels of their monster: Let them smell my blood. Let them not have the satisfaction of killing out of sight, under the structure of a building that was once a home.

And so she stood for what seemed like an age but must have been a matter of minutes. She stood as the men reboarded the casspir, as it rumbled down the street, as it left the area.

She only came to when she heard the sound of wailing from behind.

"Why did they do it?" a woman was shouting. "Why?"

Lindiwe shook herself. She turned to the woman.

"Was there anyone in that house?" she asked.

"Why?" called the woman. She had sunk to her knees and was holding her hands up to the sky as if she were beseeching God.

Lindiwe knelt down beside her. She grabbed the woman's arms and held them tightly.

"Tell me," she said, "was there anybody in there?"

The woman shook her head. "No, thank God," she said. "They all left early this morning." She raised her voice again. "But they might have been there," she wailed. "Or the casspir might have trod on my house and killed my children. And now"—as she continued she put her hand to her hair and tugged at it—"what will happen to my neighbors? Their home has been destroyed—their clothes, their everything. The authorities will not rehouse them: They will send them away."

Suddenly her eyes focused. She looked straight at Lindiwe, and her voice softened. "And do you know," she said, "who it is that commits these crimes? It is young white men. And me, I have looked after men like that. I have wiped their noses, cradled them in my arms, sat with them when they were ill. I have given them my love and my bodily strength. And then they grow up, and what do they do? They shoot at our children, they destroy our homes, they are killing us."

She got up from the ground, and she automatically wiped the dust from her skirt. "Ayiee," she muttered, "perhaps it would be better if they were killed at birth. Perhaps it would."

Shaking her head, she began to walk off down the road.

"She lost her eldest the other day," another woman told Lindiwe. She, too, shook her head. "No wonder our children take up the gun."

"I say they are right," said another voice. "I say *Viva* MK!"

"*Viva!*" The word was shouted from all around.

53

NATHANIEL, A TOOTHPICK IN HIS MOUTH, HIS HAT STUCK ON AT A jaunty angle, strolled into the bar. He glanced around him as might any new customer, and only a sharp-eyed onlooker would have noticed a special quality of alertness in his inspection. He was looking at nothing and at everything: His work, which depended always on people, had taught him much about human nature. He could have left the bar almost as soon as he had entered, and he would have still been able to describe most of its occupants.

He sniffed no danger, and so he strolled to the counter and ordered himself a beer.

There was nowhere to sit, so he stood by the bar, leaning on it as he sipped at the cold liquid. His eyes kept flicking from one side of the room to the other. Every time the door opened, he was the first to examine the newcomer.

Nobody took much notice of him. The room was crowded. Originally dingy, it was made even darker by the clouds of smoke that hovered in the air. Loud music boomed from tall speakers set high up in the walls.

Nathaniel habitually eavesdropped when he went into public places—it was an easy way of picking up the level of anger or defeat in the streets—but this bar, with its deafening disco funk, defeated him.

Well, he thought, that's not such a bad thing. If he couldn't hear others, then neither would they be able to listen in on his conversation. He picked up his beer.

He felt a hand on his shoulder, and he cursed himself for his momentary inattention. He turned around slowly. His face, when he saw the man who had accosted him, was a careful blank, although his heart was sinking.

"Nathaniel? Nathaniel Cuba?"

Nathaniel shrugged his shoulders in a gesture of incomprehension, frowned, and turned away. Perhaps that would be enough, he thought, enough to convince this old school friend that he had made a mistake.

But he was out of luck. The man, his name was Henry, Nathaniel remembered, was persistent. "You look like a friend of mine," he said in a loud voice. "Someone I haven't seen for years now, but shit, you really remind me of him, particularly in profile."

Nathaniel turned around, and picking up his beer, he took a sip while he stared at the young man.

The assuredness in the man's face faltered, and he took a small step backward. But his confidence was not dented for long; he always was a jovial character, Nathaniel remembered, even as a schoolboy. A talker, too, thought Nathaniel.

"My friend," Henry continued, "the one who looks like you, he disappeared in seventy-six." He winked, and his whole face twitched. "You know what I mean," he said.

Nathaniel took another sip of beer and narrowed his eyes.

"I often wish I'd gone with him," Henry gushed. Nervousness was making him speak faster. "I bet he's had the chance to give the Boer a taste of his own medicine. *Ja*, I'd like to be doing that, too." He took a step back and looked again at Nathaniel. "You have such a strong resemblance to him," he said. "I can't get over it."

Nathaniel put his beer down. "Why don't you bugger off," he said in a neutral voice.

"Look here." Henry's voice rose in surprised protest.

Nathaniel pushed his face close to that of the other man. "No, you look here," he said. "I come here to have a quiet drink, and I don't want you telling me who I do and don't look like. Especially—"

"Now wait a minute," Henry began.

"Especially," Nathaniel continued, "if they're some kind of terrorist." He reached into his pocket, and he brought out a flick knife. He held it low and touched it once on Henry's thigh. "You want to speak my language," he invited, "then stick around. Otherwise *voetsak* out of here and leave me in peace."

He saw his old school friend's eyes widen in horror, and he saw him take a step back. He did not put the knife away. Only when Henry turned and ran out of the bar did he pack it away, only then did he move back.

When he picked up his beer, his hands were as steady as they had always been, but his mind was working overtime as he tried to assess the situation. There was no point in panicking. If Henry was a spy, then it was too late to do anything about it. He felt in his pocket for his gun, but then he withdrew his hand.

It was sheer coincidence, he decided, nothing more than that. Henry could not have been an informer, it was the wrong approach, completely wrong. Henry was just a man who had followed his boyhood traits: who was talkative and friendly and a little bit stupid. And dangerous to me, Nathaniel thought: I must keep away from this bar in the future.

But he could not yet leave. He looked at his watch. Five more minutes. He turned so that he was facing the door. His contact entered exactly on time. Nathaniel saw him—a tall man in his middle thirties, a man in a smart gray suit—standing by the open door. The man was unhurried: He blinked and stood as his eyes accustomed themselves to the darkness. Nathaniel did not move. He glanced once at the man, then, after one almost imperceptible nod, looked elsewhere.

The man picked up on Nathaniel's all-clear signal. He strolled over to the bar, positioned himself, as if by chance, right next to Nathaniel, and ordered a drink. Only when he had it in his hand, and had taken a long slug, did he shift himself slightly so that his lips were close to Nathaniel's ears.

"Petrus," he acknowledged.

Nathaniel nodded.

The man inclined his head nearer to Nathaniel. "Our man failed to turn up," he whispered.

Nathaniel jerked his head away. He turned to stare at the clock above the bartender's head, and then, as if he didn't believe it, he looked at his own watch again. He frowned.

"He should have got there by now," he said, as he moved closer again.

"*Ja*," the man agreed. "That's why we're worried. He's got his head in the clouds, that one, but he's never done this. We have to assume the worst."

Nathaniel nodded slowly. "Take the usual precautions," he said.

The man downed his beer in one gulp.

"Next week, one hour later, at the station," Nathaniel said.

"And the legend?"

Nathaniel frowned. "Bring some money," he finally said. "You owe it to me, and I need it to catch a train. Understood?"

The man nodded. "Backup as usual?" He didn't wait for a reply. He put his glass on the counter, and he walked out of the bar without a backward glance.

He left Nathaniel standing there, a quiet, seemingly confident Nathaniel, who inside was burning up with worry. With worry and with regret.

But he had no time to dwell on either. He was, he told himself, being too pessimistic, his own mistakes had made him so. There could be a number of innocuous reasons for Boy's absence. He might have had a breakdown or temporarily lost track of the time. It was for contingencies such as these that they set up a backup meeting place.

Nathaniel took one last look around the bar, and then he strolled slowly out.

He was at the second rendezvous, a vacant lot that had been turned into a rudimentary soccer field, in good time. He stationed himself in one corner, so that he could get a view from all directions. Then he set himself to wait.

No one could have guessed that this young man who lolled against a low wall, a matchstick hanging casually from his mouth, his hat set askew on his head, was anything other than relaxed. No one would have guessed that he was counting the minutes, each one as it passed, and that his breath was held as he did so. And no one would have known when he left, at a slow easy pace, that his heart was heavy and his feet almost rebelled at each step.

"Go back!" they kept on shouting: "Wait for another ten minutes."

His mind, his will, his training, would not let him: Those were the rules. One waited only for a short time, since the failure of the contact to turn up could easily mean that the police would soon be in sight.

And so, with foreboding now prominent, Nathaniel walked away.

* * *

Lindiwe was working late. The battle in the streets had put everybody behind, and she had volunteered to stay on and clear up. She enjoyed being in the clinic alone, she enjoyed that, in the absence of a hundred conflicting demands, she could impose order out of chaos. And there was another reason she stayed late. It was better to keep working on this day, on the day that her son turned twenty-one.

She pushed the thought away and forced herself to concentrate on her paper work. But other things kept impinging. The telephone rang, and then stopped as soon as she answered it. It rang a second time, and the same thing happened. Well, she thought, that wasn't surprising: The telephone system was often erratic these days.

But it worried her slightly, it worked on her mind until she began to imagine noises. She thought she heard a car draw up, but when she went to the window, there was nothing there. She thought she heard a soft footstep, but again, when she checked, there was no one.

I'm just feeling jumpy after today, she told herself. I need some company.

But she wasn't yet ready to go home, so instead she turned on the television that stood in the corner of the clinic.

Boy was all over the screen. Not him exactly—but his corpse. They had dragged him from the kombi, and they laid him on the ground. The boxes they pulled from the wreckage. When the SABC crew arrived, the boxes had been opened: three Kalashnikov rifles, some hand grenades, and a pile of bullets were displayed beside the remains of Boy.

Lindiwe could not tear her eyes away. For a moment she convinced herself that it was Nathaniel lying there. Before the camera zoomed in, she felt as though her heart would stop.

And so, when she did not recognize Boy, she was relieved.

After the relief came shame. Somebody's son had been gunned down that day: a man who looked no older than a boy, a man labeled a terrorist, another casualty of the system. She had no right to be pleased at his death. Wearily she walked to the television, clicked it off, and began to make her way toward her unfinished inventory.

It was then that she felt a hand on her shoulder. She jumped in fright. The car, the footstep, they had all been real. And she was alone. She turned to face the intruder.

"Sorry to startle you, Mrs. Cuba," he said.

He had a gentle voice, a voice that meant no harm. Lindiwe relaxed. "The clinic is closed," she said. "Is it an emergency?"

He nodded. "It's my . . . mother," he said. "Please come."

"Perhaps she needs a doctor," Lindiwe suggested.

The man shook his head. His hand was by his trouser leg, and he moved it quickly. When Lindiwe looked down, she saw that it had formed into the shape of the old Congress salute.

She nodded.

Without another word, she went to the cupboard and pulled out the emergency kit. Then, clicking off the lights, she bolted the front door, showed the man to the back, opened that door, and slipped outside with him.

His car was waiting down a side street, and he hustled her into it. Into the darkness they sped. Lindiwe asked no questions: She had done this kind of work before, patching up people who had gone underground: In that situation it was better to know as little as possible.

She held on to the seat strap as the car took a corner on two wheels. When it stopped abruptly in a dark alleyway, she got out. There was another car waiting, she saw, and without having to ask, she crossed over to it. As she did so, a woman left the second car and rushed over to the one Lindiwe had just vacated. They were taking elaborate precautions, she thought. The person she was about to attend must be important.

Once both women were seated, the cars sped off in opposite directions. Still Lindiwe did not speak. She held her bag firmly by her side as they drove through darkened streets.

Finally the car came to a halt. They were still in the white part of Jo'burg, Lindiwe saw. She looked questioningly at her driver.

"Round the back," he said. "I'll pick you up in an hour."

He hardly waited for her to leave before driving off.

Lindiwe opened the gate and walked through the driveway. She was concentrating on the noises around her, rather than on the sights. She noticed little about the house at the end of her walk, since she was intent on avoiding it. When the drive branched, she took the dusty route, the one that she knew must lead to the servants' quarters.

She turned a corner and found herself facing a low concrete building. She went up to it, knocked on the door, and, when there was no reply, turned the knob.

The room that she entered was in darkness, but her eyes were already accustomed to the gloom. She saw that there was a man seated on the simple iron bedstead in the corner of the room. He was looking at the wall. He did not stir when she entered.

"What can I do for you, comrade?" she asked softly.

He turned then and looked at her. He smiled.

She recognized him. How could she not? Involuntarily her hand went to her mouth. She couldn't believe that only twelve hours ago she'd thought that she would not know him if she were to see him again. He was her son, after all, the flesh of her flesh.

"Nathaniel."

He put one finger to his lips, and he smiled again.

"I have been reborn," he said. "I am Petrus."

She took a step toward him, and he met her halfway. They embraced in that barren room, embraced while Lindiwe wrestled with herself. Half of her wanted to revel uncritically in this contact with her son, but the other half was registering the changes. He was so grown, she thought, so tall, and so muscular. He was Nathaniel, that was for sure, and yet he wasn't the child she had once known.

She disentangled herself, took a step back, and holding him at arm's length, she inspected him more closely. There were lines beginning to gather around his eyes, she noticed. In her memory he had never fully grown up, and yet in reality he was aging. She blinked a solitary tear away. The eyes themselves, she saw, were yet unchanged: those beautiful black eyes so full of softness, and of kindness.

"How are you?" she asked.

He gestured to himself and shrugged. "I have dreamed of this moment," he said.

"And I."

"It is good to see you."

Lindiwe blinked again. There was so much to say, she thought, and yet the very pressure made it almost impossible to start. She felt strangely nervous, nervous in front of her own son—her only son. She looked down at the floor.

Nathaniel inspected her as she did so. He saw that the deep furrows that had not even made an appearance when they were last together were now ingrained on her face. Seven years, he thought to himself, and I have not greeted her. I have asked nothing about the family. I have not even looked at her properly.

Suddenly she raised her head. She caught his scrutiny, and she smiled at him. "It is your birthday today," she said.

He did not return the smile. "I am ageless," he replied. "I have no birthdays."

"Today," Lindiwe began, as if her son had not spoken, "I was in the street, and I saw the police commit a brutal act. And do you know how the people responded? They shouted *Viva! Viva* MK!"

"*Viva*." Nathaniel enunciated slowly, as if the word were a new one to him. "It's easy to say," he concluded.

She glanced at him, puzzled.

"You know, Mama," he said, "sometimes . . ." He broke off and looked away.

"Yes," she encouraged. "Sometimes?"

"Sometimes," he said, "I get very tired."

He strode over to the window, and turning his back to her, he looked out of it. "They think of MK as a glamorous organization," he continued. "They never think of the day-to-day grind—of the traveling, the sleeping in a different hole each night, the scrabbling for food, the talking, endless talking, the weighing up, the planning, the worry about whether you have shut the door properly, the knowledge that the door might any second be slammed in your face, that . . . that . . ."

His voice faltered and died. He whipped his head around. He looked at Lindiwe as one might regard a stranger. "I don't know what I'm talking about," he said loudly. And then he smiled, somehow a grim smile, it seemed to Lindiwe.

And she realized that despite the years that had separated them, he was no stranger. "You are talking about the boy who was killed today," she said. "The one who was on the TV."

He frowned. "The boy?" he said. "Yes." He nodded his head. "Boy was his name. His mother must have christened him differently, but to me he was Boy, and to him I was Petrus." His voice deepened. "We say we are fighting for the mothers of our nations," he said, "and yet we are divorced from our mothers, and by necessity we discard the names that they gave us." He looked down at the floor. "Sometimes I wonder why it is that people like Boy have to die."

The defeat in Nathaniel's voice was so tangible that Lindiwe felt impelled to argue with it. "He was a soldier," she said. "He knew the risks."

"He wasn't a soldier," Nathaniel shouted. "He was a courier, nothing more. You know what he carried in his car? Propaganda materials, that's all."

"But the guns," Lindiwe protested. "I saw them lying beside him."

"You saw them beside him, but not in his car. They were never there. They came from the police stores. We never would have let Boy carry arms. He was too inexperienced for that."

"But they killed him anyway."

"Yes," Nathaniel replied. "They killed him anyway." He walked over to the door and opened it abruptly. He took one step out, and he seemed to be examining the yard from there.

"I'm sorry," Lindiwe said.

His head whipped around. "I'm not," he shot back. "I can no longer be sorry. My first reaction was the reaction of a computer. I did not think of Boy, but of myself and of our plans. Did he talk before he died, was what I wanted to know. Had they been following him? What happened to the woman who was with him: Was she a spy? That's what I thought about—not about Boy." He stepped inside again and slammed the door so loudly that Lindiwe jumped.

"I am a man without feelings, a man without friends, a man without family," he said, and his eyes were blank.

She would not have recognized him like this, she thought, for in his despair he had lost part of himself, the human part, the part that made him Nathaniel. She wanted to deny his words, to pull him back into his own skin. "You have family," she said. "You have me, your father, your sister. You're not alone."

Nathaniel strode over to the bed, and kneeling down, he pulled at something. "My father, my sister, you," he said, and the words came out fast, one on top of the other, "none of you are part of my life. But you're right, I'm not alone." He turned. "I have this," he said. He sprang to his feet, and in his hands he held a revolver. He waved it in Lindiwe's direction. "This is my family," he said.

She put one hand up to her neck.

His arm dropped to his side, and he let the gun go. It fell to the floor. He looked at his mother. He smiled. "This is what they mean when they say that MK cadres shoot their way out of an argument when they're losing," he said.

He looked at her, and his face was now devoid of expression. "I met Henry Musi today," he said. "Remember him?"

Lindiwe nodded.

"Henry recognized me," Nathaniel continued. "I nearly knifed him. I would have done it . . . I would . . ." He looked away. "You become part of the underground," he said, "and your whole relationship to your people changes." His eyes watered, but he blinked the tears away. "I can't afford to show my sentiments," he said. "I can't encourage Henry in his support of MK, I can't even discuss world politics, for fear of giving myself away. I'm a traveling salesman, me, a salesman." He turned to face his mother, and he tried another smile. But his face crumpled.

"My son," she said.

She went up to him and embraced him. She felt him stiffen as if he were about to reject her, but then his muscles went slack. His body shook, his tears wet her shoulder.

She held him close and let him cry until he was finished.

He pulled away from her eventually, and when he looked into her eyes, the anger had been replaced by pain. "I don't know if I can go on," he said. "Tell me. What should I do?"

"It's not my—" Lindiwe began.

Nathaniel's voice, harsh now, cut through her words. "I'm asking you," he pleaded. "Tell me."

Lindiwe's heart sank. She would do anything for her son, but this question was the one that she wished never to be asked. She knew what she wanted to say. "Yes," she would argue, "give it up, my son. Leave the country. Settle somewhere safe. We have paid enough. We owe no more."

And yet the words would not come. She thought of her daughter and of what she had experienced. Bertha had chosen the other route, had shied away from political involvement. She did this not out of preference, but because of what had happened to her in '76. She had never recovered from it, Lindiwe knew, she would always be haunted.

So her daughter lived in fear, not through any choice of her own. And her son—did he have a choice?

But even that was wrong, for this man in front of her, she thought, was not really her son: He had grown up and he had grown away, he was part of the movement.

Lindiwe wanted to tell him to look out for himself, but she

remembered her own mother. Peggy had believed that individuals could determine their own fate. Peggy had railed against her husband's involvement, she had never stopped being bitter at Moses' death.

And because of Peggy's refusal to face facts, Lindiwe had rejected her. And now, she realized, she, too, had been falling into the same trap. She had been living in the past: in the time when she had a thirteen-year-old son.

Those days were long gone. Her son was a man. He belonged, not to the family, but to the ANC.

"No," she said slowly, "you are doing what is right. We have no choice; they have not allowed us that. You must go on."

54

England: 1984

ROSA PICKED UP THE GLASS AND RAN HER FINGER THOUGHTFULLY around the rim. "What are we going to do about Martha?" she mused. She put the glass down again.

Jacob laughed. Leaning across the table, he touched Rosa softly on the nose. "What do you mean?" he asked. "She's over the age of consent, you know. She's thirty-four, in fact, even though this must be hard for a fond mother to admit."

Rosa grimaced. "Fond mother," she said. She stood up and stretched. "You know, sometimes," she said, "I think it was easier when she kept away. When she lived in Bristol and only came here on anniversaries. When we fought every time we met. At least then it was out in the open. Not like now, where all the hostility is buried in the silence." She clicked her tongue. "Fond," she repeated. "Just listen to me."

"But you are," Jacob said. "Sometimes I think you're too fond. Maybe Martha needs to find her own way in life: Maybe the fact that she can come here and scowl all over our dinner table is stopping her from developing."

Rosa picked up a plate. "Rachel's doing well," she said. "Her Peter's a nice man, even if a trifle . . ." She piled another plate on top of the first one.

"Conventional?" Jacob finished for her. He stood up beside her, took the plates from her hand, and replaced them on the table before wrapping his arms around her. "Listen to us," he whispered, "approaching sixty, and we judge our children as too staid." He raised an eyebrow. "Wanna come upstairs?" he asked.

Teasingly she pushed him away. "I'd love to," she said. "But I know you too well. The phone hasn't rung for twenty minutes, which means that as soon as we get within a few feet of the bed, the doorbell will ring, the phone will go, and twenty different comrades will insist that you get on the next plane to twenty different destinations." She turned her back on him and picked up the plates again. "So, because I don't want to tempt fate, I think we better do the washing up instead."

"Spoilsport," Jacob said. Nevertheless, he walked around the table and mirrored her actions. "You know," he continued as they methodically cleared away the debris of their family dinner, "I don't know why you put up with it. I really must be impossible to live with."

Rosa stopped and looked at him. "Live?" she said softly. "You live with me, do you? First I heard of it."

He smiled. "You know what I mean."

"Yes," she said. "I know. And yes, you are impossible."

She kicked the kitchen door open with her foot and smartly went through it.

She was at the sink, her arms immersed in soapy water, by the time he joined her. He put his tray of dirty glasses down on the kitchen table and walked over to her. He put his hands on her hair.

"You know I love you," he whispered.

"Yes," she replied. "I know that, too."

She did not shake him off, but neither did she turn. The only sound in the room was of the scraping of steel wool.

When she next spoke, there was a faraway quality in Rosa's voice. "It must be hard for our children," she mused. "Most people rebel against their parents as a way of defining themselves. But ours couldn't, because we are the ones who have excelled at rebellion."

"They could have found their own method," Jacob contradicted. "From what I hear about her adolescence, Martha did."

"I suppose so," Rosa reflected. "But I still think it's been extra difficult for them. We had it all: commitment, danger, comradeship, excitement . . ."

"Imprisonment, death."

Rosa tossed her head, forcing him to remove his hand. She turned and looked fiercely at him. "You must know what I'm talking about," she said.

He nodded gravely. "Sometimes it's hard to feel sorry for the children of white South Africans," he said. "Especially when you know what happens to the children of blacks."

"Yes, well, that's part of the problem, isn't it?" Rosa replied.

Again Jacob nodded. He went over the kitchen table, pulled out a chair, sat down, and, uncorking a bottle, poured some wine into the nearest glass. "I saw Nathaniel Cuba the other day," he said.

"Lindiwe's son?" Rosa asked in amazement, her full sink now forgotten.

"That's the one," Jacob confirmed. "He's in the army. A leading cadre, in fact. One of our best. A really nice young man."

"And?"

"I saw him twice," Jacob said. "And in the short time between the two, he had changed."

Jacob said no more, and he showed no sign of being about to speak. He stared at a distant wall as if there were moving pictures inscribed on it.

Rosa dried her hands and went to sit opposite him.

"You saw Nathaniel," she stated. "Twice. He changed. End of story?"

Jacob shook himself as if emerging from a daydream. "I'm sorry, honey," he said. He smiled and reached across for her hand. "I was trying to work it out. On the second time Nathaniel seemed more distant. Although he talked more, it was like he wasn't really there."

"Well, perhaps something happened," Rosa suggested.

"It did," Jacob confirmed. "One of his contacts was killed."

"And so? Doesn't that explain it?"

Jacob shrugged. "Oh, I suppose so," he said as he downed the wine in his glass. "It's just that I wish that these kids would have the chance to grow up normally, not to be forced up by guns, and death. I wish they could have our children's problems instead. I wish they could have some peace." Rosa picked up his hand where it lay nestled in hers, and she kissed it gently.

"And that we could have some peace," she suggested.

"That, too," he answered. The telephone began to ring.

Martha was sitting next to Stephen Archer when the phone rang. They were new at this game: They had not yet routinized the trivialities of everyday life, and as a result they occasionally duplicated each other's actions. Not for the first time, they both reached for it.

Martha was piqued to find that Stephen's reflexes were quicker than hers. She was also convinced that the phone call was for her. Stephen had, after all, only just moved in.

"Your sister," Stephen said, as he offered her the receiver.

Martha frowned. She had spoken to Rachel relatively recently, so this was not one of their duty check-ins. There was therefore only one possible reason for this particular call.

She took the phone. "Jacob," she stated.

"Right the first time," Rachel said.

"So when's he due?"

"Next week," Rachel answered. "Mom asked me to tell you."

Oh, God, thought Martha, as she detected the hint of apology in Rachel's voice, Don't they get bored with this pattern?

It was always this way before one of Jacob's visits. He would phone Rosa, who would tell Rachel, who would then make sure that Martha was the last to be informed.

Martha hated it. "How considerate of you both," she said dryly. She did nothing to repress the annoyance in her voice.

On the other end Rachel's voice perceptibly faltered. "I'm only trying . . ." she began.

Martha saw how Stephen, who was shamelessly eavesdropping, threw her a quizzical look. She moved the receiver to her other ear at the same time that she softened both her voice and her strategy. "No, I mean it," she told Rachel. "It is kind of you."

After all, she thought, it wasn't Rachel's fault that their lines of communication had become so ritualized. It probably wasn't even Rosa's fault. Rachel had, after all, done the right thing by marrying and producing two grandchildren. Their mother had more reason to keep in touch with her youngest—especially since she and Martha found it hard to spend much time together without arguing.

"Mom's doing Sunday lunch." Rachel's voice broke into Martha's reflections. "Want to come?"

"Sure," Martha replied.

"And she said to bring anybody you want to," Rachel said quickly. "Bye now, must dash."

Martha was left holding a deadened receiver. She frowned.

"I never thought," she told Stephen, "that I would have a

sister who, and I quote, has to dash so frequently."

He reached over and took the phone from her. "Too suburban for you?" he inquired. He moved it away.

He was using that familiar tone of voice—that interest mixed with sarcasm—that served both to irritate and challenge Martha. On another occasion she might have responded with a quip, but the phone call—and the prospect of another awkward Swiece meal—had set her on edge.

"I think we should work out who answers the phone," she said.

Stephen smiled. "Great idea." His voice rose enthusiastically. "We really should regularize everything," he said. "There's no point in leaving anything to chance, is there?"

"I mean it, Stephen," Martha said ominously.

Stephen was not to be intimidated. He leaped to his feet. Standing in front of Martha, he flicked at a lock of hair, the one that infallibly encroached on his forehead, and smiled. "So do I," he protested. "I'm serious. How about a shit rota, as well?"

Martha frowned. That was the trouble with Stephen, she thought; he was a law unto himself. She had been initially attracted to him because of his irreverence—at last here was a man who wasn't scared of women, who didn't treat them with a kind of deathly seriousness—but sometimes it really got on her nerves.

"Stephen," was all she said, but she managed to stiffen her voice noticeably.

He heard the warning and he chose—this time—to listen to it. His face grew serious. He came to sit beside her on the sofa, and he took one of her hands in his. "It'll be all right," he said softly. "You'll get used to me."

Martha blinked. She had not realized that she was so upset until she felt the calluses on his palms. She looked down at them and was surprised to find herself choking back tears.

Stephen put his arms around her. "I'm sorry," he whispered.

"It's not you," she replied.

"Are you sure?" Stephen asked. "We, and especially you, have taken a big step moving in together. You're bound to feel uncertain."

"It's not you," Martha repeated. She didn't know why she was so positive, since she certainly couldn't work out what was the matter with her. All she knew was that for the first time in her life she had most of what she wanted: a spacious apartment, a good job, and a man who loved her—no reason for pain. And yet she felt so terribly vulnerable, was prone to bouts of unanticipated weepiness.

Perhaps it was just Jacob's fault. She never knew how to react when she heard he was coming to London. Her pleasure at the thought of seeing him was mixed with the knowledge that she should not expect too much from him. If she did that, she was bound to be disappointed, and her disappointment would turn childish on her.

For no matter how hard she tried, no matter how she changed in relation to everything else, she was trapped within her family. She, a perfectly competent thirty-four-year-old, could be reduced to confusion by the news of her father's impending visit or driven to fury by one of her mother's offhand comments.

She looked up at Stephen. "Do people ever rid themselves of their parents?" she asked.

He shook his head. "Not really. Although they can come to terms with them. You could, if you wanted to."

Martha laughed. "Always the preacher," she said.

Stephen opened his mouth to reply, but then he changed his mind. He moved closer to Martha, he put his hand on her chin, he moved her face gently around toward his. "Not always," he whispered. "I take time off occasionally. Interested?"

Martha raised an eyebrow. "Why not?"

The abrasiveness of their relationship was reflected and refined in the way they made love. They came together as if it was always the first time, as if each had something to lose and something to gain. They were ever in motion; even when their bodies were stilled, there was an air of undefinable tension that gave off the impression of movement. And yet there was no anger in the tension, no need to punish. They joined together in passion; they were not yet fully accustomed to each other, even though they had been together for more than a year.

And yet, when it was over, peace did descend. It was one of the only times that they were together without words intervening, without challenges from one or the other, without the need for distance.

"So am I going to be presented to the family?" Stephen finally asked.

He felt Martha stiffen, but he had anticipated her response

and he enclosed her further in his arms.

"Go on," he urged. "I can't be that bad."

Martha sighed. She looked him in the eye.

"Can I?" he asked.

She smiled. "Well . . ." she began. "As a matter of fact, since you want to know . . ."

His lips stilled her. They kissed for a long, long time.

Martha emitted a whistle when he moved away. "Not bad," she commented.

"So can I?" Stephen asked.

"Sure," Martha said flippantly, and Stephen chose to ignore the panic in her eyes.

On the morning of the Swiece get-together, Stephen was surprised to discover that he was nervous. He never expected to be: He was, after all, accustomed to holding his own in company. His position as an analyst meant that it was usually other people who suffered fear of disclosure in his presence.

And yet he was nervous. He dressed himself in his most expensive suit, his convention suit, he thought wryly, which he took off after noticing Martha's expression of shocked disapproval. As he rooted through the cupboards, he tried to calm himself down by pinpointing the source of his anxiety.

He was, he told himself, infected by Martha's own insecurity. She had a strange relationship with her parents—this he had always known. She didn't see them often, but it would be a mistake to suppose therefore that they meant little to her. For Martha, he knew, had still not resolved her relationship with her mother. She spoke of Rosa with a mixture of anger and respect, and it was significant that she had kept the two of them apart.

It's not me, he concluded. I'm just feeling anxious for Martha.

But Stephen was nothing if not honest with himself. He knew that it was wrong to ascribe his own anxiety to some kind of countertransference. When he thought about it some more, he realized that the truth was that Martha's parents were both formidable people and that he had his own reasons to worry about lunch.

Although Stephen had never been introduced to Rosa, he had seen her speaking at a crowded anti-apartheid rally. She had taken his breath away. She was so incredibly articulate, so strong, so convinced and convincing, that she'd held the audience entranced. And yet her appeal was not only emotional. She had a fierce intellect, and she forced her audience to follow the complexities of her argument. After seeing her performance, Stephen no longer had to ask himself where Martha had obtained her own terrifying personality.

And even though Martha tended to avoid talking about her father, Stephen knew that Jacob must himself be an unusual man. He was, after all, one of the few whites to have obtained a high status in the African National Congress. He had withstood years of prison and come out a fighter. He must, thought Stephen, be as strong as Rosa.

And so, Stephen thought, no wonder I'm nervous. These people's experiences are so out of the ordinary. He looked at himself in the mirror, unknotted his tie, and threw it on the bed.

Martha poked her head around the door. "Aren't you ready yet?" she asked. "For godsake, we're not visiting royalty."

Stephen hurried with her out of the flat. He didn't say anything, but he couldn't help noticing that she wasn't exactly at her calmest. She insisted on driving, and then, at the top of Archway had gone in completely the wrong direction. When he'd pointed this out, she'd bitten her lips, done a three-point turn that would have raised eyebrows at a Grand Prix race, and driven the rest of the way in icy silence.

They made it up once Martha had parked outside Rosa's house in Crouch End. She was about to get out of the car when Stephen reached across and held her door fast.

"Into the Valley of Death?" he asked.

He was gratified to see her mouth twitch.

"Let's mess this up together," he suggested.

She grinned. "I don't know why I'm so nervous," she said.

"You're afraid they won't like me," Stephen suggested. "Or that I won't like them."

"Probably," Martha said. She got out and waited for him to do likewise. Then, arm in arm, they walked to the front door.

Lunch was nothing like Stephen had imagined it might be.

He was the only outsider, since Rachel's husband, Peter, was out of town. He was welcomed by Rosa and Jacob, who both showed an air of casual acceptance. He gave them full marks for sensitivity. He knew that they must have been dying to get to know Martha's man, but they managed to conceal their curiosity pretty successfully. Too successfully, perhaps, thought Stephen: One could interpret their lack of questions as lack of interest. Martha, he knew, did.

Rachel's children were ebulliently noisy, and they acted as distractions to what might have otherwise been a sticky occasion.

Thanks to them, Stephen had time to observe Martha's parents without seeming rude. They were, he thought, the model of a modern couple. It was hard to believe that they saw each other so rarely. They treated each other without rancor or fuss. They were natural, unfussy, and bordering on the cool.

With Martha they were unquestionably more tense. Rosa, Stephen noticed, paid Martha exaggerated attention, which she continually rebuffed. Their conversation was one-sided: Rosa's role was to ask questions that Martha would answer without giving much away. It was interesting, thought Stephen, that Martha was as reticent about basic information with her parents as she was with him.

Jacob seemed aware of the difficulties between mother and daughter, but was nevertheless unsuccessful in dealing with them. If he tried to prompt Martha into giving a little more information, he was rewarded with a furious look.

And in the midst of this, Rachel's family filled the silence. Rachel kept up an appearance of continual efficiency and sunniness, although Stephen thought he caught looks of frustration on her face. He wondered whether Rachel had always been the left-out one—perhaps her children were the replacement for Martha.

Lunch was interrupted three times. On two occasions the phone rang, and both times it was for Jacob. He never, Stephen noticed, took the calls in the dining room. Instead, he firmly replaced the receiver and left the room, returning, on each occasion, only after a good fifteen minutes.

The third interruption was more personalized. When the doorbell rang, Rosa got up to answer it. She returned with a man in tow—an Indian in his middle forties. He greeted the family as if they were all old friends, and smiled at Stephen as if he knew who he was. He accepted an offer of wine and he sat by the table, chatting with them all in an easy way.

But finally he rose, inclining his head once in Jacob's direction. Jacob nodded.

"Excuse me a minute," Jacob said to Stephen.

He got up, and the two men left the room together. They walked through the French doors and into the garden.

Stephen watched in surprise. It was not a day for horticultural expeditions, it was gray and drizzling—an English specialty. But the men in the garden didn't seem to mind. They walked backward and forward, engrossed in conversation, eventually stopping by the back wall, where they talked as water dripped onto their clothes.

The most surprising thing about it, Stephen thought, was the way the rest of the family reacted: or, to be more accurate, the way they didn't react. They carried on their own conversation as if nothing had happened, as if the sight of two grown men deliberately choosing to chat in the rain when the house had rooms aplenty were a perfectly ordinary one.

It was Martha who eventually noticed Stephen's confusion. "You'll have to get used to it," she said loudly. "It's a grand old Swiece habit—talking outdoors."

Rosa smiled. "It's true," she said. "It's become such a habit with Jacob that he'd probably go outside if he wanted to talk to himself."

For a moment mother and daughter were allied, the atmosphere seemed to loosen.

Stephen smiled at Martha. "So many secrets," he said. "No wonder you chose psychology."

It was a thought that he had expressed before, and so Martha's response was totally unexpected. She glared at him, as one might glare at one's worst enemy. She opened her mouth to retort.

Rosa hastily intervened. "You are the recipient of secrets, aren't you, Stephen?" she said. "Being an analyst." And with that, she steered the conversation firmly away.

Lunch did not, as in some families, turn into tea. For when they'd finished coffee, Jacob got up from the table.

"I have to go out," he said apologetically.

Abruptly Martha mirrored his action. "We must be going, too," she said. She did not look in Stephen's direction, had not for a good half hour.

He had no choice but to follow her.

Rosa saw all three to the door. She smiled, a trifle sadly, at Stephen, and extended to him an open invitation. From Jacob, Stephen received a firm handshake. Then they parted, Rosa returning inside and the others going to their respective cars.

As they were pulling out, Stephen happened to glance back. He noticed that Jacob was still outside his car. He was circling it, glancing down as if examining the bodywork.

"What's he doing that for?" Stephen asked.

Martha looked through the mirror. "Checking for bombs," she said, before speeding off down the road.

"Jesus," Stephen said. "I never realized what a strain it must be for you."

"It's not such a strain," Martha said briskly. The tone of her voice defied him to answer.

"He seemed nice," Rosa told Rachel when she came back into the room.

"Mmm," Rachel replied. She got up and began to clear the table. "Martha was her usual uptight self," she commented.

Rosa stroked Tanya's forehead. "I can't seem to get through to her," she said thoughtfully. "How should I do it?"

Rachel stopped by the door, a pile of plates in her hand. "Don't ask me, Mom," she said. "I gave up years ago."

They drove in silence, until eventually Stephen could stand it no longer.

"Okay," he started. "Tell me the worst."

"I don't know what you're talking about," Martha snapped.

Stephen frowned. "What have I done wrong?" he asked.

"As if you don't know," Martha said.

"I teased you in your parents' presence," Stephen said. "Terrible crime."

Martha's scowl deepened.

"And you might have got used to it," Stephen said, "but I think it's odd to be in the same room with a man who's so secretive that he manages to answer the phone without ever pronouncing his own name."

"You're imagining things," Martha said.

"And you're avoiding them," he replied.

Martha's face flushed. It went a kind of deep red. "What do you know?" she snapped. "What do you know?"

Stephen decided to ignore her. He looked through the window.

"What do you know?" Martha repeated childishly.

He glanced back. "I know that you're heading the wrong way," he said mildly. "You seem compelled to go toward Kentish Town," he remarked.

The level of her response was completely unexpected. Without warning, she slammed on the brakes. So abruptly did the car squeal to a halt that the vehicle behind them missed them only by inches. Its horn sounded, insistently and angrily, before its driver pointed two fingers at Martha's head, maneuvered an exaggerated circle around them, and drove off with a burst of indignant speed.

Martha slumped over the steering wheel. When Stephen reached over to touch her, she shrugged him off.

"You better move from the middle of the road," he said coldly.

Leaving the key in the lock, she got out of the car.

He shifted into the driver's seat and pulled over to the pavement. Martha, he saw, was already walking away. He started the car again and cruised up to her.

"Martha," he pleaded.

She would not look in his direction.

"Martha," he said again.

"Oh, fuck off," she snapped.

He pressed his foot on the accelerator, and he was gone.

Rosa and Jacob were in bed. They had not talked for some time, but they were both awake. They had dissected the lunch, they had agreed that Stephen was a pleasant surprise, and they were at peace with each other. But yet, Rosa could sense, Jacob was restless. She touched him lightly on the shoulder.

"Worried?" she asked.

He nodded.

"Things are hotting up, hey?" she said.

He smiled. "The country will never calm down," he said. "That much is obvious. Who knows when we will strike the decisive blow, but strike it we will." He sighed. "Still," he said, "the fact that South Africa is turning on all the front-line states— on Mozambique and Angola especially—is making it much more difficult for us."

Rosa knew what he meant: In Angola, South African forces kept invading the country, pushing forward until they were repelled, while in Mozambique they poured money into a group of murderers who went under the title of the MNR, or Renamo, and who had no policy other than the devastation of the parts of the country that they could temporarily control.

It was Mozambique that hurt the most. Its president, Samora Machel, desperate in the face of MNR atrocities that were exacerbating a growing famine, had signed an agreement with South Africa—the Nkomati Accord—that resulted in the expulsion of all ANC members from the country.

"I don't know why they believe Botha," Jacob said. "He'll never stop funding the MNR."

She snuggled in closer. "Don't worry," she whispered in his ear. "Mozambique won't put up with too many South African lies. We'll eat prawns in the Polano Hotel again."

As they lay side by side, Jacob remembered the time they had spent in Mozambique together. It had been a charmed time, a time for reflection and togetherness, amid the flurry of Jacob's work. They had been able then to both inhabit the same world— the world of Southern Africa. And they had even gone to spend a few days in Ponto D'oro, and they had walked the white beaches almost to the point of crossing over into Natal. It had been a strange sensation, standing on the deserted beach, listening to the waves pounding against it, and seeing the beginnings of South Africa just tens of yards away. They had turned away and gone back to their seaside house, laughing at the way it had made them both feel.

"We don't see each other enough," Jacob said.

"We will," Rosa assured him. "We will."

55

Mozambique: 1986

Jacob raised his arms in the air and flexed his back hard. He smiled as he felt the first layer of tension begin to leak from his cramped muscles. The meeting, he thought, had been endless: useful but nevertheless endless. It was good to be out of the stuffy room, to feel the direct heat of the sun on his back.

Taking off his jacket, he slung it across one arm. He stood for a minute breathing in the smell of the sea, looking out into its blue expanse. He reveled in his feeling of energy, in his own sense of being alive.

He was glad now that, as a security precaution, he had parked some distance away: It would be good to get some exercise. He started to walk down the Avenida Frederick Engels. It was one of his favorite Maputo streets, running as it did uphill and curving along the seafront. Rosa liked it, too. When she used to visit, they had often walked this way. It was a perfect place for an evening stroll, with its spreading jacarandas elbowing their way across the road, and its ringside view of the wide Maputo Harbor.

As he walked, Jacob remembered how Rosa had predicted that he would one day return to Mozambique. Well, he thought, she was proved right. They were back, if only on a diplomatic level.

It never, Jacob reflected, took long for the South African regime to display its true nature. Having signed a nonaggression pact with Mozambique that obliged Mozambique to expel the ANC, the South African government had proceeded to break its part of the bargain. Instead of cutting off the MNR, it had escalated its supplies of food and arms to these bandits who roamed the Mozambiquan countryside, torturing and killing for no apparent reason or policy. South Africa had been blatant in its strategy—one of its ministers going so far as to fly into the MNR's unofficial airstrip along with the supplies.

And then, when it looked as if things could not get worse, Mozambiquan president Samora Machel's plane had crashed inside South African territory, killing all but one of its occupants. It was a bad blow, and one that Mozambique could ill afford, racked as it was by war, by drought, and by the legacy of colonial plunder. But the struggle was still continuing—the FRELIMO government maintained its hold. It wasn't easy, Jacob thought, to destroy the spirit of resistance.

He carried on walking. Maputo, he reflected, was a beautiful city, with its wide, treelined avenues, its modern flats, and its gracious bungalows. It still had an aura of dignity about it, even though things had changed in the last four years.

The city was showing the strain that had come down on the country. Evidence of decay was everywhere. The streets were not as clean as they had once been, nor half as sweet-smelling: Water had become a scarce commodity, and was continually being cut off. It was even a bit risky to get into an elevator these days, since the electricity disappeared at a moment's notice. Jacob looked around him: Neglect, he saw, had not yet destroyed the essential splendor of the avenida, and yet the pavement was uneven, the wide road pitted with holes, the grass verge sprawling and neglected.

Jacob frowned to himself. The Boers will never be happy, he thought, until they have destroyed the whole of Southern Africa.

He shook off the thought. He had not time for such reflections. He had work to do. He needed to think, he had been asked to develop a new strategy for medical care of the cadres, and he found it easier to solidify his ideas while he strolled.

Of all the skills Jacob had learned in prison, the ability to cut himself off from his surroundings was the most precious. He utilized it often—on airplanes, during sections of meetings that were peripheral to his work, even sometimes during family lunches. It was this skill that enabled him to keep his productivity up despite the numerous calls on his time. It was something that he could do quite automatically. He did it now.

He was soon lost in thought, oblivious to the people around

him. He reacted to nothing; even when somebody repeatedly called his name, he did not hear.

He was thinking well and he wasn't going to let it go. He came abreast with his car completely unaware of the footsteps pounding behind him. Only when a hand gripped at his shoulder did he reluctantly emerge from his dreamlike state.

He shivered and he turned. He saw that Marcus Mkize was standing behind him, his breath coming out in great puffs. By the look of him, Marcus had been running for some time: Now that Jacob thought about it, he had heard something.

Jacob held out his hand. "Taken up jogging, have you, Marcus?" he joked.

Marcus did not smile. He did not even move.

"I apologize," Jacob said. "I was lost in thought."

When Marcus still made no move, nor spoke any words, Jacob stared more closely into his face. Marcus was a good friend: They knew each other well. It wasn't hard for Jacob to see that Marcus brought bad news.

"Something's gone wrong?"

"*Ja*," Marcus replied.

Who is it? Jacob thought. Which one now? He did not need to utter the words out loud.

"It's Petrus," Marcus said.

"Dead?"

Marcus shook his head. "No. Arrested. Section Twenty-nine."

Jacob nodded.

"We just got word," Marcus continued. "I thought you would want to know."

Jacob heard the news, but it would not sink in. Section 29— that part of the Internal Security Act that applied to treasonous acts—was infamous in South Africa. Those arrested for it tended to disappear into prisons: They were allowed no doctors, lawyers, or visitors of any kind. Its ultimate penalty was death.

It was funny, Jacob reflected, as he stood still, how one never got used to bad news. Petrus was not the first to be arrested: During the last ten years many of their brave comrades had been imprisoned, killed in combat, or hanged by unjust laws. Yet Jacob never expected to hear of another: It always came as a terrible shock.

And it was worse this time. For Petrus (or Nathaniel, which was how Jacob still thought of him) was like a son to Jacob.

They met only occasionally, but when they did, they were immediately at ease with each other. They would talk far into the night, of the old times and of the new: of Nathaniel's heritage and of the generation that had arisen in Soweto.

And now Nathaniel was in the Boer's hands. It was almost unbearable to think what might happen to him.

"I thought you'd want to know," Marcus repeated. He could see how badly Jacob was taking the news. He was at a loss as to how to console him.

"Yeah, thanks," Jacob replied. He removed his keys from his trouser pockets. He unlocked the door and slipped into the driver's seat.

"I've got another meeting," he said. He leaned over and delivered to Marcus a wan smile. "Thanks for telling me." He closed the door.

He saw Marcus hesitate and take a step toward him. He understood his friend's impulse to console, but he felt a need to be alone. He smiled reassuringly, and was relieved to see that Marcus understood and that he turned away.

Jacob put his key into its lock. He looked down the long avenida. There was a perfume in the air, a sweet, natural perfume, and he sniffed at it appreciatively. Life could be so good, he thought, the simple things so rewarding. He looked up at the sky whose blue had become a vivid orange already tinged with the promise of darkness. It was the magic hour of dusk, the time so specific to Southern Africa, the time that he and Rosa loved the best. He turned the key.

As soon as the engine sparked, the bomb exploded. It was a big device, they had taken no risks: It tossed the car up into the air, it shattered windows many hundreds of yards away. Marcus Mkize was thrown back onto a fence, where he slumped unconscious on the ground; a soldier in army fatigues tried to stop the unbearable ringing in his ears; a woman opened her mouth and no sound came out. Even the vegetation was affected: A twisted handle got stuck on the top of one of the jacaranda trees, pieces of clothing littered the uncut grass.

The bomb did all of this. And the bomb did one other thing: The thing for which it had been intended. In one decisive stroke, it ended Jacob's life.

*   *   *

Rosa and Julia were having tea together when the phone rang. With a sigh of exasperation, Rosa picked it up. She heard a satellite blip in the background, and she smiled. "Jacob," she mouthed to Julia.

But it wasn't Jacob. It was somebody entirely different: It was somebody phoning to tell her that it never would be Jacob, ever again.

She turned to her mother. "Jacob's dead," she said in a blank voice.

The man on the other end was speaking insistently, trying to find out if she was still there, if she had heard, if she had understood. And if I haven't, she wanted to shout, would that make any difference? Would that bring Jacob back?

"Yes," she said dully. "Yes, yes, yes."

She put the phone down.

"It's not true, is it, darling?" Julia asked.

Surprised, she looked at her mother. She had forgotten that Julia was there, had been there, when the telephone rang.

"It's not true?" Julia said.

Her mother was old, Rosa thought, old and frail. She looked away. She had no space, or time, for pity now. She got wearily to her feet.

"I must go and pack," she said.

"And the children?"

The children, thought Rosa. How could I have forgotten? It is I who am old and frail: It is I who will grow old and frail without Jacob. She picked up the telephone.

"I will come with you," Julia said.

"We'll talk about that later," Rosa said without emotion. "Can you remember Rachel's phone number?"

"Martha?" Rachel's voice was faint.

"Not again," Martha said in surprise. "I'm not sure I can take another family meal quite yet."

She waited for Rachel to reply, but nothing happened.

"Rachel?" she asked. She banged the receiver on the table.

When she lifted it to her ear again, she found she had missed most of Rachel's speech. ". . . tomorrow," was all she caught.

"Sorry," she said quickly. "Didn't hear that. What did you say?"

"Jacob's dead." Rachel was sobbing now. "He's dead."

Martha felt little surprise. Jacob's dead, she thought, my father is dead. They finally killed him.

"Where's Rosa?" she asked.

"At the airport. She left money for our tickets. She tried to get you, but you weren't in."

"I bet."

"I'm sorry," Rachel sobbed. "I'm sorry."

Martha smiled into the receiver. "And so am I," she said. "Look, you've got the children—I'll book the tickets."

She put the phone down and picked up her pen. "Ring British Airways," she wrote in her tidy hand on the top sheet of her pad. She got up and walked over to the door. Her lips were parched, she was desperate for water. She put her hand on the knob and turned it. Her hand slipped off, but the door was still closed. She felt her knees tremble. "Sit down," a voice said. She turned to look—there was no one in the room. She smiled. "Oh, Christ, I'm talking to myself now," she said.

She walked back to the desk and picked up the telephone. "Get Stephen for me," she said loudly into it.

"Are you all right?" the receptionist asked.

"Get Stephen," she said as clearly as she was able.

It was a sign of the changing times that Mozambique offered for Jacob what amounted to a full-blown state funeral. Every detail came under the thumb of Mozambiquan protocol. There was no need for Rosa to make any arrangements: The tickets for her and the family were provided by the government.

Rosa was on a plane within a matter of hours. She heard them all whispering about her, but she took no notice. She had been treated like royalty the whole way down. She had only to lift a little finger and flight attendants descended from every direction.

At another time this kind of overkill might have annoyed Rosa. But she had changed at the news of her husband's death: She had thrown away the habits and the reactions of a lifetime. She had been told the news of his death almost immediately after it had happened. She hadn't so much as blinked. This was, she thought, something that she had been expecting for a long time: forever, in fact.

She, renowned for her own efficiency, had allowed others to organize her. Someone had packed, someone had seen to the children, someone had driven her to the airport, someone had met her off the plane, had cleared her through customs, had taken her to a house in Maputo.

She had gone through the motions of contact with others, had accepted more condolences than she cared to count, had opened telegrams and messages of support that flooded into the country, had even shed a few tears. But she was still detached from her own grief. She was unfeeling, unwanting, numb.

Stephen told Martha that they would arrive in a couple of hours. Then she would see her father, she thought, no, not her father; she would see her mother. She couldn't imagine why she had got the two confused.

She turned to Stephen. "I don't think I ever really knew him," she said.

Stephen nodded his head. He looked into her eyes. "You knew him as well as you were able," he said. "It wasn't easy. It was never easy."

"It should have been," Martha protested. "It should have been." Her voice was childish, babyish, even, and she did not like it. But she had other things to worry about. For the first time in over twenty-four hours, her body began to thaw. Her fingers tingled, and so did her toes. I'm having a heart attack, she thought vaguely, but she knew that she was not. The ache, that ache that tore at her heart, was not physical. It was for Jacob and Jacob alone. It was for the man who had once been her father.

Her face crumpled; the tears began to fall.

Rosa awoke from a drugged sleep and realized that she did want something. She wanted to visit the Polano Hotel: She wanted to stand in the place where she and Jacob had promised each other they would once again vacation.

Her comrades looked at her strangely when she voiced her request.

"The Polano has changed," one of them ventured. "It is full of Boers these days."

"What do I care?" Rosa asked. "They have done their worst to me. What more can they do?"

They saw she would not be dissuaded, and so they drove her to the hotel. At her request, they left her alone. They would, they promised, return in time to take her to the airport to meet her daughters.

She did not immediately enter the hotel. Instead, she stood in the curved driveway and she stared up at the gracious white building, at the tall palm trees that towered above it, at the tennis courts that stood to one side.

Then she took a deep breath and walked into the lobby, past the reception desk, her heels tapping on the elegant marble, her face as frozen as it had been for days.

Inside it was as cool as her memory had told her it would be. But other things were changed. There had been some improvements in the internal arrangements—what once had been a huge and echoing room had turned into a gracious tea-serving area, a bar had been established in one corner. And yet none of these did anything to alter the essential grandeur of the building.

When she and Jacob had planned to come here, it had been the exterior, rather than the inside, that Rosa had imagined. So now she walked through the large room, through the glass door and outside to the Polano swimming pool.

She took in the sight of it all. To her left, people were still eating lunch on the patio, every dish served by waiters in immaculate white. Rosa paid them scant attention. As she passed by, she realized that indeed her comrades were right: Afrikaans was one of the dominant customers' languages.

She let it wash over her: It was incomprehensible to her—it felt as though she had never been able to talk Afrikaans, had never understood it. It was an alien language, sprung from an alien culture.

She carried on walking until she was standing at one extreme of the grounds, beside the balustrade that separated the hotel from the seaside cliff. She looked back at the Polano in its magnificence, at its fringe of palms, its gardens bright with color, its inviting swimming pool.

She stood there for a long time—just looking. She must have made a forbidding sight, for no waiter attempted to approach her. They'd been all too eager, she thought, to serve when she and Jacob had been here. But that was in the old days, when few tourists came here, when the ANC and FRELIMO walked side by side, when Jacob was alive.

Neutrally she watched as couples lounged together, as children jumped screaming with joy into the pool, as business deals were made and broken. She felt as though she had been planted there, as though she would never move again.

And then something happened to break her spell.

On one side of the Polano were the tennis courts, on the other was a sprawling house that had seen better days. It was the scene outside this house that attracted Rosa's attention.

A group of people emerged. Rosa saw them out of the corner of her eye, and she remembered she and Jacob wondering together who owned the house. Idly she wondered whether Jacob had ever bothered to find out.

The people—mainly women, they were—walked stiffly. Instead of wandering around the lawn, treading on the spiky grass, they stopped at the porch. Without speaking, they stood beside each other in one horizontal line. They were silent as they looked toward the sea. They stood as if waiting for a signal.

It came eventually—from a man who stepped in front. He raised his hand, and then he dropped it. And then the group began to sing.

Unaccompanied, they sang, their voices rising high into the sky. They picked up the beat and their bodies moved with it; they sang and they smiled and they blended together. The few men in the crowd added their deep voices to the melody, but the women rose above that. They sang, sometimes in so high a pitch that it became almost uncomfortable, they ululated, they shouted with their voices, they defied the hot summer's day.

They were, Rosa knew, just a cultural group—a collection of people who came together in their spare time to sing, and who perhaps would give an occasional performance. They were nothing special, but they were the true voice of Africa. Their voices pulled at her. Afrikaans, she thought, the symbol of South African oppression, had no draw for her. But this singing—this was the way she had once lived, this was the spirit for which Jacob had died.

She gazed away, but their voices called her back. She was unable to escape their song. And so she listened, and the tears began to course down her face. Jacob, she thought, for what must have been the first real time, is dead. He's dead, she thought—how can I live without him?

She turned and stared into the sea, but the voices pursued her, and her tears kept coming. She cried for what seemed like forever. She kept thinking that she would soon stop, but when she felt a hand tapping her shoulder and a soft voice telling her that it was time to go to the airport, she had not yet finished. She halted the outward manifestation of her grief, but inside she was torn apart by her sorrow.

She had pulled herself together by the time she found herself standing on the runway. The children, she thought, would have need of her: She must be strong for them.

But her resolve began to fracture when she saw them on the stairway. She saw, first Rachel holding on to her youngest and followed by her husband, Peter, hand in hand with the ten-year-old Tanya. Behind them came Martha and Stephen.

Rosa tried to smile a welcome, but her mouth froze. She had no control of the tears that came unbidden to her eyes. She stood there beside a Mozambiquan official, who covered his own discomfort by stretching his hand out for their passports, and she sobbed out an agony that was unending, that weeping did nothing to lessen.

When Rosa began to cry, Rachel stopped. Martha, standing behind her, experienced a moment of complete shock at the sight of her mother. She didn't know why she was so amazed, she just knew that she had never expected to see Rosa so changed, to hear her cry out so. At the back of her mind was complete incomprehension. Did Rosa really love Jacob? Was her grief not another form of trickery?

Rachel moved again, and they surrounded Rosa, hugging her.

Rosa had never felt so alone in her life. I want Jacob's arms around me! she wanted to shout. I want him, not you.

Rachel took a sudden step away. Perhaps I shouted it out loud, Rosa thought. I must pull myself together.

She took a handkerchief and dried her eyes. She smiled wanly at them all.

"You managed to dissuade Julia from coming?" she asked.

"It wasn't that difficult," Martha replied. "She didn't really feel up to traveling all this way, but she thought it was her duty."

"Duty," Rosa said. "What price has duty extracted from us?" She shivered before turning to the official. "Shall we go in?" she asked.

He nodded in relief.

56

IT WAS STILL EARLY MORNING, AND YET THE SUN WAS BRIGHT IN THE
sky. That, thought Martha, was yet another thing she could not
come to terms with: the differences between this place and the
country she had come to regard as her home.

Stephen took it all in with open eyes; he did not feel threatened
by the differences. But for Martha, it was another matter. What
annoyed her was that it all rang silent bells in the back of her
mind. She had pushed her childhood in South Africa away from
her: Now, she kept being reminded of it, reminded by the quality
of the light, the shape of the trees, the colors. And also by
something more pernicious: by the very people.

The funeral was not until the next day. Since their arrival, the
family had been staying together in a house in central Maputo.
They had hardly gone out: Scores of people had been visiting,
talking of Jacob, offering condolences, speaking of the struggle
that had claimed so many lives.

Martha didn't know how she was going to survive any more
days like these. It was all right for Rachel, she had the children
as an excuse to escape. But Martha was trapped by the visitors.
They were all kind, they were all wonderful people in their own
way, but they were from another world—from Jacob's world,
from the world that had first deprived her of her father's presence
and had now killed him.

It was a schizophrenic experience: She felt so included in their
community—and at the same time, so out of place. They came
to cook, to share the food, to clean, to sit and keep company.
They stayed for five minutes or for hours: They seemed to know
what to do, whereas she was at a loss.

She smiled at them, and then she went upstairs to cry. She had to be strong, she told herself, for Rosa was not coping well.

She kept finding her mother sitting on the bed, an array of Jacob's clothes strewn around her. Rosa would pick up an item, look at it, and then press it to her cheek. She would remove it, guiltily almost, when she noticed Martha in the doorway, but Martha suspected that as soon as she turned her back, Rosa would grab for the object again.

Martha glanced at Stephen as a man walked down the pavement toward them. He was dressed in a torn T-shirt and a pair of trousers with holes instead of knees. He could use Jacob's clothes, thought Martha.

"Do you think I should pack his clothes away?" she asked Stephen.

"No," he replied. "Why?"

With a flip of her hand, she indicated the man who was almost abreast of them.

"There's time for that later," Stephen said. "Rosa needs Jacob's belongings around her."

"Jacob is dead," Martha replied. "We can't bring him back."

Stephen stopped so abruptly that the man almost bumped into them. "*Desculpe*," Stephen muttered. The man nodded and continued down the pavement.

Stephen stared at Martha, stared at her so hard that she was forced to glance away.

He looked at her and he saw more than her: He saw in her eyes a reflection of Rosa, and before her of Julia, of a line of strong women stretching back into the *shtetl*: chains of women bound by ties of blood, of guilt, and of duty.

"Why are you being so hard on your mother?" he finally asked.

"Don't be silly." Martha bit her lip. "I'm only trying to help." She walked forward, away from him, she had to get away. "There's the hospital," she said. "I'll go in on my own."

Early as it was, the hospital grounds were already crowded. People milled about, chatting desultorily, settling themselves to wait patiently in the dry earth under spreading trees. Martha had been here once before, and she had no trouble retracing her steps. She walked briskly to the main entrance and up a flight of stairs. Then she trod the corridor until she came to the last room on the left—the private room in which Marcus Mkize lay.

She was about to go in when it happened again, that feeling in her stomach. It was the same sensation she experienced when she thought of the bomb, of the violence done to Jacob's body, of her father's death. It was a wrenching, a tearing at her guts, a dread that wormed inside her. She had felt it on the occasion of her first visit to Marcus, and now she felt it again.

Well, she would conquer it, she thought, as she pushed the door open.

Marcus was lying in the darkened room, both eyes shut. His head was swathed in bandages, his face a mass of purpled bruises. She hesitated at the door, she did not want to wake him. She felt relieved almost; this visit was like a dare to herself: If he was asleep, then she had the perfect excuse to leave.

He opened one eye: the only eye he would ever again be able to open. He smiled when he saw her. He lifted a hand and patted his bed.

She drew up a chair and went to sit on it.

"It is good to see you again, Martha," Marcus said. "How are you?"

"Fine," she answered. How should I be, she said to herself, how does he expect me to be? She regretted now this journey to the hospital. What could Marcus, a stranger, say to her to make her feel better? Just because he had been the last person to see Jacob alive, what did that mean?

"Your father was my friend," Marcus said. "And my comrade: a true revolutionary."

A revolutionary, Martha thought bitterly: not a father.

"He loved you," Marcus continued. "All of you. He carried a picture of you and your sister with him always."

A picture, thought Martha, that could never have survived the explosion.

"And he loved freedom," said Marcus.

"He loved freedom, an abstract, more than he loved me."

"It was not a question of degree," Marcus said, "or of choice. In another world, Jacob would never have left you or your mother." He paused and he closed his eye. It was a few minutes before he spoke again. "Did you see the large double doors at the end of the corridor?" he asked.

"No." The question took her by surprise: Was his mind wandering? she thought.

He smiled. "That's because they're not there," he said.

She shifted uncomfortably in her seat, eyeing the bell beside his bed.

"A nurse noticed that I jumped every time those doors banged shut," Marcus continued. "So she tried to stop the banging. In the end she had to remove those doors, because in the whole of Maputo not one doorstop exists. Can you believe that—not one doorstop?"

His mind had gone, Martha thought. Well, it was understandable, he'd been badly injured.

"And there never will be one," Marcus said, "not until South Africa is free. Every spare penny is spent fighting the apartheid bandits." His voice strengthened. "That is what freedom in South Africa means," he said. "It means spaces instead of doors in Maputo Hospital, it means starvation in Pemba, it means imprisonment in Jo'burg. And it means that heroes are born every day, and that mortals are forced to become heroes. Your father was one of them. He will be followed by others: Others will pick up the spear that has fallen from his hands."

Marcus turned his head away. His voice was muffled. "You could pick it up," he said.

"Yes," Martha answered, "I could." No, she thought, I can never do that. She got up and touched him gently on the shoulder.

"I will think of you tomorrow," he said.

The day of the funeral arrived, and the Swieces greeted it with a mixture of dread and relief. None of them wanted to see Jacob's body lowered into the ground, and yet the waiting had grown unbearable.

They took care to avoid each other's eyes: They could not afford to break now. They stood stiffly together, untouching, as they waited for the rituals of death to take over.

They were picked up and driven to a square building. Martha had enough time to wonder where they were before they were ushered out of the car. They walked as a family for only a short way, but it seemed like miles. For a crowd of people, hundreds of men and women, lined their route. As Martha walked, looking straight ahead, she wondered at that crowd. What was it thinking, she wondered, was it looking at her? The silence was immense: She could hear her own breathing, the scuff of her shoes on dust, the swish of Rosa's linen skirt.

She followed Rosa up a short flight of stairs. There was a

platform at the top, and the family stood in a row, looking down at the crowd. And the crowd began to sing.

There was a choir to one side that led the singing, but everybody joined in. Together the crowd sang. They sang of South Africa, of the struggle, of the ANC, and of Jacob. They sang, not professionally like the women whom Rosa overheard, but to expel their grief, to give to the family their solidarity, to talk of what had happened to them all.

And then the door behind opened, and the family was moved inside. It was a cool, cavernous room they entered. An empty room—except for the fact that in its center stood a coffin, and around the coffin waited men in dark suits. Martha faltered. She felt Rosa's hand link hers.

"It's okay," Rosa whispered. "I asked them to cover the coffin."

They walked around it, and they shook hands with the men—ambassadors, Rachel told Martha—who muttered embarrassed condolences. And then they were out in the light again, walking through the singing crowd, getting into the black cars, being driven through Maputo and to the cemetery.

It was a place on the outskirts of town, and it was unlike anything Martha considered appropriate. Cemeteries, she thought, were green and cultivated; but this one was brown, its earth was dry and crumbling. In Martha's imagination cemeteries looked over rolling fields, but this one was flat, surrounded by a brick wall. Cemeteries should be small and contained; but this one was huge. Cemeteries should have crosses and stones to mark the grave; but this one had only dry mounds and wilted flowers.

They were taken to a place, a place that already had mounded graves in three neat rows. Only one of them was empty.

"This is the ANC section," Rosa explained. "This is where our comrades killed in South African raids—or by South African bombs—are buried."

There was time to exchange a few snatched words, because the crowd was so big. It took a long time to line up by the grave—and when the line was complete, it was many people thick. Martha knew that she should have felt proud—thousands had come to pay tribute to her father—but her dominant emotion was anger.

What were they doing here? she asked herself. What were

they doing to her? They had come to bury a martyr, they spoke of his death as serving a cause, as never being forgotten: What they wouldn't even think of acknowledging was that Jacob was her father, and that Jacob was dead. She would never know him now.

The coffin was carried by six people, ANC members, Martha guessed, five men and a woman. It was laid into the hole.

And then the speeches began. Under the glare of a hot sun the thousands stood and listened as Jacob's life was praised. They talked of Jacob's courage, and she remembered the times she had despised him for running away from a family confrontation. They talked of his dedication, and she remembered his years of absence. They talked of his ability to love, and she remembered the awkwardness between them.

Did I know anything of him? she asked herself. Was he a total stranger?

Suddenly the talk was over. The choir had begun to sing. Hauntingly they sang, "*Hamble kahle*, Jacob Swiece—rest in peace." Sadly, mournfully, they sang, "*Senzeni*," their voices swelling: "How long? How long must we bury our comrades?" And, finally, triumphally, they sang: "We will win," they sang. "Watch out, you Boers, we are coming!"

Two long queues formed in front of Jacob's grave. Two men, each holding a spade, stood at the head. Together the men lifted their implements high into the air. The sun caught the blades, and it shone straight into Martha's eyes, dazzling her momentarily.

And then the light was gone: Quickly the men dropped their spades. They worked together, piling dry earth into Jacob's grave; they were burying him in front of the crowd as the voices gathered momentum.

The men did not work for long. They were replaced by volunteers from behind, volunteers who took the spades from them and in turn shoveled on the dirt. One after the other they covered Jacob up, this human chain: They built a mound above him— one hundred, two hundred, rushing one after the other to bury their comrade.

Among the diggers was a woman, the same one who had helped lift Jacob's coffin. Martha glanced at her curiously. Out of the corner of her eye she saw Rosa do likewise, and she heard the gasp that Rosa emitted. And then the woman was replaced by another man, and Martha's vision was obscured by tears. As the red-brown earth flew high in the air, tears coursed down her cheeks.

And then it was over. The hole had become a mound.

The men laid down their spades. The crowd began to move away, sections of it walking slowly back toward the exit, others approaching the family and lining up. They filed past, and as they left, they shook hands.

The woman who had carried the coffin was part of this group. She lined up and waited patiently until she arrived in front of Rosa. There was something unusual about this woman. She was strikingly good-looking and handsomely dressed in flowing robes of black and green, but that was not what drew Martha's eyes to her. It was something else, something intangible, something about the way she carried herself erect.

The woman proffered her hand to Rosa.

"I am sorry," she said.

She lowered her eyes and made as if to move off. Martha saw her mother grip the woman's hand.

"Lindiwe?" she asked in an incredulous voice.

The woman inclined her head.

"Lindiwe Cuba?" said Rosa, as if she could not believe the evidence before her eyes. "Moses' daughter?"

The woman nodded again.

"They will not like the fact that you came," Rosa said.

"Jacob was a friend to my son," Lindiwe replied. "You were both friends to my father. I honor the name of Swiece."

Again she tried to move away, but this time Rosa stepped in her path.

"You came here when your son is in prison," Rosa said. "You came here and allowed the security police to see you grieving for Jacob. You have indeed honored us."

"I have done only what was necessary," Lindiwe replied. "My son would want me here. My father would have wanted it, too. Do you know," she said, and her eyes became distant, as if it was only by an effort that she managed to remember. "Do you know," she repeated, "that I saw Nathaniel only once in the last ten years? We were together for a brief time, but in that short time he spoke of your husband. He told me how Jacob grieved for my father, how it pained him that he was unable to attend Moses' funeral. I did not want to carry that same pain. And so

I have come here on this day to honor Jacob."

Rosa took one step closer. She embraced Lindiwe. And then the two women hugged, each wetting the shoulder of the other. They stood together for a long, long time, they drew warmth from each other's bodies, they were timeless, unaware of the queues around them, of the sound of their own sobs.

And finally it was over. They separated. They looked into each other's eyes.

"The last time we met," Lindiwe said softly, "I cursed you for the color of your skin. I have often regretted that."

"You have no need to regret it," Rosa replied. "No matter which side we whites choose, we are still privileged in the country of our birth. There was truth in what you said."

"But now," Lindiwe protested, "Jacob has paid the ultimate price. He has given his life for us."

"Not just for you," Rosa said. "For me as well, and for himself. Jacob's thirst for justice was as strong as his thirst for love, for water, for sleep. He struggled for himself and for the society to which he wanted to belong. He was not a casualty, or a victim, he was a fighter."

"As is my son," Lindiwe said.

"As are we," Rosa replied.

Lindiwe nodded. She drew her shawl around her head. She took one last look at Rosa and then she was gone, disappearing into the depths of the crowd.

And Rosa stood still for a long time, staring at the place that Lindiwe had vacated.

57

England: 1987

MARTHA LET HERSELF INTO ROSA'S HOUSE, USING THE KEY THAT SHE had always kept, and she walked straight into the sitting room. "It's me," she shouted.

And then she stopped short. Rosa was seated on the couch, but she was not alone. Richard Crossbanks was sitting beside her. A bottle of malt whiskey lay within grasp.

Martha flushed. "I'm sorry," she said quickly, half-turning away.

"Martha—nice to see you," Richard said. His hand, Martha noticed, gripped Rosa's wrist as if he were restraining her.

"I've come at a b-bad time," Martha stuttered.

Rosa sank back into the sofa. "Don't be silly, darling," she said. "Come, take a seat."

Martha did as she was instructed, she came to sit by them. She felt out of place, but she told herself that she had as much right as Richard to be here—more in fact, she thought, warming to her theme.

"No Stephen?" Rosa inquired.

All Martha's calm evaporated. "Not everybody needs a man holding their hands at every single moment," she hissed.

She was looking at her mother, and so she saw Rosa's transformation. She saw the way Rosa's face went totally and completely white. She saw the way Rosa's eyes filled with tears. That served to further provoke her.

"Jacob is dead only one year," she said.

And then she saw something else. She saw Rosa blink back

those tears, she saw the color return, she saw Rosa's eyes harden.

Rosa got up calmly. "I am going upstairs," she said to Richard. "Tell me when she's gone."

Martha watched her mother rise and walk across the room. She watched her mother open the door. That's right, she silently screamed, run away from the truth!

Rosa reacted as if she had heard. She turned and faced Martha. "Why should I let you drive me out?" she asked. "This is my house."

"This was J-Jacob's house," Martha stuttered.

"Jacob is dead."

"And you didn't waste much time dancing over his bones," Martha said.

She felt a movement behind her and a sharp intake of breath. Come on, she silently dared Richard, see what happens if you place a finger on me.

"Leave her, Richard," Rosa said quietly. She stepped across the room until she was standing right in front of Martha. "What brought on this temper tantrum?" she asked. "What did you think we might be doing: fucking on the couch?"

The sentence hit Martha in the face like a blow. She had never heard her mother speak like this. She replied with the first words that sprang to her mouth. "You're hateful," she said in a voice that was full of childishness. She hardened it deliberately. "Even your own mother left you," she finished.

Rosa narrowed her eyes. "My mother went back to South Africa because she could no longer face her life here," she said. "Because she wanted to escape the harsh reality of her exile. Because every morning that she woke and looked out at gray skies she remembered that she was not at home, and she remembered why." Rosa turned her face toward the window. Her voice was more distant now. "Julia had an excuse," she said. "She is over eighty. But you"—Rosa faced her daughter again— "you are an ostrich just like her. You think we owe you justice— as if there is such a thing as individual justice. You wanted us to make it better for you, as if your problems were of our making. You have no excuse. You are young and strong, but you are no longer a child. Grow up, my Martha, grow up."

She walked away out of the room. Only at the door did she turn again. She looked at Martha. "Your father was right," she said. "Only you can save yourself." With that parting shot, she was gone.

Martha watched as the door swung close. The last of her mother's words echoed in the back of her brain. Grow up, said the echo, grow up before you lose them all. A solitary tear weaved its way along her cheek, down her chin, and onto the floor.

She felt a hand on her shoulder, Richard's hand. She turned her face so that she was looking into his eyes. "How can Rosa act so self-righteously?" she asked. "She never even loved him."

Richard smiled at her, smiled at her sadly. "She loved him, all right," he said.

"How could she have?"

"Your mother never stopped loving Jacob," Richard replied, "not ever. Not while he was in prison, not while he was in Africa. I should know: I hoped desperately that she would show me even half the love she felt for him. But I was unlucky: She loved me, yes, but it wasn't the same. Jacob was her man, had always been her man."

"Well, why did she live with you, then?"

"Because she was alone," Richard said. "She was lonely. Aren't you human enough to understand that?"

"She's a strong woman," Martha protested. "She wouldn't be lonely."

He stared at her. She was surprised to see that he looked almost disappointed. "I once told you that you worshiped your mother too much," he said wearily. "I see that you haven't changed. You never allowed her to be weak, perhaps because you desperately needed her to be strong. You never understood that having needs is part of being human."

He averted his eyes. "But Rosa is right," he said, "you are grown now. You're older than she was then. Put yourself in her shoes: Think how you would feel—alone with two children." He looked back, straight into her eyes. "If Stephen were imprisoned," he said, "if he suddenly disappeared, would you be faithful to him for all those years?" He smiled when he saw her blink. "Jacob understood," he continued, "and he loved her as much as she loved him. You think that you persecuted Rosa on Jacob's behalf, but you're fooling yourself. You did it for yourself. You never wanted to face the fact that your mother had needs that you couldn't fulfill, and that having needs did not make her any the less strong."

Richard sighed. "Sometimes," he said softly, "I pity you, Martha." He closed his eyes. When he opened them again, he saw that he was alone. Martha had left, left sometime in the last few minutes. He got up.

He did not bother to pursue her. She must, he thought, look after herself. Perhaps that was the trouble, that they had always misjudged her, double-guessed her, explained her away. She needed to direct her own life, make her own mistakes, and do so without blaming them. She was on her own.

He went, instead, upstairs to Rosa. He tapped on her door, and then, guessing that she might not answer, he walked straight in. He was pleasantly surprised. She was lying down on the bed, but the look of despair he'd expected was absent. She smiled at him and patted the bed. He went and sat down beside her.

"Did you chase her out?" she asked flippantly.

He'd never heard her speak so irreverently of her daughter. He looked at her to see if the encounter had driven her to the edge of hysteria, but she seemed calm enough.

He shrugged his shoulders. "She left at some point when I was giving her—advice about life and living," he said.

"Fatherly advice," Rosa said. "You can say it. You and Jacob were both fathers to that girl."

"Lot of good it did her," Richard reflected.

Rosa shook her head. "I don't know," she said. "I don't think it's all our fault. It's South Africa. She was too young, which meant that what was a great source of strength to both me and Jacob, *the* source of strength, I should say, only undermined her. She has no country, and without a country she cannot find herself." She yawned and stretched. "Ag," she said. "I'm making no sense. Come on, let's go finish that drink."

58

"READY?" STEPHEN ASKED.

Martha took a deep breath and then nodded. "As ready as I'll ever be," she said. But she did not immediately move, instead, she shot a glance at the hall mirror. She pulled a face, which turned into a half-smile as Stephen moved into vision. "Okay," she said decisively, and arm in arm they walked up the stairs toward Max Freeman's living room.

But when they got there, Martha's determination wavered. Max lived in an enormous house overlooking Primrose Hill, and she was accustomed, on her occasional visits, to walking in and appreciating the spaciousness of the living room. This time, though, it was different, because this time the room was crowded with people.

She scowled. "They said it would be a small do," she said.

Stephen shrugged. "I can imagine they had trouble restricting the numbers. Your father was a public person, you know."

"How could I forget it?" she replied. She was being, she knew, unfairly curt with him, but she was feeling the strain of the day.

It's gone on too long, she thought.

Death, or Jacob's death, had so many rituals attached to it. There'd been the funeral, the memorial meeting in London, the first anniversary, and now, when she had thought it was all over, the occasion of the publication of Jacob's prison diary. This one, she thought, was the worst, because unlike all the other times, there was no prescribed way of behaving for it.

She'd woken up early thinking about it, and had wasted most of the day worrying. The launch itself had taken place in the late afternoon, and there she'd had to tolerate several hours of smiling at photographers, of answering silly questions, of all the time biting back the tears that threatened to spill over. It had been a relief when it was over, when the public had gone home and they had made their separate ways to Max's house.

But then she saw the crowd. She had thought that this event, this private function for close friends and family, would be a more intimate one, that she would be able to experience it without having to guard her own reactions.

"Shit," she said. She couldn't help herself.

When Stephen glanced anxiously in her direction, she threw him a smile, a cursory smile, but a smile nevertheless.

"Martha! At last." Max Freeman enveloped her in a bearlike hug. "Come join Rachel and your mother," he said. "I'd like, if you don't mind, to say a few words, and the family should be together when I do."

From across the room, Rosa saw the look of distaste on Martha's face. Oh, God, she prayed, please don't make one of your fusses.

She knew that Martha must be under a lot of strain: The launch of Jacob's book, with its crush of press, had been difficult. And yet she didn't feel like either excusing or tolerating any of Martha's bad behavior. For she, too, was suffering.

She'd thought she had prepared herself for this day, and yet when it came, she had found it a thousand times harder than she had imagined. She was used to being by herself and to missing Jacob—the dark hours of night were the worst—and the ache of his absence had grown to be part of her. But to feel the agony so intensely during a time that others regarded as a kind of celebration—that she had never expected. It came upon her, and she knew what heartache meant. It was a physical sensation that tightened her chest, constricted her throat, brought unwept tears to her eyes. She'd pushed it away, but nevertheless it had left her feeling exhausted.

And so she was in no mood to cope with Martha. She threw her daughter a perfunctory smile, and turned away as if she were thinking of something else.

"Friends," Max called. "Comrades and friends."

He got immediate results: The conversation in the room died down as people turned to face the family. Martha blinked. She couldn't stand many more sympathetic eyes on her, she thought.

Max coughed. "I am not going to make a long speech," he said. "This is not a meeting or a memorial: It is instead a time for us to be together and a time for us to remember, each in his own way." He coughed again, and when he next spoke his voice was tinged with sadness. He's having trouble, too, Rosa thought.

"Although Jacob is dead," Max said, "he lives on through this book. It speaks of him—of his dedication, his patience, his thirst for justice, his love of his fellow man." Max paused and looked around the room. "I do not need to say more," he continued, "because all of us gathered here knew Jacob, and we loved him. But what I would like to do is to ask you all to raise your glasses and toast the memory of Jacob Swiece. Toast his memory and at the same time drink to his dearest wish—that South Africa will soon be free."

Max held up his glass. "To Jacob," he said.

"And South Africa," came several voices from the back.

Then they raised their glasses in the air, and in silence they drank.

"And now . . ." Max began.

"I would like to say something."

Oh, God, Rosa thought, not now. She whipped her head around and tried to catch Martha's eye, to plead with her to hold her tongue, but Martha did not appear to notice. She was staring straight ahead, her eyes focused on some point in the far distance.

"I would like to say," she started in a clear voice, "that there is another person to whom we should drink. And that person," she said, as she finally turned and looked at Rosa, "that person is my mother."

She saw the startled expression on Rosa's face.

"Max is right," she continued, "the book is Jacob's. But it is also Rosa's book. She spent painstaking months piecing together disparate sources. She used his letters, written while he was in Pretoria and once he was out, his speeches, the things he told her, the way he was—and out of all these she has structured a testimony to my father which speaks in his language, and with his voice, of the things that he held dear. In this sense it is indeed Jacob's book, but it is Rosa's as well. Each page is infused with the love she bore for him and the love he felt for her." She paused and smiled at her mother, and then she turned away.

"And so I ask you," she said, "to drink to Rosa."

She raised her glass, and she saw that the rest of the room did likewise, in unison with her. She took a sip, and she felt her mother beside her. She turned and smiled.

Rosa was crying.

Martha frowned. "I didn't mean . . ."

But Rosa cut her off. "Oh, darling," she said. "I know what you meant and I thank you for it. And now, if you don't mind . . ." She turned on her heel and fled the room. Conversation swelled to cover her exit.

Martha watched her mother's retreating back, and after her first brief moment of insecurity, she thought that she understood.

"Let her go," she said to Max, who had made a move to follow.

She herself felt an almost overwhelming desire to cry, but she would not permit that. If Rosa came back, she might misunderstand, she might feel responsible, and that was the last thing Martha wanted.

She swallowed and bought some time by going over to the table that stood in front of the full-length windows. She picked up a copy of Jacob's book, and turning it over, she looked at the photograph on the back. There he was, staring back at her, through grainy black and white, a man frozen forever in thought.

"He looks so serious," she said to Stephen, who had come up beside her.

The sentence came out spontaneously, and it caught her by surprise. Not long ago, she thought, at the funeral, in fact, all she'd concentrated on were the difficulties between herself and her father. But now, when she remembered him, she remembered him smiling, she remembered him loving her.

"That's was a nice thing you did," Stephen said.

"Why did it feel so hard, then?" she asked, and the tears came back unbidden.

"Because it's painful," he replied.

He was right, she knew he was. "It's difficult to mourn a loss," she realized. "It's so much easier to rail in anger against it."

The old Martha would have done that: She would have found a reason to argue about this occasion, she would have entered the room ready to find fault, and she would have left early in a flurry of resentment. There were some advantages to that, she thought: The old Martha would feel none of the sadness that now washed over her.

But even though the melancholy was hard to take, she did not want to banish it, she did not wish herself back in the the shell of that difficult young woman. She had learned something recently, she had finally taken it in. She realized that she had been trapped by her rage.

It was only after Jacob's death, when she had faced her mother, and when her mother had finally faced her, that she realized that Rosa was not at fault. And she had realized something else—she had understood that anger would never help her forget the unhappiness caused by her parents' political involvement and by Jacob's imprisonment. She had realized that she could in fact never forget it. The only thing she could do was face it—face it and then move on.

But it's not going to be easy, she thought. And Stephen will suffer.

She turned and smiled at him. That was another bonus of her newfound calm, she thought, the way she felt about him. She no longer found it so necessary to push him off, to build a protective barrier around herself. Jacob had got out of prison a long time ago, she realized: Her own escape was a more recent one. Stephen supplied the ladder, she thought.

She stood on tiptoe, and putting her arms around his neck, she kissed him full on the lips.

Rosa, her eyes now dry, walked back into the room in time to see the two kissing. She stopped momentarily and smiled.

Ignoring people who were trying to catch her attention, Rosa walked over to Martha.

"I'm sorry I cried like that," she said formally.

As Stephen moved discreetly into the background, Martha smiled at Rosa: an uninhibited, open smile. "You don't have to apologize," she said. "If I weren't so uptight, I would have cried as well." She looked straight into her mother's eyes, and as she did so her face became more serious. She seemed to Rosa to be on the brink of saying something, but no words came out.

"Yes?" Rosa asked.

Martha shook her head. "Not now."

It was Rosa's turn to smile. "Why not now?" she asked. "Forget the other people and pretend it's just us."

She saw Martha struggling with herself, opening and shutting her mouth, and she wanted to reach out and help. She resisted the temptation: Martha would tell her in her own time.

"I'm going to the school." Martha said the words so fast that Rosa almost missed them.

The school? thought Rosa. She must mean the ANC school in Tanzania. She raised an eyebrow.

She hates the idea, Martha thought. "I have to go," she continued, and she was irritated to hear that a childish whine, a familiar childish whine, had crept into her voice. With an effort, she banished it. "It's the only way that I'll ever find out what South Africa means to me," she said. "To me, and not just to you and Jacob."

"And Stephen?"

Martha blinked. "I have to go on my own," she said. "Stephen knows, and he supports me. He says he'll wait, whatever . . . whatever . . ." she couldn't go on. She looked down at her feet.

And this time Rosa did make a move toward her. She put an arm around her shoulder and she kissed her daughter softly on the cheek. "You're a brave one, my Martha," she whispered.

Martha looked up. "You mean you don't mind?"

Rosa shook her head. "I'll miss you," she said.

"The new me."

"And the old one as well." Rosa smiled. "Let's face it," she said, "life with you was never boring."

Martha did not return the smile. "I thought for a moment that you might resent my going," she said instead.

Rosa frowned. "Resent it?"

"Or stop me somehow."

Rosa looked straight into her daughter's eyes. "You are grown up, Martha," she said. "I couldn't stop you even if I wanted to. And I don't want to." She paused, because tears welled again in her eyes. "But I'll miss you," she said. "And now go talk to Stephen while I pull myself together."

Rosa was relieved when Martha, after a moment's hesitation, did as she was bid. She stood and watched as Martha and Stephen exchanged a special smile, the kind that only lovers swapped, she thought, and her lips trembled.

She turned away from them, picked up the first thing that came to hand and, because it was a full wineglass, took a sip. She stood motionless, lost in thought, her face set to discourage anyone from attempting to talk to her.

She hadn't, she knew, been totally honest with Martha: Part of her resented the decision taken so, without a moment's consultation; part of her did want to stop Martha from going—was it jealousy, perhaps?

Yes, Rosa thought, there's jealousy in there. I'm scared that if she moves into my world, she will do better in it than I: that she will be stronger, that her contribution will be greater.

It was a jealousy, she realized, not unique to her. Julia must have felt the same way when Rosa had grown up and begun to spread her wings. Julia must have watched Rosa do the things that she had never done, and she must have felt resentment at the freedom that her daughter possessed.

And, thought Rosa, it probably went further back than that. Julia's mother, Riva, had the hardest time of all. She had moved to a new country, but she had never settled in the new society. She must have found her daughter's expanded horizons hard to countenance. And Riva had another burden, Rosa remembered: Her mother cursed her going. That must be why Martha expected me to stop her, Rosa thought. We all carry within us the knowledge of that curse.

Rosa shook herself. She was, she thought, growing unduly fanciful. She didn't even know whether Julia had ever told Martha about her grandmother—she herself certainly hadn't, for her it had been a family myth buried back in time, an irrelevance to her daily life.

Except that it wasn't irrelevant: It was part of them. They had traveled so far, in four generations, not only in distance but in education, in possibilities, in achievement. And yet there was a continuum: Riva had left, despite her mother's curse, to find a better life. Julia, Rosa, and now Martha had in their own ways done the same: They searched for a better life, and they were prepared to fight for it, to fight against the odds.

And to die for it as well? Rosa asked herself. Like Jacob?

It was a question that she could not answer, and she did not even try. She breathed in and out again, she straightened her back, she put the wine down on the table, and then she went to join her friends, to talk to them, to smile and to cry perhaps, but more than anything to carry on with her life.

59

1988

"Here," said Stephen. He thrust a package into Martha's hands.

She looked up in surprise. "A present?"

He shrugged. "A token." He leaned against the wall and crossed his arms.

"Open it," he said. He smiled at her. "For it is a selfish present, and it needs to be explained."

Slipping her finger under the break in the paper, she removed the shiny wrapping. She found herself holding a small hardbacked book whose cover was a mass of tiny silver shreds. She lifted it curiously to the light, and it glinted at her: She dropped it and it became dark again.

She opened the book and saw that it was empty save for an inscription on the front page. "For Martha," it said. "With love."

She looked at Stephen, who had moved from the wall and was sitting on a chair by the desk. "A diary?" she asked.

"If that's what you choose."

"Then why selfish?"

He stared at her with those chill blue eyes. He rested an elbow on his desk, and he put his chin in his hand. His fingers briefly touched his lips. "I hope you will write your experiences there," he said. "And that you will one day show it to me so that I, too, can discover and understand."

She wanted to walk over to him, to remove his hand and to touch those lips herself. She wanted to, but she dared not. She turned away and placed the book gently on top of her open suitcase.

"I do love you, you know," she said in a muffled voice.

"I know," was his response.

He came up behind her, and putting his hands on her shoulders, he turned her gently around. "You are doing what is right," he said. "What is right for you."

"Then come with me," she pleaded.

He shrugged. "I can't," he said. "You know that." A finger brushed against her cheek. "And," he said thoughtfully, "I don't think that's what you want, either." He smiled at her. "Which is all right," he said.

She blinked. "I b-better ring my grandmother," she stuttered.

In her Johannesburg living room Julia replaced the telephone and frowned. "Tanzania," she muttered. "Why is she going there?"

She felt a momentary pang of annoyance that Martha had waited until the last minute before informing her of her plans. Then the resentment wafted away. After all, she thought, Martha probably told me and I promptly forgot.

It would be more difficult, she thought, for Martha to ring from her new home.

Well, what did it matter? The telephone was such an unsatisfactory instrument of communication: It emphasized rather than shortened the distance between Julia and the rest of her family. When she heard their voices, so lively, so vibrant, echoing from thousands of miles away, she realized how irrelevant they had become, how much she had begun to live in the past.

These days she spent increasing hours thinking of the old times: remembering the good times and the bad, remembering what it had been like to be young.

Painful, she thought with a smile: She did not wish those days again. No, it was peace for which she now longed—an uninterrupted peace.

She smiled to herself again. The Cyns, the Arnolds, and the Swieces were never ones for peace. Look at how they had traveled the world: first from Lithuania to South Africa, and then, within one generation, back to Europe again. And now Martha was returning to Africa.

It crossed her mind to wonder why they had all been so unsettled. Perhaps it is the fact of being Jewish, she thought. Our history has prevented us from resting: We must always change things.

But it was more than that, she thought, as her mind's eye ranged backward—it was politics.

She remembered the passion in Harold's face as he had talked of injustice; she remembered the time he had come out of jail shocked at the conditions of those whom he considered his fellow man. She remembered Rosa standing on a platform, her eyes flashing, as she spoke of the need for action. They were both doers, her husband and her daughter—she came from a family of doers.

And then she remembered Riva. She remembered how Riva had always stood aside, had watched life go by after Haim's death.

And I in my own way did the same, thought Julia. I supported Harold and Rosa as they made history. I stood in the wings.

She saw no reason to dwell on the thought—that was the advantage about being alone: One could evict uncomfortable notions. She reached out for a newspaper to distract her. She opened it at random.

Her eyes settled on an item buried among reports of the weather, of sport, of television news. ANC THREE TO BE SENTENCED TODAY, its headline read.

Julia folded the paper. I am too old, she thought, to bother about this now.

Sometimes she felt that she was the oldest person in the world, that she had become ossified in this room.

The paper dropped to the floor, and Julia Arnold slept.

Peggy Bopape lifted the lid of the pot and stared at the soup cooking within. The light was bad, and all she could see was a mass of dark-colored liquid and a few more lumpy items, which surfaced as the soup simmered. For some reason it reminded her of her childhood, of those women in the country who professed to be able to read the future in a pot of stew. She could do with that now, she thought. She'd give anything to hear the outcome of this day, not to have to wait it out.

But then the outcome was a certainty, wasn't it?

Was it stew they read, she suddenly thought, or tea? She could no longer remember, probably she never really knew. Her mother had disapproved of such superstition. "We are Christians," her mother used to say. "We put our faith in God, not in luck or ignorance."

Faith, thought Peggy. It has been my one abiding strength. And yet in the end, what has it done for me?

She shook herself. It wasn't God's fault, she thought, it was man's.

It was man who had killed her husband, exiled her from her home, isolated her from her only way of life. And it was man who was even now sitting in judgment on her grandson.

She watched a bubble struggle to the surface and then disperse back into the liquid. It would be replaced by another and another, the soup simmering until it had dried up or the heat was removed.

It was the same with South Africa, she thought: Nathaniel would be replaced by another like him, another and another until the end. God would not interfere: Man was in charge. And what man had done in South Africa, she thought, could never be forgiven. Hearing a knock on the door, she replaced the lid. She walked slowly to the door and opened it. She saw a group of women, all dressed similarly in black skirts and green shirts. She nodded.

"We have come to be with you on this day, our sister," said the woman in front.

Peggy stood to one side as the women filed past her.

Rachel stepped closer to Martha and hugged her warmly.

"I'll miss you," she said.

"I'll write," Martha promised. "And I'll be back."

Rachel let go. She smiled. "I know," she said. "But it won't be the same. It's the end of a chapter, your going. It's the final acknowledgment of our separation."

"Were we always so close?" Martha asked in surprise. "We certainly didn't act it."

"Oh, we were close," Rachel confirmed. "Bonded together in our closeness. We have shared out our feelings you and I, partitioned them together. You had the anger, and I the ability to come to terms with life. You struggled against our fate, and I embraced it. You railed against what could not be changed, while I maneuvered around it."

"Sounds like you had an easier time," Martha joked.

"I did," Rachel said slowly.

The two looked at each other, awkward now.

"I envy you," Rachel said.

The smile died on Martha's face. "Me?" she asked. "You envy me? You who are so happy in your life, whose children are wonderful, whose husband's a gem? You've got work you like, friends . . ." She held her hands up in the air, as if she could have gone on forever describing Rachel's advantages.

Rachel shrugged. She had wanted to tell her sister how she really felt, she had wanted to say that Martha was doing something they both should have done a long time ago—was coming to terms with a past that had dogged her, too. But she saw that it was too late to say that—too late, or perhaps too early. Martha was not ready. Perhaps she never would be.

"The weather," Rachel explained, "away from the gray. I envy you." Gently she propelled Martha toward the door. "Go on," she said, "before I burst into tears. As you say—it won't be long before we see each other again."

Bertha Cuba stood to one side and listened to her mother.

"I have talked to my son," Lindiwe said loudly, "only once since he was detained. That is all I was allowed." She was speaking slowly, in a measured manner. She looked around to make sure they were listening. "He does not know what the verdict will be," she continued, "but he asked me to say that it is the South African regime on trial, not he. That it is apartheid which murders, not those who struggle against it. That the bombs of poverty, of discrimination, of malnutrition, of racism, have killed a hundred thousand times more people than the bombs of the ANC, which have been aimed only at property and at the agents of oppression. He asked me to tell the world that if he is hanged, others will take his place. That he has no regrets."

The words entered Bertha's brain like steel pins with wool tips—they pierced their way in and then they stuck. She heard them, but she could not fully understand. All she could think of was that her brother was standing trial for his life.

She watched as Lindiwe dismissed the reporters with a regal shake of her head. Whatever the verdict, she knew that Lindiwe would be ready to talk to them again: to organize the maximum publicity for her son.

It wasn't, Bertha knew, that Lindiwe didn't care: it was that she had been taught how to fight. As for herself, Bertha wasn't so sure. I am not as strong as my mother, she thought to herself, or my brother.

She looked up to the top of the courtroom steps, and she shivered. Up there waited the room in which they must face Nathaniel's fate. Up there—so close and yet so far away.

She remembered another set of steps in another time. There'd been a ghost, she thought, a ghost beside her. She'd driven it way, that phantom of another age. She had refused to live with it. And now she wished that it would return. That it would walk beside her. That it would comfort her.

She felt a hand upon her shoulder. She started and turned. She found herself facing her father.

"Come now," Johannes said gently. "It is time."

Nicholas Arnold happened to be passing when the Cuba family walked up the courtroom steps. He was in his car, a string of traffic behind him.

It was stupid, he thought, to drive this way. He should have chosen another route and avoided the crush. He'd even known that it was the day of Nathaniel Cuba's sentencing. There was bound to be a crowd.

And yet even though he was in a terrible rush, he had driven this way.

He peered out the window just in time to see the family reach the top of the stairs. They stopped and turned. The older of the two women, it must be Lindiwe, he thought, looked down at the waiting crowd. The crowd responded by bursting into song.

She held up a fist, high in the air, and stood still.

It was not just any song, Nicholas realized, it was "*Nkosi Sikelel'i Afrika*"—the anthem of the African National Congress.

That song reminded Nicholas of so much: of so much he regretted and resented, sometimes in equal proportions. It was a song with which he had been brought up, which resounded daily throughout South Africa but from which his white compatriots were now shielded.

It took him back. It reminded him of those endless meetings his parents used to hold: meetings from which he was always excluded. It reminded him of the parties and the arguments, the raids and the aftermath. It reminded him of his sister, of the quickness of her tongue, a quickness that he could never match.

He wondered how Rosa was faring. He had written to her

when Jacob died, and had received only a brief acknowledgment. Since Julia seldom talked of Rosa, Nicholas had no idea how his sister was coping on her own.

Because he could do nothing, he had tried to put her out of his mind. He hadn't succeeded. Nathaniel's trial was partly responsible: During it, the name of Jacob Swiece, archcriminal to the regime, hero to the resistance, had been frequently mentioned.

Jacob was a nice man, Nicholas thought, a committed man. He had done nothing that earned him such a vicious end. But then, Nicholas sighed, neither had Nathaniel and thousands of others. It was this country, this *blerry* country. He and Jane would be well out of it.

Behind him, a car horn sounded. Nicholas put his foot gently down on the accelerator. He had only his personal drawer at the office to pack, and he was free to socialize his last days away. Well, he'd better go and get it over. Soon it would be his turn to taste exile.

It was an irony, he thought as he drove, that he would be leaving the country while his mother, Julia, stayed.

Rosa stood by the window and watched as Martha climbed into the car. There were tears on her face, but she was not grieving. She was proud of her daughter; Martha was doing the right thing, going to teach at the ANC school.

The child—and yet Martha was no longer a child, thought Rosa, she had finally grown up—needed to look through her own eyes at the struggle that had occupied so much of her parents' life. Only then could she make up her own mind.

The result, thought Rosa, might be the loss of Stephen. It was possible, likely even, that he would not fit into Martha's new world. That would be a pity. Stephen loved Martha, and Rosa could see that he was good for her.

And yet love was not something one could only restrict to a single person. Jacob had known that. Jacob had loved his fellow man too much to give it up for the sake of his family. He had participated with open eyes, fully aware of the sacrifice he was making and yet happy anyway.

Rosa turned from the window. She picked up the picture of Jacob that lay on the mantelpiece. It was an old one—he hadn't looked like that in his last year—but it was one that illustrated for her the very essence of Jacob.

It had been taken during the preparations for the Freedom Charter, when Jacob had been banned. One day, unable to bear the frustration of his enforced isolation, he had held a meeting. He had stood inside their garden apparently lecturing to the house, while his audience stood outside and listened to his back.

She smiled as she looked at the picture. It said it all: the conviction in his face, the glee at circumventing the authorities, the seriousness of his purpose.

They had had their first really serious argument, she remembered, around that time. Something to do with whether she should go to the country. She had been furious then at what she had seen as Jacob's double standard. It had taken her some time to calm down.

She looked at the picture. "You were a wonderful man," she told it, "but a man nevertheless. You never really understood what it was like for me."

Perhaps, she thought, I am wrong about Martha and Stephen. Perhaps they will find a way. The younger generation is wiser than we were. They have learned that both partners to a marriage are equally important.

As she replaced the photo, the light caught Jacob's face. He seemed to twinkle at her. Those, she remembered, were exciting days. They could circumvent the police and laugh as they did so.

Not like today. Things had got more serious. No one was playing games anymore.

She began to pace the room, her thoughts focused on Lindiwe.

Lindiwe looked straight down at her son. She smiled at him, and she saw him smile back.

He looked so handsome, she thought, despite his long incarceration.

His looks, she knew, were fueled by his own sense of conviction. He had grown stronger, not weaker, under the torturer's rule.

She glanced down at the judge in his dark robes. He was fussing with his papers, an old man with liver spots on his trembling white hands. She could not even bring herself to hate him for what she was sure he was about to do. He was a cipher, not a man, an agent of a society that had taught him that he was stronger than the young black men who stood before him.

Well, he had been taught wrong, she thought. Nathaniel was the third in his family to face death for the sake of their people. In other families the same situation would repeat itself. So how could these hands, these frail white judge's hands, dam the force of this? How could they dam the force of history? She smiled again, defiant.

Inside, her heart was breaking. Tears brimmed at her eyes but were held back by the insurmountable barrier of her own will.

Martha let out a sigh of relief as the seat-belt sign went out. She released herself from her restraint and looked around her. Everybody was settling in, assuming the kind of vacant looks that people always wore to deal with the monotony of international travel.

Well, she couldn't do the same. She was too excited.

It had all happened so quickly. She had expected to have to wait while they organized things down South. But suddenly the money had become available, and her flight was booked. She had just enough time to give her notice, pack up her things, organize her finances, and get on the plane. It was unreal—except that it was real.

She looked out of the window. Stephen, she thought, must be leaving Heathrow, making his way to London and to work. She grimaced as she thought of him. She hoped that he would wait for her, and then she wondered whether that was the right wish. Her future was ready to make a break with the past: There was no way of knowing how it would turn out.

She bent down and removed a book from her bag. Soon she would be caught up in her new life. For the moment she would revel in the luxury of being in between.

Nathaniel did not blink when the judge pronounced the verdict.

It came as no surprise.

They were sentenced, all three, to death. Death for the crime of being caught in possession of ammunition.

He was vaguely aware that the crowd was beginning to stir, that the judge had his gavel held high in anticipation, that the police were beginning to move forward. Only one thing was missing from this spectacle, one hidden ingredient.

He looked up at his parents. They were staring at him, and the pain so evident in both their eyes tore at his chest. He turned away, he could not bear their agony.

For a moment he was at a loss.

And then he knew what to do, and he knew that it was right.

He rose to his feet, rose in perfect synchroneity with his two comrades. Together they threw up their fists, clenched hard, into the air.

"*Amandla!*" they cried.

AVON ◬ TRADE
PAPERBACKS